THE LAST COVEN

THE TOME OF BILL - 8

RICK GUALTIERI

COPYRIGHT © 2017 RICK GUALTIERI

Edited by: **www.mharriseditor.com**

Cover by: **www.damonza.com**

Proofread by: ***www.bzhercules.com***

Published by Freewill Press

DEDICATION

For my wife and kids, for tolerating 5 long years of me spending countless hours writing this tale and even more spent idiotically laughing at my own jokes.

ACKNOWLEDGEMENTS

Special thanks to my awesome crew: Megan, Mallory, and Beth, for helping polish this series into something worth reading.

Additional big thanks to my fabulous beta readers: Ruby, Solace, Jenn, Evgenia, Chris, Ryan, and Cliff for stepping up to the challenge and helping me tame this monster of a story.

PART I

1

GIVING TO THOSE IN NEED

With The Destroyer dead, I thought things would get better. I was wrong and, judging by the current hail of gunfire, on multiple fronts, too.

"Jeez. How many fucking bullets do these assholes have anyway?"

"They're not assholes," Sheila chided, crouched behind the barrier with me despite being impervious. "They're just scared."

"Can we maybe meet halfway and agree that they're scared assholes?"

Had her return gaze been weaponized, it would have easily cut me to pieces.

I probably deserved it, too.

After everything we'd been through, I was still keeping secrets from her. I kept telling myself they weren't my secrets to tell, but that didn't make me feel much better about it.

Still, I'd hoped that after some food, maybe a shower, and definitely some sleep, everything would...

Hah! Would what? Get back to normal?

Normal was about as far from my reality as it could get these days. Hell, there was a good possibility what I used to consider "normal" would never grace my doorstep again.

Truth be told, I wasn't even sure I wanted it to.

Part of the reason why was on my other side, just itching to return fire.

"This would be a lot easier if we shot back," Sally remarked, casually polishing the muzzle of her ridiculously oversized handgun as if bullets weren't ricocheting around us.

"No!" Sheila turned toward us and paused, her eyes dropping to Sally's big-ass Desert Eagle for a long moment. She was probably thinking the same thing I was: talk about fucking overkill. "We're here to help these people, reassure them that the threat is over. That they no longer have to fear their loved ones being dragged off into the night."

I couldn't help but chuckle. "And who better to convince them than a bunch of weirdos wandering the streets after dark?"

Sheila's aura flared up, and I scooted back until I bumped into Sally ... who unceremoniously shoved me away. "Personal space, dickhead."

And yet I'd been happy, for God knows whatever reason, when her memories had been restored.

Sheila reeled her aura in before it could incinerate me. "We're out here after dark because it was *your* idea to do this."

Oh yeah, that.

Following the fight with Vehron and subsequent escape by Calibra, AKA Ib the first vampire, we'd been stuck in a bit of a quagmire.

While we had some idea as to where she'd gone, we had no clue how to follow. And following her was at the top of our priority list. The stone-aged bitch had kidnapped my roommate Ed, along with James, Gan, my fucking DM Dave, and nearly everyone else who'd been in the Boston complex at the time. Some people just loved to make a dramatic exit.

Christy and her coven sisters were working on tracking

Calibra, but that had left the rest of us to plant our thumbs squarely up our asses until then.

Sitting and waiting was simply out of the question. There was too much to do and I had far too much on my mind. There wasn't even a working wet bar on the premises to keep me otherwise occupied.

Turns out I hadn't been the only one antsy to do something.

The Templar who'd come up to Boston with Sheila had opted to return to the city streets. They had wanted to assess the damage Vehron had done during his rule here while also doing what they could to help anyone in need.

Though they'd professed their reasons to be entirely altruistic in nature, I had a feeling part of it was because they didn't want to wait around in the former vampire stronghold of the northeast. Oddly enough, despite being humorless shitheads of the highest caliber, it was one area where the Templar and I saw eye to eye.

I'd approached Sheila with some of my own thoughts on helping out, hoping it would also serve to break the ice between us a bit. The Templar could hand out sandwiches wrapped in Bible tracts during the day, but the night probably required a slightly different approach. There were possibly still minions of Ib about, including packs of feral zombies set loose in Boston during Vehron's reign.

Sheila had agreed with my reasoning and, after a measured pause, offered to accompany me. Score one! I'd been hoping it would give us a chance to talk. Our last conversation had ended with a nasty reminder that she and I were once again destined to decide the world's fate by way of combat. Maybe it was crazy of me, but that sounded like something worth at least a brief chitchat.

Much to my surprise, though, Sally had cock-blocked that idea and volunteered to tag along.

She claimed boredom, but her eyes said otherwise. Though her mannerisms seemed normal on the outside, I got the feeling that even though she was back to being her old self, she also ... wasn't. The way she'd acted upon her memories being returned hadn't gone unnoticed. Her tone and demeanor had been apologetic, afraid – in short, decisively not Sally.

Alex had fucked with her mind but good. Yet another in a long string of incidents I owed that asshole for, with interest piling up daily. That a truce had been called between us probably didn't mean much to either party involved.

None of that really helped our current situation, though. We'd been out for a couple of hours. Aside from a legless zombie we'd found in an alleyway, it had been slow. Slow and awkward, actually, with little more than small talk passing between us. Honestly, it was starting to piss me off.

Not exactly the dream date my subconscious insisted our threesome would be.

I'd almost rejoiced aloud when the sound of a heated argument drifted through the open window of a nearby brownstone. Needless to say, my enthusiasm had waned ever so slightly once the bullets started flying.

We'd walked over to investigate, only to be greeted by an angry face peering out from a ground floor window. "Who the fuck are you?" he'd called out, a gun barrel pointing our way giving the question extra emphasis.

Sheila's aura had sprung to life in response. Not surprising, but perhaps not the best move, as the look on the man's face quickly turned to one of surprise and panic.

A hail of lead followed his cry of "It's one of those freaks!"

Thank goodness there'd been some concrete pilings in the lot next door, an abandoned construction effort of some sort, or Sally and I would have ended the night picking bullets out of each other's ass. Kinky, but not quite a fetish I'd like to explore.

"So are we going to sit here all night?" Sally asked.

"Oh, I don't know," I replied. "It is a rather lovely evening."

She rolled her eyes in disgust and looked past me at Sheila. "You're the last defender of humanity. So do something before these fucktards need defending." As if to emphasize her point, she checked the magazine of her gun before popping it back in.

The two locked eyes for a moment, glaring at each other as if I wasn't even there, until Sheila broke contact and gave a single nod.

Before she could act, though, the gunfire ceased. "The whole neighborhood knows you freaks are out there," the man called to us.

"No shit," I whispered.

"If you want to live to see the next five minutes, throw any weapons out and then stand up. Nice and slow, and I'd better not see anything weird."

"I think he means..."

"I know what he means," Sheila hissed at me. She took a deep breath and the glow around her faded away.

"Yeah, well, fuck that shit," Sally said. "If this asshole thinks we're going to stand up and give him free potshots at us, he's..." She trailed off and cocked her head to the side.

"Finally realized the point of this wasn't a killing spree?" I asked.

"No, stupid," she snapped. "Listen."

That was easier said than done with my ears still ringing. It was probably only a matter of seconds before Doc Holliday there decided to go all O.K. Corral on us again, but I tried anyway.

Sally was right. Footsteps. No, not just footsteps ... feet marching in rhythm, a lot of them.

"What's wrong?" Sheila asked.

"We're not alone," I said a moment before two columns

of cops in riot gear came double-timing it toward us from either end of the block. About half were armed with assault rifles, while the rest...

Wait. *Definitely* not the police. Their uniforms were unmarked, completely black. Also, unless I'd missed something, silver stakes weren't standard issue for police.

Vampires.

They quickly encircled us, but from a distance – no doubt aware that getting too close to the Icon was a bad way to end one's night. Their weapons were at standby, but the meaning was clear. They could turn us into Swiss cheese before we could so much as scratch our asses.

One of them stepped forward toward the house, hands raised. "Please stand down. We have the situation under control."

"I don't want any trouble," the man called from inside, his voice finally cracking and betraying the fear beneath.

"And I can assure you, neither do we," someone answered from behind the line of vamps.

Oh no. Not him!

"Son of a bitch," Sally spat, lowering her weapon.

The line of armed vampire guards parted to reveal a familiar greasy countenance draped in an overpriced suit.

Colin smiled as he approached, a look of utmost smugness etched upon his face that had me wishing his men had opened fire on us instead.

Surely that would have been the kinder fate.

2

DICKHEADS ANONYMOUS

I expected Colin to order us to our knees and have us cuffed before being led away. All the while, that insufferable smirk of his would be practically begging for someone to wipe it off his stupid fucking face with a high caliber bullet.

I could tell Sally was thinking about it. Honestly, if she'd tried, I don't know that I would have made any attempt to stop her.

Oh, who was I kidding? I'd have helped her aim.

"Relinquish your weapons and come with us, please," Colin said.

I wasn't packing, having expected this to be a mission of mercy, but Sally was, and Sheila had her +5 sword of vamp-incineration. Two of Colin's men stepped toward us expectantly.

Now that the gunfire had ceased, I eased myself back to my feet, hoping the crazies in the house didn't decide to change their minds.

My two compatriots followed. One of the vamps in Colin's hit squad held out his hand to Sally. She glared at him for a moment, then turned over her hand cannon with a sigh of disgust. "I want that back."

The second guard was a bit more hesitant. I couldn't

blame him. His buddy had been tasked with disarming a volatile but still relatively young vampire. He, on the other hand, had drawn the short straw and had to deal with someone who could vaporize him with barely any effort.

Sheila, for her part, didn't seem overly inclined to hand over the weapon, instead looking around and taking stock of our situation.

"If it will make you feel any better," Colin said after a beat, "hand it to the Freewill. I've seen him in action and doubt he would be a threat to any save himself."

Telling Colin to take a long suck on a hard dick was my response of choice, but I instead turned to Sheila. "I won't let anyone else touch it. I promise."

Hah! I wasn't even sure *I* could touch it. Grabbing hold of it was like putting one's hands on a lit stove. Still, if it would keep us from being peppered with lead, I could risk the singed fingers.

We locked eyes and I offered my most sincere smile. Finally, she nodded, unbuckled the weapon from her waist, and held it out to me.

It was my turn to hesitate as I braced myself for the ouchies sure to come.

Thankfully, touching the leather of the scabbard wasn't the same as grabbing hold of the grip. I felt a slight tingle of warmth in my fingers, but that was it.

I let out a deep breath and turned to find Colin wearing a look that spoke of disappointment. *Asshole.*

His troops encircled us and led us away, back in the direction of the Boston headquarters. We'd only come a few blocks west before running into trouble, so there apparently wasn't a need to usher us into the back of a squad car.

I noticed about a third of the vamps remained behind as we left.

"Please tell me you're not cleaning up any loose ends," I said loudly enough to get Colin's attention at the forefront of our column. "This was our fault. Those people didn't ask to get sucked into this."

"As I am well aware," he replied without turning to face us. "My men have orders to disarm them. Afterwards, they are to provide them and their neighbors with assurances that order is being restored as well as any supplies they might need."

Wait, that's what we were out here doing. I glanced to either side. The faces of my two female companions registered the same doubt I was feeling.

"Seriously?"

Colin stopped, causing the entire column to halt. He turned and marched back our way ... albeit, he left plenty of space between us, more than enough for us to get the shit shot out of our asses if we made a move. "I am entirely serious, Freewill. You may not believe this, but the Destroyer caused grievous harm to this city and our presence within it, a presence we have carefully cultivated for over three centuries. It is my duty to reestablish some semblance of order here, and I can't very well do that by executing the citizenry. Tomorrow, those people will talk to their friends and they in turn will talk to theirs. Soon, the rumor mill will be flush with whispers of normalcy returning. That will, in turn, strengthen the effort to reestablish the former leadership and constabulary."

I blinked stupidly in the face of this all, not having expected the Draculas to do much more than repair the car wash that served as the outside façade of their underground complex.

"So you're actually trying to get things back to normal?" Sheila asked.

"Yes. At least until the First are victorious in their war effort," he said before turning around and continuing on. "After that, we shall most likely assume a slightly more proactive stance in our managerial strategies."

It didn't take us long to get back to the car wash. As we approached, Colin made a hand gesture, and the remaining guards split off in different directions, leaving us alone with him.

"Someone's feeling brave," Sally commented.

"Our façade of normalcy must be rebuilt. There is much work to be done here, but the sooner we can convince the residents that nothing is amiss, the better. That includes reestablishing the belief that this complex is nothing more than it appears. We can't very well accomplish that if it is painfully obvious we are housing a significant strike force." He turned and smirked over his shoulder. "To answer your charge, bravery assumes one is feeling threatened. I can assure you, my dearest Lucinda, that I feel anything *but* in your or the Freewill's presence."

"You fucking..."

"Lucinda?" Sheila asked.

"Ah yes," Colin continued. "I would also remind you, Icon, that the truce Lord Alexander graciously allowed is still in place. Assuming, of course, no overt hostilities are undertaken against emissaries of the First ... such as myself."

Sheila shrugged. "Wouldn't dream of it."

"I am pleased to hear that." He pulled a flip phone out of his jacket pocket, opened it, and punched a few buttons.

"Good luck getting service these days," I said.

"Our private cell towers have been reactivated," he replied dismissively before speaking a few words and ending the call.

God, what a smug prick. I couldn't help but feel especially peeved. We'd done all the work, shed all the blood, and suffered losses as a result. In the end, it had been close, but – thanks to Gan – I managed to blow Vehron's head off long enough for the rest of his body to get the hint. Despite that, it hadn't been much of a victory as we'd then had to deal with his master, the queen bitch of all vampires.

All of that, only for this brown-nosing cocksucker to

waltz in and declare he was resuming command without so much as lifting a finger.

Oh, how nice it would be to shit stomp this fucker. As much as I was admittedly a fan of nasty, sweaty sex, fucking this guy up with present company might make for an even more satisfying threesome.

Unfortunately, that wasn't going to happen, no matter how much I might want it. Colin was right about the truce. As big of a swinging dick as Alex was, there was too much at stake for us to risk breaking it – at least until a time of our choosing. At that point, well, whatever happened next definitely wouldn't be boring.

The battered exterior of the wash loomed ahead of us. One side had an odd cant to it as if something beneath the surface had collapsed. It didn't take a genius to figure out that the Prefect's office lay somewhere directly below it.

My attention was quickly diverted, however, to the main entrance of the wash's office. The door opened with a jingle. Jesus, they even had a bell on it.

Several figures stepped out. My vampire night vision compensated for the darkness, and I saw it was Christy and her small coven of witches. An unfamiliar figure, probably a vampire, escorted them out. He gave them a friendly wave, said, "Thank you, come again!" and then shut the door behind them.

"Are you fucking kidding me?"

Colin smiled in return. "As I said, Freewill, the façade must be maintained."

"At two in the morning?"

"We keep late hours. It's done wonders against the competition."

BACK TO THE BIG APPLE

"You're kicking us out?"

"Of course," Colin replied as if I'd asked a particularly dull-witted question. "If I am interpreting Lord Alexander's dictate correctly, and I assure you I am, our cease fire stipulates that we will suspend hostilities against one another, share in pertinent information, and strike jointly against our enemy when the time is right. It's possible my memory fails me, but I don't seem to recall anything about cohabitation. If it helps, though, there are several inexpensive motels within the city limits. Perhaps I can find you some coupons for a complimentary continental breakfast."

I opened my mouth to respond, but Sally was quicker. "It's fine. Too many cockroaches in this place anyway. Wouldn't want any of them trying to crawl into bed with me."

"I can assure you, my dear, that even cockroaches have standards."

Oh, crap. I stepped between him and Sally before she could make a move that would get us all gunned down. Despite appearing to be alone, it was foolish to believe he didn't have eyeballs on us.

It was all for naught, though. Sally didn't even flinch in

his direction. She merely turned her back. Yeah, something was definitely up with her. First she'd asked for permission to fire back at a trigger-happy human, and now she wasn't even pretending to want to take a slice out of this greaseball.

However, now was not the time to discuss things. Besides, I sure as shit wasn't about to let my guard down while Colin was within earshot. Instead, I comforted myself in the knowledge that if things somehow worked out in our favor – resulting in the deaths of both Ib and Alex – then that would surely at least inconvenience Colin. And, if not, then we'd be dead, in which case we wouldn't ever have to listen to him again.

That's me, a glass is half full kind of guy.

"We'll go," I said. "But how will Alexander be able to..."

"Do not doubt for one moment, Freewill, that the esteemed First Coven can find you no matter where you are."

"Uh, okay. And if we need to get in touch with them?"

"The phone lines are being reestablished even as we speak."

Of course they were. Colin was a cock, but even I couldn't deny he was an efficient cock.

Still, it felt wrong to leave without at least a parting shot at the creep. Fortunately, I had just the thing to plant a seed of paranoia in his shit-stain of a head. It was still a sore spot for me, but there was something to be said about sharing the misery.

I turned, then stopped, feigning as if something had just come to mind. "Oh, I almost forgot. That whole pertinent information thing?"

"What of it, Freewill? I have a great many matters to take care of and this discourse grows tiresome."

"Remember Starlight?"

Colin's face went blank for a moment as if he had no idea who I was talking about. Then recognition dawned in his eyes. "Ah. Alice Kessler, you mean? Former member of Village Coven. Was good enough to let me know the location of your coven's safe houses about a year back."

I gritted my teeth at the memory. "Yes, her."

"She is officially listed as missing, presumed deceased at the hands of the Destroyer."

I could feel Sally's gaze boring into me, no doubt wondering where this was going. "Well, she's not. She's one of the Jahabich now."

"Oh," Colin replied, nonplussed. "A pity, I'm sure, but I fail to see why that is a concern."

"It should because she fooled me."

"The tells of the Jahabich are well documented. Just because you didn't think to check her teeth..."

"I did, though. They were normal, like ours. She was a perfect duplicate."

"I saw it too," Sheila added.

"Starlight?"

"No. Another one. We ran into her on our way here. Normal teeth and all until she changed. Somehow, they're evolving."

"Maybe," I said before turning back to Colin. "Either way, I think that's something Alex should know. These things..." I leaned in close. "They could be *anyone*."

"Thanks for playing along," I said to Sheila as our group walked away. "He'll be going nuts with that info."

"What do you mean 'playing along'?"

"Wait, you really did see one?"

"Yes. The damn thing almost killed me."

I'd hoped maybe Starlight was a fluke, a mutation of some kind. But now, what Sheila said about them evolving ... no, that didn't seem right. Calibra had created these things. Perhaps she'd been working on improving upon her design. I didn't voice my concern, but in the back of my head, I was kind of glad I'd passed this on.

Who was to know how many of these Jahabich 2.0

existed? If so, maybe Colin wasn't the only one who should've been worried about being paranoid.

The hours before dawn found us regrouping with the Templar, or at least their unsightly leader Bernadette. Though I wouldn't have minded ditching them, we owed them one. Also, taking a steaming dump on one's allies was more Alex's modus operandi. Not exactly a person I cared to emulate.

We compared notes and discovered that nothing much had changed in the interim hours. We still had no idea what our next steps were. And without that, there wasn't much we could do except wait.

I was the one who suggested we return to Brooklyn. Hanging around in a city where our presence wasn't wanted didn't strike me as appealing. If we were going to be banging our heads against the wall, it might as well be against familiar walls. We needed to come up with some plan of action quickly if we were to save Ed, and I had a feeling we'd all think more clearly in a place we knew. At the very least, I would.

Bernadette declined to join us for now. Her knights had found renewed purpose in helping the citizens of Boston. Sure, New York was likely to be as big of a cluster fuck, but it hadn't recently suffered three months of rule by a muscle-bound madman. Also, Manhattan was currently vampire-free. Despite Colin's assurances to the contrary, Bernadette didn't trust him. Hell must've frozen over, because we finally found something we could agree on.

That said, she was still set on helping us. Fuck it. Crazed Bible thumpers they might be, but I'd take whatever I could get these days. Assuming they didn't come to blows before then, we figured we could get in touch with her through the Boston complex since the Templar planned to make it well known to the vamps they were sticking around for a while.

For a few moments, I worried Sheila might decide to stay

with them. However, she merely gave Bernadette a hug and wished her well. I just barely suppressed a sigh of relief. I mean, I didn't buy into this fate bullshit one way or the other, but the feeling that we were entering into the endgame wasn't an easy one to shake. Besides, even though she didn't need my protection, I felt better having her near. I'd already failed too many friends as it was.

That just left the getting home part, which seemed easy enough. Christy had gotten some sleep, but, more importantly, her three coven sisters – Meg, Kelly, and Veronica – had as well. Seven months pregnant and with her boyfriend, my best bud Tom, currently inhabiting the body of a cheesy action figure ... well, that was bound to leave its mark on a person. But with three fresh witches around to amp up the mojo, it wouldn't be an issue to zap us back to the Big Apple.

At least until it was.

"I can't help but notice we're still standing in this alleyway."

"Brilliant observation as usual, Bill," Sally replied.

"Hold on." Meg backed up and looked around. "One of you probably broke the circle."

"Nobody moved," I said, double-checking that I hadn't accidentally taken a step backward. For the amount of eldritch power we had at our disposal, they sure as hell had drawn a really fucking cramped magical circle.

Don't get me wrong, as the lone non-plastic male in our octet, I didn't exactly mind having so much boobage pressed against me. Add some music, cheap liquor, and a couple of jays to pass around and this would have been my idea of a party.

No, I corrected myself. This was not the time to let little Dr. Death take over. There was too much to do and too much at stake.

"The circle is fine," Kelly said, distracting me from thoughts of tits, wonderful tits.

"Try it again," Christy replied. "And this time, I'm joining hands, too."

"It's okay, you know," Meg countered. "We've got this. You can just relax."

"I wasn't asking." The tone of Christy's voice was unmistakable. She was in charge of this coven and was asserting rank. Hell, I was tempted to grab her hand, too. Sheila had a commanding iconic presence when she wanted to, but I had little doubt Christy could have given her a run for her money.

No further argument was put forth, unsurprisingly, although a tinny little voice from inside Christy's handbag asked, "Are we there yet?"

Being killed and subsequently resurrected in the body of a crappy action figure hadn't done much to put my roommate Tom out of sorts. Regardless, it was still really fucking weird and definitely at the top of our list of things that needed to be fixed. Oddly enough, he wasn't the only sentient object on her person. However, I wasn't about to say Harry Decker's name aloud and risk having to listen to the asshole.

There came another brief flash of light, but it was muted – little more than a camera flash as opposed to the normal brilliance resulting from being blown into one's base atoms and rearranged in a different location.

Once it cleared, it was obvious that we'd again gone nowhere. "You guys out of frequent apparation miles or something?"

Christy shot me a quick glare of annoyance before furrowing her brow and focusing elsewhere. I realized she was staring at Sheila. After a few seconds of this, Christy lifted her hands and turned her palms to face each other. An anemic ball of energy flared to life between them, little more than one might expect from a cheap sparkler on the Fourth of July. "Could you do me a favor and step out of the circle for a moment?"

Sheila nodded and did as asked. Almost immediately, the

faint spark of power sizzled and roared to life, becoming a crackling globe of energy that caused my hair to stand on end.

"Holy shit. Even in a magic circle?" Kelly remarked.

"It's me, isn't it?" Sheila asked. "I'm causing the problem."

Christy doused the ball of lightning. "Looks like it. That's unexpected."

"What is?" I asked. "I mean, we know she has resistance to magic."

"Yes, that's why we're using a circle. It concentrates our energy, keeps it fully contained until we're ready to let it go. I was pretty sure by doing it that way..."

"But we were all able to ... teleport, I guess, back at NORAD," I pointed out. Meg glanced at me with raised eyebrows, to which I replied, "Long story."

"Trust me, I'm aware," Christy said, looking perplexed.

Kelly nodded toward Sheila. "Maybe she's gotten stronger."

"Maybe." Christy shook her head. "Or it could have been that place itself. With all those myriad beings present..."

"Including a death god," I added.

She shrugged in response. "I suppose it's possible. That, combined with the underlying superstructure built deep into the mountain ... the metaphysical turbulence of the entire complex could have been supercharged. Whereas here, not so much."

"I have no idea what you just said," Tom replied from her purse.

"See?" Kelly turned to Sheila. "You've been beating yourself up all this time about abandoning them."

"Whoa there," I interrupted. "What? Who said anything about abandoning anyone?"

"I told you," Kelly continued, ignoring me, "you were right where you were meant to be. Almost as if fate wanted you there helping us."

"Besides, it was more like she just ditched Bill," Sally said before turning to Sheila. "I wouldn't worry about it either way. If I were a betting girl, I'd happily wager that's not the first time it's happened to him."

I was about to reply with something pithy when Kelly's words registered with me. Had things worked out how we'd planned it, it would have been a group effort to take down Vehron, with Sheila leading the charge ... the prophesied Freewill vs. Icon matchup to determine the fate of mankind.

It hadn't, though. In fact, things had worked out in such a way that she hadn't even been present for that final fight. It had been Freewill against Freewill with only one left standing in the end.

And now, here we were – the lone Freewill and the last Icon. The fate we'd been trying to avoid now stared us back in the face again. I didn't want to believe it, but enough weird coincidence had occurred to even make me begin to wonder. Still, it seemed impossible. Sheila was my ... *friend.* Things were too fucking complicated for anything more, especially with Sally firing again on all cylinders – or most of them anyway.

Regardless, we were on the same side. There was no reason for us to duke it out, and I just couldn't see what might give us cause to fight to the death.

Unless Dr. Death took over again, I considered.

That was the six-hundred-pound gorilla in my room. If that happened, hell, I might gladly let her slice and dice me.

There was also the other prophecy, the one that stated Sheila would be the end of the Magi. It was a big enough concern that Christy had sworn me to secrecy over the fact that the White Mother, a Christ-like figure to the Magi, was actually a psycho hose-beast who'd told the laws of nature to eat a dick before creating the Jahabich from the souls of the dead.

The thing was, Sheila had forced me to swear that I'd kill her if she ever threatened Christy or, perhaps more importantly, Christy's unborn baby.

That was the kicker. Present-company excluded, most

mages I'd met hadn't exactly taken a shine to me. I wouldn't shed many tears if I opened up the *New York Times* and saw a headline proclaiming that wizards and witches were being exterminated like bugs. But what if Sheila turned against Christy for some reason? And what if she threatened her baby?

I couldn't foresee that happening, but my life had taken plenty of unforeseen twists as of late. Too many for me to outright dismiss anything, no matter how absurd.

Great! As if I didn't already have enough piled on my plate.

4

HOME AGAIN, HOME AGAIN

Thankfully, I was able to push aside my rapidly darkening thoughts for the more immediate concern of how the fuck we were supposed to get home if we couldn't teleport.

Sheila was quick to volunteer to stay behind, make her own way back, but I ixnayed that and wasn't about to back down this time.

"No way. It's bad enough the Templar are staying behind ... well, fine, that's not really all that bad. I'm sure they'll make fine company for Colin. But unless there's a damn good reason, we stick together. All of us. That way, once we figure out what the hell we're going to do to save Ed, we don't have to play hide and seek wondering where everyone else is."

"Yes, but it makes more sense for you all to get back there and get to work..."

"I don't care if it makes all the goddamned sense in the world," I said, interrupting her. "The world doesn't make sense anymore, so what good is logic? Sorry, but I'm not letting you out of my sight again."

I'd been so caught up in the sentiment, I hadn't realized I'd stepped closer, well within her personal space in the cramped confines of the now-useless magic circle. What I'd meant was that we needed to watch each other's backs, but from the slight blush in her cheeks, I got the impression I'd inadvertently conveyed more than intended.

Either way, it was like time stopped for a moment as we locked eyes.

It was just for a moment, though, for just then, Tom's voice again came from Christy's purse. "What if she needs to take a shit?"

After we got home, I really needed to find some fire-crackers to strap him to.

Once upon a time, the concept of grand theft auto was nothing more than a video game to me. However, since becoming one of the undead, I've had to develop an appreci-ation for occasionally bending the law. At this point, the concept of driving around in a stolen car was barely a blip on my moral outrage meter. Of far greater concern was making sure whatever we boosted had sufficiently tinted windows to withstand the rapidly approaching dawn.

So it was that we found ourselves driving back to New York City in a couple of SUVs that Sally procured for us. Christy had handed Tom to me, then hopped into the other with her coven sisters. She wanted to discuss potential next steps with them. Left unsaid was probably wanting to discuss the issue of Calibra without Sheila overhearing. Oh well, at least she didn't give us Decker's skull, too. Otherwise, he'd have ended the day in a rest stop trashcan.

During the drive, Sheila brought us up to speed on her journey to Boston with the witches and the Templar, including how they'd knocked Bernadette's ass out with a sleep spell along the way. I didn't know Christy's new coven too well, but that immediately ratcheted them up several notches in my book.

Seems they'd also had their fair share of freaky adventure on the way up. It was a somber reminder that, despite our victory, the world as a whole was still fucked. We'd only slowed its slide toward Armageddon a bit. There was a lot of work left to do before we could consider celebrating.

Thankfully, it wasn't only vampires who had an aversion to sunlight. While not a hard and fast rule, it seemed the supernatural allies of both the vampire nation and the Feet took a step back to recharge during daylight hours.

The trip back was slow going, some parts of the road a bigger mess than mere asphalt patching could fix. However, that was the worst we encountered during the daytime portion of our drive. Though it remained to be seen what fate ultimately had in store for us, apparently it wasn't so big a cock to not throw us a little bone for having just vanquished a big scary fucker with the surname The Destroyer.

A part of me expected us to crest a rise and see nothing but a mushroom cloud where Brooklyn once stood, but thankfully that wasn't the case. Despite feeling like I'd been gone for ages, it had only been a few days since James had called to tell us to bug out or be burned out, thankfully not enough time for things to completely go to...

"Oh fuck!"

"No thanks," Sally murmured from her spot next to me in the back, engrossed in some vacuous women's magazine.

"What is it?" Sheila asked, glancing back from the driver's seat.

"Oh, nothing. Just the realization that we might be coming home to a pile of ashes."

"Shit," Tom said from where he was propped up on the dashboard. "You don't think they actually did it, do you? I mean, we left when they said to."

"Who knows? Never discount the Dracs' ability to be spiteful assholes."

"What do you mean?" Sheila asked.

"Sorry, I forgot you and Sally were out at the time ... and Sally was still out of her mind."

In response, she lowered her magazine to glare at me from the corner of her eye.

"But that's why I had to leave a note for you guys to find us at the Brooklyn safe house. We needed to get out or risk the place being burnt down around us."

"You gotta admit," Sally said, "threats from people not known for their love of bluffing do have a habit of motivating folks to action."

"Easy for you to say," Tom replied. "You were just squatting in the downstairs apartment. All of my stuff is at my place."

"Mine too," I reminded him.

"Yeah, but yours isn't worth shit. I mean, fuck, Bill, what if they carried through with it? Do you know how much stuff I'll lose? And it's not like you fuckers ever went back to get my body..."

"I'm sorry..."

"...and all the stuff I stole."

"Or not so sorry."

"You could have at least grabbed those Star Wars figures off me, y'know, to honor my memory."

"Not sure how that would have helped you," I countered. "Possession is nine-tenths of the law and, so far as I can tell, the only thing you're currently possessing isn't worth dick on eBay."

"Doesn't mean we can't try," Sally offered.

"You wouldn't," Tom replied.

Sally, in response, merely gazed back at him.

"Okay, maybe you would."

5

DID SOMEONE LEAVE
THE OVEN ON?

My worries about spending the night at the Brooklyn safe house, a dump if ever there was one, were fortunately for naught.

As the afternoon grew late and the shadows began to lengthen enough so a vamp could venture outside, we finally turned onto our block. I was happy to see the normal row of apartment buildings loom over us. Though there were far more boarded up windows than we were used to seeing before the world turned to shit, the neighborhood otherwise looked as it always did. Even better, our building hadn't been reduced to a pile of smoking rubble.

Sadly, that didn't mean it hadn't been affected by our absence.

"Motherfucker!"

"What?" Tom asked. "They fucking burned it down, didn't they? Oh, I am so sending the Draculas a bill when this is all over. Somebody turn my head so I can see what's going on."

"Relax, the building is still there."

"It's the door that isn't," Sheila added, pointing out the source of my annoyance.

"Goddamn, people suck. You can't even leave for a long

weekend without some asshole deciding to help themselves to everything you own."

"We don't know that's the case."

"Oh yeah," Sally scoffed. "I'm sure it was just a concerned neighbor deciding to check on you guys, make sure you were dead, that sort of thing."

The second car in our two-vehicle convoy pulled in behind us. If there was only one benefit to the impending apocalypse, it was that the parking situation in Brooklyn had improved dramatically. Of course, even if it hadn't, it wasn't like any of us would care much if we got towed. Heck, the only one of us who even owned a car...

Shit! I let that thought trail off as I considered Ed. Wherever he was, it was a safe bet his situation made ours look like paradise in comparison. That was something to keep in mind.

This homecoming was temporary at best. None of us could afford to get comfortable. There were too many lives at stake. Maybe it would be a good thing if we'd been cleaned out. It would give us cause to move more quickly in our efforts as opposed to letting the malaise of familiar surroundings sink in.

Regardless, if the building had been emptied, there wasn't much we could do about it. If the vandals were still around, though, well, they were in for the rudest homecoming party they could imagine.

"Let's go." I made it all of two steps toward the door when the stench hit my overly sensitive vampire nostrils. "Ugh!"

"What's wrong?" Sheila asked from behind me. Whereas in the past I'd found myself envying her Icon powers, now I couldn't help but be jealous of her human sense of smell. Ratcheted up senses weren't always a blessing.

"Smells like melted body fat," Sally said casually.

"Why would you even know that?"

"Why wouldn't I?"

"Serves them right for touching my shit," Tom said.

"Shut up or you're going into my back pocket," I warned my roommate as we crossed the threshold.

I glanced back as the rest of our contingent approached. Two vamps, an Icon, and four witches. Unless a primal god had taken up residence here, anyone still inside would be in for a nasty surprise.

Actually, it really *wasn't* outside the realm of reality for a god to have done so. I mean, shit, hadn't I already met at least one?

"What's the hold up?" Sally complained from behind.

"Just contemplating theology," I replied before forcing myself to continue onward.

Once inside, the stench became more concentrated, like a pig roast gone insanely wrong. I took another breath, letting the unsavory aroma assault my olfactory receptors. "Smells like it's coming from the basement."

"The basement?" Christy asked from near the rear of our lineup. "Damnit! Out of the way!"

"Huh?" I barely had time to open my mouth before I was elbowed to the side. The hallways of our building were fairly narrow and Christy had bulked up just a wee bit in her current pregnant state. So I found myself pressed up against the wall as she shoved her way past me.

"Where you going, babe?" Tom asked.

"Hold up," I said. "We don't know if it's safe or not."

A second later, Sheila pushed past me, too. "Don't just stand there; let's go."

Sally was hot on her heels, both of them hurrying after Christy. So much for caution. Oh well. With fingers crossed that some demon from the Abyss wasn't waiting for us below, I made my way after them.

The top of the stairs were dark, not that it was an issue for those of us with night vision. However, that changed as we made our way down. The door leading into the basement, normally kept locked, had been kicked in much like the front door.

However, unlike the front entrance, shimmering light came from inside. That's when I remembered the glowing energy ball Christy and her coven had set up in there to keep our power on while the rest of the grid suffered from increasingly common outages.

Sally's confirmation of what we were smelling, combined with that knowledge, gave me a sinking feeling in my gut. However, that was still more pleasant than the sinking feeling from my feet once I entered the basement and stepped in something with the consistency of pudding.

Sheila voiced what I was certain all of us were thinking. "What the hell happened in here?"

That was an understatement. At least five charred skeletons, maybe more – it was hard to tell – lay around the room. The bones had the consistency of a rack of ribs that had been sitting in a smoker all day. As for the rest, burned scraps of clothing lay here and there amidst the puddles of, well, what I assumed were the rest of them. Christy herself stood almost ankle deep in human soup as she studied the glowing ball of magic connected to our main breaker panel.

"Holy fucking hell!" Kelly said from behind me as she and the other two witches joined us.

"I'd say that about sums it up," I replied before focusing on Christy again. "Any idea why this place looks like a scene out of *Hellraiser?*"

"Good," she murmured, seemingly more to herself than any of us. "It's still salvageable."

I cleared my throat. "Seriously, what the fuck happened here?"

She no more than glanced over her shoulder as if she had better things to worry about. "They messed with power beyond their understanding and paid the price. They're lucky they didn't vaporize the whole building."

"Yeah, about that. 'Lucky' isn't quite the word I'd use."

She stepped past me as if I wasn't there. "We have a lot to

do, sisters. The prism needs to be stabilized if this is going to work. The rest of you should check the upstairs while we get started."

"I don't suppose we could maybe mop down here first," Kelly said from the doorway.

"I'm pretty sure I'm gonna barf if we don't," the auburn-haired member of their coven, Veronica, added.

Christy simply glared at them, a shimmer of red power crackling around her for just a moment.

Neither of them moved until Meg stepped past them and squished over to Christy's side. "You heard the lady. There's work to be done if we don't want to be reading by candlelight tonight."

"Or blown to bits," Kelly added under her breath.

Unsurprisingly, Sheila wasn't too happy at casually brushing off the deaths of nearly half a dozen people. Sure, they were probably scumbag looters, but being liquefied might have been a somewhat harsh punishment for their crime.

Still, she seemed to realize that sticking around and arguing was pointless. That, or the gnarly smell was finally getting to her. We headed upstairs to check on our respective apartments while the witches worked their mojo ... and hopefully also took Kelly's advice on mopping.

Amazingly enough, the apartments were still locked up tight, necessitating me breaking into mine since I'd lost just about all of my possessions during the trip up north. It seemed our would-be burglars decided to start at the bottom and work their way up, much to their own detriment.

I flipped on the light switch, then quickly turned it back off again after seeing how everything flickered. Though I couldn't help but think it shouldn't be her top priority, I still wished Christy well in fixing the glowing thingee.

Alas, lights or not, the place felt disturbingly empty. My roommates had been with me last time I'd been inside.

Though a cloud of impending doom hung over us, at least our number had been whole. Now, Ed was kidnapped for God-knows-what nefarious purpose, and Tom was dead.

"Let's check out my room and make sure everything is okay."

Dead, but not quite gone yet. A small miracle, but in the gloom of the apartment, it gave me hope. And so long as there was hope, we'd keep pushing forward.

"I said to check things out, not touch anything. Hands off Cheetara!"

Oh, fuck this noise. I laid out the ThunderCats figure on his dresser, then positioned Tom on top of it missionary-style.

"Dude, the fuck? Hmm, actually, this is kinda hot."

I closed the door to Tom's room behind me. Yeah, hope would keep us moving forward, but a little douchebag spite didn't hurt either.

6

DOWN TIME IN THE DUMPS

Three days ... three fucking days!

I slammed my fist onto the cheap countertop of our kitchen nook, cracking it down the middle. Hell, I was tempted to tear the entire fucking thing out and throw it across the room, security deposit be damned. Not like there was anyone around to refund it anyway.

I steadied myself and took several deep breaths. When that didn't calm me, I opened the top cabinet, grabbed the bottle of Jose Cuervo sitting in it, and poured myself a shot – a Sasquatch-sized one.

This wasn't the first time I'd almost flown off the handle since arriving back home, and that had me worried.

A part of me was convinced it was just the stress of waiting, but I wasn't sure I believed that. Dr. Death had been silent in my head ever since I tried blowing myself up in a bid to rid the world of Vehron. That act had somehow shut him up and resulted in the nice – if minor – perk of not needing to wear my glasses to see. I was hoping that last part was permanent but was still paranoid enough to carry them in my back pocket just in case I went all nearsighted again at the worst possible moment.

The thing was, what if my fraying temper was also a side effect? What if this wasn't frustration, but his essence oozing into the pores of my subconscious? He hadn't been able to win by browbeating me. What if he was trying something more subtle?

What would that mean for me? For my friends? For any innocents who happened to be around if I finally lost it and went batshit vampire insane?

The days were toughest for us. The witches had sequestered themselves in the basement. I assumed they were hard at work reverse-engineering the ancient spell we hoped to use against the Jahabich and a few other folks. At the very least, the smell of human bacon had dissipated from the place. But beyond that, I was mostly left in the dark.

Hell, Christy had even retrieved Tom to be with her, leaving me alone in my apartment with nothing but my thoughts. At least the lights had stopped flickering, meaning I could amuse myself with some single player video games, but they served as little more than a temporary distraction. Also, I lost one hard fought level at the last second and almost pounded my desktop into mush. Damn thing was liquid cooled and had cost me over a grand.

The nights weren't an issue, though.

Sheila apparently liked being cooped up as much as I did, despite having the freedom to go out during the day. She'd suggested the three of us – she, myself, and Sally – start patrolling together at night, not entirely different from what we'd done up in Boston ... albeit hopefully more competently.

Sally had demurred. I'd hoped she'd bounce back quickly once her memories had returned, and at first that seemed to be the case. However, the more time that passed, the more withdrawn she seemed to become. I also saw the way the fire went out of her eyes whenever I mentioned Starlight. I got the impression – between Alex mind-raping her and that – she was barely holding it together.

Though she kept her thoughts close to the vest, I knew from experience when someone was busy overanalyzing things and beating themselves up over it. Unfortunately, despite my entreaties to the contrary, she didn't appear to want to talk about it.

So that left the two of us – Icon and Freewill – to team up as a dynamic duo of sorts. Manhattan was currently devoid of vampires, but that didn't mean shit these days. It was a big city, full of tasty people, and there were plenty of things more than happy to treat it as an all-you-can eat buffet.

We'd taken to patrolling the seedier areas, places where the power was out and where the red and blue flashers of the police didn't seem to have a presence. For two nights we'd done so, and it hadn't been boring in the least. Monsters, both human and otherwise, turned out to be not so hard to find. Sadly, their victims were plentiful, too.

But that's also where my salvation lay. Though neither of us talked about it, the irreparably wounded or very recently deceased could still help us. With bagged blood no longer in ample supply, we couldn't afford to risk the two vamps in the house getting peckish.

It gave me a way to fill up the tank and use it against who or whatever had left those victims behind. Though Sheila's healing powers were pretty potent, there were limits to what she could fix. We'd come to an unspoken agreement of sorts during those moments. She'd turn away and let me do what I had to. I made it a point to not prolong anyone's suffering and to try to be neat about things. Unspoken agreements worked so much better when the other person didn't look like a walking slaughterhouse.

Also left unspoken was my fear of the anger inside me and the potential for me to start to enjoy this new way of life once the disgust wore off.

For now, though, it was an arrangement that bore fruit. Just last night, we'd tracked down a trio of creatures made of greasy black smoke – Wisps, if I recalled correctly. Anyway, the pyromaniac little fuckers had been having a merry old time setting homeless people ablaze before we'd arrived.

Sheila's powers worked just fine against them. As for me, thankfully, they had a solid core deep inside their burning exterior that was perfectly good for punching. Yeah, it hurt, but it wasn't like I was a stranger to being set on fire.

The problem was, the euphoria of our outings didn't last. Spending time with Sheila was great, but it wasn't the same as it might have once been. Even a month ago, kicking ass by her side would have qualified as one of my wet dreams. Now, though, we once again had that fucking prophecy standing between us as the ultimate cock-blocker. Frustration over my inability to save Ed, Dave, James, and the others, as well as worry for Sally, only compounded it.

It wasn't unlike trying to cast a wish spell during one of Dave's game sessions. Never would I have thought that being alone with the girl I used to fawn over would be so anti-bonerific, but it was. The whole saying about being careful what you wished for turned out to be apt indeed.

I swallowed another mouthful of tequila and stepped to the front window. I looked out at the sunny street below and rued the fact that there wasn't nearly enough left in the rapidly depleting bottle to get me good and shitfaced. One of the many downsides of being a vampire was a drinking constitution that would have made me the grand beer pong champion of any campus in America.

Yeah, the days were bad and seemed to be getting worse. To have so much power at my disposal – in theory, at least – yet sitting around while one of my best friends was being tortured or worse.

I barely noticed when, in frustration, I shattered the mug I was holding. By the time I looked down, the cuts on my hand were already closing up.

Movement below caught my eye and I glanced out. The

day was bright, but thankfully the sun had moved out of a position to shine directly in. A car had just double-parked down below. That in itself wasn't surprising. People typically double-parked in Brooklyn as readily as they breathed. Nowadays, with the law of the land a dubious thing, I was half surprised the entire block hadn't turned into one giant parking lot. It was more the size of the vehicle that caught my attention. Too long for even four doors – a limo, by the looks of it.

Go figure. Even during the apocalypse, some folks had to flaunt it over everyone else.

Oh well, some pretentious asshole stopping to grab a slice of New York pizza wasn't my concern, not by a long shot. I'd started to turn away when more movement below registered in my periphery: a car door opening and closing, followed by a flash of black hair.

I was just noting that they'd appeared to be heading toward the stoop of my building when there came a commotion from below. Had I been human, it would have been easy to dismiss from this high up. To my vampire ears, though, the sound of splintering wood and shattering glass was loud and clear.

We'd jerry-rigged the front door closed again shortly after arriving here, and now some asshole had just done us the favor of kicking it in again.

7

A SUNNY DISPOSITION

uck!

It's bad enough that a group of dipshits decided to liquefy themselves in our basement the second we stepped away. Now some rich douchebag was doing it in broad daylight. What the hell? It's not like we were the only building left standing in this neighborhood. Were they on a mad bender for some Grey Poupon?

Pity for them they'd caught me in a bad mood. I had a very simple rule when it came to humans: if they were innocent, I didn't hurt them. Shitheads, however, were more than qualified when it came time to dole out a beating. It wouldn't help rescue Ed, but giving some looter a broken face might distract me for a few moments.

I practically flew down the stairs. Truth be told, I wasn't overly worried about my fellow tenants. Between witches, vampires, and an Icon, whoever was waiting down below was in for a really bad meet and greet. I just wanted to get there first.

The door to Sally and Sheila's apartment was opening as I started down the next flight of stairs. I caught the barest glimpse of blonde hair and heard Sally grumble something about what she was going to do to whoever woke her up.

I was halfway tempted to slow down and let her get there first. Maybe it would snap her out of her funk.

Or maybe it would cause her to horribly murder whoever had played Big Bad Wolf on our front door. The thought caused me to speed up my steps. Hurting someone was fine, but I wasn't so far gone as to agree with tearing them limb from limb.

I reached the ground floor, noting the distinct lack of witches emerging from the basement. I mean, sure, they all had normal human senses, but they were a hell of a lot closer to the ruckus than I'd been. Also, I was fairly sure Christy had warded the doors to let her know when someone other than us entered.

I didn't know what they were doing down there, but it sure as shit must've been engrossing.

Whatever the fuck. I could yell at them later.

For now, I spun toward the front door. "Okay, asshole, you're about to learn a hard lesson about breaking and entering."

The words died on my lips and I skidded to a halt as our intruder came into view. Though the door was in splinters before her, she stood just outside of it in the direct rays of the sun, as if she didn't even notice it. But that was impossible.

Gan locked her green eyes on mine and smiled. "I knew I would find you here, beloved."

Sally's footsteps stopped somewhere above us. There was little doubt she'd heard Gan's voice and recognized it. It wasn't hard to imagine her debating whether or not to go back to bed.

However, the curiosity of the fact that Gansetseg, adopted daughter of Ogedai Khan and current Prefect of Eastern Asia, was both here and standing outside as if the sun wasn't shining down upon her, proved too much for even her dislike of the little munchkin.

"Are you seeing what I'm seeing?" she asked, stepping to my side.

"I dunno. We could be sharing a hallucination."

"I always knew there was too much lead paint in the walls of this dump."

Gan's smile turned into a bemused smirk and she stepped inside, her tiny feet crunching on the broken glass beneath them.

"I guess the doorbell was busted," I remarked more to myself than anything.

"It was locked and I didn't care to be kept waiting," Gan replied to my rhetorical statement.

"Don't take this the wrong way," Sally said, "but how the fuck are you still alive?"

Before Gan could answer, my ears picked up footsteps, a single set of them, ascending from the basement. I glanced back to see Kelly emerge at the top of the stairs.

"Christy sent me up to ask what the hell's going on." She stopped and surveyed the scene in front of us. "Um, what happened to the door and who's the kid?"

I turned towards the witch. "This is Gan. And she's what happened to the door."

It took a short while to gather everyone up in my apartment. While I waited for Sally to fetch Christy and Kelly to go wake up Sheila, Gan took it upon herself to walk back out to the limo which, upon closer look, I realized was adorned with Chinese diplomat flags. Once more, she stepped into the daylight as if it were no inconvenience at all.

When she returned, it was with two men – human thralls, judging by the way they struggled with the large metallic chest they carried.

"I thought it rude to arrive without bearing gifts," she said as they lugged it up the stairs. "Knowing your somewhat misguided proclivity against live cattle, I thought you would appreciate it."

Once they deposited it inside my apartment, Gan dismissed them with the barest wave of her hand. She walked over and flipped open the lid, revealing a full chest of ceramic jugs. I didn't need to open one to know what they contained, though. My nose instantly recognized the smell of blood.

It was more than enough to satisfy my and Sally's needs for at least a week, maybe more. Beyond that, well, if we still hadn't figured out a way to find Ed, we'd probably be so thoroughly fucked that it wouldn't matter.

More importantly, it could very well mean the difference between holding on to my humanity and devolving into what I feared most.

"Thank you, Gan." I said the words softly, more touched than even I realized.

"You are more than welcome, my love. I drained the finest virgins at my disposal for you."

And just like that, I was creeped out again. Good ole Gan. She had quite the talent for ruining any chance I had of ever growing fond of her. All in all, maybe that was a good thing, because the second I dropped my guard, she'd probably produce a shaman or something and have us declared married.

If that ever happened, I could see myself opting for the *til death do us part* clause in it.

"I had them secured in a highly insulated vessel," she continued, as if bleeding people dry was a particularly mundane topic. "I did not expect to find your home in any condition to support their storage, as ill-maintained as it normally is."

"Christy and her friends took care of that," I replied idly.

A sour look passed over Gan's face. "The witch?" Those two had hit it off on the wrong foot and had never quite gotten over it. Needless to say, if she had plans on staying, it would probably be best if they weren't roomies.

"And her new coven," I added. "They set up some

glowing ball thingee down in the basement. Keeps the lights on and all the electronics working. Also does wonders for dissuading intruders."

"I am not familiar with this *thingee* concept, my love."

"It's like a ball of energy, maybe a little smaller than a baseball." I made a circle with my hands to show her, just in case America's national pastime wasn't something that had made it to Outer Mongolia yet.

Her eyes widened slightly at my display. "White, but with shimmering colors occasionally visible?"

"I haven't spent too much time staring at it, but pretty much."

"Hmm. Such constructs are known as Xihe's Tears. Or, more commonly in this hemisphere, as Apollo's Prism."

"Um, okay."

"It is an impressive work of magic, essentially tearing a tiny hole in the fabric of reality. Very rare. I may have to revise my opinion of your witch ever so slightly."

Whoa, was that almost a compliment? It wasn't quite an invitation to be BFFs, but it was a far cry from her usual stance that Christy would be best off taking a permanent dirt nap.

"Assuming she doesn't do anything foolish with it," she added.

Oh, well, so much for that hope.

"I wouldn't worry too..."

"They are quite fragile and extremely dangerous if used ignorantly."

"Yeah, I get that. We had an incident with some home invaders..."

She raised an eyebrow. "Oh?"

"They sort of got melted."

"That is all?"

"It was pretty fucking brutal. Wait, what do you mean, is that all?"

"They were lucky."

"I'm pretty sure that's not the word I would use to describe them."

"I am talking about any remaining humans living close by."

"Yeah, it probably would have been bad had that thing sputtered out. Might have caused a fire or something."

She smiled ever so slightly at me, almost like how one might look with affection upon a particularly dim-witted dog. "Yes, it may have ... after it obliterated everything within a hundred-meter radius."

All of a sudden, being able to charge my laptop didn't seem like quite the luxury it had been.

8

IMPISH INTERROGATION

"**W**hat exactly do you mean by *obliterated*?"

"An implosion, actually, if my scholars are to be believed." Gan walked over to the bookshelf in the corner of our living room. It was covered in *Star Trek* novels and various horror paperbacks. She took a moment to look them over, then ran a finger over one of the wooden shelves. Okay, so maybe dusting wasn't exactly my strong suit. "As I said, it is a tear in reality, radiating energy from elsewhere."

"Elsewhere?"

"Another plane of existence. Should anything happen to disrupt it before it can dissipate naturally, that flow of energy would be reversed."

"And that would be bad?"

"It would be wise to not be nearby were that to occur."

We weren't supposed to play with the glowing thingee, but I'd envisioned it as more of the magical equivalent of a perpetual motion machine. I'd been too enamored with having cold beer to consider it might have more in common with a Sphere of Annihilation.

I was about to question her further about the nuke in my basement when the others arrived. Sally was first in the door.

"I see you were able to spare your whore from falling under Ib's compulsion."

Sally glared down at Gan as the others filed in. "Speaking of which, how do we know you're not still under her power?"

Gan waved her off as if that was a stupid question. However, it wasn't. When last we'd seen her, she'd been marching after Calibra, fully under her control.

"She has a good point, Gan."

"I will explain everything that I know for you, beloved."

Sally rolled her eyes before hooking a thumb toward the big cooler of blood sitting off to one side. "Grab us both a glass. If we have to sit here and listen to Rainbow Blight pontificate, we might as well not do so dry."

I tried really hard not to enjoy the blood while I watched the witches work. Despite it being quite good, I knew that whoever it belonged to was most likely no longer burdened by this mortal coil. Still, what was done was done. Pouring it down the drain wouldn't bring that person back to life. Heck, it might even save someone else if what I suspected about myself was true.

This wasn't the time for such thoughts, though, so I pushed them to the back of my head. Of far greater importance was Gan's sudden reappearance and what it meant for us. I didn't get the sense she was talking through a compulsion, her eyes bright and clear, but that didn't mean anything. Calibra was the oldest vampire of them all, in addition to being a master mage. That kind of combo meant there were certainly tricks up her sleeve we didn't know about.

There were also the Jahabich to consider. I shuddered a little at the thought. Don't get me wrong, I'd have sooner shoved a silver sword up my ass than marry the little creep, but even Gan deserved better than that fate.

Fortunately, though we might not have been privy to all of Calibra's secrets, we weren't fucking idiots either. Christy, in particular, was both cautious and not overly endeared to Gan to begin with.

She'd insisted upon a double protection circle – an inner one for Gan, and an outer one for the rest of us just in case the munchkin was little more than a distraction for an impending attack. While her sisters weaved their spells, Christy handed Gan two blades: a regular kitchen knife she'd purloined from my utensil drawer and a silvered dagger.

Gan, either understanding our precautions or playing along, objected to none of it.

I stood back near the edge holding Tom while all this went on. Sheila stood nearby, just past the outer circle, her powers being incompatible with the witches'. Though she assured me her aura was more than sufficient protection should anything go wrong, I still kept close. If something was going to happen, it would almost certainly be to the odd man – or woman – out in the group.

Finally, the prep work was finished. A bright column of purplish energy flared up around Gan, presumably trapping her where she was. A similar, if less brilliant, flash of light rose up around the perimeter of the outer circle, enclosing the rest of us in what I hoped was the real-life equivalent of a Protection from Evil spell.

Just for kicks, I tapped my finger against it, feeling a slight crackle of energy as if what was there was solid.

"Can you not do that?" Christy asked.

"Sorry."

"Dumbass," Sally said under her breath.

Christy turned back to Gan and indicated the two knives.

Gan, seeming to know what she meant, rolled up both of her sleeves. She took the first and cut a deep furrow in one wrist, then followed it up by several more slashes further up her arm. The cuts bled for a moment or two, then closed up. Definitely not a Jahabich.

"Now the other," Christy said.

Gan repeated the act with the silvered blade.

I waited for the fireworks. Silver possessed some weird incompatibility to vampire blood, the mix causing our insides to ignite like magnesium in water. In addition to hurting like fuck all, it also had the added effect of retarding our healing for a time.

However, the cuts on her arm bled normally, same as before, closing up just as quickly.

"Interesting," Gan said. "I had not expected that. One more benefit of the change."

The change?

"You sure that's not some cheap silver-plated knockoff?" Sally asked Christy.

"It's a solid silver athame," she replied while still facing Gan. "Please hand them over, hilt first."

Gan expertly spun the knives around so she was holding the blades. She held them out and their handles passed through the magical barrier. Christy stepped forward and took them. She then turned toward me. "If you will."

"If I will *what?*"

"It's time to take the Pepsi Challenge, genius," Sally said, causing Kelly and Meg to snort laughter.

Oh *that*. Yeah, I guess that would be the ultimate test of whether Gan was a rocky abomination. I was also the only one in the room, maybe the world, who could ingest vamp blood without hurling chunks.

I reached out and took the non-silver knife from Christy. No point in risking cutting my tongue and ending up with the equivalent of high-caliber Pop Rocks going off in my mouth.

"I would urge caution, my love," Gan said, drawing more snickers from the witches. They were still new to this circus. "I do not know if any incompatibilities were created in the process."

Well, that was disturbingly vague.

I glanced around and noticed all eyes were on me. Of course. "Um, the fire extinguisher is under the sink just in case anyone needs to know." I touched the tip of my tongue to the blood-streaked blade. I waited a moment for something bad to happen. When it became apparent my face wasn't going to blow off, I took a longer lick, then – before I could think of any of the thousand reasons why this was fucking stupid – swallowed.

Hmm, there was something ... different about it. I'd tasted my fair share of both vamp and human blood in the past year and this wasn't either. It wasn't far off, though. It almost tasted, it was hard to say, fizzy. Like vamp blood, but carbonated. It left a tingle on the tongue, which was to say much better than a fireball.

Then it hit my gut and there came the familiar bloom of heat, the feeling of my body supercharging itself. My strength increased, more than tripling, and with it my senses. Also, if everything else about Gan's blood held true...

Multiple voices asked if I was okay. In response, I crossed to the other side of the room faster than most of them could blink.

"Over here," I said as heads all whipped around to my new location. Well, except for Sally's. She'd seen that parlor trick before and didn't seem nearly as impressed as the others. "She's still a vampire."

"In that, my love," Gan replied, "I must respectfully disagree."

9

RISE OF THE DAY SPAWN

"Huh? What does that mean?" I asked. "What happened to you? How did you escape? How are you not dust? Is Ed okay? Is..."

"If you will please allow me, beloved," Gan interrupted, "I will answer what I can."

Okay, maybe I'd gotten a bit carried away there. "Fine, let's start with that last one. My roommate, my friend Ed. We still need to save him, stop them from doing whatever they had planned. Please tell me there's still time."

"I am sorry to say that you are far too late."

"What?!"

"His fate has already been met out."

Her words hit me like a chair to the face. "That can't be right. I mean, there has to be some sort of ritual or something. There's *always* a ritual. The moon has to be full, the stars aligned ... something, so that we can swoop in at the last moment. That's how things are *supposed* to work."

Silence met my rant for a moment and I looked around the room to see sadness and pity on everyone's faces. Everyone's, that is, except Gan's.

"I am not aware that *things* work in any such manner. Ib completed the ritual, as you call it, mere hours after collapsing the Boston prefecture. Wisely so, in my opinion. She is no fool."

"So Ed is..."

"Fully realized."

"Wait, does that mean dead?"

"No."

"But you said..."

"Exactly what I said. She forced him to drink human blood, just as Vehron had been about to when I disrupted his plans."

I opened my mouth, but Sally spoke up first. "Let those of us who speak human take a turn." Then to Gan, she asked, "So what happened after they gave him the blood?"

Gan, for her part, seemed nonplussed. She clasped her hands behind her back and appeared quite relaxed for someone in a magical prison. "He became as us, except not so. Ib referred to him as a purified strain."

"A purified strain." Sally rolled the words over her tongue for a moment. "Of vampire?"

"And what were you doing while all of this was happening?" Christy asked.

"Obeying as I had been compelled to, witch. Ib's mind is like no other I have ever encountered. My father used to compel me often so that I might learn to resist the wishes of my elders. I dare say, even the Wanderer might find himself hard pressed to command me. Not that he would dare."

"Focus, Gan."

"I am quite focused, my love, I can assure you. Ib's power, however, is immense. I could not even begin to fight her control. I suspect the same was true of any she had abducted. We were slaves to her will. But, slave or not, I was never compelled to forget and so have full recollection of all the events that transpired."

"Okay," Sheila said, her voice somewhat muffled from her place outside of the magical barrier. "Let's focus on the important part. Ed is still alive, in a manner of speaking. No offense."

"None taken," I replied. "I assume he's one of Ib's slaves now, too?"

"You assume incorrect, Dr. Death," Gan said. "Your friend may not be the most impressive specimen of our kind I have ever seen, but he remains quite immune to Ib's compulsions."

"He's still immune?" I asked, amazed. Following his miraculous, and somewhat confusing, resurrection at Sheila's hands, Ed had changed. On the outside, he was still the same disaffected guy he'd always been, but there'd been two little tidbits that stood out. His blood had somehow been infused with faith magic, making it deadly to vampires. Secondly, he seemed not only unaffected by vampiric compulsions, but pretty oblivious to them. Wish I could have said the same. Though I couldn't be controlled, they were like a sonic boom going off in my head.

"It was as if he did not even hear her commands," Gan confirmed.

"Sweet. So if she couldn't control him, then why didn't he...?"

"I did not say she could not control him. Though unique, once the change was complete, your friend appeared to have no more power than any other of the freshly turned. Surrounded by enemies, in the presence of our progenitor and trapped far below ground, where was he to go? No, Ib was not so easily thwarted. The best your friend seemed able to do was utilize his somewhat colorful knowledge of metaphor. Tell me, my love, what is a twat-waffle?"

"Um, it's an American breakfast specialty."

Exasperated sighs from around the room met my lame answer.

"Though I need no sustenance other than blood, if you enjoy these twat-waffles, then I would be pleased to sample them, beloved."

"Uh, sure. After we're done, I'll grill some right up."

"Much as I'd love to continue discussing the breakfast habits of the sad and pathetic, can we please keep some focus here?" Sally asked. "I didn't get nearly enough beauty sleep today for tangents."

"On that I would agree, whore," Gan casually remarked.

One of my kitchen chairs sailed across the room to shatter harmlessly against the magical barrier surrounding Gan. The little freak, for her part, didn't even blink.

"Hey!" I cried. "Can we not do that to my furniture? Do you know how hard it is to find matching replacements?"

"Have you tried the bargain bin at IKEA?" Sally asked contemptuously.

"Where do you think we got it to begin with?" Tom answered.

We so needed to find a different gathering place than my apartment. It was surely easier than investing in cast iron furniture.

"Okay, so Ed was turned into some sort of vampire that can't be controlled, but this Ib chick had her goons to keep him in line anyway," Meg said, ignoring all of the inane chatter and, thankfully, steering us back on course. "How does this explain you? I haven't been dealing with vamps for too long, but one thing I do know for certain is that sunlight seriously fucks with their day."

Gan's eyes barely twitched in her direction. "Up until recently, I might have considered agreeing with you, witch. I am quite learned in our history, and for as long as our kind have existed, we have been a species consigned to the darkness. So far as I am aware, The Destroyer was the only one of our kind with any sort of natural tolerance and he, being a Freewill, was obviously a unique specimen. Those he sired did not inherit this ability."

"Sucks to be them," I commented.

"Once, long ago, it was considered the highest honor to be turned by a Freewill, my love."

"And then Bill arrived," Sally added.

I casually flipped a middle finger her way, then turned my focus back to Gan. "So, Ed; can he...?"

"I do not know. As I believe I have already mentioned,

we were deep underground in the Jahabich lair. Though she appeared interested in the limits of your friend's power, at no point that I am aware of did she bring him up to the surface. I have little doubt she realized the risk in doing so."

I glanced around the room and saw the same knowing look being returned. Much as I hated to admit it, Gan was right. Taking Ed out of her personal Fortress of Solitude would have been just the move we needed to locate and confront her, a move she'd denied us. Calibra was old beyond imagining, and one didn't get that old by being stupid. "So where do you come into all of this?"

"Ib wasted no time in testing your friend's new abilities, including his viability as a sire. She had no shortage of human thralls to pick from, but she also wished to test against one who was already of our kind."

"But why you?" Sheila asked.

"I am not privy to her thoughts on the matter, but if I were in her position, I would have chosen a vampire of advanced, but not extreme age. Such a test subject would potentially yield a more powerful convert, but if the experiment failed, it would not have wasted her most potent troops."

"Makes sense."

"Additionally," Gan continued, turning toward me, "her position within the Boston Prefecture no doubt gave her access to all of their considerable intelligence. She would most likely know of our mutual fondness for one another, beloved."

"Uh, yeah. About the definition of mutual..."

"She would know that an emotion as strong as love is a potential factor in overcoming a compulsion." I was starting to fidget uncomfortably now. "In addition, you have proven yourself a thorn in her side. Those factors combined, I could see how she might think I would be more expendable than some of the others under her control. If her experiment failed, then you would be injured. If it succeeded, she could command me to infiltrate your forces."

"And yet here you are," Christy said, an edge working its way into her voice.

"Indeed," Gan replied with an increasingly creepy smile. "And Ib would have certainly foreseen the use of these precautions, as you might call them, thus rendering them impotent to one sent to act as spy ... or assassin."

She lifted her hands and began to press against the purple energy around her, causing sparks to fly. "Of course, she would have chosen the latter, for there is no need to have eyes and ears amongst your foes when they are already dead."

PINT-SIZED PROBLEMS

"Fortunately, that did not come to pass," Gan finished, lowering her now charred hands back to her side.

There was a momentary beat of stunned silence in the room. If that was Gan's idea of a joke, then her sense of humor needed serious work. I could very well imagine Christy and her friends deciding to incinerate her on her poor sense of drama alone.

"What happened?" I quickly asked.

"Ib chose me and a human thrall. Your roommate was forced to feed upon us both. I remember there being pain, much worse than I am accustomed to, almost as if fire had been injected into my veins. As this was occurring, Ib commanded me to return to her once I awakened."

"Then what?"

"Then, beloved, I died for the second time in my long life."

"Wait. What do you mean?"

"Shh," Sally hissed. "Shut up. This is the good part. Go on, Gan. Tell us about you being dead. Gives us all something to strive for."

Gan raised an eyebrow toward her but simply said, "For a time, I knew nothing. It was disconcerting, not at all pleasant." She then looked my way again, her eyes gleaming. "But I held on to my memory of you. So long as you walk this earth, I knew I would find my way back to you."

"Awww, that's sweet," Veronica replied.

"Yeah, if this were a Harlequin Romance, maybe," I groused, "and I was someone else."

"I awoke to a strange warmth," Gan continued, ignoring us. "At first, I thought a fire must have been set nearby, but as I gradually came to, I saw the light beyond my closed eyelids. I realized it was the sun shining down upon me, such a long forgotten memory."

"Bet that freaked you the fuck out," Tom said.

"Should the time of my death arrive, I shall face it with the dignity of one of my lineage. I accepted my fate and calmly waited to be consumed. But, as I believe is testament to my being here, that did not happen."

"So what did?" Sally asked, a note of impatience in her voice. It seemed the good part was over for her.

"I sat up to find myself and the human thrall on a hillside clearing just beyond a cave entrance. It was apparent that while we slumbered, we'd been carried up to the surface and left there."

"Harsh," Tom said.

"And ultimately foolish," Gan replied. "Perhaps Ib's first real mistake. Not only were we still alive under the glare of the sun, but her voice was gone from my mind. Her compulsion was erased. My will was my own again. I have no doubt it was a side effect she did not anticipate."

"So you and the thrall decided to hightail it outta there?"

"I am uncertain what 'hightail' means, beloved, but I alone sought to make contact with those loyal to me so as to find you. As for the thrall, I dispatched him."

"Wait, why?"

"Though free of Ib's compulsion, he'd no doubt been conditioned by her much longer. There was a fair chance his will was still subservient to hers. Rather than test that resolve, I thought it best to eliminate the potential loose end. Fortunately, I still retained the power of one my age, whereas he possessed strength commensurate to his own. It was over within seconds."

Somehow, I didn't find that surprising. I was more of a live and let live type of guy. She leaned more toward dusting anyone who didn't have immediate use to her. In this case, though, perhaps it was the smarter choice. "So Calibra doesn't know what happened?"

"At the time, mayhap. However, I would consider it a near certainty for her to try the experiment again, perhaps with greater precautions."

Sally leaned forward, seemingly interested again. "So you can't be compelled?"

Before Gan could answer, though, I jumped ahead of the queue. "Alex and the Draculas – do they know?"

Gan laughed, the sound high and musical as if she found my question genuinely amusing. "Do you think for even a moment that he would tolerate my existence – a vampire he cannot control? Even if he did, I would still be tainted in his eyes from my time with Ib. He would no doubt think I was still under her control and thus incapable of being trusted."

"Oh, so you came straight here from..."

"How do we know you're not under her control?" Christy asked bluntly.

"What do you mean?" Kelly replied, but I already knew the answer.

Calibra was the first vampire and thus the oldest. The thing was, I didn't even have scale to know what that meant. Alex was previously the oldest vamp I was aware of, over two millennia in age. However, the Humbaba Accord – the pact that once held the fragile peace between the vampire nation and the Feet – dated back about five thousand years. Who the fuck knew how long our first war with them had gone on for or what happened before that? Best-case scenario, Calibra was over twice Alex's age.

I'd just barely been able to snap Sally out of Alex's thrall and only after I'd gone all Hulk Smash on everyone's shit. To be able to do the same to one of Calibra's compulsions, I'd probably have to line up elder vamps around the block. Which meant that if everything Gan was saying was bullshit, the chances of snapping her out of it were slim and none.

And slim was on the first bus out of town.

"An astute observation, witch," Gan said. "Alas, all I can offer you is my word that my will is mine and mine alone." She then proceeded to tell the group pretty much what I'd been thinking.

"And if she did that much," Sally replied, "then it's safe to say she would have been smart enough to insulate you from the compulsions of others, up to and including Alexander."

"Yeah," I concurred, "and unfortunately, I don't know five thousand years' worth of vampires willing to both let me bite them and keep their fucking mouths shut about Gan's ability to tan."

"I could enter her mind," Christy offered. "When Sally was compelled by Alex, I worked with her on that, helping to unravel the strands. At the very least, I know what to look for now."

"Unacceptable," Gan replied.

"It won't be a walk in the park for me either; trust me on that."

"While the whore might have been content to allow you access to her deepest thoughts, I am not. I dare say you might find my mind somewhat more complex. Regardless, I shall not allow..."

An empty glass hit the force field surrounding Gan, where it shattered into multiple molten pieces. "Fuck you," Sally spat. "Sorry to break it to you, Pippi Shortstocking, but there's nothing overly complex about having memorized the season schedule of SpongeBob."

Her outburst gave me an idea, and not just on how to

keep her from breaking all my stuff. "Wait, what about extreme emotions? Those worked with you, Sally."

Her left eye twitched ever so slightly. Needless to say, reminding her of her time as Alex's slave was probably gonna be a sore spot for a while to come. "It worked partially," she said through gritted teeth.

"Doesn't matter. It was enough to snap you out of it at least part way. Think about it." I turned to address the whole room. "Even if it doesn't work the same, it might at least tell us if she's under Calibra's control or not."

"Extreme emotion?" Gan asked curiously.

"Yeah. Anger, pain, massively spiteful shit. Stuff like that."

"While I will admit to looking forward to the end of this interrogation, I must confess I am feeling none of those things, my darling. Your presence calms me and even if you were not here, unlike your whore, I am in full control of my emotions."

Yeah, right. So sayeth the evil munchkin who once ordered a man to commit suicide because he fired one extra arrow.

"We could try pain," Christy offered.

"I think we are both aware that my tolerance exceeds anyone's in this room by a fair margin." From the tone of Gan's challenge, I had little doubt she was reminding Christy of their first (nearly disastrous) meeting.

"Everyone has a limit," Christy replied frostily. "I think you'll find my sisters and me more than adept at testing those limits."

Veronica and Kelly looked somewhat uncomfortable with the offer. Meg, well, she just shrugged as if to say she'd try anything once.

That set off a round of bickering between Gan and Christy, pretty much centering on who could dish it out and who could take it.

"Blast her good, babe!" Tom added, doing his best to make the situation even worse.

"I think we should let her try," Sally casually remarked to me.

Sheila said something from behind us, but the energy barrier muffled it and I was too distracted to pay attention.

"Not you too," I replied absently. As much as it amazed me to be the voice of reason, I didn't want us to get caught up in some crazed torture porn – no matter how amusing it might be – not with Ed in need of saving. Still, if she was compromised, then we were in even deeper shit than we thought. Hell, if that were the case, what was to stop Calibra from sending James here next? With them as day-walkers, we would be fucked worse than a greased pig at a hillbilly hoedown.

"Listen everyone," I said, raising my voice almost to a shout. "Even if she is Calibra's thrall, there's no way to..."

My voice trailed off as the outer barrier of magic flashed in intensity and winked out of existence.

I spun to find that Sheila had stepped forward.

Her aura sprang to life around her, a blaze of white fire that cancelled out magic and did even worse things to vampires. "She's not Calibra's thrall."

"And you know this *how*?" I asked, confused.

"It's simple. Because I am."

11

YOU ONLY HURT THE ONES

Before I could so much as open my mouth to ask what the fuck she was talking about, Sheila slammed a shoulder into my mid-section. The blow itself would have barely budged me under different circumstances, but then most people didn't have an anti-vamp energy field around them. The faith magic added the force of a runaway truck to her attack. Lucky me.

Tom flew out of my hand with a curse as I sailed backward and slammed into the far wall, denting the plaster good and proper.

Sheila didn't give me a moment to breathe. She raced forward, grabbed hold of my collar, and drew me close. Her lips moved, but no sound issued forth. For a second, I thought maybe my ears had been roasted off, but then I realized I could still hear numerous protests of the "What the fuck?!" variety from the others in the room.

"Huh?" I asked, still dazed.

"By the glory of Ib, you have to die," she snarled, this time loud and clear. "Your destiny ends now!" Her fist connected with my jaw. *Ouch!*

"I don't know what she did to you, but you need to…"

She spun and kicked my legs out from under me. I went down and she jumped on top. Under different circumstances,

I'd have been sporting major wood, but the only wood I felt was my head clonking against the floor as she struck me again.

"Stop it!"

"Jesus Christ, Sheila. What are you doing?"

Despite the crowd being on my side, it didn't look like any backup would come. Magic couldn't penetrate her aura, and Sally would be burnt to a crisp as surely as I was...

Wait, I actually wasn't on fire. Sure, I was getting pretty singed, but I should have been a four-alarm blaze by now. Was her power slipping?

Another hit to my face knocked that revelation out of my immediate concern. Instead, my fangs descended. There came another blow and I was pretty sure my eyes blackened, too. Rage started to suffuse my being with every hit I took.

This bitch! She'd attacked me. Betrayed us all ... betrayed *me*. And then what? Once she was finished with me, was her plan to turn on the rest – on Sally, Christy, on Christy's unborn baby?

I spat blood, but that was fine. It matched everything else in the room as a red haze began to descend over my vision.

I had no way of knowing if Sheila had been enslaved by Calibra or if she was acting of her own free will for whatever reason, but with a slight shudder of horror, I realized perhaps I didn't care.

All the anger and frustration I'd felt building in me the last couple of days was coming to a head. I couldn't help myself, and I wasn't sure I wanted to.

Another blow struck me and a faint echo of laughter sounded somewhere. It took me only a moment to realize it was coming from inside my head. The thing was, I understood why and actually wanted to join it.

Sheila raised her fist again.

But first, there was someone who needed to be taught the last lesson of her life.

Sheila's punch struck me, but I brushed it off. She was weak. Icons; so much ado about nothing after all. Now it was *my* turn.

I reached up and grabbed her by her arms. The two-inch talons that had replaced my fingernails dug into her flesh like a hot knife into butter.

Her eyes opened wide in surprise and pain, and a moment later, her screams followed.

"Enough!" a voice commanded.

Before I could rip Sheila's arms off and bathe in her blood, Gan appeared above us. Somehow, she'd escaped her magical prison cell. In the back of my mind, I considered that should probably have been a concern for me, but it seemed insignificant, as did she in the moment.

Gan grabbed Sheila by the collar of her shirt and flung her off me, robbing me of my prize. Sheila's aura flared up in response and caught both of us in its lethal light, but I barely felt it. My own power was already busy repairing any damage the white fire caused.

I leapt nimbly to my feet, preparing to close the distance between us and finish this once and for...

"I said, enough!" Gan spun and lashed out at me with a spinning kick. As luck would have it, her size put her at the perfect height for her foot to smash mercilessly into my balls, instantly taking the fight out of me.

Down I went to my knees, just barely able to wheeze out a pained "Fuuuuuck!"

"Goddamn it!" Sally cried. "I didn't get my camera out in time. Any chance of you doing that again?"

What?!

I glanced up, tears streaming down my face, and looked around. The room was in disarray. Gan stood in front of me, her green eyes defiant and the rest of her mostly unharmed despite being bathed in the same faith aura I had been. Christy and two of her sisters were on their feet, a mix of anger and panic in their eyes. Kelly was kneeling down where Sheila had landed.

The only one who seemed out of place, mainly because she was still seated in hers, was Sally. She was putting an iPhone back into her pocket and looked to be on the verge of laughter.

The fuck?

"My apologies," Gan said, drawing my attention back to her. "Though you appeared quite intent on your course of action, I am forced to disagree with your assessment that the time for your final battle is now."

I realized the anger had drained out of me, pretty much in the same instant my manhood had been reduced to oatmeal. Clarity of thought rushed in to fill the void the rage had left behind. Staggering to my feet, I clapped Gan once on the shoulder, then stepped past her to where Sheila was just now sitting up, blood flowing freely from ten ugly puncture wounds on her arms.

Almost simultaneously, we shouted at each other, "What the hell were you thinking?!"

"Jinx," Sally called out. "You both owe me a drink."

I glanced back and forth between them, half-tempted to throw a chair at Sally for her infuriating smirk, but not sure which of them deserved it more.

"You almost tore my arms off," Sheila said. "What is wrong with you?"

"Yeah, way to go, asshole," Kelly spat.

"What is wrong with *me*? You're the one who went batshit psycho."

"Like I *said* I was going to."

"What? Have you lost your mind? No you didn't."

"Yeah," Sally said. "Actually, she did. I heard her loud and clear. It pays to have an attention span."

"And then I mouthed for you to play along, just in case you didn't hear me the first time," Sheila added.

That gave me pause and I remembered what I'd written

off as a wordless snarl. "Um, I'm not really good at reading lips."

"No shit," she snapped before turning to Kelly. "I'm okay. Let me take care of this." With that, she basically hugged herself and began to glow, the white aura washing over her and closing the wounds I'd made.

The white light, however, quickly became washed out as another glow began to suffuse the room – a red one. It was coming from Christy. "That is quite enough from all of you. The only thing I want to see moving from anyone in this room are their lips. *Is that clear?*"

Tom's exclamation of "Yeah, kick everyone's ass! Just like River Tam!" diluted her threat ever so slightly.

"Not now," she hissed.

"It's okay. I'm calm now." I raised my hands in a placating manner. "We're all calm, right?"

Nods came from around the room, except from Gan, who merely crossed her arms indifferently.

Christy pointed at Sheila. "Start explaining."

"Ib," Sheila said. "And no, I'm not a thrall of hers in case anyone hasn't figured that out yet, but we didn't know if *she* was or not." She indicated Gan, who inclined her head slightly.

Christy didn't look convinced. "I'm pretty sure we already crossed that bridge."

"Yes, we did, but we left out one very important detail."

"And what detail was that?"

"Simple," Sheila said, rising to her feet slowly. "You all forgot about love."

12

TWAT WAFFLES

I lamely covered up my gasp of surprise as a cough. Did she just say…?

"Not following," Meg replied.

"She gets it." Sheila hooked a thumb at Sally, who nodded wordlessly.

Glad to see they had their female telepathy worked out. Maybe we were in luck and their periods had synced up from living together, too. As for the rest of us, I crossed my arms and waited.

"All of this talk of compulsions and breaking them with strong emotions. You all immediately went to the negatives – hatred and pain. The thing is, that doesn't work with everyone."

Sally's jaw tightened in response.

"What we all forgot," Sheila continued," and believe me, it's really easy to forget these days, is love."

"The strongest emotion of them all," Veronica said, a wistful look on her face that told me she probably had a bookshelf full of romance novels.

"Exactly," Sheila replied. "I won't pretend to know Gansetseg very well, but it's pretty darn obvious she has strong feelings for a certain someone in this room."

"She is talking about you, beloved," Gan said, stepping to

my side. Her longing smile was more than enough to make my skin crawl.

"Yeah, kinda guessed that." I took a long step away, probably risking a fireball from Christy, but it was worth it. That's when realization struck me. I turned toward Sheila. "So if she thought I was in actual danger..."

"That might snap her out of it," she finished.

"Even if it didn't," Sally added, a bitter undertone in her voice, "there might have been a partial reaction, a convulsion or something to tell us that there was a compulsion in place."

That seemed to mollify Christy, at least enough for her death glow to fade away. A sheen of sweat remained on her face, however, indicating the strain. Pregnant, stressed, and now constantly working on something in our basement, this chick was on her way to a breakdown if she didn't remember to take five once in a while.

"Since I was kinda occupied," I asked, "how did that play out?"

"Nothing compulsion-related that I could see," Sally replied. "She broke out and then broke up your fight. So either she's clean, she didn't buy it, or she isn't into you as much as she claims."

That caught Gan's attention and her eyes flashed ... err, yellow, actually. Hmm, that was new. Still, she had the emotional stability of a stepped-on rattlesnake, so I quickly moved in front of her. "She was just testing you again, *right*?" I glanced over my shoulder at Sally, who just shrugged. "Yeah, a test. And, look, you passed. So let's get back to what we were discussing. How's that sound?"

"I don't know about the rest of you, but I could use some coffee while we talk," Kelly said.

"Works for me. A bite to eat wouldn't hurt either," Meg replied. "Right, Christy?"

Meg's eyes locked with mine for a split second and in them I saw a clear hint of worry. I didn't doubt she sensed the same strain in Christy that I had.

"Yeah," I quickly added. "We can finish the rest of this over some breakfast."

"If that is what you wish, then I agree, my love," Gan said. "Perhaps you can make some of those twat waffles you told me about. I would so love to try them."

After the chuckling had finally subsided and copious apologies were shared around the room, Sheila and Meg worked on whipping up some food for us in my kitchen nook. It was quite awesome of them since I was tits on a bull when it came to doing anything more complex than boiling water. Between me and my roommates, it was a near wonder we hadn't starved to death.

Christy volunteered to help, but the other two witches steered her toward a chair. She put up a minor protest, but once seated, it looked like her body had decided she was in for the long haul.

Finally, we were all set, plates in hand. It was syrup for most of our group, but blood for the three undead among us, albeit I had no idea whether Gan needed it to survive anymore. Nevertheless, it didn't stop her from pouring a generous helping over her food and chowing down.

"How's it taste?" I asked.

"These twat waffles are different from what I am used to, but I find them quite adequate."

"I meant the bl ... oh, never mind." The quiet snickers from around the room told me that if we had any chance of moving forward with this conversation, it would need to be on a different topic.

Fortunately, Christy was on the ball. "What Bill probably means to ask is whether you can lead us back to the cave they brought you out of."

"Of course," Gan replied. "It would do us little good, though. Ib's forces are well aware of it. I have little doubt it would be heavily guarded, assuming she did not have the

Jahabich collapse it once it became obvious what had occurred. No, there were many other entrances to their lair, some more trafficked than others. We would do far better to find one that is less traveled. Albeit, there is little chance that *any* exist that would grant us passage without running into at least marginal resistance."

"Some is better than all," I offered. "Besides, we're the beggars here. We can't be choosy. If she turns all of the vamps she kidnapped, it's gonna be bad."

"For her," Gan replied.

"Excuse me?"

"Your habit of feigned ignorance when it is obvious you heard what I said is quite adorable, my love, but perhaps we can save it for another time."

"Who said Bill's playing?" Sally asked between mouthfuls.

"Were Ib to turn all of the vampires under her thrall," Gan continued, "it would prove detrimental to her cause. If I am immune to compulsion, then it is logical to assume others would be as well. Though Vehron had many true followers in his grasp, I have no doubt that an equal number followed him out of little more than fear. Freed and with the Wanderer present to rally them, they could pose a potential threat to Ib."

I got up to refill my glass. "That's good."

"An insignificant threat, mind you."

"That's bad."

"But a threat nevertheless. Though your friend might be pure, he is not perfect."

"I could've told you that," Tom said from his spot propped up on the kitchen counter.

"What I mean is," Gan clarified, putting down her fork, "though the Cult of Ib has preached freedom in the past, it would ill serve her at this juncture. In order to topple the First, she must be able to assert a modicum of control. Without it, her odds of success are even at best, and that is being generous."

I returned to my seat and sat back down. Damn, should have grabbed myself a few more waffles while I was up. "But with her power..."

"It still would prove inadequate. The remainder of the First are even now doubling their precautions against her. It might be enough to counter her power of compulsion or it might not. However, even if they fail, that does not greatly help her."

"Why not?" I asked, getting up to fill my plate again.

"Because compulsion is finite," Sally said.

"The whore is correct," Gan replied, drawing a dirty look despite her pseudo-compliment. "Why do you think Alexander has not simply chosen to directly control the world's masses? It is because he can't. Ib took control of those present in the northern prefecture, a feat even Alexander would have been hard pressed to perform single-handedly. I would wager that even if that were not the limit of her powers, then it was close. Were the First to attack her with an army, she could potentially sway a portion of them, but not the entirety."

"What if she grabbed hold of the generals?" Sheila asked.

"A logical assumption, Shining One," Gan replied. If she harbored any ill will toward Sheila from earlier, it didn't show. "But the generals, as you might call them, would be protected by the heaviest counter-compulsions. They would also be of superior age to their troops, thus more resistant. No matter the scenario, compulsion alone cannot win the war for Ib. I suspect that is at least partially why she has chosen to remain hidden all these centuries."

"And if her troops were completely immune to compulsion, that would pretty much make the entire point moot," Sally added. "Although I doubt Alexander would be too fond of that himself. Would mean he'd have to do things the old fashioned way – lead the troops and hope they didn't decide to go the friendly fire route."

"Indeed. This new development favors Ib's strategy, but it is not yet a winning gambit."

"So we make it ours," Sally said. "We rally every vamp that's sick of this compulsion shit and make them immune once and for all."

I sat and reached for the syrup. "It has potential."

"Good," she replied, grabbing the bottle and holding it just out of my reach, "because I'm volunteering to be the first recruit."

"Wait, what?" I asked. "Let's not be hasty. We don't know what..."

"No, *you* don't know what it would do to you. You're the Freewill, and there's no telling how that would fuck up your powers ... more than they already are anyway. But for me, the choice is pretty simple."

"Yeah, but..."

"Fuck the buts!" She stopped and looked around at the wide-eyed stares. "Grow up. You know what I mean. We're talking freedom here, Bill. Do you even understand what that means for most of us?"

"Um, well..."

"Trust me, you don't. The worst you have to deal with is a migraine if someone mind-fucks you. The rest of us, we're little more than slaves. Marlene, Jeff, Alexander; they're all the same. They give vampires like me an order and we have no fucking choice but to obey. Do you know what it's like to have your will utterly subsumed? Do you know how it feels to betray people you care about without even blinking, all because someone else had a whim to do so?"

I had no idea who Marlene was, but it seemed safe to assume she was another vamp Sally knew. Besides, interrupting to ask sounded like a good way to get a punch in the face. I knew Sally was upset about what Alex had done to her, but now that it was coming out, I began to understand how badly I'd underestimated it.

"For over a quarter of a century I've been little more than

a slave, and I'm a baby compared to some. Sure, there are plenty who drink the Kool Aid, but there are so many more who don't have a choice. The whole system, both sides, could be taken down. Alex and Ib could be sent to the Hell they deserve along with any of their sycophants."

The pain radiated off her in near palpable waves. She was too tough to cry, but I could see even that was a struggle for her. So many years of building up a wall around herself, she struggled to tear it down even among friends. She needed the mother of all hugs, but, sadly for her, I couldn't.

Because she was wrong.

"It's not that simple," I said.

"What?"

"This freedom you're talking about. Sure, in the short term it might be a good thing, but in the long term it's..."

"A fucking disaster?" Tom offered.

"Pretty much."

"Now explain why," he then added. "Because I don't get it."

Ugh, such a doofus.

"Bill's right," Sheila said, all eyes turning toward her. "It would be chaos. An army of super powered beings unleashed against the world without any checks against them. No sun, no masters to order them back into the shadows. Lots of people would die."

"Lots of people are dying right now," Sally responded.

"That's not all," I said, hating myself a bit for doing so. "History has proven what happens when you have one group with more influence or power than another."

"An underclass," Kelly said. "Humanity would be relegated to a sub species – second class citizens."

"Or slaves," Sheila added.

"I can't believe we're fucking arguing this," Sally spat.

"I am forced to concur with the ... with Sally," Gan said, showing a rare display of tact. "Albeit, perhaps for different reasons."

"I kind of figured it was too good to be true," Sally replied.

"Compulsion has always been abused by the First and their delegates. It has led us to where we are today, why so many under The Destroyer's rule chose to stay there willingly."

I raised an eyebrow at her. This was the nutcase who'd ordered her men to commit seppuku for the barest of offenses, and she was preaching how much of a crutch compulsion was to the Dracs?

Gan turned to me, almost as if reading my mind – a concept I found ever so slightly creepifying. "My father taught me to use compulsion as a tool, a weapon if need be. However, it was to be used sparingly for control. My people are raised to know what it is to be loyal."

"Loyal?" Why didn't it surprise me that Gan, of all people, didn't quite see that supernatural compulsion and good old-fashioned brainwashing were the same fucking thing? Her method might be slightly less icky in the long run, but it still involved a lifetime of people being put in their place by those who thought themselves their betters. I was about to point this out, but Sally was quicker on the draw.

"Good. Never thought I'd be saying this, but we're in agreement on this one." She glanced my way. "We can discuss boring shit like ethics later. For now, we have two devils, neither of which is really the lesser of evils. They need to be dealt with and I want to be the first recruit in this new army."

Gan nodded. "Yes, we are in agreement. Alas, while this is a fascinating discussion, it is all elementary at best. The answer is no."

Sally stood up, grabbed the table she was sitting at with Sheila and Kelly, and flipped it over. As loud as the resulting crash was, though, her voice was louder. "What?!"

Holy crap. I'd never guessed Gan to side with the logic that humans shouldn't be enslaved, especially since she had designs to enslave them. Before I could say anything, however, she held up a placating hand.

"It is not because I am unwilling," she said slowly. "It is because I cannot. Whatever the process was that changed me, it has rendered me a mule, infertile. In short, I can no longer turn anyone into one of us."

13

TWO MULES FOR SISTER SHEILA

"Wait, you can't turn anyone? How do you know?"

"Is it not obvious, my love? All that we are discussing now, I realized it prior to coming here."

"You tried it, didn't you?"

"Of course. Many times, against both cattle and our kind."

"What happened?"

"The humans bled out. The vampires healed as they normally would. Alas, I am slightly embarrassed to admit that the effect of ingesting our blood has not changed for whatever it is I have become."

The thought of Gan locked in a bathroom, puking her guts out, was enough to give me cheerful pause for a moment.

That gave Sally a chance to jump back in and she wasn't happy. "Why the fuck did you let me get my hopes up, then? Why didn't you fucking say so earlier?"

"It was neither my intention nor concern to affect anyone's expectations. As for your latter question, I believe you were the ones interrogating me. So why did you not think to ask?"

I stepped between them before Sally could do something

she might regret, almost losing my footing in a puddle of syrup in the process. Ugh, that was gonna be a pain to mop up later. "But Ed…"

"Is capable of spreading this new strain, yes. In doing so, however, he renders a host such as myself incapable of siring."

"What about that thrall he turned?" Kelly asked.

"I do not know. His lifespan was tragically cut short before he was given the chance to procreate." Gan's eyes glittered, telling me she was once again attempting a joke. Thankfully, this one wasn't nearly so close to being disastrous as her last. Who knows? Maybe she was learning.

"That's a potential X-factor," Meg said.

"Yep," I replied. "But we can't worry about what we don't know. Think about it, though. Maybe this is a good thing for us." Hope started to form in the pit of my stomach. Premature, definitely, but from what I was hearing, maybe we weren't as late to the saving Ed party as I'd first thought. "Whatever Ed is, he's important to Ib and, honestly, I think I know why."

"Sunlight," Sally replied as if it were obvious.

"Yeah. An army of day-walkers changes the game, but the process isn't quite perfect. The whole compulsion thing, and now this. Calibra might be willing to create some more day-walking minions to go forth and wreak havoc, but until she can figure out a way past the limitations, she isn't going to sign up for the treatment herself. It would make no sense. Sure, she could take in a day at the beach, but she'd be incapable of controlling other vamps as well as making sparkly new day vamps."

"Day vamps," Tom said. "We should call them Damps. No, wait. Sunlight vamps, or sumps."

I ignored him. "If she did that, it would be one big step forward, but at least two steps back. What would that leave her as?"

Christy turned to me and looked as if she was about to

say something, but then glanced sidelong at Sheila and stopped herself.

It took me a moment, focused as I was on the new information we had, but then I remembered. Fuck! Everyone in the room was up to speed, except for Sheila. We'd purposely kept her in the dark about the fact that Calibra was not only the first vampire, but was also known in the mage community as Kala the White ... pretty much the real life equivalent of Merlin.

By Christy's reckoning, discovering that the vamps and Magi shared a common great-great grandma, one responsible for all sorts of nasty little acts throughout history, might be the catalyst that finally turned Sheila against them.

I didn't buy it, but arguing with a powerful witch who was both hormonal and grieving had seemed a one-way ticket to Hurtsville to me, a place I vacationed at far more than I really wanted to.

The problem was twofold. One, we all felt this was the endgame. Two, I'd seen enough B-movies to know that the best way to walk right into your bad ending was to do everything you could to avoid it. Keeping Sheila in the dark could just as easily backfire against us as anything else.

I tried to convey as much with my eyes, which I'm sure amounted to making me look like a fucking moron. A wordless battle of wills ensued between us. A subtle plea from me, an even more subtle shake of the head from her.

"You do realize, beloved, that your silent conversation with the witch is painfully obvious."

Fucking A!

Christy's eyes narrowed. Despite not saying anything, I'd pretty much spilled the beans that something needed to be said. There's a reason my mom stopped telling me what she'd gotten my dad for his birthday by the time I was five.

Oh, fuck it all. I was right in this case. Tom might have had his balls in her pocketbook, at least when he still had them, but it was time I extracted mine and screwed them back on. "We can't have any more secrets."

"Don't worry," Tom replied. "I'm sure everyone here already knows you're gay."

Gan turned to me. "I am glad to know my presence lightens your heart so."

Goddamn, I was surrounded by fucking morons.

"That's enough," Christy said quietly to her fiancé turned action figure. "You're probably right, Bill. I just..." Her hands went to her stomach.

"I know, but I promise you *nobody* here wants that to happen."

Christy's eyes met mine and in them I saw hope, but then – for just one moment – they hardened and I remembered what she'd said before we'd left to confront Vehron.

"I would kill every vampire, every Icon, every single decent person on this planet if it meant saving my baby."

She'd meant it, too. I just had to make sure it didn't come down to that.

"You want to do the honors?" she finally asked with a sigh.

"It's yours to tell," I said.

She nodded knowingly and turned to Sheila, who wore an expectant look upon her face. "Calibra ... Ib isn't just the first vampire. It's not nearly that simple."

"She's also Kala the White," Sheila replied without missing a beat. "Your law giver, if I recall correctly."

Holy shit! She'd figured it out? Someone remind me never to play a game of Clue with her. Judging by the wide eyes in the room, there were more than a few of our number surprised by this. Mind you, Gan did not appear to be one of them, little fucking know-it-all.

Christy appeared completely taken aback by this, but she quickly composed herself and replied, "She's more than just our law giver. She's the progenitor of the entire Magi way of belief. She's considered the first to have truly mastered the subtleties of magic. Everything we respect about life, nature, the balance of power..."

"Is all bullshit," Meg added bitterly, "since this bitch is apparently a total fucking psycho."

Christy glared at her for a moment but then nodded. "Unfortunately, that's true as well. Our entire existence is built upon a lie. The number one tenet all covened Magi are instilled with is that there are some lines that are not to be crossed. The circle of life is sacred." She turned and glanced sadly at Tom.

"Should I be singing *Hakuna Matata*?" he replied, blissfully clueless as always.

"No, dear," she replied with a small smile before turning back to Sheila. "Kala the White, for all of her sins as Ib, is also the creator of the Jahabich. She is the one who brought them forth. She found a way to capture the souls of her defeated enemies and enslave them in stone."

"Using The Source?" Sheila asked, one eyebrow raising.

"Okay, now this is getting spooky," I said.

"When?" Sally simply asked.

I turned to her. "When what?"

"Back in Boston," Sheila replied. "When you were all down in the ruins digging through the rubble."

"Yeah, and?"

"She was eavesdropping, genius," Sally said with an eye-roll.

Oh. Well, that kind of explained it. I'd gotten so used to doing it with my enhanced hearing, I sometimes forgot all you had to do was sneak close enough and keep quiet.

For a moment, Christy looked as if she was teetering on outrage, but then – quite suddenly – she started to laugh. I glanced at Sally, who shrugged. Even Christy's sisters seemed to be wondering if their leader had gone off the deep end.

"You okay there?" I finally asked.

"Yes," she replied, getting herself under control. "I just needed an outlet and these days, it's either laugh or cry."

"Glad it was the former."

"Me too." She turned to Sheila. "It's just that I was all set to scream out 'how dare you?' when I realized the utter ridiculousness of it. Not only was I keeping secrets from you, someone who I should trust, but I can't even say I've never tried to scry on anyone here." She then looked at me. "And with your hearing..."

"Hey, you'll notice I'm not casting any first stones," I replied.

"I can't help it if I hear well and everyone else talks loud." Sally's voice was nonchalant, but there was a grin upon her face.

"I really am sorry," Christy said. "I panicked when I found out about Calibra's true identity. All I could think about were the ramifications that would have among my people, among our position as a neutral party in this war, and..."

"And how I might think that one bad apple might mean the rest of the bunch was rotten and in need of pruning?" Sheila offered.

"Something like that."

"We shouldn't be held accountable for the sins of our forefathers, especially that far removed. While some of my former associates might prefer to think of the world in terms of black and white, I'm lucky enough to have had my eyes opened." She glanced my way for just a moment, so quickly I wouldn't have noticed had I so much as coughed. "Whoever she was or is, she's not you. I know that, and I would never hold you accountable for what she's done. And if anything ever did happen where I got possessed or somehow turned against you, I wouldn't hold it against anyone here if they did what needed to be done to stop me."

This time, she glanced my way and held my gaze, forcing me to remember the promise I'd made to her months back – that if she ever endangered Christy's child, I'd take her down. The unspoken implication was that she'd do the same if I ever went rogue.

My hope was that neither of us would ever need to call the other on their promise. Problem was, with all the chips falling into place and us seemingly being pulled by destiny, I had to pray it wasn't a hope that would prove to be futile.

14

OF FISTS AND FEET

Much hugging and such ensued.

With Gan in the room, that meant I had to be very nimble and ensure there was always a warm body between us at any given time. Not the easiest thing to do with someone as swift as she.

Sadly, despite the full stomachs and having the air cleared a bit, there was still a shadow hanging over us all. There were friends to be saved and, despite the revelations of the past few hours, we were still back to square one on how to find them.

The Source, the giant pool of Jahabich spooge, was somewhere far underground. It was both the home and former prison of the rock-encrusted fuckers. We'd originally thought it was located somewhere beneath Las Vegas, but Christy explained our folly. Vegas happened to reside over a fairly major ley line, basically the equivalent of a Magi power grid. It's why so many mages flocked there and, in general, why the place was so fucking quirky.

She'd done a little research into the legends surrounding the area and found that the Native Americans of the region seemed to be familiar with the Jahabich or creatures like them. That and the presence of the ley line suggested that perhaps the prison walls were thin there, creating a natural portal to allow both the occasional escapee and give Calibra a convenient spot to stage a full-on prison break.

Made about as much fucking sense to me as anything.

Unfortunately, Sally and me had pretty much blown the shit out of the entrance, thinking we were sealing the Jahabich in for good. Doing so had brought down the cave, and – as Christy explained – almost certainly disrupted the magic within it. Same apparently with the tunnel Calibra had used to escape from the Boston complex.

This wasn't an issue for Calibra, Christy surmised. She'd tapped into The Source to create the Jahabich. She was in tune with it. Opening a new way there would probably be as easy for her as using a GPS would be for the rest of us. Sadly, she was the only one with this particular address.

Knowing how it probably worked was one thing, but it didn't really give us anything even remotely close to a lead. Calibra was magically masking her presence. Even if she hadn't been, The Source was considered nothing more than a legend by the Magi. If it was so easy to trace back, then surely others would have done so many times in the past.

After realizing we were banging our heads against the proverbial wall, Christy and her sisters excused themselves to head back to the basement, taking Tom with them. I could only hope that whatever they were doing down there would provide us with a lead soon.

After the witches left, Sally decided to go back to bed, although I had a feeling it was just an excuse to not hang out with Gan longer than necessary. She'd rapidly lost interest in the little psycho after Gan revealed she couldn't transfer her new abilities.

Sheila said that since she was up, she might as well stay up. She stuck around to help me clean up the place, which was cool since Gan didn't seem overly inclined to do much more than gaze at me creepily.

I think she'd meant to help with the mess left from breakfast, but once we got started, Sheila began wrinkling her nose at pretty much every corner of my place. Despite the end of the world looming nigh, we spent a good chunk of the morning and afternoon spring cleaning.

Once that was done and Gan declared my apartment less offensive than normal, Sheila wanted me to come clean in a different way, namely the full story of what happened during my sojourn in Jahabich central. I figured it couldn't hurt. Between her and Gan, one of them might have some insight the rest of us had missed. Worst case, everyone in our merry group would be up to speed.

I told about how Ed had been kidnapped by the Jahabich and our journey to rescue him. I mentioned our capture – perhaps making my stand against our foes sound a bit more robust than it had been. Sadly, that only seemed to excite Gan more, so I immediately toned it back down and told the rest in as business-like of a manner as I could.

"All of those prisoners," Sheila said, rubbing her arms, "condemned to a fate worse than death."

"Some of them got away when we did. As for the rest, it's hard to say. I mean, I wasn't about to volunteer for that shit, but Mark, Sally's ex, seemed to be pretty okay with his newfound rocky outlook on life, and I didn't get the impression it was because of mind control."

"I got a similar feeling from the one I ran into up in Boston, at least while she was in her human form."

I thought back to Starlight. I couldn't shake the feeling there had been some of her talking to me despite being one of them, that parts of what she'd said were genuine. "Seems like maybe they have a modicum of freedom in their original forms. It's definitely limited, though, almost like they're on a timer to revert back and rejoin the hive mind. Say, are you okay?"

"Me?" She looked down at her arms. "Yeah. It just some-times tingles for a little bit after I heal myself."

"Listen, maybe I didn't say it earlier, but..."

"You did. Four times, to be precise."

"Well, I'm still really sorry."

"Don't be. If anything, it added an air of authenticity to our ruse."

"Not just about that, but, well, everything else ... keeping secrets from you."

"You had your reasons."

"Maybe, but I don't know if they were good reasons."

"You're a loyal friend."

"Loyal to the point of being stupid."

"I won't argue that," she said with a chuckle. "But the important part is you decided to tell me before I could confront you with it. That means a lot to me."

We locked eyes across the table, the silver in hers glinting under the light of my kitchen nook. I opened my mouth, not really sure what to say next, but maybe there was no need. Her hand and mine, both on the table, began to slowly inch their way toward each other. But *thankfully* the third wheel in the room picked that moment to place hers upon mine and spare us an actual moment.

"It is but one of the many reasons I adore you, my love," Gan said. "So honorable, noble, and yet fierce when the fires of passion engulf you."

"You know, Gan, you make it really tempting to open the window and let those fires engulf me once and for all."

Sheila covered her mouth with her hand, no doubt to stifle a laugh at my expense. I could always count on Gan to be the creepiest cock-blocker on the planet.

I quickly pulled my hand away, or tried to. Goddamn, she was strong. The table began to creak as I finally managed to slip out of her grasp. Thank goodness for sweaty palms. "Anyone want anything to drink?"

"I am quite sated, beloved," Gan said.

"I'm fine too," Sheila replied. "So let's get back to it. How'd you guys escape?"

I stood up, walked to the kitchen sink, and turned on the water full blast as I rinsed out my mug. Cleaning my glass was only part of the reason for doing so, though. Sally was downstairs and, just in case she was still awake, I really didn't care for her to eavesdrop on the next part.

"It was all my idea..."

"I am impressed," Gan said, undressing me with her eyes. Ugh! I so needed to make it a point to wear at least two pairs of underwear from here on. "To invoke the Humbaba Accord at such a time showed great foresight on your part."

"Yeah, I'm clever that way," I replied. "I mean, don't get me wrong, it didn't hurt that one of the Feet down there was Grulg."

"Grulg?" Sheila asked.

"He was the Sasquatch who'd basically acted as our host during the Woods of Mourning Summit."

"Where my love boldly spat upon the peace entreaties of our ancient enemies."

"*Accidentally* spat upon their peace entreaties," I snapped at her. "No thanks to you. Anyway, their leader Turd..." I paused as Sheila giggled. "Basically, Turd was a giant shit-stain on two legs, but Grulg turned out to be an okay guy for a giant rancid ape. He didn't particularly like us any more than the rest of them, but he was on the up and up. No tricks. So we lucked out in that Sally – I mean, *we* – recognized him. Thankfully, he remembered us, too."

"Another of those strange coincidences?" Sheila asked with a wry grin.

"I will admit, on occasion it does seem like the world is awfully small, but that's about as far as I'm willing to go. Regardless, once we cut a deal with him, the rest was causing as much chaos as we could, followed by running, lots and lots of running. That's around when we blew up the tunnel, not realizing we might need it again."

"It was a prudent course of action at the time. Yours is not a strategic mind, my love. One could not expect you to know better."

"Gee, thanks, Gan. You always know how to make me feel better."

"What happened to Grulg?" Sheila asked.

"Huh?"

"Did he come out with you guys?"

I let out a laugh. "Oh jeez, can you imagine if we'd surfaced in the middle of Pandora's Box with a Sasquatch?" Actually, considering we'd been immediately arrested upon our escape, maybe that wouldn't have been such a bad thing. "No," I continued, "once we made it to the Jahabich antechamber or whatever it was, we dissolved the truce."

"So what happened to him?"

"He ran for one of the other caves leading out of there, same as some of the other things that managed to escape. At that point, it was every man for himself."

"Did he make it out?"

"No idea. I hope so, though. He was an okay Bigfoot. With any luck, he hightailed it the fuck out of Dodge before the Jahabich got their act together enough to give chase."

Sheila was silent for a moment, a thoughtful look upon her face as if she was trying to envision the whole thing in her mind. Hopefully, her musings involved more of my heroic elaborations and less of how fucked we'd actually been at the time.

I got back up to get a refill of the blood Gan had brought. After that, I needed to step back a bit, remember that it needed to last. But damn if it wasn't tasty. Now if I could only push away the thought of how she'd likely obtained it, I would...

"Did Grulg blow up his cave, too?" Sheila asked.

"Huh?"

"You said you blew up the exit behind you. I was wondering if maybe Grulg did the same with his."

"We brought C-4. Unless he was hiding a brick of it up his ass, then I doubt it."

"The Alma shun the technological trappings of man," Gan explained.

"*Some* of them do anyway," I groused. "But as I said, Grulg was a straight shooter. I didn't get the vibe that he had a hankering for the latest iPhone upgrade. So no bombs, although who knows? I suppose he could have used magic. We've seen the Feet do some funky things with trees."

"Alma shamans are fairly rare, my love," Gan said. "Their warrior caste is far more numerous."

"Well, there you have it, then. No boom."

"Maybe that's a good thing," Sheila said, her eyes wide and sparkling.

"Not really. It means one more place where those fucking rock cocks could potentially surface from."

"That's what I mean." She stood up and leaned across the table at me.

I tried, and mostly failed, to not sneak a peek at the ensuing cleavage, but what she said next made all thoughts of boobs flee my mind ... for a moment or two.

"Think about it. If Grulg made it out, then he'll know how to get back in. If we can find him, maybe he can tell us how to get down there again and save Ed."

15

WAR AND PIECE

I couldn't help but laugh.

"Yeah, he might point out the way ... after he finished smashing my head with a rock."

"You said yourself he was an honorable man, err, ape," Sheila pointed out.

"Yes, honorable, but still a loyal member of the race that hates our guts."

"But you were able to make a truce."

"A temporary cease fire," I clarified.

"But a cease fire nevertheless. He could have attacked you guys outright, but he was willing to talk. Maybe he would be again."

"The circumstances were a bit different down there. Believe me, he made it perfectly clear he toed the party line. So long as the rest of his buddies are down with kicking our asses, then he is, too."

"But what if they weren't?" she asked.

"Weren't what?"

"Weren't hell-bent on wiping you out. It's painfully obvious the Jahabich aren't just a threat to the vampires. You said so yourself. It was a veritable Noah's ark of the supernatural down there."

"Yeah."

"So, then the ... Feet, I guess, must be aware of the threat. Maybe not to the extent we are, but we both saw it for ourselves at our trial. Some of those things turned into Sasquatches. That means they've had losses. That means they have to know there's another enemy out there gunning for them, too."

"The enemy of my enemy?" I asked. "Seems a stretch to me. I mean, you don't know these things like I do. They *really* don't like us for whatever reason. I don't know, maybe we insulted one of their mothers way back when."

Gan stood up and placed her hands behind her back. "We have been enemies for countless centuries. The reasons are lost to time. However, that mutual dislike was kept at bay for nearly five millennia by the Humbaba Accord."

"Yes, which is now null and void."

"Not entirely, Dr. Death. You yourself were able to invoke it when needed. The Accord, as you no doubt are aware, is quite lengthy – several dozen scrolls in size."

"Uh yeah. Light reading for a rainy day."

"It provides boundaries for the fragile peace that existed between our people, that much is true, but the signatories were wise. They understood our mutual nature and made sure to include provisions for breaches of that peace. The Accord was signed in blood under the eyes of ancient powers. It is not so easily dismissed in its entirety."

"So you're saying that it could be reinstated, in theory anyway?" Sheila asked.

"An argument could be made that we are simply in a state of abeyance with regard to it. In theory, as you stated."

"I'm failing to see how," I said. "I mean, we're in a state of all-out war here. Thousands have been killed. You yourself bragged how you had a mile-long line of Bigfoot skulls lining the road to your house."

"I was stating a truth, not bragging. Regardless, you are thinking of this war like a human. That is a mistake. The morality of the players involved is beyond such petty considerations. Though it is true there are many primal powers that wish to see it proceed so they might reestablish the old religions, there are just as many that wish to keep them in check."

"So there's a chance," Sheila said.

"There is always a chance, Shining One, even if infinitesimally small."

"Says the one who actually started this war," I added, letting a trace of bitterness enter my voice.

"My intentions were to make clear my claim upon you, beloved. And I make no secret that this conflict helps me forward my personal ambitions. However, I see no reason why this new development cannot also aid my aspirations."

I put my head on my hand and stared at her from across the table. "It's amazing you haven't won a Noble Peace Prize yet."

"There is also the fact," Gan continued, ignoring my barb, "that the initial aggressor of hostilities on their side is now dead."

"Turd?"

Again, Sheila snickered at my mention of his name. I couldn't blame her. If I lived to be a thousand, I doubted that would ever stop being funny. "But wait. Didn't the attack on the Khan happen before he got involved?"

Gan shrugged as if the death of her father was water under the bridge. "An opportunistic way of gaining our attention, nothing more."

I considered this. "Turd and François seemed pretty buddy buddy for a while there and, from what I heard, François did have a mad-on for your dad."

"Indeed. I have little doubt the attack was at least partially perpetrated with inside knowledge from the traitor. In fact, we have no way of knowing how long they were manipulating events to bring about the summit." She began to pace. "But they are both dead now. The Alma will have gathered to select a new leader for this hemisphere."

"You think this new guy might be more approachable?"

"Hardly. The Alma's hatred of us runs deep. However,

from what I have gathered, Turd was disgraced at the time of his declaration of war."

"Fuck yeah," I said with some pride. "Asshole had an iPod and I called him out on it."

"A bigfoot with an iPod?" Sheila asked. "That's new."

"I should have checked out his playlist. I really wanted to know if he had *Chewbacca* on it." I turned back to Gan. "Disgraced or not, he still was able to make the call."

"Yes. His influence was such that even with a shadow cast over him, the others rallied to his cry. To do otherwise would have been to admit weakness. But do not think his sins were so easily forgotten. The Alma have a long memory and even war cannot erase such a stain."

"So you think whoever is in charge now might be willing to talk?" Sheila asked. "Do something to erase the ... stain that Turd caused?"

I grinned. "Once you start, it's really hard to stop, isn't it?"

"I'm glad I don't have to meet him. Not sure I could keep a straight face."

"It's easier than you think, especially when he's busy rearranging yours with his fists."

"I believe it might be possible," Gan replied, getting us back to the point. "As with any new regime, the leaders will be eager to place their own mark upon history – whether that be war or peace."

"That's good."

"But that decision will not be made at our hands," she added.

"It won't?"

"No." She turned and pointed at Sheila. "It will be at hers."

"Not following," Sheila replied, wide eyed.

"I am a known enemy of the Alma," Gan stated matter-of-factly. "I have slaughtered them wherever we have met on the field of battle." She turned to me. "You, my love, likely possess nearly that same level of notoriety via your status as the Freewill."

"Nearly," I echoed.

"Should either of us approach them in their territory, there is an excellent chance we would be torn asunder even as we offered a flag of truce. The Shining One, however, is also known among them, but in a different manner."

"I remember," I said. "Turd tried to invoke the Icons to rally the Magi against me."

"Indeed, but his words aside, there has never been open hostility between the Alma and her kind. If anything, her status as a known enemy of our people would give her some measure of influence amongst them."

"That whole enemy of my enemy thing again," I offered.

"Yes. Should the Shining One approach them, offering to mediate peace, I do not think she would be turned away out of hand."

I stood up and leaned against the wall. "Yeah, but there's one small problem. We might get their new leaders to sit down and talk, but we'll never get ours to. Last I checked, Alex was pretty big on wiping them out."

"And who says we need him? Did you not act as the First's proxy last time? Your status as Freewill makes you an equal to them in the eyes of our enemy regardless of the reality of the situation."

Could always count on Gan to tear down three walls while building up one.

"Would that work?" Sheila asked.

"There are no official diplomatic channels between our leadership and theirs at the moment. Word would spread quickly among our allies, though, so eventually, the First would learn of it."

"And then what?"

"Unknown." She shrugged. "It has been rumored among the prefecture that Lord Alexander's ambitions for war were not formally endorsed by the majority of the First Coven."

"You think the rest of them might grow a backbone and force him to accept peace now?" I asked.

"I do not. Two of their number are dead and a third is missing. There might be some debate on the matter, but I would not count on the opposition prevailing."

"Yehoshua might make for a good argument," I offered.

"Perhaps," Gan conceded. "But the fate of Lady Theodora at the hands of the Shining One could work against supporting a peace she brokered. He was known to be fond of her."

I knew that, but at the same time wasn't sure I agreed with her assessment. However, before I could say anything, Gan continued. "Besides, it matters not. Whether the peace is real or a sham is irrelevant. What matters is that we convince the Alma it is genuine long enough for them to guide us to Ib's lair. After that, the rest is up to you, my love."

"Me?! What the hell am *I* supposed to do?"

"What you normally do. I believe your whore said it herself. You have quite the talent for, what were her words? Ah yes, fucking things up."

16

DON'T USE ALL THE HOT WATER

Sheila and I decided to forgo our nightly sojourn that evening. The plan we'd come up with had me far too distracted, not to mention I knew myself. Despite everything, I'd probably have spent the entire night apologizing for vamping out on her, which wouldn't do wonders for our vigilantism. Also, I had a feeling Gan would have wanted to tag along and her version of street justice was decisively different from ours.

After our little powwow broke up, I ran downstairs to bring the others up to speed on our plan while Sheila worked on getting a stable cell signal so as to attempt to reach Bernadette – hopefully without tipping off Colin in the process.

Sally was dubious as to our chances of success, but even she had to agree it was better than anything else we had to go on. Also, more than ever, she seemed to want to get a move on with regard to rescuing Ed. Considering what Gan had told us about what he could do, I had little doubt of the reason behind her enthusiasm. Still, one couldn't argue against having a motivated crowd.

Christy's coven seemed pretty gung ho on trying, too. Of course, the Magi weren't on the Feet's shit list, so it wasn't quite as much of a risk to them. Christy, however, barely acknowledged the plan before shuffling her sisters back into the basement and locking the door behind them.

My curiosity got the better of me and, despite knowing Christy's penchant for wards, I snuck up and tried to listen in, catching "It's now or never" before all sound inside was muted. Considering I couldn't even hear a heartbeat through the door after that, I had to assume it was magically blocked.

Jeez! What, did they have a No Bills Club going on down there? Or maybe they were doing that naked cavorting thing that witches were supposedly known for. I really needed to drill myself a peephole at some point.

Whatever the case, it sounded as if they were good with our plan. That was the important thing. In the meantime, let them do whatever voodoo they needed to. They still had a very important spell to figure out for once we were down there.

The main problem, besides forging peace with a group of slobbering troglodytes that hated me, was that we were technically under a state of truce with Alex. We'd agreed to work together to end Calibra, and part of that included an open exchange of intelligence between us.

I didn't think for one second he took it any more seriously than we did, but he had a lot more clout than us, and I really didn't look forward to another trial where our treachery would be put on display like a circus sideshow. Besides, my practical side insisted he had a whole freaking army at his disposal. Once we were ready to face Calibra, wouldn't it make a fuckload more sense to have a platoon of heavily armed shock troops to back us up?

Therein lay the conundrum. How to establish a truce, keep Alex in the dark about it, yet not have to face Calibra by ourselves.

Fuck it. That's what tomorrows were for.

I, for one, had endured enough surprise revelations for the time being. That we ended the day with far more of a plan than we had started was fucking golden. We'd failed to stop Calibra from transforming Ed into some sort of neo-vamp, but it sounded like he was still safe for the time being, at least until she rejiggered his powers to be more conducive to her liking.

Gan had returned downstairs to her waiting limo, somehow still there and ticket free, to work on rallying those loyal to her cause. That was one plus. She might have been a fucking nutcase, but she was a nutcase with a big following. I wasn't all too keen on the cult mindset, but fuck it. I could make an exception when that cult was on my side.

I decided to take advantage of the momentary quiet and lie down for a bit before the bad seed could return upstairs and try to weasel her way into my bed. She was one random monster encounter I really didn't care to have. I wasn't sure if I'd be able to sleep with everything running through my mind, but a little downtime to collect my thoughts didn't sound like a bad idea. Once on the road, luxuries such as food, sleep, and bathing tended to fall by the wayside. That latter one sucked, but those first two could prove lethal.

Why, oh why, couldn't the forces of evil muster themselves at a leisurely pace at some tropical vacation resort?

Turns out a full stomach trumped a full mind and I ended up conking out for a while anyway. I awoke nice and refreshed some time later ... and thankfully without a pair of crazy green eyes staring down at me. Most importantly, the anger I'd been feeling, the same that I'd let boil over at Sheila, seemed to have receded. Amazing what a little good news and a bit of sleep could do.

I glanced over at my clock in the dark room, but the display was out. Maybe I'd kicked the cord from the socket at some point. Thinking nothing of it, I hopped out of bed and hit the light switch. Darkness remained.

Odd, considering the Apollo what-the-fuck down in the basement. Oh well, maybe it was just the shitty wiring in this place. That I hadn't woken up in a crater told me that whatever was going on was probably somewhat less than cataclysmic. Besides, what did it matter? I could see in the dark.

The living room was quiet and likewise unlit. The power was out there, too. Unfortunately, it was the same in the kitchen, meaning the refrigerator was off. No problem; I had a backup plan. I quickly moved the blood into our freezer. Thanks to years of neglecting to ever defrost it, the walls were solid ice. Not great for the appliance's lifespan, but it made for a damn handy emergency icebox during outages.

The blood situation taken care of for the moment, I decided to grab a quick shower. Afterwards, I could meander down and ask Christy when she planned to plug her supernatural generator back in.

On the plus side, the water heater in the building was entirely gas, so my shower wasn't ball-shriveling cold. Sadly, I wasn't quite in the mood for any *me time*. The presence of Sheila and Sally had made for some good stress relief in days past. Angry jerking off wasn't quite the same as angry sex – or so I had to assume – but it got the job done. But with Gan back in the picture and in close proximity, no fucking way. The very last thing I wanted in this entire world – even less than ending up a slave, destined to kiss Sasquatch ass for all eternity – was to have Gan kick in the door while I had my dick in my hand. No, sir, I did not want that.

As if the thought of Gan wasn't enough to cause little Dr. Death to go hide in the shadows, I was just finishing up washing my hair when another unwanted guest reared his ugly head. Or skull, in this case.

You dare judge me and then perform this foul heresy?!

I guess Christy had decided to wake up Harry Decker for some reason or other. Just great. Lacking vocal cords, Decker's sole means of communication was entirely psychic – meaning that walls, doors, or fingers in one's ears didn't do shit for keeping him out.

He didn't have eyes either, but at the same time appeared aware of what was going on around him. Who knew how far that extended? Yep, any happy time was definitely out of the question. Knowing my luck, he'd start in with a play by play for the entire building to hear.

Do you think the great Kala sits on her hands waiting for us? The White marches ever forward, uniting those loyal to her cause.

I so hated getting only half a conversation, especially when that half was from a fucking nutbag.

Sadly, Decker was a necessary evil. His knowledge of magical fuckery was greater than Christy's, and she needed his help in order to modify the ancient spell we'd discovered into something that could not only stop the Jahabich, but potentially Calibra as well. If he could do that for us, I could deal with his presence for a while longer.

I could always find a convenient landfill on Staten Island to toss him into afterwards.

Despite the power outage, I was in a pretty decent mood. After I was done talking to the witches, maybe I'd stop by the downstairs apartment and check on Sally. I was hoping our new plan had snapped her out of her funk. Maybe we could shoot the shit for a while. Hell, even if she wanted to vent and spend an hour verbally eviscerating me, that would be fine. Though she would never admit it, I had a feeling she needed someone to talk to.

Of course, there was also a chance she might not be alone. That gave me pause. I'd never considered Sheila a potential third wheel. Hell, I still had no idea where my feelings were going lately. Things were definitely more complicated than ever – and not just because we were preparing for an assault against the center of the Earth.

So much for my good mood.

I got dressed and walked out, my mind full of conflicting thoughts ... thoughts I really needed to stow away for a time after the events of Armageddon had played out. Thus, I didn't immediately think anything of the familiar figure that passed me in the gloomy apartment.

"Hey, Bill."

"Hey, man," I replied idly a split second before realization hit and I came to a screeching halt.

I spun just in time to see the bathroom door close behind an impossible sight – that of my roommate.

17

MAXIMUM ADVENTURE

"Tom?"

For a moment, I was frozen in place, thinking that maybe I was hallucinating. But I hadn't imagined the door closing. And I definitely wasn't imagining the shuffling sounds now coming from within the bathroom.

That snapped me out of my funk. I stepped forward and ripped the door open, ignoring the snap of the tumbler as I broke the lock.

"The fuck, dude?!" Tom stood up from the toilet, his pants around his ankles. "In case you hadn't noticed, occupied!"

"You're..."

"On the shitter? Yes. Learn to fucking knock, oh, and eyes up here. Don't be thinking that just because the world is fucked, you can go sneaking peeks at my junk."

"But you're..."

"Seeing if it all still works. It ain't a spectator sport."

He kicked the door shut in my face. It refused to latch and slid back open an inch or so. "You fucking broke it, asshole." The door shut again and I could hear the sound of the trashcan sliding across the floor to brace it.

What the hell was going on?

Sounds from outside my apartment caught my ear —

footsteps racing up the stairs and, even more prominently, the sound of voices arguing ... female voices.

I was split between the front door of my apartment and the bathroom, indecision completely freezing me in place as my mind tried to comprehend what I'd just seen – my roommate Tom as he had been before Vehron snapped his neck. He was human again, or maybe a really solid looking ghost. I had no fucking clue.

I was totally gobsmacked. Someone might as well have walked in and showed me a birth certificate that listed Sally as my mother and Sheila my twin sister. I don't think my reaction would have been any less.

"Go back downstairs."

"No fucking way."

"I'm with Meg."

"I'm the high mentor of this coven and I say..."

"This isn't the fucking Army, Christy. You can't pull rank like that, especially since he just got up and waltzed out in the middle of the ceremony."

Christy and her sisters. The plot thickened.

The argument outside broke the standoff in my mind. There was no other egress from the bathroom, unless one counted the toilet, and if whatever was in there could do that, then I really wanted no fucking part of it. I stalked to the front door and opened it upon the trio of arguing witches. Veronica was the only one of the coven not in sight.

"Can I help you ladies?" I asked pleasantly. "Because the weirdest thing just happened."

Christy pushed her way past me. "Is he here?"

"Why, whoever do you mean? You wouldn't happen to be talking about my best friend, the one who only yesterday was still dead and possessing a plastic doll, would you?"

"Action figure!" Tom shouted from the bathroom.

Oh, Jesus Christ.

Christy walked over and pounded on the door. "Come out. We need to make sure you're stable."

"Hey, babe," he replied from the other side. "You should get in here. You wouldn't believe what's working."

She glanced back at us, a look of embarrassment on her face, before turning to the door again. "Seriously?" she hissed.

I glanced at Meg and Kelly, both of whom looked extremely uncomfortable. "This isn't a dream, is it?" Meg gave a single shake of her head. "A hallucination, maybe?"

"It's hard to explain," she replied.

"You're telling me," Kelly said. "I was down there and I still don't know what the fuck we were think... oof!" She trailed off abruptly as Meg elbowed her in the side.

The sound of the door opening behind me caught my ear and I turned to see Tom, thankfully with his pants up, step out. Christy grabbed him by the hand and began dragging him toward the door.

"I'm fine, babe. I mean it."

"I'll be the judge of that," she snapped. "This is sensitive magic. You can't just..."

"Leave without explaining what's going on?" I finished for her. "Yeah, I'd say that's accurate."

"Out of the way."

I instinctively took a half step before catching myself. Sure, she was scary powerful, hormonal, and looking just a wee bit stressed, but I was the goddamned Freewill for fuck's sake. I'd fucking killed a dude whose last name was "The Destroyer." I wasn't chopped liver. And, most of all, this was my fucking apartment.

It was time to grow a set.

And hope it wasn't immediately blown off.

I crossed my arms and leaned against the front door, blocking it.

"Move," she said.

"No."

Our eyes locked and the intensity in hers almost caused me to blink, but then I played the ace up my sleeve. I blackened mine. Not only was it pretty darned intimidating, but it did wonders to make my face unreadable. Score one for vamp powers.

Magical energy flared up around Christy and, for a moment, it looked like those points were about to be erased along with a good chunk of me. But then she took a deep breath and reined it all in. "We need to get him back into the circle. Make sure the glamour is stable."

"That's a start." I stepped to the side. I didn't want her to think she'd won, so I played it cool, but something about the way she said "stable" told me that maybe I should meet her halfway. "But I'm coming along and you can explain along the way."

I barely recognized the basement. Not only was the human sludge all gone – thank goodness – but the whole place was aglow with sigils of power as if someone had gotten stoned, installed a black light, and then gone nuts with fluorescent paint.

A large pentagram had been quite literally carved into the concrete floor, inside of which lay another circle. Cones of incense burned at all the points. It was a bit overwhelming, but it definitely beat the stench of rotting man goo.

It wasn't all wonderful, though. Off in one corner, sitting atop a pedestal, lay Harry Decker's skull. He was still missing his jaw, and a crack remained at the top where he'd been banged around during our encounter with Calibra, but the witches had polished him up a bit. Least heartening was that the purplish light emitting from him was stronger than ever.

This is a sacred place, oaf!

"To the cockroaches, maybe," I shot back. "But then you'd be right at home with them, wouldn't you?"

"I'll explain everything," Christy said to me, "but, if you're going to stay, then stay silent."

Tom walked into the room and tapped a fist on Decker's

noggin. "Want me to skull fuck this asshole, Bill? I can do that. I checked."

"Maybe later," I replied.

"The same goes for you," Christy said to him. "In the circle."

"But..."

"*Now.*"

Whatever this new body might be, a backbone apparently wasn't part of the deal. My friend sheepishly complied. Once he stepped inside, multi-hued color began to flicker around him.

As Christy placed Decker at one point of the pentagram and took a seat at another, I turned to the other witches and made a whip cracking motion with my hand. That at least got a smile from Kelly, although it didn't quite reach her eyes.

The rest then took seats at the other points.

I opened my mouth, hoping to prompt that explanation Christy had promised, but she held up a hand.

Fine. I could be patient.

Well, not really. I leaned against the wall and began tapping my fingers.

Whatever they were doing was already prepped and ready to go. There was no ceremony or stupid shit like that. They all joined hands – except for Decker, for obvious reasons. However, the witches on either side of him reached over and touched his skull. They had to stretch to do so, but once done, that apparently completed some sort of magical circuit. Power crackled in the room and when Christy opened her mouth to speak an incantation, it sounded as if her voice was coming through a megaphone.

The others joined her, speaking in something that sounded vaguely like Latin.

Thankfully, it didn't last long. After a few minutes of this, the light pulsing around Tom became steady. Finally, Christy and the others broke contact. A slight sheen of sweat shone on everyone's brow – again, minus Decker – but that seemed to be about it.

"This time, stay put until I say it's finished," Christy ordered.

"But I'm bored."

Christy fixed Tom with a stare that would have melted stone and he instantly shut up. Whatever this thing was, he sure acted like my roommate.

I stepped in and offered to help her back to her feet, which she accepted. "So about that glamour thing?"

It is a thing that should not exist!

Christy rounded on Decker. "We've already discussed this. Do you want to go back in the box?"

Well, that sounded ominous ... for someone I liked anyway. For Decker, I was kinda hoping he'd go on.

Sadly, he fell silent, the purple light he emanated taking on a sulking sort of quality. I really needed to stop attributing emotions to a stupid light-up skull.

Christy turned to her sisters, but Meg was apparently ready for her.

"I'll stick around and make sure he stays put until he's done baking."

"Baking?" Tom asked.

"Figure of speech."

Veronica stepped in close to Meg and whispered to her, too low for human ears, "Be careful."

Now I was *really* intrigued.

"I'll explain over coffee," Christy said to me.

"Might have to be over tap water," I replied. "The power seems to be out. Did something happen to the glowing thingee?" I glanced over toward the circuit panel, noting the distinct lack of an Apollo's ballsack anywhere to be seen.

"No, it's fine." Christy walked past me to the stairs. "We just had to transplant it."

"Transplant it?"

"Into the glamour," she said over her shoulder. "It's what's keeping him corporeal."

18

THE NOSE KNOWS

As the four of us made our way to the ground floor apartment the witches had appropriated, I contemplated how best to say what was going through my mind.

"Are you fucking insane?" Hmm, that had sounded a bit more diplomatic in my head.

Kelly unlocked the door, trying to hide the faint grin on her face.

Christy however simply replied, "It's okay, Bill."

"Define okay."

"Number three," Kelly said.

"Huh?"

"Not you."

While I stared in confusion, she and Veronica grasped hands. A soft white glow gathered in their clenched fists, then spread out across their bodies to their free hands. Little twinkles of light, almost like fireflies, fanned out from them, covering the room and illuminating it.

"I'm guessing you guys typically save a lot on your power bill," I remarked, following Christy into the living room while the two other witches headed into their kitchen nook. If I had to guess, whipping up some hot coffee sans electricity wouldn't be an issue for them. Also, retreating to the kitchen

107

gave Christy and me space while still keeping them in prime eavesdropping distance. Clever girls.

"I'll be perfectly honest with you, Bill," Christy said, looking me in the eye, "it's been really hard for me – seeing Tom like that." She tried to keep her voice slow and steady, but my sensitive ears could pick up more nuances than most: a slight pause here, a hitched breath there.

Though I was the last person anyone should ever come to for comfort, I wasn't a completely insensitive douche. I reached over and put a hand on hers. "Tom was ... *is* my best friend in this entire world. I understand."

"No." Her eyes began to glisten. "You really don't."

I'd known Tom since kindergarten. We'd spent more time together than most married couples, so I was willing to wager against that. However, I thought better of it and managed to keep my yap shut.

"I failed him," she said.

"No..."

"Yes," she insisted. "I failed him and, worse, I cursed him to that undeath, that living Hell."

"We had no way of knowing what that Jahabich crap would do to him, how it would affect our efforts to ... bring him back."

"Don't you think I've thought of that?" Her eyes hardened against mine and I was tempted to shrink back from them. "I've played that moment over and over again in my head almost nonstop since it happened. And you know what? I'm not sure. No matter how hard I try to convince myself otherwise, I know I didn't want him to leave. I wanted him to stay ... in *any* capacity. Their blood was the catalyst, but I was the spark and I think, even if it was subconscious on my part, that somehow I guided or nudged his soul into that vessel."

"So what if you did?" I replied. "I didn't want him to go either."

"He's not at peace."

"Have you listened to him talk? He doesn't sound like he's in eternal torment either."

"He's just being brave."

I actually laughed, probably not the best time to do so. Judging by the momentary cessation of rattling pots in the kitchen, the other two witches were thinking the same thing. "Now it's my turn to tell you you're wrong. I know Tom, maybe even better than I know myself. And I can tell you he's not one to be brave for the sake of others. I've seen him cry about his impending doom over a fucking paper cut. He's a brother to me, so please don't think I'm being cruel saying this, but he can be ... well, a self-centered asshole when he wants to be."

A part of me was certain I'd crossed a line. Though my words had been true, I was very much expecting to have to quickly duck and cover. Instead, though, Christy actually grinned. "He is at that, but he's *my* self-centered asshole."

"And I know he's happy to be that." I leaned back in. "Trust me, if he's busy yammering about mundane stuff, that's probably about as deep as it gets. Though I'm sure it sucks to be a Ken doll, I am certain of one thing. He's not suffering."

"Thanks, Bill. I can only hope you're right."

I glanced over at the kitchen where I could see a red glow coming from the stove. Ah yes, magic. Had I been given a choice, I'd have definitely chosen that over this undead bullshit. "So what did you do?"

She took a deep breath and sighed. "You're familiar with glamours, right?"

Drawing upon my D&D expertise, I nodded. "They're basically illusions, right?"

"In a sense. They come in many shapes, sizes, and intensities. At their weakest, they're exactly that – an optical illusion, nothing more. At their strongest, though, they can be a full physical manifestation – power given the consistency of actual matter. We're talking sight, smell, sound, touch; all of it. A powerful enough glamour can fool anyone, even someone with your senses, because it is essentially real for a time."

"For a time?"

"That's the caveat. The stronger the glamour, the more complex it is to create and the harder it is to maintain. There's also a personal aspect to it. I could physically change my hair to blonde and you'd never know it hadn't come out of a bottle."

"Like Sally's?" I joked.

She chose to ignore me. "I could maintain something like that almost indefinitely if I wanted to. At the very least, for weeks on end. If I were to expand it, however, and try to make everyone in this apartment building a blonde, for instance, it would be a lot tougher to maintain, especially the further you got from me."

"Okay, I think I'm following."

"So that brings us to Tom. He's essentially helpless as he was. Though what happened to him might have been similar to what happens to the Jahabich, it was indirect and on a much smaller scale. He inhabits the body of that doll, but he hasn't merged with it. It's not a full-scale possession."

"Even if it was, I'm not sure a twelve-inch bride of Chucky would be much less helpless."

"Exactly. Leaving him behind isn't an option this time. The Source is his only chance." She placed her hands over her stomach. "*Our* only chance. But taking him down there like he was..."

"Hell, even if you accidentally dropped him, that would be..." I stopped, realizing I was venturing into insensitive prick territory with that line of thought. "Sorry."

"It's okay. And you're right. How many times have we been caught and stripped of our possessions? Anything could happen to him down there and if it did, he'd be helpless to do anything except cry for help."

"Which wouldn't carry too far underground."

She nodded ruefully. I was beginning to see where this was going. What she was saying made practical sense.

However, there was a selfish aspect to it all. Not that I was about to mention it. Fuck, if given the choice between Doll-Man Tom and Illusion Tom, I know which one I'd choose to have around.

"That's when I got an idea. A personal glamour can act as an extension of ourselves. If I give myself tentacles instead of hands, they'll work as I will them, almost as if I'd been born with them."

"You didn't give him..."

She narrowed her eyes, shutting me up. "So, using that logic, a personal glamour of his original body cast around his existing one would, in essence, be as if he were whole again."

"Why his original body? Why not some six foot ten muscle jock?"

She smiled. "That's exactly what he asked. You two really do know each other a little too well. Anyway, call it personal preference."

"Understandable."

"That's what I ... ugh. Hand me that throw pillow please." I did so and she positioned it under the small of her back. "Much better, thanks. I swear I can't wait to push this kid out."

Kelly and Veronica chose that moment to join us, each carrying two steaming mugs of joe. Kelly handed me one and I took a sip. Yeesh. Magic could do wonders for heating it up, but apparently didn't do jack shit when it came to making it palatable.

"Okay." I put the cup down so as to try to steer us back on track. "So a personal glamour."

"A super tough one at that," Veronica replied.

"Yeah, but like you said, the more complex, the harder to maintain. And Tom's downstairs while we're..." I trailed off. Oh boy. "The prism."

"It was Kelly's idea," Christy said proudly.

I glanced over, and the look on Kelly's face made it seem more like she wished she'd never opened her mouth. "All I said was it was a shame we couldn't hook up a car battery or something to keep it going."

"That was enough to start me thinking," Christy continued, a slight manic gleam in her eye. "The prism is a self-sustaining power source. Hard to conjure, a group effort definitely, but worth it. I mean, it's been more than enough to keep this building humming for months now. It took a little creative hexing and we needed Harry to weigh in on it."

"Which explains why he's all happily glowing again," I muttered.

"But in the end, we did it. A tangible glamour, almost indistinguishable from his original form, but maintained by an autonomous power source."

"Almost indistinguishable," I echoed. "Wait, earlier when he was in the apartment, I didn't smell him. I mean, the place already has his scent, but ... sorry to say this, it's been getting stale. I should have noticed him."

"That was purposeful," Veronica said. She was the youngest of the bunch and seemed far more caught up in the coolness of what they'd created. "I mean, he'll pick up residual odors – like what he's wearing, what he steps in, et cetera. But he's an olfactory null."

"Let me guess; so vamps can't sniff him out."

"It's a lesson I picked up from that little bitch," Christy said. "I'm almost ashamed to admit it, but she used it effectively up in Massachusetts against those Forest Folk. Who knows? I might have to revise my estimate of her usefulness at some point."

19

WHO WATCHES THE WATCHERS?

I, of course, mentioned – as gently as possible – my concerns regarding the prism. They weren't aware that Gan had told me about its true destructive potential. Even so, I'd seen what it had done to our home invaders. Whether it was blowing us all to Kingdom Come or melting anyone in close proximity to it, I felt these were valid concerns.

Christy was pretty dismissive of it, though, citing precautions they'd taken. However, I couldn't help but wonder if there might have been a bit of wishful thinking going on there. She'd initially been aghast at Tom's resurrection as Max Adventure, cheesy seventies action figure. She'd warmed up to his situation a bit after Vehron was defeated, but there'd been a walking on eggshells feel to it. Now, though, I'd only seen them interact for a few minutes, but she already seemed much more her old self around him.

Fuck it. It wasn't like we weren't in a shit ton of danger already. Who was I to deny the poor girl a little peace of mind?

I decided I'd grilled her enough for one evening. Besides, there were other topics of magical interest I was wondering about. "What about the other stuff you guys have been working on?"

"What other stuff?" At the sight of my eyes narrowing, she actually let out a laugh. "Relax, Bill. I haven't forgotten about Kala, Alex, or the Jahabich." Her voice grew hard for a moment. "*Trust me.*"

"How's it going?"

"Slow. Harry is being difficult about cooperating. He's still hung up on Kala. But we're working on it. That's still priority number one."

I could only hope she meant it. Awesome as it was to have seen my friend in the glamoured flesh and blood, it wouldn't mean much in the long run if we couldn't stop the genocidal nutjobs behind all of this.

After a time, Christy got back up. Apparently, the spell downstairs was nearing the end of its course and it was time to give Tom the all clear. The others went to join her, but I held Kelly back a bit – feigning interest in her tattoos, which was easy because they were pretty awesome. Had she a mind to, she'd have been a shoo-in for a Suicide Girls spread.

"What do you think?" I asked, once Christy and Veronica were out of earshot.

She hesitated, clearly uncomfortable. "She's my mentor and my friend."

"I'm not asking you to backstab her. I'm just wondering what your thoughts are on this."

After a few moments, she stepped further in and lowered her voice. "What I think is we're in uncharted waters now. I've never heard of anything like this being done before. More importantly, none of the others did either, including Christy, and she studies history and shit like that. I mean, the only thing that even comes close to it..."

"Let me guess. The White Mother?"

"In spirit, not really, but if we went by the letter of the law..." She cocked her head to the side and raised her shoulders. "Still, Christy has a point. Him coming with us like this is probably a lot more useful than in someone's pocketbook. But..."

"But what?"

"The transfer seems to be stable, but don't let him fall off any high cliffs or anything."

I nodded, the meaning quite clear, then turned to follow the others down to the basement. It was time to reintroduce Tom to society.

"Wait."

"Huh?" I stopped and turned.

"What do *you* think of all of this? He's your friend after all."

"I know and I'm glad to have him back. I mean, fuck, I'm not exactly one to judge, am I? I already died once and he didn't immediately put out a room for rent sign. Would be kind of hypocritical of me to get on a supernatural high horse about this. Besides, that thing you mentioned about how this sorta resembles the White Mother."

"Yeah?"

"There's one big difference here that gives me comfort. Calibra could potentially take over the world with her creations. Christy ... well, she'd be lucky if Tom could intimidate the wait staff at a Denny's."

Whatever spell they'd worked seemingly went off without a hitch because Tom met us halfway as we were heading down. Despite the lack of a scent, he was him. It's hard to explain, but when you know someone for so long, you know the essential them. I had a feeling that's how parents could tell identical twins apart. There was a sense of "them" to each person that someone intimately familiar would just know. That's how it was now. I couldn't quite put my finger on it, but despite being a construct of tangible energy around a cheap plastic center, he was still my friend.

"I wonder if I still need to take dumps," he mused idly.

Yeah, definitely Tom.

The beauty of living in an apartment building full of people familiar with the true weirdness of the world was that they tended to take shit like this in stride. So it was that Tom got to experience the annoyance of his miraculous *resurrection* being accepted with little more than a shrug. Hell, Sally opened the door, saw him, rolled her eyes, and then slammed it shut again.

Sheila was more cautiously optimistic, though, which mollified Tom's ego a bit. Unfortunately, we stopped short of throwing him a welcome back party. For starters, this was a temporary fix at best. More importantly, we had to actually start making headway in finding Calibra, stopping her, and bringing him back in a way that didn't involve a miniature black hole powering his body.

Speaking of which, the only one of our group still AWOL was Gan. I hadn't thought much of it when I'd first awoken, being glad she wasn't trying to straddle me like a jungle gym. But now, with the excitement wearing down, her absence was most certainly noticed.

The limo that had brought her here was gone, so that probably meant she was doing more than hiding in my closet, waiting to surprise me the second I got undressed. I was torn. On the one hand, a day without Gan was almost certainly bound to be a good one. On the other, now that we had at least the semblance of a plan, I was eager to get a move on.

With Tom back, in a sense of the word, Christy seemed much more focused on the task ahead. We took some time and discussed our course of action in greater detail. I still had misgivings about the way she'd done things, but if having her head back in the game was a side effect, then it was a welcome one.

The logistics of pulling off our plan were the main roadblock. First, there was the problem of getting back to the Woods of Mourning. Last time I'd been up there, it had been a fucking slog, one where I'd gotten my ass kicked by a moose. Sadly, it seemed that was to be the order of the day again as the person upon whom this insane plan rested was also the only member of our group who was impossible to teleport.

Of more immediate concern was getting out of the neighborhood unseen. Prior to his departure, Alex had assured us that he would be in touch should he have some new intelligence to share. I had little doubt agents of the Dracs kept an eye on this place. Running out for coffee wasn't bound to raise any suspicions. All of us heading out on a road trip, however, was a wee bit different.

I didn't imagine they would buy that we were just all stir crazy and looking for a weekend at the beach.

While I brainstormed this with the witches and Tom, mostly getting nowhere, Christy and Sally took Sheila aside and gave her the Cliffs Notes version of the Humbaba Accord, both of them having far more familiarity with it than I did.

They were welcome to it. I dug ancient history, don't get me wrong, but I was more into the fun stuff like three hundred Spartans kicking ass at Thermopylae. The crap they were going over, arguing about bullshit like where the respective heads of nations should sit at a table as outlined in Section eighteen, paragraph twelve, sub-section nine, struck me as the kind of stuff that used to put me to sleep in class.

They somehow kept at it until long after the sun had come up. By then, my group was rapidly losing steam. Kelly and Meg were out cold, snoring in a chair, and Veronica was downing Red Bulls like they were the fountain of youth. Tom, amazingly enough, appeared fresh as a daisy. I actually had to remind myself that shouldn't have been surprising. Though he looked human, he wasn't.

Finally, Sally stopped talking and cocked her head to the side. "I think the Oompa Loompa queen is back."

After another moment, I heard the pitter patter of little feet climbing the stairs from the ground floor. Either Gan had returned, or we were about to be accosted to buy Girl Scout cookies.

The door to my apartment opened and the little princess

strolled in like she owned the place. She glanced around, noticed Tom, then proceeded to ignore him and walk toward me.

"Nice of you to join us," I said.

"I am happy to see you too, my love."

Ugh! I so needed to make her understand when I was being sarcastic. "Yeah yeah, whatever. Listen, we've been discussing this plan all night, going over the details, et cetera, and I still think it's a long shot."

"Indeed it is. In fact, I would argue that, were our destinies not bound for greater things, the chances of us suffering horribly at the hands of our enemies would be a near certainty."

"I can see why your people follow you. You have quite the way with pep talks."

If Gan understood I was making fun of her, she didn't show it. Instead, she walked to the middle of the room. "Gather your belongings, for it is time to depart."

"We were just discussing that," Veronica said sleepily.

"Yeah," I added. "There's the problem of Alex. If prior campaigns are any indication, he has this place covered. So, if we're going to make a run for it, we need to figure out a way..."

"He does not," Gan stated flatly.

"Huh?"

All eyes in the room, those who were still awake anyway, stopped and turned toward us.

"That is why I left," she continued. "I wished to make contact with those loyal to me to discuss our forthcoming plans."

"What's this have to do with Alex's people taking the night off?"

"Those plans, if I may be allowed to continue, my darling, included sending my assassins to silence any whose eyes might be turned our way."

"Of course they did," Sally commented.

"Surprisingly, they found none."

"Maybe they missed them," Christy said.

"Yeah," Meg added. "I mean, we're dealing with Alexander the Great here. He's not exactly a novice."

Gan sighed painfully, as if she was dealing with a group of children … like her, but far stupider. "We are not dealing with Lord Alexander, witch. To think he would take it upon himself to personally conduct surveillance is the height of both arrogance and foolishness. As for the agents of the First, I am well versed in their tactics and protocols."

"Oh, like what?"

"Like the fact that his people did not raid this place during my absence."

"Wait, what?" I asked.

"Indeed. I was fully expecting it, hence why I stationed warriors in the adjacent buildings, ready to ambush them."

"You did?"

"Of course."

"Wait," I said. "Get back to this raid part."

"Protocol dictates that this entire building be under constant surveillance, both physical and electronic."

"You mean this place is bugged?"

"From top to bottom, I can assure you."

"Hold on," Sally said. "So if you knew this, then how come you didn't warn us not to flap our lips about plans and shit?"

"Flap your lips?" Gan asked slowly. "Quite the interesting term of expression. But to answer your question, whore, I would tell you to look toward the witch."

"My sisters and I have wards up all over," Christy explained. "They're meant to discourage outside spying in a variety of ways."

"Indeed, rendering electronic means unreliable at best. However, the First would still have many eyes upon this place. Surely they would have noticed anything out of the ordinary."

"Such as you coming and going during daylight hours?" I asked.

"I was counting on it."

"Why?" Sheila asked. "I thought you were helping us."

"Indeed I am. Agents of the First operate under a great deal of autonomy during times of war such as this. Their orders would be to observe or follow, but also to gather intelligence."

"Which they'd then report to their superiors," Sheila surmised.

"In theory, yes. In practice, it is somewhat different. The First are intolerant of failure, but they also frown quite heavily on inaccurate information. My presence would raise their suspicions, but they would be hesitant to report in for further instruction before they knew more. It would make them look weak. Hence, why I fully expected this place to be infiltrated by now."

"But it hasn't been," I said.

Christy crossed her arms defiantly. "My wards would have warned us."

"And what of it?" Gan asked. "You are under a state of truce with Alexander. His people would have acted under such pretense. Had you reacted against them with force, the fault would be on your heads. But this discussion is entirely pointless now. It did not occur, nor have my men found any trace that they were ever here to begin with."

"Maybe protocol changed," Sally said.

"Even if it did, my people are trained to adapt. I can assure you, they have scoured all buildings within a three-block radius of this one."

I turned to my roommate and commented, "As if the neighbors probably didn't already hate us."

"What about the sewers?"

Sally's question received a pained sigh in return from Gan as if it were so obvious to not even be worth a response.

"So what does that mean?" Sheila asked.

At that, Gan's shell of arrogance actually began to crack a bit. She was silent for a moment, and when she finally did answer, something entirely alien was in her voice – indecision. "I do not know."

20

NORTHERN EXPOSURE

Gan explained that she was essentially in the dark. She had to be extra careful with regard to her normal contacts both within Boston and other seats of power so as to not tip off anyone that she was back. Even with her precautions, though, she should have still had enough clout to have eyes and ears just about everywhere, but for some reason, the flow of information had become little more than a trickle.

Something was up within the vampire hierarchy, but she didn't know what and was hesitant to push further and potentially reveal herself.

That was odd. Hell, it made me half-tempted to call Boston and outright ask Colin how things were going.

Mind you, I somehow resisted the urge.

Whatever the case, a gift horse had been presented to us and, rather than sit around and debate it, we decided to make use of it.

We were free and clear to pursue our plan with the Feet. There was no telling how long this window of opportunity would remain open, so we needed to act now.

Thank goodness, too. I'd felt that anger inside of me recede once we started discussing an actual plan, but it was still there. It was only a matter of time before it reared its ugly head again. If it was all the same to anyone else, I'd prefer it happen while we were surrounded by creatures that deserved a punch in the face.

Of course, that still left open the logistics of how to get there. I, for one, didn't relish another weeklong road trip to the frozen north. There was also the problem of where to go. Sure, we'd been there once, but it's not like I had kept the GPS coordinates handy. There were some waypoints you remembered and some you prayed to forget. Besides, past a certain point, one big cluster of frozen trees looked like the next.

Thankfully, Gan's indecision with regard to the Dracs didn't last long, because when I mentioned these concerns to her, she laughed as if it were one of the stupidest things she'd ever heard.

"The prior gathering at the Alma stronghold was made with certain concessions in mind, beloved," she said, a grin upon her face as if she thought my ignorance just the cutest thing. "At the time, these concessions were agreed upon because peace was still an option. However, that time is passed. Though our intentions are to reforge that peace and we will be approaching them under a flag of truce, we are still at war. Thus, a show of strength will be far more appropriate."

I considered what we had at our disposal. Icon and Freewill – check. A coven of witches, also not bad. And whatever Gan was, aka a new player at the table. On paper, it was a pretty formidable combination, enough to probably intimidate a small handful of Sasquatches. An army of them, though? Yeah, I had a feeling begging for our lives might be more conducive to our continued survival.

However, as with a great many things, I assumed wrong.

I had thought Gan was talking about our immediate group when she meant a show of strength. Maybe we'd drive up and proclaim ourselves the crème de la crème of the vampire nation. Much posturing would then ensue.

I had to admit, her plan of flying us up in a trio of unmarked Blackhawk helicopters was a shitload better than what I had in mind.

Faster, too.

Don't get me wrong. The trip was still well over a day's journey with multiple refueling stops, but Gan's people seemed to have it handled. There wasn't much to do except watch the scenery below as we flew north.

I, of course, got stuck on a chopper with Gan. There was no escaping that fate. I wasn't in any position to demand different accommodations. However, I weaseled some company in with us to make sure she didn't try to book us membership in the mile-high club, especially since our conveyances had been custom retrofitted with luxury amenities, including a divider between the passengers and cockpit.

It made sense to bring Sheila along on our chopper. As the lynchpin upon which this insane plan hinged, there was no doubt she could glean intelligence from Gan. Sally, though no fan of our diminutive host, was even less a fan of being the third wheel between Tom and Christy. She insisted on joining us, citing an aversion to vomiting for the entire ride up. Christy's coven took the third chopper.

If it weren't for the jet-black paint jobs and twin machine guns mounted on either side, our rides could've been mistaken for some millionaire's playthings. Hell, there was even a wet bar stocked with blood in ours. Gan definitely didn't believe in suffering for the cause.

Unfortunately, her presence negated any chance of serious conversation. Pity, because I had a feeling that there were a lot of things in need of saying between Sally, Sheila, and me. While we'd been in a holding pattern, it had been easy to pretend that there was more time or that someone needed space. Now that we were on the move, though, the concept of there being a tomorrow in which to do these things became uncertain. Everything did. A plan like this could set us down the path to victory, but it could just as easily go tits up.

Knowing my luck, I had the feeling that our lives were about to get *interesting* again.

"I don't suppose these things come standard with a bathroom?"

"I think that's the next model up," Sheila said to me with a smirk. "The budget didn't allow it."

"It's your own fucking fault," Sally added, far less generously. "You should have gone when we stopped to gas up."

"I didn't have to go then."

"Well, judging from the scenery below," she replied, glancing out the window, "your choices are gonna be a snowbank, a rock, or some trees. Sorry to say, but we seem to have left the land of Tim Horton's behind."

"Just so long as it's not a maple tree," I groused, drawing a chuckle from her.

Sheila glanced back and forth between us, obviously not in on the joke.

"Trust me, you don't want to know."

I already knew the chances of us running into anything resembling civilization were slim. Our last refueling stop had been the final one ahead of reaching our destination. We'd already donned cold weather gear, although, since it had come courtesy of Gan, we all looked less like backpackers and more like a group of yak herders.

Oh well, at least this time the fur coat I was wearing didn't seem to be lined with explosives. I'd take my victories where I could get them.

Thankfully, we weren't going in completely cold, minus the weather maybe. Gan, in typical fashion, had nominated some of her people to be cannon fodder in advance. Showing up in the sacred woods of the Sasquatches uninvited was asking for trouble. So, she explained, she had some of her emissaries approach ahead of time under a totem of truce, as she put it. Of the dozen she'd sent in, one had actually returned and radioed back that we were expected.

She seemed to consider this a favorable outcome. Though she could now tolerate daylight with ease, it had done nothing to give her anything even remotely resembling a sunny disposition.

"I was correct," she said as we neared the landing site. "The change in Alma leadership you forced upon them, my love, has opened a small window of opportunity. They are willing to hear us out. The presence of the Shining One will be the catalyst that gains us entry." She turned to Sheila. "You will be at the forefront of our party, sword out and raised high."

"Won't that come across as aggressive?" Sheila asked.

"Yes, but a show of strength is necessary here."

"Okay," I said. "So what about us? I assume this thing comes equipped with a weapons locker."

"Indeed it does," Gan replied.

"But we won't be using it," Sally added.

"Huh? What do you mean by that? She just said a show of strength..."

"By the Icon," she explained. "She's the big cheese of this show. The rest of us need to tuck our tails between our legs and look like our asses have been kicked."

"In a sense," Gan said. "We are to follow in supplication. Though not prisoners, we must be unarmed and carrying traditional Alma tokens of peace. A show of strength on the Shining One's part will be met with respect. One on ours will be..."

I reached up and rubbed the bridge of my nose. "Let me guess — will be met with a lot more strength than we can handle."

"Perhaps."

"Perhaps?"

Rather than answer, she said, "The witches are considered a neutral party. So long as they appear aloof to our plight, they will be treated respectfully in their role as witnesses to this event."

"Okay," I replied, resigning myself to whatever unpleasantness was ahead. "I guess that's everyone. I suppose we can suck up a bit of humility if it'll get us what we need."

"No, that's not everyone," Sally said with a sigh. "You're forgetting the meatsack."

"Good point. The Feet don't particularly like humans, so I guess he's with us."

"Except he's not human," she pointed out. "The Feet smell even better than us."

"I might debate that."

"With their noses, shit for brains."

"Oh, yeah."

"Don't think for a second they aren't going to notice he doesn't smell like a person. Hell, he doesn't smell like anything. They aren't going to like that, especially since I'm willing to bet they're well versed with that tactic your *fiancée* here used when we were trying to get to Boston."

I narrowed my eyes. "She is not my..."

"Your whore is correct," Gan said. "The human will..."

Sally leaned forward, quick as a snake, and grabbed her by the throat. "I am getting really tired of that."

Sheila's eyes widened at the attack, and a white glow began to emanate from her.

Oh shit! If she went full spotlight mode in these close quarters, we wouldn't have to worry about the Feet killing us.

"It's cool," I said to her, lifting my hands in a placating manner. "They ... err ... play like this all the time." I glanced over and gritted my teeth. "Isn't that right, Sally?"

Gan, for her part, didn't seem overly concerned that she had a clawed hand wrapped around her neck. In fact, she was so unconcerned, she slowly reached up, grabbed Sally's wrist, and pulled her off with seemingly no effort.

Sally's eyes widened ever so slightly. She no doubt remembered that, despite Gan's size, she was on the order of two and a half centuries older.

Double shit.

"That's enough, all of you!" I said, my voice lowering a full octave until it barely resembled mine at all. With a small sense of horror, I realized I sounded like Dr. Death during those moments when we had conversed in my head. I quickly cleared my throat, pretending to cough. "Sorry, frog in my throat. Anyway, that's more than enough."

"You," I said to Gan, "enough with the whore shit. Her name is Sally." I turned to Sally. "You, no attacking our gracious host." And then, finally, to Sheila, "And you, no killing us before the Sasquatches get a chance."

21

GENEVA CONVENTION 2.0

Though Gan stopped far short of apologizing, she did throw an "As you wish, beloved" at me, serving to both acquiesce to my demands and skeeve me out.

The other two were a bit more cooperative. They knew the stakes at play and the big risk we were running to even have a shot at it.

Unfortunately, there was one risk I wasn't aware of until we had landed and it was far too late.

"What the ever living fuck?"

"As I told you, beloved, we are expected to present the Alma with the traditional totem of peace to show our sincerity."

"Yeah, I get that, but why not just a white flag?"

"The Alma neither utilize nor acknowledge flags."

"But they fucking acknowledge dead skunks?"

"It is their way," Gan replied as if she were holding a bouquet of flowers instead of a stinking rodent corpse.

Of course, to the Feet – ripe fuckers that they were – maybe a dead skunk was the equivalent of a dozen roses, or perhaps a stick of deodorant. "Okay, fine, but what about the rest?"

"Only the three of us represent the nation that is at war with the Alma. The others are here as guests."

"Guests," Sheila echoed from several steps away, "that will be doing their best to march upwind of you."

She wasn't the only one. Everyone else, outside of Gan's people, were giving us a wide berth, too.

We were at the edge of the forest, where the tundra began. A large contingent of Gan's followers had met us there, having already set up a basecamp. Unfortunately, they weren't coming with us. Though the Feet were willing to hear us out, they only extended the invitation to a small group. Gan's people were forbidden from entering the forest. If they did, we'd be killed instantly. Though I'd been happy to see them, thinking an extraction force was relatively close if we needed one, in truth, we'd be on our own if anything went south.

Just wonderful.

Right as we were getting ready to go, Gan walked away to converse with the leader of her strike team. I figured it was to give instructions for him and his whole family to commit suicide if they forgot to do something minor – typical Gan stuff. However, just as they were finishing up, I noticed him hand her something small and disturbingly metallic.

My palms began to sweat. Oh fuck. It was another detonator. I was just about to tell everyone to perform an emergency striptease when she walked back and held it out to me, palm up.

A metal vial lay in her hand. "What?"

"Blood," she replied.

"Yours?" I asked.

"Yes, as well as a drop from every man you see here. If things go wrong..."

There was no need for her to finish that sentence. I realized she didn't need a bomb. She had one standing right in front of her. And I'd been right. This was a detonator of sorts, just not electronic in nature. This small amount wouldn't last for long, but it was easily palmed. Also, the results were bound to be ... interesting.

"Thank you, Gan," I said. "That's actually a really good idea."

"The anticipation of once again seeing the beast inside of you fills my body with joy."

"And the moment's over. Thanks." I put the vial into my pocket then turned to where most of the others had gathered. "Okay, let's get this over with. We get in there, present them with our dead rats, and get the hell out."

"I don't know what the fuck you're complaining about!"

I turned to find Tom stalking over to us. He seemed a bit miffed. Perhaps that had something to do with the fact that his fur coat was dripping with blood and entrails.

Though I tried to keep a stoic look upon my face, I couldn't. Gan had taken seriously our musings on Tom's lack of scent. Upon our arrival, her people had been waiting for us, complete with a slaughtered moose. Before he could so much as open his mouth in protest, they'd dragged him over and tossed him into a pile of innards.

Well, that was one problem solved. Now only a shitload more to go.

"So is there any particular direction I should be going?" Sheila asked from up ahead, her aura alight to keep her from tripping in the dark forest.

"March forward," Gan replied stoically. "We are already under observation. The Alma will present themselves at a time of their own choosing."

"It had better be soon," Tom griped. "I think I have a piece of intestine in my shoe."

He was walking with us, having been shunned by the witches marching a dozen or so paces behind, their magic lighting their way and making them easily seen despite the foliage.

I stopped abruptly and spun, not-so-accidentally

smacking my friend with the skunk in my hand. "Y'know, a positive attitude would probably do you well."

"I never liked you."

I grinned back at him, then turned and continued walking. "I can't see why not."

"I'm not really liking anyone right now," Sally said. "I can't believe I volunteered to come back up to this God forsaken place."

"Adversity makes for strange bedfellows."

"Hah!" Tom chuckled. "Like how you and Sally..."

In a flash, she grabbed him by the greasy collar of his bloodied coat and dragged him down to her level. "What did we discuss about that?"

Uncertainty flashed in my friend's eyes. "Um ... that we were never ever to mention it again?"

"Yes, and what would happen if you did?"

"You'd melt me down into a pile of suppositories and pass me out to crackheads."

"Same rule applies up here, except I might have to substitute our hairy soon-to-be friends instead."

"Mention what?" Sheila asked from up ahead.

"Nothing," Sally replied, still glaring unblinkingly at Tom. "Just a tiny incident that happened on the road to Boston." She glanced at me sidelong. "A *very* tiny incident."

I stuck my tongue out at her and continued on my way. It was probably something we needed to discuss at some point, although up until now, Sally had purposely blown me off. She didn't seem to think it was a big deal – one of those things that happened between vamps. Me, I wasn't quite so certain. I mean, my alter ego Dr. Death had forced himself upon her with the intent of killing her when he was done. It was meant to be the ultimate slap in the face to me, the last thing I saw before being shunted into my own subconscious forever.

Pity for him, it hadn't quite worked out that way.

Even so, neither Sheila nor Gan knew about it, as far as I was aware. And, quite frankly, I thought it best to keep things that way. Gan might flip out and do something Gan-like. As for Sheila...

Oh, Jesus. I had no fucking idea there anymore. Talk about getting mixed vibes. Albeit, in all fairness, I was probably giving them off myself. In truth, I had feelings for two women, either of whom was both a wonderful prospect and a potentially dire mistake at the same time.

I glanced quickly at Sally by my side, then forward again toward Sheila.

There would have to be a reckoning soon between us all. As for what that would mean, I had no idea.

No. All I knew was that I was a doofus marching through the woods, searching for Bigfoot with a dead skunk in my hand – the plot of a romantic comedy if ever there was one.

Fortunately for me, as tended to be the case during times when I really should have been paying attention, fate decided to spare me from such deep thoughts.

I have little doubt the others noticed it first. They'd stopped walking, causing me to almost saunter into Sheila's backside, a not so great thing with her aura up. As I backpedaled a few paces, I noticed my footsteps on the cold, hard ground sounded very loud. All sound, save that which we made ourselves, had ceased in the woods.

"And here we go again," Tom muttered. "Try not to shit on any sacred trees."

"That wasn't me."

"Would you both shut the fuck up?" Sally hissed at us.

"I am forced to agree," Gan said quietly. Then, more loudly, "Shining One, *now*."

Sheila glanced back, uncertainty in her eyes ... strange, considering the force that powered her.

"You can do it!" a voice further back cried – Kelly's.

Sheila nodded, then turned to face the darkness before her. She drew her sword, and it blazed white fire as she lifted it over her head, becoming an unmistakable beacon in the night. "I am Sheila O'Connell of the..." She hesitated for a second. I couldn't really blame her. This next part was kind of stupid. "Of the Silver Eyes. I have come here to parlay between the two great warring nations as set forth in the Humbaba Accord."

"*Accord broken*," a gravelly voice replied from somewhere up ahead. Even with my enhanced night vision, I couldn't see the source. However, it probably wasn't a stretch to imagine the owner was very large and smelled terrible.

And there it was. One moment there was nothing, save the stench of Tom and our peace offerings. The next came an odor that made me want to bury my face in the skunk's ass and breathe as deeply as I could.

Sheila coughed a few times, but thankfully kept her composure. Sadly, the witches behind us weren't quite as magnanimous.

"Dear goddess!"

"I think I'm gonna hurl."

Oh well, hopefully their status as a neutral party held.

"A sword which is broken can be reforged," Sheila said, her voice tight but loud. I had little trouble imagining her eyes were watering something fierce right now, but she held it together. "So too can a broken accord."

The crunch of dried pine needles beneath enormous feet could be heard all around us. Where a moment ago there was nothing, now massive shapes moved between the trees. We were surrounded.

If things went badly for us, we would be fucked in the ass as thoroughly as if we were under contract with Vivid Video.

Maybe it was a trick of the light, but the trees immediately in front of Sheila seemed to bend away from each other, revealing the massive form of a Sasquatch. Over nine feet tall, he approached to just outside her aura and stood looming over her. The look on its face was one of ... well, these things always looked pissed off, so that wasn't really anything new.

It occurred to me that none of us really had any clue whether an Icon's power could work against the Feet. I mean, they were basically spirits given flesh ... really big flesh, that hit really really hard when it wanted to. Then again, hadn't

Alex once said something about vampires originally being like that too before something happened to cause us to adopt our current forms? I couldn't help but wonder if maybe that something had a name that started with I and ended with B.

Still, that was speculation best saved for another time. No matter what the Feet actually were, it would be a particularly lousy time to learn that Sheila's powers didn't do jack shit against them.

The two beings, both of them supernatural wonders in their own right – the legendary Icon and fucking Bigfoot – stood there staring at each other. A Mexican standoff in the woods of Canada.

And then, without a word between them, the impasse was broken.

22

C IS FOR COOKIE

Sheila's sword blazed furiously, casting a ghostly light on the monster in front of her. Its eyes flashed red and its lips pulled back in a snarl.

Then she drove the tip of the sword into the frozen ground between them and took a step back.

The ugly fucker in front of her glared down for a moment, then nodded as if it liked what it saw. At last, it opened its mouth and spoke. "*Silver Eyes great warrior. Cunt honored by your presence.*"

Wait, what?

No. I did *not* just fucking hear that.

I turned to Tom and saw his eyes widen with surprise as he no doubt wondered the same thing.

"Excuse me?" Sheila asked. "I'm pretty sure I didn't hear you correctly."

The Sasquatch turned its head and blew out a wad of snot, perhaps the Bigfoot equivalent of clearing its throat, then addressed her again. "*Great Cunt, leader of the Northern Clans, welcomes you.*"

"Don't do it!" Sally warned us, her voice barely audible.

Tom snorted beside me and I couldn't help myself. I raised my hand to my mouth so as to not audibly lose my shit – hoping beyond hope that maybe the stupid fucking apes thought I was just caught up in the moment. Oh God, and I thought Turd was bad.

Sally shook her head and sighed. "We are so fucking dead."

"*Yes*," the Sasquatch replied. "*T'lunta who stupid enough to enter this sacred place die. You here, so must be very stupid.*"

Oh shit, I forgot these things had senses to rival our own.

"My frien..." Sheila began, then caught herself. Yeah, putting it out there that she was buddies with their sworn enemies was not something she wanted to do. "I mean, these tuh-luntas have come here with me at great risk to themselves. They have approached me with humility. Their nation has suffered great losses at your hands. They have asked me to broker a new peace with you, oh mighty..."

She trailed off and then glanced back at us, panic in her eyes as she bit down on her quivering lips. Well, at least it was good to know I wasn't the only one who found these fuckers to be as ridiculous as they were terrifying. A small part of me wondered if whoever had first translated their language to ours hadn't been a smartass of the first degree.

"Oh come on," Meg shouted from somewhere behind us. "He's a big cunt. This isn't so hard."

Christy could be heard grumbling something under her breath in response.

Oh yeah, this was going well.

Thankfully, it didn't appear as if this Bigfoot had much more in the way of brains than his predecessor did, as he replied, "*Magi acknowledge Cunt with honor. Cunt welcome you as witnesses.*"

"Sorry," Sheila quickly added. "I was overcome with ... emotion at this historic undertaking."

That seemed to mollify the monstrous ape. He turned his eyes from her to my group, specifically me. "*Freewill T'lunta,*" he spat, "*we know you. You vanquish Turd.*" He said that last part with a growl.

Oh crap, what if this guy was Turd's bestie or maybe his

brother? If so, quite the family nomenclature. But still, his eyes bored holes into me. I took it as my cue.

I stepped forward, holding the dead skunk in front of me as if it were some sort of magical talisman against even worse smelling things. "I am sorry for your loss. Turd fought bravely, but you have to realize he attacked me first and..."

The ugly fucker lifted his head to the sky and roared, utterly drowning out my rambling apology. The sound echoed among the trees for several seconds. I couldn't help but think that maybe I'd said the wrong thing. Perhaps I didn't sound sorrowful enough. Perhaps I...

"*Turd traitor! Breaker of our sacred ways.*"

"And that's why the motherfucker needed to die," I quickly amended.

"Yeah!" Tom added. "Bill punted that fucker's ass for a field goal."

I glanced his way and sighed. "Thanks."

"Anytime, bro."

I already missed being able to shove him into a pocket.

"*Must be mighty warrior to vanquish Turd,*" one of the Sasquatches off to the side commented.

After a year of dealing with this bullshit, I was beginning to get a sense of how these things worked. When someone higher on the food chain gave you shit, you were expected to swallow it and compliment them on the flavor. But when a nobody talked smack, you threw it right back at them. "I am the motherfucking Ty-D-Bol man, asshole. And if you want to find out why, I suggest you step up and find out."

Internally, however, I was really hoping he declined.

"*Thought you come to make peace,*" Cunt said from up ahead. "*Yet you challenge my k'tun to combat?*"

"Um, k'tun?"

Gan stepped up and nudged me in the side. "You may wish to know, Dr. Death, that means father in their language."

Oh Jesus Fucking Christ! "No. That was just smack talk."

"*Smack talk?*" Cunt asked. With that, he backhanded the sapling next to him, shattering it into splinters.

"Different type of smack," I clarified. "It's ... a T'lunta custom, where we say inappropriate things to people we have great respect for." That's right, Bill, dig yourself in even deeper.

"You are such a pussy," Sally muttered.

"*I see,*" the Sasquatch said. "*Much like your mate talk to you now. Stupid custom, but Cunt understand.*"

Sheila spun back toward us, one eyebrow raised, but I mouthed "Not now" to her.

Forget forging a new peace. We'd be lucky if we made it past the next minute or two.

Fortunately for us, the Sasquatches had continued in their fine tradition of electing complete morons as leaders. The whole "strongest must lead" trope might have made for a good caveman movie, but in actual practice, it ensured that the folks sitting at the other end of the negotiating table were a few quarts short of a gallon when it came to brains.

Cunt nodded and two more of the monsters stepped forward from the shadows. I guess they were dignitaries or the welcome wagon. Or, fuck, maybe they just liked the taste of skunk, because they took them from me and Sally. When they got to Gan, however, they wrinkled their noses.

"*Not T'lunta,*" one of them said, sounding confused.

The other took a long sniff, snorting up what sounded like a gallon of snot in the process. "*Not know. Look like T'lunta warrior others claim to fight, but smell different.*"

They grunted a few syllables to their leader, to which he asked, "*Why this one offer peace? This one not at war.*"

"I will have you know, I have slaughtered..."

I stepped in front of Gan. "Yes, she's slaughtered many cows. Little bugger just hates them. Anyway, she's one of our allies, just signed a treaty with us, so we figured we'd bring her. But aside from that, she's new here. Never even met a ... whatever is the polite term for you guys. She just has one of those faces. You know how it is."

We were finally making progress but, for whatever reason, I didn't think letting slip that the vampire nation had a whole new strain, one capable of withstanding sunlight, was a great idea. For all I knew, this would cause our hosts to freak out or demand we offer her as a gift for dissection.

Don't get me wrong, a world free from the fear of waking up chained to Gan's bed was something I strived for, but that didn't mean I was willing to sell the micro-demon down the river for it.

Cunt nodded toward the Bigfoot closest Gan. He grabbed the dead skunk from her hands and tossed it away, back over our heads, eliciting a quick "Gross!" from Veronica as it hit her with a wet splat.

Oh fuck it. That was kinda funny.

Just as the two Feet were about to step away, one of them glanced back and cast an eye on Tom.

Oh no, not again.

However, it simply gave a sniff before turning away.

"This human smell nicer than others."

23

THE NEGOTIATING TABLE

Much like during our last foray into the Woods of Mourning, we were escorted to a Sasquatch village and deposited into a crude hut until such time as they were ready to talk.

The place was large enough for us all, but that was pretty much the end of the creature comforts. It might have been clean by Sasquatch standards, but even sitting at the crude stone table in the middle of the place had me wishing I'd brought along a gallon of hand sanitizer.

But hey, at least they left us some *snacks*. The frozen corpse of a hiker was propped up in one corner and the table was covered in bowls ... some of them containing nuts; others full of things that still wriggled.

"Brings back the memories, eh?" I asked Tom.

He flipped me the middle finger.

Sheila looked at us quizzically from across the table, and I explained how we'd tricked him into thinking he'd been zombified.

It was all we could do. The non-witches, especially Sheila, had been relegated to the center of the room while Christy and her coven hastily etched sigils into the four corners of the hut.

"There. We should have some privacy now."

"Are you sure?" Sally asked.

"Only one way to find out," Meg replied before shouting, "Hey, Bill! When you finally kill that fucking Cunt, make sure it hurts!"

What the...?! I stood up. "Are you fucking insane?"

She raised her hand to her ear with a grin. "I guess not."

Sally poked me in the side. "I like her."

"You would. Oh, by the way, Gan, sorry for interrupting you back there."

"While I have no desire to hide my many victories over the Alma, perhaps it is for the best. The machinations of Ib are our business to deal with. The Alma, being our eternal enemies, are best left in the dark." She waved a hand like it was nothing and then scooted over closer to me.

I took that as my cue to get up and pace. "Yeah, learning that an army of vamps with much more *sunny* dispositions than usual was in the works could really throw a monkey wrench into our talks."

"I see what you did just there," Kelly said to me with a smile.

"Then you're going to love this, because up next, we need to discuss the six-hundred-pound gorilla in the room."

"I'm pretty sure most of them weigh more than that."

"Yeah, well, I don't want to test that by having any of them sit on me," Tom said. "The way that one said I smelled good kinda creeped me out."

"Sorry, man." I clapped him on the shoulder. "But since you're basically the magical equivalent of a RealDoll now, I think we should keep that possibility on the table as a negotiating chip."

Tom's eyes opened wide in horror. Dead, alive, or somewhere in between, he was just too easy.

"What I really meant was..."

"Let me guess," Meg interrupted. "The big problem is that the leader of these fuckers ... sorry, Christy, I mean the leader of the Forest Folk has a name that's gonna be almost impossible to negotiate a peace against without laughing at."

Sheila nodded. "My power can instill a near stupid level of confidence in me, but this is completely different. Even I'm not sure about that one."

"It's just a word," Sally said. "Get over it."

"I know it's just a word, but it's..."

"The nuclear option?" I offered.

"Yes!" Sheila replied, throwing her hands up.

"I do not see the issue," Gan said. "It is simply a translation from one inelegant language to another."

"Trust me, I get it," I replied. "In case you hadn't noticed, I'm kind of loose with my tongue."

"Pretty sure it's not just you," Tom added.

"Yes, I know. But what I mean is, in a world of lots of fucks to give, his name just happens to be the one under glass that you only break in case of fire. In other words, only if you really really mean it."

"Gee," Sally said with mock concern, "and here I had you pegged as someone who definitely had a friend named Mike Hunt."

"Fuck you, cunt."

As a trio of Sasquatch escorts led us to where the talks would take place, I considered the ridiculousness of the situation. Here we were, trying to stave off the end of the world, and yet our immediate concern was not losing it and laughing at a giant gorilla with a stupid name.

Ah yes, life was strange some days.

"Wow," Sheila said as we came to the hollow, at the bottom of which lay a large table that appeared to have been grown more than built.

"You should have seen it last time," I replied, noting how empty it was.

"Yeah," Tom remarked. "Bill almost punched out a snack cart vendor."

I flashed him a dirty look. Not one of my finer moments.

Still, it was amazing how different it seemed now. Before, it had been noisy, full of all sorts of oddball life. In a way, it had felt sort of like the paranormal equivalent of Woodstock, up until the point where the crowd had turned on me.

Now, though, it had a sort of peaceful quality to it. I could imagine taking a hike in the woods and stumbling upon this place. It would seem like something out of a fairy tale, at least until you realized this was sacred Bigfoot ground and they ripped off your arms for trespassing.

Their leader was already seated at one end, with a couple of other Sasquatches around him.

"Is Grulg one of them?" I asked Sally in a hushed whisper.

"Not as far as I can tell."

"These things need name tags."

"You'd just piss yourself laughing."

"Yeah," I mused, "you're probably right."

We were led down to the table. There, one of the Sasquatches pointed out a raised seat in the center. "*Your place, Silver Eyes.*"

"Congrats," I said to her. "You get to play the role of the big glowing ball of death this time."

"What?" she asked, eyes wide.

"Inside joke. Good luck; you'll do fine."

I flashed her a thumbs up and she smiled, albeit there was uncertainty behind it. Jeez, put that girl in a fight and she was all kick-ass and take names. Ask her to look one giant ape with a stupid fucking name in the eye, though, and suddenly there was an issue.

"*T'lunta and mate sit there,*" one of the beasts snarled. I couldn't help but notice its tone was ever so slightly less respectful toward us.

Gan immediately stepped forward – presumptuous little minx – but the squatch held up a hand. "*No! Table only for T'lunta.*" He spat a hock of nastiness on the ground at her feet. "*You and witches sit there.*"

"I am not one of *them*," she replied indignantly. "I am here in the capacity of..."

"*Not care. Sit.*"

"She's ... my advisor." I didn't want Gan's feathers to get ruffled and for her to start any fights we couldn't win. More importantly, she knew what the fuck she was doing. Last time I was here, I'd had to sit at the head of the table, but it had originally been as a figurehead position. The reason was simple: I wasn't a fucking diplomat! I doubt I'd be able to even tell the parchment that stupid accord was written on apart from something I'd wiped my ass with.

The big ape snarled at me. "*She advise from there, then.*" He pointed a large finger at the spot right next to Christy.

I glanced over at Cunt, hoping maybe he'd say something, but he was busy with important matters involving an itch on his ass. Finally, I nodded. "It's okay, Gan. It's not like there's a crowd to shout over if I need you."

"As you wish," she replied curtly. Glad to see she wasn't letting a little thing like ego get in the way. Just to add a little extra oomph to her pouting, though, she left a wide gap between her and Christy when she finally sat down. Oh yeah, she might claim to be three hundred years old, but she had the attitude of a preteen down to a science.

Christy, for her part, opened her bag and placed Decker's skull down between her and Gan. Just great. He'd been quiet on the walk over. I think Christy had whammied him into silence, but even so, I couldn't help but feel uncomfortable with his eye sockets looking my way.

Finally, I turned to Sally. "Shall we?"

"Can I get a proper introduction, or should I just carry your laundry for you?"

"Oh, sorry." I turned to our escort, albeit not before allowing myself a small grin. "This is Sally. She's my partner."

The beast cocked its head to the side, making it possibly look even stupider. "*Part Ner?*"

"Yeah, she's not my mate."

"Nor am I applying for the position," she added, because why not kick me in the balls when I was trying to help her?

I glanced up and saw Sheila watching us intently. Hopefully, she found as much amusement in this as our hosts.

The squatch shrugged. "*Okay. Sit with servant.*"

"She's not my servant. She's my partner. It means equal."

"*She female T'lunta.*"

"So?"

The Sasquatch turned to his side of the table and grunted a few times. After a moment, they all burst into laughter. Not really a confidence builder, I might add.

When they were finished, Cunt spoke up. "*T'lunta funny. Now sit.*"

"Yeah, but..."

"*SIT!*"

I planted my ass firmly in my chair. After a beat, Sally slid in and took the seat next to mine.

I leaned over to her. "I'm assuming that women's suffrage hasn't quite caught on here yet."

"Ya think?"

"Just try not to start a war." She glared at me. "I meant another war ... or a worse war."

Oh yeah, we were off to a great start.

24

A PIECE OF PEACE TAKE TWO

"**L**et's see if I get this right," Sheila said with a nervous chuckle.

I took some slight amusement at her discomfort. In a way, it was also nice to see. Though Icons and vamps were like oil and water, it seemed the transformation into one or the other had at least one thing in common: a change in attitude. The majority of vamps I knew were predators. Most of them didn't even try to maintain their humanity. For Icons, however, the change was a bit more positive, but a change nevertheless. Seeing her nervous like this reminded me of the old her, the one I'd fawned over for three years.

Being members of warring species, I'd thought the rift between us too wide to cross. Now, however, seeing her vulnerable like this, I began to wonder if perhaps I hadn't been too hasty in my judgment.

"We, the gathered, are here to bear witness..." she began.

I smiled. They were the same words that had kicked off the last summit. Although back then they had been mind-beamed into us all by some glowing ball of magical energy that served as mediator, not to mention judge, jury, and executioner. All in all, I considered our current host to be a considerable upgrade.

Of course, far cuter than a floating globe of death or not, the official opening statement was still boring as fuck. Goddamn, I so hated ceremony. Why couldn't we just get on with it?

"...the leader of the Northern Tribes..." Sheila paused for a moment, composing herself. "Big C."

The Sasquatch leader looked up at that. "*Huh?*"

It had been our little compromise back in the hut. She just wasn't comfortable saying his name, at least without dissolving into giggles like she was a little girl caught swearing. It was kind of cute, but ultimately not the best thing to do during life or death negotiations.

"*What say?*" he asked.

"My apologies," she replied as we'd rehearsed. "Among the Silver Eyes there is a tradition to honor great warriors. We give them a nickname of respect that all will tremble before. You, mighty ... Big C," she sputtered, almost losing it for a moment. "I was so impressed upon our meeting, that I thought to convey such an honor upon you. I am sorry if I was wrong, though. I will stop..."

"*No!*" the Sasquatch roared, then softened its voice, as much as it could anyway. "*Cunt is mighty warrior. Mighty Cunt indeed.*"

Oh crap, I could see the corners of her lips trembling.

"*You honor me, Silver Eyes.*"

She turned to me, panic on her face as she struggled to keep from laughing. Oh crap. What to do?

Oh, wait. What I did best ... play the part of the asshole.

I pounded on the table. "All right, enough of this shit. Let's move on!"

The Sasquatches at the other end all glared at me. Definitely a social faux pas on my part and probably not a great thing to do while trying to bargain for peace, but it worked. The impending bout of laughter fell off of Sheila's face and she flashed me a look of gratitude before simply stating, "I similarly welcome, representing the vampire nation, the reborn Freewill Bill Ryder."

"*HAH!*" the Bigfoot leader shouted, smashing his fist into the table much as I'd done, if a lot more effectively. "*No honor for you from Silver Eyes!*"

I opened my mouth to say something, but Sally silenced me with an elbow to the side.

"Don't do it," she warned. "This is a good thing."

Once I gave it a moment's thought, I realized she was right. Though our word game was meant to keep the inappropriate giggles to a bare minimum, by doing so, Sheila had inadvertently proven her neutrality to the Feet, maybe even convinced them she leaned slightly in their favor. If the stupid shit monkeys thought she was on their side, it could make these negotiations much easier.

"That will be enough," Sheila said, moving smoothly into the next part of her role. "These are to be respectful negotiations."

Hah! That was a good one.

To help emphasize her point, she drew her sword. It flashed brilliantly, lighting up the hollow. I couldn't help but wonder if maybe she was putting a little extra oomph into it just for show. Regardless, she laid it down on the table. "I need not remind either side that, as mediator here, it is my duty to both move these negotiations forward and enforce that the dictates of neutrality remain in place. Any who violate those dictates will be dealt with swiftly and with finality."

That last part was the big question. I wasn't too worried about myself or Sally. The worst we would probably do was some verbal sparring, something that fell somewhat short of an executable offense. The other side was far more likely to let their fists do the talking, the problem being that none of us – not even Gan – had any idea whether Sheila's powers would be effective against them.

All we could do was hope for the best and that they didn't call our bluff.

"Big C calls your bluff, stupid T'lunta!"

I couldn't help but notice the big ape had adopted his new honorific. It didn't make him sound any less stupid, but at least it kept us from cracking up every time he talked in third person.

"There is no deception here," Sally said. "All Bill was saying was that there have been losses on both sides. It's a war. That's common sense."

The Sasquatch on Big C's right spoke up. I guessed he was an advisor, but so far, most of his advising had been to remind me of how weak and stupid I was. *"Freewill T'lunta lets his mate speak for him. What else he let her do?"*

"He's gonna let me kick your ass if you piss me off."

Did I say the Feet were the only ones we'd have to worry about threatening violence? Silly me.

I stood up and placed a hand on Sally's shoulder, partially as a show of support, but mostly to keep her from leaping across the table and trying to rip off any Sasquatch junk. "For the last time, she is my partner, my equal. I would ask you to respect that our ways are different than yours."

"Go, Bill!" Tom shouted from the sidelines. "Show these cocksuckers you're a badass Susan B. Anthony motherfucker."

I almost had to laugh. Who'd have thought I would ever find myself the voice of reason in a place like this? My normal method of debating consisted of how big my dick was and how badly I was gonna bang someone's mom with it. Yet here I was, arguing about women's equality with Sasquatch. What a fucking world we lived in.

Sheila stood and turned to the Feet. "I would remind you that I am also a female. So if we could please acknowledge everyone at the table as having a valid..."

"Not female," Big C said dismissively. *"Silver Eyes. Mighty warrior. You fight T'lunta, not sit back and let cubs suckle you."*

There came a snort from my side. It was really not the

time to let Sally's catty bitch side out to play. Sheila, for her part, stared at the Feet with her mouth open and her face rapidly reddening.

"I'll have you know," I said, trying to help, "she looks really good in a skirt."

And just like that, her aura flared up around her as she turned to glare at me – expanding until it was so close I could have fried my arm off had I reached out.

"Um, well you do," I added sheepishly.

"If you were the last virile man on earth, you'd still find a way to die alone," Sally muttered with an eye-roll.

Three hours later, we'd finally managed to establish that girls were good and war was bad for both sides. Jesus fucking Christ! At least the last time I'd been here, I had the option of zoning out and letting the real diplomats do their job. At this point, if someone wheeled in a barrel of shoe polish, I'd have gladly drunk it all just to make the boring go away.

Fuck me, but I almost wished Ed was here taking a shit under one of their sacred trees again. I was half tempted to call for a break just to do it myself. Ritual combat would probably get every bone in my body broken, but it was still debatable as to whether that might be the lesser torture.

It seemed the Feet wanted to argue with us at every turn. If it weren't for the fact that it would come back to bite me in the face even harder, I would have said, "Fuck it. You win. We surrender" just to get us there faster.

Finally, right before we'd need to break for dawn, requiring us to wait here another day only to start right the fuck over, I saw a potential opening. Thank goodness, too, because daylight was sounding mighty tempting.

"*Tribes not aggressors here,*" Big C said, coming to the end of some long story about how we'd been mean to them for the last several thousand years. "*Sought to respect great Humbaba and the peace he set. T'lunta spit upon that. Hand of friendship offered, but then Freewill T'lunta kill ceremonial bride.*"

Oh, this shit again? I was sorely tempted to point my fingers at Gan and throw her to the wolves ... err ... apes. Especially since I glanced her way when he said it and all she did was smile at me.

Yeah. That would be a good idea. Let her pay for her crimes. Let them tear her limb from limb. She deserved it. It would also rid me of her once and for...

"Uh, Bill, are you okay?" Sally asked.

"Huh?" I was about to ask what the hell she was talking about when I looked down. At some point, my talons had extended and I'd dug eight long furrows into the table with them.

"You need a break?" She put a hand on my shoulder and my first instinct was to deck her.

The fuck?

Oh shit! It was happening again. Before, it had been the frustration of waiting. Now it was the boredom. Again, that same anger was seeping to the surface. "Goddamn it, Dr. Death!"

All eyes in the glade turned my way. Had I actually said that aloud?

Oops.

"Bill..." Sally and Sheila both began expectantly.

"*What a doctor death?*" one of Big C's advisors asked.

Oh crap.

I stood up, not entirely sure if I was going to speak or tear across the table at him. Thankfully, my lips started moving before my legs. "Um ... it's just an expression. I sometimes say it when I ... err ... point out a gross inaccuracy of the facts. Yeah, that's it."

"You do?" Sheila asked, forgetting herself for a moment.

"Yes, I do," I hissed. "All the time."

"*What gross inacc ... that word?*" Big C asked.

"It means falseness," I explained.

"*Big C know that! Big C not dumb!*"

Fuck that noise. I'd known some dumb cunts in my time, but none as big as him. Pointing that out wouldn't be in our favor, though. So, instead, I took several deep breaths to get my runaway emotions under control. "My apologies," I said. "What I meant was the inaccuracy of stating that I started this war."

"*You deny killing Turd's cub?*"

"By my hand, yes." I hated to throw Nergui under the bus posthumously. If there was an afterlife for vamps, hopefully he understood I was doing it for our entire benefit. "Another of our party did the deed without my consent."

"*He one of you. You leader. His actions your actions.*"

There was some logic to that, in a Neanderthal sort of way.

"Perhaps," I offered, "but the only reason we were up here to begin with was because of Turd's treachery."

The mention of Turd caused a lot of teeth to be bared on the other side. What I said next was either going to be my winning hand or would work them up into such a froth they'd beat me into a senseless pile of goo.

Time to remember my gaming roots. What would Kelvin Lightblade do? Why, he'd trust in the dice, that's what.

"Turd liked technology, your great taboo. There were many witnesses to that. The only reason he wanted us up here was to force a business arrangement, one that would have robbed you of the nectar of your sacred trees and given him money to buy even more technology. Before you know it, he would have been living large in a mansion, sitting in a hot tub and snorting coke off of hooker's asses while his million-dollar sound system played in the background."

I stopped and saw three blank expressions staring back. Glancing down at Sally, I asked, "Too much?"

"The hookers might have been a wee bit over the line."

"Gotcha."

Okay, time to dial it back a bit and put my cards on the table. "I argue that the Humbaba Accord was never in danger. It was treachery that brought us all to the Woods of

Mourning. Though I regret the death of Turd's daughter, any insult caused was entirely on him, not the rest of you. Our people have been fighting, dying, for no reason other than the selfishness of a few. All we need to do is acknowledge this and we can end this massacre once and for all."

Holy shit, that wasn't half bad. I hadn't done anything that good since I bs'd my way through a fifth grade oral lecture on the Civil War.

Judging by the looks of those at the table, and the witnesses sitting in the stands, I'd have gotten at least a B+ on this one. Fuck yeah! I'd take it.

I locked eyes with Sheila for a moment and she gave me the barest of grins before forcing a look of neutrality back onto her face.

Hell, even Big C looked thoughtful, or as thoughtful as he could. I hadn't really spent a great deal of time conversing with any members of the Feet, but I got the impression deep thinkers were a rarity amongst their number. Even so, when he finally spoke, I was half amazed to find it wasn't to argue with me again. "*Freewill T'lunta speaks ... wisely.*" Talk about having to choke out a word. "*Conflict is Turd's fault. Deaths are Turd's fault. Everything is Turd's fault!*"

I'm not quite sure I'd say *everything*. I mean, François had just as much a part in it, but thankfully, that wasn't too widely known. Also, that asshole was dead too, so it wasn't like we had to worry about him.

"*Insult was against Turd and his cub. Restitution must be made as such,*" Big C added, using an awfully big word for one with such primitive brain cells.

"Restitution?" I asked, throwing a quick glance Gan's way. She, for her part, seemed completely unfazed by the implication. "As in payback?"

"*Life for life. It is way of things.*"

"Well," I said, "in theory, that's already been paid for. I mean, the vamp who killed Turd's daughter didn't walk away from it."

"*Servant does not equal leader.*"

Yeah, except it was Turd's daughter, not Turd we were talking about. Considering their attitude toward Sally for the entire proceedings, I was tempted to throw back in their faces that, according to their logic, they probably ended up owing us in the exchange, but somehow, I didn't think that would work in my favor. Logic wasn't really their strong suit.

"*Life for life*," Big C repeated. He pointed a hairy finger at me. "*You and mate have cubs?*"

"Are you fuckers deaf or what?" Sally spat. "I am not his mate!"

"*Big C not deaf, she-T'lunta. Just not believe you.*"

Oh God, it was happening again, wasn't it? We were so close to signing a peace treaty with these assholes only to have it completely and utterly fucked up. I considered the vial of blood in my pocket. If things turned to shit, at least I'd have a shot at taking a bunch of them with me.

I glanced toward the witches. The expression on Christy's face was unreadable, but I knew the Magi were neutral parties under the Humbaba Accord. I had no doubt whatsoever she and her coven would step in if things turned bad for us, but the repercussions could be dire. By her doing so, she could potentially drag her entire race into the war.

Fuck that. I at least needed to make a futile attempt to salvage this before Sally could...

Big C held up a hand as one of his advisors leaned in and grunted something at him. The two chattered back and forth for several seconds, giving me time to attempt to calm her down. At least she hadn't brought her fifty-caliber hand cannon with her to the table.

Finally, Big C stood up and said, "*Bring Plug!*"

Plug?

What the fuck? My mind turned to the only thing I could think of ... a Bigfoot-sized butt plug. Ye gods, the horror. Was that their compromise for me not having any cubs to kill? If so, hopefully they chose Sally to wear it, because I was willing to do a lot of things for peace, but even I had to draw the line somewhere.

25

THE BROWN WEDDING

Another Sasquatch marched into the hollow, taking the steps two at a time, obviously double-timing it at his commander's request.

I won't lie. I was extraordinarily relieved to see him walking in empty-handed.

"Oh, it's this guy again," Sally said.

"Who?"

"Him," she replied. "Can't you ... oh, never mind. Why do I even bother?"

"Because I'm such a likable fellow?"

She glared at me. "When we get back, I'm locking you in a room with nothing but jars of their fur until you can tell them apart by scent."

"You wouldn't."

"Try me."

"Do you two need a time out?" Sheila asked.

"Nope. All's dandy here."

"Good." She turned back toward the newcomer, then paused for a moment as if remembering her lines. "Who dares interrupt these proceedings?" She then picked up her sword and pointed it at the Sasquatch. "You have not been recognized."

Hmm, no offense to her, but when the green ball of

death had done that, it had been intimidating. When she did it, it was kinda cute. Probably not what she was going for.

Even so, there was protocol to follow.

Before we had to discover if her powers were worth a fig against giant stink apes, their leader stood and said, "*This Plug, war party wolf. Once served Turd. Now serve me.*"

Wait a second.

"*He capture Freewill not long ago.*"

That was this guy?! Plug ... of course, why not? I hadn't thought to get his name at the time, considering my first impression had been of him stomping on the back of my head. Maybe that was for the best. It was really hard to take a beating seriously once you learned what these things' actual names were.

"*Tell them!*"

The raiding party leader stepped forward and grunted toward Sheila in what I guessed was meant to be a respectful manner. For her part, she put the sword back on the table and sat down. "You are recognized, Plug."

"*Plug thanks Silver Eyes. Plug war wolf. Lead other warriors to battle after shaman make trees grow.*"

"Make the trees grow?" Sheila asked.

"Sasquatch magic," I replied.

She turned toward me and grinned. "You are not recognized."

"Sorry."

"I'll let it slide this time."

Rough chuckles came from the other end of the table. Bunch of dicks. A summit to determine the fate of the world this might be, but damn if it didn't have the feel of a high school pep rally at times.

"*Plug capture Freewill T'lunta. Mighty Plug!*" He took a moment to raise his arms and beat his chest. The thumping echoed through the hollow.

I opened my mouth to comment, but Sally put a hand on my arm. "Just don't."

She was probably right. I could eat crow for a bit.

Arguing semantics with Sasquatches was ultimately self-defeating. Besides, he *had* captured us.

"*Plug capture other T'lunta. Plug capture T'lunta mate.*"

Sheila raised an eyebrow and indicated Sally.

"*No! Plug say his mate.*" He pointed a finger at Christy. "*That one.*"

All eyes in the glade turned toward her. Some of them in curiosity, most of them in surprise. Gan's, however, was the one I was most interested in. I could see the claws on her hand momentarily lengthen. Oh, crap.

"Something you want to tell me, babe?" Tom asked, glancing between us.

A yellow crackle of power shot from her fingertips, causing him to jump back.

"Ow!"

Guess that glamour was pretty damned good after all.

"It was all ... a misunderstanding," she said with a tone of annoyance.

"*Magi and T'lunta?*" Big C asked.

Plug turned back to him and nodded.

"And the point of this?" Sheila asked, a look of utter confusion upon her face.

"*We capture their cub, too.*"

Not that again! For Christ's sake! Was there a stupidity plague rampant among the Feet or something? I stood up. "Listen, guys. That cub was named Ed and he was a fully grown..."

Sally grabbed me by the sleeve and dragged me back into my seat. Before I could say a word in protest, she said, "Sorry, the Freewill is still distraught over the whole affair with his beloved ... son."

I stared incredulously at her, to which she mouthed just two short words. I couldn't read lips for shit, but this I understood: "Zip it!"

Um, okay.

Sheila blinked at us, as if maybe we'd grown a few extra heads, but then she turned to Plug. "Please go on."

Plug spared one snarl in my direction before continuing. *"Plug capture funny smelling Freewill T'lunta cub. Plug present cub to Turd as prize. Much glory heaped upon Plug!"* And again with the chest beating. I was half expecting to see Cheetah swing in from the sidelines.

"What happen?" Big C asked.

"Turd adopt cub as his own. Try to train it."

"Cub not here now. Cub die?"

"No. Cub escape."

"Cub escape Turd?"

"Yes."

Wait a second. I was beginning to see what Sally meant here.

Big C stood up and slammed a fist onto the table. *"Turd get revenge. Capture Freewill T'lunta cub. But Turd stupid and let it escape. Fault of no one but Turd."* He turned and locked eyes with me. *"Honor is served."*

And just like that, we'd won.

Well, winning is a relative concept, but I'd been coming up short in that column lately. I'd take what I could get.

The big ape wasn't finished anyway. *"Turd stupid and selfish. Get many of our kind killed for dishonor. Let the War of Turd end. It die with him. Let the Peace of Cunt begin!"*

Sheila completely lost her shit at that. I had to stifle a fake coughing jag as well. She had it worse, though, not having been previously insulated against the raw fucking idiocy that was the Feet. She folded her hands on the table and put her face down on it. After a few moments, she could barely breathe.

Fuck it. There hadn't been a lot of laughs the last few days. The poor girl had earned it.

I turned to Sally. "Who'd have thunk it? The legendary Icon laid low by..."

"Don't say it," she warned.

"Fine. Too easy anyway." I lowered my voice. "By the way, how'd you know where he was going with this?"

"Never discount ego or new management taking an opportunity to make the old management look bad."

"Sounds a lot like corporate America."

"With maybe a bit less hygiene," she added.

After a few minutes, Sheila got herself under control and lifted her head. Her eyes were puffy and a few tears were still present on her face, which she quickly wiped off. "Sorry," she said in a shaky voice, as if it wouldn't take much to set her off again. "I was just ... overcome with emotion at this historic occasion."

"*Understand*," the giant ape replied with a nod. "*Very moving to be in presence of the great...*"

"Big C!" I shouted, before he could send Sheila into another laughing seizure.

Not only did it spare her that, but it seemed to mollify the stupid baboon even more so. "*Yes! Big C!*" he shouted, then began to repeat it until the other Sasquatches in the room joined in with the chant.

"*Big C! Big C! Big C!*"

Ah yes. Music to my ears.

As hoped, once things settled down, talks turned to the terms of the peace itself. It was agreed that since the Humbaba Accord had been broken by treachery, it was still valid and could be reinstated by both parties. Thank goodness, too. Considering how long it supposedly was, if they insisted on drafting a new treaty, we'd be here until long after Alex and Calibra had finally hashed things out.

I did have one moment where I suggested that maybe we rename it the Cuntbaba Accord, in favor of the new Sasquatch leader, but that drew a painful shot in the arm from Sally. Hey, can't fault a guy for trying.

Unfortunately, that brought us to the part we all knew was coming.

"Peace has been brokered in accordance with the terms set forth in the Humbaba Accord," Sheila said as we all stood at attention. She glanced once at me as if to ask if I really wanted to go through with this next part.

The answer was no, but I didn't really have a choice. Besides, if things worked out in our favor, we could deal with the consequences later. Hell, they'd probably be a cakewalk compared to the horrors waiting for us at the pool of magical spooge. I gave her the barest of nods.

"Very well," she said. "As was done before, during the original signing of the Accord, the leaders of both parties will take a mate from the opposing side as a show of fellowship. The exchange of vows will take place immediately to seal the pact."

Now came the tricky part.

"*Freewill*," Big C said, "*I offer you Turd daughter.*" He let out a roar, and I sensed movement at the top of the meeting place. I glanced up to see a seven-foot-tall Sasquatch with saggy tits that reached down almost to its knees come loping in to join us.

"Hope you're a boob guy," Sally whispered to me with a smirk. Bitch!

"Um, I thought Turd's daughter was, well, you know..."

"*Turd have many cubs*," Big C replied. "*One die to start war. Make sense for one to take her place.*"

Heh, yeah, and would also spare Big C from having to introduce his ugly new son-in-law at any family gatherings. Different ape, but still an asshole.

Whatever the fuck. This was all just for show anyway.

I hesitated for a beat. We'd discussed this beforehand, but there was still no way of knowing if Gan might decide to let her catty side out to play.

Fortunately, the Sasquatch female's chest remained knife free. I glanced over and saw that Gan's expression was unreadable. She definitely wasn't happy, but she was playing along. Now, as also discussed previously, it was her turn.

"Thank you," I replied. "I'm sure she will make a fine mate and give me many ... cubs." Turd's offspring apparently found this prospect as appealing as I did based on the grimace she made. Well, she needn't have worried. I'd made a few deposits in the skank bank back in college, but even I had standards. "Now, I would like to offer you, from our side, Gansetseg. She will make a fine mate for you. Though she may be short in stature, she is large in ... spirit."

Gan stepped forward, a neutral expression still on her face. Yeah, remind me to never ever play poker with her.

Big C, however, backed up a step as if aghast. "*What this?!*"

"Huh?"

"*This T'lunta treachery?*"

Hah! Who'd have guessed? The Feet might have been shit-covered, bug-eating morons who considered females a lesser species, but apparently they had qualms about those females being little girls.

"I can assure you. Though she appears young, she is..."

"*Not T'lunta!*"

"What?"

"*That not T'lunta!*" he repeated, getting extra huffy, snot running out of his nose in ropes thick enough to climb. Eww.

That's when I remembered. Oh shit! They'd refused Gan a place at the table. I hadn't argued the rule before because of the day-walker thing, and also because I was glad not to sit next to her for hours on end. Now it was coming back to bite me. Fuck it all.

"Yeah, but she's..."

"*Bride must be T'lunta,*" he growled. "*Only T'lunta! Or pact not sealed.*"

"The only other vamp we brought is Sally," Tom helpfully pointed out.

Sally turned and fixed him with the gaze of death itself.

"*Yes*," the ugly ape replied. "*Big C take that one.*"

The crack of knuckles could be heard. I looked at Sally and saw her fist clenched so tightly blood dripped out from between her fingers.

"You can't have her," I said, trying to think quickly.

"*Why not?*"

"Um ... because she's my mate."

"*Huh?*"

"And as much as the thought of a wife swap is interesting, I'm thinking the logistics just won't work. I mean, I live in Brooklyn. You live..."

"*You say she not mate. Spend entire time at table claiming she not mate.*"

"Well, I was being shy and..."

He turned to Sheila. "*Silver Eyes, did him not say so during sacred meeting?*"

Shit! He had her and she knew it. She couldn't just outright lie to him.

"Yes," she replied after a beat. "The Freewill did claim multiple times that she was not his mate."

"*Then she now Big C's mate,*" the monster gorilla replied with finality.

I turned to Sally, a look of desperation on my face. "It's not..." I couldn't say it with them in earshot. "You know. We need this. *Please!*"

Finally, after a long moment, she nodded and stepped close to me. "I know. It has to be done. I understand that." Thank goodness. "But you should also understand," she said, lowering her voice to a pitch even I could barely make out, "that the second we're alone, you are so fucking dead."

As if I didn't know that already.

26

SHOTGUN HONEYMOON

The Humbaba Accord had some stupid rule that the marriage vows would take place in accordance with each species' personal beliefs.

I had no idea what constituted a vampire marriage. Whatever it was, it probably involved a lot of biting, and no goddamned way was that happening. So I opted instead for a traditional city hall type ceremony with Sheila forced to officiate.

Since she wasn't an ordained minister, an elected official, or a boat captain, I took some small comfort in knowing that whatever was said wouldn't be legally binding. Even if it was, dragging a Sasquatch down to the hall of records in Manhattan was not something I'd be doing anytime soon.

Mind you, it really didn't help that she took great amusement in the "Do you, Bill Ryder, take Muld to be your lawful wedded wife" part.

When the chips were down, everyone wanted to be a comedian.

Oh, and now I had a spouse whose name sounded like mold. Fitting, considering I think she had some growing on her.

Sally's ceremony was at least slightly more amusing. It involved a lot of screaming, roaring at the sky, and generally acting like she was an extra in a King Kong remake. Less amusing was the death glare she gave me with every new debasing thing she had to do.

Far more tragic was what she was likely going to do to me once she realized I'd palmed my phone and secretly recorded the whole thing. Sure, the world might end and we might all die horribly, but I'd meet my maker knowing there would soon be a couple million views on my YouTube channel. Small victories really did make or break a day.

And, hey, Sasquatch weddings had one thing in common with human ones: there was a customary throwing. Yeah, it wasn't a bouquet and there was no fucking way any of us wanted to catch a giant lump of shit, but it served to show how truly small the world could be. If we all tried just a little harder, we could all find a common ground to stand on.

Of course, now that all the peace bullshit was done, we needed to get ourselves to a common underground, and to do that, we needed Grulg.

Once the ceremonies had concluded, Big C turned to all those present and declared the truce in effect along with the hope that peace would lead to many cubs for both of us.

That's when I made my move.

"Mighty Big C," I said as reverently as I could, which wasn't much. Sally stood by his side, and it was all I could do to withhold comment on what a blushing bride she made. "I know the peace has just been established, but I wish to ask a favor of you."

"*Favor?*" he asked dubiously.

"Though I can't wait to consummate the marriage to my *beautiful* wife, I am afraid it must wait. I have a matter of honor that must be satisfied first. I cannot in good conscience make..." I glanced back at the butt ugly Sasquatch female, standing there picking her nose. "...cubs until this matter is satisfied."

"*Matter of honor? Tell Big C.*"

"Do you know of an ape ... I mean, warrior named Grulg?"

He thought for a moment, then nodded solemnly. "Yes, Grulg. Honorable war chief. Fight well. Lead well."

"Yes he is, or does, whatever." Sally rolled her eyes at my sputtering. "You want to do this?"

"Oh, no," she replied. "It's always fun watching the master at work."

"Anyway, me and my partner, your new *wife*," I put an extra big grin on my face as I said that, "were both saved by Grulg some weeks back."

"*Saved?*" he asked, raising his sloped brow.

"Yes, we were both imprisoned by an enemy known as the Jahabich."

"*Not know that word.*"

"Ugly rock fuckers who can turn into people or others of your kind."

That he apparently understood because he bared his teeth. "*In'luh. We know of them. Enemies to all.*"

"You can say that again. Anyway, we were all trapped, and then Grulg offered a truce as per the Humbaba Accord. We didn't trust him at first, but his actions proved themselves and he led us to safety." It was stretching the truth, but truce or not, it wouldn't hurt to butter up these assholes a bit.

"Yes," Sally added. "Grulg acted honorably that day, despite our unworthiness. It would mean a lot to us to find and express our gratitude. In fact, I really don't think I could truly give myself to my new..." She gritted her teeth. "*Husband* with that dishonor hanging shamefully over my head."

Hell, I didn't think I could give myself to my new beast even if I taped porn to the inside of my eyelids. But, with any luck, we wouldn't need to.

The ugly monster appeared to consider this. I just had to hope he wasn't a horny fucker like Turd. Sally was a grade-A piece and, quite frankly, if I was in his position, I'd have probably said, "Fuck this noise. You can do that shit in the morning."

"*Walk with me,*" he said at last. "*Words not for females to hear.*"

Sally looked insulted by this. Muld just continued to look dumb.

"Why don't you two ladies bond or something? We'll be right back."

I followed Big C as he wandered off into the trees. Though he could have lost me in an instant and double-backed behind me before I'd know it, he kept a slow pace, as if being mindful of my much shorter legs. A small part of me feared he was leading me off so as to beat the shit out of me away from prying eyeballs, so I kept one hand in my pocket on Gan's vial of ass-kickery. But, instead, he eventually stopped and turned to face me.

"*Grulg not here.*"

For a moment, I felt a sinking pit form in my stomach. "Um, he's not dead, is he?"

Thankfully, he shook his head. "*Nuh. Grulg mighty warrior. Hard to kill.*"

"Oh, that's good, then."

"*No.*"

"No?"

"*Freewill T'lunta has acted honorably today.*"

I had? Good thing he didn't realize I had every intention of ditching my marital duties both now and forever. "Thank you, Big C."

"*Big C confess that expected this to be trap. Planned to spring trap instead.*"

"Wait, you're saying this was all an ambush?" Why the fuck was there a need for an ambush? His people had my small group outnumbered by dozens to one. Sure, we had Christy's coven and Sheila as our surprise allies, but that would have merely delayed the inevitable.

"*But now we at peace,*" he continued cryptically, or was that cryptidly? "*Not all at peace, though.*"

"Well, yeah. I mean, word has to get out." I wasn't looking forward to that. Once Alex found out we'd signed a peace treaty without his say so, he'd go through the fucking roof. That part was bound to be tricky, especially since it might make him less likely to let us lead him to his death, as we'd been hoping.

"*Not what Big C means,*" he replied. "*Big C only say this. Beware Magi.*"

"The Magi?"

"*They come to watch, but maybe not just watch.*"

I had no fucking idea what he was talking about. Did this idiot actually think that Christy and her coven were on his side? What? Had he been counting on them to go all hippy dippy and declare us enemies of the trees or something? What a fucking idiot. "Thanks. I'll be sure to keep an eye on them."

That seemed to mollify his stupid self, because he changed subjects back to the one I was truly interested in. "*Grulg far away. He near place of big human huts. Place of T'lunta power.*"

Place of power? "Wait, Boston? You mean he's near Boston?"

He appeared to consider that, probably having never seen Google Maps. "*Hear that word before from captured T'lunta.*" He nodded. "*He sent to lead troops, new allies. Lead them to great victory that others fail at.*"

"Okay." That didn't really help much. New England was still smaller than Canada, but finding one Sasquatch was bound to be a needle and haystack exercise. "So, any idea how we make contact once we're there?"

Sadly, I didn't expect to be given his cell phone number. There was also the small problem of what would happen if the Sasquatches several hundred miles south hadn't yet gotten a messenger pigeon to let them know peace had been declared.

"*Trees will take you,*" Big C said.

"The trees?"

"*Magic.*"

Oh, yeah. The Feet had used that trick to sneak up on us

many times. One minute, there'd be nothing but forest and the next, a small platoon of them would step out from behind a tree. It was unnervingly creepy. I hadn't realized they could also use it as a sort of express train if need be. "And how do we do that?"

"*We help. Shamans grant you temporary passage.*"

That was good. It would be a fuckload easier to step out of a tree trunk right where Grulg was. Of course, this could be tricky if C expected us to kiss Grulg's ass and then immediately get back here and make with the fucky-fucky time.

Big C stepped up close and leaned down, almost as if reading my thoughts. "*Take all time T'lunta need,*" he said. "*Not wish to say so she-T'lunta wife hear, but Big C find her ugly. Not looking forward to making cubs.*"

27

HITCHHIKER'S GUIDE TO CANADA

We were allowed to gather back at our hut to ready ourselves, which also allowed us to take advantage of the wards keeping prying ears out.

It gave me a chance to bring them all up to speed on what I'd learned, including the Sasquatch chief's offer to send us. I left out, however, the part about him finding Sally about as attractive as a wasp-infested knothole.

Hmm, actually, for all I knew, these fuckers might've been into that.

"So he's not too far from where we were just a few days ago?" Sally asked.

"That's what I gathered," I replied. "Hard to understand Captain Caveman there, but reading between the lines, I think Grulg may have been sent to take command of the invasion Turd fucked up. It's probably a good thing we showed up here when we did. I have a feeling an offensive with him in the lead might be slightly more effective."

"Is that such a bad thing?" she asked with a smirk. "I mean, Colin is in charge again."

"This is a good point."

Gan stepped forward and proceeded to ignore our pettiness. "It would be dangerous to approach Boston airspace the way we came up. The First Coven's agents would most certainly notice and investigate. The offer by the Alma presents both an opportunity to circumnavigate this challenge as well as a means to do so more quickly."

I nodded. "Oh, by the way, Gan, thank you for showing such restraint during the negotiations. I ... very much appreciate it."

She waved it off as if it were nothing. "I would move mountains for you, my love, or let them crumble to dust at your say so. Regardless, this was all agreed upon in advance. If I thought for one moment that you had any intention of returning the Alma's affection, I would ensure she was dealt with accordingly."

Affection didn't quite describe the look on Muld's face every time she looked my way. Still, her meaning was clear.

"I don't suppose you'd throw my loving husband in as a two-for-one deal," Sally said.

Gan glanced her way and a sour look came over her face. "I must ... apologize. I did not consider the Alma would refuse to acknowledge my status. You performed admirably in my stead."

"Was that a compliment?" Sally asked, one eyebrow raised.

"It was. Know that I do not hand them out lightly."

Tom stepped forward and put a hand on both my and Sally's shoulders. "Well, just to be safe, I'm buying you both a package of fur-lined condoms when we get ... Oof!"

Sally elbowed him in the gut. I held my breath for just a moment, knowing what was inside him. I really needed to pull her aside and tell her not to do that.

For now, though, it seemed a plan was working itself out, one where we'd find Grulg and hopefully get him to point out the hole he'd used to escape the Jahabich lair.

"We still have one problem," Kelly said.

"What?" I asked. "Believe me, I'm okay that nobody got us any wedding presents."

Most of the group chuckled, even Kelly for a second, but then she pointed a finger at Sheila. "Our esteemed MC. This tree transport that these monkeys use. It's still magic. How do we know it won't fizzle out the same way?"

Sheila glanced at her and gave a slight nod. "Yeah. Hate to agree, but so far I don't seem to have much luck volunteering to go up on stage to be sawed in half."

"Probably a good thing, considering some of the players on the field," I replied.

"It still presents a problem. I'm stuck doing things the old-fashioned way. With me around, that slows you guys down considerably. Without me, you guys can do this much faster."

"We're not leaving you behind."

"Hear me out, Bill. Time is of the essence. We know Calibra has Ed, that she needs him for some reason. But he's not the only person she has. You have other friends in need. We can't take the long way around, counting on the fact that she's doing nothing but waiting for us."

Damn it! She had a point. Dave, James ... even Starlight. I didn't know if there was any way to save her now that she was a Jahabich, but that didn't mean she didn't deserve us trying. James, in particular, was a member of the Draculas. Calibra knew that, having pretended to be his subordinate for God knows how long. He was a VIP, a very important prisoner. Sooner or later, she'd play that card to our detriment.

Still... "It's a bad idea. First rule of D&D is that when you split the party, you get fucked. Hell, you saw how things went south when we invaded Boston."

"We ... you still won," she said, averting her eyes for a moment.

"Yeah, well, we almost didn't. We got lucky and it had nothing to do with our plan working. We need to stick together."

"I can catch up to you."

"That's a lot of catching up to do."

"Those choppers we came up in are still there."

"No offense, but..." I glanced around. This wasn't really something I wanted to say in front of certain company. "But I really don't feel comfortable with you flying alone with..."

"With my men?" Gan asked. "Though they are loyal to me and will not strike without my authority on pain of death, I am forced to admit it is a valid concern."

"It is?" I asked, surprised she was agreeing with me on this point.

"The Shining One strikes fear into the hearts of many. Fear can make even the most loyal soldier act foolishly."

I hadn't expected Gan to side with me on ... oh, who was I kidding? The little nutcase was obsessed with me. If I told her the moon was purple and the oceans full of hamster piss, she'd agree. Now if only I could convince her there were other fish in the sea, ones that weren't utterly skeeved out by her advances.

Yeah, little chance of that happening.

"There has to be a way," Meg said. "That's one of the fundamentals of magic. Energy can be manipulated, and faith magic is simply another form of it."

"Well aware," Kelly replied with a lopsided grin for some reason.

"It's not that simple," Christy said. "The energy we manipulate is intangible, fluid. An Icon is basically that energy in corporeal form." She turned to Sheila. "Sorry, not trying to talk about you like you're not here."

"I used to be an administrative assistant. I'm used to it."

I, for one, never ignored her, but it was probably not particularly helpful to bring that up. Ah, how I missed those simpler days.

"Maybe Sasquatch magic works differently," Sally offered. "I mean, we won't know until we try. What's the worst that can happen – we step around a tree and end up on the other side?"

"She has a point," I said.

"The Forest Folk manipulate that energy differently than the Magi," Christy explained. "They're forest spirits, so they're in tune with that power in a way that's difficult for us to understand, much less match. But fundamentally, it's still energy manipulation, no matter how you package it."

"Shit!" For a second, that frustration within me boiled to the surface before I was able to stamp it down again. "I hate to say this – I mean, I *really* hate to say this – but what about Decker?"

Christy looked dubious at the prospect.

"Yeah, I know. He'll probably just say we should kill her. He's a broken fucking record that way, but maybe we should at least ask."

Having said it out loud, I now saw what a terrible idea it was. Disembodied, he was potentially even more annoying than he'd been in life. At the same time, Christy had confided in me that he knew his shit when it came to magic. She was fucking badass, but she was also our age. Sometimes you had to defer to experience in these things, even if that experience was wrapped up in an asshole enchilada with dickhead sauce.

Christy, for her part, narrowed her eyes at me for a moment. No matter what he'd done to us, deep down, a small part of her still looked at him like a father figure. Stuff like that was hard to shake.

"Might be worth a try," Veronica offered.

"Worst case, I can show off my new body to him again," Tom said. "Fucker was seriously jealous."

Tom grabbed the bowls off the rough table in the middle of the hut to make room while Christy retrieved Decker's skull from her backpack. She placed it in the center and then ran her index and middle fingers over the top of it, leaving behind a slight trail of yellowish energy.

As she did, the skull began to glow with that purplish light that told me its annoying owner was awake again.

Tom flicked a cashew in one of its eye sockets. "Two points!"

Christy turned and glared icily at him, but before she could say something, Decker spoke up.

What you see in this imbecile I will never know.

"He's an acquired taste," I replied.

Ah, I see I am surrounded by fools again, each stupider than the last. The light pulsing from the skull momentarily brightened. *Where have you brought me? This is neither that putrid apartment building nor the illustrious Kala's lair.*

"We decided to go camping," Sally said. "Figured you'd make a good bug zapper."

Christy slammed a hand on the table. "That's enough, everyone. I didn't wake him up to trade abuse."

So this is what I have been reduced to? Decker asked with a sigh ... interesting to hear in my head since he didn't have lungs. *Am I but a mere magic eight ball, to be brought out when it is convenient for everyone's amusement?*

That seemed to catch her off guard and her eyes softened for a moment. "I'm sorry. It's not like that."

Gan, however, was having none of his shit. "Enough with the games, maapamba. You have been summoned for a purpose."

Murderer!

He might as well have told Gan she had black hair for all the emotion she showed at his outburst. "We have need of your knowledge, wizard, regarding the Shining One."

My killer and the destroyer of our way of life in league with one another? How fitting.

"I didn't ask for any of this, Harry," Sheila said.

I know, my dear, but a dog doesn't ask to be bitten by a rabid animal. Yet, when it happens, it must be put down before it can do further harm.

"Enough of this," Christy said, taking control again. Decker's outburst had seemingly given her the steel to push aside her feelings. "We want to know how to make Sheila susceptible to teleportation magic."

She would be quite susceptible were she dead.

"That's not what I meant and you know it."

If there were an easy way then we would have done so, he snapped. *Sent her to the bottom of the ocean or perhaps into a live volcano before she realized her true potential.*

"She's not going to kill us!" Kelly snapped. "Just knock it off with that shit already."

Ah, to be young and naïve again.

"And with skin?" I added, unable to help myself.

Christy held up a hand. "Can we please all concentrate?" The annoyance in her voice was easy to hear. "Darling, please go grab me that chair over there."

Tom did so without hesitation. Once she'd eased herself into it, she turned back to the skull. "You said if there was an easy way. That means there's a hard way."

You were always an astute pupil.

"I want to know what that is. We don't have time to play games." She glanced around. "You said it yourself. The Source could be used to help Tom. Maybe we can use it to help you, too."

Dangling a carrot? Very astute.

She lowered her voice. "It's the truth and you know it."

When the time came, I hoped we could put it to a vote, because bringing Decker back to the land of the living rated a huge fucking no in my book. However, there was probably a better time for that argument to be made, so I kept my mouth shut.

Very well, Decker mind-blasted. *Icons, foul creatures that they are, are living, breathing generators of faith.*

"Nothing we don't know already," Christy replied.

Think of them like a live wire. Dangerous to touch, so long as the energy is flowing through them. But remove that energy...

"You're talking in riddles, Harry."

Decker's skull made a derogatory sound, then continued. *Or weaken it enough so that it isn't as potent.*

"Weaken it how?"

The same way you kill her kind.

What?!

"The Black Tngri," Gan said in a low voice.

"What is...?"

She looked up at me. "He means the ritual of Baal."

28

BLADE OF CHAOS

"Wait, you mean whatever the fuck they do to make those black blades?"

As usual, Freewill, your stupidity astounds.

"Fuck off, chrome dome."

I remembered what Gan had told me about it. It was a spell that invoked the god of heretics – apparently also the god of contradictions, as that made no fucking sense. Somehow, the weapons were steeped in some sort of evil blood, which in turn corrupted them enough to cut through Sheila's otherwise invulnerable aura.

"It needn't be the entire ritual," Gan clarified. "That would take time we do not have and be most inefficient with regard to the resources at our command." The way she eyed Christy's sisters made me think that whatever this ritual was, it involved a lot of hosing off afterwards.

"I'm gonna assume it's not particularly bystander friendly."

Such an insightful observation. Rare for one as dull-witted as you.

Mother fucking cock! It was all I could do to not down Gan's vial of pimped out blood and see how far I could throw his stupid fucking skull.

This talk, combined with the bowling-ball-shaped asshole

in the room, wasn't doing wonders for my temper. I could feel my fangs trying to descend almost as if they were fighting me. Not good.

Still, from what Gan said, it sounded like this wasn't a five-minute ritual either. "We don't have time for this."

"Indeed, as I was saying, my love. However, if I am interpreting the revenant totem correctly, then the full ritual would not be necessary; just the end result."

The corrupting blood of the damned.

"I think I saw that movie on Cinemax a few months back," Tom commented.

Christy fixed him with a stare, but otherwise ignored him. "The only place we've seen that blood is on those weapons the vampires used during our trial."

"And in Boston," Meg added.

"Exactly," I replied. "Neither of which are places we're currently at. So, since we don't have one, this entire discussion is..."

"That's not true."

I turned toward Sally, who was leaning against one of the far corners of the hut. "Excuse me?"

"I said, that's not true." She picked up the bag she'd packed for the trip and opened it. After fishing around for a few moments, she pulled out a short dagger, a dagger with a jet-black blade.

What the hell?

"Is this what you need?" she asked as if a neighbor had knocked on her door to borrow the lawnmower.

I took a step toward her. "Where the hell did you get that?"

"I picked it up before we left Boston."

"More important, *why* do you have that?"

"Souvenir," she replied blithely. "What does it matter? We need it. I have it." Calm and collected, she stepped past me and placed the blade on the table. Maybe that's what bothered me the most – how nonchalantly she'd done so. "Will this work?"

To plunge into the creature's heart? Yes, assuming any of you have come to your senses.

"That's enough, Harry," Christy warned, yellow lightning dancing on her fingertips.

So be it, Decker replied with enough disgust that I was surprised spittle wasn't dripping out of his skull. *It will serve our purposes.*

Sheila had been quiet during all of this, her eyes on the knife and her expression unreadable. Finally, she took a deep breath. "What do we need to do?"

"Are you fucking insane?" Kelly asked. "This shit is bad for you, as in you'd better be carrying your EpiPen while kicking a beehive bad."

"You think I don't know that?" Sheila gave a humorless grin. "Again, what do we need to do?"

"Harry?" Christy prompted.

Scrape the blood off of the blade. Rehydrate and dilute it. Save enough to coat a syringe needle with and...

"Where the fuck are we going to find a syringe up here?" Tom asked. "Freebasing Chewbaccas would be a fucking awesome band name, though."

I could have hugged my roommate. He'd managed to put the brakes on this stupid idea once and for all.

"I think I have that one covered." Veronica retrieved a small handbag from her backpack, opened it, and pulled out two sealed syringes. I raised an eyebrow, to which she said, "I do a lot of heroin." After listening to the shocked silence that ensued, she added, "It's a joke. Lighten up a little. I'm type 1. As the credit card commercials say, don't leave home without it."

Son of a bitch.

"Okay, that'll work," Christy said, taking one. It was hard to tell what was going through her mind as she spoke. I'd be lying, though, if I didn't suspect a small part of her wondered if Harry was right.

Fuck it. I stepped back to the table next to Sheila. "You don't have to do this."

"I know," she said. "But it's either this or the long way around." She looked down at the dagger. "I already let you down once. I'm not going to do it again."

"You didn't let anyone..." Kelly began.

"What are you talking...?" I simultaneously blurted.

She cut us both off. "I ask again, will it work?"

The theory is sound, Decker replied. Maybe I was projecting, but I could have sworn he had a slight cadence of amusement in his voice. *My pupil injects you with the diluted blood and it should dull your powers enough for spell casting to take hold.*

"How long will it last?"

Who can say? This time, the glee was unmistakable. *So far as I know from both my earthly studies and my time beyond the great veil, such a thing has never been attempted. Suffice it to say, whenever an enemy has gotten close enough to an Icon to use such a weapon, they have not done so with the intent of merely wounding.*

"That will be enough, Harry," Christy said. "Thank you."

Wait, I...

Christy ran her fingers over his skull before he could say anything further and he immediately fell silent again. At least I could be thankful the fucker came with an off switch.

"I think the next several hours will be difficult enough without listening to Harry's dogma," she told us all.

Though I seriously doubted anyone in our group was about to be swayed by his insane ramblings, she probably had a point. Well, okay, I had assumed nobody in our group would be swayed. But then, Sally had produced the knife. Suddenly, I wasn't so sure.

"Are you certain about this?" Kelly asked. "You'll be vulnerable."

"No," Sheila replied with a laugh. "But I enjoy the irony

of not being certain. Besides..." She turned and looked each of the group in the eye, finishing with me. "I'm surrounded by good friends who won't let anything happen to me."

"Damn straight," I said.

"I agree," Gan replied, stepping between us. "It would be dishonorable to allow any harm to come to you under such circumstances."

"Thank you, G..."

"Besides, I prefer you to be at full strength when you finally face my beloved. I will be quite disappointed if your final defeat is not most glorious."

29

A WALK IN THE WOODS

The Sasquatch shamans were attempting to make contact with Grulg in advance of their sending spell, mostly to make sure his people didn't immediately try to smash our skulls upon our arrival.

The witches were likewise busy following Decker's instructions. Gan, despite her dislike of Christy, offered her advice as they worked. Yep, wouldn't want any harm to come to the Icon before I could tear her limb from limb in a fair fight. Whatever floated her boat.

That left the rest of us a few minutes of down time.

"Let's go for a walk."

"It's daylight out," Sally replied, leaning against a wall well away from where the others were gathered.

"We're in a fucking forest." I tossed her the bottle of spray-on sunscreen I'd just liberally applied to myself. "There's plenty of tree cover. And it wasn't a request."

I locked eyes with her and a battle of wills ensued. It wasn't something I was used to winning against Sally, but that anger inside of me had been bubbling up to the surface big time ever since she'd produced that knife. It was all I could do to not throttle her right there. If she thought I was backing down this time, she had another thing coming.

"*Now,*" I snarled, my voice sounding lower and more menacing than intended.

For a moment, she looked as if she had something snarky to say, but after a beat simply replied, "I guess I could use some fresh air. The meatsack is starting to get a little ripe anyway."

She did have a point about Tom. Hopefully, wherever the Feet sent us, it was next to a YMCA, lake, or garden hose. He could definitely use ... no! Enough with the stupid shit. This was serious, and I didn't need to be distracted until I got some answers.

"Everyone else stay here. We'll be back."

The witches and Gan barely glanced my way. Sheila looked at me questioningly, but I gave her a single shake of my head. As usual, only Tom seemed oblivious.

"I wouldn't mind stretching my legs."

"Dear, could you come over here for a second?" Christy asked to my eternal gratitude.

I grabbed hold of Sally's arm and guided her out. Though spots of sunlight filtered down here and there from above, the Sasquatch village was only slightly less wooded than the surrounding forest. The fuckers liked their trees and, right now, that was just fine by me.

A few of the creatures milled about, but with the peace treaty and us now respectably married, we were all one big happy family. Okay, maybe not. Most of them still looked like they'd sooner shit on our corpses than talk to us, but whatever. Either way, they left us alone.

Except for one, who started sniffing the air as we walked by.

"*What smell funny?*"

"Cool coconut tropical sunrise scent, asshole," I replied as I led Sally away into the forest.

I wasn't stupid enough to think we'd find any privacy from the Feet out here. We were in their fucking backyard, for Christ's sake. However, just about when I was ready to stop and round on her, Sally took the lead.

Curious, I followed her.

She kept walking, the tree covering getting denser all the while. I was beginning to suspect she was avoiding the confrontation she no doubt knew was coming when we stepped out into a clearing of sorts. The trees all leaned inward, blocking any direct sunlight. An odd place, but vaguely familiar, too.

"Is this...?"

"Grulg's secret place," Sally said, stepping in and taking a seat upon a moss-covered rock. "The spot he showed us when he spilled the beans on Turd."

"How'd you find it again?"

"It's because I pay attention, ADD boy."

"Fair enough." My tone was neutral, but deep down I was impressed. I couldn't have found this place again had I marked it in my GPS. Maybe that was her ploy – drag me out here and then hope I didn't find my way back.

"I assumed you didn't want prying ears."

"You assumed correct." I stepped over and faced her. "So, want to tell me about it?"

"About what?"

"Don't play stupid, Sally. That's maybe the one thing I understand better than you."

She smiled slightly.

"Why did you have the knife?"

Rather than answer the question, she replied, "Do you think Ed will be happy to see us?"

"I think Ed will get more pissed off every hour we leave him there, but yeah. I'm expecting puppy-dog let out of a hot car levels of gratitude from him. But that doesn't have anything to do with..."

"And what do you think he'll say when I ask him to bite me?"

"What?" We were back to that? "Considering the few times you've bitten him, I think he'll be highly amused at a little payback."

"Maybe. I know the prospect frightens me a little, but I find it exciting, too."

"Your sex lives are your business."

"Not like that." She waved a hand dismissively. "The thought of facing down Alex, Ib, hell, even James without being afraid that they'll take over again. You really have no idea what that's like."

"Wait, James?"

"Don't get me wrong. I'm not worried about him. He's a friend. He's always been a friend. He's the one good thing that happened to me as a vampire..."

"He's a good..."

"Before I met you."

"Oh." And just like that, the anger that had nearly boiled over was gone. Talk about instantly disarming a booby trap.

"But even so," she continued, seemingly oblivious to the loop she'd just knocked me for, "there's always been that shadow, even with the good ones. Knowing they could do that to me, it gives them power. Hell, even you can when you're hopped up on blood."

"You know I'd never do that."

She waved me off. "Yeah, yeah, but it's still there. That sense of inequality, of subservience, of knowing you're only free due to the other person's good graces. It sours you after a while. Turns you hard. Combined with the bloodlust, that nearly overpowering need to hunt and kill that's been there ever since I woke up like this..."

"Dressed like a prostitute?"

She glared sourly at me. "As a vampire."

"I hope that's not the only reason you're helping me rescue him."

She stared back with a look that said her opinion of me was rapidly dropping several notches. "Don't be stupid. You know I was on board long before the munchkin kicked in the front door."

"Sorry. Yeah, I know. And also, I'm sure you're eager to save him. After all, you and he…"

"You're about as subtle as a rhino in a china shop."

"I thought it was a bull."

"You're even worse." She leaned back and took a deep breath. "I don't know. He's a nice guy, and I respect that he had the balls to ask me out even knowing what I am and what I could do to him. You don't see that often."

"Desperation makes a man brave."

"You would know."

"Touché."

"But things kind of hit a brick wall. First, there was when you disappeared on your mad jaunt into crazy town. Then afterwards, when we learned his blood could make vamps go boom. Who knows, maybe I have a little ADD myself because I tend to get distracted easily."

The last of the anger gone, I sat down next to her.

"Then there's what happened between us after you killed Turd."

And I hopped right back to my feet again. "Um yeah. Still remember that, eh?"

She tapped the side of her head. "One of the loopholes of compulsions. Unless you're specifically told to forget, you don't."

"That wasn't me. Not exactly."

"I know that now. Didn't know it at the time."

"Sort of … complicates things a bit."

"Welcome to life, Bill. It tends to be that way. Apparently, it gets even worse after you're dead."

"Tell me about it."

"I often don't," she said cryptically.

"Huh?"

"We've been joined at the … well, fist mostly, since I ran into you on that subway car. Yet you really don't know me at all."

"I think I do. And..." I stepped back, not wanting to catch the aforementioned fist to my face. "I've seen you open up more than you think you have. I know you and Starlight were friends. I know you and James have history. I know that when I met you, you'd have gutted most people sooner than talk to them, yet just a few months later had become a patron saint to the homeless back at Pandora."

She nodded thoughtfully.

"I know you and Christy get along and that you've gone out of your way to protect her."

"Those are all good things. What about the bad?"

"Well, I know you're a psycho mass-murdering bitch when you want to be. And I mean that as a compliment – I've seen your dark side and it still hasn't scared me off."

She raised an eyebrow. "Did you know I was once like you?"

"Awesomely cool?"

"The opposite, dipshit. I was a dork, a bookworm back in grade school."

Okay, I was willing to believe a lot, but this strained the boundaries of disbelief. "You're shitting me."

"It's true. I spent my days in the library. My sister Linda was the glamorous one. She had the looks, the popularity, the boys."

I couldn't quite stifle a laugh. "Hold on. Linda and Lucinda?"

"Yes, my parents were assholes," she snapped. "Especially Dad."

The bitterness in her voice stopped me short. I'd heard things like this before. "Hold on. He didn't..."

She rolled her eyes at me. "Relax. This isn't one of those types of confessions. He never laid a hand on me. He was just a chauvinistic ass and he made it known all the time. He's the reason I eventually rebelled, ran away from home, made some bad decisions that led me to this life. Who'd a thought little bookworm Lucinda, who dreamed of being a businesswoman on Madison Avenue, would end up like this?"

"Well, if it helps, you filled out quite nicely."

"Don't think I'm not aware. Being a vampire under Jeff was tough, but it did wonders for my self-image."

"So why are you telling me all of this?" I asked, then remembered why we were out here. "And what does this have to do with the knife ... or is it Sheila?" Yeah, I was tossing the bait out there, but fuck it. Can't be a pussy all my life.

"I'm telling you because this is it. It's the end game. I'm not gonna lie. I'm pretty certain not all of us are coming back from this one. So I figured you deserved to know that much. As for the rest..."

"Yeah?" Now we were getting to the interesting part.

"It's because you wouldn't."

"Wouldn't what?"

"Kill her, if it came down to it."

"Wait, what are we talking about?"

"You said it yourself, I have a fondness for Christy. I consider her a friend. Never thought I'd say that out loud, but she is. I like her. Hell, I might even go so far..."

"As to say you like Tom, too?"

"More like tolerate him to a small degree. A *very* small degree."

"Okay, fine. I'm sure he'd be good with that. But why do you think I need to kill...?" I promptly shut my mouth as realization set in. "The prophecy?"

"Ours and that goddamned one the Magi have."

"You don't really think..."

She stood and threw her hands in the air. "What the fuck does it matter what I, you, or anyone else thinks? We're dealing with magic here. It doesn't follow the rules of logic. I can't say I believe in destiny, but if I did, I sure as shit wouldn't want to know about it in advance. The fact is we do, though, and it seems hell-bent on happening. That scares the shit out of me."

"She doesn't want that. Sheila, I mean. She's not a baby killer."

"Do you think I don't know that? I've lived the greater part of my life with people who are. After a while, you begin to develop a knack for spotting the type."

"Okay then. But even assuming fate throws us a monkey wrench and we learn Christy's kid is destined to grow up to be Ming the Merciless, I made Sheila a promise that I'd stop her if it came down to it."

"And that's the problem, Bill. You're not a killer either. Sure, you do what you need to do, but you don't enjoy it."

"I might've enjoyed it with a few of them."

"You wouldn't enjoy it with anyone who didn't deserve it."

I took in the silent forest around us. One might have thought we were the last two people left on earth at that moment. Problem was, if we waited here long enough, we might end up that way. "You said it yourself. I do what I need to do."

"Not this time. You're too close. Too conflicted with any of us. What if it turned out that killing Ed was the only way to stop this? What would you do?"

"I ... I'd make like Captain Kirk and the Kobayashi Maru. I'd find a new choice."

"No. You'd hesitate, try to talk your way out of it. Maybe you'd even manage it, but maybe you wouldn't. Know what I would do? I'd kill him."

"He's your friend, too."

"I know. But here's the thing: I'm already a killer. I gave in to the darkness a long time ago. It's a part of me now, and that's why I had the knife. So if push came to shove, I could kill her so you wouldn't have to."

"Wait, you did this for me?"

"You truly are a fucking moron when you want to be, you know that?" She turned and gave me a shove. Of course, a shove from a tiny vampire was pretty much the equivalent of a four-hundred-pound wrestler putting their all into it, so

I ended up landing on my ass about ten feet away. "When this all started, it was all about me. I won't lie. You were a means to an end. Nothing more. But then you and your goddamned humanity ended up being contagious, like some sort of disease."

"Hadn't quite thought of it that way," I replied, getting to my feet and dusting off the seat of my pants.

"It's like one day I woke up and suddenly I believed in you. Well, here's the thing. I still do. You're one of the most clueless assholes I know, but you're a good person inside."

I stepped back over to her, but cautiously this time. I'd meant to drag her out here to chew her out, not get beaten up. "I don't know about that."

"Whatever that thing inside of you is, it's not you. It can act like you, but it isn't and, here's the thing – you're stronger than it. You proved that when you didn't let it kill me. You proved it again when you blew the shit out of Vehron and took over, even if it was just for a short time. You may not believe it, but you are."

I considered my recent mood swings. I still wasn't sure I could agree. However, hearing of her faith in me didn't exactly hurt. "Thank you."

"Fucking idiot," she replied offhandedly.

"But that still doesn't explain the knife. I mean, if you think destiny is that strong, then Sheila and I still have to face each other in some final apocalyptic battle."

"Yeah," she replied, lifting a hand and... Holy crap, was she wiping her eyes? Hell, I'd barely ever seen her shed tears of laughter, but this... "You're going to lose, you know."

"Huh?"

"Just what I said. You're going to lose that battle."

"I might not be the best fighter in the world, but..."

"But you're going to lose it on purpose." She held up a hand. "No, don't try to argue it. You will, because that's what you'd do for anyone you loved rather than have to hurt them. You'd do it for her. You'd do it for Ed. You'd do it for that idiot Tom."

"I'd do it for you." I paused at the realization of what I'd just said. "Um, what I meant was..."

"I'm not a fucking idiot, Bill. I know."

"Oh."

"Believe me, I know." She stepped up and placed a hand on my cheek. I looked her in the eye and finally saw her. The mask that she always wore had fallen away and, in her eyes, I saw the pain of a life forced to live as a monster against her will. "But I'm not as generous as you. I'm a selfish person. I can't promise I would do the same."

"You might surprise yourself."

"You might want to think twice before betting on that." She blinked and her eyes turned soullessly black for a moment before resuming their normal green color. "I can promise you one thing, though."

"What?"

"I'd sooner kill that girl and have you hate me, than watch you do it and hate yourself."

PART II

30

EJECTING THE WARP CORE

Had my life been a romantic comedy, our time alone in Grulg's secret place would have culminated with much kissing and rolling around in the dirt.

Sadly, we were in the middle of Armageddon, and fate — whether or not it existed — didn't quite like me that much.

I did manage to pull Sally into a big hug that she returned for maybe about four seconds before threatening to knee me in the balls if I didn't let go.

Despite all she'd said, I still didn't believe her. Yeah, on the outside, she projected an aura of gold-digging that would have put any reality show family to shame, but inside, there was a solid core of goodness.

I'd mentally put my feelings for Sheila on the shelf back in Boston, or tried to anyway. After our talk, I realized I had to do the same with Sally as well. Right now, all of us needed friends we could count on far more than anything else.

For once, I was letting my brain do the thinking over my dick. Maybe this was that whole growing up thing everyone talked about.

If so, it kinda sucked.

As we walked back, I happily realized if either of them happened to offer me a pre-end-of-the-world good luck fuck,

I'd still gladly accept it. Maturation might have infected me, but it was nice to see it wasn't a fatal dose.

"Are we cool?" I asked as the rancid smell in the air signaled that we were nearing the Sasquatch village again.

"We were never not cool," she replied with a smile. "Well, you probably weren't."

"Too late; you already called me cool."

"Don't let it go to your head."

"Also too late."

"I'm still worried about what's coming."

"Worried about the end of the world? Nah, you don't say."

"No, I mean who we have to face. Either of them could snag control of me in an instant. If that happens..."

"I'll do what needs to be done," I replied. "Although, know that will mean knocking your ass out, nothing more."

"You mean *trying* to knock my ass out."

"I thought you had faith in me."

"I do, but I have more in me."

"Fair enough. You're still not getting the knife back, though."

"Hah! As if I couldn't get another."

We arrived to find our friends ready to go through with the power dampening.

Yeah, that was a nice way of saying it. The reality was more to the tune of injecting Sheila with dark magic that would leave her vulnerable in a way an Icon wasn't meant to be. I really wasn't comfortable with it, but it was her choice to make. I had to respect that, even if I didn't like it.

She was sitting on a bench with her sleeve rolled up. Kelly held her hand while the other witches were finishing up on their end.

"I see the whore survived your admonishment," Gan

said, stepping away from the group and approaching us. "I am pleased by that."

"Really?" we both asked.

"Of course. She still has uses, even if only as cannon fodder."

I leaned down. "Gan, Sally is my friend. She's not cannon fodder."

"If you say so, my love."

"Speaking of love," Tom added, also strolling over, "how did your little *walk* in the woods go?" He added a hip thrust for good measure.

"Do that one more time and we're going to find out if that glamour of yours has intestines," Sally warned.

It was good to see nothing had changed in the interim, in a sense anyway.

"Go on," Sally said to me with a nudge. "I think someone else could use a friend right now." I raised an eyebrow and she simply nodded.

Tom stepped in to continue talking to Sally, so I excused myself from that idiot sandwich to ask Christy how things were going.

She held up a syringe filled with a dirty dark grey fluid. "We're as ready as we're going to be. One of the Forest Folk popped in a while back to let us know we were a go on their end, too. They're ready to send us whenever we are."

"Arboreal apparating. Cool."

She narrowed her eyes at me for a moment, but then lightened up. "I will admit a little bit of curiosity to seeing how it works."

I pointed at the syringe. "So is that stuff ... safe?"

"I don't think anyone can answer that," Sheila replied with a smile that didn't reach her eyes.

"We diluted the mixture as much as we thought possible while still leaving it effective," Christy said.

"Yeah, I made the calculations," Meg added. "As best I could, anyway."

A glance passed between her and Christy, not an entirely friendly one either. Trouble in witch paradise, perhaps?

I turned back to Sheila. "Are you sure about this?"

"No, but I don't think we have much choice."

I took a seat on her other side. "You always have a choice."

"I don't know if I can believe that."

"Sure you can. Just have a little faith."

The smile turned real and she laughed. After she was finished, she looked up at the witches. "Let's do this."

Kelly stood up to make room for the others. Christy stepped forward, but Veronica offered her hand instead. "Let me. I've done it enough times I'm almost a pro."

Christy nodded and handed over the needle.

Kelly stepped to the side and Sheila raised her right arm. Barely realizing I was doing so, I grabbed her free hand and squeezed it. It trembled slightly, then she squeezed back.

"Let's do this before I chicken out." Sheila glanced at me as she said it, making me wonder if she was actually talking to Veronica.

"Any preference where you want it?" Veronica asked, holding up the syringe.

"Whatever's convenient," she replied with a chuckle. "Just do me a favor and make it fast. If you're going to try doing the distraction thing, don't. I always hated that."

Veronica smiled and nodded. "Me too." Then she inserted the needle.

31

TAKE YOUR MEDICINE

At first, there wasn't much to note – just a tiny wince from Sheila as the needle sank into her upper arm and Veronica depressed the plunger.

"I guess that wasn't so..."

She didn't get a chance to finish, as her back arched suddenly and she squeezed down on my hand with surprising strength. The rest of her began to shake uncontrollably and her eyes rolled into the back of her head.

"Damnit," Christy snapped. "Someone help Bill."

Kelly and Meg grabbed Sheila from the other side. Together, we tried to get her into a prone position so she couldn't hurt herself.

"Quick," Veronica said. "Put something between her teeth so she doesn't bite her tongue in half."

Fuck! There wasn't anything in reach, at least not that I thought hygienic enough to chew on. Oh, the hell with it! I shoved the flat of my hand into her mouth until something better could be found.

And, of course, she promptly bit down hard. God fucking damn!

"Not what I had in mind," Veronica chided. She was starting to get a deer in the headlights look in her eyes.

I turned to her and said in my best calm voice, "Well, if you'd be so kind as to find something else, then."

"Hold on," Christy said. She'd retrieved a backpack and used her magic to sear off one of the straps.

"Good idea. That oughta to be thick enough to..."

Minor things, like words and coherent thought, were immediately cut off as Sheila's aura erupted from her body. It washed harmlessly over the witches. For me, however, the effect was slightly less *fun*.

White fire burst from my skin where we made direct contact. Both of my hands blazed up as if I'd dipped them in lighter fluid and held them over an open flame.

My concern wasn't for my own safety, though. Well, okay, not entirely for my own safety, because, fuck me, it hurt a lot! At the same time, I couldn't let go. Kelly and Meg were just barely holding down the fort on Sheila's other side. If I backed off, she could seriously injure herself.

"Beloved," Gan said from behind me. "Perhaps it would be best if you..."

"Oh, the hell with this." Sally stepped past Gan with a snarl and made to drag me away.

"No!" I roared, despite wanting nothing more than to curl up in a ball away from the hurty magic. My hands were really starting to feel charred and...

Wait, it was just my hands. Not the rest of me as it should have been.

I was about to point this out when Veronica cried, "Look!"

Sure enough, the glow around Sheila was fading. Had this been any other time, I'd have been burnt to a crisp. I would have had to spend the rest of the day growing back my skin, and that's only if I had gotten supremely lucky. But now, yeah, my hands were going to mostly be useless hunks of meat for a while, but the damage pretty much stopped at my wrists.

I removed my hand from her mouth and replaced it with the backpack strap, but the danger appeared to be almost over. Slowly, the convulsions began to lessen. Finally, her body went slack.

Meg put two fingers on Sheila's neck to make sure she had a pulse, but it was unnecessary. I could hear her heart beating and the sound of her breathing. Both were a little fast, but nothing dangerous, or so I hoped. It wasn't like I was a trained paramedic or anything.

Sheila let out a groan and her eyes began to flutter. "Ugh, why do I have the taste of barbecue in my mouth?"

I put my hands behind my back and leaned over her. Her eyes opened and I smiled.

"What?" she asked weakly. "See something you like?"

"You." Her eyes opened wide, and I quickly added, "I mean, you're back. The old you, that is. Oh jeez. Anyone have a mirror?"

"I don't see anything different," Meg replied.

"Hold on, Romeo," Kelly said, then she fished out her phone, took a picture of Sheila, and showed it to her.

"My eyes, they're..."

It wasn't quite as dramatic an effect as what a vamp could do. Hell, only someone intimately familiar with how she looked could have told. And yes, I'd Facebook stalked her enough to be able to give a sketch artist a near perfect rendition of her features. Sue me for being desperate.

Regardless, just a few moments before, her eyes had been a brilliant silver in color, almost as if her irises were made of metal. Now, though, they were a light grey, the same light grey I'd seen nearly every day at work for three years.

"More importantly," Christy said, pushing her way past the rest of us. "How do you feel?"

"Like I just got over a bad cold. Ouch..." She sat up and placed a hand over where she'd been stuck with the needle. A small bruise was forming and a tiny drop of blood could be seen on her skin.

"Oh, sorry. Let me clean that up," Veronica said.

"No need." Sheila closed her eyes. A second later, she gritted her teeth. The faintest of glows appeared around her hand, only visible because the interior of the hut was fairly dim. If we'd been standing outside in the daylight, you'd have never noticed it. Finally, she let go. "I take back what I said." She looked at me. "That's all the juice I've got in me."

"Think it'll be enough to get you through the Stargate?" I asked.

"There is only one way to be certain," Gan said.

Before I could question what she meant by that, she was across the room. By the time I had spun back around, Kelly and Veronica had been abruptly knocked to the side.

Of far greater interest, though, was Gan and the hand she had around Sheila's throat.

32

THE HIDDEN MENACE

Sheila's eyes opened wide and she instinctively tried to ward off her smaller foe. She grabbed Gan's hand by the thumb to force her off, but Gan countered expertly, maintaining her grasp.

Stunned silence met this in the hut. I had learned to expect the unexpected from the little runt, but this was insane. All of her talk of wanting to see destiny play itself out. Had that been little more than a ruse, a chance to get close enough for something like this?

That broke the impasse. I reached into my pocket and grabbed hold of the blood vial still there.

I wasn't the only one on the move. Little more than a blur herself, Sally raced past me ... only to catch a back kick from Gan that came up so quickly you'd have sworn her foot teleported.

"That will be unnecessary, whore," she replied before releasing her grasp on Sheila and backing up a step. "I have seen enough. The Shining One is capable of making this journey with us."

Her words registered in my ears, but I wasn't listening. Anger flooded through me and I ripped my hand out of my pocket and took a swing at the little monster.

She caught me by the wrist as if I'd been moving in slow

motion. "I believe it would be unwise to waste that, my love."

It was only then that I realized I still had the vial grasped in my fist.

"What the hell?!" I screamed at her, before turning to Sheila. "Are you all right?" I then remembered Sally. I glanced back and saw Tom helping her up across the hut. "Are you *both* all right?"

"Nothing a good orthodontist couldn't fix," Sally said, spitting out a wad of blood.

"She really fucking nailed you," Tom said.

Sally glared at him, then shoved him away. Yeah, she was fine.

"You?" I asked Sheila, who appeared shaken but otherwise unhurt.

She nodded, then turned to Gan. "You scared the crap out of me. Why did you..." Her voice trailed off. For a moment, I was afraid she was hurt worse than she realized, internal injuries maybe, but then – amazingly enough – she began to laugh.

Looks of confusion were passed back and forth among the occupants of the room.

"You get hit in the head a little too hard there, Sheils?" Kelly asked.

"No." She got the laughter under control, but still had a big grin on her face. "Don't you get it? She frightened me. I was actually afraid."

"I don't get it."

"Think of it like being underwater too long and then finally breaking the surface for air."

Collectively, we stared blankly at her.

"I mean, I can still feel fear, but it has to be something big. Something deep."

"Like?" I asked.

She averted her eyes for a moment. "Just something big. But physical conflict, normally that's nothing. More of a rush than anything. But what she did right there, it scared the ever-living crap out of me."

It took me a moment for this to sink in, but then I got it. Primal fear was supposed to be alien to an Icon. Getting a dose of it must have been for her what feeling the momentary warmth of the sun might feel like for a vampire ... albeit maybe a tad different. Even so, give a deaf man back his hearing for a day and I'm sure the most annoying sound in the world would seem like music to his ears.

"Your reflexes and combat skills are still intact, I see," Gan replied.

"Yeah, intact," Sheila replied dubiously. No doubt she'd noticed how easily Gan had countered her.

"Enough with the tests," I said.

"C'mon, man, this is the fun part."

I spun to glare daggers at Tom. "No comments from the peanut gallery, especially you." My roommates' idea of fun had, in prior days, typically involved me in various stages of on fire.

Tom gave an easy shrug as if to say he had to try.

I turned my attention back to Sheila. "So, how are you feeling?"

She was quiet for a moment as if running an internal diagnostic. "Pretty normal, and I mean normal me, not normal Icon me. Maybe a bit queasy, like something didn't quite agree with me, but decent. Well enough to give the magic carpet ride a try."

Good enough for me. "Okay, folks, grab your bags. It's time to check out of the Sasquatch Hilton. Be sure not to steal any towels along the way. I hear the penalties for doing so are a killer."

That got them all moving, albeit there wasn't much to pack. We hadn't come up here with the intention of moving in. And, truth be told, I hoped to never ever see this place, or my new wife, again.

Now to hope that was one fate I could avoid.

The supernatural world could be so mundane when it wanted to be. Typical vampire society was more like a frat house than anything, while their higher up operations wouldn't be alien to any middle manager in corporate America. There were glimpses of the fantastic here and there – Gods, weird monsters, the various ceremonies that Christy's magic seemed to favor.

It was that latter I was thinking of, so of course I was slightly underwhelmed when the Sasquatch shaman threw a hunk of ... let's just pretend it was mud ... against the trunk of a tall pine tree, pointed a grimy finger, and said, "*T'lunta walk there. All walk there.*"

"Walk where?" I asked. I didn't see any shimmering portal, black hole, or magical opening in the tree.

"*There.*" It pointed again. "*Behind tree. But first...*"

"Oh fucking A, man!" I yelled as the glop of shit splattered against my chest. "Was that completely necessary?"

The creature opened its mouth in a broken-toothed grin. Fucking asshole.

"You might want to look up this thing called fluoride," I replied lamely.

"*Shaman mark you,*" Big C said. He'd joined us to see us off and maybe get in a goodbye smooch from his blushing bride. Too bad so sad, but my *lovely* wife was nowhere to be seen. Ah, what a heartbreaker. "*That way Grulg and others know not to kill T'lunta.*"

Oh. "Well, thank you, then."

He turned to his shaman, chattered something, and they both broke out in mirthful hoots. Somehow I got the sneaking suspicion it was the ape equivalent of "The dumb rube fell for it."

"*Big C wish you well, mate,*" he said to Sally. "*Return soon so that we make many cubs.*" The tone he used, however, was anything but eager. The big idiot was probably more likely to throw a party if Sally was returned to him as a pile of dust.

Heh. Maybe, once this was said and done, we could actually come to an agreement in which neither us had to dip our wicks anywhere we didn't want to and still keep the peace.

Still, that was probably a moot point as there was a good chance we wouldn't see each other alive again. One could always hope.

"Not gonna give your sugar daddy a kiss goodbye?" I asked.

Sally gave me the stink eye, then stepped around the tree ... and didn't reappear on the other side.

Okay then.

I made to move forward, but a big paw fell upon my shoulders. Uh oh, this was what I feared. I glanced up, expecting to see a fist headed my way, but Big C simply said, "*Let Magi go.*"

I shrugged. "Whatever. I mean, sure, ladies first and all."

Kelly looked at me, then at C as if wondering what that was all about. Finally, though, she stepped through.

Christy and her other coven members followed. Tom was next, then Gan after I promised I'd be right behind her.

That left Sheila and me as the final two.

"I should go last," she said. "Make sure you're okay."

Her meaning was clear. The apes could just as easily pummel me into paste once the others were gone and nobody would be the wiser. Under normal circumstances, I'd agree, but this was anything but normal.

"You first. We need to make sure this works. If it doesn't..."

"If it doesn't, the Forest Folk will escort me back to Gan's people."

"Where you'll be both surrounded *and* powerless. No deal."

"I'm not arguing."

"Neither am I." I scooped her up off her feet.

"Hey!" she protested. I could feel her aura flicker to life, but it was still weak as a kitten, barely enough to singe even my coat.

I carried her over and said, "You can yell at me once you're safely there," then unceremoniously dropped her back to her feet and shoved her behind the tree. With one step, she was still there. With the next, it was like she dissolved into nothingness.

It had worked.

"Yes!" I allowed myself a congratulatory fist pump, then turned and found Big C and his shaman standing there. A small contingent of Feet were behind them, supposedly gathered to watch our departure, but they could just as easily serve as my impromptu executioners if they wanted.

There was no way I could fight them all, but the vial of happiness in my pocket could at least ensure I made them regret trying. Heh. Small comfort to the doomed.

I steeled my voice as best I could. "So, are we going to have trouble now?"

Rather than answer my challenge via way of tearing my limbs off, though, C actually raised his eyebrows in what appeared to be mock horror.

"*Big C honorable,*" he said. "*Honor treaty. Honor truce. Ask you to stay so you have chance when you step through.*"

"So I have a chance? You said you told the others the war was over. Hell, you said you marked me." Okay, maybe that last one was a stretch.

Big C took a step forward until he loomed above me. Oh crap. I'd stepped over the line.

Instead of punting me into next Tuesday, however, he looked down and solemnly said, "*We did. Will honor truce. Not need worry about us. Others you need worry about.*"

Well, if that wasn't ominous sounding, I didn't know what was.

33

SHIFTING OUT OF NEUTRAL

Bigfoot teleportation was weird, but a lot less disconcerting than traveling via mage express. Rather than feeling like I was being blasted to pieces, shunted to nowhere, and then reassembled incorrectly, this was like trying to walk up the stairs four at a time. It's hard to explain, but for a moment, one of my feet was back in Canada while another was touching down a thousand miles away.

And then it was over and I was stepping out from behind a totally different tree in different surroundings and in weather that was – thankfully – a shitload warmer. Gan's helicopters had the advantage of luxury accommodations, but this was a hell of a lot faster. I'd take it.

Speaking of Gan, the little demon doll was there waiting to step into my personal space and give me a great big hug, strong enough to knock the wind out of me. "I am glad to see the Alma did not resort to treachery, my love." She looked up at me with her big green eyes. "Though, if they had dared, I have little doubt you would have prevailed."

I glanced around and saw the others had likewise made it through unscathed, including Sheila, thank goodness. Even with her temporary vulnerability, I was afraid shit would still go awry and she'd somehow end up teleported into the middle of the Pacific. Nice to see that Christy knew her stuff. Well, fine. It was Decker's plan, but it would be a cold day in Hell before I acknowledged him as anything other than a cockmeat sandwich with all the fixings.

I peeled Gan off as best as I could, shedding the thick Mongolian fur coat in the process. I tossed it over the evil munchkin, giving me a moment to step away as she freed herself from it.

That's when I realized we weren't alone. Large shapes loomed over our party from every direction. I could only hope they'd gotten the memo about the treaty – I didn't fancy getting my skull stomped in.

One of them, an eight-foot-tall monster covered in scars and missing patches of fur, stepped forward. "*This place of peace*," it said, turning and scanning all of us with its beady eyes. Finally, it settled upon Christy. "*No fighting here.*"

Though I had no way of knowing if I was right or not, I decided to take a chance and address him. "Hey ... Grulg."

The beast stepped toward me, glowering down. Oh great. I'd gotten it wrong and now I was gonna get dick-slapped for it. "*Grulg see you remember, Freewill T'lunta.*"

"I did? I mean, yeah, of course I did." I quickly turned to Sally and pointed a finger at her. "In your fucking face!"

"Blind squirrel, dickhead," she shot back.

Grulg grunted disapprovingly. "*Blind squirrel not live long in woods. Too many things to catch and eat it.*"

"Not what she meant. It's, well ... never mind. Just a dumb saying anyway."

"We've been looking for you," Sally said. "We need your help."

He frowned, albeit that seemed to be a pretty common expression among his kind. "*Grulg hear of treaty. No more war. But T'lunta never be allies, friends. T'lunta always enemies of the tribes.*"

Oh yeah, there was that. I needed to remember that treaty or not, the vamps and the Feet really couldn't stand each other. A piece of dried up parchment and a few sham weddings weren't going to bridge that gap anytime soon.

"*Still,*" Grulg continued, "*T'lunta and mate have acted honorably in past.*"

Sally made to open her mouth to say something, but I held up a hand. Fuck it, let this guy believe what he wanted. It didn't matter so long as he gave us the directions we needed.

"*Grulg will help if Grulg is able.*"

"Awesome..."

"*But know this. If trick, then Grulg will smash T'lunta with rock!*"

"Hey," I replied, holding up my hands in a placating manner, "if we're lying, we're dying."

"Wonderful choice of words," Sally commented with an eye-roll.

"*Grulg see she still have fire.*"

"Oh yeah, she's a pip, all right," I said. "Anyway, let's get right to it. Remember when we..."

The words were caught in my throat as Grulg's massive hand covered my face. For one horrible second, before I could close my lips, I tasted his palm. Oh God, the humanity!

He quickly let go. "*No talk here.*"

"A simple shhh would have sufficed."

"*Enemies present. Grulg honorable. Not allow war here. Listen to T'lunta alone.*"

I looked around, seeing nobody besides our group and a bunch of Sasquatches, most of whom weren't looking upon us with any great amount of kindness. Were there factions present that didn't want peace? Not a big stretch of the imagination with this bunch. Either that, or we were surrounded by invisible demons ready to kick our asses – just my luck.

Whatever. "All right, Grulg. Lead the way. Everyone else, try to keep up."

Grulg looked down at me as if I'd gone insane, his brows raised in surprise. "*You bring along?*"

"What? Of course…" Oh wait. I think I got what he was saying. "Sheila … the Silver Eyes. She's agreed to a temporary truce. The enemy we seek is an enemy to all."

Grulg looked confused *"Who?"* I hooked a thumb back at Sheila. He stepped past me and gave her a sniff. *"Smell like human."*

"Long story. Listen, can we…"

"Not talk about human, stupid T'lunta," Grulg growled, rounding on me.

"Why argue?" one of the other Sasquatches asked, stepping forward. He was a bit taller than Grulg and was giving me a stink eye that almost made the rest of him smell good in comparison. *"Let allies do as want. Not matter to us."*

"Not allies. We no longer at war," Grulg spat back.

"T'lunta still enemies," the other one argued. *"Magi not enemies."*

Okay, none of this was making any fucking sense. "Yeah, we know the Magi aren't enemies," I said. "They're here with us."

That stopped Grulg and the other Sasquatch dead in their tracks. Grulg turned to me. *"Not prisoners?"*

"Of course not."

"Slaves?"

"You tell me. Hey, Kelly, fetch me a beer."

"Do I look like a fucking Budweiser Clydesdale to you?"

After the chuckling had died down, I turned back to Grulg. "See? They're my friends."

He leaned down until he was almost face to face with me. Grulg might have been the closest I came to having a favorite Sasquatch, but that didn't mean he wouldn't have benefited from a handful of breath mints. *"Not friends."*

"Okay, enough of the riddles," Christy said at last. "What's going on?" Then, almost as an afterthought, she added, "As neutral signatories of the Humbaba Accord, I and my sisters request to know the circumstances which seem to be hampering our progress here."

"Neutral?" After a few seconds of silence, during which

Grulg appeared to be processing this, he stepped back and waved his hands to seemingly indicate her and her whole coven. "*Not know?*"

"Not know what?" Meg asked.

Grulg opened his mouth to answer, but then shifted his focus and brought his teeth together in a snarl. "*This place of...*"

He was cut off as a purplish dome of energy crackled to life around us, surrounding me and my friends.

What the fuck?

I turned to Christy. "I didn't know their magic could do this."

She looked around, an unreadable expression upon her face. "That's because it's not their magic."

"Grulg!" a human-sounding voice yelled from somewhere behind us. I turned to see several Sasquatches stepping to the side to allow a bunch of hooded figures in white robes past. I'd seen similar such garments before when I'd been up in the Woods of Mourning the first time. They were Magi.

The woman at their lead spoke again. "As allied signatories of the Humbaba Accord, I and my coven demand that you hand over the vampires and their traitor allies."

And with that, any hope of my day becoming less complicated evaporated in a puff of logic.

34

MEET THE NEW CULT, SAME AS THE OLD CULT

"Um, anyone have any idea..."

Christy shut me up with a glance. Whatever was going on, she was as much in the dark as I was, but the look on her face said she planned to find out.

"This is unexpected, my love."

"Not now, Gan," I hissed.

I held my ground, trying to not make any moves that might set off a wave of fireballs in our direction. Christy, however, didn't seem inclined to the passive aggressive route. "What is the meaning of this? I am Christine Fenton, Mentor of..."

"We know who you are," the woman replied. "And you can drop the formalities. They won't help you here."

"I see," she replied, putting her hands on her hips. "Very well. Who do I have the *honor* of speaking to?"

The mage in question removed her hood, revealing her to be middle-aged in appearance, perhaps of Mediterranean descent. Long brown, braided hair containing streaks of grey fell to the middle of her back. Her eyes, even darker brown than her hair, held a no-nonsense look about them as if she wasn't about to tolerate any bullshit.

"High Mentor," Christy said with a polite nod of her head.

"I see you remember. Good."

"Care to clue the rest of us in?" Sally asked.

"I don't speak to your kind," the witch replied.

Meg stepped forward. "How about me? Same question, lady."

"Ah, Christine. You haven't taught your students much in the way of manners, I see. I suppose that's to be expected."

Christy, for her part, played it neutral. "Meg, you stand before Agnes Zema, esteemed High Mentor of Northern New England."

"And how does my cousin's favorite pupil fare these days? Heavy with child, I see."

Wait a second. *Cousin?*

"Hold on," Tom said. "You mean this bitch is Decker's cousin? Small world." So much for keeping my mouth shut, especially when Tom was around to fuck things up for me.

The witch's eyes narrowed at him. "I'd heard the Freewill had a tongue that could only be silenced if it was cut out. Do not tempt me, vampire."

"Oh, I'm not ... oof!"

He was silenced by Sally quickly stepping in and elbowing him, again making me flinch. Maybe it was time to bring her up to speed on the whole Apollo's Prism thing. "Don't say anything else, *Bill*," she said. "She doesn't deserve the satisfaction."

What?!

"What is this, Christine?" Agnes asked. "Some sort of glamour around him? Silly girl. That would have worked a lot better if you'd included his lackeys. I'd have thought Harold would have taught you better."

It was good to know that my picture wasn't circulating around the entire supernatural world. Seemed everyone and their mother could usually sniff me out. However, maybe that was the key here. Mages had their magic, but their senses were no better than anyone else's.

As subtly as I could, which wasn't much since we were surrounded by witches, Sasquatches, and a magic force field,

I took stock of our group. Thankfully, Tom seemed to be the only one looking confused by this. Hell, even Gan shot me back a neutral glance, proving she could act with the best of them.

That left only...

"*Grulg protest!*"

Uh oh.

"*T'lunta enemies but granted free passage by great leader Cunt.*"

By the way Agnes arched an eyebrow, and the hushed snickers of her coven that followed, I got the sense the idiocy of the Feet wasn't lost on her either. But I had to give credit where credit was due. The big ape hadn't ratted me out.

"I would remind you, Grulg," she replied, "what you have is, at best, an armistice with them. We have forsaken our time-honored neutrality so as to ally with your people. What means more to you, the request of those who are friends or a shallow promise made to an ancient enemy?"

Grulg didn't have an immediate answer.

Thankfully, Christy didn't let the silence pan out for long. "You dare to call me a traitor when you just willfully admitted that you've broken our neutrality? The Magi have stood silent witness to the machinations of the other races since before recorded history, tending only to our own affairs. Yet you and your coven casually throw that away and expect..."

"You think this is only us?" Agnes asked, sounding surprised. "You and your coven have truly been blind these last few days."

"What do you mean?"

"What I mean is that our most revered mother, Kala the White, has returned from the mists of time. She has returned and covens all across the world have flocked to her calling."

Well, goddamn it all. Talk about check and mate.

❖

While we'd been busy trying to figure out how the fuck we were gonna spelunk our way back to her homestead, Calibra hadn't been sitting on her hands. Somehow she'd gotten word out, even as she blocked our efforts to scry her, that she was back and it was time for the Magi to fall in line.

Apparently it had worked, too. And why shouldn't it have? Hell, she was the giver of their laws, the maker of all they held dear, a Christ-like figure in her second coming.

"You don't know what she's done. Who she really is," Christy said, a hint of desperation in her voice.

"The White has prepared us for your lies. Do you think she hasn't told us there would be those who would speak out against her – those who would willingly betray their covens?" She shifted her glance toward Christy's stomach. "Those who would consort with our enemies, lay with them. Bear their bastard seed."

"Hey," Tom said. "You better not be talking about my kid."

A smile appeared on Agnes's face. No fucking way! First, Turd believed Ed was my child, and now this nutcase thought Christy's was mine, too. I swear, it would be a near miracle if I wasn't hit with multiple paternity suits before this whole thing was over.

Still, maybe there was a chance to worm in some doubt. I mean, hell, you can't tell me that Jesus appearing in the middle of modern times wouldn't incite at least a little skepticism.

"Did you know your high and mighty Kala created abominations against life?" I asked.

Christy spun toward me so fast I was certain she'd give herself whiplash in the process. She raised her eyebrows, but I simply smiled back at her. I had this one. Besides, the smug bitch outside the force field struck me as someone who needed to be taken down a peg or two.

"What would you, an abomination of life, know of this?" Agnes asked.

"It's funny you should say that," I replied, clasping my

hands behind my back. "Didn't you ever wonder how your beloved Kala just happened to show up now, after being missing for the last several thousand years?"

"She's a living goddess. Her knowledge of magic transcends ours many times over. Perhaps she slept. Perhaps she was reborn."

"Perhaps she's a fucking vampire just like me."

That hit a nerve. If it hadn't been for the magical shield between us, you'd have thought I'd slapped her in the face. Cries of "Blasphemy!" could be heard from her coven mates.

"Yep, you guessed it, kiddies." If I could get these magic users riled up enough, then maybe their concentration would falter. "Old Kala is a fang-faced bloodsucker."

Christy turned toward me, wide-eyed, but I ignored her. I was on a roll.

Regardless, it didn't make sense to do this stupidly. I glanced around, taking stock of all the witches and wizards I could see, ready to dodge at a moment's notice. I wasn't an idiot. A pissed off magic user was a sloppy magic user, but that didn't mean they wouldn't do what they did best – fire off Disintegrate spells as fast as they could say them. "Not only that, though..."

"I am warning you, vampire."

"But your best bud Kala isn't only a vampire; she's the first..."

I saw the shot coming. For all their power, it seemed mages had to charge up a bit for their more lethal spells in a way that would have made any character on Dragonball Z proud.

A wizard on the side closest me had apparently heard enough. He let fly with a bolt of red-hot magic that effortlessly passed through the purple construct, but I'd seen him before he shot his load. I sidestepped just in time for it to hit the ground where my feet had been a second earlier, leaving a nasty scorch mark.

I'd correctly guessed he would be conservative in his aim. There were too many in this force bubble, too closely packed.

Had we all been vamps, surely a shooting gallery would have been declared, but we had a coven of witches with us and, traitors or not, the Magi had never struck me as the kind to wantonly execute their own kind.

"Gerald!" Agnes shouted. "That will be enough. You have not been given permission to..."

"He dared profane the White," a witch on the other side protested.

More chimed in, mostly in favor of melting me into goo despite Agnes ordering them to stand down. Uh oh. I'd forgotten that Magi covens weren't like vamp covens. The master, or mentor, didn't have absolute control. Hell, Christy was living proof of that.

I took a quick look amongst my own group. They likewise appeared to be coming to a similar conclusion. Agnes seemed a bit of a bitch, but she was apparently a bitch who wanted to capture us alive. The rest, not so much.

"Good job as usual," Sally said, adopting a defensive stance.

I glanced back at Grulg, but he seemed to be at a loss. For once, *he* was the neutral party. Go figure.

"Everyone get close to us," Christy said as more angry red glows rose up in the peanut gallery.

"I think not, witch," Gan replied. "Your strategy is short-sighted."

"Fine, you're on your own," Christy stated without looking her way.

"That is enough!" Agnes roared, trying to regain control. In response, the dome around us began to shimmer. She was apparently the architect of this particular spell.

I was debating between Christy and Gan while this happened. Not personally, mind you. That was an easy choice in any state of mind. But Gan had a point regarding defense. The witches, Sheila, and Tom would do best collectively fending off spells. Gan, Sally, and I, however, would be better served using our speed and agility.

With Gan around, things were bound to get bloody fast,

but right then, I was having a hard time thinking of reasons to ask her to hold back.

"Be ready, my love," she said, as if picking up my thoughts. Eww, creepy.

"Stop!"

The voice carried with it the unmistakable cadence of command, and all eyes on the would-be battlefield turned Sheila's way.

The bulk of her powers might have been in the shitter for the time being, but she still managed to convey a commanding presence. A part of me wondered if it was one of her Icon powers or just her.

She placed her sheathed sword on the ground and stepped to the forefront of our group, her hands raised. "There's no need for this."

"Get back here," Kelly warned, but Sheila paid her no heed.

"We are not here to wage war against the Magi," she said, her tone authoritative yet placating enough to not be aggressive. "Nor are we here on behalf of the vampire nation."

"Who are you?" Agnes asked.

She didn't know? First me and now Sheila. Either this chick was out of the loop or we just weren't as cool as we thought. Still, perhaps that was a good thing – far too many of the Magi had already tasted the kill the Icon Kool Aid.

Now, to just hope Sheila didn't ruin it by introducing herself.

"These are my friends," she replied, keeping it nice and neutral. Smart.

"Your name, child?"

Before Sheila could answer, one of the other mages ratcheted it back up to DEFCON 2. "She's a thrall. Don't listen to her!"

A beam of pale blue light lanced out before Agnes could reassert control. Sheila's aura flared up in response to it, or tried to.

Shit!

For a moment, a weak glow surrounded her, but it was nothing compared to the spell. It plowed through her defenses, lifted her from her feet, and sent her careening backward across the dirt.

I was by her side in a split second, kneeling and swearing to myself that if she wasn't okay, there were going to be a lot of dead mages littering the woods by the end of the day.

She coughed and blinked her eyes – stunned but still alive. These mages might be thralls to Calibra in their own right, but they still had their basic sense of morality about them regarding humans.

"Did you see that?"

"She glowed white."

"Dear goddess, it's the Icon!"

Or at least they did a second earlier.

I looked down. "Can you run?"

It was a stupid question because, right then, she couldn't even speak.

Unfortunately, running was probably not an option at that point. All around us, angry red glows of magic began to sprout up.

35

WIZARD SORTING

This was starting to turn into a shit's creek without a paddle scenario.

Agnes's coven outnumbered Christy's by at least three to one, and there was no telling how many more mages were waiting to come rushing to their aid. Then there was Grulg and his band of abominable apes. There were about half a dozen Sasquatches in sight, but if this was the force that Turd had previously commanded, there could be hundreds more lurking about. Sure, we weren't at war with them anymore, technically, at least. But we were on their turf. Any of them could easily use that as an excuse, especially in the cause of aiding their new allies.

Despite Agnes stupidly thinking Tom was a glamoured-up me and Christy and her witches still having a pass against lethal force, my main concern was Sheila. With her full faculties in place, she was as close to magic-proof as it got. I could only hope that blood concoction wore off soon. Until it did, though, she needed help, whether she wanted it or not.

"Stay with Tom," I shouted to Sally.

She raised an eyebrow but stepped over to him anyway.

I grabbed Sheila and hoisted her over my shoulder in a fireman's carry. Her power tingled uncomfortably against my skin, but it was still easily ignored – not much more than being zapped with a joy buzzer.

Sally shrugged, then decked Tom square in the face ... catching him the same way as he fell forward. Not quite what I had in mind for her to do, but any port in a storm.

And a storm it was because, at that moment, the bulk of the mages cut loose.

I jumped to my left just as a smoking crater opened up where Sheila had been lying a second earlier. Another nearly took my toes off before I sidestepped.

The mages were playing it safe, aiming low. But now they knew the prize I held in my arms. I had a feeling their restraint wouldn't last long.

Fuck! Out of the corner of my eye, I saw a blast coming at me. I turned too late, my only option to put my body between Sheila and harm's way. I braced myself for the feeling of a foot-wide hole being arc-welded through my chest, but at the last moment, the blast was deflected by a purple wall of energy.

I turned to find Veronica and Kelly close by, having worked it in the nick of time.

"You're welcome," Kelly said with a grin before concentrating on fending off more of those blue bursts.

Enough of this shit. Those red beams of energy might be easy to see coming, but this game of bobbing and weaving wasn't one I could win in the long term, especially not carrying cargo that was starting to snap out of it.

"Put me down," she ordered.

"Sorry, princess, not in your condition."

"I'm fine," she protested, which I dutifully ignored as I leapt up and over two other blasts coming my way.

I'd definitely had enough of this shit. I dug my free hand into my pants pocket and ... remembered I'd left the vial of blood in my coat. The same one I'd promptly discarded the second I got here. Fuck my life!

Where was Gan when I needed her?

Just then, a cry of pain rose up from amongst the ranks of the mages, quickly turning to a gurgle before falling silent again. Guess that answered that question.

Now for...

I spotted Sally still carrying Tom, who was very much awake, by the way. She'd attempted to retreat into the forest, but two Sasquatches had stepped in front to bar her way. Damnit!

They weren't hurting us ... yet, but they certainly weren't helping either. Not good, especially since... Fuck!

"Sally, look out!"

Tom saw it coming, too, from over her shoulder, because he started yelling at the same time. One of the mages had seemingly remembered that the *Freewill* was in the battle as well and *he* was nearly as tempting a target as the Icon.

Sally spun around, but rather than a look of panic on her face, I saw her grin for a split second before diving to the side with my roommate.

What the...?

Confusion instantly turned to understanding as the lance of red-hot power slammed into the two Feet instead, gouging chunks of flesh out of their abdomens and setting them instantly ablaze. Shit-stained fur was apparently flammable. Who'd a guessed?

A primal roar of anger echoed across the clearing, momentarily causing the blasts flying back and forth to cease. It was Grulg, I think anyway, and he did not sound like a happy camper.

I caught momentary sight of Agnes in the chaos and actually felt some pity. The look on her face said that things had spiraled out of her control. I didn't feel too sorry for her, but I got the sense that whatever she'd meant to accomplish this day, this wasn't it.

Alas, I didn't have much time to commiserate because the

mages recovered quickly. More screams rose up from their ranks, probably Gan's handiwork. Music to my ears at that moment.

Now to see if Sally's ploy had any effect on...

"Uh, Bill..." Sheila called from over my shoulder just as I felt a slight tremor beneath my feet.

I turned my head in time to see the Feet charging into the fray.

Yes!

Or make that no. Grulg came straight at me, moving disturbingly fast for something so big. Crap!

He roared again, deafeningly loud in such close quarters.

I shouted out, "It was them!" but he didn't seem to be in a listening mood, so I decided that getting the fuck out of the way was the safer option.

Only I didn't.

From out of nowhere, that rage in me flared up again. With it came an overwhelming urge to throw Sheila down in Grulg's path, to watch him trample her and be done with it.

Wherever that feeling had come from – and I had a pretty good idea where – it caused me to hesitate, rooting me to the spot long enough to catch a backhand fist that nearly spun my head around. The next thing I knew, we were both airborne. I had just enough sense left to try to spin my body so as to shield hers from the impact, but then I slammed headfirst into something harder than my skull and a sensation of nothingness washed over me.

"C'mon. Get up," a voice – female – said from somewhere outside of the peaceful darkness I was enjoying.

Fucking bitch!

The stab of anger from deep inside woke me up far more than the nudging from whoever was shaking my shoulder.

"Let's go. He didn't hit you that hard."

For a moment, I wanted to lash out, but I managed to

hold myself in check – easy to do since my limbs felt like they'd been broken, set badly, then broken again. "I beg to differ," I croaked weakly, daring to crack my eyes open. Thankfully, the anger retreated as consciousness took hold.

Sally was staring down at me, her face smudged with dirt but otherwise looking no worse for wear. That figured. If there was a true survivor among my friends, it was her.

"Um, she's not looking too hot," Tom said from somewhere close by, worry clouding his voice.

I raised a hand and Sally dragged me back to my feet. I was a bit wobbly but trusted in my vampire constitution to take care of that in due order.

My eyes easily cut through the gloom of the forest to find Tom, kneeling down over ... oh no!

I pushed past Sally to where Sheila lay on a bed of moss. One of her arms was bent at a bad angle, and there was a smudge of fresh blood at the corner of her mouth.

Her eyes were closed and she appeared to be out cold. Or at least I hoped she was. "Is she..."

"She's alive," Sally said, "but banged up badly."

"*Grulg apologize.*"

I came close to shitting my pants at the sound, spun to find him standing right behind me, and came a lot closer.

Though he was more than two feet taller and looked strong enough to bench press a truck, I somehow managed to collect myself and not back down. I searched deep inside of me for that anger, for whatever it was that Dr. Death kept feeding me, and found it ... dragged it kicking and screaming to the surface. "What the fuck did you do?"

Grulg actually backed up a step at the sound of my voice, again deeper than I usually spoke.

"I swear to whatever gods are out there, if you hurt her..."

"He didn't." Sally grabbed my arm, and it was all I could do to not backhand her in the mouth. I only paused when I looked down and saw that my claws had extended. "Listen to me. He saved her. He saved *us*."

It took a moment for her words to register, so transfixed

was I by my body's defenses seeming to have taken on a mind of their own.

"Huh? What? Then why is she lying there like..."

"*Silver Eyes said to be strong. Said to be hard to hurt. Grulg not know.*"

"He explained it to me while you were out," Sally said. "His hands were tied with the witches. They're allies now. At some point, while we were playing footsie back in Brooklyn, the Magi took a side, declared war on us. He couldn't blatantly help us with them there. But once the Feet were forced to intervene..."

"After you almost got us blasted," Tom complained.

"You whine like a bitch," she replied before addressing me again. "Anyway, Grulg had to act the part. He knocked your ass out while I ran with the meatsack here. That's when he grabbed you both and followed under the pretense of chasing us down."

I sat next to Sheila and took hold of her hand. I brushed a strand of hair out of her face, then looked up at Grulg. "Is that what happened?"

He nodded.

"Why?"

"*Grulg, Freewill T'lunta, and mate all honorable. War with T'lunta over. Grulg remembers what you do for him. Debt of honor must be paid.*"

I offered up a weak smile. "While still appearing to toe the party line?"

He grinned down at me. "*Grulg honorable warrior, but Grulg not dumb.*"

36

BAKED BEANS AND BROWNSTONES

When it came to tending injuries, Tom and I were next to useless. Hell, I could barely put a Band-Aid on straight.

I could follow directions, though. My roommate and I fashioned a crude litter out of branches and vines ... with maybe a bit of help from Grulg. While we did this, Sally did her best to help Sheila.

"You know how to splint an arm?" I asked.

"James's suggestion," she replied. "He said I knew how to break them, but maybe it wouldn't be a bad idea to learn how to set them, too. So I practiced on some of the Pandora vamps while I was out there."

"I bet they really *appreciated* that."

She smiled in a sweet yet somehow creepy way. "One of the beauties of being a coven master is not needing to give a shit. And with some of them, I gave a shit far less than with others."

While we worked, Grulg used the trees to communicate with some of his more trustworthy troops. Hopefully, there were a few other Feet with his sense of honor because, if not, we were gonna find ourselves bent over facing the wrong end of a magical wand.

Speaking of which, he gave the bad news. Christy and

her coven had been captured after we'd departed the fray. However, from the sound of things, they'd surrendered and no further harm was done to them. Again, I mentally added the caveat *for now.* Whatever morality Agnes had, I knew for a fact Calibra didn't share it.

That left Gan. Unsurprisingly, her whereabouts were unknown. I didn't think for a second she'd gotten vaporized. Not her. She was the very definition of a bad penny that kept showing up. It was only a matter of time before she sniffed us out, probably right when our asses needed saving again, which really wasn't something I should have been sneering at.

There was one upside. Grulg felt really bad about what happened to Sheila. He promised to do what he could to protect her until she was back on her feet. Another of those debts of honor, I supposed. However, that was more than welcome. She needed all the help she could get in her current state.

"How is she?" I asked, trying to keep the worry out of my voice.

"Broken arm. I'd say several broken ribs too, but that's about the extent of my expertise."

"If you had to take a guess," I prodded.

Sally stood up and put a hand on my shoulder, the cold gleam instantly fading from her eyes. "Her powers need to come back, or we need to find a hospital right away."

"*What is hospital?*" Grulg asked.

I was tempted to round on the big ape, but held myself in check. This wasn't his fault. He'd helped us when he didn't have any reason to. "It's where sick humans go to get better, Grulg. Sadly, I don't think we have much chance of finding one way out in the woods."

"*It in place of tall huts?*"

"Tall huts?"

Grulg looked like he was at a loss for words for a moment. Finally, he said, "*T'lunta place of power. Place Destroyer ruled from.*"

"You mean Boston?" I asked. "Sure. I mean, I'm not from there, but there's bound to be plenty of hospitals."

Sally glanced at me, an eyebrow raised. Then she turned to Grulg. "How far are we from Boston, Grulg? Do you know?"

He nodded. I expected an answer expressed in how far a squirrel could travel in a day, but he simply said, "*Not far.*"

"What do you mean 'not far'?" I'd been under the impression Turd's forces had been in retreat after his death and that Grulg had come down to take command and lead them back north.

"*When Magi come, we call upon the trees. Many new trees. Place of power not far. Come, we go.*"

That was surprising, but I wasn't about to turn my nose up at the opportunity. I wasn't sure about making my presence known in Boston, especially escorted by a creature most vamps would try to kill on sight. However, my concern for Sheila's well-being trumped my own. Worst case, the Boston complex had medical facilities and I threw myself on the mercy of Alex's truce to get her help.

We padded the litter with more moss, then lifted her as gently as we could onto it. Tom and I grabbed hold on either side and began to pull it while Sally stayed in the rear to make sure Sheila was okay and didn't fall off.

That would have been the height of incompetence – to find a doctor, only to look back and realized we lost the patient somewhere miles behind us.

By unspoken consent, we tabled the purpose of why we'd come looking for Grulg until a more opportune moment arose. Tom tried to bring it up a few times, but Sally kept changing the subject – or pelting him in the back of the head with acorns – until he finally got the hint. The Sasquatch army's new allies had turned out to be an unexpected complication to our plan of tracking down and killing the person who just so happened to be their patron saint.

Nothing could be straightforward and easy, could it?

As we marched along, we began to see signs of civilization – utterly destroyed civilization, that is. Broken asphalt, billboards covered in vegetation, completely overgrown brownstones. Eventually, the shadows loomed long around us, and it wasn't just the trees. The buildings became denser, all of them looking like a scene from some post-apocalyptic movie set hundreds of years in the future. The Feet had gone all out with their magic on this one.

We saw no people, although at this point we knew enough about Sasquatch magic to understand what had happened to them.

Sheila woke up a couple of times, bouts of semi-consciousness in which she mumbled for a few moments before passing out again. It was mostly incoherent, but I caught a few bits and pieces, including her talking to an imaginary Jim, our former manager at Hopskotchgames, prepping for some all-day meeting we were getting ready for. I couldn't help but smile when she mentioned ordering lunch, but then argued against Jim's apparent suggestion by telling him, "We can't order from there. Bill doesn't like their menu."

Sally kept an eye on her as we walked, having us stop a few times so she could readjust her field dressings and check to make sure we weren't making things worse. Aside from that, though, conversation among us was few and far between. I was too worried to do much more than trudge on. Even Tom, someone who death itself had trouble silencing, was unnaturally quiet.

More than once, I wanted to stop and question when the hell that goddamned cursed blood was going to wear off, but that was a question nobody in the group could answer.

Dragging the litter kept me focused on a task. That was good, because the anger was slowly coming back, lurking just below the surface. I wanted to lash out – punch trees, throw rocks, slice Grulg's fucking face off – anything violent. Staying the course, reminding myself who we were trying to help, kept me sane. It was my silent fuck you to Dr. Death, still somewhere inside me and seemingly more hell-bent than ever on turning me into a monster.

Or so I hoped it was him. That this might be coming entirely from me was a thought too terrifying to consider.

A break in the trees ahead caught my eye. The sun was setting, which was good news for Sally and me, but I could also see unmolested buildings and a city street beyond.

As we got closer, though, an eerie sense of familiarity began to set in.

No way.

"Sally?"

"Keep marching. Uber doesn't make house calls to Tarzan. You can rest your feet when we get there."

"Not that," I replied, pointing. "Look up ahead. Does that seem sorta familiar to you, or am I just imagining things?"

"You're probably just delus..." She paused for a moment. "Holy shit, I think you're right. That's the place where that asshole opened fire on us. There's those concrete pilings you hid behind."

"*We* hid behind."

"No, it was my idea to shoot back. It was yours to hide."

"Whatever," I replied, frustration edging into my voice.

"How many trees did you guys grow, Grulg?" she asked, turning serious again.

"*Many*," he replied. "*We grow many trees.*"

Grulg wasn't shitting us. Once we moved out from the tree line, we were able to turn back and get some perspective. The entire city seemed to end at a wall of vegetation. Within the space of a few steps, Boston, one of the major cities in the American Northeast, ended and a primeval forest began.

Sure, some buildings towered over the trees, evidence a modern city had been here a few days back, but they were overgrown with what looked to be centuries of vegetation.

It took a bit of back and forth with our *tour guide*, as the Feet's concept of measurement was different than ours, but eventually, we were able to conclude that a spear of forest, perhaps half a mile wide but several long, had been grown down from the north into the heart of the city. Had we not been otherwise occupied, I'd have conceded that was some combination of ballsy and impressive.

Grulg, amazingly, offered to continue along with us even after the trees petered out. He seemed genuinely sorry about what had happened to Sheila. The Feet apparently held the Icon – the so-called Silver Eyes – in high regard, partially because of their warrior prowess, but mostly because they tended to fuck up vampires wherever they went.

I was happy to not lose track of him again, don't get me wrong. I'd gone to the ends of the Earth and gotten hitched just to find his ass. I didn't want to have to do that all over again. Even so, vampire or not, I was a bit weirded out to walk down the middle of a city street with an eight-foot-tall monster ape by my side. Shit like that might've been ignored in Manhattan, but up here, I had a feeling someone was bound to notice.

Except there was nobody around.

When Sheila, Sally, and I had gone out on patrol, the streets had been empty too, but signs of life remained. That and it was easy for someone with vampire senses to tell when people were hiding behind closed doors and looking through openings in their blinds. Not so now.

"Kinda creepy," Tom commented.

"Each of us here is a creature straight out of a horror movie, and I still gotta agree with that." I glanced back at Sally. "You sensing anything?"

"A lot of nothing."

"*Grulg not smell humans.*"

"Did your magic...?"

"Probably not," Sally interrupted. "Think about it. If you saw a wall of trees advancing upon you, like they did here, would you stick around to pick up pinecones?"

"No, probably not."

"I might," Tom offered.

"Yeah, but you're a fucking moron," Sally pointed out. I started to laugh, but she shushed me pretty quickly. "That's not all that's wrong, though."

"What do you mean?"

"Take a closer look."

At first, I didn't notice much. I mean, buildings, streets, some cars parked on the side. A decent amount of garbage blowing around. Looked like the place had fallen under a bit of disrepair during Vehron's reign, but...

Then I began to see what Sally meant.

Cars riddled with bullet holes. Chunks of pavement missing from the street that didn't look like ordinary potholes. Gouges in the facades of the buildings and what I thought to be grime wasn't. There seemed to be scorch marks everywhere.

"Looks like a dump to me," Tom said. "There goes the neighborhood."

"This isn't urban decay," I replied softly, suddenly aware of how loud our voices sounded in the twilight-lit street.

"No," Sally finished for me. "This is a war zone."

37

PARANOIA WILL DESTROY YA

"Fuck this noise." I stopped and pulled out my cell phone. "I say we call 911 first and investigate second." Sadly, it proved a moot point as I couldn't even get a blip of a signal. "Goddamn it!"

"Maybe we could break into one of these buildings and use the phone," Tom suggested.

"Not bad, meatwad," Sally replied, "but I think we need to be a bit further in. I'm seeing a lot of downed lines. Even if we did manage to get a dial tone here, I'd be willing to bet you're not going to find anyone willing to come this close to the green zone." She hooked a thumb over her shoulder toward the trees.

"We could still try," Tom said.

"You just want to see if you can find more toys to steal, don't you?"

He grinned like a jackass. Such a douche.

I turned back to Sally and asked, "How is she?"

"No worse than she was."

I sighed wearily. "Fine. Let's head in further, toward HQ. If we can get a signal before then, we use it. If not..."

"Don't think Colin won't see this as an opportunity," Sally warned.

"I know, but we have the weight of Alex's word to back

us up and he's a fucking weasel when it comes to name dropping."

"And if he still tries to fuck us in the ass?"

"Then I start biting every vamp I see and make him regret it."

Normally, I'd have expected Sally to laugh at my threat, idle as they often were, but something in the tone of my voice must have convinced her otherwise.

She simply nodded and waved us on, for better or worse.

As it turns out, I'd have had a better shot of sending up smoke signals than getting cell service. The closer we got to the aboveground car wash that served as the entryway to the Boston Complex, the more pronounced the destruction.

Cars were smashed into charred wrecks. Entire sides of buildings had collapsed. Piles of rubble lay everywhere, some still smoking.

Maybe it was a result of the debris everywhere, but I couldn't help but notice the layers of dust lying atop everything. Perhaps it was just shattered concrete, but my nose insisted differently.

"Son of a bitch," Tom remarked. "Did World War Z happen while we were out?"

"Pick a different letter," I said. "Pretty sure this wasn't zombies. Besides, I don't see any abandoned office supplies lying about."

Tom glanced at one burnt out SUV partially sticking out the side of a nearby building. "This must have been a hell of a paperclip fight."

"Whatever the case," Sally replied, "it was costly for our side, or their side... Fuck, I don't even know what side I'm on anymore. Either way, looks like a lot of vamps ate it."

"I don't see any other bodies."

"Me neither," Tom said, lack of night vision notwithstanding.

"There wouldn't be," Sally replied. "Standard cleanup procedure. Vamp dust blows away, but in a major hub like this, they wouldn't want to leave a mess behind."

"Even during the apocalypse?" I asked.

"Some vamps are slaves to process."

I chuckled, knowing who she meant.

Through it all, Grulg was silent. Hell, I almost forgot he was with us until I turned and saw the big wall of fur walking alongside Sally. Speaking of which...

"We're getting close to the complex, Grulg. Lots of unfriendlies there to all of us, but I think they might have a special place in their black hearts for your kind. Can you hang back?"

"*No reason*," Grulg replied softly. "*But Grulg do as asked.*"

I was about to question what he meant, but he stepped into the shadows of the closest building and it was suddenly like he wasn't there. I might have thought he'd actually ditched us, but I took a quick smell of the air and coughed when I caught his ripe odor.

Yeah, I really had to stop doing that.

We continued onward, the only sound the scraping of litter in the breeze against the asphalt. It wasn't much further now, just around the next corner.

Vehron had done a good job gutting the surrounding neighborhood of obstructions under his rule. Even if he hadn't, cameras were hidden everywhere. There was virtually no chance of sneaking in. So, I tried to steel myself for a session of kowtowing to Colin. Ugh, maybe I should have taken a bigger whiff of Grulg. It would have better prepared me for the brown-nosing to come.

"Okay," I said as we rounded a bend. "Let's do this..."

The words died in my throat as I beheld the destruction before me.

The parking lot was a mess of shattered asphalt and concrete. Dark stains covered much of it, easily detectable by scent as blood. That in itself was shocking, but nothing that should have blown anyone's mind where vamps were concerned.

It was the complex itself that stopped me in my tracks ... or the massive crater where it had once stood. The car wash itself was gone, completely leveled. The sinkhole went down farther than I could see from my vantage point. But even if I was standing at the lip, I doubted I'd have too clear of a view. Smoke still billowed out from it, as well as remnant wisps of flame – green flame.

"My God," Sally whispered, stepping up beside me, any trace of attitude gone from her voice. All that remained was hushed awe. "They did it. They actually did it."

"The witches."

"I don't know. If so, it would have had to been a fuck load more than we saw back in the forest. And even then, Boston was equipped to deal with these things."

"Apparently not well enough," Tom remarked.

"You really have no clue," she replied. "The place looked like an office, and that's how it functioned most of the time, but it was a fortress ... built to act as a base of operations for an offensive or repel just about any invader you can imagine. Hell, from what James told me, a nuclear strike would have been a minor inconvenience to anyone on the lower levels."

"What are you saying?" I asked.

"What I'm saying is this shouldn't have happened even with an army of witches, Feet, and a few primal gods backing them up."

Yet it had.

Or maybe that was what we were meant to believe. "Stay here," I said.

"What?"

I was on the move before Sally could finish. It was a long shot, but when Harry Decker's bunch had leveled Village Coven's loft, they'd created a realistic illusion, a powerful glamour of the place still standing. It was only when you got close enough that you realized it had been blown to hell.

Maybe the vamps had a contingency similar to that, but in reverse. It was worth investigating.

There was a good amount of heat radiating from the area, but nothing my fast healing skin couldn't compensate for. If this was an illusion, they'd gone all out.

I glanced off to the side and saw the remains of two burnt out firetrucks. Someone had responded to this mess, or at least tried to. That should have been my clue that I wasn't going to step past a barrier and suddenly find the car wash intact with Colin sitting outside sipping a mojito. No idea why I was imagining him doing that, but whatever. Sometimes my mind was a strange place.

I reached the edge of the crater and looked down, my eyes watering from the thick black smoke. Still, I had to know for certain. If there was even a chance this was a trick and we could get Sheila help inside, I had to take it.

Stepping gingerly, I got to the very edge, balanced myself, and reached out with one foot to see if there was solid ground where my eyes were telling me there was only a chasm.

And, of course, that's when the asphalt beneath me crumbled. I was in free fall for a second, panic completely overwhelming me. Then, somehow, my hand grasped a finger hold on the edge, leaving me dangling over the abyss of a burning hell.

Okay, I was convinced. Definitely not an illusion.

"Bill!" Sally called from back in the direction we'd come from.

Ah, it was nice to see she cared.

"What the fuck are you doing, idiot?!"

In a manner of speaking, of course.

I didn't often give thanks for my vampiric powers, but at that moment, I'd have signed over my paycheck to whatever deity saw fit to get me bit. I reached up, hoping this section of the sidewalk held, and managed to grab on with both hands so as to pull myself up.

Just in time, too, as I was starting to smell singed cloth.

With everything going on, no way did I need my clothes burning off, too. I hauled myself to the top and double-timed it away from the edge.

I guess that was what Grulg meant when he said there was no reason to check. He knew, but he probably also realized we needed to see it for ourselves. Or he wanted to laugh at our despair. I mean, honorable or not, he *was* one of our ancient enemies. I needed to remember that before I sent him a friend request.

Dusting myself off, I walked back to where Tom and Sally stood.

Sally glared at me, one eyebrow raised. "Care to explain why you felt the need to jump into the big gaping hole?"

"I could ask your former clients the same thing." Okay, perhaps that wasn't helping much. "I wanted to make sure it wasn't another glamour."

Tom stepped up and put a hand on my shoulder. "You know I'm your best bud, right? Well, I say this with all brotherly love, but have you gone fucking stupid?"

"So says the walking illusion," I replied. "It was a long shot, but I had to try. Never know what weird-ass tricks people have up their sleeves."

"Sounds like a stretch to me."

"Save that for your dick," Sally said before turning to me. "It was actually pretty clever that you thought of it. Moronic in practice, but impressive that you considered it. Who knows? Maybe there's hope for you yet."

Whoa, an actual compliment, and in front of witnesses, too. We were indeed living in the end days.

"Stranger things have happened, but enough of that. I'm not going to shed any tears for this place, and we still need to find a hospital." I paused to cough the last of the smoke out of my lungs, taking a deep breath. At first, all I noticed was the scent of burnt buildings, dried blood, and assorted debris, but then I noticed another scent buried beneath it. I took another sniff and realized it was getting stronger.

Sally's eyes opened wide. She'd noticed it, too.

"We need to move *now*."

"And where will you go, Freewill?" Colin asked, stepping from an alleyway a few buildings down. He was dirty and disheveled, his expensive suit in tatters. It was the first time I'd seen him looking anything other than a poor excuse for dapper. "If indeed that is who you are."

"What the fuck are you yammering about?"

I let the accusation go as I realized he wasn't alone. More vamps, wearing riot gear and pointing guns our way, stepped out from their hiding spots. I counted at least a dozen before I stopped bothering.

"By order of Lord Alexander, First of the First," Colin said, speaking as if he were wearing regal finery as opposed to rags, "I place you under arrest."

38

THINNING THE HERD

We weren't in much position to fight. No guns, no vamp blood, and only two of us in any shape to put up much resistance.

I didn't doubt Colin's men were packing silver bullets. Even if they weren't, Sheila wouldn't have lasted two seconds against mundane gunfire, much less anything else. Seeing our choices were limited, I lifted my hands into the air.

"We have wounded," I said, hoping against hope.

"I am neither inclined nor in a position to care," Colin replied. "As you can see behind you, I have more important matters to deal with."

"The place has definitely seen better days," Sally said. "Good job managing things while we were gone."

Colin, normally unflappable, flashed his eyes black. Dude was definitely having a bad day. "One more word from you and we will skip the test and get straight to the execution."

Hoping the threat against Sally didn't hold true for me too, I asked, "Test? And here we are with no study guide."

"Do you think this is a joke?"

Tom opened his mouth to reply, but I quickly shook my head. I still had, or used to anyway, some clout with the vampire nation. He, as a presumed human, had about as much leverage with these guys as a damp sponge.

I gritted my teeth and prepared to metaphorically bend over, swallowing a wave of anger that commanded me to feed him his teeth. "Sorry, *Prefect* Colin."

"Better, Freewill," he replied. "Although I am not certain whether your ability to prostrate yourself when it suits your need is a plus or minus in your favor."

I glanced over at Sheila, still unconscious and far too pale. We didn't have time for this shit. "Can we cut to the chase? We have no idea what happened here and no clue what this test is you're talking about."

"So much for your sense of propriety. You say you don't know what happened, you who are known to consort with witches?"

"I'm pretty sure Bill hasn't consorted with anyone recently," Tom replied. "Dude's dick is drier than the Sahara."

Okay, maybe one or two bullets wouldn't be such a bad thing for him.

"And you claim to not know the test I speak of," Colin continued as if Tom hadn't spoken. "Yet you yourself were the instrument of its design. So far, it is not looking good for you, *Freewill*." He held up his fingers in a mockery of quotations. "I'm afraid that's already two checks against you. One more and I may have to cast summary judgment. What a true shame that would be."

One of the vamp guards at his side leaned in and whispered something. It was a bit too low to catch all of it, but I caught one word that I knew would damn us.

"Is that so?" Colin asked the trooper with mock surprise before addressing us again. "Well, it seems this good man is telling me that you were seen entering the city limits with one of the Grendel. I seem to recall a little something about them being our blood enemies, yet you were looking quite cozy with the creature." I made to reply, but Colin wasn't finished. "Perhaps it was one of the number who came to our doorstep allied with an army of Magi." His voice took on a cold edge. "It was almost as if they knew we were weakened by the culling. As if they knew it was the perfect time to strike."

His eyes locked upon me. "As if someone told them exactly how to hit us."

"You're probably not going to believe this, but that's all just an unfortunate coincidence."

"Culling? What do you mean by that?" Sally asked.

I took a slight step to the side, away from her. She noticed and rolled her eyes.

Thankfully, Colin didn't seem inclined to follow through on his initial threat to her. Perhaps because it had been a serious question with no snarky subtext attached to it. "The Jahabich."

"What about them?"

"Your friend there, as well as..." Colin paused, seemingly noticing Sheila on the litter for the first time. "Well well, is that supposed to be the Icon, lying there prone? Let me guess, some misfortune befell her and now she's helpless as a baby? Convenient. Too convenient. I'm afraid it is looking very bad for you."

Shit. No matter which way you looked at things, I'm sure our sudden appearance in the wake of the complex's destruction looked suspicious. That our judge and jury happened to be someone known to go out of his way to fuck us over didn't help our cause. As if to echo my thoughts, the vamps around us began to take aim.

"Let's back up a sec," I said, quickly trying to think of something. "You said the Jahabich. Did they attack again? Did they manage to infiltrate..."

Wait, infiltrate! That's when I remembered how Starlight appeared to be an evolved form of Jahabich, one capable of blending in anywhere. I'd only told him that as a joke, a way to take the edge off his asshole smugness, but now it had come around to bite me in the ass.

Sally turned to me, and I could see in her eyes that she'd come to the same conclusion. "Good job, Bill."

"Starlight," I said aloud.

A grimace creased Colin's face at the name. "Perhaps a point in your favor," he grudgingly admitted.

"What happened?"

I didn't know if it was a rare moment of humility, or because he knew he had us at his mercy, but he held up a hand and the troops around us relaxed their stances ... by maybe a millimeter.

"Unlike some," he spat, "and that number seems to be growing every day, I am loyal to our cause and our leadership. I serve the First proudly."

I glanced around and could see both Sally and Tom had a crack to make about that one. Hell, I did, too. Thankfully, we all seemed to sense that now was not the time for show and tell.

"Though you told me about the former Village Covener with your typical degree of flippancy," Colin said, "the Icon's words added weight to yours. I dutifully relayed this news to the First."

Oh boy, I had a bad feeling about this.

"It was Alexander himself who ordered the purge. Any who may have been in contact with the Jahabich. Any who'd gone missing and returned. Any who he couldn't be one hundred percent certain of."

"Holy shit. Are you saying he declared open season on his own people?"

"Do not make light of this!" Colin snarled. "Many who had been recently assigned to this facility had come from a garrison charged with fending off a recent Grendel incursion. They had been in the woods to the north for days, operating independently. There was no way to ensure their loyalty. The Jahabich cannot be compelled and the beast that is Ib could easily insulate those who could."

I shared a glance with Sally and she returned a knowing look. That's how the witches were able to take this place. Even the most impregnable fortress needed an adequate number of defenders and, thanks to Alex pulling a Stalin on his followers, the Boston Complex didn't have that. If the witches and the Feet had hit them fast and hard enough, they wouldn't have stood a chance. Hindsight seemed to support this theory.

It also pointed toward why Gan hadn't been able to find any trace of Drac agents watching our apartment. If they were busy either culling or being culled, then that would explain their absence.

Colin, of course, managed to make it through this all right. No surprise there. Dude probably had every backdoor exit tattooed onto his eyelids. Still, that opened the door to doubt.

"And now here you are, Freewill," he continued, "miraculously showing up on our doorstep from the unnatural forest beyond with a Grendel, a wounded Icon, and a conveniently resurrected human following you." I glanced Tom's way and Colin added, "Of course we noticed. We have kept thorough tabs on you and your associates, even the more buffoonish ones. He was killed by The Destroyer. His body was recovered and subsequently burned, yet now he stands by your side again. What other power, save the Jahabich, could do such a thing?"

"Hold on. You fuckers burned my body?" Tom asked.

"Only after harvesting anything useful," Colin replied. "Waste not."

"Like my action figures? Because those things were worth..."

I stepped in front of my friend before he could say anything else stupid. "He's not a Jahabich."

"Oh?" Colin asked, as if he found that terribly interesting.

I was thinking of a way to explain his presence, but

before I could, Colin waved a hand and one of the vamps at his side opened fire.

39

ASSASSINS IN ARMANI

It was only a single shot, but it echoed through the empty urban valley like thunder.

My first instinct, asshole that I am, was to make sure Sheila was okay, but Colin's interest hadn't been directed at her. I forced my eyes to turn my friend's way, fearing the worst.

"Motherfucker," Tom said with an air of indignation. He was looking down at a gash in his pants around mid-thigh, through which I could see the bullet hole in his glamoured flesh. "You almost shot my nuts off."

Oddly enough, he sounded far more put out than in pain. As for the wound itself, there was no blood. After a few seconds, the area where the bullet had penetrated shimmered and then reappeared as whole, pants and all.

"Holy shit, Bill! Did you see that? I have a fucking healing factor, too!"

I seriously could have decked the moron.

"You see?" Colin remarked smugly. "And you dare insult my intelligence by claiming he's not one of them."

All around, I could sense fingers tensing on triggers. Shit!

"Wait!" I held up my hands. "There's an explanation." Thinking quickly, I extended the claws on one hand and slashed my wrist with them. Fuck me! I so hated having to do shit like this just to prove a point. "Look at this! I'm bleeding. What about that? And I can't be compelled either."

"True enough. Alas, your loyalty has been in question since day one, Freewill. You have proven time and again to be as reliable to our cause as, well…" He waved a hand in the direction where Sheila lay. "As for your other companion, I doubt she required much effort from Ib. Our dear Sally is more than susceptible to control. One might call it her natural state since she was but a child."

What the…?

I dared a sidelong glance in her direction, expecting to see her glaring daggers of galvanized death. What I didn't expect were tears in her eyes and a look of such hurt that I'd have thought she'd been shot instead. "Sally?"

She wiped one hand across her eyes, then her gaze hardened. "If I'm going to die today, it's going to be with my hands around your throat."

"Doubtful," Colin replied. "Such wasted potential. You always did have a habit of choosing the wrong path. Now is no different. But at least it's fitting that you die as you lived, on your knees. Take out her legs first."

Fast as we were, there was no way we were going to dodge in time to make a fight of it. But we didn't need to. A few of Colin's lackeys had made the mistake of aiming at Sheila's prone form.

"*No hurt Silver Eyes!*" A roar of primal rage sounded through the urban decay around us in the split second before we were cut down. The war cry seemed to be coming from all around us thanks, in part, to the acoustics of the surrounding buildings.

Nervous heads forgot about us for a second and looked around, trying to home in on the source. They needn't have bothered. Grulg leapt from a nearby stairwell. One moment there was nothing but a pool of shadows, and in the next eight hundred pounds of angry ape knocked three vamps aside like bowling pins.

Thank goodness for his guilty conscience. Sure, he was technically violating the peace by helping us, but Colin and his goons didn't know that. Ignorance truly was bliss at times.

Sally, never one to look a gift horse in the mouth, was already on the move, using Grulg's distraction to launch herself at one of the gunmen and her claws to quite literally disarm him.

I needed to follow her lead, but I couldn't leave Sheila lying in the middle of the street. One stray bullet. Hell, one *not so* stray bullet...

"Go," Tom said, kneeling by her side. "I got this."

"But..."

"Dude, I'm fucking bulletproof. Let them do their worst. I'll keep her safe."

His definition of bulletproof didn't quite match mine. That and I still wasn't sure what would happen if he got shot in the wrong place. Still, beggars couldn't be choosers, and right then I was standing in the gutter with an empty change cup. I flashed him a grateful smile, but I needn't have bothered. He knew. We both did.

"Try not to get shot in the balls," I added to ensure the moment wasn't too gooey, and then I was off to join the fray.

I had to give Colin's vamps credit. With their base of operations destroyed and a newfound sense of paranoia invading the vampire nation, you'd have thought they'd be a twitchy bunch, especially being attacked by a monster gorilla. I expected panicky gunfire all around – not a great thing for us, but not exactly wonderful for our enemies either. Not so, though.

At least half of their forces formed ranks in front of Colin, weapons at the ready, while their comrades engaged

Sally and Grulg in hand to hand combat. Still, I didn't expect the stalemate to last long. Vampires were backstabbing motherfuckers as a whole. The moment it looked like one of their enemies might be getting the upper hand, they'd open fire and take out the whole lot – friend or foe.

We needed to increase our odds before that happened, and I could only think of one way.

I ran toward where Sally engaged three of the vamps. She'd gotten her pound of flesh, but it was easy to see she was outclassed. These were trained soldiers and older than her. It was only a matter of time.

My plan was simple – jump in, start biting, and get stronger.

Sadly, that was pretty much the only strategy in my playbook and Colin knew it. Several shots hit the dirt in front of me, stopping me in my tracks.

"I think not, Freewill."

Shit! I looked his way to find almost a dozen guns aimed at me.

"Yeah, asshole?" I shouted back, knowing that any moment I was going to be turned into Swiss cheese. "Well, what do you think is going to happen to all of you when this is done? You survived a massacre that others didn't. You've been hiding here, out of sight from your superiors. You said it yourself. Anyone who Alex can't be one-hundred percent certain of gets the axe."

"That's it?" he asked, sounding confused. "That's the best you've got right now? Perhaps I was wrong and you *are* you after all."

Pathetically enough, that actually *was* the best I had. I was out in the open, covered by vamps who knew how to shoot, and with no other edge in my favor. I glanced around. Grulg was being swarmed. Strong as he was, he was outnumbered and outgunned. Several shots were fired, which he took like a trooper, but it wouldn't last. Sally was on her knees. The vamps she'd tried to fight were busy smacking her around with the butts of their guns.

One cracked her on the side of the head, sending her face first onto the asphalt. A fresh wave of anger surged through me at the sight. Weapons or not, I wanted to feed these assholes their own intestines.

"Uh uh, Freewill," Colin chided. "No interfering."

I turned back his way and hatred filled me. And that's when I realized perhaps my wit wasn't the only thing in my favor after all. No, I had something inside of me that was far sharper.

I'd been biting my lip for days now, forcing the anger back down, bottling it up. The impotence of not being able to help Ed, Dave, or James. Tom's fate. Christy's despair. Sheila's helplessness. And now Sally. All the negativity inside me was begging to come out and pay the universe back thrice-fold.

I didn't know what it meant. Would I still be me like when Vehron died, or would I be letting the evilest of genies out of the bottle again? Did it matter so long as Colin got what was coming to him?

At some point, while I considered this, the greys of the dark city street had been replaced by red in my vision. Whatever was going to happen, it would be soon. I just needed to do one thing first – make sure my friends were safe.

I turned back and found Tom standing in front of where the litter lay – obscuring it from my view.

"Run!" I growled, my voice taking on a deeper cadence.

To my surprise, though, he smiled at me. Goddamn, what a moron! Did he not realize this wasn't some wrestling match he had ringside seats to? No, actually, knowing him, he probably didn't. Next time Christy hexed him, she really needed to see about maybe whammying up a clue.

The redness retreated from my vision and I realized my thoughts were interfering with my plans, driving back the rage while I contemplated what an idiot my best friend in this world was.

He then inexplicably gave me a thumbs up and stepped to the side.

The litter was empty.

The hell?

Was it possible?

A flash of white light, a small beacon in the darkness of the street, ignited in the corner of my eye. I turned in time to see Sheila launching herself at Grulg's attackers. Okay, it was more a lurch than anything. She was moving far slower than normal with one hand clutching her side, but the glow around her was steady if somewhat fainter than it should have been.

Fainter, but enough.

She plowed into the group, and the two vamps closest to her burst aflame. Fuck yeah!

Grulg roared, but it was in pain as the fur on one side of his body also ignited. Shit! Guess that answered the question as to whether her powers worked on the Feet. Hell of a fucking time to find out the answer.

Fortunately, it was a glancing ... err ... sear. He stepped away from her and back into the shadows, allowing her to engage the remaining vamps with her powers.

"Kill it!" Colin screamed.

The men in front of him all trained their weapons her way. They opened fire in a thunderous explosion of sound, but I was already on the move.

Getting shot sucks, even when you're a vampire, but there was another target more appealing than me on the battlefield now. I tried not to be insulted that I wasn't at the top of their hit list. Being number one wasn't always a good thing.

Sheila cried out, although whether in fury, fear, or pain, I wasn't sure. Sadly, I could only hope her powers were strong enough to protect her. In order to win this, I had to erase the edge Colin's men had and I couldn't do that while standing there holding my dick.

All thoughts of trying to summon the beast within fled my mind at the sight of her up and mobile again. However, I must've still had some residual adrenaline in my system because I hit the first vamp in the lineup like a runaway freight train.

He went careening into the two buddies next to him, and so on like a row of dominos. Oh yeah, that was more like it.

Some victories you savored like a fine meal, others you got your ass back into the game immediately. This was one of those latter.

I let my momentum carry me forward, landing atop the vamp I'd plowed into. His body armor seemed a bit daunting to chew through, but fortunately he had no gloves on. I didn't know where this guy's fingers had been, but I knew where they were going.

I grabbed hold and bit down with everything I had.

Rather unsporting of me, especially since I chomped off his trigger finger, but sometimes you gotta do what needs to be done.

The taste of gunmetal and blood filled my mouth, but I focused on the latter, taking a swallow and letting it do its job.

Oh yeah. I began to power up. "It's over 9,000, mother-fuckers!"

Well, okay, maybe not that much, but it was still a couple hundred years of vamp strength added onto my own. Even better, it allowed me to drag another in before anyone could stop me. This was more like it. Kevlar was closer to paper with the added boost. I ripped open his sleeve and dug in for another bite before the troops could rally themselves.

Gun butts slammed into my back and ribs from above, but they were too late. Two vamps weren't going to be enough to blow this one out of the water, but it helped solidify me as a solid threat to these assholes.

Rough hands dragged me back to my feet, away from the vamps I'd already savaged. I didn't do anything to stop them. As any gamer will tell you, fighting while prone was a good way to find your ass in need of a Breath of Life spell. Since we were a bit short on clerics, that wasn't a particularly sound strategy.

I came up and kicked out in front of me, nailing a couple of vamps who'd been all set to rearrange my teeth. They went flying, and then it was my turn.

I used the extra oomph in my legs to launch myself and the two soldiers still holding me into the air. We landed on our backs, with me on top. But these guys were a persistent bunch. One tried to wrap an arm around my neck, but I caught him with my teeth instead, tearing out a big chunk of fabric and an even bigger chunk of flesh.

Now we were cooking with gas. I'd have to remember to thank Colin.

For good measure, I broke the arm holding me, then scrambled back to my feet.

It was time to...

Notice everyone had realized I was now the biggest threat on the playing field.

I stood up to find every weapon in sight trained in my direction. Colin stood behind his men, a smug grin on his face as if he was a kid who'd just woken up on Christmas morning. His smile said it all: I'd finally given him an excuse to get rid of me once and for all.

And the day had been going *so* well up until then.

40

DWARF TOSSING

I was debating which way to leap: up, to the side, anywhere that would result in the least amount of bullets perforating my body.

I'd been expecting the deafening sound of gunfire, so I was caught by surprise when one of the vamp troopers instead said, "Sir! I think he's the real deal."

"What did you say, soldier?" Colin asked, sounding amazed that one of his lowly dogs decided to pick that moment to bark.

"Sir, I think he's really the Freewill. Did you see what he did?"

Well, what do you know? I had me a fan in the crowd. Maybe if I managed to survive this, I'd autograph his gun.

Colin's face flushed all sorts of red. Can't say I didn't enjoy it ever so slightly. It also gave me a split second to take stock of my friends.

Sally was out of it, but alive. Two vamp soldiers were holding her up, but she appeared to have been worked over pretty good.

Sheila was down on one knee. She didn't look particularly great either, but she was still with us. I didn't see any blood, at least. Her shield had held.

"Fuck 'em all up, man!"

Yep, Tom was fine. That left Grulg. I didn't see him, but maybe that was a good thing. He'd proven a distraction before. With any luck...

"I did not ask your opinion, child," Colin said to his underling. "I am well aware that he is..."

"The guy who's working for Lord Alexander?" I interrupted, adding a little extra fuel to the flames.

Doubt flashed in several of the eyes before me. Ah yes, if there was one thing the coven system instilled in the unwashed masses, it was an appreciation for name dropping.

Colin realized it too, because he was quick to add, "By order of the First Coven, I am Prefect here and I declare these ... *creatures* to be enemies of our great nation." I almost laughed, because it came out more a whine than an edict. Unfortunately for us, the next part did not. "***I ORDER YOU TO EXECUTE THEM ALL, STARTING WITH THIS FOOL!!***"

Shit! I'd never known Colin to make with the compulsions. In the past, he'd always been the type to enforce the orders of his betters, not make them himself. Hell, I'd known him as an armchair general, a piss-poor one at that.

All doubt and independent thought faded from the faces of the troops in front of me as their eyes glazed over one by one. I heard movement behind me and glanced back to find the two vamps I'd landed on boxing me in with their guns. I was surrounded. This was Colin's winning hand, and it was a hard one to...

Hold on. I wasn't exactly a slouch at the moment either. Some days I am so stupid I even surprise myself.

"***NO!! KILL THAT FUCKER INSTEAD!!***"

Colin's compulsion had been a mighty shout, but mine was a fucking bullhorn. Sure, it wasn't the most eloquent way of putting forth my desires, but sometimes you gotta be direct.

A ripple passed over the crowd of vamps. They swayed on

their feet and a few grabbed hold of their heads, but Colin remained irritatingly bullet free. The fuck?

The arrogant cocksucker raised his hands and brought them together in a golf clap. "Nicely done, Freewill. Even I have to admit to being impressed with you for a rare change. Who would have thought you'd ever develop the competence to accomplish ... anything, really?"

The soldiers in front of him appeared to have been knocked for a loop, but they still hadn't ventilated this asshat. Why?

"Don't tell me you've forgotten already. Ah, I suppose that is to be expected from a lesser mind such as yours. I'll give you a hint: Insulation."

Oh crap. He was right. James had told me himself. Prefects, office workers, shock troops, anyone who worked for the vampire hierarchy received a series of compulsions by older vamps. Folks like Vehron or Ib were ridiculously old and could force their way through most of it. Me, I hadn't quite sucked down enough blood to be that effective. Shit!

Still, even if they hadn't blasted Colin's head open like a ripe melon, the power in me – coupled with the doubt some of them seemingly felt – had been enough to slow them down. Which meant...

"Fine, you win the game of compulsion tag. Here's your prize, asshole." Fast as I could, I grabbed hold of the vamp nearest me before he could resume his regularly scheduled programming and launched him into the air, over his buddies, and right into Colin's smug face.

I couldn't control his troops, but I could scramble their circuits for a couple of seconds. Sadly, in doing so, I had a feeling any lingering doubt they had toward killing my ass was gonna be erased real quick.

We needed an edge and this time one that would stick. We needed...

Grulg!

He stepped back out of the shadows, a few paces behind

where Sheila was pulling herself to her feet. I let a smile play out on my face, but it immediately turned to a look of horror as he grabbed her and lifted her from the ground. What the fuck?

Her aura flared to life around her as a look of shock replaced the one of pain on her face. Grulg's hands ignited, but before the rest of him could, he let out a roar and threw her.

My own predicament was forgotten as I watched her tumble end over end through the air from a dozen yards away. What the fuck was that stupid monkey doing? We'd trusted him and he'd...

Thrown her straight at the group of vamps threatening us.

Okay, then.

What he'd done was stupid as fuck and dangerous as all hell, considering how hurt Sheila was, but rational thought wasn't really a Sasquatch forte. On the other hand, there was probably no better way to protect someone than to take out their enemies. She was basically the living embodiment of the holy hand grenade of Antioch.

And she was heading this way.

I instinctively stepped forward when something plowed into my blindside. It was a weak hit, nothing against my current power level, but it had caught me unaware. I stumbled and went down, my attacker atop me.

My first thought was to remedy that situation. I rolled over and prepared to throw off ... Tom?!

"You'll thank me for this," he said, still scrambling to cover me. "Oh, but just in case ... no homo."

A blaze of white light erupted around us. I couldn't see much, but I could hear screams, ones that cut off quickly as their owners immolated. Sheila had landed and, though I had no way of knowing if she'd been injured even worse in the impact, it was plain to see her power washing over us.

The exposed parts of my skin sizzled where it touched me, but Tom took the brunt of it, protecting me with his own body.

He truly was the best of friends.

Sadly, he was also a complete idiot. His body was currently made entirely of magic, and if there was one thing the power of faith did, besides turn vampires into charcoal, it was negate other magic.

Tom grinned down at me, but it changed into a look of surprise as his form began to shimmer under the onslaught of white light. His face began to droop almost as if he were made of melting candle wax. With some horror, and a serious sense of being weirded out, I realized he was liquefying atop me.

I tried to push him off, but my hands sank right into his chest – an odd sensation: dry yet yielding at the same time. My analysis of his body composition came to an abrupt end, however, when I brushed up against something inside of him that felt akin to touching a live wire.

All thought of being burned by Sheila's power fled my mind as a jolt of magical electricity traveled up my arm, causing every muscle in my body to contract way past the point of breaking. Crackles of multi-hued lightning blotted out my vision, and I could smell my tongue beginning to smoke.

A flash of memory stirred in my mind – stepping into the puddle of human fat in our basement. All at once, I understood what had happened. Not a fun way to go.

I blinked steaming tears and saw a figure rise above us. He was wearing body armor and was aflame from Sheila's power, but he still refused to give up. He raised the gun he was holding, rapidly turning red hot in his grasp. So I did the only thing I could think of.

I shared the love.

Though every muscle in my body felt like it had a mind of its own, I somehow tore one of my arms free, reached out, and grasped hold of his ankle.

The result was nearly instantaneous. Between the power of faith and a generous jolt of Apollo's junk, the vamp turned white hot from the inside out and immolated.

Sadly, I was going to be next. The only thing saving me was the combined strength and healing of three vamps, but I had a feeling I'd just about reached my limit in this game of pass the shock ball.

I was, quite literally, sinking into my friend as he melted around me ... very likely the weirdest fucking thing I had ever experienced. I couldn't push him off me; he was too ... err ... goopy for that. The flaming vamp had given me an idea, though, one that was better than anything else that came to mind. I had already stopped and dropped. Now it was time to roll.

Stuck as he was to me, Tom came along for the ride.

The contractions in my muscles were getting worse. Much more and I'd shatter my teeth just by biting down. Adding to it, that first roll exposed my backside to Sheila's power. Oh yeah, burning and frying, quite the combo.

But I kept going – over and over, across the asphalt, away from her power, until I thought I had enough momentum to give a heave.

Distanced from Sheila's aura, Tom's body regained just enough coherency for me to get one hand on his chest and shove with everything I had.

He went flying off me, pulling away with a disturbing *schlup* sound as if I'd just unclogged a toilet with my fist.

Speaking of which, it was a good thing I was right handed, because my left was a mangled mess of exposed bone and gristle.

Still, it wasn't over yet. I'd probably burned through –

pun definitely intended – most of the stolen power in me, but there was a bit left. I rolled to my feet, my healing already starting to mend my injuries, and took stock of the situation.

Grulg had engaged the vamps who'd been working over Sally. They were keeping him at bay, but not for long. She was on her knees behind them, but conscious again. She glanced my way through one eye that wasn't swollen shut and gave a single shake of her head, the meaning clear – these assholes were hers. With Grulg helping her out, I decided to give her this one.

Sheila was likewise down. There was a sizzling aura of white power around her, but she otherwise didn't look too hot. Thankfully, she'd gotten the job done. All around her, discarded weapons and body armor lay amidst piles of smoking ash.

I hobbled over, feeling my flesh regenerating with every step.

She looked up as I approached, but her eyes had a dazed look about them.

"Hey," I said gently and a bit slurred as my tongue was still repairing itself. "Turn off the light show. It's me."

She blinked, gave her head a shake, and then spat out a wad of blood. Finally, her power fizzled and then collapsed in on itself.

I stepped up and offered her my good hand. "Are you okay?"

"Not really," she replied weakly. "Wasn't ... expecting that."

"Yeah, Grulg played dwarf toss and unfortunately, you got to be Gimli."

I got the feeling my joke fell flat with her, but she smiled anyway. "At least ... these guys were here to ... cushion my fall."

"That's the spirit," I replied. "Now we just have to..."

I didn't get a chance to finish. The words were lost in my

throat, but even if they hadn't been, the sound of gunfire this close would have rendered them unheard.

That was okay. What I had to say wasn't important anyway, especially not compared to the ragged gunshot wounds opening up along my torso and the searing pain that followed. Yes, indeed, Colin's men had been armed with silver bullets.

Well, at least that question was answered.

41

A COMPELLING ARGUMENT

I was knocked off my feet and landed roughly on the back of my head. I thought I saw stars, but then realized it was just the fireworks erupting from where the silver touched my blood.

So ... pretty.

I spied Colin standing with a gun in his hands, wearing a look of distaste as if he was irked he'd been forced to get his hands dirty. Poor baby.

He aimed it at Sheila, still on her knees, then seemed to realize the futility of doing so. Instead, he spun the rifle, grabbed it by the barrel, and swung it like a baseball bat.

Her power flared up, but only at a fraction of its normal intensity. The aura appeared to mute the blow, but didn't stop it fully. I heard the thunk of it connecting with flesh and then Sheila was knocked back, rolling with the blow and holding on to her ribs.

Colin was left slightly singed by the encounter but otherwise got the better end of that deal. At least his suit was in even worse shape than before. Small victories and all.

I lifted my head as best I could to check on Sheila, my insides screaming in pain as the silver worked its magic. She was down on the shattered asphalt. Her aura flared around her, fizzled, then flared again. It was plain to see she wasn't fully purged of that goddamned Baal blood and that, what-ever she'd given in the last few minutes, it was all she had to give.

Thankfully, we weren't alone.

Sally turned from where she and Grulg were busy dismembering the last of Colin's troops. Bloodied but unbowed, her eyes turned black as coal as she laid eyes on him. A mix of disgust and hatred crossed her face and she snarled, "I'm gonna enjoy this."

"Of course you will," Colin replied, casually sauntering Sheila's way as if he had all the time in the world. "You've always been so adept at following the orders of your betters. ***KILL THE FREEWILL, MY DARLING LUCINDA!!***"

Oh shit.

Sally froze in her tracks. Her eyes glazed over and she turned my way. She took one step, then stopped, her body shaking and her teeth gritting so hard blood began to drip from her lips.

"Well, isn't this surprising?" Colin raised a finger to his chin as if contemplating the situation. "Don't tell me you actually have feelings toward this lout."

Sally struggled, her eyes beginning to slowly clear as she fought against the compulsion.

"Huh. You *do,* and strong ones at that. And here I thought our mutual friend Jeff had beaten such silly concepts out of you. Your lack of taste aside, I suppose I can work around that. It looks like the Freewill isn't going anywhere. Perhaps a more suitable target will keep you busy. ***KILL THAT THING!!***" He pointed toward Grulg, who'd just dispatched his last foe and looked eager to leap back into the fray.

Though he was the one Bigfoot we were sorta on amicable terms with, he was far from being on either of our BFF lists. A compulsion to kill a neutral party would be far harder to fight than a friend. Sally's eyes re-glazed, she turned, and launched herself at the giant ape.

"Don't ... hurt..." The rest of my words were lost as the

breath in my lungs turned to steam. In another couple of minutes, I was going to be fit to be served as Thanksgiving dinner.

My body was just barely keeping up. Accelerated as my powers were, silver tended to fuck with our healing abilities, in addition to flash-frying us from the inside out. There was also the small problem of me running out of gas pretty soon. When that happened, it would be sayonara.

To think we'd come all this way, beaten as many foes as we had, and yet, after everything, Colin was the one poised to be our undoing.

Yeah, fat fucking chance of that.

No goddamned way was I going to the afterlife knowing that greasy shit had sent me there.

A dull thud sounded, and I glanced over to see he'd laid into the side of Sheila's head with a boot. Again, her power saved her, but it was getting weaker by the minute. Soon he'd be able to throttle her with his bare hands.

Gritting my teeth, I extended my claws as an idea formed. This was not going to be fun. The flames escaping my open wounds only added to the thrill that was self-surgery.

Before my rational side could talk me out of it, I dug my fingers into my own flesh, experiencing a pain that made me wish Colin had hit me with a headshot.

The beauty of previous horrendous wounds, and I seemed to have gotten a lot of them since turning into a vamp, was that I could mostly concentrate on the important things, like screaming. After all, in most cases, there wasn't much else to do save curl up in a fetal ball and hope I either passed out or my healing took care of things. Digging around in my own innards, though, required concentration. I needed to be fully aware of every turn my fingers took and every obstruction they encountered so as to make sure I actually extracted a bullet and not, say, my pancreas.

I yanked my hand back with a wince, then let the metal slug slip out of my bloody fingers and onto the ground. That was two. One more to go. I dove back in, touching myself in ways that even I found inappropriate.

Even after I yanked them out, my wounds continued to bleed. Sure, my blood was no longer ablaze, but I was getting pretty goddamned woozy all the same.

Grulg was doing his best to fend off Sally, but I could tell he was getting frustrated. Sally was quick and not averse to taking cheap shots. A few scratches to his arms were one thing, but I had a feeling Grulg was going to be a lot less friendly if she managed to slice his ballsack off.

Colin had picked up a piece of rebar and was using it to work Sheila over. She'd managed to recover enough so as to be able to focus her waning power in time with his strikes. Still, she was barely fending off his attacks. It was only a matter of time. I needed to get this shit out of my body and somehow rejoin the fight.

Yeah, easier said than done.

"Grul ... HOLY FUCKING SHIT!" I let out an incoherent scream as I pulled the last bullet free, puncturing something I was fairly certain I needed. For a moment, the world went grey with pain and the mouthfuls of blood I coughed out compromised my ability to speak.

Despite the grievous wounds I'd suffered, there had been no inkling of Dr. Death since I'd been shot. Normally, he acted as a sort of defense mechanism against near fatal wounds, but not now. Interesting ... or it would be if every nerve ending in my body didn't feel like it was on fire.

I cleared my throat and managed to say what I'd been trying to. "Grulg, throw her this way!" It came out as more of a squeak, but that was fine. He heard me.

Unfortunately, I picked the wrong moment to distract him, as the second he turned his head Sally kicked out with one heeled boot and caught him squarely in the nuts. The big monster went down to one knee with a look on his face that was all too familiar.

He wasn't entirely out of it, though. Before succumbing to the pain, he managed to backhand the compelled Sally, sending her careening my way. Not quite what I had in mind, but close enough.

She landed about five feet short and skidded the rest of the way, erasing the skin on her exposed arms. Painful, but she'd live.

Using what little strength I had left, I grabbed hold of her dazed form before she could recover and dragged her in.

"Sorry," I whispered in her ear, "but I need this more than you do."

Before she could wriggle free, I bit down on her neck, taking an extra-long pull from the artery I'd torn open. I released her and she tried to get back to her feet, back toward where Grulg was cradling his unborn children, but then she dropped to the ground and lay there panting. My attack had taken the last of the fight out of her.

Now to see if I'd been right. Silver somehow retarded a vampire's healing, but I'd been hoping maybe a boost from some untainted vamp blood might counter it a bit.

Sally's strength flooded my muscles. A modest increase, but anything was better than nothing at that point.

C'mon, work!

After a couple of seconds, though, it became obvious that ploy was a bust. I was still bleeding badly, but at least I had a little extra jolt in me, enough to pull myself back to my feet.

"Hey, asshole," I said weakly. "Come get some."

Colin ceased his assault upon Sheila and faced me – just in time, by the look of it. The glow around her was barely visible, a mere spark, and her eyes were as glazed as any compelled vamp's. Blood dripped from numerous wounds where her power had failed to protect her. None of them looked fatal, but added up, it wasn't good.

The smug asshole dropped the now bent rebar and

straightened his ruined collar. A natty dickhead to the very end.

"Let's finish this," I said.

"Very well, Freewill." He glanced around at the battlefield, my downed friends, and then back at me. Even now, the arrogance radiating off him was enough to power a small town, made even worse when he smiled my way.

I balled my fist and prepared to charge him, unsure of how I was going to pull this off, but hoping maybe a lucky bite would even things up a bit.

Before I could move, though, he held up his hands.

"This battle is over. As Prefect of the Northeastern Covens, I declare your identity confirmed. By edict of Lord Alexander, first of the First, I uphold the truce that was declared and offer any assistance I might."

42

POLITICAL ASYLUM

"Hold on, what?!"

"You heard me, Freewill," Colin replied. "As to whether you understood me, I am certain that is debatable. However, it will have to suffice that at least one of us is in possession of the intelligence to do so."

"Hold on a second there, Hoss. I was just about to kick your ass. You can't just..."

"Also debatable, but I can and I will. Though you may think yourself an exception to our rules, you are not. You are governed by the edicts of the glorious First, as am I. Lord Alexander's orders cannot be questioned."

"But you attacked us and..."

"And beat all of you quite soundly?" It was like the fuck-face was feeding off of my annoyance. The angrier I got, the more he seemed to like it. "I can assure you, that is a memory I shall cherish for eternity, all of you laid low and on the precipice of defeat by my hands. I only wish I had thought to capture it for posterity. Regardless, as I have already mentioned, that was Lord Alexander's edict as well. Any who could not prove themselves were to be purged. Fortunately for you, though, I am now convinced of your and the Icon's identities. As such, his other orders now take precedence."

My eyes narrowed. "Just ours?"

Colin sighed and held his hands out as if he thought himself magnanimous. "Very well, our dear Sally, too. As for your other friend..."

"Tom isn't..."

"Yes, yes, Freewill," he replied dismissively. "I have seen the Jahabich in action. They fight ... competently, a word I cannot use to describe your friend's actions. For now, we shall consider him an anomaly under your charge. I will warn you to keep a short tether on him, though." He must have seen the look I was giving him at the implied threat because he added, "Oh, and lest you think otherwise, I will point out that the terms of your truce swing both ways. Neither you, the Icon, nor any of your other friends may lay a hand upon my person, lest you anger our lord and master."

"Is that so?" I glanced over to where Grulg was getting back up, one meaty hand still grasping his, well, meat.

Colin may have been a dirtbag, but he was a perceptive dirtbag. He understood my meaning. "Though I do not believe it was originally Lord Alexander's intent, as Prefect I am allowed the freedom to make field decisions. He will have the final say, of course, but for now I declare your ... err ... *acquaintance* privy to the protections laid forth in your agreement. Let's call him an ambassador of sorts. Again, the reverse holds true."

"Of course," I replied through gritted teeth. Oh, how tempting it was to let Grulg smash this twat's skull like a grape. But knowing my luck, despite his assurances otherwise, we probably were being taped. Killing Colin might be the most worth it thing in this entire universe, but we needed Alex's help until such time as we were ready to betray him. "Stand down, Grulg. Please stand down, that is. Colin is..." The words burned even as they formed in my mouth. "...a *friend*."

"*Friend?*" the big ape asked, the look on his face suggesting he thought I'd gone soft in the head. "*Grulg find T'lunta customs very strange.*"

"Strange to me, too, buddy," I replied. "Strange to me, too."

I dragged a sofa from one of the nearby ruined buildings, then helped Sheila onto it. She tried to insist she was okay, but didn't put up any fight once I insisted she stay put for a while.

Sally needed some alone time after the battle. After she woke up and I explained what happened, she was pissed with a capital P. Don't get me wrong, she had every right to be. If she could have killed Colin with her thoughts, she would certainly have done so slowly and painfully. Alas, it would have put us right back where we started and at an even worse disadvantage, I noted as I glanced around at the armed vampires guarding the street.

Turns out Colin had kept some men in reserve, just in case. They'd made their presence known shortly after the greasy shit-stain had declared us all one big happy family again. I didn't think for one second these guys wouldn't plug us with but a single word from his mouth, but for now, they held themselves in check. I'd take what I could get.

Sally decided to go hunting to both blow off some steam and replenish the fluids lost in the fight. I should have gone with her, but I wasn't about to leave Sheila alone with Colin. No fucking way was that happening. Tom offered to watch her for me, the glamour of his body having reconstituted itself, but that seemed a bad idea. One flare up from her and all he'd be able to do was melt into a puddle of ectoplasm again.

Besides, I wasn't in shape to do much of anything. The bullet holes in my stomach and chest had finally scabbed over but, thanks to the silver, that was about the best I could hope for anytime soon. I was trying to put on a brave face for my friends, but it was all I could do to not fall on my ass.

At least we had plenty to keep our minds occupied with,

trying to figure out what our next move should be. The circumstances had changed on us too quickly for us to adequately adapt. As much as I hated to admit it, we kind of needed the time out.

I just wished it was with better company than Colin.

I managed to glom some bagged blood off of our hosts, desperately needed after my extended session spent digging bullets out of my own body. It wouldn't help me heal quicker, but I'd settle for not passing out. Fortunately, there were a few more Freewill fans among Colin's remaining troops and they were more than happy to share in exchange for a bullshit story on how I pimp-slapped the shit out of The Destroyer.

"If you're finished listening to the Freewill's fairy tales," Colin said, strolling over after I was finished, "I want a flat area of at least ten thousand square feet cleared post-haste."

The guards gave me a look that said they knew shit duty when they were assigned it, but didn't dare question their superior. Ah, yes, it was rare to meet a vamp who didn't jump when told by an elder.

As they ran off to do whatever the fuck he needed them to do, Colin turned to me. "While I imagine this is an alien concept to one such as yourself, I must remind you there are those of us who work for a living. I would ask that you neither distract my people from their duties nor waste rations that could be put to better use."

Some things never changed.

In my current condition, this prick could have easily creamed me, so I realized it might be wise of me to mind my tongue.

Pity that wisdom was the dump stat of my last D&D character. "And what duties would that be? Sweeping out the crater that used to be your office? Because I think you might need a few more men."

"The Magi hit us at an inopportune moment and with little warning."

"You should have kept some of Vehron's men on the payroll, then. They seemed to be pretty good at keeping an eye open for him." We glared at each other, the night quiet save for the sound of scurrying vamps and settling rubble. "Speaking of which," I said, looking around, "aside from your people, I haven't seen any signs of life at all. I'd imagine there'd be emergency crews, people trying to get back home, maybe someone brave enough to wander into the woods for a souvenir tree branch."

"Mandatory evacuation by the National Guard once the attack began."

"Convenient."

"Not really," Colin replied. "Who do you think ordered it?"

I raised an eyebrow. "Huh, who'd have thought you had a soft spot for humans?"

"I do not. I do, however, seek to draw as little attention to our kind as possible, even during these *interesting* times. As much as I appreciate cannon fodder for what it is..." His eyes flashed black. "I do not appreciate the attention such an attack would surely draw to a building that is supposed to remain clandestine to the populace."

"And a giant smoldering crater is clandestine?"

"An act of terrorism," he replied with a shrug. "We will ensure some silly group or other claims responsibility once the media picks up on it."

"Terrorism ... against a car wash?"

"These are strange days we live in, Freewill. Do not discount the ability of cattle to believe what is spoon fed to them."

"You're a real humanitarian, you know that?"

"I am loyal to the establishment I serve. You could learn a thing or two about that. Despite my assurances earlier, I have little doubt Lord Alexander will be quite interested to know why one of the beasts that helped perpetrate this attack is currently among your entourage."

This was more like the Colin I knew. Despite his actions earlier during the battle, he was always one to let others do his dirty work for him. Still, he did have a point. Were our positions reversed, I'd hopefully be less of a suck-up, but it would probably look pretty bad for the poster boy for the war effort to be hanging out with the enemy. Kinda like if Captain America came waltzing into camp hand-in-hand with the Red Skull.

I took a subtle look around, mostly to make sure Grulg wasn't in earshot. "Not so strange to be offering asylum to a defector."

Colin raised one eyebrow dubiously. "A defector. That's your story?"

"What? No one has ever switched sides in the history of our war?"

He let out a pained sigh. "There were reports in the sixties of some covens going native, but so far as I am aware, no Grendel has ever crossed the so-called Bridge of No Return."

"Oh, well, there's always a first time."

Yeah, it was weak. There was also the problem of what one would do with a Sasquatch defector? Put them in a zoo and have them pretend to be an overly large monkey?

I also had no idea how Grulg would react at being asked to play along with my lie.

All in all, it was a few more shovelfuls from the grave I seemed intent on digging for myself.

43

HAIRY PALM AND HIS FIVE SISTERS

awn was rapidly approaching. Sally still hadn't returned from her walkabout, which meant she was either really pissed or busy wrecking wholesale slaughter upon some human stragglers she'd found. Regardless, I was beginning to get worried.

The good news? Sheila was on the mend. Her powers continued to grow stronger as the tainted blood wore off and she was able to begin healing herself. Reasonably certain the danger to her had passed, I decided to wander back to the tree line of the unnatural forest. Grulg had professed to being more comfortable there and had returned to it. Since we appeared to be in the eye of the proverbial hurricane, it was time to tell him why we'd been seeking him out. The alternative was to shove my thumb up my ass and pretend it would all be fine in the end – a strategy that hadn't worked out too well for me in days past.

I stood at the very edge of the forest, looking in. Though a sniff of the air told me there wasn't a group of Feet waiting for me in ambush, that didn't mean anything. Their magic could be tricky, and I'd gotten enough woodland ass-kickings to put me off the idea of camping for the rest of my life.

"You there, Grulg?" I asked, my voice perhaps lower than

intended, but with good reason. Should anything unfriendly answer, I was in no condition to fight back.

After a minute or two of feeling like I was ringing the doorbell to an empty house, I was about to turn around when the shadows a couple of yards in seemed to solidify, taking on a far more solid form. Even though I recognized Grulg, the sight still caused me to catch my breath for a moment. After my dealings with these guys, I'd probably never be able to view *Harry and the Hendersons* as anything other than a horror movie.

I forced a casual tone to my voice. "Just hanging out?"

"*No,*" he replied. "*Needed to tell others.*"

"What?" Oh shit.

He held up one of his massive hands in a placating manner. "*Told others Grulg still hunting T'lunta. That Grulg must hunt alone, otherwise Grulg's honor be disgraced.*" He actually winked at me. Either that or a flea had bitten him in the wrong place. Regardless, I was happy to hear it.

I turned and took another sniff, this time back the way I'd come, making sure I hadn't been followed. "I think it's time I came clean with you."

"*Clean? T'lunta always smell funny. Wish to smell better?*"

I backed up a step before I could be pelted with anything foul. "No. Just a figure of speech. It means it's time I told you why we were looking for you. Before I start, though, I want to ask one favor of you."

"*What?*"

I considered their new alliance with the Magi. "If you don't like what you hear, at least give me a sporting head start."

I reminded Grulg of our time spent underground as prisoners of the Jahabich. From the snarl on his face, I gathered he wasn't overly fond of the memory. Then I dropped the bomb that their creator was Calibra, aka Kala the White, aka Ib the first vampire.

As I got into the nitty gritty, his face became unreadable. I could understand. It was like learning your best friend and your worst enemy both had the same dad.

"*T'lunta and Magi same?*" he asked. "*Neutral was trick?*"

"No. So far as I'm aware, the connection isn't widely known and I'm not sure the people in power would want it to get out anyway. So far as the Magi are concerned, Kala the White is the ultimate hippie chick of goodness and us vamps are still sewer scum. I sincerely doubt she outed herself as vampire numero uno to them. The thing is, not only is she the progenitor of both races, but she's the creator of the Jahabich as well."

I went on to explain how Sally and I had collapsed our escape tunnel behind us, sealing it. "That's why we need you, Grulg. You escaped, too. We were hoping you could show us the way back."

"*To kill In'luh ... Jahabich?*" Our word for them was a big one for his kind, and it came out sounding like he was gargling gravel.

"More than that," I explained. "To kill Ib. She's too powerful and evil to let live. She kidnapped some friends of mine. Also..." I took a moment to debate whether I wanted to place all my cards on the table, but then concluded we were simply too far along to do otherwise. I needed to let the dice roll and accept the outcome. "We're going to kill the leader of the First Coven, too, so we can end this war once and for all."

Unsurprisingly, that garnered me a raised eyebrow and a snot-filled snort, which I just barely sidestepped. "*War already over. Peace now.*"

"Yeah, about that..."

I laid everything out to him, including how our peace mission was neither sanctioned, recognized, or even known by the Draculas.

This was extremely risky. Far as I could tell, Grulg was the equivalent of a battlefield commander. He didn't quite rank up there with the Turds or Big C's of the world, but he had a goodly amount of pull. If he decided I could take my story and shove it up my ass, we could be looking at a second offensive. Between the Feet and the Magi, there was virtually no chance of stopping them from leveling the entire city if that happened.

It was a good thing breathing was no longer a vital function for me, because I held my breath as Grulg pondered my confession.

"Tell Grulg if he understand right. Freewill T'lunta make false peace to find Grulg, so Grulg lead to enemies, so enemies can be crushed, so real peace can be made?"

"In a nutshell, more or less."

He raised a hand and I flinched, but he simply placed it upon my shoulder. *"Clever T'lunta."*

"You're not mad?"

"Lies happen in war. Who to blame? Enemies or those who fall for lies?" He shrugged as if to say shit happens. *"Lies to cause harm to Grulg's kin bring much rage. Lies to bring peace, Grulg understand. Many die in war. Maybe they not need to."*

Wow, that was actually pretty deep for a creature that liked to bathe in its own shit. "Yes, Grulg. That's my hope, too. Just remember, the other vamps still think we're at war. We have to keep up the ruse for a short while."

"Grulg deceive T'lunta leaders? Grulg like that. Much honor to Grulg."

I had to stifle a laugh. I could only imagine, in the near future, Grulg sitting around a fire with the other Feet passing around a cup of ... err ... grubs, I guess, and bullshitting about how he'd managed to punk the Dracs. Not a bad picture, if I did say so myself. I could get behind something like that.

"Awesome to hear." I turned and glanced up at the sky. It was starting to grow light in the east. Time to head back. I didn't relish the thought of being cooped up for the day with Colin, but thankfully I had friends to mock him with. "Oh, yeah, almost forgot," I said, looking over my shoulder at him. "I also told them you were a defector, so you'll have to play ... URK!"

Grulg grabbed me from behind, basically engulfing my head in his gigantic hand. "*You tell T'lunta that Grulg traitor?*"

Uh oh. When he put it that way...

"It was ... ugh!" I choked as one of his fingers slipped into my open mouth. That was really not something I had wanted to taste *ever*.

He gave my head a shake. "*Grulg not traitor! Grulg honorable warrior!*"

"It's ... just ... a..."

"You will put him down *now*."

The voice startled both of us. I couldn't see very well between Grulg's massive fingers, but I didn't need a line of sight to know who'd said it.

"Don't be hasty," a second voice, equally familiar, purred. "I kind of want to see where this is going,"

Gan had found us, and she had Sally with her.

44

DEFECTIVE DEFECTION

Grulg began circling, dragging me along by the face. Judging by the sound of foliage snapping, I assumed Gan and Sally were doing the same. Or, at least Gan was.

Okay, this was getting fucking ridiculous. Any second now, these two were going to go at it with me smack dab in the middle. I didn't fancy being used as either a club, shield, or tug of war rope. I dared to open my mouth again, praying my taste buds forgave me. This time when Grulg's finger slipped in, I bit down, just hard enough to get his attention.

He growled and released me, finally getting the hint that this gnat could sting. I quickly stepped back out of his reach and spat out whatever was in my mouth. Guh! It was almost enough for me to consider going vegan when this was all over.

For now, though, I stepped between the two wannabe combatants, hoping I didn't get pummeled for my trouble. "That's enough!"

"This creature dared to attack you, my..."

"Don't say it, Gan." I glanced over and saw Sally leaning against a tree, a look of amusement on her face. "Control her, please."

"You're not the boss of me," she replied with a grin.

Assholes, all of them. I quickly turned my attention back to Grulg. "It's another deception. We know it's not true. Remember what you said, a lie to bring peace was worth it."

"*Lie destroy Grulg's honor.*"

I could kinda see his point. I personally didn't care if the Dracs thought I was a piece of shit. Hell, most of them did anyway. But Grulg wasn't me. This was a guy who was proud to be part of the system. Heck, he was like a more tolerable version of Colin, just for the other side. What I was asking him to do was for the benefit of his people, but at what cost? If word got out, Grulg could, in all likelihood, never go home again.

Goddamn it. I hadn't thought of that. In truth, I didn't know shit about him. For all I knew he had a wife and kids, or cubs anyway. Turd may have been a pile of crap, but that didn't mean the rest of the Feet didn't understand the concept of friends, family, and love.

"I'm sorry, Grulg. I spoke without thinking how it might affect you. It was selfish of me."

"Aw. This moment so needs to be on Maury."

"Not now," I growled at Sally.

Fortunately, my words seemed to have reached the big gorilla. He still kept an eye on Gan, but some of the tension went out of his massive arms. I took a risk and locked eyes with her, then gave a single nod and she immediately relaxed, looking again more like a preteen girl and less a one-woman wrecking crew.

"Are you okay?"

"I would think that would be obvious, beloved." She smiled sweetly at me, obviously pleased that I'd asked.

"I meant from earlier, with the witches."

"I am in far better condition than many of them," she replied smugly.

"What about...?"

"Taken prisoner. After you were removed from the field of battle, your friend the witch mentor saw the futility of our situation. Even with my skill, the odds were too against our favor. She offered a compromise, her surrender in exchange for her coven not being harmed."

"Her coven and you, you mean?"

She shrugged. "Her omission did not go unnoticed." Yeah, she and Christy would never be on each other's Christmas card lists. "I made good use of the momentary cessation of hostilities and escaped."

"With a souvenir," Sally added. She inclined her head toward the sheathed sword lying at her feet.

"Awesome! I know a certain Icon who's going to be pleased as punch to see that."

"You should have expected no less," Gan replied. "I wish the Shining One to be at full capacity when you finally dispatch her. It will make your victory all the sweeter."

"Uh, yeah, sweeter. Maybe not quite the word I'd use. So, why didn't you catch up to us sooner? I'm sure you could have..." I was so going to regret saying this. "I'm sure you could have followed my scent."

"Indeed I could, for an eternity if need be."

Yep, I regretted it. Creep factor ratcheted up to eleven.

"The Magi were persistent, though, as were a handful of the Alma." She turned toward Grulg. "Some of your soldiers recognized me despite my scent."

He raised an eyebrow. Great, just what we needed – a reveal that Gan had a whole collection of squatch skulls.

"Never mind that," I quickly replied. "So what happened?"

"They were diligent in their pursuit. More than once, they thought me boxed in."

"So what happened?"

"What do you think happened?" Sally asked with an eye-roll. "You remember her first visit to the Office, right?"

Yeah. It hadn't been pretty. She'd basically put the fear of God into the entirety of Village Coven.

"Once they were *dissuaded*," Gan continued, "I followed your trail here. Rather than announce myself to the Wanderer's former assistant, though, I chose to circle around, scout the surrounding area. That is when I came upon your whore."

"What?" Sally spat. "Did we not just talk about that?"

"I believe you were doing a great deal of the talking," Gan replied. "It was quite tiresome to listen to. That you mistook my disinterest for compliance, however, is a failing on your part, not mine."

I could see Sally eyeing the sword, pondering her odds. Such a happy little family our group was.

Looking to diffuse the situation, I turned back to Grulg and changed the subject. "You've been awfully quiet during all of this."

"*T'lunta like to chatter,*" he replied. "*T'lunta mate and cub chatter much.*"

"She is not our cub," Gan replied without any sense of irony whatsoever.

"He didn't mean ... never mind." I massaged my temples, willing the stupidity headache away. "You and ... our cub just pipe down for now, please."

I resumed my conversation with Grulg before Sally could voice her opinion on that. "I know it's a lot to ask of your honor, but will you help us?"

He crossed his massive arms over his barrel of a chest. "*No.*"

What?! Shit like this wasn't supposed to happen. I mean, hell, in the movies, you fuck up, say you're sorry, and then go and defeat the bad guys. It's practically a mandatory trope.

"*Grulg not defector. Not act like defector. Grulg honorable, loyal. All Grulg's people know this.*"

I meant to reply with a quick primer on the concept of acting, gleaned from my single semester with the NJIT drama club, but before I could do so, Grulg raised his head to the sky and let loose with an ear-splitting roar.

Shit! I really hoped it wouldn't come down to this. I

didn't exactly like Grulg, but I definitely despised him less than his filthy brethren. Also, if we had to kill him now, we'd be thoroughly fucked. He hadn't told us what we needed and without Christy around, there was no chance of a Speak With Dead spell.

As I tensed myself for what was to come, Grulg opened his hand and slapped a nearby tree three times, shaking it to its roots and producing a hollow booming noise certain to echo for miles.

Once I could hear myself think again, he bent down toward me and bared his teeth in a snarl.

A few moments later, I realized I had no choice in the matter.

As we struggled with Grulg's unconscious form, I realized the irony of our situation – two vamps, both vulnerable to sunlight, racing against the clock to drag our foe back to where Colin's men awaited. All the while, the one among us who could sunbathe with impunity hid back in the trees. Yeah, this made a lot of fucking sense.

Heavy as he was, though, at least I could handle the load now. Following the brief scuffle, Gan had noted my piss poor condition. She had wasted no time in slitting a wrist and shoving it into my face. Even had I been at full strength, I'd have been hard pressed to fight her off, at least until I got a couple of sips. Not only did her blood pep me up, but it had an added bonus. In addition to sunlight, she'd apparently also picked up a resistance to silver as part of her transformation. Unlike the sunlight thing, which sadly didn't seem to survive the transfer of blood, I seemed to have gotten a little bit of that silver immunity, evidenced by my wounds finally knitting themselves shut. By the time we approached the building Colin was using as a temporary base, I was feeling like myself again.

I glanced down at the bruised form we were carrying,

noting that I'd come out of this latest scuffle in much better shape for a change. Grulg had gotten a pounding, but it had been necessary.

We needed to know what he did and he was going to tell us – one way or the other.

45

WOOD VERSUS WOOD

Tom and Sheila met us upon our return, helping us get to the shelter the buildings provided. I could tell they had questions, but thankfully, they held their tongues until we were out of the sun. That was good of them. I so hated being interrogated while on fire.

"Damn, Bill. You kicked his ass," Tom said as we laid the unconscious ape on the floor.

"Something like that," I replied.

Sadly, Colin was also waiting for us. At some point, he must've sent some hapless lackey to salvage his wardrobe because he was once again dressed like he was ready for a corporate power lunch.

He approached the battered Sasquatch and gave it a contemptuous kick before pulling out a handkerchief and wiping off his shoe. Seeing no reaction from us at his petty assholishness, he grinned, showing off straight white teeth that I really wanted to kick in. "I thought you said this creature had defected."

"He changed his mind," Sally replied. "Must've been the company."

"True class is lost upon lesser beings," Colin sniped back before turning to me. "May I inquire as to why it is still living? It has seen our..."

287

"Awesome defenses?" Sally interrupted. "Yeah, bet he couldn't wait to get back to his buddies to see if they could round up three cubs to take this place."

"He has information we need to know," I explained. "Things Alex needs to know."

That caught his attention and he immediately lost all interest in trading barbs with Sally. "You presume to know the mind of Lord Alexander, Freewill? That is arrogant even by your standards."

"I only presume because I haven't heard of Calibra's head being given a place of honor in his closet yet."

Colin's eyes narrowed. He wasn't too keen on me speaking so flippantly about the guy whose boots he shined with his tongue. It probably killed him inside to know that I'd had more interactions with the Dracs in the last six months than most vamps did in half a millennium. "The First Coven are not in the habit of lauding their victories to children."

"And yet this *child* has an actual truce in place with him, one that calls for the free exchange of information." I didn't like this fucker at all, but I really enjoyed knocking him down a peg or three. I casually strolled up and put an arm around his shoulders. "Like it or not, buddy, you're in the presence of not one, but two beings who are prophesied to be the key players in this conflict. We may not be as old as some of the players on the field, but we're badass enough to hang with the cool kids."

Sally's mouth turned up at the corners. Good to see she was enjoying this.

"Fate truly has a sense of humor," Colin remarked bitterly, shrugging me off as if I had cooties. "As for Lord Alexander, let him and his glorious brethren be the judge as to how worthy this beast's so-called information is."

"Hopefully you can get a signal in this dump, because I sure as shit haven't seen a single bar on my phone. If not, email might have to suffice."

"You misunderstand me, Freewill, as seems to be

commonplace." The smug grin returned to his face. "There will be no need for you to relay this information remotely. You may do so directly to Lord Alexander himself."

"Huh, what?"

"Did I fail to mention it? Oh, dear me. Well, since you seem so eager to speak to our lord and master, I should let you know he is on his way and will be arriving shortly."

"He is?"

"Oh yes, and from my last communique with him, he seemed quite eager to speak to you."

I hadn't been expecting that. Sure, we needed to eventually loop in Alex with some carefully spoon-fed bullshit, but I figured for now he'd be off doing whatever a would-be world conqueror did during their downtime – like dusting all those pesky non-conformist covens.

"Oh, did I not tell you?" Colin asked after a few moments of stunned silence on our part. "I reached out to him as soon as our debacle was concluded. He seemed quite intrigued by the circumstances surrounding your arrival." He leered at Sheila. There was nothing sexual about it, though. Colin seemed the type who would only get a boner if the orders were signed in triplicate.

No, his look was that of a pure predator who knew his prey had been cornered.

Shit!

Back while we'd been waiting for the Squatch shamans to prepare their tree teleporter, I'd casually asked Gan about those black bladed weapons, mostly to keep her off the subject of planning our wedding. Encouraged by my feigned interest, she'd told me about the freaky-ass ritual needed to produce them and why it was mostly done with daggers or specific pole arms. Something long and thin like a sword would effectively be like swinging a glass rod instead. Just for shits and giggles, I asked why not projectile weapons, too.

Turns out that, over distance, arrows would disintegrate mid-flight. Bullets were even riskier, as they'd often blow apart in the barrel of the gun first, causing it to backfire. The blood was that caustic.

I hadn't been paying a great deal of attention at the time. Now, though, I found myself considering the implications.

A weapon coated with that shit could injure her, but injecting it directly into her bloodstream actually neutralized her powers for a time. In some ways, it wasn't entirely unlike what silver did to vampires

If they could figure out a way to load it into a dart, make it gaseous, or even poison an Icon's food with it, then it would be game over. They'd need never fear them again. The checks and balances of the supernatural world would be kicked to the curb.

Colin had seen Sheila vulnerable. He had to have guessed something happened to make her that way. It didn't take a genius to figure out those of us with her probably knew what that was. The asshole was probably chomping at the bit to spill his guts to Alex about all of this.

It was yet another chip for the pile already sitting in the middle of this dangerous game of high-stakes poker we seemed to be playing. Between this and The Source, it was rapidly becoming the ultimate jackpot.

It was a game we couldn't afford to lose now more than ever before.

"We need to take a shower."

"Excuse me?" Colin asked.

"What do you mean, *we*?" Sally added.

"I meant we all need to clean up a bit. We can't be scummy for Lord Alexander's arrival. Wouldn't do."

"No, it would not," Colin replied, looking dapper in his fresh threads. "But I assure you, he is quite used to it from the rabble." He smirked, probably still pleased to have ruffled my feathers with his revelation. Dude was a world-class prick.

"No doubt, but if it's all the same to you, we'd like to try."

It was a pathetic lie, and I didn't expect Colin to buy it for a second, but he didn't stop us as we covered up against the daylight before presumably trying to find a place with running water.

Before stepping out, I glanced down at Grulg, still lying on the floor.

"Fret not, Freewill," Colin said. "We shall keep him safe."

"Just keep him in one piece," I warned. "I'd hate to be the one to tell Alex that his new toy got broken before he got a chance to play with it."

The smile faltered on Colin's face, and I walked out before it could reassert itself. Always leave on a high note.

Despite the bright sunshine, there were several figures milling about – vamp soldiers outfitted for the day with body armor and tinted helmets, all in all far superior to the meager protection Sally and I wore. You'd think my status as their legendary warrior might warrant me at least a parasol, but no dice.

Bloodthirsty cock-faces, all of them. Even if we won and left Calibra and Alex dead under a thousand tons of rock at the center of the Earth, we'd still need to contend with the rest of the vampire nation's shit for all of eternity.

Oh well, one problem at a time.

I led us to a nearby building and kicked in the door. I wasn't being particularly choosy because it didn't really matter. We just needed to be out of earshot for a few minutes.

Once inside, I instantly felt less singed around the edges. I headed upstairs, the others following, then opened the door of the first apartment I came to.

"You weren't serious about the showers, were you, Bill?" Tom asked. "Christy is pretty open minded, but she might have a problem with all of us..."

I rounded on him. "Seriously?! That's the thing you're most concerned about? Sally, compel him."

"What?"

"You heard me. Compel Tom." Then, before she could open her mouth, I added, "Nothing lethal, please."

"Such a killjoy," she mumbled.

"What are you doing?" Sheila asked.

"Testing something," I said. "Please, now, while we're young."

Sally flipped me the finger, but then I felt the slight tingle in the back of my skull that told me she was doing as asked. ***"GO DRY HUMP THAT BANNISTER!!"***

Okay, that was certainly an interesting choice.

I instinctively stepped in to catch her, knowing the toll compelling humans took, but she remained steady on her feet.

"It's okay." She waved me off. "That didn't take as much out of me as I thought it would."

"Maybe you're getting used to it."

"More likely it's because he's not human anymore. Not that he ever really was."

I hadn't considered that, but it sounded as logical as anything else.

"Um, guys..." Sheila pointed to the stairwell, where Tom was busy making sweet love to the wooden bannister at the top. From the look on his face, he was getting into it, too.

"If you're joking with us, you can stop now."

He ignored me, though, and kept at it. "Yeah, bitch! My wood or yours! Let's see whose wins!"

I turned to the others. "He's not joking."

"No," Sally replied thoughtfully. "It would appear he is not."

"Was kind of hoping he'd be immune in his new form."

"What was that saying?" she asked. "Something about the Force being able to control weak minds? Yes, I do occasionally go to the movies, dipshit."

"I didn't imply..."

Sheila stepped between us, pointing with one hand and covering her eyes with the other. "Can someone please stop him? I ... think he's almost, you know, done."

Eww, she was right. He was more anatomically correct than I'd have guessed. I had to hand it to Christy. This was one hell of a spell.

"*YOUR DICK IS AS LIMP AS YOUR BRAIN!!*"

The compulsion rushed out from Sally and I caught a piece of it, feeling it reverberate in my brain for a second or two.

A confused look came over Tom's face as his eyes cleared. He glanced down in horror, then gave two more thrusts against the wooden railing before giving up. "That is so not cool."

"Get over it," I said, wishing I had a gallon of brain bleach.

"No, seriously. You can't do that to a guy." He pushed past me into the open apartment. "Excuse me."

"Where are you going?"

"There are some things you just can't start without finishing," he replied, then disappeared into the bathroom.

"All in favor of breaking into a different apartment?" I asked.

Sheila shrugged, obviously uncomfortable with what had just taken place. It was kinda cute. "Joking aside, was there a reason for that?"

"I'm glad you asked. It's because..."

"Fuck me!" Tom cried from inside. "It's not working now!"

"Christy stays with him willingly?" she asked.

"Love is truly blind, and oh so tolerant."

Okay, enough of that. I needed to focus. Sally's compulsion wasn't super loud, but I was fooling myself if I thought none of the other vamps in the area hadn't picked up on it. We didn't have much time before someone got curious as to why Tom was first fucking the decor and now was a blue-balled, limp-dicked sad sack. "Sally, you need to take Tom and run."

She rolled her eyes at the suggestion, but I was pretty certain it was less what I wanted her to do than who she was supposed to do it with. She was a stick of dynamite and Tom was a walking, talking lit match. Her tolerance of his shit was low on a good day.

"Why do they need to run?" Sheila asked. "I thought you said we should all stick together."

"It's Colin," Sally explained. "You saw the way he looked at you back there."

"He's not really my type."

"I'm pretty sure he'd creep out Ilsa She-Wolf of the SS, so it's good to know you have some semblance of taste, but that's not what I meant. Compulsion. The meatsack is vulnerable to it, probably more so than most." She paused, disgust evident in her voice. "But so am I."

Understanding passed through Sheila's eyes. "It's me, isn't it?"

"When we got here, you looked like you were at death's door," I said. "Don't think Colin didn't notice. Hell, at first I actually think he might have believed you weren't you, but then he saw you in action. Despite that, he managed to beat you badly. That's something he's not about to let go as a fluke."

"It wasn't *that* badly," she replied defiantly, her eyes flashing silver.

"Is that you speaking or the Icon?"

She looked taken aback by my question. After a few moments, though, she lowered her eyes and nodded.

Sally, in a rare gesture of camaraderie, put a hand on her shoulder. "Don't feel bad. The prick stopped me in my tracks with a few words. The problem is a loser like him shouldn't be able to touch you and live. He knows something was wrong. He knows you were a lot weaker than you should be. And you can bet that if he knows, Alexander is going to know, too."

"From the mouths of assholes," I said.

"Don't think for a second Alexander isn't going to force the issue. He won't let something significant like this drop. For all his bluster, he knows you beat Theodora in a fair fight. That's not a small feat. You need to remember the stuff you learned in history class."

"Not really my best subject," Sheila admitted. "Although lately I seem to be getting a crash course."

"Alexander of Macedon is one of history's great conquerors," Sally said. "He led via a combination of charisma and cunning. If anything, he's gotten smarter over the years. If he can gain an advantage over a foe, he's going to. The first thing he's going to do is try to weasel it out of us using that truce of his. Don't forget, we're supposed to be sharing information."

I nodded. "We can try playing stupid, but..."

"Bill's specialty." Bitch. "But that won't cut it, not when there are two of us he can make squeal via brute force." Sally gritted her teeth as she spoke, no doubt remembering her time as Alex's meat puppet. "We can't let that happen."

"I'm not afraid of him," Sheila said.

"We know you're not," I offered supportively.

Sally shot me a withering look, then turned back to Sheila. "You should be, though. He won't just have an advantage when we go after Ib. He'll have an advantage for the end game as well. Think of it, that goddamned prophecy."

I made to protest, but she held up a hand. "I know your thoughts on this, but let's pretend for a moment that it's not bullshit. That somehow destiny will twist and turn us so that you two have to face off in some sort of climactic battle. If Bill wins, you're out of the game, but he's not out of the woods."

"Yeah," I replied with some annoyance. "Alex has already proven he's more than willing to remove Freewills from the equation. I don't want my noggin ending up as his paperweight for all eternity."

"I doubt anyone does," she replied. "But what if the

opposite holds true? If the Icon wins, the darkness is supposed to be dispersed. The world stays in mankind's hands. Except Alexander won't like that at all. And if he has the means to take you out right afterwards, well then, who knows what'll happen? At that point, he can make his own history."

"So he can't know," Sheila concluded.

"No. It's too dangerous, which means we have to make sure he can't force the issue. Even if he tortures you both, without compulsion, he can't know for certain."

"Which hopefully means he won't bother with the torture." I'd been on the receiving end of Alex's manhandling. The guy was a maestro of pain, and I really didn't care to be his fiddle again.

"But what will you two do?" Sheila asked.

Sally smiled. "I'm thinking a nice stroll in the woods will do just..."

"The first thing she's going to do is get rid of this compulsion," Tom snapped, stepping out of the bathroom. "I can't go out with a non-functioning dick."

"Why not?" Sally replied. "You've been doing just fine with a non-functioning brain. Besides, just talking about your dick makes me want to gargle industrial strength mouthwash."

"Don't worry about them," I said to Sheila, putting what I hoped was a bit of false positivity in my tone before lowering my voice to a bare whisper. "Assuming Sally doesn't kill him first, we're not alone. Trust me when I say, we have small friends in big places."

46

DRACHAWK DOWN

As expected, it wasn't long before Colin's guards came looking for us. They found Sheila and me alone in one of the apartments, looting the closets of the former owners for some new clothes. Despite my earlier lie to Colin, we both really did look like hell after our recent battles.

Though I couldn't have cared less about being presentable for his high and mightiness, there was something to be said about walking around without having to worry about your clothes disintegrating right off your body. Though I wouldn't have minded it with present company, I didn't want to give the wrong impression and suddenly have Alex break out the wrestling oil again.

"Where are the others?" one of the guards snapped.

"The others?" I asked, testing the fit of a pair of fairly new jeans. Not bad. A bit long in the leg, but probably handy in case I happened to lose control and transform.

"The vampire and the human."

"Not here," Sheila said, stepping out from the bathroom wearing slacks and a silk blouse. "How's this look?"

"Goes with your eyes."

The two guards were starting to get agitated. Probably best to not let this go too far. Despite their superior age, I was fairly certain we could take them. But where would that leave us? We'd still have to deal with Colin and, soon enough, much worse.

"Those two?" I asked with a sigh, while double checking to make sure I hadn't left anything behind. "Serious fuck buddies. Can barely keep their hands, and other parts, off each other. Thought they were gonna bone right here in front of us. Finally told them to get a fucking room. Guess they listened."

I'd been betting on the fact that, even with Colin's reserve troops, he didn't have the manpower to keep anything but a fairly small area under constant surveillance. With the power out, there were no cameras to act as extra eyes. Sally and Tom had simply slipped out a back window and made a run for it, but these two dickweeds didn't need to know that.

One of them grumbled to himself, then turned to the other. "Search the building. If you find them, bring them back."

"And if I don't?"

The first guard shrugged, then turned to us. "You two with me. I am told ... the First shall be here shortly."

"Nervous much?" I asked with a grin.

He didn't answer, which made me smile even wider.

In truth, I knew exactly what he was feeling.

Knew it and felt it several times over.

I grabbed both an umbrella and a hooded jacket from my unaware benefactor's closet, and then we followed the guard back out into the street.

Once outside, his focus seemed to be more on getting back than watching us, allowing us to fall back several paces.

"Fuck buddies?" Sheila whispered with a grin.

I smiled from behind the oversized aviator sunglasses I'd swiped. "If you're gonna lie, might as well go big."

"That is one way of doing it. Speaking of which, what is it with Sally? I mean, between the two of you..."

I held up a hand as a sound reached my ears. A few moments later, she heard it, too. Helicopters – more than a few, I'd say.

Saved by the Dracs. I swear, I'd get a more accurate reading from the women in my life with a cheap plastic mood ring. That she'd even thought to ask had me curious, however. When we'd started this crazy journey, I'd sort of resigned myself to the fact that it wasn't meant to be. There'd been a new coolness between us that seemed to signify that door was now closed. Oil and water, I suppose.

I couldn't lie, though. As we'd progressed, that wall of ice between us seemed to melt bit by bit. Maybe it was old habits dying hard, or maybe I was just fooling myself. I'd pined for her since first setting my eyes upon her, so to settle on being nothing more than friends? A bitter pill to swallow.

Or maybe I should concentrate on the here and now and worry about those things later, I considered too late. I had absentmindedly turned my head toward the sound of the choppers and exposed my face to the sun, just long enough to remind me what a bad idea that was.

"Oh my God! Are you okay?"

"No," I replied with a hiss of pain. "But considering the company about to join us, I have a feeling okay is a condition we're not gonna be familiar with again for a while."

So *this* was what Colin had put his men to work doing. We were close to the ruins of the Boston Complex again. Colin had his men set up several large pavilion tents that formed a covered passage from the open area to the brownstone a block away, which served as a temporary headquarters.

I had to give them credit. Vamps might be assholes, but with the proper motivation, they could apply themselves like busy little bees. Sadly, proper motivation was usually in the form of compulsion, death threats, or worse.

Still, Colin had somehow made the most of a shit situation. Pity, there was still the wee fact of there no longer being a functioning vampire stronghold in the Northeast. Listening to him try to weasel out of that one ought to be interesting.

It didn't look like we had long to wait. I looked up – remembering to shield my face this time – and saw four attack choppers escorting their much larger brother. The big helicopter looked how you might expect Marine One to appear if it was decorated by The Cure. All of them were matte black in color with no markings. If I didn't know better, I'd half expect Will Smith to step out when they landed and wipe all our memories.

"Is it rare for them to travel during the day?" Sheila whispered in my ear, sending goosebumps up and down my arms. She'd apparently forgotten about the whole super hearing thing.

Forcing myself to attempt adult-like behavior, I leaned in, pausing just long enough to sniff her hair, because deep down I obviously wanted her to think I was a creep. "It's probably rarer for them to make an appearance to the unwashed masses. From what I hear, the waiting list for an audience is at least a couple centuries long."

"I guess we should be flattered."

Yep, flattered, as well as terrified. My prior dealings with the Dracs hadn't always fallen on the win side. Sadly, the one supporter in the bunch that I could almost always count on was currently among the missing.

Oh well, as tempting as running and hiding was, there was relatively little chance of me making it far. It was time to do what I tended to do during times like this – put on some false bravado and bullshit like my life depended on it.

Go figure – it probably did.

Two of the attack choppers landed first, dispatching heavily armed vamps in head to toe obsidian-colored armor that looked thick enough to stop a grenade. Big guns were the order of the day – no silver stake bullshit for these fuckers. Two of them sported miniguns, making me wonder how badly three thousand rounds a minute of silver-jacketed love would mess up a fella's day.

They formed a wide outward-facing circle as the big helicopter descended, leaving the remaining two choppers hovering above. The wash from the blades kicked up a lot of dirt and dust from the cleared area, but the vamps standing guard didn't even flinch in the downdraft. I had a feeling these were the Draculas' elite – the guys who, in another universe, would be draped in red and guarding Emperor Palpatine. As tough as Boston's finest had looked back when the place wasn't in shambles, these guys had an aura about them that said it would probably be best to avoid getting on their bad side.

Oh yeah, this was gonna be fun.

The big helicopter touched the ground and its engines began to power down. They were still spinning, though, when the hatch lowered, revealing Alexander. The dude was definitely not one for waiting. Even so, I had to admit to a smidgeon of grudging respect. At least he was at the head of the line, firmly in charge. An asswipe like Colin would have been the last one out, no doubt after a lot of pomp and circumstance.

That was as far as my admiration for Alex went, though. The guy was dangerous, power-hungry, and a serious douchebag.

His hair was blown about by the downwash of the rotors. Annoyingly enough, it made him look more rugged than disheveled. That made me hate him ever so slightly more.

Alex surveyed the scene from the hatch of the helicopter for a few moments, then reached one hand out and tapped it impatiently against the side. I caught movement in my periphery and couldn't help but smile at seeing Colin in a near panic, gesturing to some of the vamps near him.

His men raced out toward the chopper, carrying a portable canopy with them. Couldn't let the Dracs get a sunburn, could we? Maybe he thought Alex would do the reasonable thing and wait for the engines to completely stop.

The rotors were slowing but still creating enough wind to throw the vinyl tarp into disarray. One thing most outsiders didn't realize about vampire society was that it was only possible to live forever so long as someone higher on the food chain decided to let you. Fucking up in high-ranking company was a good way to ensure that didn't happen. After all, why bother giving someone a second chance when you could just bite another and give them a turn at being competent?

The amusement of Alex's slight annoyance when he finally walked down the steps to the ground, not giving the guys shielding him from the sun the barest of acknowledge-ment, slightly muted my terror.

I really hoped Colin was wearing an adult diaper, because I sincerely doubted the smell of him pissing himself would be a point in his favor.

Next out of the helicopter stepped an unexpected, but very welcome sight – Yehoshua. Though I didn't quite dare to put as much trust in him as I had James, he'd proven himself a straight shooter. Not only was the guy firmly against Alex's warmongering, but even after we'd accidentally killed his friend Theodora, he'd still opted to give us a chance rather than see us summarily executed.

Now to only hope he wasn't still pissed about Thea. I mean, the chick had been a bit of a stuck up bitch, after all.

My breath caught as more figures followed him. I didn't know most of their names. The last time I'd seen them, there hadn't been any formal introductions, but I recognized their faces. It was the rest of the First Coven, the entirety of the vampire ruling counsel.

Holy shit, they were *all* here?!

Well, not all, I suppose. The First Coven was normally thirteen strong. However, two of their number – François and Vargas – had recently met their end, while James was still MIA. I could only guess that with the insanity of the last few days, there hadn't been time to choose replacements yet.

Or maybe that was purposeful. With Theodora and James out of the picture, so too were some major voices of opposition to Alex's plans. Yehoshua was still there, but I had a feeling the rest would fall in line with their leader's wishes if push came to shove.

Ten of the most powerful vampires in the world strode forward, led by Alexander of Macedon. All around us, the remnants of the Boston prefecture dropped to one knee. I was tempted to do the same, but glanced to my side and saw Sheila standing there, watching this all. Yeah, I'd probably lose a few cool points if I did that, assuming I had any to begin with. Besides, we all knew I was on these guys' shit list. Kissing their asses now wouldn't count much in my favor.

Almost as if his hearing were acute enough to pick up on my thoughts, Alex briefly turned my way and locked eyes with me. He allowed a slight grin to cross his face. Ever since we'd met, he'd purported to find my attitude amusing. Of course, it still hadn't stopped him from fucking me up the ass at every opportunity, but it was nice to know he held me in the same regard as most people did a puppy.

"Who's that?"

"Huh?" I thought she was asking about one of the Dracs, which struck me as odd as she'd seen them all before, but then I followed her gaze. A final occupant was climbing out of the big helicopter. What the...?

The runners with the canopy had departed with the First Coven, not daring to let a single ray of sunshine fall upon their regal asses, but that didn't seem to matter. I'd joked about imperial guards, but this guy really rounded out the illusion with his black cloak and hood. He was hunched over, so all I could see of him was a white beard that hung almost to the ground.

Clipped to his waist was a two-pronged silver dagger, the points just far enough apart to poke out a person's...

"You've gotta be kidding me. Not this fucking clown again," I said, louder than intended, even with the two choppers still circling above.

The last vamp looked up, having almost certainly heard me. Though I knew he couldn't see me, he turned my way regardless and bared his teeth below the ragged and bloodied sockets where his eyes should have been.

47

EYEBALLING THE COMPETITION

Fortunately for me, the Draculas were still the stars of the show. For all I knew, the eyeless weirdos who hung out in the drug cave beneath Chillon Castle in Switzerland weren't even known to the general vampire populace.

Regardless, Colin and his people mostly ignored the head seer in favor of the Dracs. I watched as the ass-kisser bowed deeply before Alex, then to the others, almost as if they were an afterthought. Way to win brownie points, dickhead.

No words were exchanged so far as I could tell, just him leading the way toward the temporary headquarters he'd set up. In the chaos, Sheila and I were nearly forgotten ... nearly.

Not that we really had anywhere to go. Besides, our presence would hopefully mean our friends' absence would be ignored. No offense to either of them, but they didn't have prophecies hanging over their heads, at least so far as I knew. Maybe eye-scream boy would have something to say to that.

Speaking of the weirdo, just as he reached the cover of the canopy, two guards – the same who'd fetched us earlier – approached and told us our presence was required as well. It wasn't quite an order, but it definitely wasn't a suggestion. Unfortunately, thanks to the pace the seer was hobbling along at, we caught up to him fairly quickly.

305

Once we were within ten feet, he stopped and spun, quick as a mongoose. I had to remember, this guy might look frail, but there was no telling how old he was. If he was in charge of the freak show from which the vampire nation's end of the world predictions flowed, chances were he was no spring chicken.

He sniffed in our direction and smiled, revealing chipped and ragged fangs.

Sheila and I both stopped as he took a long pull of the air and hissed something I didn't even remotely understand.

"You catch that?" Sheila whispered, as if it would do any good.

"Nope. Didn't take crazy in high school."

The freaky geezer continued to face us, either not knowing or caring that the rest of his entourage were leaving us all behind. As our Mexican standoff continued, something strange happened. I mean, it shouldn't have been weird, knowing what I knew about vamp physiology, but it still was. The bloody pulp inside his eye sockets began to pulse and bubble. Had this been Halloween, I'd have thought it a neat effect. In this context, though, it was halfway between freaky and gross.

"Are you seeing this?" Sheila asked.

"Interesting choice of words," I replied as the oozing mass began to fill out the open wounds in the vamp's face. The bloody liquid inside them began to clear and brown irises formed, followed by pupils. The newly formed eyes dilated once, then focused directly on us. There was no kindness behind the foul gaze as the ancient vamp glared at us for a moment before cackling out a laugh that raised the hackles on my neck.

Who knew how long it had been since this guy had seen anything? Decades, centuries, more? So I figured it only right that he catch an eyeful of me flipping him the bird.

I'd no more than raised a one-fingered salute, though, when his newly regrown eyes exploded into a shower of fresh blood. He'd drawn his dagger and blinded himself again, so quickly I hadn't even seen his hand move.

Despite what had to be excruciating pain, the seer continued to laugh even as he turned away and continued onward.

I glanced back at the two guards who'd been escorting us, similarly frozen in place. "It's not just me, is it? That dude is creepy as fuck, right?"

The looks on their faces said they agreed, but duty prevailed and the one on the left merely said in a shaky voice, "They're waiting for you. Please keep moving."

We did, going extra slow so as to give Grandpa Munster a wide berth.

"What the hell was that about?" Sheila asked after several seconds.

"I don't know. Maybe that blouse doesn't go with those pants after all."

I was beginning to think we should have followed Sally and Tom out that window. The First Coven were scary as fuck, but their guest struck me as the kind of crazy one didn't turn their back on. Hell, an eternity as Gan's pool boy sounded preferable to five minutes alone in a back alley with Dr. Cyclops there.

I remembered back to my first meeting with him and his buddies, when I'd accidentally opened my mouth at the wrong time and sent them into a murderous rage. Even Alex had almost seemed worried, but at the time I'd dismissed it as either a trick of my imagination or a side effect of those guys being high as balls on the fumes they sucked down all day.

Now I found myself wondering if perhaps I hadn't imagined it after all. A man with a plan was one thing, but a crazy motherfucker who wanted to watch the world burn was a whole other issue.

Weirded out as we were, though, Sheila didn't appreciate my suggestion that we set him and Bernadette up on a blind date. I caught an elbow to the ribs for that. But it did serve to bring up the question of where the Templar were and what had happened to them since we'd last seen them. All we knew for certain was they weren't here now. Good thing, too, because I had a feeling shit was gonna get real.

Colin had ordered everything but the load-bearing walls knocked out on one floor of his temporary command. This left a space that was open but still dark thanks to the blacked out windows.

As Sheila and I entered, a vamp guard snapped his fingers and a few lights were lit, the hum of a gas generator audible somewhere nearby. I guessed they realized if it were too dark, Sheila would need to ignite her aura to see. That would almost certainly have ended badly.

In the center of the space sat a line of ten chairs, a true mismatch cobbled together in an obvious panicked haste. A couple of dining room chairs, some bar stools, a beanbag, and a La-Z-Boy recliner in the middle. It was a far cry from the regal thrones upon which the Draculas had sat during our trial. One would have almost thought we were being gathered to discuss this year's family vacation instead of far more serious matters.

I stifled a smirk as I caught sight of Colin, embarrassment etched so deeply onto his face that it almost looked tattooed.

The Dracs were all seated, looking none too pleased at the trailer trash level of décor. Heh! If I didn't think I'd be summarily executed, I would've pulled out my phone and snapped a picture.

Behind the Dracs stood their honor guard, one for each of the First present. At opposite ends of the lineup were the big guys with the miniguns. Though I couldn't see their faces through their mirrored helmets, their stances gave me the impression they were itching for an excuse to ventilate someone.

Colin's vamps all stood at attention in neat rows, their dress ranging from near perfect to "Can you spare some change, sir?" The greasy douchebag was at their forefront, almost directly opposite Alex. I almost felt sorry for Colin, for about a nanosecond anyway. I was far more sorry Sally wasn't here to see him like this. She could have used a pick-me-up of this caliber.

That was everyone, everyone except ... ah, there he was. The eyeless creep skulked in the shadows off in a corner, his robe making him nearly invisible. Only a quick gleam off his bloodied dagger gave him away. I made a mental note to keep track of him. No way did I want to turn around and find him standing right there behind me. Lack of heartbeat notwithstanding, I didn't think that was a system shock my poor body could withstand.

"I must admit, Prefect Kennelsbeth," Alex began, "I am somewhat taken aback by the condition upon which I find the Boston Prefecture. Was it not intact mere days ago?"

Kennels... oh, whatever the fuck. It stood to reason the douche had a last name. What was more important was that Alex wasn't focusing on us yet. For now, I might as well enjoy the show.

"My lord, if I may?" Colin replied. Alex gave the barest of nods. "You are aware of the ... sub-optimal conditions upon which we reclaimed the facility, yes?"

"Of course."

"The Destroyer left the defense grid in a state of disrepair. Between that and the edict to cull the untrustworthy, we were left in a vulnerable position."

"So you are laying the blame at our feet?"

The look on Colin's face was priceless. If I'd had the means, I'd have captured it for posterity's sake and wallpapered my entire apartment with it.

"It appears to me that the Prefect was a victim of circumstance," Yehoshua said from Alex's left. "I do not think it necessary to..."

"I would prefer the Prefect answer for himself, brother," Alex interrupted.

"Agreed," a short woman of Polynesian descent said from a few seats to Alex's right. "The Boston Prefecture was the jewel of this continent, the seat of power from which our dictates flowed. It has influenced events here since before this country was officially established and never once been bowed or broken. Yet now we find it laid low in the span of a day."

"Indeed, sister Zyra," Alex replied.

I leaned toward Sheila and whispered, "I'm trying to picture the pilgrims landing here and finding a car wash waiting for them."

"Thank you for that insight, Freewill," Alex said.

Damnit! Should have known better.

"Suffice it to say, the facade of the prefecture has changed significantly with the times."

"Yeah, I kinda..."

"Do shut up, boy," another of the Dracs spat, a middle-aged lady of seemingly indeterminate European origin. "Need I remind you..."

"Need *we* remind you who we are?" Sheila interrupted, causing all heads in the room to whip in her direction, mine included.

My first instinct was to back up and deny any connection to the person crazy enough to mouth off to the Dracs. These guys were badass to the extreme. Still, that probably wouldn't have raised anyone's opinion of me.

Sheila spared a glance my way and raised the corner of her mouth in a half smile. Fuck it! These were the end days. If I was gonna get my ass killed, I might as well give people a good reason to do it. Fortune favors the bold, after all.

"She's right. We're not here as your prisoners today. There's no trial going on, no audience to impress and, quite frankly, we're doing this all in a fucking dump that makes my apartment look regal by comparison. So what say we drop the formalities just this once?"

I flashed a smile of my own toward Sheila, to which she

shrugged uncomfortably, her meaning clear – I might have gone a wee bit overboard.

The sound of chambered rounds and disengaged safeties seemed to agree with that assessment as we suddenly found a whole lot of firepower aimed at us.

Despite the old saying, I had a feeling it would be a lot more painful to burn out than fade away.

48

STOMPING ON THE FEET

Sheila stood frozen by my side, staring at the weapons pointed our way by the First Coven's honor guard. I grabbed her hand, forgetting for a moment that being in contact with her might be a bad idea once the lead started flying.

Fingers tightened around triggers and I resigned myself to the fact that the next couple of seconds were going to really suck.

"I need not remind anyone that the Shining One is currently under protection of truce."

The guns couldn't have lowered any faster had their owners dropped them. I heard a deep sigh of relief at my side that I was tempted to echo, save that Alex hadn't included me in his proclamation.

"As the Freewill was the one responsible for *negotiating* this truce, I will allow his impertinence to be struck from the record." He then turned my way. "Would it be too much to ask that, if you are not capable of keeping this hearing formal, that you at least remain civil?" Despite the edge in his voice, his eyes sparkled. Fucker was enjoying this.

"My apologies," I replied. "Armageddon has me a bit on edge."

"As it does us all," he said, his tone implying it didn't in the least. "I have appraised my brothers and sisters of the situation, as well as my trusted advisors. All others present, ***YOU WILL FORGET THE DETAILS OF WHAT IS SAID HERE ONCE WE ARE FINISHED!!***"

The compulsion washed over the room. The sheer power of it caused the walls to creak, plaster to fall from the ceiling, and my eyeballs to almost pop out of my skull. Goddamn, that guy had some firepower at his disposal.

It gradually died down to a dull roar in my head. Once I was sure nothing important in my brain was going to rupture, I took a look around. Save for the Dracs and Sheila, everyone else in the room stood at attention, their eyes glazed as the compulsion took hold. Heh, even Colin was caught up in it. If I didn't think it would violate Alex's definition of being civil, I'd have taken advantage of the moment and cock-punched the weasel.

Hold on. Creepy eyeless guy seemed to be fine, too. If anything, he appeared to be cackling soundlessly at everything playing out. Why was there always one nutjob in the crowd?

"Now, where were we? Ah, yes. Prefect Kennelsbeth, I believe you were offering your explanation as to the events that transpired."

Colin's eyes cleared, the glaze replaced by panic. "Y-yes, my lord," he stammered. "The culling left us understaffed. I had to order the remaining men to triple their efforts in the repairs."

"And you did not think to postpone the culling until after the repairs were finished?" an ugly, grey-haired troll of a Drac with warts on his nose asked. I was glad to see not everyone in the room was a fashion show reject.

"I ... interpreted Lord Alexander's orders as being of utmost importance to carry out immediately."

"You thought to interpret orders as you saw fit? You..."

"That will be enough, Gaius," Alex interrupted. "Indeed that was my intent."

"It was perhaps a short-sighted intent, brother," Yehoshua said. "How many were culled that didn't need to be?"

"The threat of Ib is not to be taken lightly," Alex fired back. "We have already been made fools once by her. I will not sit back and let our ranks be infiltrated by her minions because we were too soft-hearted to do what needed to be done."

Soft-hearted? The Draculas? Holy shit, if that wasn't a paradox worthy of ending all life in the universe, I didn't know what was.

"Prefect Kennelsbeth is the Wanderer's protégé, is he not?" Alex continued. "He has served us honorably for centuries. I would trust his instincts in carrying out..."

"Was not the deceiver Ib also pretending to be a student of the Wanderer?" Troll-Faced Gaius asked. "Hers was a cancer that grew in our midst unseen for eons. Why should we offer this creature any quarter knowing he might be in league with her? For all we know, he himself opened the gates to the Grendel and invited them in."

"No!" Colin cried out, then, no doubt remembering he wasn't protected by any truce, quickly added, "My apologies. I meant no disrespect, my lords. I would never do such. I would have defended my post to the death had it come to it."

"Then why did you not?" Gaius asked. I got the impression this guy didn't like Colin too much. I wasn't quite ready to team up with him, though. Dude looked pretty ornery, the sort who didn't really like anyone. Still, even I was curious how the fucking greaseball was gonna weasel his way out of this one.

"The attack came with no warning," Colin replied, looking a bit desperate. "Had it simply been the Grendel, we would have held, I assure you. But the Magi; they came from out of nowhere. They struck from all sides. Our defenses were smashed before we could properly respond. I myself set the facility to self-destruct, prepared to perish along with our secrets. It was my men who pulled me out." He gestured toward a group of guards to his left, maybe a third of the people at his disposal. "They disobeyed my orders and dragged me to safety."

"Is this true?" Alex asked them.

Colin's minions seemed at a loss for words at having been thrown under the bus. Me, I wasn't surprised. I had little doubt Colin was the first one out the door once things went bad.

The vamps in question looked nervously at each other, as if hoping one of their number would speak up. Talk about being between a rock and a hard place. It was either take a bullet for your boss or rat him out and hope he didn't survive.

That was assuming they could even do so. Fucker could have compelled them to keep their pie holes shut so that...

My thoughts scattered to the wind as what sounded like a chainsaw echoed throughout the room. It was only when the vamps in question all burst aflame from the inside out that I realized it had been the roar of one of the miniguns.

"You ... you killed them!" Sheila cried.

"Indeed," Alex said. "Our way is one of absolute obedience."

"But you didn't even give them a chance."

"Mercy is a privilege these days, one that is not to be doled out lightly." He turned back to Colin. "I have given you the benefit of the doubt as per your station of Prefect and will consider the matter closed for now." He turned to address the rest of his coven. "Our intelligence has confirmed a decrease in Grendel hostilities worldwide since this incursion. This is curious considering the recent offensive by the Magi, up until recently considered a neutral party. Our enemies should be primed to strike a critical blow against us, but they have not."

"It is possible they are taking advantage of the zealotry of their new allies, utilizing them as fodder so as to conserve their own strength," the sour-faced bitch who'd talked smack to me earlier said.

"Perhaps, sister Kathryn," Alex replied. "The declaration

of war by the Magi has been sporadic, however. Some cells have reasserted their neutrality, while others have engaged wholeheartedly in this mad affair. They have to know that a non-unified front will simply not work against us, even now. The Grendel, too. A coordinated, global effort on their part, all striking simultaneously, would have been disastrous for us. Instead, they allowed the element of surprise to pass."

Yehoshua lifted a hand to stroke his beard. "Do not dismiss them as a threat so lightly, brother. The loss here is a significant one, and many other covens are reporting casualties as well."

Alex dismissed that with a wave of his hand. "Scattered attacks at best, many of which have not been particularly strategic in nature. It is chaotic, the work of novices. Our ancient enemies might be lesser beasts, but they have played this game long enough to have grown cunning. I see none of this at play now." He turned back to Colin. "Which brings us to why we are here to begin with. I believe you said you had information that could be of use."

Colin spared a momentary glance my way, a grin replacing the panic. He'd no doubt noticed my earlier glee at his dilemma and decided payback was gonna be a bitch.

This time I was ready for him, though.

"Yes, my lord," Colin began. "Earlier this day, we observed figures emerging from the unnaturally grown woods nearby – what appeared to be two vampires and a human dragging a third injured party. They were accompanied by one of the Grendel."

"Prisoners?" Yehoshua asked.

"Or traitors," Gaius added. Oh yeah, let the ass-fucking begin.

"Unknown at the time, my lords," Colin replied. "I wisely told my men to hang back and observe. We watched as one of them approached the ruins of our once great fortress and then leapt inside as if in search of something."

Oh yeah, that. Not my finest moment.

"Did they find what they were looking for?" Zyra asked.

"I do not know. You will have to ask the perpetrator yourself." Almost as if on cue, Colin pointed a finger at me. How surprising.

"The Freewill?" Alex asked with mock horror. Goddamn, these assholes loved their spectacle.

"I..." No. Telling them I lost my footing wouldn't exactly help my standing here. "I was searching for survivors, as I'd like to think any loyal servant of the Boston Prefect would." And the crowd goes wild as Bill Ryder returns the volley over the net!

"Very well," Alex replied. "A judicious answer."

"Thanks. I've been trying to pay better attention."

"But that doesn't answer the question of the company you were keeping or what you were doing here. I thought we had agreed to share information. I would hate to think I am the only one upholding our arrangement."

Before I could answer, Colin jumped back in. He was probably sensing a noose around my neck and hoped for a chance to kick the chair out from beneath me. "The other vampire was Sally Sunset, member of Village Coven and former master of the no longer extant Pandora Coven. The human is an associate of the Freewill's. There is something odd about him that we may wish to..."

Alex waved his hand in a hurry along motion. Hah! As if mere humans were worth his time ... even ones that melted when exposed to Faith magic.

"Sorry, my lord."

"The final member of their party? The injured one?"

"The Icon, my lord."

"Truly?" Alex replied, tenting his hands beneath his chin.

"How is that possible?" Yehoshua asked. If he was still miffed about Thea, he wasn't showing it, at least not at the moment.

"That was my question as well," Colin replied. "I naturally assumed them to be imposters and set my men upon them. It was only some time later, after we'd suffered even more losses, that I realized their identity was true. I, of course, immediately deferred to your standing orders of cease-fire."

"Good man, though I would expect no less," Alex said, earning a pleased grin from Colin's smarmy mug.

"Of course not."

Alex turned toward us. "Are you injured, my dear? Do you require medical assistance?"

She glanced my way for a second, a questioning look in her eye. She hadn't been expecting that. "Um, no. I mean, I'm okay now. Thank you for asking."

Alex's mouth spread in a smile. It was probably meant to be comforting, but he'd drawn his fangs, thus giving it a predatory leer. "I am thankful to hear that. Know that so long as we are bonded by our word, I will do all I can to assure your safety. Alexander of Macedon brings death to his enemies, but forever stands by an ally."

Sheila gave him an uncomfortable nod back.

"Perhaps I will ask one of our physicians to examine you nevertheless, just to be certain. I, of course, insist." Before she could say a word, he turned back to Colin. "This is all very interesting, Prefect, but what does it have to do with furthering our cause?"

Colin appeared miffed that two of his potential brownie points had been seemingly glossed over, but he quickly composed himself. "I was just getting to that, my lord." He clapped his hands and addressed his remaining men. "Bring forth the final member of their party. Bring forth the Grendel."

49

OPEN MOUTH INSERT FOOT

Grulg was only semi-conscious as they dragged him in. Despite being surrounded by enough vamps to make escape nigh impossible, they weren't taking any chances. Thick chains bound him and heavy manacles hung around his wrists and ankles. It wasn't dissimilar to how a human prisoner might be shackled for transportation, except that his restraints looked about a hundred pounds heavier.

The floor creaked beneath the big ape's weight, reminding me this was all happening in some poor schmuck's former living room and that Grulg was about to be judged by folks sitting on IKEA furniture. Just a wee bit surreal.

As he passed us, Grulg shook his head as if clearing the cobwebs. He turned our way and we locked eyes. I couldn't help but feel guilty. A member of the race who most hated us in this world or not, I hadn't wanted this. All the same, we had friends who needed saving. There was never really a choice.

A snarl crossed Grulg's face and, despite his sorry state, he lunged at us. The guards escorting him were all armed with cattle prods, though, and he fell to his knees twitching before he could take more than a few steps.

319

"This is wrong," Sheila said quietly, turning away from me.

"I know." I reached out to put a hand on her shoulder, but then thought better of it ... only partially because of the company in the room. "But remember what I told you. This is our world now, and it's not a very nice place."

She glanced over her shoulder and gave me a sad smile. "I seem to remember throwing that back in your face not too long ago."

"Yeah. I think maybe it's something we both need reminding of."

Grulg was brought before the First Coven. At that point, Colin's men stopped and looked around, seeming confused. That's when I realized they were trying to find something to secure him to. Hah! Good luck. It would take a lot more than some drywall anchors to hold him in place.

"That will not be necessary," Alex said with a sigh after a few moments. He waved them off, then stepped forward. Grulg growled and tensed his legs – as best he could anyway – as if to attack.

"You know who I am?" Alex asked, sounding almost bored.

Grulg snarled, then spat a blood-soaked loogie at Alex's feet.

If this was meant to intimidate the once and would-be future conqueror, it didn't. He took another step forward, well inside Grulg's limited reach.

"Lord Alexander?" Colin asked, but Alex shut him up with a sideways glance.

"Know this, beast," Alex said, "I am Alexander of the First Coven. I have slain thousands of your kind with my bare hands. The exact number is unimportant, but know I could drown you in a river of the blood I have spilled from your brethren."

If Alex was trying to goad Grulg, he was doing a hell of a job. The Bigfoot's eyes opened wide in rage and he bellowed a roar that shook the floorboards. He reached out with his cuffed hands and grabbed Alex by the throat.

Much as I felt guilty, I still took a small measure of enjoyment from it.

That is, until Alex peeled Grulg's hands off with seemingly little effort. It was quite the sight to watch. Alex wasn't a particularly tall guy – a bit below average, actually – so watching him power an eight-foot gorilla to its knees was pretty damn mind-blowing. Sally had proven time and again that size meant nothing in the supernatural world, but that didn't mean seeing it happen would ever stop surprising me.

Once Grulg was down to eye-level, Alex bitch-slapped him for good measure. The sound was like a crack of thunder in the enclosed space. Grulg's head whipped to the side and he spat out a tooth. Ooh!

With that, Alex turned and walked back to his lounge chair. "Know that each of my brothers and sisters is capable of the same. I say this so you know that escape is impossible. Have I made myself clear?"

Grulg stared at Alex with hateful eyes, but Alex stared right back until Grulg broke contact.

Finally, acknowledging that he'd been beaten, Grulg said, "*T'lunta clear.*"

"Good. That was not so hard, was it? Remember your station and this need not end badly." He then addressed Colin. "You said he was with the Freewill, did you not?"

"Yes, my lord."

Here it comes.

As expected, Alex turned my way, that bemused look reappearing upon his chiseled mug. "Please enlighten us, Freewill. I always look forward to your unique take on circumstances."

I was sorely tempted to tell him to take a flying fuck off the nearest church steeple at high noon. Instead, I told him the truth ... or at least a heavily edited version. Hey, I was trying to cover my ass. Discussing the unsanctioned peace conference was probably best saved for another day.

I told them of how Sally and I had been captured by the Jahabich during our time in Vegas. How Grulg was a fellow prisoner with whom I'd formed a temporary truce in order to escape.

"Calling upon the provisions of the Humbaba Accord despite it being in abeyance?" Alex asked. "Resourceful."

"*Grulg should have died,*" the Sasquatch moaned. "*Then at least T'lunta die, too.*"

Colin waved a hand and one of his people jabbed Grulg with a cattle prod, shutting him up.

"That will be enough, Prefect," Alex said well after the fact. Quite the merciful fellow. "If I may be presumptuous for a moment, Freewill, shall I assume you and this creature followed separate routes to freedom?"

"Bingo," I replied. "We caved in our escape tunnel with explosives, but I'm willing to bet monkey boy here hadn't thought that far ahead."

"And why are we just now learning you have seen the lair of the enemy with your own two eyes?" Gaius asked. That guy was starting to annoy me a bit. He'd been mostly silent during our trial, but now seemed to find his voice. Apparently someone shit in his cornflakes this morning and he was here to take it out on the rest of us.

"For starters, at the time, we didn't realize the significance of it. I mean, the Jahabich incursions up to that point had mostly been localized. Later on, well, we were busy being tried for our lives and then carrying out our sentence. Nobody seemed particularly interested in seeing our vacation photos while that was all going on."

"I am not Alexander, boy. I do not find you amusing. You would be well advised to mind your tone."

I mulled that over for a moment. The safe thing to do would be to apologize respectfully. But there was no safe anymore, not really.

The dull anger that had been threatening to take over reared itself in the back of my head. There was no way I was letting it out now. Not with this crowd. Even with Dr.

Death's power, that was a losing strategy. But I let some of it seep in regardless.

"How about you mind my dick and use it to go fuck yourself instead?"

And with that, all eyes in the room were on me. Ah, gotta love the spotlight.

Stunned silence met my response. Heck, from the look on Gaius's face, you'd have thought I'd walked up, dropped my pants, and cock-slapped him right there.

Even Sheila's mouth was agape.

I realized I probably should keep going. If I insulted this asshole and left it at that, I was dead. A cherry needed to be put on top, one that ensured I walked out of here alive – a position I'd just put into considerable peril.

Throwing Sheila a quick wink, I turned to the front of the room before they could sentence me to immediate execution. "Let's get something straight, guys. You're the ruling council, I accept that. But right now, I'm under protection of truce and the reason for that is because you need me."

"Need I remind you, Freewill, the truce you speak of was between the Shining One, the Templar, and a small coven of Magi," Alex said. That infuriatingly bemused grin was still on his face, so that meant I probably had a few seconds to dig myself out. "You were simply its proctor. However, in light of the recent actions of the Magi, I may need to rethink..."

"My friends aren't a part of that," I interrupted. "They want to stop Ib as much as any of us."

"How can we know this?"

"You can't," I replied, steeling myself. "But I can. They're *my* friends. They won't betray us. That is, *unless* something happens to me. You want to kill me for mouthing off, fine, but if you do, you're guaranteed they'll be standing against you."

"And what of it?" Zyra scoffed. "Are you seriously trying

to tell us that Ib the First cannot be vanquished without the help of a handful of children?"

Again, I turned Sheila's way. She gave me a supportive nod to go on. I wondered if she'd have done so if she knew I was making this shit up as I went.

"I'm not going to pretend we're going to march in there and win singlehandedly. But I do know one thing. I'm the Freewill. I'm the lone vampire on this planet who is capable of fully resisting her will."

Yeah, between Gan and Ed, that was bullshit, but the devil was always in the details.

"Standing by my side is the Icon, the only person alive who Ib's magic can't touch. Our allies are the Templar, and though you may scoff at them as little more than mere humans, they are warriors devoted to their God. They bring..."

Someone coughed. I turned my head and saw it was Colin. What the fuck? Was he making "Bullshit" sounds into his hand? What a prick.

"Anyway, the Templar bring with them the power of faith, a potent weapon against our foe. Finally, there are the Magi. Though they are small in number compared to those who now fight for Ib, they are wise to the ways of their people, a strategic advantage you'd be foolish to turn away."

Damn, that went better than I thought it would. Even I was impressed by the bullshit I was able to spew when I got my panties in a bunch.

"Well said, Freewill," Alex replied after a moment. "You do put forth a compelling argument. But even so, I believe you may be overstating your importance to this mission. Still, I will allow this presumption if the others agree."

"You would let this lout insult us and pay no price?" Gaius roared. He stood and pointed a finger my way. "Are we not the First? Are we not above reproach?"

"I take it you do not agree?" Alex asked, his tone even.

"I would have this fool's life. We have survived for over half a millennium without the Freewills. Their time has passed. We no longer need them. Let us send this child to whatever Hell the rest of his kind now rot in."

"You do that and you're fucked," I shot back. Hmm, perhaps not the most eloquent way of putting things, but sometimes you gotta play to your strengths. "I meant, you can kill me if you want. I doubt I could stop you."

"You doubt..."

"Fine, I *highly* doubt it. Whatever." I remembered a passage Dave had once read us when we were about to assault the Ice Troll Fortress at Frozen Corpse Pass. "But the truth remains, you will only be sealing the pact of your own doom if you follow this dark path."

"You think yourself that important?" Zyra asked.

"Let him finish," Yehoshua said. "I am intrigued by this show of fortitude."

"Thanks," I replied. "It's simple. I don't think I'm that important in the grand scheme of things. I'm just a programmer from Brooklyn who got caught up in all of this. Fate, however, seems to think differently. You are all aware of the prophecy, yes?"

The various members of the Draculas mumbled among themselves for a moment – all except Alex, who continued to stare at me with his mismatched eyes. I caught some movement in my periphery and saw I even had the blind weirdo's attention. He'd actually moved forward, his head cocked as if listening. Made sense. After all, he and his asshole buddies had been the ones to make the stupid prophecy in the first place.

"It states," I continued, "and I paraphrase, that in the very last days of this war, the Icon and Freewill will do battle. Winner takes all. I win, and the world is cloaked in darkness. She wins, and goodness, light, and baby bunny rabbits prevail." Okay, maybe that was spreading it on a bit thick.

Gan had already pointed out that was complete rubbish. Alex had also once confided in me that he'd manipulated events so as to make them match the prophecy. The rest of this group, however, I was willing to bet weren't privy to those plans.

Time to see if my bluff skill was up to snuff.

I stepped forward, addressing Gaius ... fucking stupid name anyway. "I can see you know what I'm talking about. Well, genius, kill me now if you want, but if you do, you're handing victory to the Icon. Vehron is dead. I'm the last Freewill. Without me, it'll be sunshine and happiness, and the rest of the First Coven can thank you for that. So what's it gonna be, Baltar? I ain't got all day to die."

And there it was. I'd either cemented my rep for any doubters present or given them a nice epitaph to put on whatever urn they swept me into.

50

THE GATHERING STORM

Gaius was fit to be tied. I don't think any vamp had ever mouthed off to the assembled Draculas in recorded history and lived to tell the tale.

And you could be sure as shit I was gonna tell people. No way was Sally not getting an earful of this. Even better, I had a witness to back me up.

The rest of the room stared in wide-eyed silence. It kinda made me sad I'd sent Tom away. He might've been a doofus, but he appreciated the awesomeness of knocking assholes down a peg. Oh well, spilt milk and all that bullshit.

I continued to stand there unmolested as the seconds drew themselves out, all eyeballs on me – albeit not all of them friendly.

Finally, Alex turned toward the back. "Seer of the Mists, what say you?"

The hooded weirdo stepped slightly forward from the shadows.

"Yeah, about that," I said. "Why exactly is Sierra Mist here again? I thought he and his buddies were all about sucking fumes in their cave."

Alex's frown turned upside down. "It is interesting that you bring up the prophecy in your defense, Freewill, because that is exactly why he is present. It is the seers' belief as well

327

that the time of prophecy is nigh. Though it goes against the edicts of his order, he has requested to be present so as to record its passing. I allowed such."

I gave him a thumbs up, then promptly shut it as the blind guy began to speak in his dead language, pausing to cackle with every other breath. There was a dude with a serious case of the crazies.

After a few minutes of this, Alex said, "The seer and I are in agreement that the Freewill makes a convincing argument. Mind you, it is **ONE NONE HERE SHALL EVER SPEAK OF!!**"

The compulsion hit me in the face like a pile driver. I flew back into a group of Colin's people, scattering them like dominos. When my vision cleared enough for me to look up again, I saw Alex standing over me.

"While I commend you for your rousing speech and surprisingly impeccable logic, I think we can all agree that word of this spreading would be counterproductive. The First are above reproach, after all."

I had a feeling another compulsion like that at close range would knock me out cold, so I simply nodded. Fine, let the babies have their bottle.

Alex took his seat as if the last few minutes hadn't happened. "I believe you were telling us about the Grendel, were you not?"

Alex wasn't stupid by any stretch of the imagination. He was able to put two and two together. Obviously, my goal in tracking down Grulg had been to learn how to find Calibra again. I shared this information, thus keeping my end of the bargain. Thankfully, he chose not to question that.

"Prefect Kennelsbeth claims you seemed to be on amicable terms with the Grendel," Alex said.

I stepped forward, keeping about ten feet between me and Grulg. "It was a necessary ruse to..."

Grulg suddenly snarled and pulled at his restraints. "*Enemy of the peace!*" he bellowed. "*Enemy forever! Die, T'lunta!*" There came a groan of metal and, amazingly, he managed to break one of his arms free.

Though his legs were still shackled, he was able to bend his knees enough to launch himself at me before his handlers could get him under control. He cocked his free fist back so as to smash me into pulp.

This was gonna hurt.

I was right, but in a different way.

While everyone else had been transfixed by what was happening, save the Draculas who probably thought they were too good to help me, Sheila dove forward for the save ... sorta.

She stepped in between me and Grulg and ignited her aura.

Grulg screamed in pain as the resulting crackle of power caught us both. It was a glancing blow, but I nevertheless found myself hurtling through the air. Thankfully, my fall was broken by someone unlucky enough to have been in the way.

Before I could breathe a sigh of relief, a clawed hand grabbed hold of my throat and flung me nearly the length of the room. I slammed into a kitchen cabinet hard enough to turn it into kindling and then crashed to the floor, dazed.

"Enough!" a voice roared, rudely rousing me from the dreamland I'd been headed toward. "Remove that beast from this place now. We will extract what we need from him afterwards."

The cobwebs began to clear and I realized it was Alex speaking. Hope he wasn't talking about me, because that would just be plain rude.

"Bill! Are you okay?" asked a voice that was definitely not Alex's. "I'm so sorry."

Sheila stepped to my side a moment later and helped me extract myself from a pile of Tupperware bowls. "Never a matching lid when you need one."

"What?"

"Huh?" I asked her, then shook my head. "Never mind. Thanks for the assist."

"I didn't mean to blast you." She lowered her voice. "Or knock you into that Gaius fellow."

That figured. Asshole had probably considered it a gift from heaven. He'd gotten his pound of flesh. Hopefully that made him happy for the moment. "Grulg?" I asked.

"Angry, but alive."

I nodded, and got back to my feet just in time to see him being dragged out. He looked pretty singed, and pissed as all hell, but he was definitely still kicking. Once again, I had to remind myself it was either him or Ed.

A few minutes later found me standing in front of the Draculas again, a new chair having been procured for Gaius, who continued to stare venomously at me. Guess he wanted two pounds of flesh.

"You alone defeated the Grendel?" Yehoshua asked as I finished telling Alex how I lured Grulg here under false pretenses.

"My friend Sally helped."

Alex leaned forward. "Where is she?"

"Not here."

He and I locked eyes. It was a losing proposition for me and I knew it. I never could hold someone's gaze without laughing, even as a child. Still, I tried.

"Tell me..."

"This Grendel," Zyra said, interrupting Alex. "He is one of their war chiefs, is he not?"

"I ... guess so."

"His name?"

"Grulg."

"Interesting. Prior to our arrival here, I received some inquiries on him through our diplomatic channels."

"Diplomatic channels?" Alex replied. "I thought they had been severed."

"They had been. They were re-opened without warning, questioning why he had been taken hostage."

Uh oh.

"Questioning?" Alex asked. "They do realize we are in a state of war, do they not?"

"I did not have a chance to request clarification," Zyra replied. "Our mission here took priority."

"Just as well," Alex replied dismissively.

"They know," I said, sensing a potential opportunity.

"Know what, Freewill?"

"Grulg's a loyal soldier," I explained. "I learned that much up in the Woods of Mourning. He's all into their dogma."

"And we should care why?" Kathryn asked.

"We shouldn't," I replied, "except that whatever he knew, he no doubt told his superiors. Think about it. They just signed the Magi to their side, a big win if ever there was one. Well, the mages didn't join up because of any hippie shit involving nature."

Alex nodded. "Our intelligence suggests Ib revealed her presence to Magi covens a few days ago."

I hesitated for a moment, not really wanting to divulge more than I should, but then remembered the minions here had all been compelled to forget everything. As for the Dracs, hopefully Alex had brought them up to speed. If not, they were about to get a crash course.

"Calibra, Ib, the White Mother ... all the same person. We know this, but I'm willing to bet she omitted the Ib part when she revealed herself to all those mages. She had to know doing that would make it less the second coming and more a remake of *Fright Night*."

"Yes, Freewill. As I said, we had surmised as much."

"That's why the Feet are asking about Grulg. He knows how to find Ib. The Feet know we have him. What he knows jeopardizes their new alliance. So of course they're going to be desperate to get him back." I almost had to smile. Such a nice web of bullshit I'd weaved. Now for the coup de grace.

"And if they can't get him back, they're going to make sure he can't talk."

I stood there enjoying the silence for a moment. Sparing a glance toward Colin, I grinned, putting every ounce of smugness I could into it.

Goddamn, some days being petty felt so good.

I was just about to ask Alex if he had any further questions when the room around us began to rumble. Nothing major, more like what one would expect from a large truck driving outside.

Except there wasn't any traffic of the sort last I'd been out there.

A booming sound came from outside that rattled the windows like a thunderstorm passing overhead. What the...?

The rattling grew worse until a set of windows on the north side of the building shattered just in time for something big to come falling out of the sky past them – something big and metallic. Kind of like a helicopter, one that was engulfed in green flame.

The fuck?!

Being petty felt good, but lately being right felt a lot less so.

The deafening squeal of metal crunching into more metal sounded from outside, and everyone stepped back as more flames – these the normal color – raced up from below where the copter had crashed.

That stuff I'd said about our enemies wanting Grulg dead if they couldn't rescue him had been complete bullshit – a fabrication I'd made up on the spot. Yet there was no denying it.

The Magi had returned.

Sadly, there wasn't much time to contemplate this as the entire building began to shake. Cracks appeared along the walls and plaster fell from the ceiling.

Shit!

"We need to get out of here!" I yelled, stating the bleeding obvious. Yeah, I was useful like that.

Colin's men began to scramble. So too did the majority of the Draculas. Based on Alex's reaction, or lack thereof, you'd have thought nothing particularly exciting had occurred.

He pointed a lazy finger Colin's way and the lackey froze in his tracks.

"My lord?" he asked tentatively. "The Freewill is right. We must vacate the premises now."

Kudos for me. Pity I wasn't going to be able to enjoy them buried under several tons of rubble if this building collapsed around us.

Still, I found myself mesmerized by Alex's calm demeanor.

"Come on, Bill!" Sheila grabbed my arm and tried to pull me along. As much as I appreciated it, she also wasn't the best person for a vampire to stand next to if the ceiling came down, but it was the thought that counted.

I held up a finger and mouthed "one second" to her. I kind of wanted to see what Alex was up to.

"Tell me, Prefect," Alex said in a voice as calm as a summer day. "Did you, by any chance, properly ward this building prior to our arrival?"

All the color drained out of Colin's face, quite the feat for someone who had a tan rivaling that of the Pillsbury Doughboy.

All at once, I understood. They weren't here for Grulg. No. A far more appealing target were all sitting in the same unfortified room – the entirety of the First Coven, with us as a bonus.

The mages couldn't scry Sheila, that much I knew, but the floor Colin had cleared was big enough so that her power didn't hold sway over it all. It was nothing more than dumb luck that she and I were here now.

Just great. We were going to die, too, as little more than the bloody icing on Ib's cake of death.

Alex's eyes continued to bore into Colin as more magical explosions rocked the building.

Finally, the little weasel stammered, "Forgive me, my..."

Before he could finish the sentence, Alex was across the room and standing in front of him. "Your incompetence grows tiresome," he said softly, barely audible to my ears over the din of battle.

With that, he backhanded Colin, the sound like a thunderclap even with what was going on outside. The greaseball went flying as if he'd been shot out of a cannon, slamming into one of the outer walls and then straight through it where I lost sight of him in the dust and smoke beyond.

Ooh, bet that hurt.

I turned to Sheila, a smile on my face. "*Now* we can go."

51

WATCHING THE WORLD BURN

W e ran for the exit. None too soon, as it felt like the place was shaking apart around us.

"Once we're outside," she said as we practically flew down the stairs together, "get behind me. Not too close, though. I'm going to draw their fire."

Good idea, except for one little thing. "What if they have us surrounded?"

"Then find a place to hide."

Even better.

I didn't like the idea of her wading into battle while I holed up like a pussy, but she was far better equipped to deal with magic users, especially now that she was back to her full capabilities. No way was I going to allow anyone to inject her with that Baal shit again, not if I could help it. Next time, we'd just take the long way.

We reached the outside door, and Sheila cried out for me to duck. I hit the deck just as a beam of red-hot death lanced toward us. It fizzled harmlessly against her power, but there was no doubt she'd painted a big white target on herself. Whichever entity faith magic originated from really needed to be taught the value of subtlety.

"Oh, crap," she muttered. "We need to move *now!*"

I threw the hood of my jacket over my head as she

doused her aura. Multiple beams of energy struck the side of the building, the strategy obvious. If they couldn't blast her, they'd try to bury her.

Not on my watch.

I whisked her off her feet and out the exit before heading left. Though it might've gotten me a kick to the nuts when this was over, the reality was she might be magic-proof, but I was a lot faster.

I dove behind an abandoned car on the far side of the street just as the building began to crumble. It came down in a rumble of debris, the immediate area filling with smoke and dust.

"Cover your mouth," I said. "Pretty sure the Surgeon General would call this shit hazardous to your health."

I wasn't too worried about getting asbestos-related cancer myself, but I did the same.

The one upside to this debacle was the cloud created by the building's destruction provided us with instant cover – from both the Magi and the sun. Despite the smoke, though, multiple beams of energy lanced out in all directions, telling me that death by daylight was currently the least of my concerns.

A dark shape appeared out of the gloom close by, wielding a massive weapon. The vamp holding the minigun pointed it our way for a moment, then apparently recognized us. He turned away and started returning fire toward anywhere a spell seemed to come from.

Soon, others joined him.

"Stay down," I warned Sheila, crouching protectively over her before realizing how ridiculous that was.

However, she apparently wasn't in on the joke, because she didn't try to stop me. All she did was sit there with a wide-eyed look on her face. I guess I couldn't blame her. It felt like we were in the middle of a blindfolded turkey shoot. Both sides fired wildly at where they presumed the enemy was, hitting mostly nothing in the process, but creating a shitload of crossfire.

Bullets ricocheted off the asphalt just a few feet away and I cried out, "Shoot at *them*, numbnuts! Not us!"

Fucking trigger-happy assholes.

"We might need to…"

To my surprise, Sheila shirked away from me, her eyes staring at where the gunfire had just hit.

"Um, are you okay?" After another moment, I added, "Hey!" She finally focused on me. "Are you all right?"

She gave me a shaky nod. "I'm fine."

"You didn't get hit, did you?"

"No, it's just…"

"Just what?" I recognized the look on her face. Hell, I knew it well. I'd seen it staring back from the mirror enough times. She was afraid. "Shit! You still have some of that crap in your bloodstream, don't you?"

"What crap?" she asked, still cowering.

"I'm sorry. I didn't think. I figured the last of that shit cocktail was out of your system."

"No. It's gone. I can feel it. I'm…" She shrieked as the car we were hiding behind was peppered with bullets.

Goddamned idiots. I swear the Dracs' honor guard wouldn't be happy until everything in a three-block radius looked like Swiss cheese. Right now, though, I had more pressing concerns, like an Icon who was apparently still going through withdrawal.

Despite knowing how potentially disastrous it could be, I moved closer to her. She immediately threw her arms around me and buried her face in my shoulder.

Comfort wasn't my strong suit. Worse, with her holding on to me, I could feel my old insecurities bubble to the surface. All of a sudden, words, so freely flowing just moments ago, began to get all jumbled in my head. "Um, it'll be … okay. As soon as that crap is out of your system you can…" Oh wow, she felt good pressed up against me. So warm, so alive.

Focus, moron! Any second now, we could be hit with a

Flamestrike. This was not the time to turn into a tongue-tied imbecile.

"You don't get it, do you?" she said, looking up at me, her eyes moist with fear. "This *is* me. That blood wore off."

"It can't be. You ... well, you look terrified."

"I am," she replied timidly.

"Since when?"

At that, her voice hardened. "Since that bastard Remington put a bullet into my head."

Holy crap. I'd never considered that. I had gotten the ever living shit blasted out of me more times than I cared to admit. But it was more the overarching task of trying to save the world that frightened the shit out of me. Remington was dead, out of sight out of mind, as far as I was concerned.

But the thing was, we'd thought Sheila had died in that incident, too. Now that I considered it, though, wouldn't something like that be harder on an Icon? Hell, I was accustomed to losing. After a while, you brushed that shit off and moved on with your life. But an Icon's entire power delved from their singular belief in themselves. It was a belief that empowered them up until the point of their death.

But what if they didn't die? What if an Icon was only badly injured? What could something like that do to their unflappable belief?

"I didn't know," was all I could think to say.

"I didn't want you ... *anyone* to know," she replied bitterly. "I'm not supposed to be like this, not now when the world is counting on me."

"So?"

"What?"

"So you're scared? So what?" I said. "Trust me, I'm pretty sure the only way I can fall asleep most nights is by passing out from sheer exhaustion."

She pulled away from me, albeit not so far that she was exposed. "You don't get it. I'm not *supposed* to be scared."

This was really not the time to be having this discussion. Almost as if to drive home the point, a beam of green flame lanced out from the smoke and hit our cover, melting the front half of the car into a slurry of steel and burning rubber. I almost pissed myself but, oddly enough, Sheila just kept glaring at me, ignoring what had happened. I didn't begin to understand. I mean, guns freaked her out, but a fucking death ray was no big deal? On the flip side, if I started adding up all the things in my life that didn't make any goddamned sense, I'd be working on it well into the next century.

Fuck it! Sometimes you gotta be direct.

I grabbed her by the shoulders and looked her in the eye, hoping she didn't pick that moment to ignite. "Who says you're not supposed to be scared – heroes who died thousands of years ago? The Templar, maybe?"

She didn't answer.

"Well, here's the thing. Fuck them all. You know what the difference between you and all of them is? That first group is dead and the rest are assholes. You're neither."

And that was about as much of a pep talk as I was capable of giving.

At first, I thought I'd pushed too hard and she was going to tell me to take my advice and go fuck myself with it, but then her gaze softened and a smile crept across her face. "Anyone ever tell you the world lost a great motivational speaker when you got bitten?"

"Truthfully?" I replied with a laugh. "Not really."

I didn't know a lot about phobias, PTSD, breakdowns, or any of that shit. Psychology wasn't one of my better subjects. Even so, I was pretty sure you didn't shake stuff like that just because a doofus wearing stolen clothes told you to get over it. It was a long process to heal, preferably away from places being torn to shreds by a firefight.

Thankfully, the vamps started to get their shit together. Fewer stray bullets came our way. Despite neither of us being at the top of this group's friend list, they seemed to be smart enough to realize plugging their so-called allies with friendly fire wasn't a winning strategy.

I heard rubble shifting nearby, back toward the ruined building. The smoke had cleared just enough for me to see vague shapes digging their way out of the rubble. Not too surprising. Most of the Dracs weren't going to die that easily. That was fine. Right then they were the lesser of evils, even if just barely.

"Can you flare up?" I asked Sheila.

She still had a wide-eyed look about her, but nodded.

"Good. Do so after I step back. Draw fire from the mages. Maybe give the others a chance to take out a few so we can make a run for it." Sue me for being a realist, but I didn't have any delusions of winning this.

"There will be no running. Not by us, anyway."

I turned toward the sound of the voice and saw Alex walking our way. His clothes were ripped and he was covered in dust, but he was very much alive. What a surprise.

"They're..."

"Right where I want them, Freewill," he replied. "Did you not stop to consider that I would have anticipated such a move?" Alex reached into his pocket and pulled out a cell-phone, somehow still intact. He pushed a few buttons on the number pad, then tossed it over his shoulder.

Well, duh. I could have told him he wouldn't get any reception. This whole section of town was a fucking disaster. It ... what the...?

"Do you feel that?" Sheila asked.

I did, a rumbling beneath my feet. That wasn't all, though. Whatever was causing it was getting closer.

Oh no, not them. Not now!

52

COUNTERINTUITIVE ATTACK

I stood amidst the rumbling with a look akin to terror on my face. Had Alex just called the Jahabich? Oh shit! Had Ib actually replaced him with one of them?!

He stared back, one eyebrow raised, before finally saying, "If I were you, I would retreat to the sidewalk post haste."

The rumbling grew stronger, but rather than the street opening up beneath our feet and a horde of orange-eyed monsters spewing forth, I heard the throaty growl of engines – powerful and numerous.

I looked toward where they seemed to be coming from, the exact opposite of where the magical forest lay, and began to make out large shapes in the gloom. They looked like...

"No fucking way."

Sheila grabbed my arm. "I think he's right, Bill. Maybe we should stand back a bit."

No shit on that, I considered, as the column of tanks advanced toward us.

That's when I remembered what Colin had said about the National Guard. Although, judging from Alex's pimp-slap, Colin wasn't the one responsible for this. No, this was too strategic in nature for that ass kisser. Alex had to know the risks flying in here, but he seemingly also had considered what was to be gained. They couldn't lose Boston so easily

341

without being seen as weak throughout the supernatural realm.

And he'd known the perfect bait to set his trap with: he and his coven.

The tanks rolled past us. A few took hits from errant magic, but the mages' offensive had turned clumsy. I imagined our attackers were every bit as surprised as I'd been. But this time, I had the advantage of not being the target.

"*LEVEL THE FOREST AND EVERYTHING IN IT!!*"

This close, there was no need for radios or walkie-talkies. Alex was content to let his compulsion do the talking for him.

Holy shit! I mean, I knew covens had dealings with the local police to keep annoyances such as murder investigations out of their hair, but I never imagined...

Hah! That was on me, though. I should have. The Draculas controlled the entire fucking nation of Switzerland, for Christ's sake. Not to mention I'd accidentally chowed down on one of the US Government's Joint Chiefs of Staff during my trial.

I'd thought Alex's mad culling party a stupid decision, disastrous even. But maybe he didn't need those troops after all. Sure, both sides had allies in the supernatural world, but whereas the Feet shunned technology, the Draculas embraced it. Tanks, planes, and guns were Alex's secret weapons all along. The entry of the Magi into the war had simply escalated his gambit.

Whatever mages were LARPing around in the woods were fucked. Yeah, they were potent, but guns could be reloaded a lot faster than they could replenish their energy.

One thing nearly all creatures of power had in common was runaway egos. The Magi had given the vamps a bloody nose by crushing the Boston complex. They were no doubt overconfident of an easy victory here, meaning I seriously doubted they expected a heavily armored mechanized division to bear down upon their wooded haven.

Wait a second... "Shit!"

"What's wrong?" Sheila asked, then realization seemed to hit. "The woods!"

"Tom and Sally," I confirmed. "Gan too."

The three of them – well, okay, Sally and Gan at least – were survivors. Regardless, there was simply no way I could resume our mission without knowing if they were okay. It was stupid of me not to trust in them and pure idiocy to leave now, especially when we still didn't have the information Grulg did. It was the height of naïvety to think Alex wouldn't notice us running off and assume the worst.

In short, just another day in my life.

"Let's go!"

This was a mistake, a stupid, stupid, stupid fucking mistake!

It was easy to overtake the tanks. Once we got past them, though, it was like walking into some bizarre Terminator-esque future. Cannon fire on one side, death rays on the other.

And once we entered the forest, there were falling trees to contend with, too. That would be just our luck, to dodge the worst the Magi and Draculas could throw at us only to get crushed by a falling maple.

What an ending that would make for all the prophesies and proclamations. "*The end of the world was nigh. The Icon and Freewill disappeared into the forest ... and then the next day, they were found dead under a log. The end. Now go the fuck to sleep, kids.*"

"Are you okay?" I asked as we both slipped past some thick foliage while explosions rang out all around us. We ducked beneath some cover, then got moving again once the debris raining down upon us had settled.

"Surprisingly, yes," she said with a smile.

"Even with all the cannon fire?"

"Go figure; not quite the same thing. Maybe they're too

big, or too surreal, but I'm doing okay. Let's just hope nobody jumps out from behind a tree with a handgun."

If she was able to joke about things, then she was probably all right, for now anyway. I didn't see any of that wild-eyed fear in her from before.

"Any luck tracking them yet?" she asked.

Sadly, I couldn't be as positive as she was. I gave my head a single shake. "Needle in a haystack. Tom's scent is neutral and there's no fucking way I know dead moose well enough to track it. I sort of made it a point to never remember Gan's scent, and we seem to have picked the one fucking day out of the year when Sally decided to not wear that overpriced perfume she likes to waste money on." My frustration boiled over and I backhanded a nearby root that was poking out, snapping it.

She placed a hand on my shoulder. "It's okay to be worried. I know she ... they mean a lot to you."

"She does," I replied, realizing my Freudian slip a moment too late.

Sheila nodded once, then turned away. Shit!

Before she could scramble out of cover, though, I caught her arm. "She's not the only one, though. You should know that, just in case."

She put her hand over mine. "We really pick the worst times to do this, don't we?"

"Seems to be our fate."

"When this is all over, maybe the three of us should sit down and have a good long talk."

I grinned. "Ooh, a threesome. Now you're talking."

She swatted my arm, putting a little faith into it for good measure. "And the moment is over. Shall we continue?"

I let out a laugh, cradling my now smoking hand. "I don't get it. Lines like that always work in the movies."

"You need to watch better movies ... uh oh. Down!"

I pulled back just in time for a trio of angry beams of magic to meet the white brilliance of her power.

The energy pouring off the attack was enough to singe

my eyebrows. The foliage all around us hissed from the heat. Thankfully, this was new growth; otherwise, we'd be standing in the middle of a rapidly expanding five-alarm blaze.

Movement registered up ahead, but when I tried to focus on it, all I saw was more vegetation. I thought it might be my mind playing tricks on me, but then it happened again. The third time, I popped my head up to get a better look and saw an odd undulation of sorts, like the bushes became blurry for a moment. A blast of green energy shot out from that same spot, barely missing me as it whizzed by and burned a hole in the tree behind me.

I finally realized what was going on. More fucking glamours. Apparently, there were some *Predator* fans among the mages. Slick, but maybe not as smart as they thought. I took a sniff of the air. These weren't nearly as complex as the one wrapped around Tom. It was just a visual distortion, probably to save power better spent trying to kill us. I turned toward Sheila and tapped the side of my nose. "Got those motherfuckers."

She nodded once, then stood up, her aura a beacon even in the thick growth. "Is that the best you've got?!"

It wasn't, as more lances of power struck out. Some of it fizzled harmlessly off her shield, but a few of our attackers were smarter than their coven siblings. One blasted a crater at Sheila's feet and she stumbled. Another took out a tree, sending it careening down where it slammed into, then bounced off of, her faith-based aura. Nice try, but no dice.

Sheila began to advance upon them and I realized what she was doing. She was the bait. That meant I was supposed to play the part of the hook.

I was no Sasquatch, but forest fighting tended to favor those who could move quickly and strike hard. I'm sure silence played a part in it, but with the various explosions going on around us and the haze of smoke starting to settle in, I liked my odds.

Control was what I needed to remember. The people out there were glass cannons. You could punch most vamps as hard as you wanted. The Feet, too. So far as I'd ever seen, though, mages weren't any more physically imposing than a normal person. I needed to rein myself in and not let my temper get the better of me. These people might be frothing at the mouth lunatics now that their progenitor had returned, but I wasn't so callous as to opt for wholesale murder.

Also, I kinda liked the stolen jacket I was wearing and didn't want to get blood and brains all over it.

I took off perpendicular to Sheila, keeping low but accelerating as much as the forest floor would allow. Angling my movement, I started to curve around back to where I'd sensed the group of Magi. There came the sound of wood splintering nearby and I turned to see one of the mechanized monstrosities knocking over a tree as it advanced. Alex wasn't fucking around.

And still no sign of our friends. Fuck!

This whole plan of ours had long since graduated from shit show to complete fuck-up. If things got any more out of hand, I might have to give up on the elaborate schemes and start spelunking down caves until I got lucky.

First things first, though. If we could capture a mage or two, maybe we could get a lead on freeing Christy and the others. Maybe we couldn't find Sally and Tom in this chaos, but they certainly could. Yeah, that sounded like it had potential.

There! Just up ahead, judging by the spacing of their shots, was a fairly tight knit group. A poor strategy, but one didn't need to be a trained soldier when one had magic dust in their pocket.

I crouched down and prepared to make my move. If I attacked them from the side and got lucky, I could take them all down before they knew what hit them.

They fired off another volley at Sheila, the flash of her aura visible even from where I stood. Subtlety thy name definitely wasn't Icon.

And it was about time it wasn't mine either. I took off at

full speed while they were distracted, spreading my arms wide so as to tackle the shit out of as many mages as I could.

Ten yards to go.

Five.

Another few steps and...

The world seemingly exploded just as I reached the mages. A wall of fire rose up where they'd been standing, followed by deafening sound and a shockwave that launched me at far greater velocity than I'd been running.

Shrapnel tore into my body as flames washed over me.

I landed in silence, my eardrums blown out and the broken asphalt of the forest floor doing little to cushion my fall. I tumbled end over end until finally skidding to a halt.

Pain racked every inch of my shattered body. When the bliss of unconsciousness finally called out to me, I gratefully let it take me away.

PART III

53

ALTARED STATE

"He's waking up."

"What should we do?"

"We gave our word. It is our bond, so we will follow it."

"But this ... this..."

"Be at peace. This is but another test of our faith. We shall weather it as we have all that have come before."

Faith? Was that ... no. The conversation had started out low, hollow, barely audible, but it gradually gained volume and clarity. Sheila's voice didn't have a low raspy quality to it. This one sounded like the owner had spent a lifetime chain smoking Pall Malls.

Wait, I knew that voice – Bernadette?

"Look at all the blood. I ... I can't take my eyes off of it."

"Turn your thoughts to Heaven, brother. Draw strength from it. Resist the temptation, great as it might be."

Shit! There were only a few things that tempted the Templar where I was concerned, and they all involved staking my ass six ways to Sunday.

My eyes popped open, painful consciousness returning to every inch of my bruised body. Guess my healing was still playing catch up from that tank shell. Nevertheless, it was

351

best to get my ass back in the game before this debate took a slightly more lethal turn.

Smoke and haze filled the air of the forest, but it wasn't nearly thick enough to hide the circle of red-robed zealots staring down at me ... an odd mix of disgust and over-eagerness filling most of their faces.

Bernadette stood directly over me, her plump legs to either side of my head. Thank whatever gods there were that she wasn't wearing a skirt. I've seen a lot of disturbing things, but there were some memories I didn't want haunting me until the end of time.

Despite being in prime position to shove a cross down my throat and stomp it in nice and deep, she took a step back and actually offered me a hand.

"Um, thanks," I replied, feeling my jaw snap back into place. Rapid healing; it never stopped being weird.

I let her help me to a sitting position, then almost screamed when I looked down at myself. I was covered head to toe in gore, like I was a victim in a *Saw* movie. It was sorely tempting to ask if any of the Templar might be good enough to dial 911 for me, until I realized I felt a hell of a lot better than my appearance suggested.

The blood wasn't mine.

That's when I remembered I'd gotten hit by the shockwave of a tank round, and apparently the messy fallout, too.

I let out a bark of laughter at the realization, which the Templar duly frowned at. Humorless fucks.

Climbing gingerly to my feet, I glanced around, a frown of my own forming once I saw who was or, more precisely, who *wasn't* with us. "Sheila?"

"Be at peace," Bernadette said, averting her eyes from mine. "She fights still, over yonder."

"Good," I replied, relief evident in my voice. "We should go help her."

"The Blessed One requires no help from ones such as us."

"What?"

"I mean, she is best equipped among us to deal with the treachery of the Magi. It is her destiny, after all."

Oh, not this shit again.

Problem was, Bernadette had a point. Sheila hadn't started out with a grudge against mages. Hell, even taking recent events into account, I still didn't see how her attitude could change so drastically to wanting them wiped out, but even I couldn't deny things had taken a disturbing turn with regard to that particular prediction.

"They're spread out in the forest," another Templar said, a guy by the name of Vincent or Victor ... V something. He seemed to be Bernadette's second in command from what I'd seen when last we'd all been together. "I think those tanks caught them by surprise."

"They're not the only ones," I replied, my ears still ringing.

He looked me up and down, seeming to take measure of me, then too averted his eyes and spoke as if I were sitting somewhere else. Bunch of weirdos. "What I meant is that we would best serve the Blessed One by doing the same, so as to better engage them."

While I didn't like the idea of leaving Sheila off on her own, what he said made sense. If we bunched up together, it would only serve to give the Magi a chance to take us all out at once. Hell, depending on what Alex's orders were, one of those tank jockeys might give it a go, too.

"Fine," I said. "Time to put those paintball skills to use, but first..."

"What are you doing?!"

Oh, Jesus Christ. We were in the middle of a goddamned supernatural war zone. Not the best time for them to act like fucking prudes. I stopped licking the blood off my fingers long enough to reply, "Waste not. *Comprende?*"

Figured I might as well grab a snack since I was covered with enough of it. Hmm, not too bad, but a bit of a burnt aftertaste.

We could still hear tank fire, but it was falling behind. Between the forest and the Magi wising up, Alex's tactics had limitations.

That said, I wasn't sure whether his intention had been to destroy them outright or give them a bloody nose and drive them back. If the latter, he'd succeeded, mission accomplished. If not, though, if he truly meant to level the entire fucking forest and everything in it, then it was only a matter of time before phase two got underway. That could be bad. If Alex had access to tanks, there was no telling what he could call in next.

I, for one, didn't care to be napalmed in an airstrike.

The Templar must've been thinking the same thing because, much as I liked to make fun of them, they kept up with me. Swords and guns at the ready, they moved through the forest both adeptly and quietly. Vampire powers were great, but one should never discount actual training.

Even Bernadette managed to surprise me by keeping up. I'd have bet good money that the tubby Templar would have stopped for an Oreo break long ago.

Mind you, not all of this was a good thing. Though we were technically allies in this endeavor, I knew where I stood with them. I kept looking over my shoulder just in case one of them decided baby Jesus wanted me dead after all.

Still, that they hadn't abandoned my ass and flocked to Sheila for some righteous ass-kissing was admirable. Who knows? Maybe the holy rollers were finally beginning to realize I wasn't a piece of shit from Satan's toilet, waiting to splash my havoc upon the innocent asses of the world.

Don't get me wrong. It was still gonna be a while before I offered to pick up the bar tab for this group.

I took a sniff of the air. Crap. There was too much smoke. Everything smelled like burning. Of course, that might have just been me. Boston was surrounded by rivers. Despite not wanting to swim in the waterways of any major

American city, it might not be a bad idea to take a dip and clean off before...

"Bill!"

Huh? I spied some foliage moving off to my right barely a moment before Sheila pushed through. I hadn't noticed her closing in. Served me right for daydreaming. At least this time, I'd gotten lucky and it had been a friend as opposed to a foe.

A big smile crossed her face, then she doused her aura, ran up, and gave me a hug. Oh yeah, so much better than a punch to the face.

"Thank goodness! With all the magic and the tanks, I lost track of you. I thought maybe, well..."

"Nah," I replied cockily. "These losers take me out? No way."

She stepped back and crossed her arms, looking me up and down.

"Okay, fine. I got the shit blown out of me. But thankfully, your God-squad buddies were around to help."

"You mean the Templar? You found them?!"

"More like they found me. Points to them, though. They didn't immediately stake me and bury the ashes."

"Be nice," she chided. "Bernadette can be a little ... intense, but she's a good woman. Her heart is in the right place."

"Hey, so long as *my heart's* still in the right place."

She chuckled. "Where are they?"

"They were right..." I looked around, noting the eerie stillness of the forest. "They can't be far." I took another sniff of the air to no avail. "They said something about spreading out, not wanting to give the Magi a good target by bunching up."

She appeared to mull it over. "That makes sense. I'm just glad to hear they're all right. After seeing what happened back there, I was kind of worried."

"Bad pennies always turn up."

She slapped me lightly in the arm. "Still, it's a good plan. I would have said the same thing."

Yeah, it *was* a good plan. Pity we weren't following it, standing there and talking as we were. If anything, we were making ourselves a good target in the process.

So, when a group of Magi dropped their glamours right in front of us, we had no one to blame but ourselves.

I knew the drill. Jump back and let Sheila's power act as a magic sponge. Only this time, I wasn't quite fast enough. That, or the Magi were getting wise to it.

I backpedaled, but one of the mages anticipated it and sent a bolt of red-hot death my way. It grazed my side, knocking me on my ass and making my ribs feel like they'd been barbecued.

Three wizards attacked Sheila simultaneously from different sides, each striking the ground just outside her aura with explosive force. I wasn't sure what they hoped to accomplish until I saw the very earth collapse beneath her feet. She dropped into the sinkhole and was lost from sight. Shit! I'd forgotten that we weren't actually fighting in a forest. Just a few days ago, this had been northern Boston.

The witch who'd seared me wasn't content to let the others have all the legend-killing fun. She let loose a multi-beamed volley my way just as I scrambled back to my feet. Off balance as I was, I barely managed to stay ahead of it.

The others turned their power upon the trees surrounding the hole they'd created, sending them toppling down upon it. I didn't know how much weight Sheila's aura could support, assuming she hadn't been hurt in the fall, but the mages seemed intent on burying her alive.

Shit! Where the fuck had the Templar gotten off to?

No. I couldn't wait for them to pull our asses out of the fire, as if they even could. I was the only one here who could turn this around and quickly.

I gritted my teeth both from the pain and now with anger, once again feeling that darkness stir within me. Letting it out was stupid. I could end up causing a bloodbath before I got it under control again. But maybe that was what needed to be done.

Thanks to my association with Christy, I'd developed an aversion to killing mages. In my mind, they were as human as anyone else ... just capable of doing some extra weird stuff. It was hypocritical, though. Had these assholes been vampires, I'd have had no problem dusting them.

I didn't have to like it, but it was time to take the kid gloves off. If I didn't, there was little chance of walking out of this mess.

First, I needed to take out the witch who had a bead on me, then go after the others. Yeah, that was the ticket.

I waited for her to let loose another volley of energy. The moment she did, I ducked beneath it and charged forward with everything I had. Head down, shoulder out, I slammed into her with enough force to ensure she'd be eating through a straw for weeks to come. She went tumbling head over heels and landed unmoving.

Now for...

A light blue glow enveloped me before I could get moving again and every nerve in my body seized up. It was like being hit by a taser hooked up to a lightning bolt. Guess the other mages hadn't been as focused on Sheila as I thought.

I was pretty sure my eyeballs were beginning to smoke when the spell abruptly ended and I fell to the ground in a useless twitching heap. Residual sparks of energy continued to course through me.

The wizard who zapped me stepped over, a look of pure rage upon his face. "You killed Melinda."

I wanted to correct him in that it was very possible she'd survived. That, and also tell him I'd fucked his mother. Sadly, my tongue didn't seem to want to do much more than hang out the side of my mouth.

Energy began to gather around him. Oh, crap. This was gonna hurt.

"For the glory of The White Mother, I send you to the Hell you..."

Red flashed before my eyes, but rather than hitting me, it slammed into the mage. At first, I thought maybe one of our friends had escaped and was sending this asshole a taste of his own medicine, but then I realized I wasn't seeing a spell. It was a cloak, the crimson cape of a Templar.

And not just any Templar.

I could do nothing but watch wide-eyed as Sister Bernadette bent the mage's head to the side. Her eyes turned black as coals and she sank her teeth into his neck.

54

HOLY MOLARS

"Wha da fuh?"

That was the best I could manage as two more of the Templar joined Bernadette in taking care of the mages that had been focusing on Sheila.

Limbs were broken, necks snapped, and bodies drained as sharp teeth sank into them.

At what point had I stepped into the fucking *Twilight Zone*?

Okay, maybe that was a stupid question. It was painfully obvious what had happened. More important was when, why, and who had done so; all questions I wasn't going to get answered lying helpless on the ground.

Finally, the eldritch stun gun effect began to wear off. "Um..." I still had no idea where to begin. "Guys, I think you got them."

My entreaties were ignored, however, as the Templar leader and her two knights continued to feed. Soon it was difficult to tell where the color of their robes ended and the blood of the now quite dead Magi began.

I'd seen this before. It was bloodlust, something most freshly turned vamps couldn't fight. Once they got their first taste, they didn't want to stop. It was why so many of us were little better than monsters.

I pulled myself to my feet. We didn't have time for this, not with Sheila trapped under several tons of lumber.

"Come on, that's enough ... whoa!" I stepped back as Bernadette snapped at me, dragging the mage out of my grasp. Guess somebody hadn't ever been taught to share. "I don't want your..."

This was pointless. There was no trace of humanity in her eyes as she continued to chew on the wizard, desperately trying to get every last drop. Jeez, I could only imagine how many bags of potato chips had suffered a similar fate at her hands.

At least this explained the Templars' odd reaction to me waking up covered in blood. They hadn't been disgusted at my appearance. They'd been barely able to keep themselves from licking me clean.

I paused as I pictured that. No way was I sleeping soundly anytime soon with that thought in my head. Eww.

Shit. I had a feeling that compelling these assholes to knock it the fuck off wouldn't win me any favors in their eyes. Sadly, it seemed like that was my only option, but then an idea popped into my head.

"Come on, guys; the *Blessed One* is in danger. She needs our help."

"Blessed One?" Bernadette gurgled through a mouthful of blood. A moment later, she blinked and her eyes returned to their normal dull brown color. It was an improvement, however slight. She dropped the dead mage like a sack of potatoes, then backed up with a look of horror upon her face. She looked at me, then toward the two other knights still busy tucking into their not-so-happy meals. "What have we done?"

Despite our mutual dislike, I felt bad for her. Being turned hadn't been a bed of roses for me, but I'd been a gamer and horror geek before. As a result, I'd adjusted relatively quickly. For the Templar, however, it had to be like having helms of opposite alignment unwillingly put on their heads. They'd become the things they hated most. I truly felt sympathy for her plight. "You turned a trio of wizards into your own personal Slurpees."

Well, okay, maybe I didn't feel *that* much sympathy. Bernadette had always gone out of her way to treat me like a pile of shit. I wasn't above rubbing it in a bit.

But perhaps I'd save the rest for later.

"As I was saying, Sheila got attacked. I could really use your help." I pointed out the pile of trees lying atop the sinkhole in the ground, then took a couple of steps toward it before realizing she wasn't following. I glanced over my shoulder and found her staring at the other two, still feeding like there was no tomorrow.

Without a word, she walked up to the first, picked up the sword he'd discarded, and then beheaded him in one clean cut.

"What the fuck?!"

The first Templar barely had time to turn to dust, when she did the same to the other.

Bernadette then turned the point of the sword toward herself. That finally spurred me to action. I jumped in and kicked the weapon out of her hand before she could commit some half-assed version of hari-kari.

"I repeat, what the fuck are you doing?"

"Did you not see them?!" she cried. "They were no better than animals, beasts. When we awoke like this, we all vowed to God under Heaven not to partake in the hunger that was eating away at our insides. They broke that vow ... as did I. I am unworthy to be in the presence of the Blessed One. I am unworthy of life itself."

With Sheila in danger, I was running a bit low on sympathy. "Get the fuck over yourself already. Besides, isn't suicide a mortal sin?"

"It is. But so is murder, and I have done that as well. My soul is already damned. Nothing can save me now."

"Uh huh. Yeah, I'll freely admit it sucks. Been there, done that. But we have a friend in trouble, and – as much as I hate to admit it – I need your help to save her. So we can discuss your unworthiness later on. For right now, put your fucking faith where your mouth is and get moving."

She looked as if I'd slapped her in the face, something I also wasn't above doing. After a moment, though, her eyes hardened as she hopefully remembered what a reprehensible beast I was supposed to be. Finally, she gave me a single nod.

"Good."

"The mages?" she asked as I turned away.

I remembered what James had said after Calibra outed herself as Ib. Under normal circumstances, mages couldn't be turned. "Don't worry about them. They aren't going anywhere except a shallow grave."

Turns out Bernadette was far more useful than she would have been if she'd still been human. The wizards had done a job of things, requiring a lot of muscle to clear enough debris to open a hole. I won't pretend I wasn't worried sick the entire time. In a way, Bernadette's death wish was a good thing, as it kept me preoccupied with making sure she didn't break off a branch and impale herself on it. I swear, with some people, it was nothing but drama.

Finally, we cleared enough that I was able to see down below. My field of vision wasn't very wide, but I saw melted asphalt, broken rebar, and a lot of debris.

What I didn't see, however, was a white glow of any kind.

Damnit! We redoubled our efforts, alternating between digging and calling out Sheila's name. Well, *I* did anyway. Bernadette still kept up with her Blessed One bullshit. In retrospect, it was probably a good thing she hadn't been around to watch us inject Sheila with the blood of Baal. She might've objected ever so slightly.

Of course, had she been there, she wouldn't have ended up sucking off any mages, so perhaps my wish was a wee bit selfish at that.

Footsteps approached and I turned to find more of the

Templar joining us. They were all dirty, and most of them looked like they'd been at least partially singed by magic, but none had the dipped-in-gore look Bernadette wore. "I'm gonna cut right to the chase. Are all of you..."

"Filthy denizens of the night?" Bernadette's second in command replied, disgust practically dripping out of his mouth. "Aye. We are all damned."

"Not all, Brother Vincent," Bernadette said. "Did you stay true to your bond?"

"Yes, though it was difficult. The call is strong, hard to resist. And you?"

Bernadette turned away without saying a word and got back to digging. Okay, whatever. I didn't pretend to follow their logic. Though they all seemed intent on bemoaning their fate, I considered it a good thing to have some extra firepower backing me up, at least for now. In the long run, I'd have to see about getting these guys assigned to a coven as far away from me as possible. An eternity of bible camp didn't sound particularly appealing.

"Let's go," I ordered. Fuck it, if they were vampires now, then technically, as a former coven master, that made me their superior. "Play time is over. Start digging."

That didn't fly with them. I had to tell them who we were trying to save before they did anything but glare at me like I was a bag of dicks. Once they understood the stakes, though, we all got to work. Half of the group fanned out. There were still mages running around, and I could also hear tank fire in the distance. The haze had gotten thicker, too, making me think Alex was far less concerned with forest fires than Smokey the Bear. The rest of us removed debris as quick as we could until we'd opened up a hole wide enough for me to squeeze down.

Caution warred with my need to know. Much as the forests had been hostile territory to vampires for centuries, so too had become the underground in recent days. I needed to keep an eye open for Sheila's white glow, but at the same time be mindful of any orange ones.

Fuck it! My safety came second to my friends', albeit a close second.

I sat on the edge and kicked off right as I heard a voice cry out, "Thank goodness you're all right!" I dropped down into the darkness just as Sheila stepped out from the undergrowth.

The fuck?!

It took a few minutes for me to climb back out. The Templar abandoned their posts the second they saw her, leaving me to my own devices. Goddamned pack of overly righteous undead assholes.

Sheila was waiting with a confused look upon her face once I managed to extricate myself. The Templar were standing around her defensively, although I couldn't help but notice none of them were making eye contact or speaking to her.

"Are you okay?" we both asked simultaneously.

I held up a hand. "How did you get out?"

"The hole dropped me down into a subway tunnel." She hooked a thumb over her shoulder. "Turns out there's a station exit maybe a block that way."

"But you're not hurt?"

"Some scrapes and a twisted ankle. Nothing I couldn't take care of," she replied before turning to Bernadette. "I'm happy to see you're okay. I was worried."

When Bernadette didn't answer, Sheila eyed her more closely, no doubt noticing all the blood. "Are you hurt? Do you need healing? I can help you."

"Yeah, about that..." I commented under my breath.

"I am unworthy of your touch, Blessed One," Bernadette said, turning away.

"Don't be silly. If you're injured..."

She put a hand on Bernadette's shoulder and the Templar flinched as if she'd been bitten by a snake. She leapt back, out of Sheila's reach, a good ten feet. When she looked at us again, her eyes were blackened.

Yep, safe to say that cat was out of the bag.

"Do you not see this?" Bernadette cried. "I ... all of us. We have failed. We have failed you. We have failed God. And I am the worst offender of them all."

A faint glow of faith magic emanated from Sheila for a moment, probably the shock of seeing Bernadette hopping around like a howler monkey, but she quickly reeled it back in until it dissipated around her. "I'm sorry. I didn't mean..."

"It's not your fault," Vincent replied. "It is what you do, your calling. God still smiles upon you, and the glory of his light is meant to burn the unclean ... such as us."

"Jesus fucking Christ," I muttered quietly, forgetting for a moment that the Templar now had super hearing. I'd need to watch my tongue around these assholes. Oh, the hell with this. "I will remind you dickheads that I'm a vampire, too, so if we can please keep the self-loathing to a minimum, I'd appreciate it. You're all giving me a complex."

Sheila was a bit more diplomatic. After giving me a pained look, she stepped toward Bernadette and held out her hand. The Templar leader shrank back – pure misery etched on her face. Sheila, however, was persistent and eventually Bernadette stopped backing away. After several more moments, the Templar leader lost it and collapsed blubbering into her arms.

Despite the gore covering Bernadette, Sheila embraced her tightly. "It'll be okay. Tell me what happened."

It took Bernadette several minutes to get herself under control. In that time, a few more of the Magi found us. Vincent dispatched his men to counter them, reminding each to hold true to their vow before sending them off.

Thankfully, the damage that had been wrought trying to bury Sheila had left us a defensible area with cover. We needed to get moving soon, though. Nowhere in this tree-ridden hell was safe, and we still hadn't seen hide nor hair of our missing friends.

Bernadette clenched her teeth as she spoke, the bitterness chasing the grief away for the time being. Maybe that was a good thing. Anger could be molded, used. Self-pity, not so much. "It had been barely a day since you left when they took us. We thought ourselves vigilant, but our focus was turned away, seeking more of the so-called Destroyer's revenants."

"Zombies," Sheila explained to me.

"Aye," Bernadette said. "We hunted them as well as helping those in need. There was so much work to be done that I thought nothing of it when our patrols were late in returning. Contact in the city was spotty at best and there were many mouths crying out for help." She threw a dirty look my way. "They came under guise of friendship, surrounded us before we realized it. I protested, citing the truce, but even then I knew our fates were sealed. For what is the word of a beast, even a silver-tongued one?"

"Silver tongued?" I asked.

"The leader of that house of sin."

I let out a heavy sigh. "Colin."

"I know not his name," she replied. "I only know that his men fell upon us before we could mount a defense. It was my fault. I should have known better, should have been on my guard. But I am old and my faith is weak."

"No you're not," I said. "Well, okay, you are old. I'll give you that."

Both Sheila and Bernadette glared at me.

"What I meant is there's nothing wrong with your faith. Alex gave his word. Even I didn't think they'd turn on us so quickly. I should have considered that Colin is a fucking backstabbing prick. I'm sorry."

Don't get me wrong, I didn't particularly like Bernadette, but I did feel sorry for her. Alex would eventually fuck us all up the ass, but the fucker didn't even wait for the ink to dry on his bullshit ceasefire.

At this point, all bets were off.

"What happened after that?" Sheila asked.

"We were controlled. His voice in our head, too strong to deny."

"Compulsion," I explained.

"Whatever it is called, it is a living nightmare. To be stripped of one's will, to be forced to do another's bidding."

I thought back to what Sally had been through. "Can't argue there."

"We were hidden away. Ordered to the deepest depths of that den of devilry. But then the Magi came. The leader, Colin, took us with him when he escaped. Said we might prove useful yet."

"Sounds like him, all right," I replied. "So where have you been all this time? We've been here a while now and..."

"Once the vampire leader saw who you were, he ordered us away to guard the furthest perimeter. To stay out of sight." She turned to Sheila. "Indeed, I think he planned to use us against you. To make us the serpents in your garden."

I had to stifle a chuckle at the thought of a fat Bernadette-shaped snake sneaking up on anyone.

"He returned our weapons and trappings to us to complete the illusion, all save our crucifixes, rosaries; anything we truly held dear."

"The implements of your faith," Sheila said. "I hate to say it, but that's probably a good thing. Those would have been lethal to you now."

Bernadette nodded sadly. "Each of us was given a black blade, no doubt meant for your heart."

Sheila nodded ruefully. "But that didn't happen."

"Yeah," I added. "Unless you're planning on attacking her now, after telling us all of this."

A look of sheer horror crossed Bernadette's face. "Never! I would sooner die. I would..."

"I think Bill is just explaining things badly," Sheila said, giving me a look that was a definite prompt to agree with her.

"Yeah, nasty habit of mine."

"We discarded those accursed weapons the moment we were freed," Bernadette said fiercely. "We..."

I held up a hand. "Wait, freed? They let you go?" That didn't sound good.

"I know not," Bernadette admitted. "All I know is that around the time the Magi struck again, we awoke, our wills our own again."

I considered this. "And Colin was the one pulling your strings, right?"

"The well-dressed one? Yes."

I turned to Sheila. "Remember when Alex punted his ass through the wall?"

She nodded. "Hard to forget. That must have been it."

It had to be. If there was one thing that could fuck up a dude's concentration, it would be that. Still, why beat the shit out of Colin and risk him losing control of the Templar? Bernadette was right. They could've made for a hell of a nasty surprise against us.

Sheila coughed. The smoke was definitely getting thicker. We needed to get moving again soon.

"Once freed," Bernadette continued, the act of telling the story seemingly making her feel better, "many of my brothers fell to despair. I ... I committed a sin so as to give them hope. I told them there was still a chance to save their immortal souls. I made them vow not to partake of any blood save that of Christ. It was all I could think to do to once more rally them to the cause."

"You told a lie to save them," Sheila said. "I'm pretty sure any loving God would understand that."

"Except I was weak." Bernadette's tone again became desperate. "I could not stop myself. The pull was too strong. I fear the others, seeing me fallen, will soon follow."

"Can't be helped," I replied matter-of-factly.

Both of them turned and looked at me, wide-eyed.

"Not trying to be an insensitive prick. It's just biology. If they don't eventually feed, they'll go crazy."

"Their faith will..."

"Mean nothing if they're starving and feral."

"How long do they have?" Sheila asked me.

"They've gotta be hungry now," I replied. "Hunting pokémages like this isn't going to help them much either. Sorry to say, but that *Lost Boys* bullshit of not turning unless you feed is utter crap. It's a matter of when, not if."

Bernadette dropped her gaze. "Then all hope is lost."

"You do realize that, up until recently, I had a job, a relatively normal life, all while being a vampire, right? It's not the end of the world."

"For one who was already a sinner, perhaps," she shot back. "For the faithful, I fear it will eat them apart from the inside until they become little more than demons given flesh."

Arguing with Bernadette was about as fruitful as banging my head against a brick wall. I didn't want to come across as a total dick, but the reality of the situation was that some of her people were probably going to be able to handle it just fine. The rest would most likely do what other vamps did: become total raging dicks. Unless the order of the Templar decided to really relax their membership standards, though, all of them would need to come to grips that their days in the clubhouse were over.

My eyes met Sheila's and I could see she was probably thinking the same thing, either that or "Why does this weirdo keep staring at me?"

The thing was, this was neither the time nor place for an intervention to convince them that life goes on. And, the truth was, it was best to save that discussion until this was all over anyway. We needed them as proud warriors right now, not sad sacks wallowing in self-pity.

For the duration of this ordeal, let them be Templar and let them do what they did best: destroy the forces of evil.

55

BUSTING THOSE BUNKERS

Bernadette didn't like my plan, didn't like giving her people hope where none existed, but she agreed anyway. The stakes were simply too high. We needed all the help we could get, and right now, the Templar could offer a lot more than they could as humans.

That was good because there wasn't time to debate it. The sound of tank engines had grown distant, but the smoke continued to thicken. Off in the distance, back the way we'd come, I could just make out wisps of flame. Alex had meant what he said.

Vincent joined us right as we were about to break cover and move out. "Sister Bernadette!"

"Yes, brother?"

"The Magi. They're on the move. We believe they're retreating."

Not a second too soon, then. The mages weren't stupid. They got greedy earlier, fell into a trap, and knew it.

But maybe opportunity lay in the chaos, something that would allow us to rescue our friends.

There'd been no sign of Sally or Tom. We could either keep combing the woods and hope we ran into them, or follow the mages who we knew were definitely holding Christy hostage. As much as I hated to play Sophie's

Choice with my friends, it seemed the logical course of action.

Mind you, if the Magi idea of regrouping was to teleport a thousand miles away, we'd be fucked, but I had to hope that wasn't the case. The mages who were out here had been using a lot of power. They probably wouldn't be in much shape to zap anywhere. Hopefully, we had a shot.

Problem was, we'd also be heading into Sasquatch territory to do so.

Still, it was either that or turn around and slink back to Alex. Yeah, I'd sooner risk the Sasquatches. At least those fuckers knew how to uphold a truce, assuming they hadn't figured out it was bullshit yet.

Fuck that. One issue at a time. At this point, all of our plans had turned to total shit anyway.

Maybe we'd have better luck winging it.

Earlier, I'd thought it best to split up and let Sheila draw the mages' fire while I circled around and fucked up their shit. Hadn't worked out so hot. Now, after discussing it with her, Bernadette, and Vincent, we decided on the opposite course of action – a close grouping.

For starters, powerful as she was, Sheila was still the slow-poke in the group. Her powers were great for defense, but not so much for cross-country sprinting. I offered to carry her, but she gave me a withering glare in return that would've made Sally proud.

The second line of reasoning was far more practical. Her powers messed with magic. Sure, if she flared up while we were all around her, we'd be toast, but even without her aura, she was essentially a black hole to the mages. They couldn't scry her and their wards would fizzle in her presence. They'd need to spot her in the woods the old-fashioned way – a diffi-cult prospect in a burning forest, at least so long as she didn't ignite her powers like a road flare.

From that perspective, we had the advantage. Yeah, there were potential glamours to deal with, but again, that took power; power that might be in short supply following an extended battle with a column of tanks.

It was the best we had to work with.

We had the Templar stow their robes for the time being – no point in them looking like Christmas ornaments among all the greenery. Then we took off in pursuit.

Thankfully, it was hard to get lost in this forest. The wooded finger that had been shoved up Boston's asshole was maybe a half mile wide. With a fire on our tail, that made it relatively easy to keep on the straight and narrow.

Then there was scent. It was hard to sniff out the mages with all the smoke, but the residual reek of Feet was another thing entirely. All the smoke in the world couldn't perfume their unwashed asses.

Our course set, there was only one slight issue – what to do once we got there, wherever *there* was.

Retreating Magi or not, there were bound to be a lot more of them than us.

Even if I bit all the Templar and powered up – something I doubted they'd be too keen on letting me do – it was still going to be a cluster fuck of trying to dodge dozens of fireballs at once.

On that, I had no answer.

Even my old character Kelvin Lightblade would have been hard pressed with that one. He was good, but not that good.

I would need to be better.

"Be careful," I hissed as one of the Templar accidentally strayed into a ray of sunlight streaming in through the trees. Doofus had apparently forgotten that his days of sunbathing were over. Fortunately, he only got singed enough to give him a good reminder.

"God no longer smiles upon us," Bernadette muttered to herself, because that was exactly what we needed to keep our morale high. Bunch of killjoys.

At least the air was clearing up. We'd crossed over the Charles River, I think, at some point. The magical forest had torn the manmade bridges all to shit, but it left a swampy, but passable, crossing of interconnected roots, logs, and broken concrete. Whatever fire had been on our asses seemed to have been stopped there.

Far more pressing, however, was how thin the coverage was starting to get. When Grulg had led us this way, it had been only a few steps removed from jungle. Now the trees appeared shrunken, withered. Soon enough, we were able to see the ruins of civilization through their branches.

"Alexander's doing?" Sheila asked.

"No. Not unless he had a bunch of anti-druids in his employ or a shit-ton of weed block. It's the Feet."

"How so?"

"I think they're pulling back, taking their magic with them."

"Are you sure?"

"Fuck no," I replied with a laugh. "But if they're holding to the peace, then it makes sense. This place, even on the outskirts of the city; they hate shit like this. They're forest spirits, so they're going to want to get back to where they belong."

"I thought you said they were allied with the witches now," Bernadette said.

"Yeah, I did. But, and don't quote me on this, the Humbaba Accord, the treaty that kept the peace for thousands of years, is a pretty big deal to both sides. This alliance with the Magi strikes me as more a back alley deal than anything. If they'd joined the war under the Accord, they'd have to pull back, too." Or so I assumed. Nevertheless, my nose seemed to support this. The reek of Bigfoot in the area was residual at best.

"You thinking this Calibra person isn't too big on the paperwork?" Sheila asked.

"That's the funny thing. All this time, her disguise was a by-the-book office drone. Hell, the first time I met her, she came across as so tight-assed, I figured she could crack walnuts between her cheeks. Now, though, I have a feeling she couldn't care less about due process. The Feet do, however, and the Accord holds weight with them. Mind you, it's a fair bet they'll be cheering the Magi on from the sidelines."

"At least until they figure out it was all a sham."

"There is that," I replied. "There is definitely that."

"Looks like we're in Bunker Hill," one of the Templar said, pointing out an overgrown sign.

"Awesome," I replied. "If we're gonna party, might as well level a historical landmark while we're at it. What's a few extra thousand lost karma points?"

Sadly, I wasn't joking. If shit was going to happen, it was going to be soon. With the air clearing and the stench of Squatch dissipating, I could pick out other scents up ahead – human or, more likely, close to human. I couldn't really differentiate between mages and people like Gan could yet, but it seemed a safe guess. After all, who else would be hanging around? Far as I knew, every last living person in the immediate vicinity had been turned into a shrubbery by those ugly-ass apes.

I glanced around and saw several noses twitching. The Templar were beginning to come to grips with their newfound abilities.

"What on God's green Earth could smell so foul?" one of them asked.

"That would be Bigfoot," I replied. "Be thankful. If you're ever unlucky enough to take a good long whiff when they're around, you'll regret it. Trust me. For now, concentrate on moving beyond that. Filter out their scent, the trees, everything else, and focus on what lies beneath it all."

I could see many of the Templar closing their eyes and trying what I'd just said. It was almost enough to make me laugh. Me, perhaps one of the worst excuses for a vampire on the planet – at least according to Sally – mentoring the next generation. Oh yeah, these guys were doomed.

"I smell ... something," Vincent said. "People, maybe?"

"Mages," I replied. "Has to be."

"Do you think our friends, Kelly and the rest, are unharmed?"

Friends? That was new. Go figure, a Templar with an open mind. "No idea." We were still too far away, and there were enough scents on the wind to make it impossible for me to pick and choose. "But we're going to find out. Unpack your cloaks. It's time to raise some hell."

Perhaps a poor choice of words as, again, most of the Templar glared at me. I really needed to sit them down and discuss how vamp hierarchy worked. For now, though, I swallowed what little pride I had and turned to Bernadette. "If you wouldn't mind."

She gave me a single sour nod, seemingly the only expression she was capable of. "Unpack the garments of your faith, my brothers. Hold them dear. God's love may yet shine on us again through our deeds."

I was sorely tempted to point out her hypocrisy. I mean, I wasn't a bad fella, but they'd never said inspirational shit like that to me. It was all spawn of Satan this and damned to Hell that. Well, fuck that shit. Sad to say, but you couldn't buy your way into Heaven, at least not according to John Constantine.

Now was not the time to kick these guys when they were down, though. There'd be plenty of time for that later.

"Is it a good idea to do that?" Sheila asked, hooking a thumb at the Templar, all busy pulling their capes out of backpacks and bags.

"Yep. You'll notice I said out, not on," I replied, smiling.

"Not following."

"I may not be a military genius like Alex, but I watch a lot of movies."

So far as I could tell, the mages had turned the Bunker Hill Monument itself into their personal base of operations. We didn't even need to get close to figure it out. They'd put up one of those purplish energy domes around the entirety of Monument Square. The energy itself seemed to be flowing from the top down, so it was a good bet there was at least one mage, maybe more, up top. That was one mystery solved.

Normally, the monument would give a pretty good view of the surrounding area. However, despite the forest beginning to thin out, it hadn't fully given way yet. Another couple of hours and we'd probably be fucked, but for now, we had a chance, however small.

I found myself actually longing for the Feet or the Jahabich. Dangerous as they were, they mostly needed to get up close and personal to tear your head off. The Magi were distance fighters, the artillery of the paranormal world. If we could close the gap, they were vulnerable in hand-to-hand combat, but getting close enough was the trick.

Thankfully, I had years of gaming experience to fall back upon. Hell, wasn't this just another wizard's tower waiting to be stormed? Sure, we'd lost a lot of those battles thanks to Dave's fondness for TPKs, but those losses had taught me a lot, and not just that my DM was an ass.

Most importantly, it had given me the realization that all spell casters had at least one weakness, whether they were newbs or twentieth-level badasses: their egos.

Sure, real life wasn't a one-to-one correlation, but arrogance seemed almost a prerequisite for supernatural entities.

The mages might've been full of themselves, but that didn't mean they were necessarily idiots. Case in point, there were scouts in the woods beyond the perimeter of their defenses, as well as wards on every tree for dozens of yards.

Thankfully, we had a moveable anti-magic field.

With the Icon's powers, aided by vampire senses, we were able to get the drop on the half dozen or so sorcerers who'd gotten unlucky enough to pull scout duty. As expected, strong in the Force they might be, but glass in the jaw they also were.

Those taken care of, I had the Templar hang back so as to prepare. Sheila and I made a wide circuit around the square, well out of sight of the monument. The goal was simple – fizzle out enough wards to give our people safe paths to follow, but leave enough active that the Magi didn't sense anything awry.

We walked in silence, her fizzling while I used my claws to mark our passage for the others. I think we both realized that if we started talking, we might get caught up in it. This was neither the time nor place.

Once that was all done, we met up with our allies again a few blocks away. The Templar said a prayer while we readied ourselves. Then it was time to move.

The second Battle of Bunker Hill was about to begin – except this time, with the exception of one of our number, there were no whites in our eyes to be seen.

56

RABBIT UP MY SLEEVE

"**D**on't think like a human anymore. Imagine you're in the Matrix. Some of those old rules can be bent, and some can be broken."

I got the impression my instructional session was lost on nearly everyone present. Fuck it.

"You're vampires now. You're faster and a lot stronger. You need to remember that and use it, because if you don't, you're fucked."

That wasn't much better, but it was the best I could do on short notice.

Besides, the Templar were trained warriors, whereas I was a former game programmer from Brooklyn. The irony of trying to tell them what to do wasn't lost upon me.

My *pep talk* finished, Bernadette dispatched her men into the forest. "God's grace be with thee, Blessed One," she said just before disappearing into the woods herself.

"Good luck, Bernadette." Sheila said, but the Templar was gone by the time she finished.

"Once more unto the breach?" I asked.

"Seems to be the story of our lives lately."

"Better than those boring exposition chapters."

She smiled at that. "Good luck."

"You too. I'd give you a hug but..." I looked down at myself.

"Trust me, I get it." She turned toward where the monument lay. "Bill, what if they're not there? What if they're...?"

I put a hand on her shoulder. "I can't believe I'm gonna say this to you, but have a little faith."

Now if I could only find a bit of that myself.

As the most experienced vamp in the group – and someone not nearly bright enough to avoid sticking his nose where it shouldn't be – it had been decided in advance that I'd be the guy to light the proverbial fuse.

It was probably an unnecessary step. Away from Sheila, the mages could easily pick us up if they were actively scrying. Chances were they already knew we were there.

But if they didn't, they were about to.

Moving before I could think better of the idea, I raced off the safe path we'd marked, straight ahead toward the purple barrier. I put every ounce of speed I could into my gait, despite the foliage.

It was necessary.

When I first learned of what Christy was, I'd paid an uninvited visit to her apartment. There, Sally and I had gotten a firsthand lesson that magical wards weren't just an invention by dungeon masters looking to blow their players into tiny chunks.

Christy's had been fairly benign – defensive, but meant more to dissuade than outright kill. But that didn't mean they couldn't be juiced up if the mage in question was in a mood.

One moment, I was just a fool running through the woods. The next, I was a fool running through a magical minefield. Explosions rang out around me as I set off the magic that had been inlaid into the trees. I didn't know what each symbol meant, but I had a feeling they were all some variety of "Fuck you!"

In some cases, the ground blew out from beneath where I'd been a second before. In others, trees simply exploded, sending wooden shrapnel everywhere before toppling over. In all instances, I somehow managed to stay one step ahead of whatever nastiness happened.

As I neared the barrier, I heard more explosions ring out; some close, others distant. The Templar were on the move.

Just before I reached the force field, I veered hard left and doubled back, setting off more of the magical traps. A flash of heat from off to my right caught my attention and I turned my head just in time to see a red beam of energy dissipate.

More joined it, searing into the forest from the direction of the monument – some from above, others at ground level. A few came close enough to make me want to shit myself, but none hit the mark.

Hopefully, the Templar were having similar luck.

I'd hate to think we'd all taken a filthy mud bath for nothing.

I knew the mages could scry us coming, but I'd been willing to bet that once the shooting started, they'd rely more on their senses than some spell that probably required them to sit in a circle chanting.

I'd started us off, but now the Templar were drawing fire, too, or hopefully their bright red cloaks were, easily spotted propped up on trees or bushes while their owners ran amuck.

The mud had been my idea, the thought popping into my head as we crossed the swamp that had been the Charles River. It was one half camouflage, helping us to blend in with the surrounding forest, but it also served as a makeshift sunblock in spots where daylight couldn't be avoided.

I kept dodging and weaving, the dust and debris from the explosions making up for any cover lost as trees were felled. Though I wouldn't pretend to even remotely like them, I still found myself hoping things were going as well for the Templar. This was not a situation where I wanted to find myself the sole survivor once the smoke cleared.

The goal was simple: trip their traps and draw their fire from all sides, hopefully both confusing and panicking the shit out of them. All of this, while hopefully drawing attention from the grand finale, which, if timed correctly, should be happening any moment now.

There!

The purple dome turned a deep angry color as its power fluctuated. As planned, Sheila had made her way forward while we were drawing fire, then ignited her aura right before stepping into the magical barrier.

Come on!

The force field continued to strobe, the mages at the top of the monument no doubt putting their all into maintaining it, but a flash of white fire somewhere below fought back with equal or greater effort.

The dome flared, darkened, then winked out of existence.

Yes!

Pity for the mages that vampires were particularly good when it came to coordinating. All it took was a single word.

"*NOW!!*"

The compulsion was weak and broadcast wide, but that was fine. It wasn't meant to control. I wasn't that much of a dick.

No, I'd save that for later if Bernadette managed to piss me off with her fire and brimstone rhetoric. For right this moment, though, I did what hopefully every Templar still standing did – rushed the monument with the intent of hitting these enchanted assholes as hard as we could.

I was right. The multi-pronged assault had sent them into a tizzy. Mages ran back and forth, shooting at shadows, a few even taking shots at one another before realizing their mistake.

Two wizards spotted me rapidly closing the distance. I didn't have anything to return fire with as they unleashed their powers – the few guns we had were better spent in the hands of the Templar – but I did have memories of snowball fights as a child to draw upon. And the one harsh lesson from those was the person who won often was the prick who wasn't afraid to fight dirty.

I reached down, scooped a couple chunks of broken concrete from the sidewalk, then leapt into the air with everything I had. The first burst of red fire hit low and I landed safely past it, throwing my projectiles with abandon. Sadly for the wizard, what was headed his way was a bit harder than some slushball.

Amazingly enough, I hit home. He doubled over screaming as I reached his friend and unloaded with an uppercut destined to put some orthodontist's kid through college.

Teeth and blood flew in every direction and the mage went down hard.

Hah! I was so used to fighting creatures who outclassed me physically that I almost felt guilty fucking these guys up.

Almost.

Unfortunately, my hit had the unintended consequence of rubbing most of the mud from the back of my fist. I caught some daylight and my hand started smoking.

Shit! No matter how many times I found myself on fire, it never ever stopped sucking. Adding to that mouthful of ball sweat was the first mage. He'd recovered from my shitty rock throw – it was no wonder I was always picked last for dodgeball – and was powering up again.

Fuck that noise.

I stepped up to him and threw a haymaker with my burning hand. "SUPER KAIO-KEN!"

Sadly for him, he was more Yamcha than Vegeta.

Taking a moment to glance around and beat out the flames on my hand, I saw other *mud men* charging in. At least some of the Templar had survived Phase One along with me. Swords were swung, guns fired, and several mages dropped.

"Remember your faith!"

It was Bernadette, looking like a fat turd in her mud covering. She was screaming at a few of her men who'd fallen upon their victims. Yeah, that was gonna rapidly turn into a shit show. Hopefully, they could come to some peace with their need to feed.

At least one of the Templar was beyond listening, tearing into a witch like she was the main course at dollar burrito night. Sadly for him, he got caught up in the blood and ignored the warnings shouted his way. A moment later, a bolt of green energy slammed into the ground from above, erasing him from existence.

The magi held the high ground, but I knew the interior was cramped and, while the view was pretty awesome, the line of sight directly below to the square wasn't all that great. My parents had dragged me here one year on vacation instead of Disney World. Walking the Freedom Trail might have been historically relevant, but compared to Space Mountain, it sucked goat balls.

I hoped the rest of the Templar took the cue that dinnertime could wait. They needed to keep moving. So long as they did that, the folks up above could only hope to get lucky with potshots. No point in making their jobs easy for them.

I spied one of the Templar; hard to tell with the mud, but could have been Vincent. He was apparently thinking the same thing. He took cover behind a tree and aimed his gun at the monument entrance. Smart. What went up, must come down, and he'd be there to fill them with lead when that happened.

Oh well, there were plenty more mages on the ground floor to deal with and they were beginning to get their shit together – forming ranks, taking cover, and measuring their shots rather than going off half-cocked.

It was to be expected. It was also why Sheila had hung

back. After the shield came down, she had extinguished her aura and taken cover in the trees, letting the rest of us take the lead.

Now it was her turn again.

She'd used the trees to circle around. Now, she broke cover and made a run for the side of the lodge next to the monument, straight toward a group of about a half dozen mages.

I dare say, a few wizard robes were probably soiled as she ignited her aura and leapt into their midst. Two were taken down before they had a chance to do much more than gape. The rest engaged her in hand to hand, seeing that their magic wasn't worth dick now.

That was gonna prove to be a mistake on their part. As for myself, I focused on the front of the lodge. It wasn't a huge structure by any means, but it was certainly large enough to serve as a base of operations and – I hoped – perhaps a makeshift prison, too.

Getting there was going to be tricky. There was a lot of magic between me and the door. There was also the itty bitty question of what was waiting inside. Stepping through the door, only to get blasted by a dozen Magi, wasn't quite how I wanted to end this day. Besides, been there done that, or at least a barbarian I ran in one of Dave's games some years back had. I didn't care to LARP some of the less spectacular character deaths I'd suffered.

Oh well, I'd deal with it when and if I got there. For now, there was still more of the herd to thin out.

I spotted a trio, two witches and a wizard, just as the Templar knight they'd ganged up on blew apart into dust. It was too late to help him, but I could ensure his killers would be focusing less on their spells in the coming weeks and more on relearning how to walk.

"No! This isn't the way!"

I glanced toward the sound of the voice to see the front of the lodge was now open and a woman stood in the doorway, facing the interior and blocking the exit. What the...?

The distraction was ill-timed, though, so I forced myself to ignore her for the moment as I accelerated and took a flying leap.

"Booga-Booga!" I yelled as the trio turned their wide eyes skyward just as my mud-encrusted self fell upon them. Hah! It truly was hilarious how easily unnerved some supernatural beings could become. I mean, we *were* the monsters under the bed, for fuck's sake. You'd think the weird and unusual would be old hat.

Pity for them, they didn't have a chance to do more than fire a few sparks my way. It was a clumsy attack on my part, doing little more than knocking them all into the pile of dust that had been the Templar, but that was fine so long as I made sure they didn't get back up.

"Fuck you, you wand-sucking bitch!"

What the...?

That sounded like *Tom's* voice.

I spun back to the lodge where that woman was still blocking the entranceway. She had long brown hair peppered with grey. Wait, was that Decker's cousin from before? Agnes, wasn't it? If so, what was she...?

A nimbus of blue energy surrounded the woman and she was flung to the side, twitching. That stun gun spell again. Oh well, better her than...

Hold on, maybe not. With her out of the way, my view inside was now unobstructed. There were three other mages in there and they were in the process of dragging my roommate outside.

What the fuck was he doing in there?

Sadly, it was a particularly poor time to stop and speculate on Tom's sudden reappearance. One of the mages I'd tackled managed to get up to his elbows. Before I could rearrange his jaw, he got off a shot of red energy.

Thankfully, he hadn't had time to charge up, or I'd have joined the dead Templar as a fine mist of particles in the air. It was, however, more than enough to knock me off him, cooking the mud still clinging to me until it felt like I was being fired in a kiln.

"Shit, Bill!"

I hit the ground and the hardening mud began to crack, leaving me partially exposed. That was the least of my worries, though. I looked up to see Tom racing toward me. That wasn't so much my concern as the mages who'd been manhandling him just seconds earlier.

They all wore humorless smiles upon their faces as they gathered explosive green energy around them.

That's when I realized they knew. They knew what Tom was, what he was made of. Of course they would. Their leader, or former leader anyway, was some kind of mage prefect.

Worse, I got the impression the magic they were powering up was meant for him, not me.

If I was right, they were planning on winning this fight with one shot, enough energy to vaporize anyone in the square – including themselves.

Surely they couldn't be that fucking insane.

One of them cried out, "For the glory of The White Mother! May she reign eternal!" as the power coalesced around him and I realized I was about to be proven dead wrong on that point.

57

GIVE ME LIBERTY

"**G**et down!"

Even as I screamed out the warning, I tensed my legs for action. There was no time for anything but to hope I could knock him out of their line of fire in time.

Their friends were ready for that, though. My shadow elongated beneath me for one horrifying moment and I launched myself to the side just as a bolt of magical energy slammed into the ground where I'd been, creating a shock-wave that sent me tumbling end over end.

No!

I rolled to my feet, expecting to see a mushroom cloud followed by white hot oblivion.

Instead, Sheila dove between Tom and the magical assault right as it reached him. Simultaneously, a rotund blob of sludge-covered Templar tackled my roommate from the other side, using her ample body to shield him.

Way to go, Bernadette!

Sheila's aura activated just in time to cancel out the sizzling hot magic, but, airborne as she was, the recoil of her power meeting that of the Magi's sent her careening through the air to slam into a tree with a dull *thunk*. She slumped down to the ground, stunned or worse.

Goddamnit! Two of the people I cared most about in this world were sitting ducks and I was being forced to choose between them.

I glanced over at Sheila. If things ever did work out between us, surely this moment would come up as a sore spot in couple's counseling. She had her power to keep her safe, though, whereas one stray blast could potentially turn Tom into a briefcase nuke. Besides, I had faith in her abilities. Tom's, a bit less so.

Bernadette was already dragging him to his feet. He had a dazed look about him but otherwise appeared unhurt. Unfortunately, there were at least three groups of mages, two on the ground and one up in the monument, who had a bead on him.

Before I could move, however, there came a scream from above, rapidly getting closer.

A moment later, a body slammed face-first into the ground. Considering the ensuing blood splatter, I had to assume whoever had just taken up skydiving wasn't a vampire. I didn't think the mages were into using their own as living water balloons, so who...

There came a sound, like wood splintering, followed by a blur of movement that just barely registered in my eye. I turned to find the three Magi I'd tackled were back on their feet. I expected an all-out assault from them, but they stood silent and unmoving. That's when I realized their bodies were facing forward, but their heads were each turned a hundred and eighty degrees. They remained where they were a moment longer, then crumpled to the ground dead.

Any of the Templar present would have been strong enough to do that, but none of them were nearly fast enough.

Unfortunately, there wasn't time to consider the implications, as there was still a group of Magi standing at the entrance of the lodge.

They were each powered up with their hands spread as if

preparing to deliver as much damage in as short a time as possible.

Before they could release their stored up energy, however, there came a crackle of power and the red around them turned to blue as they all crumpled in a heap.

Behind them sat Agnes, her body still twitching, but one hand held out and aglow.

This battle had just gotten ever so slightly more interesting.

The Magi resistance was broken. Those still present on the battlefield, seeing their friends killed and their leader seemingly switch sides, took off. Most ran for it, but a few had enough juice left in them to apparate away in flashes of light. We'd won, but it would be a temporary victory if we didn't act quickly. For all we knew, those who'd zapped away would return with fresh reinforcements. If that happened, we were screwed.

Tom was complaining about the mud as Bernadette helped him to his feet. If he could still whine, then he was okay. Vincent shouted orders to his men to regroup and not give chase. I didn't bother to stop and see if he was successful.

Instead, I ran back to where Sheila was just now pulling herself to a sitting position. Thankfully, the sun was on its way down by then, enough so that the long shadows cast by the trees provided more than enough shade.

I bent down and put an arm around her, heedless of the danger. "Are you okay?"

"Just ... got the ... wind knocked out of me," she said, taking several deep breaths. "Ever been in a car accident where the airbag deployed?"

I helped her to her feet. "No."

"The airbag will save your life, but it'll still break your nose. Never been caught mid-air like that before. Didn't realize my aura would kinda work on the same principle."

"Good to know if you decide to go cliff diving."

She let out a weak laugh, then set to work healing the bumps and bruises she'd taken. I dutifully stepped back to allow her this, as I didn't care to get fried.

Speaking of cliff diving, though...

I turned and started back toward the monument, passing the greasy spot on the lawn that used to be a mage. I glanced up. No way did this guy fall out. He'd either gone suicidal mid-battle, or...

"I gotta admit, there's a killer view up there," Sally said, stepping out from the entrance. "Just watch that first step."

Her hands were covered in blood, leading me to suspect that any other mages stationed up top were probably no longer a consideration.

Fuck it! I ran up to her, joy overtaking me, and made to give her a big-ass hug. She, however, stepped back out of my reach. That's when I remembered my somewhat grimy state. I looked down at myself, then shrugged.

"I don't think so," she said. "Let's save the warm welcome for a time when you look less like a walking shit pile."

"Says the girl covered in wizard guts."

"This?" She held up a blood-soaked hand and ran her tongue across the index finger. "Just a snack for the road."

Sally's reappearance cemented what I already suspected about the neck snappings from a few minutes prior. Almost as if on cue, I heard soft footsteps coming up behind me. "Hi, Gan."

She squealed in delight. "It does my heart..."

"Yeah yeah." I held up a hand. "I get the point. Thanks for the save back there."

"It is always my pleasure, although I am certain you would have dispatched them yourself."

Sally let out a derisive snort of laughter. I gave her a glare, then turned around. Gan was wearing a bright yellow sweat-shirt. In fact, everything she had on was bright yellow – pants, shirt, shoes, all of it SpongeBob. "Um, nice duds."

"We found a mall after we met up with her," Sally explained. "Someone decided she needed to accessorize."

"And you let her?" I asked.

"Do I look like Polly Pocket's nanny to you?"

I decided to let that one slide. Way too easy. Besides, we had more important matters to discuss. "So, what happened? Was this some kind of half-ass trap you guys set?"

"The only ass here is your fucking moron of a roommate," Sally replied. "Idiot got himself captured."

"Indeed," Gan replied. "I own yaks that have more survival instinct than he."

"Okay, let's back up a bit." I explained to them what happened after they left: Alex, Grulg in chains, the rest of the First Coven.

"Aw, you mean I missed out on meeting one of those blind nutjobs you were telling me about?" Sally asked.

"Yeah, lucky you."

"The head seer has not left Chillon Castle during my lifetime," Gan said. "If my father was to be believed, it did not happen during his either."

"Maybe the asshole wanted some sun. One can only hope," I replied before telling them about the Magi assault, Alex's response, and meeting up with the now-turned Templar.

"And you didn't get any video of Alex bitch-slapping Colin?"

"Sorry," I replied.

"Is he dead?"

"Colin? No idea."

"I hope not. Always wanted to dust that asshole myself."

"I guess we'll see," I replied. "I have a feeling we're not finished with that bunch yet. What about you guys? How did Tom get captured, and how did you all end up here?"

"We got out of Dodge like you wanted us to do.

Doubled back to the forest where Princess Sunshine here was waiting."

"I thought it best to scout out the Magi," Gan said. "I did not think it likely the earlier coven was their full force in the area. Once your whore told me of the First Coven's arrival, it was a simple matter to deduce that an attack was imminent." Sally shot her a glare, but she ignored it and continued. "I suspected it would be an optimal time to slip behind their lines and discover their base of operations. Alas, Dr. Death, your *human* friend presents a rather challenging hindrance for a stealthy approach. After a time, I found him somewhat ... vexing."

Yeah, that sounded like Tom, all right.

"Don't worry, Bill," Sally added. "Turns out he's pretty hard to hurt. You pop him in the jaw and it snaps right back into place. Hell, I had to stop myself before it became habit forming."

"Your self-control is truly awe-inspiring," I replied. "So how did you guys end up here and he wind up with them?"

"After we found out where the mages were holed up, we backed off," Sally explained. "Found a building nearby to hole up in until sundown. Figured we'd double back under cover of darkness. It seemed safest that way since this forest appears to be dying."

"The Alma have left the area," Gan said.

I looked down at her and nodded. "I kind of figured. So what happened?"

Sally shrugged. "I grabbed some shuteye and the next thing I knew there were explosions and all sorts of shit going on. Oh, and your idiot friend was nowhere to be found."

"He decided to go for a walk around midday and was captured within minutes," Gan added in a conversational tone.

"And you know this how?" I asked.

"Because I saw it happen."

"And you didn't stop it?"

"Of course not," she said dismissively. "I am not overly inclined to care about the human's fate."

"Perhaps the one thing we have in common," Sally commented.

"However, once it became clear the Magi were under assault and you were the one leading the charge, I immediately sprang into action."

"How noble of you," I replied sardonically. "It's so good to know…"

"No, please! We surrendered," a voice cried out.

"Dear God, what are you doing?!" another pled.

The commotion was coming from around the corner, near the historical lodge's front.

I ran around the side to find the Templar standing in a semicircle before the entrance. Sheila was at the back, trying to push her way forward but having trouble. She obviously didn't want to use her aura, now lethal to her former brotherhood, and the knights present didn't seem too inclined to let her through. They all appeared entranced with what was going on in front of them.

Bloodlust had apparently gotten the better of three of their number. They had fallen upon the mages, who'd been stunned and were ripping them to bloody shreds.

Two more of the Templar held a struggling Agnes at bay, but their eyes were more focused on the slaughter than her. Vincent stood at the forefront of the audience, barking orders for his men to stand down, but I saw the look in his eye. He clearly wanted to join them. Every second that passed probably felt like an eternity for the poor hungry fool.

Sally stepped to my side and let out a sigh of disgust. "Newbs."

"I think it's a bit more complicated than that," I replied quietly.

"With these guys, no doubt," she said. "Just make sure none of them get assigned to any covens we're part of."

"Please!" Agnes cried out again. I'd gotten the sense from her earlier that she wasn't quite as zealous as some under her charge. What her coven members had tried to do to Tom was apparently the last straw for her. She'd probably been hoping to parlay with us, but it was obvious she hadn't been expecting this.

I started forward, but Bernadette was faster.

She bounded to the front of the line, quite the fascinating display from a woman who looked like she couldn't do a sit up if someone stapled Twinkies to her shoes. She then stepped up to the two men holding Agnes and slapped them both, getting their attention.

By her command, they dragged the master mage away, out onto the lawn, while she turned to the three Templar still ignoring everything save the feast before them. She drew the dagger she wore at her side. "I am sorry, my brothers. Forgive me." Before Vincent or any of the other knights could react, she dusted the three in quick succession.

"Her resolve is impressive," Gan said from my other side, where she'd slithered up next to me like a SpongeBob-obsessed snake.

"Not quite the word I'd use."

I expected to see shock or condemnation on the faces of the Templar still present, and indeed Vincent seemed to have been snapped out of his spell by what she'd done. Many of the rest, though, continued to stare greedily at the still oozing corpses of the mages.

"To your duty, knights!" Bernadette ordered. "Secure this area."

Sheila finally managed to push through the crowd. She stepped up next to Vincent and stared sadly at the Templar commander. "I'm so sorry, Bernadette."

Bernadette wasn't having any of it, though. "Brother Vincent, take control of your men. Remind them of their faith. Hold them to it. If they should falter, take action. Save their souls if you can."

She turned and walked past them, out onto the lawn where the two knights were still holding Agnes. "Release her." Then to the mage, she said, "I am truly sorry about that."

I started heading toward them, gesturing for Sally and Gan to follow. "Come on, we need to get some answers before she zaps away."

"I never meant for this to happen," Agnes replied, her voice low and ashamed. "When the White Mother appeared to us, I was joyous, elated. Everything I'd ever believed in was suddenly proven true. I joined her readily. Nearly all of us did."

I stopped next to Bernadette. "Our friends, where are they?"

If Agnes heard me, she didn't give any indication. "But from the start, what she asked of us, it didn't seem right. If anything, much of it seemed to go against the teachings we all held dear. And then, when some dared to question her..." She paused for a moment. "They were taken, and then ... how they came back to us."

Uh oh. Mages couldn't be turned into vamps, but I had a sinking feeling that didn't mean they couldn't be turned into other things – things with soulless orange eyes that obeyed their mother without question.

"But still we followed. We did as asked, certain that this was our reward, our destiny." Her eyes sought ours, desperation in them. "You have to understand. Hundreds of years of persecution. Driven nearly to extinction in some parts of the world, our organs sold on the black market in others." Her eyes locked with Bernadette's. "Your people forever hunting us in the name of your god. Well, now we had our god and she..."

"She's not a god," Bernadette said, stepping forward. "She's a devil." She put a hand on the mage's shoulder. "My God is one of forgiveness, though, and mercy."

Agnes looked at me. "I truly am sorry. Your friends, they were taken to her. Christine ... Kala seemed especially eager for her. Called her a traitor. I kept them with us for as long as I could, thought perhaps I could convince The White to offer her penance or perhaps simply bind her power. But I could sense her anger, the petty spite behind her visage. I know now this is not the Kala I was raised to revere."

"You have no idea," I muttered.

"I couldn't stop them, though. My people no longer listened to me. It was only a matter of time before I was brought to her, too, brought down below..."

"You are free now," Bernadette said softly. "I can hear the repentance in your voice. A greater power than us all is listening. I cannot forgive you in his name, not as I am now, but I can assure the demoness will hold sway over you no longer."

Agnes lowered her eyes for a moment, but then nodded once before looking up again and smiling.

She was still wearing it on her face when Bernadette reached out, quick as a greased pig, and snapped her neck.

58

SHUT YOUR HOLE

Sheila stormed over. "What have you done?!"

I echoed the sentiment. "We needed her!"

The witch could have zapped away from here at any point, but she hadn't. She'd seen enough and wanted out. Just not in that way.

"My God is one of mercy," Bernadette said, backing away from us. "But there are some sins that cannot be forgiven. I have taken her life so as to spare her the ravages of Hell, same as I have done with my brothers. I do not know if I have succeeded. That is only for Him to know, but I needed to try. They deserved that much, even if in doing so I have damned myself."

She continued backing up until her foot reached the edge of the shadows, an area where the setting sun continued to peek through the shade of the trees.

"What are you doing?" Sheila asked.

"Protect my brothers, Blessed One. Remind them of their vows. Help them be stronger than I was."

"Wait! I don't understand."

"I think I do," I said. She'd been the first to waver, her thirst getting the better of her, and now she was doing what she could for her friends ... just as I would for mine.

"Aye, Freewill," Bernadette replied. "Wicked though you

may be, I know. I just pray you have enough decency left within you to make the right choice when your time comes. The Blessed One's destiny lies before her. The path is laid bare. Will you be yet another obstacle on it, or will you too step into the light when your time comes?"

She lifted her hand to her forehead, made the sign of the cross, then stepped into the sunlight where her skin immediately began to bubble and blister.

"Sister Bernadette!" Vincent barreled past Sheila, shoving her to the side, but it was too late. I grabbed hold of him and held fast as his former commander burst aflame.

It was over quickly, as it tended to be with us vamps. Soon, there was nothing left but dust in the wind. I hadn't liked her much, but nevertheless hoped she found peace wherever she ended up. I mean, creatures from my Monster Manual were real, so then why, too, couldn't a concept as simple as Heaven exist? Who was I to say? After all, faith magic had to originate from somewhere.

Vincent rounded on me once it was over. "Foul beast! How dare you stop me from helping her?" He pulled out a makeshift cross, two sticks he'd tied together at some point, and shoved it impotently in my face.

I slapped it out of his hand like it was nothing. "She chose her path. Now it's up to you to choose yours. We can either do this now, and believe me, you'll lose, or you can get your shit together and keep your people on the straight and narrow until we rescue our friends."

That seemed to get through to him. "Do you really think Kelly ... I mean, do you think they're still alive?"

His Freudian slip wasn't lost upon me, but I decided to let it slide ... this time. There'd be plenty of chances to make jokes about him sticking his crucifix in her magic circle later on, or so I hoped.

Sadly, I couldn't do much more than offer my own hopes with regard to their current status. "If they are, we'll rescue them and send that bitch to Hell. If they aren't, then we'll send her there twice as hard."

Fortunately, we weren't given much chance to wallow in our plight. No sooner had I asked Sheila if she was okay than Sally called over to us from the lodge. "I hate to interrupt date night, but you might want to get your asses over here."

I, for one, welcomed the interruption. What happened with Bernadette had sucked, but the bigger danger was to our morale. I got the sense the remaining Templar were on the verge of losing it, assuming they didn't go feral with hunger first. If any of the rest of us, especially Sheila, gave in to despair, that would be it for them.

Sally drummed her fingers against the doorframe, looking impatient as we walked over.

"We're coming," I said. "Don't get your granny panties in a bunch. It's not like you don't have all of eternity."

"I might, but in case you haven't forgotten, genius, the world probably doesn't." She hooked a thumb inside. "Let's go. You need to see this."

"I didn't realize you had such a hard-on for U.S. history," I replied, stepping past her. Any other comments I might have made, however, died in my throat as I saw what lay inside.

"I don't," she said from behind me. "But I *have* taken a sudden interest in spelunking."

I'd been here when I was a kid. The main attraction had been a statue of some dead guy whose name I'm sure my history teachers would have bitched me out for forgetting. I must've somehow missed the big honking sinkhole at the far end. Maybe I'd been too busy playing my Gameboy, or maybe, just maybe, it was a new addition.

The rest of the structure had been redecorated in early American witchcraft – a large pentagram on the floor, candles, incense, and arcane symbols burned into every wall.

Gan was already inside, viewing it all with a studious eye. Tom was there, too, standing on the edge of the hole, looking down.

I fished my phone from my pocket, still intact, if barely. Thank goodness for militarized cases. It still had a few percentage points of battery left, so I unlocked it and snapped some photos of the place.

"Think Christy will be interested in seeing this?" Sheila asked.

"Huh? Maybe." I put it back in my pocket. "It's more for Dave once we rescue him. Never a bad idea to scout out new campaign ideas."

Sally clapped me on the shoulder. "Planning ahead for future dateless nights? Good. Gives me hope that you think we're going to win this."

I ignored her barb as I refocused on the gaping maw in the floor. "You guys thinking the same thing as me?"

"Hell yeah," Tom said. "If we all take a piss at the same time, it might hit that Ib chick right in the face."

"I've never been much of a churchgoer," Sally replied, "but in Christy's case, I'm gonna hold out hope for a virgin birth."

"I might join you in that," Sheila added.

Stifling my agreement, I stepped over and joined my roommate in peering over the edge. It was pitch black inside, but my night vision cut through the murk enough to see that it wasn't a straight shot down. The shaft eventually bottomed out. It seemed as though the path continued at a somewhat gentler downward slope. Thank goodness. Even prepared as they were, I doubted the Templar had enough rope for a descent as deep as we'd gone the last time we'd visited Jahabich Central. I, for one, didn't really care to free-fall all the way.

"If we can get past that first drop, it looks like it might be walkable ... for a bit anyway."

"I have already ascertained as much, my love," Gan replied, continuing to study the magical desecration of this once mighty tourist trap.

"Never hurts to get a second opinion." When she didn't reply, I asked, "See anything interesting?"

"Quite. The nuances of magic were one of the more fascinating areas of study I undertook at my father's insistence."

"Was always more of an early Renaissance poetry girl myself," Sally commented.

"I am impressed you know what that is," Gan replied offhandedly. "The whores my father kept were barely literate. He saw little value in educating them beyond the services they provided."

Sally produced a handgun and pointed it at Gan's back. "How about I show you all the things I learned in chemistry class about explosive reactions?"

I put my hand over the barrel and gently lowered it. "Here's an idea. Why don't we wait until this is over to sign each other's yearbooks?"

Sally glared at me for a moment before putting the weapon away with a grudging nod.

"Good. Now if we can stop sniping at each other for a moment, is there anything you can tell us, Gan?"

Without answering, she walked over to the northern wall, extended the claws of her hand, and raked them through some of the symbols. "It is fortunate that we have the Shining One with us," she said. "Otherwise, we would almost certainly be under observation. This is old magic, however. It is possible that even her presence might not be enough to block it for long. Beloved, kindly order the freshly risen to destroy the rest of these. This is work best suited for servants."

"The Templar are not servants to beasts such as yourself," Vincent growled from the doorway. "We..."

"We need to knock it the fuck off is what we need to do," I snapped. "Don't make me compel you guys to take a chill pill."

"As if you could, if you wanted..."

"***SHUT IT!!***" Sally commanded. Vincent immediately stopped talking, to which she added, "So much for that theory."

Sheila and I both turned to stare at her.

"What? He practically dared me."

Being that her Highness considered herself too good to vandalize a national monument, Sally and I worked on defacing the magic on the walls. Once that was done, I stepped to the circle on the floor, intent on drawing a giant dick in the middle of it, when Gan grabbed hold of my wrist.

"Leave that be, my love."

"Why? Is it going to explode?"

"Hardly," she replied. "I believe this circle is charged with displacement magic."

"So ... what?" I asked. "Half of me will end up somewhere else?"

She smiled. "Truly your ignorance of such matters is endearing, but no. Did not the mentor say that your friend was taken to Ib?"

"You heard that?"

"Is it not obvious?" I somehow managed to keep from decking her as she continued. "If what we are led to believe about the Jahabich lair and the methods of entry are true, I suspect this may be helping to power a means to access that lair."

"Okay, that explains the big gaping hole in the floor. I mean, I kinda figured they didn't dig it to bury pirate treasure, but why not open a portal directly there? Why the big effort to ensure we have to play tomb raider?"

"I do not know," she replied after a moment, an annoyed look on her face. Apparently, little Miss Perfect wasn't too keen on being in the dark on something.

"As much as I love hearing that," Sally said, "any guesses?"

"Perhaps it has something to do with what powers the Jahabich. Perhaps there is something about the surface that disrupts the process. The Templar were hasty in dispatching the mage. She could have enlightened us. For now, all we can do is guess."

"Which is probably pointless anyway," I concluded. "The important thing is, we found a way in."

"The downside is that some of the Magi got away," Sheila said. "What are the chances of them not telling anyone?"

"Slim to none, which means we don't have time for this shit. We need to get moving now before that tunnel fills up with a Jahabich welcome wagon."

"Fuck yeah!" Tom cried. "It's about time we taught that Babylonian bitch she can't mess with my woman."

"That settles it, then." I turned to Vincent. "Gather your men. It's time to end this."

He opened his mouth to reply, but nothing came out.

I glanced over at Sally. "Seriously?"

"Sorry. Must've forgotten to release it in all the confusion."

Once she had, Vincent muttered a few unkind words under his breath as he turned to gather his men.

Before he could go, however, Gan spoke up again. "I do not believe it will be that simple."

"Nobody ever said this would be simple," I replied. "I mean, we are talking about the oldest vampire in the world who also happens to be a master mage."

"Not that, my love. I meant this circle."

"What about it? You said we shouldn't break it. We didn't. Everything is cool."

"Displacement magic works both ways," she explained. "It is a doorway to the ether. We cannot destroy it without destroying the way. However, there is nothing to stop others from stepping through to here."

"You mean Ib could send reinforcements?"

"I mean, any Magi made aware of this place and what we have done here could do so. If what I suspect is true, this is not a natural waypoint to the Jahabich's lair. It may be entirely controlled by this circle, which means if it is tampered with after we leave..."

"They could send us into the fucking sun if they wanted to," I concluded.

"Well, then we just hurry the fuck up," Tom said.

Sally shook her head. "Not that easy, meatwad. Last time Bill and I went down, we were walking for hours."

"You don't know..."

"No, we don't. The actual crossing could be right at the bottom of this thing, or it could be miles beneath us. That's the problem. We have no goddamned idea how this thing works. Hell, I doubt the mages who set it up do."

"I am forced to concur," Gan replied. "This is advanced magic, possibly combined with knowledge unknown to any save Ib. The risk is great. We might be better served by returning to the Prefecture and ascertaining what knowledge the Alma has to share with us."

Grulg. Unfortunately, there was no way of knowing if he was even alive following the Magi attack.

"What if some stayed behind to defend this location?" Vincent asked. "Gave the rest time to find this portal to the underworld?"

"Too risky," Sheila said to him. "If the Magi return, they'll return in force."

"Then we'll meet them with force. We have already done so, taking this place from them."

"Agreed with Sheila," I said. "We caught them tired and with their pants down. If those dickheads who zapped out of here bring back friends, though, you can bet they're going to be fresh."

"Perhaps," Vincent replied. "But the sun is setting. Whatever it is that I and my brothers have become, that will play to our advantage. We are creatures of the shadows now and can make use of the night."

"It's a suicide mission," Sheila said.

"And storming the gates of Hell isn't?" Sally asked. "Seriously, let's keep things in perspective here. Nowhere is safe. Anyone who's looking for a calm retirement for their old age signed up for the wrong mission."

"I never thought I would agree with a harlot of darkness," Vincent said, "But it's true. This is a choice we're making, a choice to buy the rest of you the time to end this."

"I can't let you stay here alone," Sheila said. "I can help…"

"No." Vincent held up a hand. "Your destiny lies below. I know it. You are destined to return the world to light. Once that happens, there will be no place for the likes of what I and my brothers have become, but perhaps therein lies our salvation – giving you enough time to do what you must. The Lord is merciful, sometimes even to the damned."

"I…"

I put a hand on Sheila's shoulder. "He's right. Well, maybe not about everything, but this is our best, maybe our *only* shot at rescuing our friends and fucking up Calibra's plans … whatever they are."

"I agree with the Templar," Gan said, stepping to my side and putting an arm around my waist. "Our fate and our future lie before us on this path."

I really didn't like the way she said "our future," but before I could comment, it was Tom's turn. "I have a kid on the way and I sure as hell don't want Christy giving birth in a bathtub full of orange jizz. So let's do this shit."

Ah, as eloquent as ever. I next turned Sally's way.

"What?" she asked. "I'm here and not three thousand miles away hiding in a fallout shelter, aren't I? We've gone over this already."

"Sounds settled to me," I said, smiling. "It would seem that perhaps we all have a date with destiny tonight, and I don't think it's going to take a raincheck this time."

59

BELOW

There wasn't much time to spare. Every moment we fucked around was another that an army of zealot mages could zap in and level this place. That might be awesome to watch, but a lot less fun to experience.

We offered Vincent our assurances that we would do our best to rescue the others, then thanked him and his men for watching our backs.

It was time to equip ourselves as best we could. The Templar gave us whatever supplies they could spare, enough to hopefully get us to our destination. We weren't going to be the best equipped rescue party to ever go into hostile territory, but we'd make do with what we had and improvise the rest.

About twenty minutes later, we were ready to depart when I realized Gan was missing.

"Maybe she met a sixth grader and they decided to run off together," Sally suggested from the edge of the sinkhole.

"I can only hope," I replied, "but I have a feeling I'm not gonna get that lucky."

Tom laughed. "I'm aware of your dating life, bro. You couldn't get lucky if you…"

Thankfully, before I could give his ass a shove, the door

to the lodge opened and Gan stepped through holding something that caused a certain Icon's eyes to light up.

"My apologies, Shining One. In the excitement of post-battle discovery, I neglected to return this to you." She drew the sword and expertly twirled it around a few times. The weapon didn't glow in her hands, but it didn't burn her either. "Not quite as balanced as I prefer, but a competent weapon nevertheless." She laid the blade over her arm and presented the hilt.

Sheila reached out for it. Once she touched the grip, the blade instantly began to glow. There came a sizzle of hot steel against flesh and a small wisp of smoke rose from Gan's arm, which she didn't appear particularly put out by.

"Thank you, Gansetseg," Sheila said, holding it aloft before taking the scabbard and buckling it on.

Gan merely nodded before turning my way and throwing me a knowing grin.

Her motives might've been self-serving, but if it would help us cut down a few more of the bad guys, I'd take it.

That done, Tom, the least physically adept of our small group, climbed onto my back while the remaining four of us grabbed hold of the ropes and began to lower ourselves down to whatever awaited us in the dark confines of the underworld.

I was still kinda cruddy from my mud bath before storming Bunker Hill, so the general dirtiness of the cave didn't bother me – at least until a foul-smelling water began dripping in from above, leading me to think the witches had stupidly excavated beneath sewage lines.

Fortunately, I was right, and the cave at the bottom of the drop sloped downward at a walkable incline. Eventually, the packed dirt gave way to rock walls, the sides oddly smooth, almost glasslike. I'd seen this before when we'd been below Vegas. The witch we'd been with at the time had ventured to guess the passage had been carved by fire magic. I wasn't inclined to disbelieve it then or now.

Should I ever end up with a house in the suburbs, I'd definitely be calling Christy to help with the excavation of an in-ground pool.

We needed to rescue her first, though. I stifled a sigh. The list seemed to be getting longer and longer. By that point, I wouldn't have been surprised to get a letter from Ib stating she had my parents, too, just for good measure.

Fortunately, they were safe in the relative mundanity that was Scotch Plains, NJ, one of those pockets of humanity the apocalypse appeared to have overlooked. I kind of envied them their spot, watching the end of the world unfold from the comfort of the overpriced leather sofas they bought last year.

Assuming I survived this, I would need to pay them an overdue visit, show them how much I appreciated them. And, if Mom just so happened to do my laundry and feed me while I was there, who was I to say no?

I shook the thought from my head, letting go of it reluctantly. The utter impossibility of it all hadn't quite gotten to me yet, which was a good thing. Sure, we were descending through the earth toward a giant well of magic owned by the most powerful vamp-witch on the planet, but it wasn't all bleak. I mean, I had some of the best friends in this world by my side, two of which weren't exactly hard on the eyes. Sure, there was Gan, too, but her tactical genius made up for her creepiness, mostly.

Yeah, things could have definitely been worse.

"Hey, Bill?"

I glanced up from my woolgathering and saw Sally facing my way. "Yeah?"

"Any reason why you're shuffling along with a stupid grin on your face?"

"I just realized I had a little bit of hope that we might actually make it through this."

"Oh." She turned to Sheila and held out a hand. "Pay up. I told you he'd gone off the deep end."

Ah yes. Hope indeed.

"How will we know when we've crossed over?" I stared at Sheila for a moment and she added, "Maybe a poor choice of words?"

"Been there," Tom said blithely. "It kinda sucks."

I turned toward Gan, which she sadly noticed, giving me her big puppy dog eyes. "Tell me if I'm wrong, but we'll know by smell."

"Dr. Death is correct." Gan smiled like I was a prized pet who'd just learned to roll over. She paused and took a deep breath. "The scent of the Magi is still overpowering."

"I don't suppose you can tell us if Christy or her coven were taken this way?" I asked hopefully.

"Her coven, no. I am not familiar enough with them. The witch, however, yes. I can scent her and her fetus."

"Wait," Sally said. "You can smell her unborn baby?"

"Of course."

"Jesus Christ. I've gutted men for looking at me the wrong way and I still find that disturbing."

"I'm sure you've also gutted them for stuffing small bills in your G-string," I added.

"That wasn't nice," Sheila chided.

Sally grinned. "Yeah, Bill. That wasn't nice. Apologize or I might cry."

"Fine. I'm sorry." I lowered my voice to a pitch that was just barely audible and added, "Bitch."

Sally shot me a snotty look, then turned to Sheila. "Anyway, Wonder Woman, what I think the munchkin is getting at is that so long as we only smell mages, we're still on this side. It's when we notice other things that we'll need to start paying a lot more attention."

"Other things," Sheila repeated.

It wasn't a question, but it hung in the air between us all nevertheless.

"We should discuss our plans for dealing with the First Coven once Ib and the Shining One are disposed of," Gan said idly after several minutes of tense silence in which I did little more than breathe through my nose, dreading any change in the residual smells we picked up.

"Wait, did you say 'Shining One'?" Sheila asked from her spot near the rear of our lineup.

"Of course," Gan replied. "I believe I am not the only one who feels the time of the prophecy draws near. First, you will eradicate the Magi, and then you will lose to my beloved in single combat."

"Oh, this ought to be good," Sally muttered.

"First of all, I'm not killing the Magi, even if I wanted to, which I don't, trust me." Sheila looked pointedly at Tom, who flashed her a thumbs up. "Besides, it's not like every witch in the world is going to be there waiting for us."

"We do not know what will be waiting for us. However, I, for one, am certain some mechanism of fate will present itself."

"Even if it did," Sheila argued, "you're still assuming Bill and I are going to fight. Hate to break it to you, but I don't have any reason to do that."

"Spend some more time with him," Sally said. "He's bound to open his mouth eventually."

Tom laughed and held up his hand for a high five which, of course, she ignored.

"It is fate – nothing more, nothing less," Gan replied calmly. "It cannot be denied. There will come a reason for you to face each other. Once that has come to pass, the world will be ours. Dr. Death and I shall ascend to the throne that is my family's birthright. There, we will rule as husband and wife."

I glanced her way. "Just for argument's sake, what if I don't want to?"

"And what makes you think I'll lose, even if this does happen?" Sheila asked Gan.

"Simple," Gan replied. "I have faith that my beloved shall overcome you. Take no offense from this, Shining One, but I have seen the doubt in your eyes. I have none. Mine is a belief that is unwavering. This..."

I stopped dead in my tracks. "Holy shit."

"Oh, relax, Bill," Sally said. "It's not like this is the first time she's driven off the road and ended up in Crazy Town."

"Not that," I said. "Doubt."

"What about it?"

I turned to Sheila. "The only way to get to Ib is by passing through some unseen magic portal. Except you can't do that."

Sally stopped and punched the wall with a growl. "Not that shit again. No offense, sister, but it's like trying to backpack across Europe with a friend who doesn't have a passport."

"It's not for lack of applying," Sheila replied.

"We do not know that for certain," Gan said.

"What?" I asked.

"This portal or passage. We do not know that the Shining One will be barred entrance. This is mere speculation."

"Based on lots of experience," Sally shot back. "Or have you forgotten all the times she's been zapped by magic, only to soak it up like a sponge?"

"I forget nothing, whore, least of all when I am spoken to with impertinence."

Sally flipped her off. "Respect this, pipsqueak."

I stepped between them. "Okay, enough with the lip flapping. Sally's right, Gan. What evidence do you have that this time will be any different?"

"No evidence, my love. Merely speculation. It stands to reason the sending we are seeking is unlike others the Magi use, otherwise why bother at all? If passage to the lair of Ib were so mundane, why not do so normally?"

"Go on," Sheila said.

"I need no permission, just so we are clear," Gan commented before continuing. "I have been considering that, as well as why crossings such as the one we seek are deep underground. It is my speculation that the so-called Source the Magi revere is a breach between worlds, a well-spring from which power flows. However, that very power is so immense as to be disruptive to normal levels of magic. That is why it has remained hidden all these centuries."

"Not following," Tom said.

"What a surprise," Sally replied. "I get it. Think of it in terms of electronics. One massive piece of machinery putting out a lot of EMF can fuck with other smaller items nearby."

"Interference," I said, catching on. "So basically, this Source is so intense that in some ways it works like an Icon's power, futzing with regular magic."

Sally nodded. "Maybe. At the very least, I think it might appear as a sort of dead zone for any wizard GPS they might use to try to find it."

"Okay, so how does this all tie together with these underground portals?"

"Ley lines," Gan replied. "If The Source is the vast ocean of power, then ley lines are the rivers and tributaries that run from it. Their power can be tapped from the surface, much like drawing water from a well, but they themselves exist deep underground. Perhaps one needs to tap directly into a ley line, draw from its power, in order to return upstream..."

"To The Source."

"Exactly, my love."

"And me?" Sheila asked.

Gan turned to her. "A temporary distraction for my beloved. Sadly for you, fate has decreed it to be nothing more."

A momentary silence descended upon the cave, save for

some quiet chuckling from Tom, then Sheila replied, "I meant, how does that affect me stepping through?"

"Ah, I understand now. A ley line, in theory, would possess far more magical energy than a mere sending. It may be enough to overcome even your immunity."

"And if it doesn't?"

"Then we're fucked," I replied.

"No," Gan said. "If so, then we simply resort to more drastic means."

"We start digging?" Tom asked.

"This golem grows tiresome."

"Yeah, we know," Sally said, then turned to my roommate. "How about you go find a nice shiny rock to stare at while the grownups talk?"

"What kind of drastic measures?" I asked. "You don't have another of those fucking blades, do you? Because if you do..."

Gan produced something from one of her pockets. It was a syringe, about a third full with a dirty black liquid. "We have no need of the blades of Baal when we already have the essence we require."

Son of a bitch!

60

MEETING UP WITH OLD FRIENDS

"What the fuck do you have *that* for?"

Gan shrugged as if she'd shown us nothing more interesting than a pen.

"Bill, don't overreact."

"Overreact?" I turned to Sheila. "We saw what that shit did to you last time."

"Yes, and I survived."

"Barely. Answer me, Gan."

"I do so love seeing your fire."

My eyes turned black. All at once, that anger inside of me was practically begging to be let out. "You really don't want to go there, because this is one fire that will burn the shit out of you."

"Way to grow a set, man!" Tom exclaimed, pretty much ruining the mood.

"Do you mind?"

"Once the witches were finished administering it in the Woods of Mourning," Gan replied casually, "I took it upon myself to retrieve what was left."

"Yeah, but why?"

"A precaution."

"Against?"

"Should your final battle with the Shining One not go in your favor."

"What?!" Sheila cried out.

"Hold on; you were going to cheat to help me win?"

"Of course."

"What was all that bullshit, then, about having faith in me?"

"I do, beloved." Gan's voice took on a coldness I'd only seen her use on her subordinates, "but know that I am a descendent of the great Temüjin, heir to his throne. I believe in you with all my heart, but I am no fool. I do not plan my campaigns on faith alone. Fate cannot be denied, but that does not mean it cannot be manipulated by those with the foresight and spine to do so."

Whoa.

Tom nudged Sally. "What was that you were saying a few minutes ago about Crazy Town?"

"Yep, I think we're past vacation and well into having her mail forwarded there."

I stepped up and held out my hand. "Give it to me, Gan."

"I do not believe you are thinking this through logically, my love."

"Hand it over, or so help me..."

"No." Sheila stepped between us. "Give it to me."

"What?"

She rounded on me, her eyes glowing white. "You heard me. Gan is right. The second she hands it over to you, you're going to smash it against a rock or something."

"Pretty much."

"I can't let you do that."

"Yes you can."

"Wrong. I was late to the party with Vehron. Because of that, you had to face him alone. I won't do that to you again, to any of you."

"You don't know Calibra."

"And you do?"

"Well, no, but I've seen her in action. She's unlike anything either of us has ever fought before. Neither of us can face her with anything but our A game. She is the best of both worlds, vampire and mage. If you're vulnerable to either one..."

"And you're not? What about him?" She pointed to Tom and then toward Sally. "Or her."

She had a point. Truth be told, all of us combined might not be enough. Even so, it was a stupid risk for her to wander directly into the lion's den prozacced-out on that shit.

"This is my choice," she said at last, holding out her hand to Gan.

I stepped in front of her. "And what if I say no?"

Her free hand dropped to the hilt of her sword, drawing the blade an inch. "Then we do this final battle right here and now."

"You can't be serious."

"She looks pretty serious to me," Sally said rather unhelpfully.

"Are we taking bets?" Tom asked. "Because no offense, dude, but..."

"Oh, shut the fuck up already," I snapped.

"I'm coming with you no matter what," Sheila said slowly and with finality.

Fuck me! I swear, in the next life, I am making friends who aren't so fucking stubborn.

After a few moments, Gan handed over the syringe. "Well said, Shining One."

Sheila took the needle and pocketed it. "I'm still mad at you."

Gan shrugged as if she expected no less.

"So much for your grand plans," I said with a bitter smirk.

"Worry not, my love, for much like Alexander, I am more than capable of modifying my strategy in the field."

That's what I was afraid of.

One moment, we were walking down the dank tunnel, Sheila softly glowing so as to light the way for her and Tom. The next, we were engulfed in pitch darkness.

"Ow! Fucking wall!" Tom cried out.

The sudden darkness wasn't an issue, but it caught me by surprise, so much that I missed what my other senses were screaming out.

"Oh shit," Sally said. "We're here."

"I believe you are right," Gan replied.

"What are you...?"

That's when it hit me. The scents had abruptly changed along with the lighting. I could still sense the residual smell of the Magi, but there was more ... a plethora of aromas, like a zoo populated by creatures straight out of a nightmare. Beneath it all, almost like a fungus, was a familiar earthy aroma, not much different than the walls around us, but just enough to set off my "Oh Fuck!" alarms. The Jahabich.

"Good thinking dousing the lights," I said. "How did you know to...?"

"Um, Bill?" Sally asked.

"Yeah?"

"Notice anyone missing?"

That's when I realized Sheila hadn't quelled her powers. Our group had somehow become one fewer in number.

"Anyone care to explain for those of us without fucking night vision?" Tom asked. "Or should I just shove my thumb up my ass until someone produces a flashlight?"

"Why should now be any different than at home?" I replied, looking around.

"Oh, for Christ's sake!" Sally shrugged off her backpack and began rooting around in the supplies we'd gotten from the Templar. After a moment, she shoved a Maglite into Tom's hands.

A second later, the cave was aglow again.

"Can you not point that at my face?" I snarled.

"Sorry, man."

I blinked and waited for the spots to disappear before resuming my search. She was just gone, with no trace of what had happened.

"We have crossed over," Gan replied. "The Shining One did not. It would seem I was in error."

"Ya think?" Sally asked.

"Sheila!" I cried out.

Sally smacked me upside the head. "Why not just ring the doorbell, fucktard?"

Oh, shit. "Sorry."

However, a moment later, I thought I heard my name called. It was faint, probably only audible to those of us with super hearing.

"Did you guys...?"

"Yeah," Sally said. "Weird. It's like it came from right here, but far away at the same time."

Right here, but far away ... was it possible? "Hold on; I'm gonna try something."

"Should I duck and cover?"

"Oh ye of little faith."

I turned and began walking back the way we came. For several steps, the tunnel looked no different than it had moments earlier. Suddenly, it all changed, though. The glow from Tom's flashlight was replaced by one of purer white. I turned to find Sheila standing right there behind me. All at once, the smells of creatures from a dozen different mythologies faded away.

"Okay, that was weird."

"You're telling me," she replied. "It's like you guys just winked out of existence. If I didn't know something like that could have happened, I'd probably be questioning my sanity right now."

I looked at her and then had to do a double take, for what I was seeing was seriously fucking trippy. She was there, but so were the others, too, all of them looking my way. They were all standing in roughly the same spot, except there was a double image quality to it, flickering back and forth. One second Sheila seemed real, whereas the rest of my friends looked like ghosts, then it would reverse itself.

"Are you seeing any of this?" I asked.

"What? I don't see anything except you and more cave."

"Guess your powers futzed with the magic after all. But you heard me call out?"

"Yeah, just barely. It sounded like you were at the other end of a bad phone connection."

"I think I know why. It would seem that right about here..." I waved my hand in front of me, and judging by the looks I got from the other three, they saw it, too. "...is the portal, passage, or whatever the fuck it is."

After a moment, Sheila nodded. "It's weird, but I think I knew it was coming."

"You did? How?"

"For the last couple hundred feet, I've been feeling this odd buzzing in the back of my teeth. I thought maybe I was getting a headache. Guess not."

I considered what Gan had said earlier. "It might be the power from the ley line. You could be subconsciously picking it up, like radio interference. I don't know. Hold on a second. Hey, Sally!"

Sally looked directly at me. "Is there a fucking reason you're yelling again when I just told you not to?"

"Wait, you heard that?"

"Loud and clear."

"And what about the last few seconds?"

"We've been listening to you talk to yourself."

"Are you talking to the others?" Sheila asked.

Okay, this was getting weird.

"I must be standing right in the portal," I explained – hopefully to everyone. "I can see and hear all of you, and you can see me, but not each other. Sound about right?"

"Right, if not particularly sane," Sally replied.

"Good enough. Stop fucking around, Tom. It's obscene. She's standing right there."

Sheila's lips narrowed. "What's he doing?"

"Don't ask. Just being an asshole."

"This is fucking cool," he said with another hip thrust.

"It's going to be a lot less cool," I warned, "if I ask her to power up and melt you into a pile of goo again."

"Beloved?"

I let out a sigh. "What, Gan?"

"Please tell the Shining One I would highly recommend she commence with our plan."

"Why?"

"Because I believe we have been noticed."

I didn't hear anything, nor feel any movement from the ground, but judging by Sally's reaction, she did. Maybe I was slightly more on Sheila's side of reality than theirs.

"Oh, shit," she said.

"I'm coming."

Sally held up a hand before I could move, though. "No! Stay where you are. In fact, get behind her, wherever she is."

"Get behind her? What the fuck are you...?"

"I can see you," she hissed, "but I can't smell you. I'm willing to bet neither will they, but the jig will definitely be up if these fuckers can eyeball you standing right there."

"Your whore speaks wisely," Gan said. I think it was meant to be a compliment, but Sally threw her a nasty look regardless. "Do so ... *now*."

I was still confused, but the insistence of Gan's voice got me moving. I backed up a few steps and beckoned Sheila to follow. Thankfully, she didn't waste time on questions. She did as asked, reining in her power enough so I wasn't immediately burnt to a crisp. Over her shoulder, the images of our friends began to waver, taking on that ghost-like quality again. It was Sheila's powers messing with the passage. It had to be.

The sound from the other side grew faint, barely audible, leaving me with a distorted view that more closely resembled an old Charlie Chaplin film than real life.

"Tell me what you see," Sheila said.

The others turned away from us and faced down the tunnel. "I think there's something coming."

"Is it..."

"Yeah, the Jahabich."

An orange glow approached from up ahead. A few moments later, the forms of at least a dozen of the ugly monsters appeared, three wide and several deep.

"Shit! We need to help them. There's no way they can fight off that many."

"Maybe they're not planning to," Sheila said, still blocking my way.

"What do you...?"

That's when I realized what Sally had meant. Neither she nor Gan had taken up defensive positions. They both held their ground, almost casually, as the rocky abominations closed in. Only Tom appeared worried.

"Um, you guys are gonna do something, right? Oh fuck this shit." As the Jahabich closed to within a couple of paces, Tom apparently lost his mind and raced forward.

"Suck my mega-cock, motherfuckers!" He threw a punch, which landed right between the eyes of the first of the creatures and, unsurprisingly, did absolutely nothing.

"What the fuck?"

"What's going on?" Sheila asked.

"Um, hard to describe."

The line of Jahabich halted as Tom continued to rain blow after ineffectual blow on the one he'd decided to attack. It was impossible to attribute emotions to the Jahabich when in their rock monster forms. They didn't have too many other expressions aside from creepy staring. However, if they did, I'm certain the one in the lead would have been expressing embarrassment for my roommate.

It opened its mouth and let out a noise that almost sounded like a sigh, before shoving Tom to the side and approaching the others.

My roommate, for his part, wasn't so easily daunted.

"Yeah, you like that? There's more where that came from. What's the matter, too badass for you?"

"Are they okay?" Sheila asked, her voice barely a whisper. She couldn't see what was going on, but she could probably sense something was wrong.

"For the moment," I replied, my voice just as low.

"*We have been expecting you,*" the Jahabich rumbled. "*Mother has been expecting you.*"

The others behind him echoed the sentiment. "*Mother.*"

"These fuckers definitely have mommy issues," I said. "I guess they weren't loved enough as..."

The words died in my throat as the Jahabich in front began to change. Its rocklike features softened, then became almost fluid-like as its skin flowed and reshaped itself, becoming taller and leaner.

Clubs became hands and the armored skin took on a more refined texture, akin to that of an expensive suit. Finally, the orange holes in its head filled out until a pair of familiar beady eyes stared back at my friends with a mixture of both hostility and triumph.

"Well well well, if it isn't my two favorite ladies of the night," Harry Decker said with a grin. "The trollop and the murderer."

61

IN THROUGH THE BACKDOOR

"S on of a..."

"What is it?"

"It's Decker," I said. "He's alive. I have to..."

Sheila continued to block my way. "Don't."

I made to move around her. Seeing a dead dickhead risen from the grave had that effect on me. All I wanted to do was wipe that smug grin off his face and send him right back to the land of the talking skulls.

She continued to stand between me and the passage and then, finally, when I tried to push my way past, she ignited her aura. It was only a momentary flare up, but it had the desired effect of sending my ass flying back down the cave the way we'd come.

I landed, a bit crispy on the outside, but still in charge of my own faculties.

"Don't give us away," she hissed through gritted teeth, as if being blasted had been my idea.

I was about to voice my thoughts on this when I realized Decker had stopped his gloating to look in our direction. I'd forgotten the magical wall between us was thin enough for some sound to carry through.

Thankfully, he didn't seem to see us. He continued to stare for a moment longer, but then turned back to my friends and commenced monologuing. "Just you two? Curious."

"Yo, dude, I'm here, too," Tom said.

"Speak to me not, fool," Decker spat. "You are the cause of this all, the one who turned my beloved pupil against me."

"Don't blame me, asshole. Once a fine lady knows my cock, there ain't no other she wants to rock."

Oh God, he did not just say that.

"How the fuck have you not died a virgin?" Sally asked with a pained grimace.

"What's going on?" Sheila whispered.

"Oh, the usual. Tom's talking about his dick."

Decker ignored Sally's comment and continued to direct his spittle-flinging fury at my roommate. "And look what it has wrought you. This mockery of life. You are no man, merely the illusion of one."

"Pot calling the kettle black."

Decker smiled again and, this time, I noted his very human-looking teeth. He was another like Starlight, a Jahabich 2.0, a perfect doppelganger. "What I am is blessed, fool. The White Mother has smiled upon me, embraced me, made me whole again." He made a gesture with his hand at my friend, but nothing happened. He looked at it and frowned. Interesting. No magic. That could be useful. "Almost whole, anyway. But soon, once she triumphs, she will fix that. The Source shall wash over me and I shall be reborn as I once was."

"I see death has not made you any less delusional, maapamba," Gan said. "Or are those the words of Ib seeping through your lips?"

Decker hauled off and backhanded her. Her head turned to the side from the blow and a small trickle of blood seeped from the corner of her lips, but that was all the effect it had on her. Impressive. Even though the Jahabich could appear human, they still hit like a ton of bricks. Tough little girl.

"Speak not any of the names of the White Lady, little

murderess. None of you may dare speak of her. You know nothing of her power, her glory, her benevolence."

Tom started moving his fist up and down in a jerking off motion. When he noticed Decker looking incensed at him, he said, "What? I wasn't speaking about her."

I got the feeling it was going to be a race to see who could punch him in the face first – Decker or Sally.

"If you must flap that never-ceasing tongue of yours, then it should be about something of value. The Freewill and the Icon whore. Where are they?"

"What's happening now?" Sheila asked.

"Harry just called you a whore."

Yeah, maybe my play by play left a little to be desired.

Sheila's aura sparked around her, no doubt from annoyance. Couldn't blame her. It wasn't enough for Decker to be an evil prick. He had to be a cock about it too.

"Not here, obviously," Sally replied to him. "Unless you think maybe they're invisible. Hell, they could be right behind you."

Decker actually looked over his shoulder. Dude was seriously paranoid, even if what Sally said was true in a sense.

"We thought it best to split our forces, find another way," Gan said. "It is my hope they had more luck than we did. Perhaps even now they are within Ib's lair, slitting her throat."

"Nonsense!" Decker roared. "Do you think me a fool?" Amazingly enough, Tom let that one slide. "We were made aware that the coven guarding the breach in Boston was compromised, that the Icon and Freewill were both present. Do you honestly expect me to believe they would send you three in their stead?"

"And yet here you are having a conversation with us," Sally replied, adding a generous dollop of smarm, "while who knows what is happening back at your happy little homestead."

That was apparently too much pressure for a nut like Decker to handle without cracking. "We will take them back to the White Mother."

"*Mother*," the Jahabich all echoed.

"Should any of them attempt even the slightest resistance, kill the tramp and the child."

"What, no love for me?" Tom asked. "Not that I'm complaining."

"I am aware of what you are," Decker replied, narrowing his eyes. "I helped create you. That means I can unmake you. But perhaps I shall do so in front of my lost daughter so that she might know the folly she has wrought."

Uh oh. That didn't sound good.

Decker motioned to some of the Jahabich standing in formation. "Go further down the tunnel. Make sure these wretches are not some sort of pathetic distraction so their friends can double back on us. If they are waiting on the other side of the breach, kill them. No, on second thought, just kill the Icon. Leave the Freewill alive, but don't hesitate to hurt him ... *a lot*. Collapse the tunnel when you are finished."

That sounded even less good.

Decker's form wavered and transformed, widening into that of a Jahabich.

Our friends were surrounded and led away from us. Four of the Jahabich then broke ranks and started walking our way.

"Shit!"

"What is it?" Sheila asked.

"Trouble incoming."

"Fight or run?"

I debated for a moment. Running would be useless, as we'd just need to come back anyway, something that would be impossible if they caved in the tunnel. That would put us back to square one and leave Calibra with even more hostages. Fighting was the better option. I had little doubt we could take these assholes together, but if even one got away, it would alert Decker to our presence and we'd be swarmed. With the portal to their backs, the advantage was theirs.

So maybe we needed to remove that advantage.

"Quick," I said. "Turn down your power to the very barest of minimums. Enough for it to be there, but not enough to hurt me."

"Why?"

I looked up and saw the Jahabich shamble forward. "Just do it!"

The light in the cave dimmed as Sheila reined in her aura until she was just barely aglow, as if she were surrounded by flickering candlelight.

"Hold it there."

I stepped up to her, pressing myself against her back and grabbing hold of her waist. There came a tingle, her power reacting against my presence ... but it was low, like licking a nine volt.

"What are you doing?"

"Now walk forward," I whispered. "Quickly!"

She did as told and we both walked forward together while I did my best to ignore the tingling from other parts of me as I rubbed up against her. Oh the things I did to save my friends.

The situation could have quickly gotten a wee bit awkward, but thankfully we had the supernatural equivalent of a cold shower bearing down upon us with their soulless orange eyes.

We neared the Jahabich. "Keep moving."

A couple more steps and we were face to face with them. I sure hoped this worked.

Then, with another step, we walked through each other, the Jahabich passing us as if they were nothing more than ghosts. Yes! I'd been right. Sheila's power was incompatible with the passage, but it had worked in our favor this time, essentially letting two realities exist in the same place.

"Weird," she whispered back. "Felt like I just stepped on my own grave."

"You have no idea."

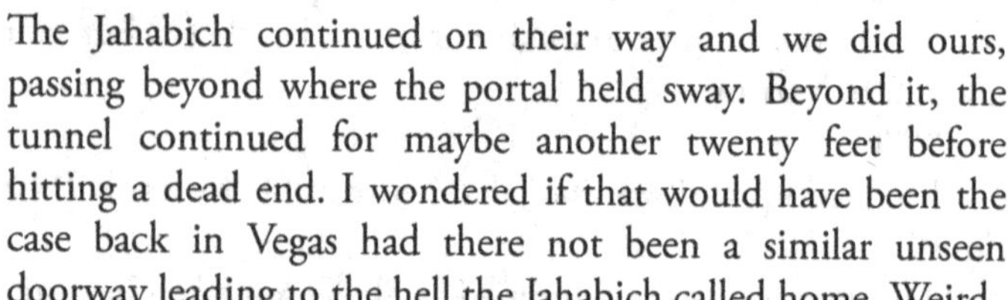

The Jahabich continued on their way and we did ours, passing beyond where the portal held sway. Beyond it, the tunnel continued for maybe another twenty feet before hitting a dead end. I wondered if that would have been the case back in Vegas had there not been a similar unseen doorway leading to the hell the Jahabich called home. Weird.

Even weirder, though, there was light here beyond what Sheila was generating. A soft reddish-orange glow suffused the cave wall, coming from seemingly nothing, unseen from the other side, but clearly visible here. One might have thought the walls were red hot from the look of things, but there was no heat.

"You seeing this?"

Sheila nodded, but said nothing.

"It must be the ley line Gan mentioned. The mages must've magically drilled until they hit it. That's where they set up the passage."

"Um, how long are we gonna stand like this?"

Oh yeah, I was still pressed up against her, and though my mind might've been distracted by the magic around us, my body wasn't. I was sporting some serious timber down below.

This was definitely not the time. Had this been a bad Cinemax movie, this would be the gratuitous scene where the two heroes fucked each other's brains out while hiding from the monsters. Not a half bad idea, but that wouldn't do much to help our friends.

I backed up just enough so that little Dr. Death wasn't painfully obvious. I was probably a few seconds too late for that, but it was the best I had.

"Wait for it," I whispered, guiding us in a circle until we were facing back the way we'd come.

"Wait for what?" she asked, her voice cracking.

"Err, not that," I quickly added before pointing a finger over her shoulder.

The Jahabich had their backs to us, shambling slowly in the other direction. We were hidden from them by the magical doorway we were now apparently standing behind.

"I can see them," she said. "Four, right?"

"Yep. That means they're through the passage and on our side now."

We gave the Jahabich a few more steps, enough to clear the portal and make room for us. Then we doubled back the way we came, in the same close quarters so as to ensure the magic didn't affect me. The tingling continued and I began to smell wisps of smoke rising from my clothes, and not because my dick was trying to bore its way out of my pants either.

Just a few more feet.

Sheila took another step, and the Jahabich turned toward us, seeming to hear the crunch of gravel beneath her feet. We were through and now they knew it, too. Pity the realization came a bit too late for them to save themselves.

Or so I hoped.

I stepped away from Sheila, allowing her to more properly ignite her powers as well as draw her sword.

"Looking for us, assholes?" I gave them a toothy grin before rushing in.

The two in front were my target and I hit them with everything I had. Ugh! It was like ramming my shoulder into a fucking brick wall.

It had the desired effect, though. I sent those two stumbling backward into their buddies at the front of the procession, the added mass knocking them prone.

"Your turn," I wheezed, leaping back to catch my breath and let my strained ribs heal.

"With pleasure," Sheila said, stepping past me.

Though a normal sword would have been worth dick against monsters made of stone, the aura of faith made hers more akin to a fucking lightsaber. I let out a yell of triumph as she bisected the head of the first of the creatures, sending a shower of orange goo splashing onto his friends.

Unfortunately, the cave wasn't quite wide enough for proper Errol Flynn type antics. She was forced to back up, parrying as the next creature reacted with frightening speed, swinging its club arms with enough strength to turn our noggins into a fine red mist.

"Duck!" I yelled, and she did. She swung her sword low while I dove over her shoulder and tackled the thing high.

Its legs came off, and I landed atop it.

Before the rational part of my brain could speak up, I reached into the Jahabich's maw of a mouth and grabbed hold of two of its stalagmite-like teeth. I yanked hard, putting my back into it, and they snapped off, leaving me two handy dandy stone daggers, which I then helpfully gave back to its owner by way of its eye sockets.

I pounded them in until the monster stopped squirming. Unfortunately, whereas my hands might have been a claw hammer, the Jahabich's were fucking Mjolnir by comparison. The two up front had recovered and one caught me square on the chin, sending me flying back while spitting teeth.

I landed and skidded along the rocky floor, clonking my head a few times to make sure I was good and loopy. Fighting these fucking things was so much easier when I was hopped up on vamp blood.

No! Screw that kind of thinking. I didn't need a boost to deal with base level losers like these ... hopefully.

Unfortunately, the Jahabich didn't acknowledge my time out. The tunnel rumbled around us and there came the groan of rocks giving way under pressure. That roused me from my wool gathering. I sat up and saw Sheila engaged in combat with one of the two remaining creatures.

This fucker was seemingly smarter than its friends. Rather than going for the kill, it fought defensively, parrying Sheila's sword strikes so they did minimal damage. Its rocky skin had been chipped away in half a dozen places, allowing the orange glop they called blood to dribble out, but it still seemed to have plenty of fight left in it.

Another micro-tremor struck and I realized why the change in tactics.

Oh, fuck!

It was defending the last one, which was busy clubbing away at the sides of the tunnel. The Jahabich didn't need to win. It only needed to stall Sheila long enough for its friend to bring the whole fucking thing down on our heads. I had no idea how far beneath the earth we were, but it was a safe bet it was more than enough to crush us into paste.

The other Jahabich, the one playing a life-sized game of *Dig Dug,* slammed both its granite clubs into the wall again, and the entire place started to shake as cracks formed along the previously smooth surface.

I scrambled to my feet. "We need to go *now!*"

"I can beat them!" Sheila growled, her tone practically daring me to try and stop her.

Fuck! It was that goddamned Icon self-assuredness taking over again. She'd told me about it, about how little things like common sense stopped being important when there was a fight to be won.

As if to punctuate the point, a massive boulder nearly half as wide as the cave itself came crashing down next to her, kicking up a plume of dust, yet she kept battling the creature as if nothing had happened.

Beyond the Jahabich doing the demolitions work, I could see even more debris falling, rapidly filling up the only way out of here.

No. It was the only way out of here for *one* of us.

That red hot anger inside of me leapt at that thought from seemingly nowhere and grabbed hold of it. It chomped down, using it as fuel, and I realized escape was easy. All I had to do was back up.

A few steps and I'd be elsewhere. There'd be no coming back this way, but that was fine. I could figure it out as I went.

My fangs elongated at the thought. Watching Sheila's lithe form battle the creature, I realized that victory from the accursed prophecy was at hand. Gan would get her wish. I would win, the darkness would take over, and humanity's days in the sun would be numbered.

What the fuck was I thinking?!

I raised a hand and slapped myself, dispelling those thoughts.

Not all of them, though, I realized as I struggled to catch my breath and get my emotions back under control.

The passage behind us was a way out for me, but it didn't need to be that way.

My hands plunged into my pants pockets until they closed upon ... no. That wasn't it. Where the fuck? Oh yeah, I wasn't the one who had it. Shit!

Nevertheless, I had no choice but to remedy that.

I had no fucking idea what I was about to do. Usually, whenever Dave stuck me for the purpose of drawing blood, I was too busy bitching him out to pay attention.

Oh well, time for a crash course.

Sadly, whatever happened next was almost certainly going to hurt me as much as it did her.

I stepped behind Sheila, just outside her aura. The rumbling of the tunnel grew worse, and I realized we had seconds at most. Come on...

The creature parried a thrust from her sword, putting her slightly off balance. It swung at her, but she jumped back at the last second.

Now!

Bracing myself for the hurt to come, I stepped in before she could attack again and grabbed hold of her.

"What are you doing?!"

The fires of faith immediately reacted to me, but I held tight and dug my hands into her jacket. Where the hell was it? The pain was rapidly becoming unbearable and I knew we were seconds from one of two scenarios: either I'd burn to a crisp and we'd be buried, or I'd lose control and we'd be buried.

Fuck that noise.

There! My hands closed upon the syringe and I yanked it free. With no time to waste, I ripped the cap off with my teeth, then, figuring it was as good a place as any, jabbed the needle into her ass.

White fire, rocks, smoke, debris, and a terrible roaring overloaded my senses, causing me to lose track of my surroundings.

It didn't matter.

I knew where I was.

Wrapping my burning arms tightly around Sheila, I spun and kicked off with everything I had left, sending us both flying just as the world crumbled around us.

62

THE BELLY OF THE BEAST

One moment there was the roaring of the cave as it collapsed, the next there came a terrible shriek of pain and betrayal.

I reached up and cupped a hand over Sheila's mouth to stifle the sound. "I'm so sorry," I whispered into her ear.

Already the fire was dying down as her body convulsed, each tremor causing her aura to shrink more and more until it finally winked out entirely, leaving us in darkness.

The air was still filled with dust, some of it having no doubt drifted through the passage, but gone was the rumbling that had signaled the tunnel's destruction. We wouldn't be leaving the way we'd come in, but we'd made it.

We lay there for several minutes – her in the throes of whatever that shit was doing to her insides, me healing from the damage I'd taken saving her.

At last, her body went slack, save for the heavy breathing against my hand. I was about to check to see if she was conscious, but then she bit my finger.

"Ow!"

I pulled my hand back and let her go. We both got back to our feet, albeit she did so a bit shakier than me. While she caught her breath, I turned and looked down the tunnel

Decker and his crew had retreated down. At the moment, nothing was coming our way.

"Bill? Are you there?"

Oh crap, I'd forgotten she was effectively blind down here right now. "I'm here."

"Are you okay?"

"I should probably be asking you that question."

"You first."

"A little crisp around the edges, but I'll live. You're probably a bit pissed right now, but believe me I..."

"I understand," she replied, holding up a hand in almost my direction. "That stuff, it feels like liquid fire in my veins, and my butt hurts a bit, but it definitely cleared my head. Sorry I bit you, by the way."

"That's all right. I enjoy the irony of someone biting a vamp for a change."

"Better watch out; maybe you'll turn into one of me."

"Oh no, not that! Whatever will I do with an extreme amount of confidence?"

"I could think of a few things."

"Like going to Atlantic City and hitting all the tables?"

"Not quite what I had in mind."

"Oh." Pity I didn't have her powers, because I might've had an answer to that. But I didn't, and we really needed to get moving. "Can you walk?"

"I might not be doing any front flips for a while, but I can manage. Seeing might be another issue entirely."

"Not much of a view. Rocks, rocks, and more rocks. Got any juice left?"

She closed her eyes and appeared to concentrate, but the darkness remained. "Nothing," she said. "I'm tapped. Wait a second." Her hands reached down to her empty scabbard and a moment later panic appeared in her eyes. "My sword! Where's my sword?"

"There." I pointed, then realized the idiocy of what I was doing. "Hold on. You dropped it after I injected you, but thankfully it was on this side of things." I took hold of her hand and guided her down to where it lay ... just barely on this side of the passage. The thick layer of dust covering it seemed to confirm this. Luck or fate; one of them was on her side.

Though I was reluctant to do so, her grasping hold of the weapon's grip was the perfect impetus for me to let go of her, as a dull white glow began to suffuse the blade.

"Better?" It wasn't much, about the same one might get from those shitty outdoor solar lights my dad liked to line his driveway with. But it was enough to allow someone to walk slowly down a dark tunnel.

"You have no idea."

"Stay behind me," I said. "You're in no shape to fight."

"And you are?" she replied with a chuckle.

It was meant as a joke, but I could feel that dull anger rising again nevertheless. A voice whispered in my subconscious that I could end this, finish the prophecy right now.

And then marry Gan and end up being her bitch for all of eternity? I thought back at it. *No thanks, asshole.* Aloud, I said, "I'll make do in a pinch."

"How many of those things do you think are down here?" Though she tried to hide it, the tone of her voice was unmistakable – fear. With her powers suppressed, there was nothing to keep those feelings at bay.

No, that wasn't entirely true. "Don't worry about it. You've got this."

"I'm not sure I believe that."

"I do. Look at you. Most people would be shitting themselves right now, but you're holding it together."

"Barely."

"Join the club. I'm serious. You're a lot stronger than you think you are, and it has nothing to do with being the Icon."

She smiled back at me, the glow from the sword lighting up her face. "You're not so bad yourself."

"I have my moments." I grinned back, then turned to lead the way.

"You didn't answer my question," she said after a few moments of walking.

"Heh, I thought the answer would be obvious," I replied. "All of them."

I'd been hedging my bets that we wouldn't run into another Jahabich patrol for a while, but it had nothing to do with luck or sound strategy.

No, it was because Harry Decker had been in charge of the last group. Though I knew the Jahabich had a hive mind when in their rock forms, there was still some influence from their original personalities. Unless Mommy Dearest took complete control of the reins, they appeared to have the ability to make their own decisions. Based on what I'd seen of Starlight, this new batch, the upgraded models, seemed to be even more inclined toward independent thought.

That was good for us. Decker was both an ass-kisser and a flaming egomaniac. I was willing to bet he'd been paranoid enough to send that patrol out looking for us, but his ego would demand no others be allowed to double check his work.

Sure enough, we walked for what seemed like miles without seeing or hearing anything. They were there, though; my nose confirmed it, along with lots of other *things*.

It wasn't a matter of *if* we'd run into something. It was a matter of *when*. Decker's arrogance had merely postponed it long enough for us to get close.

"Put your sword away," I whispered.

"Why?"

"I don't think you need it anymore ... at least to see."

She did as asked, revealing a dim light that remained even after the weapon was sheathed. A faint glow was coming from the walls – that bioluminescence I'd seen the last time I was down here. It wasn't much, but it would allow us to continue onward without the risk of her sword drawing attention to us.

"It's beautiful," she said, studying a section of wall that was home to a multi-colored collection of glowing crystals.

"You ain't seen nothing yet. It's a really pretty place, housing some really ugly tenants."

"Fate has a sense of irony."

"It would seem so."

We continued onward. The glow from the walls grew stronger, albeit never much more than a child's nightlight. Nevertheless, it told me we were getting closer.

"How are you feeling?" I asked.

"I should have worn different shoes."

"I meant your powers."

"Let's just say I've wanted to puke ever since we got here, but I'm not sure if it's nerves or that shit you injected me with."

"Probably a little from column A, a little from column B. Still beats being buried alive."

"I'll give you that, if barely."

"Give it a few. I'm sure the real horrors haven't even begun yet."

"Your confidence is reassuring."

"And I don't even have Icon powers. Go fig ... stop!"

"What is it?"

"Hold on." I halted my advance and peered ahead, my eyesight cutting much further into the gloom than Sheila's. That'd teach her to roll up a character without at least low-light vision.

Once more, my mind was compensating for the mind-numbing fear by shunting into gamer mode. Hell, if I didn't think it would've burned my fingers off, I'd have asked to borrow her sword to complete the illusion. It was definitely preferable to pissing myself.

Now if only the dice would prove to be in my favor...

What had caused me to stop was the proverbial light at the end of the tunnel. Up ahead, the passage ended and a brighter glow shone through. I had a sneaking suspicion I knew what we'd find once we emerged. Problem was, that was when the tricky part began. The first chamber of the Jahabich lair was massive, so it offered some wiggle room in case we chickened out and decided to run for our lives. However, it wasn't particularly great when it came to hiding spots.

Of course, that was just the ground level. I wasn't quite as adept with my claws as a certain psycho princess, but I had them. Maybe that was our strategy right there. Sheila would go low, then I'd strike from above.

Batman, eat your heart out.

I turned to her. "Here's the plan. We..."

"Come out, Bill. I know you're there."

The voice wasn't particularly loud. It didn't need to be. Nevertheless, I spun back toward it quick enough that even Sheila let out a little whoop of surprise.

I glanced down the tunnel again to where it opened up. This time, a figure stood right outside, silhouetted by the soft light behind it.

We weren't close enough for me to pick out many details. Regardless, I knew that voice and it definitely didn't belong to Harry Decker.

The figure started to walk toward us, alone but sure in its steps.

It didn't take long for me to be able to make out details — feminine curves, long dark hair, a generous bust.

Running was pointless. Where would we go? There'd been no side tunnels or forks in the path. Even if we did run, she would certainly hear our footsteps retreating.

I glanced back at Sheila and let out a sigh of defeat. So much for plan A.

I'd fumbled my sneak roll. Withdrawing wasn't an option. And going straight into initiative seemed a poor plan. Thankfully, I had one fallback. I'd always been big on pumping up my bluff score, no matter my character class.

"Hey, Star," I said casually. "You're looking well."

63

WELL, THAT WAS EASY

"How did you know it was us?" I asked my former friend turned Jahabich slave.

I hadn't been lying; she did look good. Last time we'd met, Christy had accidentally taken off the top of her head, but I was happy to see it had grown back. Either that, or someone down here had a concrete patching kit handy.

Starlight put her hands on her shapely hips and inclined her head. "Decker came marching out a little while back with Sally and Gansetseg in tow. He told us he'd taken precautions against you following, but I had a feeling you wouldn't be far behind."

"Let me guess, you realized Decker has shit for brains?"

She smiled. "He hasn't been with us for long, but I remembered the things you told me about him."

Smart of her, and also giving credence to my theory that these new and improved Jahabich had even more of their sense of self than the old models. Maybe it was something I could use to my advantage.

"We've met, haven't we?" Sheila asked from behind me. "Bill's *sister*, right?"

Starlight nodded. "Simpler times. Safe to say we've both changed."

"For better or worse?" I asked.

"I'm still me, Bill," she said.

"I wish I could believe that."

"That's why I'm here. I could have sent in an army to flush you out, but I was hoping I wouldn't need to."

I considered our options. We could take Star, I was sure of it. But then what? Also, I wasn't certain I wanted to. Despite my assertion otherwise, I believed her. She was still in there. Problem was, if push came to shove, she could be dragged back into the collective. That had already been proven when she'd sold us down the river to Vehron.

"Sally?" I asked.

"Unharmed. They only arrived a few minutes ago. I got the impression, based on what I could hear, that she and Harry spent a good deal of the trip sniping at each other."

"Who won?"

Starlight laughed, the sound way too cheerful for such a dark place. "I think we both know the answer to that one."

She turned and led the way forward. Not seeing many other options, we followed.

"Not going to demand our weapons?" Sheila asked as we neared the cavern entrance.

"Harry told us everything, what was needed for you to step through the passage. You're no threat to us."

"How do you know we didn't find another way?"

"Even if you had," Star replied, "my statement still stands."

She stepped aside for us, revealing the outer chamber of the Jahabich lair, still as fucking huge as I remembered it. However, it was a bit less empty.

Last time, the welcoming party had consisted of Sally's ex and a few of his close buddies. Now, the extended family was here. We're talking hundreds of Jahabich, maybe thousands, and they weren't alone, albeit it was difficult to tell which of the other creatures present were those rocky fuckers in their alternate modes. I saw humans, vamps, Sasquatches, four-armed imps, winged monstrosities, piles of living goo – you name it. At first glance, I thought they were all wandering freely, but then I saw the pens. Scores of the Jahabich, standing side by side, forming living walls around the creatures held captive. Nobody I recognized yet, but this place was enormous and I could see only a small portion of it from my vantage point.

Starlight held out an arm as if welcoming us in. "You're free to wander. Explore as you please, just so long as you do not try to leave or disturb any of the ... *enclosures*. Ib will summon you when she so desires."

I turned to Sheila. "Welcome to the party. Feel free to mingle."

"Oh, and Bill," Starlight said, sounding so much like her old self that it was almost painful to listen to. "A word of advice."

"Yeah?"

"Be careful. You're not among friends here. There are ears everywhere and Ib's temper is not to be trifled with."

I recalled the fight at the Boston Prefect's office, when Calibra almost popped me like a zit for mouthing off. "Noted."

Movement caught my eye and I saw a group of the rock-faced fuckers headed our way. Our tour guides, maybe?

"*What are they...*" The Jahabich in the lead changed form mid-sentence. "...doing here?!"

"Hey, Harry," I replied. "Bang up job you did of catching us. You really haven't lost your touch, you know."

"How did you ... It matters not." He turned to the group he'd led over. "Kill the Icon and ensure the Freewill's tongue is in no position to continue its ceaseless flapping."

The other Jahabich, however, didn't move.

"Did you not hear me?"

"They did, as you well know," Starlight replied. "Mother has dictated differently."

"*MOTHER!*"

The word rumbled through the cave as if it were thunder,

the product of hundreds of vocal chords, Harry's included, crying out in unison.

Once it passed, I saw embarrassment clearly etched on his face.

"So that's the magic word, eh?" I remarked. "Pity it's not 'dickhead.' That one better suits you."

"Laugh while you can, fool, for I can assure you that you shall soon join the cry with the rest of us." He grinned broadly. "That stupid moniker of yours, Freewill, shall become the ultimate irony once that transpires. I do not pretend to know the will of the White Mo..." He hesitated, perhaps knowing he'd set off every fucking Jahabich in the place again. "Of the mighty Kala, but I am certain of one thing: you will never set foot from this place again as anything other than a slave."

He stepped past me, glowering at Sheila. "As for you, vile beast, foul temptress of the Apocalypse, know that I am beyond the touch of destiny now. Nevertheless, I will sacrifice all that I have to ensure yours never comes to pass. The Magi shall live and they shall remember my name as the one who sent you to a well-deserved grave."

Sheila locked eyes with him. For a moment, I was certain she'd draw her sword, which I had a feeling would end very badly for us. Instead, she simply said, "Just so you know, even if none of this had happened, there was no chance of you ever getting a second date."

With that, she stepped past him and grabbed my arm.

"Let's go find our friends."

I didn't know what was creepier: being captured or that our hosts were so secure in their power they didn't feel the need to take us captive.

I tried to ask Starlight where our friends were. Hell, we couldn't have been far behind Sally and the others. But she'd apparently reached the limit of her *me time*. She transformed into the shape of a Jahabich, scarring still visible on the top of her head in this form, and then melted into the crowd. I had a feeling we weren't going to find her again until she wanted to be found.

"This is almost too much to take," Sheila said quietly from my side, her eyes darting every way. Her standoff with Harry had been an act, her Icon powers still suppressed. Now that we'd made it a point to get the fuck away from him, she was beginning to become unnerved.

Couldn't say I really blamed her.

Imagine being in Hell's petting zoo, except the attractions really weren't anything you'd ever want to pet. I was tempted to call out to Sally via compulsion, but I was kind of afraid that might violate the terms Starlight had given us. She hadn't specifically said I couldn't, but it was probably wise to walk on the proverbial eggshells just this once. "How the hell are we going to win this?"

It was mostly rhetorical, but Sheila replied, "I'm not sure we can."

"Well, this is new."

Things had changed, but not in a good way. We'd been making our way forward, my goal being to see if they'd let us into the inner chamber, home of the orange goo pool, when shimmering light from above caught my eye.

Though I couldn't be certain we were in the exact same place as last time, I had a feeling we were close. Gone was the massive cave painting that had once dominated the wall.

No, gone was the wrong word.

It had been changed. The rock wall bore signs of being scoured clean, much of the surface now shimmering like glass. This only served to enhance what had been put in its place – a giant effigy of the white mother. The image, outlined in more of that bioluminescence, had to be at least fifty feet high. It was still crude – the Jahabich were a lot of things, but awesome graffiti artists wasn't one of them – but it was similar to other depictions we'd seen of her, glowing white with her arms outstretched.

It was safe to say this chick had a bit of an ego.

"Wow," was all Sheila said.

"That's a word for it," I replied, taking it all in. "It's changed. The spell, the one we'd hoped to use to stop the Jahabich, it's been wiped clean." I explained to her what we'd seen, since I hadn't shown her the pictures I'd taken from last time. "Here's the funny part. When we first saw it, we thought it was you."

"Me?"

"Well, an Icon anyway, because of the white glowing and shit."

"Guess you were wrong."

"No shit, Sherlock," I muttered.

We stood there, arm in arm, staring at the massive effigy for probably longer than we should have, but it was hard to look away. It was both beautiful in its simplicity, shining down upon the cavern, but at the same time carried with it a foreboding, as if the person depicted was unto a god. A scary thought, especially considering she probably was.

"It's about goddamn time," a voice said from behind us, startling us from our reverie.

We both spun to find a sight for the sorest of eyes staring back at us, looking quite annoyed.

"If I may be so bold as to interrupt date night," Ed continued, "could we maybe get on with the fucking rescue already?"

64

THE NEW BREED

I might've been a wee bit too enthusiastic in my response to seeing Ed. I threw myself at him, only realizing too late I was exerting enough pressure to shatter his ribs.

Except I didn't. He caught me and returned my bear hug with surprising strength. Oh yeah. I'd almost forgotten what Gan had said about him being not quite normal anymore.

I stepped back, allowing Sheila to step in for a hug.

Once that was finished, I said, "So ... you're looking well."

"You really are a fucking asshole, you know that?"

"It's part of my charm."

"Which explains your love life," he added.

"Seriously, are you okay?"

He looked down at himself. "Do I look okay?"

It was only then that I realized his clothes were in tatters, filthy ones at that. Speaking of which, he smelled ... not good.

"In case you're wondering," he replied to my unspoken question, "there aren't any fucking shower facilities, unless you want to take a bath in that orange shit next door."

"As fascinating as your hygiene is, what the fuck is going on?"

"What I think Bill means to say," Sheila said, "is we

446

planned on a lot of scenarios, but not finding you here ... like this."

"Walking around freely?" Ed asked.

"Yeah."

"Where the fuck am I gonna go? When I first got here, there wasn't shit I could do anyway. Sucks being the weakest guy in the room, let me tell you."

"Something you should be used to," I said.

Ed flipped me the finger. "Then, after *this* happened..." He opened his mouth, revealing fangs. "They kept me caged up for a while, but thankfully your friend, that woman from your coven..."

"Starlight?"

"Yeah," he replied. "She convinced the queen bitch there wasn't any way for me to escape. Said so long as I cooperated, I should be allowed to wander freely."

"Cooperated?"

"She keeps mixing up shit for me to drink, but mostly I get to suck people on command."

I raised a fist to my mouth and made a back and forth motion.

"Not like that, dipshit."

"Have you..." Sheila tried to suppress a grin, but failed. "Had to suck on a lot of people?"

"You too?" he asked with a pained sigh. "I see you've been spending too much time with this one."

I shrugged. "What can I say? I rub off on people. How many, though?" I looked around, as if this new breed of vamps was even remotely conspicuous.

"Don't bother," he replied. "Seems to be a pattern. I bite someone, then never see them again. That is, until about ten minutes ago. I could have sworn I saw that little nutcase."

"Gan? Yeah, she's here, too."

"Just fucking great. Well, she might not be for long. Calibra and her lackeys seem to have forgotten I picked up those vampire ears you're always bragging about. She hasn't been happy with the results, whatever that means. Keeps bitching about one failure after the other. I kinda got the impression those others weren't long for this world."

That jibed with what Gan had told us. Ib was looking for a way to purify the vampire race, but so far her experiments had two failings: the new converts were mules and they couldn't be controlled. I had a feeling that latter one was the bigger sin in her eyes, but there were too many unfriendly ears present to bring Ed up to speed.

"Wait; you said she had you drinking stuff," Sheila said. "What kind of stuff?"

"I feel like a total tool saying this, but I'm pretty sure we're talking magic potions."

"Cure light wounds? Invisibility?" I offered.

Ed let out a bitter laugh. "I'd already be home if it was that last one. More like potion of tastes like shit."

"I don't think I've seen that one in the Player's Handbook."

"We're talking some nasty stuff here, man. Like, I spent most of yesterday puking my guts up, nasty."

"Tasty."

"You don't know the half of it. Whatever I was regurgitating actually ate through solid rock."

"Shades of Alien."

"Tell me about it. No idea why she decided to choose me as her personal food taster, but I wish she hadn't."

Sheila and I shared a knowing glance. Ib was experimenting, trying to modify Ed into her ideal of a perfect vampire. All of the powers and none of the weaknesses, save the one most important to her: susceptibility to compulsion.

He backed up a step and crossed his arms over his chest. "You guys know something."

"Huh?"

"I'm not a fucking idiot, Bill. The meaningful glance you two just shared was about as subtle as your poker face, which is to say not at all."

Goddamn it! "The walls have ears," I said quietly.

"Well aware," he replied. "It's cool. I just hope it's something that'll help get us the fuck out of here."

On that, I honestly couldn't give him an answer.

"Have you seen the others?" I asked.

"Aside from you two and Gan?"

"Yeah. Tom…"

"Tom? Wait. What was that shit you were telling me about him being…"

"A Barbie doll? He got better."

"In a manner of speaking," Sheila added.

"But yeah, him, and all the others, too. Dave, James, Sally, Christy, Christy's coven…"

"Jesus fucking Christ, man, did you let everyone get captured?"

"Don't judge me."

He lifted a hand and massaged the bridge of his nose. "No offense, Bill, but you seriously suck when it comes to rescues."

"Oh yeah? How about when I saved your ass from Remington?"

"I got bitten."

"What about when Vehron thought you were an abomination?"

"My new car got trashed."

"Um, when Turd kidnapped you?"

"They tore my clothes off, painted me with shit, and then I got captured by Vehron again."

"You're a bit of a negative Nancy, you know that?"

He turned to Sheila. "At least you're here."

I lowered my voice to a whisper and leaned in. "About that. She's kinda powerless right now."

"Please tell me it wasn't thanks to you."

"Well…"

He held up a hand. "You really do make switching sides

sound like a good idea. To answer your question, though, I haven't seen anyone else who was captured recently, but this place is huge and packed. It's like trying to pick someone out of the crowd on 7th Avenue."

"Shit."

"That doesn't mean I can't speculate. Calibra has her own spot in the inner chamber. It's where she keeps counsel with her most favored minions and tortures her least. Needless to say, I don't get too many invites on that first roster, and I've been trying my best not to qualify on the second."

"What about the vampires she kidnapped?" Sheila asked.

"Some of the vamps down here are on her side. They swallowed the fucking Kool Aid. As for the rest, she keeps them compelled." He turned to me. "Pretty sure your friend James is in that latter group."

"That would make sense. He's too powerful to let run loose and probably too valuable as a hostage to kill. Dave?"

"Firebird has him."

"Wait, Firebird?"

"That redhead from your coven, the one you were always complaining put out for everyone but you."

I could feel Sheila's eyes boring into me. "I know who she is," I snapped, "and I'll have you know I was always a perfect gentleman to my coven members. But, uh, anyway, what was that about her having Dave?"

"Just like I said," he replied. "Word got out that he was a friend of yours, so Firebird asked if she could keep him as a plaything. I got the sense she was kind of burning you in effigy through him, except I suspect with more fucking than actual fire."

"Is he okay?"

"Haven't seen him in a while. Don't know. All I can say for certain is I didn't bite him."

"Lucky you."

"Lucky him, too, considering."

He had a point. Vampires who could act freely during the day and couldn't be compelled were dangerous all around. Even those devoted to her would be suspect. Vehron had spoon fed me some bullshit about how Ib's teachings were all about freedom. Problem was, there was already a vampire hierarchy in place to be overthrown. Even he had to admit some revisions to their dogma might be necessary until such time as they prevailed.

"First things first," I said, lowering my voice, for all the good it would do. "We focus on any friends in immediate danger. Christy managed to piss off Calibra big time. From the sound of things, she isn't going to be too big on Gan's continued existence either. And, if Decker has his way, I have a feeling Sally might be in for it, too."

"We need to find them all," Sheila replied.

"I know, and like Ed said, this place is enormous."

"So what do we do?"

"I hate to say this. It goes against every gamer instinct I have, but I don't think we have a choice in the matter." I looked them both in the eye. Sheila was powerless, and we'd gone through so much to find Ed. It wasn't fair to have to say goodbye so quickly, but it needed to be done.

"We need to split the party ... again."

65

SEEING THE SIGHTS

"**S**ally might be with the rest of the compelled vamps," Ed said. "I'll check there."

His reasoning for going after her was probably slightly less than platonic. However, he knew this place better than us. It would allow him a decent shot at finding out for certain quickly.

"It's over that way." He pointed toward the far end of the cavern.

"Fair enough." I turned to Sheila. "You check out this end."

"What about you?"

"I'm heading further in."

"I should be the one to..."

"No!" With her powers at full, she was a paragon of self-assurance, an iron will that could not be overcome. Right now, though, she was just herself. Hell, she actually jumped back at my interruption. "I've been here before. I know the way, mostly."

"But Calibra is in there somewhere."

"Yep, and if she is, I'll deal with her best I can." I held up a hand. "At least, until you're ready."

"But I am."

"No, you're not." She opened her mouth to argue, but I

talked over her. "Stick to the rules while you're searching. Look, but don't touch unless you absolutely must. If you find our friends and they're okay, come looking for us. If not..." I glanced down at her sword. "But only if you have to. Keep it sheathed otherwise. If they're good to their word, they won't hurt you."

"You're not the boss of me," she replied.

"I technically outranked you at Hopskotchgames."

"We don't work there anymore."

"Fine. I'm the Freewill and, right now, you're a puny human. Don't make me compel you."

"You wouldn't."

"Try me." It was a pathetically idle threat, but she didn't need to know that.

We stared each other down for a long moment, but in the end, she looked away first. Oh yeah! Who stared down the Icon? This guy!

"This conversation isn't over." She turned and stalked away.

I was actually glad to hear that.

It meant she was planning on living long enough to bitch me out.

It's not uncommon for me to get that feeling of being watched. Oftentimes, that's no more than bullshit on my part, except of course when it isn't. It was quite the opposite here, though. Creatures – Jahabich, humanoids, other things – all passed me by, none of them looking my way. Heck, I tried a friendly "Hi!" a few times to no avail. It was almost like being invisible. At the same time, I knew the second I took a shit without asking permission they'd swarm me mercilessly.

It really was the perfect prison – the illusion of freedom, but unescapable at the same time. Well, unescapable at the moment. Personally, I was counting on that infamous supernatural arrogance to expose a few cracks in the armor of this place. No idea what I'd do once I found them, but, whatever happened, there would be plenty of chaos to go around.

For now, though, I was walking through a tunnel that looked sorta familiar – as familiar as tunnels that all looked alike could be anyway. The main thing was, it was headed in the direction I remembered being right.

As the soft light of the crystals in the wall gave way to a brighter glow from ahead, one that suffused everything with a bloody haze, I found myself rethinking the wisdom of splitting up. I could have used some of Ed's complaining to lighten the mood. Sheila was still recovering from the effects of the cursed blood, but she had her sword and that made her potentially dangerous.

The person I was really missing, however, was Sally. We'd walked into nearly every hellacious situation imaginable together. Sure, I'd managed to defeat Vehron without her. Even after that, though, even after proving to myself I could stand alone, it still didn't mean I wanted to. They say perception is nine-tenths of reality. Well, my perception was that we, as a whole, were greater than the sum of our parts.

Albeit, Sally did have some tasty parts.

Yeah, that was more like it. When in doubt, tits will always trump terror.

Mind you, as I stepped out into the massive cavern, even the thought of luscious breasts wasn't quite enough to keep my jaw from dropping open in awe.

"Holy shit."

Calibra had been busy. Much like Alexander, it seemed her favorite subject was none other than herself. On the far end, I spied the pool of orange goop – the supposed Source. It colored everything in sight with its glow, giving the place a serious horror movie vibe.

When last I'd visited, there'd been a time-weathered statue of the White Mother overlooking it. Now, three much newer and larger statues stood around the perimeter. The glow from the pool painted them all a sinister blood red.

Fitting, considering what a psycho hell-bitch she'd turned out to be.

There were even more living pens of Jahabich here. Prisoners of myriad races stood inside of them. A few still looked defiant, but many more appeared to have given up hope.

Hell's concentration camp wasn't the only sight to see, though. Scores of white-robed figures took up almost every space free of Jahabich. The Magi, more than I'd ever seen in one place. Some were chanting, others meditating. Many writhed on the floor, their arms entwined around each other and their robes pushed to the side to allow access to the goodies beneath.

Ooh, a sorcerer gang bang. Guessing Calibra subscribed to the Thulsa Doom method of doing business. A happily fucking crowd was one less likely to ask questions.

I wandered a bit closer to one such cluster of half-naked flesh to get a better look … y'know, to make sure it wasn't anyone I knew. A witch who was being energetically plowed by some dude's wizardly staff saw me and hissed in my direction.

"Works much better when you have fangs, babe," I replied, quickly retreating before the fireballs could start flying.

Good job, Bill. Piss off the natives before you've managed to cobble together any resistance.

Now where to start? I glanced around, then stopped as my eyes took in another new addition to the place.

A massive structure stood on the far end of the cavern away from the pool. It was partially obscured by all the various entities milling around, but my first impression was of the pueblo dwellings I'd read about in American History class. It appeared to be made of the same stone as the rest of the cavern. Where those were squarish in shape, though, this architectural monstrosity was all curves and domes. It didn't look built so much as melted off the wall and then reformed before it cooled down.

As I focused on it longer, I realized it looked less like a

Native American dwelling and more like some infernal fortress. Dave had once taken us on an adventure through the nine hells, and his description of the city of Dis could have easily applied to this.

I would definitely need to check that out, assuming I was allowed. If there was one place down here that looked like it was a seat of power, that was it. Calibra was most likely in there.

If what Ed had told me was true, then so was Dave ... currently playing muff-slave to Firebird. Some assholes had all the luck.

Had some of my other friends been brought there as well?

It was definitely a possibility, but first I needed to check out the holding pens.

A part of me felt like a kid walking up and down the lines at the dog pound, trying to pick my lost puppy out of the crowd. Most of the holding cells were easy to dismiss, containing *things* that I was pretty certain I'd never met.

Last time I'd been here, I'd been one of the *attractions*, far more focused on escape than sightseeing. Now, I found myself losing focus as I stopped to gawk. I mean, shit, they had a fucking *dragon* in one – the size and shape of a Tyrannosaurus, but with two sets of wings that looked big enough to attach to the side of a passenger jet. It wasn't going to be flying anytime soon, though. It was stuck fast to the floor, massive boulders pinning down all four of its wings while a living chain made of Jahabich was wrapped around its neck.

I wasn't here to throw peanuts at Smaug, however, so it was with some reluctance I forced myself to turn away and keep moving.

There! I spied a pen of vamps. Though I didn't recognize their faces, their uniforms stood out. It was some of the guys Alex had brought to Boston after I'd beaten Vehron. He'd sent them on a search and destroy mission, mostly that latter. They'd been in the process of mercilessly mowing down all the vamps in the Prefect's chamber when Calibra had made her grand entrance.

I didn't actually know these guys from a hole in the wall, but it was nice to finally see something recognizable.

Things had definitely changed, though. Last time, we'd seen other vampires here too, but they'd been feral. They'd been starved and had turned on each other while their uncaring captors did nothing to stop it. New security protocols had obviously been instituted since then, quite possibly as a result of my meddling. These vamps looked hungry, pale, and gaunt. They'd seen better days. But they weren't attacking each other. They weren't doing anything at all, as a matter of fact.

They stood in precise formation inside the walls of their living cage. It didn't take a genius to realize they'd been compelled into obedience. Interesting. They'd almost certainly been insulated against betraying the Dracs, but Calibra was no idiot. A neutral compulsion, basically telling one's victims to do nothing at all, required far less effort. Considering the size of this place and the number of prisoners I'd seen, it made sense. As Gan had told us, even the most powerful vampire in the world could only control so many.

This was her cannon fodder, no doubt waiting for her to perfect whatever she was doing to Ed.

I heard footsteps approach and turned to see a column of Jahabich walking my way. Marching four wide, they took up almost the entirety of the row where I was standing.

I'd stepped to the side so as to not get trampled when I realized they weren't the only ones in their little parade. There was an open space in the middle of their column where other figures were being herded along – a Sasquatch, a couple of imps, and one or two other figures I didn't recognize. I was just about to turn away when I spied a wisp of what I thought might be blonde hair, just barely visible even over the somewhat short statures of their Jahabich captors.

No, what were the chances?

Nevertheless, I had to be certain. I stood up on my tiptoes so as to make sure ... OOF!

One of the Jahabich in the lineup abruptly stepped away from his buddies and slammed a club arm into my side. Confusion gave way to pain as my ribs cracked and I went down to my knees. The fuck?! I hadn't interrupted anything, at least not yet. I'd just been looking.

Sadly, this particular blockhead didn't seem to have gotten the memo. It raised the same arm again and then brought it down across the back of my head.

I guessed that meant the show was over as my sight exploded into a mass of stars followed by blackness.

66

FIRST IN LINE

I couldn't have been out for long. I knew how hard these things could hit when they wanted to, and this hadn't been anywhere close. If anything, it had seemed to pull the punch at the last second.

Feeling bruised and a bit trampled, I opened my eyes and sat up. Next to me stood the wall of Jahabich still acting as both warden and jail cell for Alex's vamps.

"No, it's okay. I don't need any help," I said to absolutely no reaction. Humorless fucks.

Forgetting myself for a moment, I tried to use one to pull myself back to my feet and got a lacerated hand for my troubles. Yeah, I really needed to remember to look, but not touch, around these jokers.

I stood up, dusted myself off, and prepared to continue with my sightseeing. If this pen housed Alex's men, then perhaps I was getting closer to where I might find some trace of my friends. Still, I hesitated. There was something about the Jahabich who'd clobbered me. He hadn't merely brushed me to the side. It had felt ... deliberate.

Then there was that wisp of blonde hair I thought I'd seen. If there was even a chance, however small, I had to know for certain.

Letting curiosity get the better of me, I turned and walked back in the direction they'd been headed.

I reached the end of the aisle and looked around. At first, I saw nothing but more mages involved in their hippy-dippy shit, although if any wanted to send any free love my way...

No! Enough of that. I was here for a reason, not to take a ride on the magic bang bus.

Tearing my eyes away from one couple fucking each other's brains out three feet above the ground, I turned the way I'd come in. Nothing there to be seen. I then glanced back toward the glowing jizz pool. Looked like the Jahabich were lining up prisoners to take the last bath of their lives. Poor fuckers.

I spied several creatures in the lineup, including a petite redhead. Sadly for them, I couldn't help without...

That's when I did a double take. The woman's hair wasn't red at all. It just looked that way due to her proximity to The Source. I started that way, focused on her.

Her head just barely cleared the Jahabich around her, so it was hard to tell. But then she shifted her stance ever so slightly and I caught a glimpse of her profile.

It was Sally.

Shit!

She was third in line – no, make that second. I watched as a Jahabich up front dispatched some sort of two-legged slug thing, then threw its body into the pool. I didn't wait to see what happened next. I'd already been to this matinee once before. No need for an encore, especially when one of my closest friends stood in a line that definitely didn't lead to the concession stand.

I put on speed and raced toward them.

Thankfully, the path to The Source was fairly clear. It was either off limits, considered sacred, or everyone in this fucking place was smart enough to know there were friendlier shores to sunbathe upon. I made it there just as the next in line, a vampire I didn't recognize, was clubbed in the head like a baby seal. The Jahabich who'd done it shifted back to human form so as to catch the ashes in the cup of his hand.

God fucking damn!

Harry Decker grinned my way as he tossed the vamp's remains over his shoulder into the pool, where the surface immediately began to bubble.

"Sally!" I cried to no avail. She stood there, still as a post, waiting her turn. Fucking compulsions! Sadly, I had no way of telling by who. If it was Calibra, I'd have a better chance of fighting off this whole place by myself than breaking it.

That didn't mean I wouldn't try.

Two Jahabich stepped up to either side of her and began to nudge her forward toward Decker, shithead that he was.

All the while, he watched me coming at them, his grin growing wider with every step I took. I expected him to shift back into his rock monster form, but instead, he remained as he was. As I closed in, he reached behind his back and produced a wooden stake.

The meaning was clear – this was personal, and he wanted me to know who did it.

Thankfully, I had a little more to give and put it all into my legs as I rushed forward at a speed that would have made even my fourth grade gym teacher stop giving me shit. I lowered my shoulder, braced for the hurt to come, and slammed into the Jahabich on Sally's right – cracking my collarbone but sending it tumbling end over end until it landed in the goo pool with a splash.

I didn't stop to gawk at what two dips would do to these cocksicles. Instead, I stepped between Sally and Decker. "Nice try, asshole. But, much like your last marketing campaign, this scheme of yours is gonna fall flat on its fucking face."

Decker's eyes narrowed at me as Sally bumped into my back, still trying to march to her doom.

"A failure?" he asked. "I wouldn't call two million views on YouTube plus over fifty thousand Facebook shares something to sneer at. If anything, the shoddy code of that game caused its downfall, or have you forgotten the privacy debacle that followed?"

"Fuck you! I told Jim people would freak out if we harvested their browser histories, but I got shot down."

"So that's your excuse? You were merely at the mercy of the whims of others?"

"Whatever works."

"True enough. Pity for you, history is doomed to repeat itself."

"How so?"

"Do you really think I care anything at all about your trollop? She is as far below me as I am beneath the glory that is the White Mother."

Cries of "*Mother!*" rang out.

Goddamn, that was starting to get annoying.

"No," Decker continued, twirling the stake like he was trying out for high school marching band, "I simply wanted to draw you in."

"Well, it worked. So what now, magic man? Gonna dazzle me with a card trick?"

"I wasn't finished. I wanted to draw you in, so you would *interfere.*"

Oh, shit. I'd forgotten all about the one rule that had been dropped in my lap upon arrival.

I looked around, and, sure enough, all the Jahabich in the immediate vicinity were closing in on my direction. And here I was, still stuck trying to keep my friend from marching forward.

"Sorry, Sally. Please try to understand." I spun, quick as I could, and decked her in the jaw with an uppercut. She landed on the ground, dazed. Okay, that was one problem solved. No way could I defend us both, especially with her intent on taking a swim.

"So tell me, Freewill," Decker said, "how does it feel to know that, once again, you are a victim of nothing more than your own stupidity?"

I tried to keep an eye on all directions at once. Sadly, all of them looked equally bad.

"Hold him," Decker ordered. "But feel free to rough him up first."

Shit! There was only one option so far as I could see. I'd wanted to save it, but now it looked like I had no...

"Enough."

The voice wasn't loud – or at least it shouldn't have been – yet it seemed to cut across everything, somehow drowning out every other sound in the cavern.

Almost as if a switch had been thrown, all of the Jahabich who'd been approaching me stopped in their tracks.

The voice had seemed to come from nowhere and every-where, except it hadn't been psychic like a compulsion or how Decker had talked in his much more preferable skull form. I'd definitely heard it, though. But where...?

Movement registered in my periphery and I turned toward it, putting my back to Decker, which was probably the stupidest thing I could do. However, no stake pierced my heart, or my ass, as the figure approached us – a flowing dress around her, somehow still a brilliant white despite the glow from The Source.

Once again, the Jahabich called out in unison, "*Mother.*"

Calibra seemed to almost float toward us. Hell, for all I knew, that was exactly what she was doing. She was a witch, after all.

I'd never put much credence into the whole Clark Kent / Superman transformation, but she was living proof how much difference a few changes could make. She couldn't have stood out in greater contrast to how I'd first met her if she tried. Before, you'd have thought she ate coal and shit diamonds. She had been pretty, as just about every other chick I'd seen in the vampire world up to that point was, but everything about her had been severe – from her prim office attire to the strict bun of her hair.

Now her hair was down, jet black in stark contrast to her dress, and she was wearing makeup to suggest perhaps she'd managed to kidnap Sally's ex-hairdresser Alfonzo, too.

Despite her beauty, though, there was something sinister, predatory, about her gaze. I had little doubt that as far as she was concerned, we were all cannon fodder or less.

Never let it be said that makeovers were necessarily a good thing.

Regardless, if she'd deigned to make an appearance now, then my odds had just gone from almost nil to fucking laughable.

"What is this?" she asked softly, her voice again rising above everything else as if this were a badly mixed soundtrack.

Before I could offer my opinion on the myriad ways she could go fuck herself, Decker stepped past me and dropped to one knee. "White Mother."

"*Mother.*"

He wasn't quick enough to suppress the sigh that escaped his lips. Glad to see I wasn't the only one who found that increasingly annoying. "Mighty Kala," he began again, "the Freewill has broken your covenant, spit upon the generous boon of peace you offered. I was merely seeing that he be duly punished."

"Oh?" she asked. "How so?"

"The Source. He would make an excellent slave. Compliant, yet truly joyous to torture."

"I see," she said with a smile.

Perhaps sensing he'd won some primo brownie points, Decker rose to his feet. From the look of things, it was a visible effort for him to keep from humping her leg. Fucking pathetic. "Your will is my own."

"And yet," she replied, "here you are subverting it."

"Glorious one? I do not understand."

"Oh, Harold. You claim to be one of my most loyal

servants, a devout student of my teachings. Yet here you stand, feigning ignorance of my commands, pretending you did not purposely goad the Freewill into attacking you. Truly I had hoped that in remaking you, perhaps you would show promise. Instead, I see the petty concerns of your former life still hold sway. Yet another disappointment, as are all your siblings."

"*Mother*," the Jahabich all sounded off, unbidden.

"All of you are the same," she said, her tone oozing disgust. "Such low creatures, unworthy of the new dawn approaching."

"But..."

"I may be in deep shit, Harry," I interrupted, "but it looks like you just waded in next to me. It's always more fun to swim with the buddy system."

"Spare me your tiresome prattle, Freewill," Calibra said. "You will find no receptive audience here."

"Can't blame a guy for trying."

"Harold." She turned back to Decker. "Know that my power here is absolute, but that does not mean I am without mercy like those pretenders who would claim title to the First. I offer you this: face the Freewill in single combat. Defeat him and all shall be forgiven."

Decker turned toward me without any hesitation. I had to assume she was exercising her will upon him. I'd never known the dickhead to be the first into a fight, at least not unless the odds were heavily stacked in his favor. Sadly, they still leaned his way. The Jahabich were tough, hard to hurt, even harder to kill for a vamp my age. Each of them weighed more than a quarter of a ton and was covered in razor sharp shards of stone.

Still, the odds were a fuckload better than they'd been seconds earlier, and the fact that it was Decker's smug face I'd be punching added a little extra zing to my step.

"Know this, Freewill," Calibra added. "I am not without mercy for my enemies either. Defeat Mr. Decker and I shall release your friend from my thrall." She said that last part with a bitter undertone. Obviously, she hadn't forgotten how Sally had mouthed off to her back when she'd thought her to be nothing more than a vampire Prefect. One of the most powerful beings on the planet she might be, but her accusation about Decker's petty concerns was little more than the pot calling the kettle black.

"Fight well, little men," she said, "for the winner shall know my favor, whereas the defeated only the cold embrace of oblivion."

67

DECKER THE HALLS

Harry Decker, former wizard and VP of marketing at my old company, was not entirely without a sense of sportsmanship.

Of course, that might've been unintentional.

He telegraphed his attack from a mile away. I'd watched enough professional wrestling to know when someone was pretending to pay attention to someone else only to turn and do a surprise chair shot. Albeit in this case, substitute stake for chair.

I caught him easily. The Jahabich were quick for beings made of living rock, but they couldn't hold a candle to vampire reflexes. I grabbed hold of the stake, wincing as I picked up a good many splinters, snapped it in two, then tossed away the pointy end.

"Uh uh, Harry," I said. "Not going to be that easy."

"Fool!" he bellowed as he held out his hands toward me. His fingers were contorted in what I assumed to be some sort of arcane hand sign, but since nothing happened, it just came across as a bad secret handshake.

I was happy to oblige.

"Oops, looks like wizard needs food badly!" I grabbed his wrist and fell back, dragging him with me. Once I landed on my behind, I kicked out with my legs. Harry might've looked human, but he had the weight of a Jahabich. Fortunately, I was expecting that. He went flying over me, skidding to a stop just short of goo lagoon. From the wide-eyed look upon his face, and the fact that the Jahabich I'd sent into it hadn't emerged yet, I got the feeling that being double-dipped in shit wasn't a good thing.

Decker rushed me clumsily, proving he was about as adept at hand to hand combat as I'd been during my first months as a vamp. I waited for the right moment, then wound up and swung, wanting to see how far I could send his teeth flying.

Sadly, I'd gotten cocky. He transformed as I threw the punch, completing the change far quicker than I'd ever seen happen before, and caught my fist in his rocky teeth.

He clamped down and I expected to find myself short one hand, but instead, his teeth dug in to my wrist, pinning me in place. I could have sworn I saw a flicker of mirth in his soulless orange eyes, but then his club arms began to pummel me, distracting me ever so slightly from those thoughts.

I defended myself with my free hand as well as I could, but it was two against one. He caught me a good one with his right, and I spat up blood as my ribs cracked. Fuck me!

Much more and I'd be pounded into a bloody smear. Worse, if I lost, there would be nothing to stop this corporate fuck from sending Sally skinny dipping into the primordial ooze behind him.

No fucking way!

Two could play at this game.

I leapt into Decker's grip, wrapping my legs around his wide torso. He still had my arm pinned fast, but I'd robbed him of the momentum needed to beat the shit out of me. Mind you, that didn't mean he couldn't bear hug me to death.

Sadly for him, I still had one free hand, which I shoved into the nearest eye-socket. Using my claws, I began to dig for whatever passed for a brain in his head.

Harry wasn't overly appreciative of that. He opened his mouth to let loose a roar of anger, freeing my trapped arm. It was mangled pretty badly, but still attached.

If only he had another eye to keep it nice and warm while it healed.

Oh wait, he did!

"AWAKEN!!"

What the fuck?!

The compulsion washed over me, subtle, yet with an underlying power that caused my teeth to rattle. I was in no real position to spare it any thought, though. Decker and I were pinned together, him seeing how much pressure it would take to make me pop, and me trying to reach the candy center of his face.

It was a race to see who got to the finish line first and, judging by how much blood I felt running down my ruined back, it was gonna be a close one.

Still, I simply couldn't live with myself – even in the afterlife – knowing I'd let Decker beat me. Fuck that noise. I closed my eyes and gritted my teeth, digging for all I had.

All of a sudden, I felt Decker's grip loosen.

I opened my eyes and saw Sally staring at me over his shoulder, somehow back in the game. Her claws were embedded in his arms and she was prying him off me. "Need a hand?"

"Could use two," I replied with a smile. I had no idea why Calibra had released her, but I wasn't about to argue with it.

She dragged Decker backward, pulling him off balance. He lost his footing and she stepped out of the way just as he tumbled over onto his back with me on top. My hands pulled free, but before I could dive back into my work, he transformed back to his old self, a look of panic upon his face. He knew he'd been beaten.

"Stop! Have mercy!"

"No, it's supposed to be in the name of love. Pity for you, you're not my type." I hauled off and clocked him in the jaw.

It was like punching a concrete wall, but whatever. I'd heal. He wouldn't, at least not when I was finished with him.

"This is unfair!" he screamed as I continued to pummel his stupid face. "Mother!"

"*Mother.*"

Sadly, aside from the Jahabich answering in stereo, no help came his way. A moment later, Sally joined me in feeding this asshole knuckle sandwiches.

We only stopped once there was nothing left of his head but a crushed pile of gravel. Good riddance to a bad wizard.

My hands looked like bloody chop meat and Sally's weren't in much better shape. Nevertheless, I threw my arms around her and hugged her hard.

After several long seconds, she bent her head and whispered in my ear, "Thank you."

"Anytime, always."

"But you still owe me a new blouse. These bloodstains aren't going to wash out."

"Bitch."

"Anytime, always," she replied happily as she got to her feet and offered me a hand.

I took it, wincing a bit, and pulled myself up where we both took a few moments to stomp on Harry's former noggin, just for good measure.

"There is something so satisfying about killing an asshole who deserves it," she said at last.

I lowered my voice to the point where it was barely audible. "Then let's hope there's a lot of satisfaction left to come this day."

"That is one of the few aspects I admire about you, Freewill," Calibra said, obviously overhearing us. There would be few secrets spoken around her. "You always think big, far bigger than one would presume your talent allows for."

"That's me, a dollar and a dream," I replied warily. We were definitely not out of the woods yet, not by a fucking mile.

Decker was small potatoes compared to her, by several orders of magnitude. It was like arm-wrestling Aunt May only to find your next opponent was the Hulk.

"Thanks," Sally said. "I guess."

"Spare me your false gratitude, child," Calibra replied with barely concealed annoyance. She turned on her heel and began to walk away, although her voice still carried as if she were facing us. "Decker defied me for a petty squabble. I released you for that reason and that reason alone. I allow my servants a measure of freedom, but he overstepped his bounds and got what he deserved."

I glanced at Sally and shrugged. We hadn't been invited to follow, but we hadn't been not invited either. That she hadn't killed us immediately was a good sign.

We both tagged along, watching as the crowd parted before her while sycophants of varying races pledged their loyalty and love to her. It was good to be the queen.

Oh well, she was either going to vaporize me for impudence or not. No point beating around the bush. "I thought Harry was one of your more ardent supporters."

"What of it?" she replied, not bothering to face me.

"Well, petty squabble or not, why choose Sally over him?"

"I would choose any of my favored children over his kind." This time, she did look over her shoulder at us, just long enough to give Sally the stink eye. "Even ones I do not favor at all."

"So why bother?" Sally asked, flipping her off behind her back.

"Do that again and I will remove your arm," Calibra replied. "But to answer your question, girl, I do not waste fodder when it can still be put to use."

"How so?" I asked.

"Do not play the fool, boy. I know that Gansetseg made contact with you after escaping my clutches. The girl considers herself wise, yet thinks two dimensionally."

"She still escaped," I offered.

"A simple error on my part. I assumed the pure one's brood would be perfect. It seems there are still imperfections to work out."

"Speaking of Gan..."

"She is mine."

"So she's alive?"

"I will humor you, Freewill, but only because you somehow managed to best the most favored of my children."

"Decker?"

"The Destroyer. Your paramour will live until such time as I deem her usefulness at an end. I have decided that perhaps I have been hasty in terminating my experiments so early. Where magic fails, perhaps science can produce results."

I waited for her to elaborate, but she stopped to let a group of Magi bow at her feet, conveying a bored blessing upon them that I doubted gave them even a plus one to hit.

The mages had looks upon their faces that I imagined weren't much different from that of teens in the sixties upon meeting the Beatles. Calibra, however, acted as if she were forced to deal with them only because she was under contract. I got the impression that if any of them tried to get overly chummy with her, she wouldn't hesitate to have them skinned alive. So much for being a loving goddess.

Still, I decided to hold my next question until we were well out of earshot. No point risking a stray lightning bolt from a miffed mage.

Calibra turned down one of the aisles flanked by Jahabich pens, when I finally opened my mouth. "Earlier you mentioned favored children."

"So I did."

"Well, then unless my friend here learned some card

tricks in the time since her capture, is it safe to assume you mean vampires?"

"It is never safe to assume anything around me, Freewill. There is only what I have said and what I have not."

"Okay, then I'll change that to a question. Did you mean vampires?"

"Yes, child. I did."

I struggled to find the right words. "So then how do the three races ... um ... how does this work? How did this all happen?"

"What I think genius here means to ask is, where do vamps, mages, and Jahabich all fit into the food chain?" Sally added.

Calibra turned back toward me, seemingly ignoring her. "You truly have no idea of our history, our struggles, or the spirit inside of you trying to open your eyes to your potential – any of it, do you?"

That caught my attention. "Huh? Wait, what do you mean spirit inside of me?"

She looked away, a wistful expression upon her face. "No, I suppose not. Such knowledge is lost to time, a combination of malaise from my children and the usurpers trying to rewrite history to suit their image."

"Hold on. What do you know about Dr. Death?"

Sally snickered under her breath. "Oh, this ought to be worth the price of admission."

"Bite me."

If Calibra took offense at our back and forth, she gave no indication. Instead, she merely waved her hand and the legions of Jahabich before her parted as if she were Moses, revealing a view of The Source again. From the look of things, the Jahabich at its shore had resumed turning hapless victims into rock-encrusted slaves.

"I found this place roughly six thousand of your years ago," Calibra said, that wistful expression still on her face as if deep in a memory. "It was such a different world back then."

"I'm sure it was," I replied. "All the mastodon burgers one could eat."

"You joke, but I have beheld them with my own eyes. They used to roam the plains in herds." She glanced toward me, her eyes glittering. "But they were the least of the wonders one might have once seen. Dragons flew through the skies in those days. Leviathans and Kraken would battle upon the seas, their struggles sending tidal waves which would wipe out coastal villages in an instant. Gods forced men to build the very first wonders of the world – shrines to their greatness." She appeared to consider something for several moments. "Gather close, children, and I shall show you."

She waved her hand again and the air in front of us shimmered. Images began to form – people. Heck, I was half-expecting one of them to turn our way and tell us Obi-Wan Kenobi was their only hope.

They weren't alone, though. We watched as things came from the darkness – monsters, demons, nasty shit like that – all with a hankering for human flesh.

Sally grunted dismissively. "Not bad, but my surround sound system is better."

I chuckled before turning back in time to see an army of what looked like ghosts chasing a group of hunters from a forest.

"We were at their mercy, the lowest of the low," Calibra said. "Cattle who existed to be slaughtered. For you see, in those days, the walls were thin indeed. Other realms bled into ours and with them came beings of power, the least of which made us seem as nothing but ants."

I turned to a Jahabich who was standing close by, still as a post. "You getting all of this?"

"But, as it turned out, we were not as helpless as we thought. There were those born among us who could tap into the powers from beyond the veil, use them."

"The first Magi?" Sally asked.

"Indeed. I was proud to call them my brothers and sisters."

The scene before us shimmered to show a group of people fighting off winged gargoyles with magic. The image zoomed in to reveal Calibra. She looked a lot different, plainer – this was obviously before Revlon was a thing. Her hair was shorter and shirts apparently hadn't been invented yet, but it was definitely her.

I took a moment to admire her Cro-Magnon boobs before turning to Sally. "Holographic pornography will be a thing one day, mark my words."

"But powerful as we were, we only slowed the inevitable," Calibra continued, caught up in her story enough to ignore my stupidity for the moment. "There were too few of us and, even with selective breeding, we could not guarantee that those we birthed would have the gift."

"Recessive genes are a bitch," Sally said.

"*SILENCE!!*"

Sally immediately ceased her commentary. Guess she'd pushed Calibra's buttons enough for one day.

"This is not a joke," Calibra warned. "I lost many – brothers, lovers, children. It was a brutal time to live. Forget what the human histories have taught you – that humanity spread like a plague, conquering everything in its path. Many times, the world as you know it came close to being wiped out before it could even gain a toehold. What humans today foolishly call myth and legend was my reality, save there were few heroes to fight against the oncoming tide."

I was busy waving my hand in front of Sally's face, but she was caught tight in the compulsion. There wasn't much I could do for her at the moment and I had a feeling that if I ticked off Calibra too, then story time would be over and hurting time would begin. "What about Icons?" I asked. "I thought they were the heroes of ancient history."

"We have very different viewpoints on what defines antiquity," she replied. "This was all before their time. Had they existed in those days, events might have played out ...

differently." She turned and glared at me. "Wishful thinking perhaps, but no more than foolish fantasy. We were pushed to the very edge of extinction, barely holding on. But all tides eventually change and so too did ours. We began to push back, to assert our dominance over this world."

"What changed?"

"Is it not obvious?" She gestured at the cavern around us. "I found this place."

68

ORIGIN OF A SPECIES

"I was out gathering berries, a simple task, far below the station of one who could wield the power primordial, but one I'd enjoyed as a girl."

If she was about to go off on a tangent on the finer points of pie baking, I was gonna get a running start and preemptively throw my ass into the jizz pond.

"It was then I discovered the cave, quite by accident. It was a one in a million chance – one of the few natural tunnels that lead here." She smiled, as if enjoying the memory. "It still exists, the entrance hidden in the sub-basement of an ancient mosque in Damascus. I should have gone back, gotten the others, but I was young, certain of my power, and curious. I followed the tunnel for hours, perhaps days, ever downward. It's hard to explain, but I felt drawn. I should have been terrified. After all, the way was not unguarded. Soon, I was fighting my way through hordes of fell beasts, many of them seemingly drawn as I was."

The image changed again to something right out of a dungeon crawl. The only difference was Calibra was a party of one, and she wasn't wearing armor. Hell, she wasn't wearing anything but tatters as I watched her blast a pair of giant glow-in-the-dark scorpions. Hmm, a naked cave

477

woman fighting off monsters ... why the hell hadn't HBO picked that up as a series yet?

"Had I faced such odds on the surface, I would have surely fallen, but not down here. The further I walked, the stronger I felt, so I kept going until I came to this place."

Now things got trippy with the magic hologram, for we were looking at a view of this place superimposed over the same spot. The difference was that back then, it wasn't being manned by the Jahabich.

Several incorporeal forms danced around the pool, seeming to come from it. Many of those forms touched upon the ground where they became solid, took on new forms. They grew in size, until they were over eight feet tall and covered in fur – Sasquatches. "Son of a bitch."

"I took this place by force," Calibra continued. "Claimed it as my own."

She did at that. Nasty as some of the things in the cave were, the Feet seemed to be minding their own business. It was a lot like the village I'd seen in the Woods of Mourning, except replace the crude wooden huts with mud ones, and give it an overall less warlike feel.

It didn't last. One moment there were happy groups of squatches prostrating before the pool, seemingly worshipping it, and the next Calibra came charging in all set to kick ass and chew bubble gum. Pity for them, bubble gum was still several millennia away from being invented.

I could only watch as she blasted her way through their ranks regardless of their age or sex. It wasn't an attack so much as a slaughter.

"This used to be their home?"

"Yes. Used to be," she echoed. "I doubt even they remember. They were unworthy guardians, so I drove them out and lost myself in the wonder of this place."

Ah, it was the montage portion of the show. Time passed. Little by little, Calibra learned how to tap into The Source, use it. She changed her name to Gollum and started calling it *my precious.*

Okay, maybe I'm making that last part up. But even so, one could see the young girl who would become the monster called Ib slowly losing herself to this place, even as she mastered its power. At last, her training apparently complete, she summoned energy directly from the pool. A tendril of liquid goo flowed out of it and around her, flashing bright and becoming a dress of pure white, not dissimilar to what she wore in the present day.

"After so much time in the dark, I was ready to return to my people. But it seemed The Source had one more wonder left to show me."

The Calibra in the image, though obviously thousands of years younger, was already showing shades of crazy – utilizing magic from The Source, blowing shit up, laughing like a loon. Then, she looked down upon something. It was a massive skull – one of the Sasquatches she'd killed many years earlier. She gave it a contemptuous kick and it went rolling down the embankment until it landed in the pool with a splash. She made to turn away, but then noticed what was happening on the surface. I knew what came next.

The pool bubbled, turning angry red for a time, until finally, the fully reconstituted form of a Bigfoot strode out of it. Calibra raised her hands defensively but then it changed, shrinking in on itself until it resembled a crude rock-like monster with glowing orange eyes – a Jahabich.

"The first of my eternal children," Calibra said. She stepped over to one, standing statue-still nearby, and ran her hand lovingly over its head like it was a dog. Her fingers healed almost instantaneously from the shredding they took, so quickly I didn't even see any blood escape. "Such disappointments."

If her words hurt the rock monster's feelings, it didn't give any indication. Who knows? Maybe it was crying on the inside.

"You're losing me," I said. "Right, Sally?" I looked and found her still frozen in place. "Can you, you know ... uncompel her? She'll be good. I promise."

Calibra waved a hand dismissively, not even looking our way, and Sally's posture suddenly relaxed ... for all of a split second, anyway. Her eyes flashed black and she opened her mouth, which I promptly slapped my hand over.

I pointed a finger at her. "Be good or you go back into the box."

She narrowed her eyes, first at me, then at Calibra, but gave a single nod. No point in aggravating the person who could hand out impromptu swimming lessons at the center of the Earth.

"Anyway, as I was saying, I don't get it. The Jahabich are strong, durable, hard as fuck to kill. They can blend into a crowd and, excuse me for saying so, they seem to love the shit out of you. That's pretty much the perfect foot soldier right there."

"You are correct, Freewill," she said, still rubbing the creature like this was Satan's puppy mill. "They do love me, but I cannot always be there to guide them. Powerful as I am, this world is large. The Jahabich, alas, are beings of chaos. Though they are possessed of remnants of their individual will, they are always called back to the whole."

"A hive mind."

"Exactly. And that mind is ever geared toward destruction. They cannot help themselves. A part of the void beyond lives within their shells, the entropy which exists between the many planes of existence."

She waved a hand and the image changed to show the surface world again. The Jahabich were defending a walled city from an army of Sasquatches pouring out of the nearby woods. The scene shifted to after the battle where the Jahabich, without provocation, turned upon the humans they'd been protecting and proceeded to trash the city themselves.

The image before us pulled back and we saw it wasn't a lone incident. Cities, forests; all of them burned from the onslaught of the Jahabich.

"My beloved children." A tear slipped down the side of

Calibra's cheek as she watched history play out. "Nothing more than rabid dogs in need of putting down." She turned back toward us and her eyes hardened. "So I did. The only way to contain them was to draw them back to the source of their creation, the very womb of life."

We watched mages fighting off the Jahabich, slowly pushing them back toward the hole in the earth. Then, down below, Calibra was casting magic, calling out to her creations, beckoning them back. Finally, she sealed them in using the very source of magic that had created them.

"The prison wasn't perfect. There were occasional escapes, but it held the bulk of them for thousands of years."

"Why didn't you just kill them?"

Calibra rounded on Sally. "Could you slaughter your own children?!"

Sally glanced at me and I remembered what she said about her sister. If I were Calibra, I wouldn't be so certain of that.

"Though The Source was sealed off, it had left its mark upon me, touched me with its power. Years passed and though my brethren withered, the vitality of youth stayed with me. In time, they were gone and what had come before passed into myth."

"But still the threats remained. I refused to let history repeat itself, so I set about teaching young mages, imparting to them what I had learned of magic from my long life. The memory of my failure haunted me. Thus, I strived to educate my pupils with a set of principles so they would not make the same mistakes I did."

And so the myth of the White Mother began. She showed us scene after scene of her teaching covens of mages. This was the Snow White part of the story, before we got back to the wicked stepmother shit again. In reality, we had no idea if this magical slideshow had been heavily edited or not; however, what we saw seemed to indicate that perhaps once upon a time she was legit in her reasoning. But, as Sally and I were both aware, this movie had a dark sequel.

"So what happened?" I asked.

"Time," Calibra replied. "For centuries, I passed on my knowledge, my wisdom."

Oh yeah, this chick wasn't at all full of herself.

"But eventually, I felt my body changing. I was slowly beginning to age again. The Source, its touch, began to ebb from my body." She turned to face us, and her eyes blazed with power. "But I never stopped hearing its call, always there, always reminding me of what I had once grasped in my hands."

"So ... what?" I asked. "You found a vampire bat and..."

"I am imparting upon you a great gift, showing you this. Do not play the fool."

I held up my hands. "Sorry. No offense intended." Yeah, that was a fucking lie, but thankfully, she decided to skip her sense-motive roll this one time.

"Busted," Sally whispered under her breath. Bitch.

"I could not return, not without unleashing my children back upon the world, a world I had spent ages rebuilding, defending. But still, flawed as they were, for a time the Jahabich helped defend humanity against its myriad enemies ... enemies that once again tested their strength against us. My time upon this world had left me powerful, learned. I decided to try again."

"Try again?" Sally asked.

"But this time, I vowed to not repeat my mistakes," Calibra said, ignoring us. I couldn't help but notice a manic edge worming its way into her voice. Oh yeah, we were getting to the cray-cray part of the story. "The Source is infinitely powerful, touches innumerable worlds. To attempt to tame it is madness itself. So instead, I sought to recreate it, rebuild it in my own image."

I glanced sidelong at Sally and she shrugged as if to let me know she was thinking the same thing.

This tale was about to take a dive off the deep end.

Indeed, it did. Calibra showed us her efforts to sequester herself away from the world while she worked her magic to try to force open a new door in reality. But, time and again, she met with failure. There would be a massive flash of energy, only for it to fizzle out.

"I eventually realized a catalyst was needed, beings who had weathered the passage between worlds, whose energy could stabilize it."

And that's when we saw it. As much as the Feet would have probably disliked Calibra for evicting their ancestors from their lakefront property, what we saw before us cemented why they kinda sorta hated us. She was experimenting on them – and not just a few. Scores of them, chained up and used as guinea pigs as she tried to suck the very essence from them – the spirits that were their native forms when not being giant sacks of shit-flavored fur. Robe-wearing apprentices assisted her in the torture, although whether mages or human servants, I couldn't tell.

"It was working," she said, a look of avarice upon her face as she lost herself in the history playing out before us. It would have been the perfect opportunity. Oh, if only we were armed ... and not surrounded by thousands of creatures who would die at her command before they'd so much as let us sneeze.

So, we watched with her. Maybe there'd be something, anything, we could use. If not, well, at least this wasn't one of those boring historical documentaries.

Some kind of grand experiment of mad sorcery was afoot. Beneath the light of a full moon, Calibra commanded her servants to slit the throats of dozens of captives at once. Their spirits were pulled from them through the wounds, leaving their bodies dried, withered husks. Those spirits, glowing yellow under the light of the moon, began to swirl in a circle, their energies melding together as Calibra worked her magic.

Faster and faster they flew in ever tighter formation until they lost their sense of individuality, becoming one massive floating circle of power. The yellowish color began to pulse, growing darker, until it turned an angry red. The surface began to bubble and appeared to become less energy and more physical matter – not entirely unlike the massive pool in this cavern, save smaller in size and floating on its side in mid-air like some sort of half-assed Stargate.

Hah! I realized that's exactly what it was. She'd ripped open a doorway. To where? I didn't know. Perhaps I didn't want to know.

"The breach began to stabilize," she said. "Began to draw power from beyond to be self-sustaining, but then betrayal struck."

Betrayal wasn't quite the word I would have used. One of Calibra's human servants, an older fellow with a long white beard that almost reached the ground, was too busy staring in awe as his master orchestrated her shit storm. A large male Sasquatch managed to break his bonds while this guy's attention was diverted.

It bellowed a challenge and raced forward. The servant saw it but reacted too slowly. He stabbed at the creature with a double-bladed dagger, but it was only a glancing blow.

Calibra turned and saw it coming. She raised a hand and red fire flew forth from her fingertips, but she was also too late. The flame consumed the squatch, but he still managed to drive the bulk of his dying body into her, sending her flying.

She hit the swirling, glowing portal and everything went to shit.

The power within it began to pulse different colors, quickly becoming chaotic as whatever spell she'd been weaving began to unravel. Calibra herself screamed out, stuck to the portal as if it were made of flypaper and she a giant bug. Arcs of energy, resembling clawed hands, reached out and began to grab at her. Though I couldn't know for certain – and I had a feeling it was probably not a good idea to outright ask – it seemed to me as if the spirits she'd corrupted were attempting to get their revenge.

Calibra fought back, though, using her magic to try to free herself until the entire thing fucking exploded.

I tried to stifle a laugh, but it was tough. I didn't consider myself a cruel person, but I wasn't a saint either. If enjoying watching an evil asshole get creamed was a crime, then send me to jail.

The show wasn't over, though. No, that was just the warmup act.

An explosive shockwave tore through the prison camp, flattening minions and prisoners alike. Of that latter group, many were freed from their bonds to retreat to the woods around them, although a few were curious enough to stop and watch from cover what happened next.

And what happened next was apparently key.

When the dust cleared, gone was the nascent portal to whatever Hell it led to, but it had left something behind. Calibra lay on the ground unmoving, her white dress mostly burned away, but the scraps that were left were now black as soot.

Fitting, because when she finally opened her eyes, so were they.

69

MONOLOGUING FOR
FUN AND PROFIT

And thus it came to pass that we witnessed the birth of the first vampire. They say the road to hell is paved with good intentions and, holy shit, they're right. Calibra had started out trying to do good, but had slowly been corrupted from her path. She was kind of a less whiny, but no less douchey, version of Anakin Skywalker.

What happened next was nothing I couldn't have predicted. The first person to her side was the bearded fellow who'd caused all this shit with his worshipful neglect. Within moments, his white beard was stained red as she turned upon him and tore his throat out.

His buddies all followed in quick succession as Calibra arose, angry and apparently quite hungry.

The image before us dispersed and we were once again in the here and now.

"I became what I am today," Calibra said. "Though I didn't know it at the time, my servants would soon rise as the first of this new race, driven by the hungering spirits inside of them to eternally seek mortal blood for survival."

"Hold on ... what do you mean spirits inside them? You said that earlier, too."

Calibra turned away from me and began to walk toward

the castle of rock. She didn't tell us to take a fucking hike, so we again followed her.

After a few moments of uncomfortable silence behind her high and mightiness, she finally spoke again. "The Jahabich are weak, captured souls imprisoned within stone and empowered by the magical energies of The Source. Though I failed to recreate its power, I succeeded in creating a superior race, but not a perfect one. The sun burns our bodies. Faith, a magic I once wielded with impunity, now turns us to ash. However, despite our failings, we are far above the Jahabich – not one soul, but two, and not in a false body, but in the original, strengthening it beyond belief."

"Two souls?" Sally and I asked.

"Yes," she replied, "in each of us, even myself – the creature who disrupted my spell, as a matter of fact. The multiverse has a sense of irony, after all. I'd thought the magic of my conjuring dispersed, but I was wrong. It persists, a little bit in all of you, the way opened at the time of your becoming." She stopped and turned toward us, causing me to back up a step. Sorry, but crazy and powerful was a combo I didn't care to get all too close to. "When the undead pass along their gift, what they leave behind draws in a primal spirit from beyond."

"Pass along their gift?"

"The venom, boy," she said as if explaining to a particularly stupid child.

"Wait, you mean from our fangs? Holy crap, Dave was right."

"Right about what?" Sally asked.

"He had this crazy theory about us secreting venom like a rattlesnake. Milked me for a sample." Even as the sentence left my mouth, I realized it was a poor choice of words.

Sally couldn't help but smirk. "Doesn't surprise me. So, how often did you two *milk* each other?"

"Fuck you."

"Guess I'm not your type after all."

"David?" Calibra asked. "This wouldn't happen to be the same..."

"The one you gave to Firebird? Yeah, same guy."

I could feel Sally's eye's boring a hole into the side of my head at the mention of that name. Safe to say, Firebird was at the bottom of her list of people to show mercy to.

"He has proven surprisingly ... useful," Calibra replied before once again resuming her pace.

Dave? Useful? Oh yeah, things were definitely getting weird now.

Calibra went on to explain that when a vampire bit a human, it wasn't so much the person dying and being reborn as it was them being possessed. Seems that was part of the reason the Feet hated us as much as they did – y'know, aside from her using them as her personal guinea pigs. The Feet were spirits made flesh through their own abilities. A vampire was a less natural merger, an extra-planar spirit drawn into a body – kinda like with a lure – then fused with the soul still in possession of that body, essentially creating a new being.

I remembered what Christy had told me when she'd been mucking around in Sally's mind, how she'd felt like she was being watched. All of a sudden, that made perfect sense. "So, you're saying that a human soul and some sort of ghost thing merge and form Devastator?"

"The spirit thrives on the life force of others, but much depends on its strength of will compared to that of the human host it inhabits."

"Life force?"

"Blood," Sally said. Gone was the snark. Calibra had her full attention now.

"Indeed, child. If the spirit is stronger, so too is the need to feed. It is why so many are born feral. It is why so many become that way."

"And if the human is stronger?" Sally asked.

"Then they might not even notice the change. They may very well think that it is they and they alone inhabiting the shell of a body, the thirst merely a byproduct of their transformation. If their will is strong enough, the other within them can become little more than a slave."

"But the need to hunt, to feed, to kill..."

"Do not underestimate human nature," Calibra replied. "We are predators every bit as they are. They simply enhance one's natural proclivities, bring out the beast inside."

"They turn us into monsters."

"That is a very narrow way of thinking."

"Oh? When I was growing up," Sally said, "I never hurt anyone outside of calling them names. After ... that's when I moved on from people's feelings to hurting the rest of them."

"Perhaps you were one of the weaker souls."

Whoa. Those were fighting words. Before things could devolve, I stepped in front of Sally and warned her, "You can't win this."

"Indeed she cannot," Calibra replied. "I am older..."

"And thus stronger," I finished for her.

"Incorrect. I am more whole."

"Come again?"

"We do not get stronger as we age, foolish boy. It is the merger that becomes stronger, allowing us to draw more and more upon the energies of the being to which we are bonded. When we are first born, we are comparatively weak. Two souls fusing is traumatic. It leaves both debilitated. It takes many centuries, longer even, for that damage to fully heal."

She was arguing semantics. Fine; maybe a new vampire was essentially a gimp with a lot of rehab ahead of it, but the end result was still that an older vamp was faster, tougher, and a hell of a lot stronger.

But that still didn't explain me.

"All of this is fascinating, but it doesn't jibe with what's going on in my head. That whole soul merger thing. It didn't take. I can talk to my ... whatever the fuck it is. And it tends to talk back."

"That is because you are a Freewill."

We'd reached the gates of her palace, much larger up close than it had seemed when I first entered this cavern. One wouldn't think such a subterranean world would be possible outside of stories like *Journey to the Center of the Earth*. It was too large, too open. But then again, it also had the magical energies of the multiverse coursing through it. That was probably enough to keep the place from caving in on itself.

Calibra turned and approached me, putting a hand upon my shoulder. I had a feeling it wasn't be convey brotherly love. "You are to be my crowning achievement."

"Wait, what?"

"We are talking about Bill here, right?" Sally asked.

Calibra looked me in the eye. "Tell me, child, do you think I have told you all of this simply for your own edification? Do you believe you are owed answers for your existence when so many who have come before you have died ignorant of their true nature?"

"Um, maybe."

She actually chuckled, although I had a feeling it wasn't because I was a funny guy. "Consider yourself a beneficiary of happenstance, nothing more. I am the First, and so can appreciate the amusing symmetry of telling this tale to the very last Freewill."

Somehow, I didn't find her words particularly comforting.

"Alexander, too, realized what you represent. He sought to destroy your kind because he knew you were a threat to his power." Her grin widened into a leer. "Yes, I know all about his machinations, as I know he had the heads of all the others destroyed not long after my servant was freed."

"So much for reinforcements," I muttered.

"He did so out of ignorance and fear. If one could be

reborn as Vehron was, so too could they all. But in doing so, he foolishly presented me with a boon."

"A boon?"

"Yes, because your kind are the ultimate obstacle to overcome. Through the freak occurrence of circumstance and your very nature, being dormant catalyst Magi, your kind possess powers others do not, most important of which is the ability to overcome the orders of those stronger than yourself."

"What the fuck is a catalyst Magi?"

She ignored me. "Your friend, the pure one, thinks he possesses this gift, but I do not believe he does. I believe he is simply different, much as we are from humans. I seek to learn, to understand that difference, to overcome it, and once I do, I will build my new following, one that is not harmed by the sun or the petty beliefs of either humans or Icons."

"Yet one you can control," Sally said.

"Your friend sees far more clearly than you do," Calibra said, indicating Sally with the barest nod of her head. "Control is key."

"I thought the..." I held up my fingers in quotes. "*Glory of Ib* was all about choice, freedom to be the hellions God intended us to be."

Calibra let out a laugh, loud but somehow cynical. "Once perhaps, but not now. That is a harsh lesson my own children taught me when they usurped my power and erased my name from the very history I created."

Sadly, if I was hoping to be shown that part of the past, I was in for disappointment. I guess that was the bonus gag reel that came with the deluxe Blu-ray edition.

"First I will crack the code, reintroduce compulsion to the new breed as it was meant to be. But before I ascend and undertake the change myself, I will make sure that what makes you special is overcome, so that never again will a Freewill rise to challenge its betters." She cocked her head and looked thoughtful for a moment. "In a way, I should thank Alexander for his dogma. For so long, I hid among his ranks, hating him, biding my time, but eventually I came to see his point of view." She looked past me at the sea of Jahabich standing guard. "Chaos can win the world, but it cannot hold it. There must be order."

"If you admire the guy so much, maybe you should marry him." Yeah, it was lame, but it was all I had.

"Alexander will not share power. Though his ideals regarding the First Coven are not entirely misguided – I know that now – he will not be the one to lead this new race into the sunlight. That honor is reserved for me and me alone."

"What a surprise."

"And once I wrest control, I will have you to thank for at least a portion of that victory."

What? Okay, now that really was a surprise. "Not following."

"My new children, I know you've seen them."

"You mean the Jahabich 2.0?"

"An interesting way to refer to them, but in a sense correct," she replied.

"And you're thanking Bill for that?" Sally asked.

"Once I saw the signs of war, that destiny was at hand, I released my children from their eternal prison to once again sow discord. Alas, it soon became obvious their gift for infiltration, once their greatest asset, was no longer what it once was."

"Yeah, I'm sure the invention of toothpaste went a long way toward that."

Thankfully, she ignored my smartass remark for the moment. "With The Source once again at my command, it was within my power. Sadly, their ability to blend in seamlessly comes at a price."

"Greater individuality," I said.

"Indeed. My plan had been to introduce them among the First's number, gradually surround Alexander with those under my control, and whittle down those truly loyal to him until an easy victory was assured. When in their original forms, however, enough of their old selves remains that such a tactic would have eventually been found out. It was doomed to failure." She pointed a finger my way. "But thanks to your words, spreading like a cancer through their ranks until they reached the ears of Alexander himself, I achieved all that I hoped for with barely any effort at all."

My words? Oh wait. Yeah, I'd been the one to tell Colin about the upgraded Jahabich. In retrospect, perhaps not my best decision.

"Thousands of those loyal to the First, forces that could have given me grief once it was time to strike, now lie as dust. Between my Magi, my children, and the new breed that shall soon rise, I will strike the face of this world like a monsoon, washing away all who would stand against me."

Sally turned and clapped me on the shoulder. "Good job as usual, Bill."

I ignored her as I tried to process everything.

There was an underlying madness to Calibra's pontification, but all the same, it seemed that once upon a time she'd had nothing but the best of intentions ... albeit perhaps not where the Feet were concerned. Still, she hadn't set out to become a world conqueror. It was more a case of falling into the job.

I'll be the first to admit, I'm a sucker for a sob story, thus I actually found my overall dislike of her slipping, even if her plans involved destroying the one thing about my powers that made being a vampire not suck.

In short, I fell for the benevolent God act. It was a stupid mistake on my part.

I didn't have the experience that some did, but I liked to think I wasn't a complete fucking idiot. Yet at the same time, her tale caused me to momentarily forget that the most nefarious despots in history were capable of appearing benevolent in public. Behind closed doors, though, things were often far different ... as I was about to be reminded.

Calibra led us inside her fortress, away from the eyes of

the adoring masses gathered outside. There must have been some sort of magical barrier erected, because one moment there was nothing more than the background noises of the cavern and the creatures within it.

One step, however, changed that all, because that was the difference between silence and screaming.

70

THE HOUSE OF PAIN

"What the fuck?!"

"Oh that?" Calibra asked, her voice magically projected above the cries of pain. "Alas, there are some things that are best dealt with in private."

Another shriek sounded, too incoherent to understand, but the pitch, it almost sounded like..."

Sally stepped forward. "What have you done to...?"

Calibra was so fast I didn't even see her hand move. I simply heard the crack of bone and then Sally fell to the floor, her head rotated almost a hundred and eighty degrees. It was like how Vehron had killed Tom. The effect was instantly sobering for me. My breath caught in my throat and for a moment, I found myself unable to do anything save stare at what she'd done.

"That is for speaking out of turn," Calibra said.

I dropped to my knees at Sally's side and almost cried out in relief when her eyes turned and focused on me. What was fatal for a human wasn't so much for a vampire. Thank God!

Calibra looked down upon us with barely concealed contempt. "Prepare her. She will be the next test subject after the vivisection is completed."

Her words barely registered with me, nor did the figures approaching from an adjoining hallway – vampires, from

495

their scent, not that it mattered. There was only one person in this place I was focused on at the moment.

I launched myself with reckless abandon, but Calibra caught me by the throat with ease. "You can't be serious." Her tone bordered on boredom.

The thing was, I'd been expecting it, hoping for it actually.

Her hand around my throat, squeezing so hard I could feel my own vertebrae creaking beneath her fingers, but all it did was serve to help my cause.

Learning what I was – that the thing inside me wasn't me, but some alien entity pulled into my body after I'd been bitten – had been shocking to hear. At the same time, there had been a comforting element to knowing I hadn't gone crazy. Two souls merging – it explained a lot about vampire nature, how a relatively normal person could be bitten and then immediately turn into a bloodthirsty asshole.

My circumstance as a Freewill was different, though. Somehow, that spirit was trapped inside of me, yet still separate. All this time, I'd thought I'd been suffering from some bizarre split personality, but it had been this creature fighting me for control. Maybe that was how I became so strong when it took over. Calibra had mentioned the transfer was traumatic on a spiritual level, leaving both souls weakened.

But what if that wasn't the case with me?

What if, by Dr. Death remaining a separate entity in my head, that meant he'd been pulled into my body whole, as it were, allowing him access to his full potential? Whenever he took over, my personality was pushed to the back. By doing so, that also allowed him to tap into the monstrous power he naturally possessed.

The thing was, we weren't as separate as either of us wanted to believe. Whenever he'd been in charge, I was still there ... subtly influencing things, keeping my friends safe.

The opposite was true as well, him whispering nasty ideas in my ear when I was in the driver's seat.

That had all changed, however, when I tried to blow myself up to take out Vehron. I woke up with Dr. Death's power, but I was still running the show. We'd been battling for control up until that point, but only now did I realize the war was over. In that moment, I'd won. I'd become the dominant soul.

Dr. Death was capable of a lot, but apparently not self-sacrifice. By doing so, I'd inadvertently played a winning hand. He'd been forced to irrevocably hand over the reins so as to save his own ass.

That was why he'd been quiet since then. He wasn't asleep or sulking. He and I were now one being, with me in charge. As for the anger I'd been feeling, that was his residual influence, all he was now capable of. It was something I'd have to learn to live with, to control ... but maybe not right now.

All of this passed through my mind in the time it took Calibra's hand to clamp down upon my neck. I ignored her, though, focused on Sally, lying there paralyzed, helpless to do anything ... except maybe roll her eyes.

She was my friend, my partner, perhaps more. I loved her and she'd been laid low by this prehistoric bitch as if she were nothing.

Now that I knew the truth, I no longer feared Dr. Death taking over. I no longer feared the anger welling up inside of me. I no longer feared being the Freewill of legend.

A red haze descended over my vision and I felt the sleeves of my shirt begin to grow tighter. Calibra was paying attention to the two vamps she'd summoned, busy scooping Sally up to take her God knows where.

I compressed my right hand into a hammer of a fist, hearing the knuckles crack. There was no time to wait.

Distracted as she was, it was hard to miss someone putting on six inches in height and a hundred pounds of muscle.

Now to only hope this worked.

Oh well, there was only one way to find out.

Calibra either didn't see it coming or judged me no threat. Either way, my fist connected solidly with her face. Her nose crunched satisfyingly under the blow and, for a split second, I was able to enjoy the look of her eyes widening in surprise. Then she was airborne, sent crashing through the far wall.

Booyah!

The two vamps who'd been in the process of dragging Sally out didn't stand a chance. I tore through them before they could mount a defense, leaving me covered in their dust.

When I looked down at myself again, the change was complete. My clothes were an absolute mess – note to self, invest in Spandex – but I was definitely not. Sadly, this was not the time to stand there gawking at my awesome biceps.

I bent down to help Sally. "Sorry, this might hurt a bit." My voice came out sounding gruffer than usual, almost as if someone had run my vocal chords through an action movie filter. I could dig it.

I grasped hold of Sally's head, and, gently as I could, turned it back the right way. It was going to be a while before she was walking again, even with her fast healing, but she managed to mouth "thanks" to me.

That was all the time we had for meaningful conversation. I scooped her up and tossed her over my shoulder, her weight barely a feather to me. Oh yeah. It was like that time Kelvin Lightblade had donned a girdle of giant strength, only better because I wasn't wearing a girdle.

I'd caught Calibra by surprise, but didn't fool myself into thinking she'd be out for the count. If anything, she was gonna be pissed. Freewill or not, she definitely had the advantage.

Thankfully – well, not really – but our next choice was made easy by the shrieks of pain that still sounded through the halls. My hearing, now amplified a good ten times past my normal limit, easily picked up the direction it came from. Sadly, I also came to the same conclusion Sally had right before she'd been snapped like a toothpick. Though there were no words, the pitch was a familiar one

It was Christy and, whatever was being done to her, she was in agony.

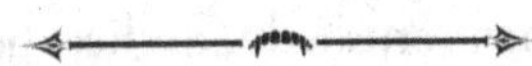

After determining her direction, I knocked down the wall behind us, hopefully buying a few extra seconds, then took off.

This place was packed. The scents alone told me that – Jahabich and vampires, mostly. That made sense. Zealots they might be for their reborn White Mother, but most witches and wizards had a sense of right and wrong. If Christy was indeed being tortured, I had to think at least some would have questioned it. Still, that meant no fireballs to the face for the time being. I'd take it.

The Jahabich were the first to respond, seemingly connected to Mommy's whims. However, they presented no challenge. Heads rolled, quite literally. Three came at me and I took them down in quick succession, never losing my grip on Sally.

Christy's voice seemed to be coming from somewhere below. Go figure – even at the center of the Earth there was a basement.

"Mistress? Is something wrong?"

I turned to see a familiar sight: Firebird stepping around a corner heading my way. She saw me and skidded to a halt. "Who the hell are you?"

Her eyes focused on who I was holding, then back to my face. They widened in surprise, then, without further preamble, she took off running in the opposite direction.

Sally moaned questioningly from where I held her. She was gonna be pissed, and I couldn't blame her, but we didn't have time for the traitorous redhead right now.

"Sorry, wrong number," I said, then let my ears lead me once more.

I found a set of stairs and leapt nimbly down them. I could get used to this shit ... minus all the enemies and the unbeatable witch-vamp who'd no doubt be hot on our asses soon.

More of Calibra's forces met us at the bottom. I dusted one vamp and then crushed another between a pair of Jahabich. "Sorry, but I forgot the mayo for this asshole sandwich."

"That was pathetic," a weak voice said from over my shoulder. It was good to see Sally's healing was starting to kick in.

I strode past the remains of our enemies and kicked in a massive obsidian door that lay beyond their broken bodies.

Now all we had to do was...

I stopped dead in my tracks. "Holy shit."

"What is it?" Sally asked. "I can't see dick back here."

"That's because my dick isn't back there," I replied idly, my gums doing little more than flapping as I took in the sight before us.

The sub cavern was big, probably extending further than the structure sitting above it, and it was absolutely crawling with Jahabich. Dozens of them stood side by side, still as statues, forming the walls of makeshift rooms.

I guess it beat putting up drywall.

I took a sniff and then gagged. This place was ripe, and not because of the Jahabich either. Piss, shit, sweat, and with no cross breeze to air it out. Whoever was down here, they'd been left to rot.

That bioluminescent stuff lit the entire place, but in greater concentration than above. However, the glow it provided was mostly offset by the sizzling ball of energy that floated at the far end – jet black, like a sphere of nothingness, waiting to consume all around it.

The screams were coming from inside of it.

Before I could step forward, movement caught my attention. I tensed myself to take out the two Jahabich nearest me, but they paid no heed to my presence. They simply stepped apart, like a living automatic door, revealing four more of their brethren. These were carrying what looked to be a stone table. That in itself wasn't particularly interesting so much as who was lying upon it. Gan! Her eyes were closed and stalagmites pinned her arms and legs down.

My gaze was torn, however, between her and the familiar face standing just behind.

"It's about fucking time." He looked up from a notebook he'd been busy jotting stuff down in. "Put her over there. I'll be ready for her just as soon as I finish dissecting this one."

"Dave?"

71

MAGIC CIRCLE OF LIFE

"Yeah?" my former DM asked. "That's my name, Mongo. Now do as you're told, otherwise the boss lady is gonna be pissed. We both know you won't like that."

What the...? Oh yeah, I only looked like myself in the vaguest roided-out sense.

"Please tell me that's not who I think it is," Sally said.

"Pipe down," I told her. "Adults are speaking. Dave, it's me, Bill."

"Bill? Bill who?"

"Kelvin Lightblade," I replied. "You know, the character you sacrificed to a fucking demon orgy."

His eyes opened wide. "Bill? No shit? When did you discover exercise?"

"Um ... never mind that. We've come to rescue you ... and some other folks. What exactly *are* you doing, by the way?"

"Oh, you know, just what I was told to do. The glorious Ib has commanded me to aid her efforts to discover the secrets of the pure one."

His eyes glazed ever so slightly as he spoke that last sentence. Shit! He was compelled, although apparently not too deeply since he still seemed to be him. That made sense.

The more you were opposed to something, the stronger a compulsion would need to be. But ordering Dave to perform insane medical experiments? That was a slow Tuesday for him.

"What do you mean, aid her?"

"She's been making shit progress with magic to figure out what makes Ed tick. As if that would have fucking worked. I suggested that maybe it might make sense to add a little science to the mix."

Sally growled from over my shoulder, "You *suggested?*"

"Hey, is that Sally?"

"Never mind her. Well, actually, yeah, what she said."

"Oh, that? I was just thinking out loud after she made him put the bite on some unlucky asshole. Guess she overheard."

"We can kill him, right?" Sally asked.

"No."

Dave was an asshole, but he was still a friend, a compelled one at that. Douchebag or not, I knew him well enough to know he was in this game for himself and himself only. He wasn't the type to help anyone else take over the world out of the goodness of his own heart.

"*SNAP OUT OF IT!!*"

The compulsion rang throughout the cavern, causing the place to shake slightly from the power of it. Whoa. I'd forgotten how strong I actually was for a moment there.

"Holy shit!" Sally cried from behind me. "Was that you?"

I ignored her and focused on Dave. Though my command caused him to pause for a moment, he simply replied, "No can do, buddy. The glorious Ib commands it."

I should've guessed. Calibra was the most powerful vampire ever. Badass as I was, it still wasn't enough to undo her orders ... especially given Dave's proclivity toward following them.

Unfortunately for me, the compulsion did have one unintended side-effect. All of the Jahabich in the immediate vicinity turned their pumpkin-sized heads in my direction.

Oh boy.

So far, they seemed to be aware of me knocking and hadn't made a move to open the door and clobber me, but it was only a matter of time.

"Um..." I sputtered, trying to figure out my next move. Strong as I was, there were *a lot* of enemies in here. There was also the question of how long my hulked-out boost would last. I'd achieved it by giving in to the anger, feeding upon the rage buried deep inside of me. But right now, I was far more weirded out than pissed.

That was the sad truth of the matter. I wasn't normally an angry guy. I didn't like being ticked off. It might be easier now, with Dr. Death tethered up and contributing, but it just wasn't me. "So, Dave, what's going on with the giant glowing ball of death over there?"

"Oh that? The glorious Ib is torturing a witch who pissed her off – that one who was fucking with your head last week. Remember when I drew Ed's blood and was gonna use it to blow you to...?"

"Yeah, I remember." Oddly enough, his tone was putting me back in the right frame of mind. I swear, if I didn't know he was compelled, I'd have knocked his fucking head off.

"Anyway, it's pretty fucking brutal. She basically created a magical feedback loop."

"Not following."

"Of course not, because you're a dumbass." That was all him, no compulsion needed to make him a dickhead. "The glorious Ib is channeling all of this chick's magic through her unborn baby ... pretty much turning it into a living time bomb."

"WHAT?!"

"Put me down."

"Huh?"

Sally repeated, "Put me down. I can handle this twit. You help Christy."

"Are you...?"

"NOW, dickless!"

Without further hesitation, I lowered her to the floor. She seemed wobbly, her spinal cord no doubt still iffy after being twisted into a pretzel, but she held her ground.

"Much better, thanks," she said before looking me up and down. "Huh! You actually don't clean up too badly."

"Thanks. I don't work out."

"What a surprise. Now, if you'll excuse me..." She turned to Dave.

"Hey there. You know, we have an opening at the table on Sundays if you're ever interested in..."

His words were abruptly cut short by a fist to the face. With Calibra's compulsion strong in his mind, Sally couldn't compel him to take a nap, but that didn't mean she couldn't dissuade him the old-fashioned way.

"I'd get moving if I were you," she said to me over her shoulder as the Jahabich dropped the table upon which Gan still lay.

It wasn't just them either. Not all of the Jahabich responded. Some of them still kept playing wall, but enough disengaged to give me cause for worry. We needed backup, but thankfully, some might've been at hand.

I stepped in and took off the head of the first Jahabich with a backhand. Goddamn, this was awesome! I felt like a comic character who'd just gotten a massive upgrade. I grabbed the next and flung it over Sally's head, into a group that was heading our way, doing a decent job of slowing them down.

The other two were likewise dispatched without much worry. I marveled at how my skin flayed as I punched through their stupid faces, only to heal before I could even begin to bleed. Just call me Logan!

"Get Gan back on her feet."

"You don't have to tell me," Sally replied, slapping Gan across the face with an audible crack. "Get your ass moving. We'll be fine."

I took off with everything I had, which was a lot more than I was expecting. I moved so fast that I slammed into a pack of Jahabich before I could ready myself. A bit weird, but the results were definitely promising. Though they weighed a quarter ton apiece, a good half dozen of them went flying from the collision.

It was pretty goddamned impressive, if I did say so myself, but it really wasn't the most efficient way to reach the far end. Thankfully, I could do better.

As the next group disengaged from their spot as living wall panels, I tensed my legs and then leapt.

And once again underestimated the power at my disposal. I slammed into the rocky ceiling headfirst – pretty much the exact same thing I'd done during my first five minutes as a vampire. Heh, guess those who failed to learn from history really did relive it. Thankfully, I was made of sterner stuff this time around.

I came down, along with several hundred pounds of rock that I'd dislodged in the impact. A couple Jahabich were caught in the mini cave-in, so bonus points for that. I was unhurt but made a note anyway to be more careful. There was a whole palace above us and, tough as I was, I didn't care to test if I could handle it all dropping on my head.

My next leap was a bit more cautious, aiming for length instead of height. I flew about thirty feet, my tattered shoes just barely clearing the tops of the heads of the Jahabich. I landed, spun, and decked the one closest to me, putting out its lights for good.

"Hey!"

What the...?

"Over here! I can help you!"

Kelly's voice rang out from off to my left, seemingly in another makeshift Jahabich room. Though I needed to help Christy, it might be a hell of a lot easier with some firepower.

Calibra might have had the keys to this cell, but in my current state, the walls weren't much of an obstacle. I was a one-man wrecking crew.

There! She was chained to the actual wall of the cavern.

Her eyes widened as she saw me approach. "Please tell me you're friendly."

"You could say that. It's me, Bill."

"Really?"

I can't say I wasn't flattered by the way her eyes drank in my musclebound form. Still, it was a poor time for flirting, especially once I took a breath. She must've seen my nose wrinkle because she said, "Sorry, the bathroom facilities here kinda blow."

"Offhand, I'd say this whole place does." I took out a few more Jahabich, then stepped in and snapped her chains. I'd been expecting those magic-sapping manacles I'd seen vamps use before, but these were pretty run of the mill. "Why didn't you just blast your way out?"

"Long story. I'll have to tell you some day," she said dismissively. "Veronica should be on the other side. Get me to her and we'll bring the pain."

"But why...?"

"Do you want to stand here debating or do you want me to fucking help?"

Point taken. I let her climb onto my back, arms around my neck, then took off for the opposite end of the cavern.

This time, I took extra care about the ceiling, being mindful of my cargo. No point in reducing a potential ally into goo.

"Nice pecs," she said as she held on. "Whatever happened, I dig it."

I let a smile creep onto my face as we landed and sent the first Jahabich in the immediate area flying via a whirlwind of fists.

"I definitely dig it," she said, dusting some rock chips off herself. "V!"

We spied Veronica, similarly trussed up where Kelly had indicated she'd be. She looked out of it – semi-conscious and with not nearly as much fight left in her as Kelly had. I took care of more of the Jahabich while Kelly ran over to her coven sister and melted her chains away.

"It's okay, V. I'm here."

Veronica offered her a weak smile but remained slumped against the wall.

When Kelly next turned to face me, an angry red glow had begun to suffuse her body. "And now comes the pain." She winked at me, then let loose, sending a wall of magical flame into a quintet of our foes.

Another combatant added to the mix, the rocky assholes were forced to split their forces between us. It was the break I needed and just in time, too.

Another cry of pain came from the floating sphere o'doom.

"Shit!" Kelly said. "Go; I've got this."

"On it!"

"You need to redirect all that power elsewhere," she shouted after me as I once again took off.

Redirect it? How the fuck was I supposed to do that?

Oh well, hopefully I'd think of something. That, or I'd be melted into a pile of sludge.

Either way, something interesting was about to happen.

72

CROTCH FRUIT

The Jahabich surrounding the massive ball of negative energy – best way I could think to describe it – kept their distance. Whatever it was, they didn't seem all too eager to be in close proximity to it.

Mind you, that didn't mean they were kind enough to step out of the way and let me through. No, that required some *persuasion* on my part. I took on about a dozen, doing my best to use them as weapons against their buddies when I could. Go figure – the Jahabich made for good clubs against other Jahabich.

By the time I'd cleared a path, I was starting to feel a bit winded. Worry for Christy outweighed any anger I felt. That, and I'd been expending a lot of energy with no snack breaks in sight.

The sphere itself was pitch black, almost a void. There was no reflection of light or anything else from its surface. It just gave an impression of *nothingness*.

Mind you, the cries coming from within were definitely something.

Trusting in my accelerated healing, I reached out and touched the surface. Amazingly enough, I wasn't immediately incinerated. There was an odd tingling in my hand, a rather unpleasant one, but that was about it.

The cries coming from inside suddenly raised in pitch to a shriek, so I quickly pulled my hand back.

Odd. It was pale ... well, okay, even paler than my normally pasty skin. Just to make sure it wasn't a trick of the light, I held both of them up side by side. Sure enough, it was almost like my right hand had gotten a reverse suntan. Weird as fuck.

Oh, the hell with this. I remembered past dungeon crawls with my former gaming group. There were two ways to go about things: the safe way, checking for traps every five feet while taking two hours of real time to travel down one hallway. Then there was the method I employed once the hour got late and I grew tired of rolling my D20 every thirty seconds – just do whatever the fuck you're going to do.

This was one of those latter times.

Bracing myself for the fortitude save of a lifetime, I took a deep breath and leapt into the nothingness.

Though the sphere was of the advanced darkness sort on the outside, inside was different. Multicolored lights seemed to flow around me, distorted as if we were moving really fast. It was kinda like being at warp speed in *Star Trek* – minus the explosive decompression.

Wait, I was wrong. The light wasn't flowing around me. It was all going in the same direction, toward the center of the sphere and the person floating there – Christy! Her arms were held out to either side in kind of a magical crucifixion, a mockery of Calibra's favorite pose. Her eyes were open but unfocused, and a grimace of pain twisted her face.

All at once, I began to tingle all over, sort of like licking a nine-volt battery with my entire body. Whatever was happening to me wasn't a particularly wonderful feeling, but it was seemingly far worse for Christy. Her cries rose to an ear-piercing pitch, causing me to cover my ears with my hands as I floated in the weirdness.

At last they stopped and Christy's head flopped forward. She was still breathing, thankfully. Whatever that was, it had knocked her out, perhaps mercifully.

I tried to swim toward her, but it was tough going. The closest I'd ever come to experiencing weightlessness was on a roller coaster, so I mostly ended up flailing about.

That feeling of tiredness doubled. My tank must've finally hit empty. Fatigue began to set in and suddenly I wanted nothing more than to take a nap. I blinked several times and then did a double take. Maybe it was the exhaustion, but it seemed as if light was escaping from my body, the same multi-colored hues as I'd seen floating around in here. They were flowing from me toward Christy, swirling around her until they were drawn into her midsection.

What the fuck?

Christy likewise seemed to be a source of the lights. They trickled from her outstretched hands almost like water, floated aimlessly for a bit, then were seemingly sucked back into her stomach.

The realization of what was happening dawned on me.

Holy shit! Dave had been right. Somehow, this sphere was redirecting Christy's magic – sucking it out of her and then force-feeding it to her unborn child. And now it was seemingly doing the same to me, sending my energy into her.

Almost as if in answer to this, Christy's stomach began to glow from within. The light became brighter, causing her skin and clothing to become translucent, and making the tiny silhouette inside visible. I hadn't been around too many expectant mothers, but I was smart enough to know that wasn't normal.

It was like a live ultrasound picture, but from the inside. As I watched, the baby kicked. My ears – now supercharged like the rest of me – easily picked up the little heartbeat inside, fast and frantic, and picking up speed.

It must've been my power. The feedback from Christy was enough to keep her in torment. I had no idea what that energy was doing to the baby, but it couldn't have been good. Now, though, with me here, the flow had easily doubled.

Dave had said something about it becoming a bomb. This had to be Calibra's punishment for Christy standing up to her, defying her. Calibra was all into her White Mother bullshit, so what better revenge than to fuck up an enemy's motherhood – turn their baby into a living weapon that destroyed them both?

What a cunt.

That was an argument for later, though. I had to somehow fix this and it had to be done *now*. Problem was, how the fuck did I do that?

Kelly had said I needed to redirect the power. Okay. Not super helpful.

Sadly, I didn't see any convenient switches labeled "Reverse" anywhere.

How did one redirect magical energy anyway? Did I need a spell? A magic wand?

I mean, if Christy was a computer and I had a length of copper wire and a good heatsink I could have...

Wait a second. Maybe that was it.

I let out a heavy sigh in the emptiness. Some days you installed the heatsink, and some days you *were* the heatsink.

I doubled my efforts to get to Christy, kicking with my arms and legs until I somehow managed to flop close enough to grab hold and pull myself in.

She was still out cold, no doubt from the pain. Sadly, I didn't think there was time to wake her up and have a rational conversation about what I was about to try.

My theory was simple. What did you do when anything had too much of something in it? You let it out, whether it was heat from a processor or too much air from a balloon.

Surely magic worked the same way, right?

Yeah, well, it was the best I had to go on. She was as good as dead otherwise.

Putting one arm around her, so she couldn't float away again, I used my other to undo the bottom buttons of her maternity blouse. Pushing the material to the side, I exposed her stomach, heavy with child.

"Sorry," I whispered in the magical void, my voice oddly distorted as if the sound were being sucked away along with the power inside of me.

My claws extended. The tips were like razors, able to part skin like a hot knife to butter. What I needed more, though, was a bit of finesse, not something I normally cared about when carving a bad guy's face off. Christy's stomach glowed again and I got a good look at where her baby was positioned inside, as weird as that might've been.

That was as good as I was going to get.

I positioned my hand, placed the tips of my claws against her skin, then sank them in as deep as I dared to.

Holy fucking hell!

It was like cutting into a power cable while standing in salt water. Energy raced through me, causing every muscle in my body to seize up.

My arm felt like it wanted to vibrate out of its socket and it took everything I had to fight it. I needed to maintain control that I no longer had. My claws had just barely pene-trated Christy's skin. I couldn't let them sink in any further, not without badly injuring her or the baby.

I wasn't sure I had much choice in the matter, though. I seemed to have about as much control over my body as Sally had when Calibra snapped her neck, giving her a good view of her own shapely ass. A searing pain exploded in my mouth as I bit through my own tongue – a sensation best described by words I mercifully could no longer mutter.

Christy's stomach ceased glowing and, a moment later, wisps of light began to escape from the wounds my talons had opened. It was working!

Pity that it was killing me at the same time.

I tried to scream, but was too busy *enjoying* the taste of my own blood.

The pain from the feedback increased ever more, like a thousand angry hobos had invaded my body and set trash fires in all of my organs, but still, I held on.

It felt as if my blood was heating up to the boiling point, cauterizing me from the inside out. I couldn't take much more. A few more seconds and...

I felt a hand take hold of mine.

It was Christy's. I looked up and found her eyes open and her smiling at me. Hopefully, it wasn't because I was about to become the punchline of some great cosmic joke.

She gently pulled my other arm from around her shoulders, all while keeping my claws in place upon her stomach. She took hold of my now free hand, steadied it, and folded the fingers until only my index and middle fingers were still pointed. Even if I had wanted to stop her, there wasn't anything I could do with my nerve endings on fire. I had to trust she knew what she was doing.

She pointed that hand down toward where I thought the floor was and then closed her eyes again.

After a moment, a brilliant blue light suffused her, then spread until it covered me as well. I had no idea what she was doing or how that would help us, but then a torrent of white-hot energy shot out from my hand toward the floor.

I opened my mouth to cry out, partially in pain, but mostly because it was fucking cool to watch. Pity I hadn't been in control of my own faculties because I'd have definitely shouted out, "Kamehameha!"

Oh well, at least I thought it.

As the brilliant energy hit the blackness of the orb around us, the two began to cancel each other out. Where before there was nothing but the void, I could now see the rocky earth beneath us.

Better yet, I began to regain control of my body as the excess power was siphoned out.

The hole in the void beneath us opened wider, almost a

third of the diameter of the sphere and then Christy threw both her arms around me. Before I could question why, gravity took hold and we fell out to the floor, me landing first with her atop. Guess that explained it.

Oh well, I couldn't begrudge the poor girl a softish landing after what she'd been through.

Once we were outside, the rest of the spell collapsed and the black sphere above us winked out of existence, leaving no trace it had been there at all.

"Thank you," Christy whispered. Sweat stood out on her brow and she looked beat to all hell, but she was alive. Now to keep her that way.

"Rest for a few. We'll..."

"No time." She pointed over my shoulder.

I probably should've guessed we weren't alone. I turned to find a column of Jahabich advancing upon us. With the sphere of baby annihilation gone, they no longer had any reason to keep their distance. Fine by me. If they wanted some more, then I was happy to serve it up for them with a side of hurt.

"Come on!" I balled my hands into fists and raised them up ... then, just as quickly, wished I hadn't. Gone were the mounds of muscle and the extra-long claws. I looked down and saw no sign of those awesome pecs Kelly had been admiring.

In short, I was me again.

Yeah, this could be a bit problematic.

73

THE VIP ROOM

The diabolical brilliance of Calibra's trap wasn't lost upon me. It had sapped my power just as surely as it had been draining Christy's. I had a feeling it would have done so to anyone – mage, vampire, or other – who tried to rescue her. In order to stop the sphere, one had to be inside it. But if one was inside it, one got juiced like an orange.

Not helping matters was the exhilaration of having saved Christy. An odd thought to have, perhaps, but right then a little unrestrained rage would have gone a long way.

"Stay behind me." Even powered down, I was still a vampire. With any luck, I could bust a few heads before they shit-stomped me into paste. There was no way I would ever claim to be a brave man, but I valued my friends and was just a wee bit too stupid to know when to quit.

Sometimes that was enough.

And sometimes it wasn't even necessary.

Something shoved me back and flashed past at incredible speed. When I looked up again, the faces of three of the Jahabich had been erased, gouged out by the claws of a rather smallish hand.

"Never thought I'd be glad to see her," Christy said wearily from behind me.

"Perhaps one day I will be able to say the same of you, witch," Gan replied, stopping just long enough to put her fist through another Jahabich's chest.

She cocked her head, then quickly sidestepped as a lance of red power cut through two more of the monsters. As they went down, I saw Kelly and Veronica standing behind them and looking eager for a scrap.

"The cavalry has arrived!" Kelly gleefully announced.

Indeed it had. I took a moment to catch my breath and look around. It seemed that our newly released friends had been busy while I'd been practicing my zero-g maneuvers. The place had fallen into chaos. Scores of dead Jahabich stood fused to the ground where they'd been blasted. Even more lay in dismembered piles of rubble. They still had the numbers advantage, but my friends were doing a hell of a job playing catch-up. Never discount payback as a good motivator.

"Bill!"

I turned toward the sound of Sally's voice calling from elsewhere in the cavern, although I couldn't see where from my vantage point.

"It would appear your whore is summoning you." Gan's tone was conversational. Hell, she wasn't even breathing hard. Little show off. "I reiterate, you should consider having her whipped for insolence."

"Here in the states, we call that foreplay," I replied. "I hate to ask, but..."

"No harm will come to the witch until such time as you wish it, my love."

That was probably as good as I was going to get from her, which wasn't all that comforting, actually. Christy's sisters were in close proximity, though. I doubted they'd let anything happen to her even if Gan's attention wavered.

I took off toward the direction Sally's voice had come.

"My love," Gan called after me, "perhaps now would be an ideal time for you to use..."

"Hold that thought," I yelled over my shoulder. "I'll be back."

At least I hoped I would.

I won't lie. I really missed my buff form. He – err, I – was badass. Not to mention, I'd finally gotten my wish from my early days as a vamp. I'd finally become sexy.

Oh well, there was no use crying over spilled biceps. I was lucky to still be upright after the job Calibra's power-sucking sphere had done on me. My healing was finally catching up, but my tank was starting to run dry. At the very least, the idiot light was on.

Thankfully, the Jahabich in the room had rightly concluded that Gan and the witches were the bigger threat right then and let me through. I still had to dodge and weave past them, but, oddly enough, it was much easier to fight when your strategy was to run away.

"Any year now!"

And yet I was actually running toward her voice.

Most of the Jahabich had broken formation once the shit hit the fan, but at least one group had remained as they were – standing together, forming the walls of a prison cell, inside of which I could see several figures.

There! Sally was standing right outside. There were a few dead Jahabich at her feet, but the ones currently playing living dollhouse seemed to be ignoring her.

I skidded to a halt by her side, just about out of breath.

"Took your sweet time."

I flipped her the bird. "One for you and one for the high horse you rode in on."

Rather than sock me one, she gave me the once-over. "Back to yourself, I see."

"Yep. Saving Christy left me a bit deflated."

"Pity. I have a thing for guys who are ... well, the opposite of you. Christy okay?"

"Not sure on that point, but she's alive." I looked around. "Dave?"

"Over in the corner nursing a broken face. Physician, heal thyself."

I gave her a single nod. Good enough. "So what's up?"

"Follow me and see for yourself." With that, she leapt over the heads of the Jahabich standing guard. "I'd hurry if I were you," she warned once inside.

Story of my life. I followed, although it took more effort than I'd have preferred.

As I was airborne, though, I saw the Jahabich beginning to stir. That's why she wanted me to move it. There was no way to perform a jailbreak without setting off the alarm.

And a jailbreak was apparently what she had in mind.

Several vampires sat inside, unmoving.

I landed and looked around, noting the glazed expressions. Compelled. That made sense. Now why were we...?

That's when I saw Sally and, more importantly, the person she was standing over – James.

"Help me with him."

She didn't need to ask twice.

"This must be the VIP wing," she said. "Here, let's get him up."

I got an arm under James and dragged him to his feet. He stood on his own, but that was it. All around us, orange eyes turned our way. Time was short.

"How do we wake him up?"

"We can't compel him awake," she said, glancing my way. "Especially not now. So, let's try the old-fashioned way."

She slapped him across the face, hard enough so that it echoed in the cave. Had he been mortal, she'd have both cleaned and broken his clock. As if was, his head barely turned to the side from the impact. Unfortunately, that was it. He didn't wake up. Fuck! That usually worked to snap vamps out of neutral compulsions, but we'd never tried it on someone as powerful as James. I had a feeling a punch to the face wasn't going to get through to him.

No, not to the face...

"Buy me a minute," I said as the Jahabich closed in on us.

"Isn't it the guy who's supposed to be protecting the girl? Never mind. Forgot who I was talking to for a moment." With no further hesitation or snark, she threw herself at our enemies. "Make it count."

I intended to, grabbing hold of James and sinking my teeth into his neck. There was only time for a quick sip, but that's all I needed.

His power became mine the instant I swallowed. Then, before I could talk myself out of what was surely a suicidal move, I brought my knee up into his crotch.

My logic was simple. A slap to the face was a good way to get someone's attention, but there was simply no better method to ensure you had a guy's full focus than smashing the shit out of his nuts.

James grabbed hold of his crushed junk and sank to his knees with a whoop of pain.

"Did you just kick a member of the Draculas in the balls?" Sally asked, momentarily diverting her attention from the Jahabich.

"Not my first choice among their group, but yeah." Now to hope it worked.

There was no time to wait and find out, though. The Jahabich swarmed us, clubs swinging. Thankfully, I had a shitload more power than I did a minute earlier.

I put my back to Sally's. "Mind if I have this dance?"

"Takes two to tango."

I readied myself to kick some ass, but before that could

happen, a pair of Jahabich in front of me were tossed to the side, revealing a sight for sore eyes.

"Perhaps we should consider something more suited to a threesome," James said, dusting himself off. "The Electric Slide or even the Macarena. I always did favor that one. Never understood why it went out of style."

74

THE MORE THE MERRIER

His shitty taste in dance crazes aside, James helped turn the tide, telling us to wake up the other vampires in a similar fashion while he tore through the ranks of the Jahabich surrounding us.

Management-sanctioned kicks to the balls. That was a first. I tried not to enjoy myself too much. Sally didn't even bother hiding her glee as she cracked some nuts.

I'd been right. This was where Calibra kept the prisoners she either deemed important, dangerous, or just really didn't like all that much. James was the only Drac in the bunch, but there were some other heavy hitters in here. Judging by what Calibra had said earlier, I had little doubt these guys were meant to be the front line in her new army of UV-resistant vamps.

Thankfully, they directed whatever anger they felt at their rude awakening toward their jailers. This was one area where Calibra and Alexander were alike. They both seemed to have forgotten vamps under compulsion might be loyal, but only because they had no choice in the matter. Turn that off, though, and you'd have nothing left except some royally pissed off vampires.

Vehron might've been a tool, but at least he'd seemed a true believer to her original teachings about freedom. I briefly wondered if, had he lived – and not killed my ass – whether he'd have fallen in line with her new way of thinking.

Maybe one day I'd pick up a Ouija board and ask him. For now, I helped in mopping up the rest of the Jahabich down here.

Once that was finished, James and Gan directed the other vamps to blockade the door with the bodies of our foes. It was the only way in here, or out, for that matter. We'd have to use it eventually, but all of us needed a few minutes to get our bearings before continuing on. There was also the fact that Calibra could simply ensnare most of this group again the moment she saw them.

While they worked on that, I returned to the far end of the cavern to check on Christy. Sally was already there with her, as were Kelly and Veronica.

Christy, for her part, looked like shit, but she smiled when she saw me approaching.

"How are you doing?" I asked.

"We're just finishing patching her up," Veronica said.

"Go figure," Kelly added, "magic works a bit better than iodine and Band Aids. She's still pretty banged up, though."

"At least that answers one question," Christy said weakly.

"About what?"

"About my baby." She put her hands on her stomach. "I'd been wondering if it was going to be a..."

"She," I said.

"Excuse me?"

"She. Back when your stomach was glowing, I kinda got a pretty good look. Didn't see any ... y'know ... between her legs."

"Can't help scoping out the dicks, eh?" Sally asked.

Before I could reply, Kelly smacked me upside the head. "Spoilers, asshole!"

"What?"

"I was really hoping to wait until ... *she* was born to find out," Christy replied, a tinge of annoyance in her voice, "but it's okay. Will make it easier to finish her room. Hah. Two big revelations in one day. We're having a little girl, and she's going to be a witch."

"Hold on," I said. "That was in question?"

"It's no better than a fifty-fifty shot where a Magi and a human are concerned," Kelly replied. "Not much different than being born with blue eyes or brown."

"So how do you know for sure?"

"That bitch," Christy growled, a crackle of red energy passing before her eyes. "She created a feedback loop, channeling my power into my baby. Said she would teach me respect through pain of loss. If it ... sorry, *she'd* been human, there was no way she could've survived."

Sally knelt and took Christy's hand. "She did, though. That's the important part."

Christy flashed her a look of gratitude.

Kelly stepped to her other side. "If she could handle all that and more, then she's gonna be a real corker. Might need to bind her before she burns down her crib."

The witches shared a laugh at that. Guess it was an inside mage joke or something. Speaking of witches, though... "Aren't we missing someone?"

"Oh yeah, that mouthy brunette," Sally said. "I kinda like her."

"Meg," Veronica replied. "We don't know."

"What happened?" Christy asked.

Kelly threw her hands up in frustration. "You know Meg. She just couldn't zip it. Needless to say, Kala wasn't too pleased."

"Did she ... hurt her?" I asked.

"Like I said, we don't know. Kala had her taken away. Said she needed to be taught the meaning of respect."

"Respect?"

"Yep. Said she was unworthy of her power and needed to be taught to respect her mother or some crap like that."

"Shit!"

"What is it?" Christy asked me.

"Calibra gave us a bit of a history lesson when we got here. Long story short, she seemed hung up on the whole motherhood thing, especially when it came to some of her kiddies."

"Goddamn it!" Sally said. "The Source. She's going to turn Meg into a Jahabich."

Kelly stood up. "We need to get moving, then."

I stepped in front of her and held up a hand. "Not so fast."

"What do you mean? Get out of the..."

"What I mean is that we're fucked if we go marching out that door all half-assed. I probably don't need to remind anyone that Calibra is pretty much all powerful down here. Not to mention she has an army of both Jahabich and Magi."

Veronica stepped up. "We're not alone, though. We can..."

"I am afraid I must concur with the Freewill on this."

I turned to find James and Gan heading our way, while the other vamps continued to work at the far end of the cave.

It embarrasses me to say this," James continued, "but Calibra ... Ib..." There was a note of disgust in his voice as he said her chosen name. "Her powers of compulsion are like nothing I have ever seen before." He hooked a thumb over his shoulder. "As formidable a force as these fine fellows might be, they ... *we* would be helpless before her. You, too, my dear Sally. Only the Freewill has the power to resist her call."

"That is not entirely true, Wanderer," Gan replied.

"Oh?"

"Yeah," I added. "Gan's immune now. She helped us get down here."

"Really?" James raised an eyebrow. "I had assumed the Freewill had simply awoken you a few moments before me. But how..." He paused for a moment, then turned and looked at me. "Your friend?"

"Yeah, the not-so-pure one."

"Intriguing. It seems there was a reason she wanted him after all. Tell me, does Lord Alexander know of this?"

"I should say he does not," Gan replied. Though James was a member of the First Coven, the ruling body of the vampires, and the guys you absolutely did *not* fuck with unless you wanted to end up as dust, Gan talked to him as if he should've been filling her wine glass.

I had to admit, I wasn't quite sure where to place my money if things got ugly between them.

However, James was not your typical vamp. "All things considered, perhaps that is for the best. I do not suppose you are able to share this new ... gift?"

Gan averted her eyes and gave her head a single shake, looking almost embarrassed.

"So far, Ed's the only infectious carrier," I explained.

"I see." James narrowed his eyes at me and turned serious. "This is news that should not leave this room if you wish for your friend to continue breathing. Fortunately for us all, there seems to be some residual effect of Ib's compulsion on my short term memory."

His meaning was clear – he was willing to forget we'd ever mentioned it. As I said, he was a good egg among bad guys.

Awesome as that was, Sally decided to drag us all back to reality. "That's great and all, but it still doesn't change the fact that we're fucked the second that bitch decides we are."

"Maybe not," Christy said.

"What?"

"Before all of this, when I was still trying to get your memory back, I started working on a spell."

"Hold on," I interrupted. "You're in no condition to..."

"Please continue, Christine," James said, the authority in his voice making it clear I should ixnay my outhmay.

"I hope your short term memory loss counts for this, too," she replied with a grin. "When I was in Sally's head, I was also studying what Alexander had done to her. Powerful stuff, not easy to undo, but I learned a lot about how compulsion works. Bill was telling me all about them, how there are two kinds – focused and wide."

James glanced my way, a bemused smirk upon his face. "Why do I not find that surprising?" Oh yeah, I was definitely gonna be on the receiving end of a lecture for this one.

"What I was working on might not be so hot for the focused ones," Christy continued, "but I think I came up with a way to insulate ... that's the word you guys use, right? Anyway, I came up with a spell, combining what I learned with my knowledge of mind magic, that could insulate other Magi from a wide compulsion, no matter who might throw it out."

"And?"

"And, I have no idea how well or how long it would work, but I think it could be effective in shielding vampires, too."

"You *think* it could be effective?" James asked, his face unreadable.

"It isn't much to go on, I know."

"It is much more than we had before," he said. "If it fails, we shall be no worse off. If it succeeds, however..."

"We can give that bitch a bloody nose she won't forget," Sally finished.

"It would give us a chance to escape," he clarified. "I am sorry to say, but I have no confidence in our ability to defeat Calibra with our current resources."

"I must disagree, Wanderer," Gan said. "My beloved is here. If I am to assume correctly, then that means the Shining One is, too." She looked at me expectantly, a knowing smile on her face that I so wanted to erase with my fist.

Instead, I replied, "Yeah, she's here, too. Somewhere outside. But she's..."

"Do you not see?" Gan asked James. "The prophecy is nigh. These are the end times that were spoken of. The Shining One will lay low the Magi while my beloved destroys

Ib. Then he will strike her down, paving the way for our future."

"Um, not to nitpick," Kelly said, "but as one of the Magi in question, I kinda take issue with some of that."

"Destiny cannot be denied," Gan replied, as if discussing the weather. "I would suggest you prepare yourself in whatever manner you find most dignified."

I stepped between them before things could further devolve. "Okay, enough of this bullshit. Let's get something straight. Sheila isn't going to destroy the mages and I'm not fighting her. The only one I'm here to end is Calibra."

"So you say now, my love."

"Will you please shut the fuck up? Did you ever think that maybe your precious fucking prophecy has been interpreted wrong?"

She, James, and the rest all stared at me expectantly.

"Um, for starters," I began, not entirely sure where I was taking this, "maybe it's not an Icon I'm supposed to face. Calibra seems to think she's walking around in a perpetual white wedding. Well, couldn't those blind assholes have seen her in her stupid dress and misinterpreted it?" I was grasping at straws, nothing more, but it kinda made sense.

"Go on," James prodded.

"And she's a mage, too, their so-called White Mother. If Sheila were to, for instance, shove her sword up that bitch's ass, wouldn't she be sort of killing the mages' belief system, their way of life?"

"And the part about the final battle?" Sally asked with a smirk. She seemed to be enjoying the grave I was digging myself.

But, with a flash of insight, I realized I was ready for her this time. "That makes sense, too. If I win, things go on as they have. We remain creatures of darkness, so our world just continues as it is and we rule it from the shadows, not much different than we do now. If Calibra wins, however, she fucks with Ed and makes an army of sunlight-loving vampires.

They stride out into the light and conquer the world. See? It's all open to interpretation."

James, for his part, seemed amused at my trying to rewrite a prophecy that had probably been studied for thousands of years. Oh well, fuck it. They could've all been wrong.

"I still believe our best plan of action is escape," he said at last. "However, if fate is indeed nigh, then it may not be possible, regardless of whatever interpretation we give it." He turned to Christy. "How long would it take you to put your spell into effect?"

Shit! My whole point in speaking out was to keep that from happening, yet as usual, I got fucking sidetracked. "Christy is in no shape to do card tricks, much less muck around with every head in the building."

"I understand your concerns for your friend, Dr. Death," James replied. "However, I believe our options in this are limited."

"Then we'll find another..."

"No," Christy said from behind me. I turned to find her back on her feet. "We're going to do this."

"You're in no condition," I said.

"Can't believe I'm saying this," Sally added, "but Bill's right."

"I appreciate the concern." She smiled at both of us. "I really do. But this is my choice." Before either of us could protest, her voice hardened. "Everything I ever believed in is a lie ... *everything*. Not only that, but Kala tried to kill my baby. There is nothing I will not do to repay that bitch threefold."

Whoa. Even the other witches backed up as Christy stepped forward and came face to face with James.

"I don't know whose interpretation of this prophecy I agree with anymore, but I stand with those who say its time is now. I'll perform this ritual, this spell, but not for those who choose to run. This ends here and now. If you stand with us, I will do everything I can to help you. But I swear before all the gods, I will have no mercy on any who stand between me and Kala's end."

James and she locked eyes for several seconds. If he took this the wrong way, as the other Dracs certainly would, it could end very badly for her. After a few moments, though, he grinned. "Well said, Christine Fenton. You shame me with your words, but perhaps I needed to be reminded of my station. I have lived a long fulfilling life, with few regrets. If I am destined to die, it could not be with better company."

"Awesome," Sally said with a shrug. "Now if we're done with the feel goods, let's get a move on. I, for one, am tired of people fucking with my brain."

"There's just one small problem," I said.

"Just one?" James asked.

"No, but it's a big one. All of this talk about stopping Calibra and the Jahabich ... how are we going to do that?"

Christy looked at me knowingly. "We've already discussed this."

"I'm well aware, but..." I tried to be mindful of present company. James was a good guy and I had no doubt he was on our side, but he was still one of the Draculas. It was probably best to keep our plans for Alex out of this discussion. "I hate to tell you this, but Harry is dead."

"I..."

"I mean, really dead this time."

Christy looked down at the floor for a few moments, then let out a deep breath. "He chose his path. It doesn't change anything."

"But the spell..."

"Spell?" James asked.

"Err..."

"To stop the Jahabich," Sally said, bailing me out. Her ability to massage the truth with a straight face outclassed mine several times over. "Last time we were here, we discovered a spell. We think it can be used to lock the Jahabich away for good. Maybe Calibra, too. Christy's been working on it."

"That is excellent news," James replied.

"With some uncooperative company," I added.

"I have what I need," Christy said. "The plan hasn't changed."

"But I thought you said he was..."

"I also once told you I was good with mind magic." Again, her voice turned to steel. "I got what I needed from him."

Her meaning was clear. She'd forced his secrets from him at some point. Goddamn, this chick was hardcore when she wanted to be.

"Preparing both spells is going to take some time," Christy added, breaking the uncomfortable silence. "And I'm going to need my sisters' help."

"What about Meg?" Kelly asked. "We can't just leave her..."

"I'll go."

Sally turned to me. "You're kidding, right? No, of course you're not. This is both stupid and suicidal, two of your fortes."

"You know me so well." I reached out and pinched her cheek. "It's kinda cute."

She slapped my hand away. "I'm pretty sure the welcome wagon has been recalled in favor of the war party by now."

"No doubt, but we still have friends out there and at least I can't be compelled." I turned to Christy. "Just don't take all day."

"I will go too," Gan offered. "My beloved and I stand as equals in this regard."

"Awww, and you didn't even get her flowers for your date."

I shot Sally a withering glance. Sadly, Gan was right. If there was one vampire who was ideal to join me in this, it was her. Oh, well, maybe it was for the best. With her by my side, constantly reminding me of our future together, I would almost certainly not fear death.

"Just one problem, genius." Sally hooked a thumb back

toward where the vamps were still building a giant barrier of dead Jahabich. "Even if we open the front door again, you're going to have a hell of a time fighting your way out of this place."

She had a wee bit of a point there. I glanced at the ceiling. No, probably not. There was no way of knowing how deep beneath the other cave we were. Besides, I didn't favor playing undead gopher.

"We can send you with our magic," Christy offered.

"Hold on, I thought this whole cavern was warded against people zapping in unannounced. That's why we had to go to all that trouble finding a tunnel leading in."

"The entrances, maybe, but not once you're inside. I can feel it," she said. "Too many Magi here anyway. Even with Kala spoon-feeding them her dogma, they'd get antsy if they were too restricted."

Veronica leaned in. "Also, a lot of mages really don't like to walk if they don't have to."

"That is potentially disturbing to hear," James said. "It begs the question of why Ib has not opted to simply appear here in this place and retake control."

"Holy shit, you're right. She could..."

"She won't," Sally said.

"What do you mean?" I asked.

"Because of you, stupid. Think about it. She purposely told us she plans to eliminate Freewills from the equation. That might have just been idle speculation on her part, but then you had to go and prove you were actually dangerous by popping her one in the face."

"Is this true?" James asked.

"Hell yeah. Bill buffed out and sent her through a wall."

He turned to me. "So you have finally mastered your powers?"

I shrugged. "Mastered is such a strong word."

"Anyway," Sally continued, "she's not an idiot. She has to know by now, especially since our corpses weren't dragged back up, that we've managed to free her VIP prisoners.

Zapping in here would be dangerous for her. There are two vampires she can't control, one of whom is physically a threat." She looked at me, then sighed. "In theory, anyway. Not only that, but we have witches with us. She'd probably still kick all of our asses, but I'm willing to bet there's just enough doubt there for her to rethink how best to handle things."

"Good enough for me, but how does that help once Gan and I are gone?"

"We'll take care of that," Christy said. "This place isn't warded right now, but it will be the second we finish sending you."

"Will that keep her out?"

"Not forever, but we don't need it to. Just long enough for the insulation to take hold."

"Good enough," I said, even though I wasn't certain of it. "Let's do this. Send us to Meg."

The three witches looked uncomfortably at each other for a moment.

"What? Did I say the magic word or something?"

"It's not that simple, Bill," Christy said at last. "There's too many Magi up above, not to mention The Source. It would be like trying to scry a needle in a haystack."

"I'm gonna assume that means it's difficult."

"Quite a bit."

"Shit. Sheila's a fucking magical dead spot. So that's no good." At least I hoped she was. There was no way of knowing if ... no! I couldn't allow myself to think that way. She was fine. She had to be. Regardless, sticking around here wouldn't do dick to help her. Difficult as it was, I forced myself to focus on the task at hand. "Ed maybe?"

"I wouldn't even know how to look for him now," Christy admitted. "Unless you maybe plucked a hair from his head or something."

"Wasn't the first thing on my mind, sorry."

"Wait," Sally said. "Dead spot. That might be it."

"What do you mean?"

She ignored me and turned to Christy. "If this place is filled to the brim with magical static or whatever it is, could you maybe find her by trying to filter in reverse?"

I clapped her on the shoulder. "Good idea. If you can find a hole in the magic, that's gotta be Sheila. That at least gives us a landing point. Then we can fan out and look for Meg."

"It's a burden to be so brilliant, but I somehow live with it."

Christy appeared to mull it over for a moment, then nodded. "That actually might work."

It was probably the best we could do with what we had, and time was running short for new options.

"Let's do this, then."

75

SCARY MONSTER ALL-OUT ATTACK

Kelly and Veronica managed to locate a very small magical *dead zone* somewhere above us. Crossing my fingers that was Sheila, Gan and I stepped into a hastily drawn circle in the dirt and they zapped us out of there.

I had a momentary fear of a Fly-like transporter accident in which we'd reappear as one fused Bill-Gan freak, but thankfully, their magic wasn't privy to the whims of science fiction horror.

The whims of a nervous Icon, however, were a bit different. After a brief moment of disorientation in which it felt as if every molecule of my body was being stretched like taffy, we appeared in a flash of light. The first thing I saw once it cleared, though, was a sword swinging my way.

Loath as I might be to admit it, thank goodness for Gan. Her reflexes put mine to shame and she dragged me out of the way before I could even think to react.

"Oh my God! I'm so sorry," Sheila cried once she realized who we were.

"No problem," I replied in a voice that was far calmer than I felt.

"What are you two ... how did you...?"

Gan stepped forward, apparently nonplussed by any of

this. "It was my beloved's idea. He told the witches to find your hole and send us to it."

Sheila turned to me, both eyebrows raised questioningly.

"Not quite like that," I said sheepishly.

"I hope not. Doesn't matter, really. I'm just glad to see you both. Wait, you said the witches. Did you find..."

"Yeah. Just in time," I replied. "Kelly and Veronica, too."

"Is Kelly okay? I mean, are they?"

"They're fine. So are Sally and James. We found Dave, too. I think he's going to be all right, albeit maybe not in the head, but he never really was."

"You're rambling, my love."

I glanced down at Gan. "Thanks."

"I find it endearing."

"Of course you do."

We were off in a corner of the antechamber cavern, the one with the massive White Mother mural. We'd materialized behind a Jahabich pen housing some beaten down lizard men. A few of them glanced our way, but otherwise we didn't appear to have been noticed. "How are you feeling?"

"Better," Sheila said. "Maybe about fifty percent. Not good enough, though. I had no idea there would be so many Magi."

"Did any of them recognize you?"

"No idea, but I didn't take any chances. Thankfully, it's easy to lose yourself in the crowd here."

"What about Ed?"

She shook her head.

"Okay, we'll have to trust that he's still Calibra's golden child. Of everyone here, he's probably in the least danger."

"Where are the others?"

"They are currently preparing for battle," Gan replied.

"So we have a plan?"

I hated to be a Debbie Downer, so I sugarcoated things. "Working on it. For now, I need you to stay here. Gan and I have to go find Meg and try not to get killed in the process."

"No way."

"You're in no shape to..."

"And you are?" She looked me over, no doubt noticing the fact that my clothes were ripped to hell.

Amusingly enough, wardrobe aside, I was better than I had any right to be. Before leaving, Gan had suggested I bite all the vamps in the room. Problem was, the Jahabich sucked balls as jailers. Apparently, the feeding schedule was timed to coincide with the 12th of Never. Old they might have been, but even I could tell the vamps we'd rescued were just barely hanging on. The fight with the Jahabich had further drained what few reserves they had left. I felt bad for the first wizards they came across once it was time to go on the offensive.

Well, okay, not really.

James, however, had insisted I take some more of his blood, pulling rank and reminding me how things tended to go for those who told the First Coven to go fuck themselves.

Gan, Sheila, and I continued to bicker for a few more moments, but then – as luck would have it – the decision was made for us.

"Ssssstrangers! Look out."

It was one of those lizard dudes, and we didn't need to wait to see what he was talking about. A section of the wall penning them in had turned around and disengaged, heading our way. Guess word had gotten out that the Freewill was no longer on the guest list.

Normally, the phrase "there were only four of them" wouldn't exactly be a comforting thing to hear where the Jahabich were concerned. But between the three of us, we made short work of them.

Pity that more were on the way.

"Guess that settles it," Sheila said with a grin.

"So it does," I remarked snidely. "Try to keep up."

I glanced back toward the lizard men, but they stayed where they were. We could have used their help, but they had the look of prisoners broken enough to cower even when their cage door was wide open. So be it. "If anyone asks, tell them we went that way." I pointed in the opposite direction we were headed and hoped for the best.

I remembered my last time down here. Though the Jahabich might be creatures of chaos, they tended to react slowly when confronted with it – their methods of attack more in tune with their hive mind. Thus, it was time to introduce some bedlam to the mix.

We were in the outer chamber and needed to get back to where The Source was. Even if Meg had been spared a quick dip up til now, I didn't doubt Calibra was the type to bump her off out of spite. Ancient evils from the dawn of time tended to be assholes that way.

"Follow my lead."

"To the ends of this Earth and beyond," Gan replied.

Sheila laughed as I threw the little hellion a sour look. Yeah, she'd definitely roomed with Sally for one day too many.

"Just do as I do," I said. "The name of the game is tag."

I spied a nearby wall of Jahabich standing guard around something big, slimy, and with a lot of tentacles. Perfect! I ran up, grabbed one of its jailers, and flung it into his buddies, sending them tumbling. "Tag! You're it!"

A trio of monstrous yellow eyes opened up on their prisoner's mucus-covered ... err, body, I suppose ... and stared down at me.

"Yo, Cthulhu! Don't just sit there looking pretty. Get your fucking ass moving."

I had no idea whether it understood me or not. Honestly, I hoped to never have anything remotely resembling a meaningful conversation with something that looked like it. However, even if it didn't grok what I was saying, it began to struggle against the stalactites pinning its many appendages in place. With a tremendous heave, it tore itself free and attacked its tormentors.

Okay, that was one.

I turned to find Sheila had just done the same for a group

of captive Wisps. Not a bad choice, all in all. Like many of the other prisoners, these things were in pretty sad shape. Yet it was amazing how motivational a little bit of hope was. They immediately set to work fusing Jahabich in place, raising the temperature in the immediate area uncomfortably.

Sheila ran over to join me. "I think I kinda like this game. So how do we win?"

"We don't die," I replied, spotting Gan.

As usual, she had to make the rest of us look bad. She'd released some winged gargoyle-looking things, a pack of maniacally cackling gremlins, and a group of feral vampires. That last bunch was probably as likely to attack us as our enemies, but beggars couldn't be choosers.

Our strategy wasn't a winning one. If I knew the Jahabich, they'd regroup quickly and brutally. Those fighting back would also mostly be trying to escape. It was only the truly pissed off or the insane who would want to stick around to see how this ended.

But that was fine for now. Every Jahabich that got smashed was one less to pound our heads in.

"This way!" I led us in the direction of the caves that would get us further inside. That was going to be the tricky part. They were narrow and didn't have any prisoners in them to free. We'd be on our own and with a shitload more Jahabich, not to mention mages, waiting on the other side for us.

Yeah, this oughta be fun.

"You can put me down now."

"Are you sure? Because it might be dicey once we're in..."

"I believe the Shining One's legs are quite sufficient to carry her," Gan said. Normally, she was pretty magnanimous with regard to me and Sheila, confident that one day we'd rule the world as queen and whatever the fuck slave title I'd get, but today she sounded a bit snippy. Music to my ears. Glad to see the little nut wasn't entirely crack-proof.

Several Jahabich battling a group of four-armed imps had blocked our way. Much as I would've liked to have stopped and helped the multi-armed guys, we had places to be. So, counting on the fact that her powers were still weakened and less likely to blow me to bits, I'd scooped up Sheila and gotten a running start before leaping over the fray.

One of these days, I really needed to invest in one of those GoPro cameras because I was pretty sure it looked cool as all hell. I even stuck the landing.

"There!" I said. "The cave is right ahead, right past those..." The fuck? I put Sheila down, barely realizing I was doing so.

"Bodies?" she finished for me.

There was maybe half a dozen of them, all human – in appearance at least. It was painfully obvious this wasn't done by the Jahabich. My first clue was that their heads hadn't been caved in. The blood seeping from the wounds on their necks was my second.

But who...?

A familiar figure stepped from the cave entrance, leaned against the wall, and folded his arms impatiently.

Ed was trying to look cool, but that illusion was immediately dispelled once he doubled over and puked his guts out all over the floor.

We raced over to him, taking care not to step on the corpses littering the place.

"Are you okay?" I asked.

"Yeah. Damn vampire blood. Always does that to me. Don't seem to have a taste for it like you do."

I helped him up. "That's because you're a fucking pussy."

"I hope there's a plan behind all this chaos," he said after nodding a greeting to Sheila and then pointedly ignoring Gan. "Because otherwise, we just stirred a major pot of shit for no reason."

"We?"

"Who do you think did all this?" He pointed toward the bodies.

"Why?" Sheila asked.

He dropped the bullshit act. "Relax. They all volunteered. Once I heard the commotion at the far end of the cave, I figured shit was happening, so I punched out the closest Jahabich. By the way, have I mentioned how awesome that is to do?"

I motioned for him to hurry up. "Fascinating. We're on a timetable here."

"Fuck you. I guess I'm still on their do-not-hurt list because his buddies all stood by and let me do it. They were guarding some vampires who jumped in once they saw what I was doing. After we were finished, a bunch of them asked if I'd put the bite on them. Guess the rumor mill works even down here."

"So you did?"

"Yeah. I mean, these guys were pretty much fucked otherwise. This way, maybe they'll wake up in time to help us out a bit."

"Ready-made reinforcements," Sheila said. "Not a bad idea."

"See, told you I was a good pick to run your company."

"Uh huh," I replied. "Be sure to give him some stock options when we get back. Unfortunately, we can't sit around and wait for these guys to turn. We have a witch to save and a bunch of other stuff I have no idea how we're gonna pull off. You in?"

"I've tagged along this far. Might as well see how the rest plays out."

"Sounds like a plan. Follow me and I'll show you how a real vampire does it."

"Good," he replied. "Now we just have to find a real vampire."

Such an asshole.

I wouldn't have it any other way.

76

BRINGING A WAND TO A FISTFIGHT

If the Jahabich were smart, they'd have simply caved the tunnel in on us and been done with it. I mean, there we were – the Freewill, the Icon, the progenitor of a new breed of vampires, and Gan. Four for the price of one, and it would have almost certainly saved them a lot of trouble otherwise.

But either they were idiots or Calibra had too much ego at stake. So we raced unmolested down the tunnel toward the cave that held The Source.

For a few moments, I thought our transition between the two caverns was going to be easy, but then I spied a lone figure walking our way from the other end – Starlight.

I held up a hand for my group to stop. "Let me handle this."

"A foolish course of action, my love. You would do best to dispatch her immediately."

I was sorely tempted to turn and clock the little princess. With my current power level, I actually had a fairly decent shot of hitting her. But this was probably a poor time to test the limits of our relationship. "I said I have this." I walked away from the rest of the group and approached my former friend.

"Ib is angry," she said.

"I kind of figured."

"No, I mean really angry. She's going to make an example of anyone you haven't gotten to yet."

"Then I guess I need to keep moving."

"You do."

I folded my arms in front of my chest and locked eyes with her. "Are you going to try to stop us?"

Starlight hesitated for a moment, then gave her head a single shake.

There it was. She was still in there somewhere. I had to at least try. "Help us."

"It's too late for me."

"Obviously it's not."

She turned away and struck the wall of the tunnel in frustration. "Yes it is. She's in here, too." She pointed to her head. "Always. All the time. It never stops. I can hear the rest of them, never ever shutting up. The only peace I get is when I give in. Even now I can feel it. She's ordering us all back to our ... other forms. We're more susceptible that way, less likely to do our own thing."

"Like Decker did?"

"Excuse my saying so, but he was an asshole." She looked past me toward where the others stood. "I'm glad you killed him. The first time, anyway."

Gan, obviously eavesdropping, replied, "The pleasure was entirely mine."

I turned back to Star. "So now what?"

"Now you get moving that way, and I keep going the other way ... for as long as I can. I don't have long. I can't fight her. I'm sorry."

"Not as sorry as I am for letting Vehron take you."

"You got him. That's the important thing." She lowered her voice. "Just don't let anyone else around here know I said that."

I let out a small laugh. "Your secret is safe with me."

She stepped up next to me, preparing to walk past. "Good luck, Bill. I mean it."

"I'll do my best."

"Just don't worry about what happens to me. Promise?"

I let out a long sigh and finally replied, "I promise."

"Good ... oh, and if you see Sally, tell her I said I always considered her a friend."

"I will."

"Even if she was a bitch most of the time."

"Are you okay?" Sheila asked after Starlight had passed us.

I didn't answer her, but Ed did. "I think we'll all be much better after we ice a certain white-wearing witch."

"Amen to that." I turned to Sheila, "How are you doing?"

"Nothing a blood transfusion won't cure. Seriously, I'll make do. At least nobody in there is likely to point a gun at my face."

"There is that."

"The end of the tunnel is up ahead," Gan said. "Do you still possess the Wanderer's strength, beloved?" After a moment of silence, she added, "Beloved? I am speaking to you."

"I don't answer to that."

"You are being childish."

"Look who's talking," Ed muttered.

"I will remind you," Gan addressed him, "that, despite my love's fondness for your well-being, I am quite aware that ending your existence will foil Ib's plans."

"And I'm shutting up now," he replied quickly.

"A wise choice." She turned back toward me with an expectant look upon her face.

"Fine. Yes, I still have James's power. Not sure for how long, but good to go for now."

"And what about...?"

"That too," I hastily replied. "Saving it for a special occasion."

"Good," she said. "Then you and I will strike first and

fast. Wade into the throng of Magi, use them against each other."

"And us?" Sheila asked.

"This one..." Gan indicated Ed. "Will not be harmed. None of Ib's thralls will risk her wrath. Use that to your advantage."

Sheila glanced sidelong at Ed and he replied, "Let me guess. Demoted from president to meat shield?"

"Something like that."

"Story of my life."

As far as plans went, it wasn't much to go on. But then, from a tactical perspective, we didn't have a lot to work with. We were in a mostly straight tunnel that opened up right into the belly of the beast. The chances of us casually walking in unnoticed were somewhere between nil and don't make me fucking laugh.

Fast and painful it was, then, just like most dates I'd been on.

Speaking of which...

"Wait a second, Bill." Sheila approached me, then stopped and looked down at Gan, who'd stepped right in front of where I stood. "Excuse me."

Gan, however, did nothing of the sort. Oh yeah, the claws were definitely coming out now that we were finally reaching the endgame.

"Fine, whatever." Sheila stepped around her to face me. She held up a hand, hesitated, then looked embarrassed for a moment. After a beat, she kissed her own palm, then pressed it to my lips. "Here. For luck."

I raised an eyebrow.

"Probably not a great time to accidentally set you on fire," she said sheepishly.

I meant to agree with her, but instead found myself saying, "I'm willing to risk it."

With that, I stepped in and ... bumped into Gan, who had helpfully inserted herself between us again.

"The Shining One is correct," she said frostily. "This would be an inopportune time to act foolishly."

The moment definitely over, we prepared ourselves. Gan and I were the shock part of the plan, whereas Sheila and Ed would hopefully bring the awe.

"Use all of the speed at your disposal, my love," Gan said. "I will be barely a step behind you."

"Okay, let's do this before anyone else steps into this tunnel and fucks it up."

"Good luck, man," Ed said from behind me. "You too, Princess Cockblocker."

I blew out an annoyed breath and then I was off.

Oh, how I envied James. To be able to do this at will, moving so fast the world slowed down around you. And he didn't even have to bust out of his clothes to do so.

The tunnel entrance rapidly grew wider as I approached, then, like a flash, I was through. There were about thirty feet of open space in front of me ... and a whole lineup of angry mages beyond, all apparently waiting for my stupid ass to come barreling out.

Fast as we were, we weren't nearly quick enough.

Before I could close the distance, a purplish globe of energy surrounded me and lifted me off the ground. My feet were still moving at a pace that made them little more than a blur, but my actual forward momentum abruptly halted thanks to the magical hamster wheel I was now trapped in.

Fuck me!

I turned to shout a warning to Gan, hoping I provided her at least a small cover bonus, but she was nowhere to be seen.

What the fuck? Had they vaporized her?

Beyond, Sheila was approaching the tunnel mouth, albeit at a far more human pace than I had. One of the witches shouted a warning at her appearance.

About half a dozen mages powered up in an angry red glow and then let loose as she set foot outside the tunnel entrance. She'd been expecting that, though, and abruptly side-stepped, revealing Ed.

Judging by the look on my roommate's face, he shit an industrial-sized brick. Can't say I didn't do the same as the torrent of power raced toward him.

Come on!

Yes! As we'd hoped, the blasts either fizzled out before they could hit him or were harmlessly diverted into the cavern wall. I doubted if any of the Magi present understood what Ed was or how Calibra planned to use him in the grand scheme of things. However, their Jesus-witch had deemed him untouchable and they weren't about to risk getting on her bad side.

The distraction caught them off guard. Sheila's aura sputtered to life around her, not nearly as brilliant as it should have been, but hopefully enough. She drew her sword as she raced toward me and then actually sliced through the spell.

The blade passed dangerously close to my face, but it did the job. The next thing I knew, I was back on the floor as the power of faith fizzled out the spell in its entirety.

Ed, finally remembering he had vampiric speed, caught up to us, ruining any other shots the mages had been preparing to unleash. Indecision shone in their eyes. Oh yeah, Calibra had definitely put the fear of God into them but good. Bad for them, good for us.

I took advantage of this and slammed into their front line before they could power up again. The idiots, secure in their power, had packed themselves in like sardines ... or more like dominos. Sadly for them, I was in no mood to be gentle with my toys.

Cries of pain rang out as bones snapped and bodies got knocked aside. Gan, wherever the fuck she'd gotten off to, had been right. The middle of this massive group was perhaps the safest place to be. Even as I picked up one wizard and used him to bitchslap his closest buddies, I could see the confusion in their eyes. Mages, as a whole, didn't like hurting their own kind ... some sanctity of life bullshit or such. With the kind of close up fighting going on, more a vampire's specialty than anything, they were finding it hard to hit me with anything strong enough to stop me, at least without also killing their far more fragile brethren.

Soon I was deep among them, punching, slapping, maybe a little hair pulling, too. I didn't know if Calibra had set up an emergency room in between all the castle raising, but if so, it was gonna be full tonight.

A spell slammed into my back and knocked me slightly off balance, but it had been one of those stun blasts I'd felt before. With James's power coursing through me, it barely registered. Unfortunately, the boost was starting to wear off and I wasn't even a third of the way toward where I wanted to get. I couldn't even see The Source yet from my vantage point surrounded by angry sorcerers.

I needed to use what I had while I could. My normal power level was maybe a bit beyond the very peak of what a human athlete could do. One on one, I could hand any of these mages their asses, but together they could easily take me down.

Or maybe they didn't need to. The crowd in front of me parted slightly and a big musclebound goon with mystical tattoos up and down his ripped arms stepped in. Guess this guy hadn't gotten the memo that magic users were supposed to be about as physically imposing as puppies. Either that or he'd decided to multi-class.

This guy was a beast and, considering the stance he adopted, he knew how to fight. That was a lesson I'd learned before. I was normally at the low end of the vampire spectrum, so a human at the high end could clean my clock. Pity for him, I still had a bit of badass left in me.

He threw a punch, which I barely sidestepped in the crowded quarters. I knocked down a witch in doing so, then used her as a step stool to launch myself onto the big guy's back. He slammed an elbow into my gut, almost driving the wind out of me.

Yeah, I was fading fast. Too bad for muscle mage here, it wasn't fast enough.

Physically overpowering opponents was definitely one way to win a battle, but never discount the advantage of psyching your foes out. I took a quick look around to ensure I had everyone's attention, then sank my fangs into Conan's neck.

He screamed as I ripped his flesh open, then tried to dislodge me with a judo throw, but I'd been ready for that. I sank my claws into his skin, effectively stapling myself in place as I took a satisfying swig of the red stuff.

Thankfully, wizard blood was pretty much the same as human when it came to being a part of this nutritious breakfast. It not only served to freak the ever-living fuck out of everyone around us, but made for a very convenient and much needed lunch break.

Some of the big guy's friends tried to pull me off, but I was stuck tight as I forced him to his knees.

Savoring the rush of blood, I got to thinking that if this freaked out his buddies, just think what would happen if I snapped this fucker's neck like a matchstick.

For one moment, it was tempting. Hell, shredding my way through these assholes would be a lot more useful in the long run than a few concussions. I could turn most of these mages into confetti if I wanted. I could...

Fuck! Dr. Death's goddamned influence was working on me again. Having him a part of me was going to be even more dangerous than hearing his insults as a separate voice.

A lot of the faces staring back at me were young, barely my age. I tried to remember that mages by themselves weren't a bad lot. These guys had chosen poorly in their messiah and they definitely deserved a good ass kicking, but wholesale slaughter? No. That wasn't my way.

I let the big guy go and he dropped to the floor, beaten but alive.

As expected, though, I'd scored a big psychological advantage, which was what I'd been hoping for. The eyes looking my way were angry, frightened, but best of all, hesitant. That was good, because I was almost back to being just me.

I again started forward, heading the way The Source lay. This time, the mages in front of me stepped to the side like I was a celebrity on the red carpet, one known for punching out any paparazzi who fucked with me.

I finally caught sight of The Source's shores again. Goddamn, I wasn't sure I'd ever get used to seeing that, especially now that I knew it wasn't just some big radioactive bukkake pool.

Sadly, the spectacle quickly became a secondary concern to me. The Jahabich were once again marching prisoners to the edge, preparing to make more of them into Calibra's slaves.

I caught sight of a head of raven-colored hair near the front. Shit! We'd been right. Calibra, in a snit at having her nose-bloodied, had stepped things up.

I didn't know Meg very well, but she'd stood by our side when everything about her belief system told her to do otherwise. That counted for a lot in my book. Hopefully, Sheila and Ed could distract the rest of the Magi because, right then, I needed to move.

Powerful as vamps might be, though, we don't have eyes in the backs of our heads. I'd thought the mages in front of me had been making a path out of fear, but they were also making sure their brothers and sisters had a nice wide area to target.

I didn't see which backstabbing cocksucker got off the spell. All I felt was a searing flash of red-hot pain that slammed into my ass and knocked me down just as the Jahabich began to close in on the hapless witch.

77

ICONIC DEFEAT

Either I still had a residual bit of James's power in my veins or the spell wasn't at full strength. Otherwise, the next thing I saw would have been the Pearly Gates opening to let me in.

Even so, it was enough to turn my backside into a charcoaled mess and send me skidding face-first across the rocky ground.

Worse, it would embolden the rest. And with me lying there taste testing the dirt, I would make an extra easy target.

"Bill!"

From the sound of things, Sheila wasn't far behind. Pity it was probably far enough that it wouldn't matter if...

An animalistic scream of rage sounded from far above where I lay. It was as if someone ran a mountain lion over with a lawnmower. Most importantly, I knew that cry. Barely a week went by in which I didn't wake up in a cold sweat, listening to it fade away from a dream that, more often than not, offered horrific visions of a future wedding.

I flipped over onto my back, my eyes turned toward the ceiling – the same as just about everyone else here – in time to see Gan dropping down. So that's where she'd gotten off to. Letting me race in as her stooge while she climbed like a spider monkey on meth. I so needed to kick her ass for that, but maybe later.

Her eyes flashed yellow and her claws extended as she landed among the assembled Magi and was immediately lost to my view. It was easy to tell where she was, however, from the spray of blood erupting up and outward. Gan definitely didn't share my thoughts on being merciful.

That darkness inside of me flared up in admiration of her handiwork, tempting me to give in to the rage and join her. Together, we could turn this place into a fucking bloodbath.

With some effort, I pushed my inner psychopath back down and told it to go stand in a corner somewhere while I physically forced the rest of me back to my feet.

I stood just in time to see Sheila closing the distance, her aura protecting her. She used the flat of her sword to break a mage's nose while Ed followed right behind her, punching out any Magi she happened to miss.

"Yeah, you like that? Oh, you want a piece, too?"

Ah, the lame trash talk of one fighting with total impunity. Oh well, let him have his fun while he could. It wasn't often one found themselves in a pitched supernatural battle against foes who wouldn't fight back.

Between them and Gan, the mages had more than enough to contend with. In fact, many of them, already unnerved by my attack, broke ranks and ran for it. Others apparently decided their own skin was worth far more than their coven buddies and began firing off spells into the crowd, seemingly heedless of who they hit.

In short, it was utter chaos, which meant I had a shot at saving our friend.

Reining in the desire to let loose, give in to the anger, and see how many corpses I could decorate the place with, I took off in the direction of The Source – barreling through any mages who got in my way. I finally broke from the crowd and once again caught sight of my quarry. Sadly, the stony assholes had been busy. She was now queued up while a freshly minted Jahabich emerged from the other side of the pool. Shit! "Meg!"

She turned unseeing toward the sound of my voice, shackled and beaten all to hell. Both of her eyes had been blackened to the point of being swelled shut.

She raised her hands in a warding gesture, but nothing happened. The manacles she was wearing were obviously of the magic dampening variety.

"Run!" I shouted. "Toward the sound of my voice!"

The head of the Jahabich closest to her spun nearly a hundred and eighty degrees to face me, its jack o'lantern eyes blazing with malicious intent.

It opened its mouth and said, "*Mother,*" which every Jahabich in the place immediately echoed, the sound bouncing off the walls of the cavern and seeming to come from dozens of directions at once.

The creature raised its club arms; all the while, its gaze never wavered from mine. I put on every ounce of speed I had, but it wasn't enough.

I had only covered maybe half the distance between us when it crushed Meg's head with a sickening crunch, instantly snuffing out her life.

Three of the Jahabich disengaged from the lineup to intercept me as I closed in, intent on revenge. These fuckers were gonna wish they'd gotten jobs as garden gnomes instead.

My anger at them was merely a displacement of the disgust I felt with myself, though. I had the means to save Meg, but had chosen not to use it ... instead waiting for some bullshit *right time* that's a cliché in almost every fucking movie.

I ducked and sidestepped, throwing a punch of my own that knocked out a few stalagmite teeth. In the background, the first Jahabich, blood still dripping down its arms, stepped up to Meg and kicked her corpse into The Source, which began to bubble and take on an angry red hue as the unholy transformation took place somewhere beneath its surface.

I'd seen this before. Soon, Meg would surface again ... miraculously whole. However, just when you thought it was going to be okay, the true horror would begin and she would cease to be her. She'd transform into one of them, becoming another puppet under Calibra's control. Within seconds, she'd be lost to...

Wait! Maybe there was still a chance.

Truth be told, I had no fucking clue what I was doing or whether it would work. Meg had proven herself a friend, though, and if there was anything that could be done to help her, then I had to try.

But first I had to stay alive.

The Jahabich I'd decked had staggered, but was very much still in the fight. My other friends had their hands full with the Magi. So that left four against one.

Fighting them was an issue, but dodging was another thing entirely. I feinted one way, then took off in another, sidestepping the rest until I came to the line of prisoners waiting to be Jahabich'd.

"Run!" I shouted. Who knows if they understood or not? I mean, shit, the first creature in the lineup appeared to be made mostly out of tongue – bet he was a hit with the ladies. My meaning, though, was apparently clear. Two of the three creatures still waiting to be clubbed like baby seals turned away from me, obviously too broken to care. But the last, a red-skinned troll with a circle of teeth where its face should've been, made a break for it.

Two of the Jahabich immediately broke off to chase it down, which evened the odds against me considerably ... at least until all their buddies elsewhere in this place got the memo.

There! The bubbling in the pool became pronounced and concentrated. Something was moving just beneath the surface toward the shore. I kicked out and managed to trip one of the Jahabich still hounding me. That just left the asshole who'd clubbed Meg. It lowered its head and charged. That was fine by me. It went low, but I went high.

The Jahabich weren't particularly tall. I jumped and cleared it, striking it with the heel of my sneaker in the back of its head. That, combined with its momentum, sent it staggering away from The Source where a figure broke the surface.

The orange goop covering it fell away as it climbed out, revealing Meg. She was naked at first, but then her skin shimmered and the clothes she'd been wearing reappeared around her. She walked up onto the shore holding her head before finally noticing me.

"Holy shit. That was really fucking weird. It's like..."

"Sorry about this." I lashed out with everything I had, driving my fist into her unsuspecting face. If there was any chance of this working, assuming it did at all, it would need to be before she first turned.

She looked like Meg, but felt like she'd been given an adamantium skeleton. I was pretty sure I broke most of my fingers, but it worked. Her eyes rolled into the back of her head and she went down like a ton of bricks, quite literally.

The important thing was that she stayed her. As I said, I had no clue whether anything could be done, but I had to try. More importantly, I had to find Christy and the others so they could try ... something at least.

I had a feeling continually knocking her out wasn't really a sustainable plan for the long run, but for now, I kicked her in the jaw to make sure she stayed out for a while. Fuck! My poor toes. But if this worked, it would be well worth it.

I picked her up, hoping to make a run for it, but then remembered she was a lot denser than she looked. Ugh! My encumbrance immediately went from light to heavy, which meant I was gonna be lucky to walk, much less jump over these things.

That was gonna be a problem, because the two Jahabich I'd tripped up were back on their feet and several more of their buddies were marching over to join them.

Looked like we'd used up our surprise round.

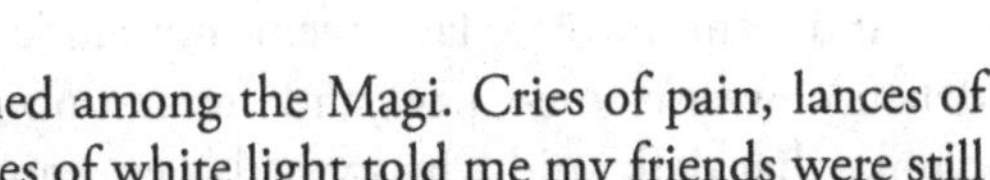

Chaos still reigned among the Magi. Cries of pain, lances of power, and flashes of white light told me my friends were still doing their damnedest to keep them occupied. Sadly, a column of Jahabich that grew larger by the second cut me off from them.

However, rather than charge, they began to form a wide semicircle around me, with The Source at my backside. Talk about being stuck between a rock and a hard place. I didn't want to leave Meg, but I couldn't escape with her either, at least not as I was.

But maybe I didn't need to stay that way. I'd taken a good long drink from one of the mages a few minutes earlier. I was actually feeling pretty okay – not quite recharged, but good enough. If so, then maybe I could once again unleash my inner hell beast.

I glanced down at Meg's unconscious form ... sentenced to a fate worse than death, all because she refused to bow before one person's arrogance. I remembered what Calibra had tried to do to Christy's baby. I had more than enough to make me good and angry.

I laid Meg down at my feet and when I stood up again, the Jahabich had taken on a reddish hue that had nothing to do with the pool of power behind me.

All at once, my skin felt tight. Oh yeah, this was more like it. When I was finished, these freaks were gonna look like they were made out of talcum powder. There was gonna be enough gravel to pave a road between here and...

I suddenly felt lighter on my feet. For a moment, I assumed it was just the effect of my leg muscles becoming a shitload stronger, but then I realized it was because I was actually floating a good six inches above the ground.

Okay, *that* was new.

The transformation completed itself, and I took a

moment to admire my biceps. This was so much easier than a gym membership, and cheaper, too. It was time for a workout nevertheless. I crouched and leapt at my foes.

And went nowhere fast. Seems my sudden bout of gravity defiance wasn't some new and interesting power after all. Unlike that dark void Christy had been imprisoned in, there didn't seem a way to propel myself forward. Swimming against the air did little more than make me look like a fucking idiot.

This wasn't good.

There came a flash of light from within the semicircle and Calibra appeared before me. As expected, she seemed decisively less friendly than last I'd seen her. Hers was the countenance of someone who had invited guests into her personal Garden of Eden, only to catch them shitting all over her prized petunias.

The Jahabich all did their annoyingly creepy "*Mother*" routine. Bunch of broken records from Hell, those assholes. At least the Magi were a bit less mundane about it. They let loose with a chorus of cheers and whistles. The ones not occupied by my friends feeding them their own teeth, that is.

Calibra glanced toward where Meg lay unconscious at my ... beneath my feet and allowed herself a smile. "What's that phrase? A day late and a dollar short, isn't it?"

"Come a little closer and I'll give you change," I growled, made somewhat less menacing by the fact that I was now floating sideways.

"All of that power in one so young," she said, pretty much ignoring my impotent threat. "Freewills have always yielded interesting results. But you, able to fully merge with the spirit inside, able to heal the damage of integration and tap into all of the power flowing to you from beyond ... it is truly impressive. If it could be harnessed, controlled, just think what I could accomplish and in so much less time than it has taken so far."

"Yeah. I mean, I could shove my fist up your ass at light

speed and all my friends could join in. Sounds like a hell of a party."

"Kill it!"

"Destroy the monster!"

I got the impression the mages weren't exactly rooting for me.

Calibra, for her part, seemed to consider their request. "All of that power," she repeated, "yet in the hands of an insufferable fool lacking the intelligence to know his place in this world. Yes, I could accomplish much by controlling you, but I see now that isn't to be. You are far too much of a wild card, Mr. Ryder."

"My reputation proceeds me," I replied as I twirled upside-down in midair. God, talk about embarrassing. The only way this could be worse would be if she invited all the mages to line up and take turns hitting me like a piñata.

"You are unworthy of my rule, unworthy to serve me, unworthy even as a slave," she growled. Her eyes were still normal and I didn't see any fangs. If anything, she was probably relying on her magic alone because we had an audience, but the vampire attitude was definitely there.

Whatever force was holding me aloft became visible, forming an angry reddish sphere around me. In an instant, the air inside went from comfortable to boiling, like sitting atop an electric stove someone had decided to turn to high.

Cries rose up from the mages watching us. Oh great, just what we needed: a cheering section. Maybe Calibra would be nice and let them toast some marshmallows over the open flame that was going to be my body if this kept up.

It was an interesting sensation, taking a breath, feeling my lungs char from the inside out, then healing in time for me to do so again a moment later.

The pitch of the cheering mages rose. Glad to see they were enjoying the show. But then it changed, became commingled with cries of pain, surprise, and – yes – warning, too.

Calibra turned in time to see a white glow rising up

behind the Jahabich that surrounded us. Multiple blasts of magical energy converged on the spot, but the glow held true.

Faith magic.

I allowed a smile to form on my charred lips. A moment later, Sheila hacked her way through the wall of Jahabich with Ed hot on her heels.

She pointed her weapon at Calibra. "Let him go."

Ed, being more inclined to one-liners, cracked his knuckles and said, "I am really going to enjoy fucking up your shit."

Eh, I'd heard worse.

I didn't see hide nor hair of Gan, but the screams and continued chaos coming from the herd of Magi told me she was still busy turning them into magical coleslaw. Probably a smart move. If given a chance to get their shit together, they could have made short work of us. Also, I kinda got the impression Gan wasn't all too fond of mages.

The temperature around me decreased to a somewhat less scalding level as Calibra's attention was diverted elsewhere. Sadly, I still found myself spinning helplessly in midair. Go figure, Levitate was a shit spell in real life, too.

Ed stepped forward. "Let's do this."

"Let's not," Calibra replied. "Know your place, child." She waved her hand and an arc of sky blue energy lanced out and hit him square in the chest. Dude really needed to learn how to duck if he was gonna survive in this world. He went flying back into one of the Jahabich, taking it out in the process, before falling to the ground, stunned.

I couldn't help but let out a pained sigh. For all the value placed upon him, Ed was like some rich dude's prized Pomeranian – useful for breeding purposes, but aside from that, he was just a yappy runt trying to run with the big dogs. And yet he'd dared mock me as a vampire.

Calibra turned her full attention to Sheila. "The last Icon, I presume."

"That's me." She glanced over to where Ed lay twitching. "What he said about enjoying this, double that."

She charged, her aura steady if not quite back to one hundred percent yet. Calibra, however, sidestepped easily. Though I doubted the wickedest of witches would show her full prowess in front of the mages, Sheila needed to remember this chick had more than enough speed and strength to spare.

The mages, the ones not being torn new assholes by Gan anyway, cheered her on. Dicks.

But maybe they didn't need to be.

I might not have been able to do much in this fight physically, but that didn't mean I couldn't ruin things in my own special way. "She's a fucking vampire, you idiots!"

Calibra spun toward me, her eyes flashing black for the barest of moments. Ooh, looked like I hit a nerve. Pity for her, that gave Sheila an opportunity to step in and aim for something a bit more vital.

The tip of her blade burst through the front of Calibra's dress, bloodying her right side good. It wasn't a fatal hit – she'd managed to partially dodge at the last moment – but it looked like it fucking hurt.

What damage the blow didn't do, however, the faith magic pouring through it made up for. White flame burst from the wound, cauterizing it from the inside out.

Several of the Magi screamed as they watched this, but I was a bit more interested in the battle at hand and whether I'd be joining it to finish off this bitch.

True enough, I felt the power around me waver and I dropped several inches.

Right before I hit the ground, though, the magic stabilized again and I found myself once again floating around like the world's most pissed off helium balloon.

Calibra looked up at me and the grimace of pain on her face turned to one of predatory glee. She turned, quick as living lightning, and ripped the grip of the blade from Sheila's hands by sheer virtue of her speed and strength.

One half of her body still ablaze, she turned to face the Icon. Sheila, for her part, did her best to cover up the look of surprise on her face, but I couldn't blame her. Even with that Icon power feeding her self-esteem, the fact was Calibra had just performed a pretty hefty mind-fuck by not acting like a good little vampire and dying like she was supposed to.

Calibra laid a finger on the point of the sword and pushed it out of her body. Even I had to admit that was pretty fucking badass. The weapon slid out of her back, where it clattered to the ground, the blood upon it still sizzling.

By the time I looked up from the sword, Calibra's wounds had already healed. She stood between Sheila and her blade, almost daring the Icon to make a move.

Then, much to the cheers of the Magi bearing witness, Calibra raised a hand. I caught a flash of light from my periphery and turned my head to see a thin column of energy rising from The Source. It traveled through the air, snaked around Calibra's arm, then down her body. When it was finished, her white dress appeared whole again, unburnt and unbloodied.

"Well, isn't that just fucking brilliant?" I shouted at her. "You have all the magic on the fucking planet at your disposal and you use it for dry cleaning."

Calibra flashed a look of annoyance my way, but I simply smiled, floating as I was. I was just a distraction, one she'd fallen for hook, line, and sinker.

Sheila stepped in, her aura continuing to blaze. She ducked down, spun, and swept Calibra's legs out from under her. Then she rolled atop the downed master vampire, wrapped her legs around her midsection, and delivered a faith-powered punch to Calibra's jaw.

The Jahabich stood unmoving, apparently content to let Mommy work out her issues. One of the Magi, however, had apparently gotten a wee bit antsy watching what was going on and shot a beam of energy over their heads.

Thankfully, it fizzled harmlessly against Sheila's aura.

Unexpectedly, though, it seemed to really piss Calibra off.

Her body burning from where the aura encompassed her, she nevertheless spoke. "You would dare make me look weak in front of my children?" Calibra's hand shot up and grabbed hold of Sheila's throat. Using her superior strength, she forced her way back to her feet, dragging Sheila along for the ride until she held her several inches off the ground by the neck.

The faith aura continued to eat away at Calibra, but she seemingly ignored it. Even as the flesh of her hand melted away under the assault of faith magic, the charred bones beneath it refused to give way.

Sheila began to turn blue as the unearthly strong vampire crushed her windpipe.

Shit!

"Yo, Ib!" I shouted, hoping for another distraction. "Why don't you try that on someone in your own weight class? Or are you afraid that once I'm finished, you'll have to change your title to..."

Motherfucker! "No!"

Calibra ignored my baiting as she lifted Sheila high over her head with both hands. She brought her down onto her knee like she was Bane and her foe Batman. There came the sickening crack of bone as Sheila's spine was broken.

Oh my God!

Sheila didn't scream. I wasn't sure she even could. The look on her face was one of surprise, pain, and shock. She slid off Calibra's knee onto the hard rocky ground and lay there, her limbs twitching.

"I swear I'm gonna..."

"Oh come now, Freewill," Calibra purred, turning toward me. "You're a bit too late for ineffectual posturing, wouldn't you say?"

From somewhere beyond the wall of Jahabich came the sound of cheering.

"The prophecy is ended!"

"Long live the Magi!"

"All hail the White Mother!"

If Calibra cared, though, she didn't show it. She continued to smile triumphantly at me while I could do nothing but glare back. But then her smile faltered and she looked down. "Are you still trying?"

I followed her gaze. Broken as Sheila was, she'd dragged herself by her fingertips to Calibra and was even now trying to reignite her aura. The effort it must have taken was incredible and I felt ashamed that all I could do was float helplessly in the air.

I needed to get out of this, needed to help her. And then I really needed to finish off this bitch. But how?

Calibra reached down, grabbed hold of a handful of Sheila's hair, and dragged her back up. To her credit, Sheila didn't cry out. Calibra then spun her around to face me. Our eyes met. In them I saw many things: defiance, pain, but also regret. She mouthed, "I'm sorry" right before her head was tilted to the side, leaving her neck exposed.

Calibra's eyes blackened and her fangs descended, wicked sabers sticking out from an otherwise flawless smile. "I want you to watch this."

Sheila's aura sparked to life weakly, but not nearly enough. Calibra grinned at me as she opened her mouth and lowered her head.

From beyond the Jahabich, the cheering ceased, replaced by confusion as at least a few of the Magi began to put two and two together. I couldn't have cared less, though. I was entirely focused on Sheila, on Calibra, and on my helplessness to do anything.

"Please!" I begged as her lips brushed across Sheila's throat. "I won't fight you anymore." It was all I had to bargain with.

"Is that what you called it?" she asked with some amusement. "Don't flatter yourself. You and your friends have been an annoyance to me, nothing more. Gnats to be swatted."

Her teeth sank slowly, almost lovingly, into the side of Sheila's neck. Calibra's throat worked and she took a swallow.

Smoke escaped from between her lips and she shuddered, although whether in pain or enjoyment I couldn't tell ... mind you, I was really hoping it was the former. Watching her blow apart into chunks wouldn't have sucked either.

She pulled back and gritted her teeth for a moment, but then she opened her eyes and smiled at me. "A magnificent feast. Fit for a queen."

Fuck it all! I put everything I had into lunging forward, finding some purchase with which to get to this bitch and tear her to shreds. But there was nothing. I might as well have been floating in the infinite vastness of space for all the good it did me.

"Now the last Icon dies," Calibra whispered in Sheila's ear. "And your stain shall forevermore be erased from this world."

A part of me died as she lowered her head again, preparing to finish what she'd started.

And she would have, too, if the wall of Jahabich beyond her hadn't picked that moment to explode in a massive fireball.

78

THE BIG BOYS WITH THE BIG TOYS

I couldn't do much more than shield my eyes from the blast, floating around as I was. Even so, what the fuck? I mean, last I checked, the Jahabich didn't tend to explode if left to their own devices.

Whatever was happening wasn't finished, though. A brief whistling noise sounded, then something slammed into a group of Magi and blew up, sending dismembered bodies flying.

Next came the sound of machine-gun fire. Had James and the other vamps been armed? Maybe they'd found the armory and...

Those thoughts were broken up by screams of both pain and rage. Beyond the Jahabich – those still in one piece, anyway – just barely visible through the smoke, I saw figures charging in. Fire erupted from one in a cone about thirty feet long, catching more of the Magi and probably convincing them they should've sprung for the fire-retardant wizard robes. It didn't look like magic, though. It looked like ... a flame thrower?

Calibra, for her part, seemed slightly put out by the interruption. Aside from some dust on her dress, she was fine. She continued to hold on to Sheila, who bled freely from the side of her neck. "Who dares?!"

She held out a hand in front of her, then began to slowly turn, almost as if scanning the cavern. After a few moments, she stopped and pointed back toward the tunnel we'd used to enter this place. "You!"

I spied a line of figures through the smoke headed our way. The closer they got, the more familiar they became. A large contingent of warriors on either side of them had engaged both the Magi and Jahabich, clearing the way forward.

"Did you really think this reckoning would not happen?" Alexander the Great asked from his place at their forefront. "A foolish and unwise presumption where one such as I am concerned."

Alex?! But how did he...?

The answer became obvious a moment later. The rest of the First Coven, as well as that creepy eyeless guy, flanked him on either side. Behind them, though, looming over their heads, stood Grulg. He was still in chains and looked like he'd gotten intimately acquainted with Alex's fists, but he was alive. He'd known the way down here and had apparently decided to share at some point.

Alex and his buddies weren't alone either, not by a long shot. Men still poured into the cavern from the tunnel beyond. Some of them wore camouflage fatigues and carried assault rifles. Others were dressed in the black body armor that vampires preferred. So a mixed force ... smart.

That wasn't all, though. I spied what looked to be a platoon of reptilian humanoids, all wielding wicked curved scythes. Before I could wonder what they were doing here, something coalesced next to Alex ... a nightmare creature covered in scales, with four eyes and multiple horns upon its head.

Druaga.

I had to give Alex credit where credit was due. He'd one

upped Calibra's status as mage messiah by inviting an actual god to the party. Clever guy, assuming Druaga didn't decide to either eat us all first or morph into a hundred-foot marshmallow man.

"I believe you are holding an ally of mine," Alex said. His tone made it clear he didn't really care if Sheila lived or died, but that he didn't immediately applaud her defeat was at least a minor checkmark in our favor.

"Siding with the Icon, Macedonian?" Calibra asked with a barely concealed laugh. "You truly have brought our great race to ruin. I should have made certain you didn't survive your infancy among our people. As for this trash, I think it's time to dispose of it."

What?! "Wait!"

But I was too late. With a contemptuous swing of her arm, Calibra flung Sheila toward The Source. I watched, helpless, as she flew through the air. Maybe it was a trick of my imagination, but I could have sworn she threw me one last smile as she soared by overhead ... that warm smile which I'd fallen for the first time I'd seen it. The same one that had greeted me every time I'd come to the office where we'd been coworkers. It was a smile I'd once hoped to see every day for the rest of my life.

And then both it and she were gone. Viscous as it might appear, the alien waters of The Source greedily swallowed her up with a splash before becoming still again.

She was gone.

"You fucking whore," I snarled. "I'm gonna enjoy killing you slowly." That was all Dr. Death speaking now, but I let him take the ball and run with it. The rest of me was too busy processing the shock and grief of what I'd just witnessed.

It seemed so unreal, so impossible.

Her, the prophecy ... it didn't make any sense.

No, it didn't, and it wasn't fucking fair either – two of life's harshest lessons for the price of one.

Calibra raised an eyebrow at my idle threats, then smiled.

All at once, the heat from before returned, this time set to broil. Behind her, the Magi and the Jahabich engaged Alex's forces.

If I was destined to join Sheila, then at least I had one solace: despite the power of Calibra's forces, it appeared they were fighting a losing battle.

Dozens of Alex's vamps had brought sledgehammers, flails, or maces to the party, which they used to split open rocky heads left and right. As for the Magi, between the chunk my friends had taken out of their considerable numbers and the shock of still trying to figure out what to make of their so-called goddess, they didn't appear to have their full hearts in the fight. Pity for them, because Alex had seemingly given orders to take no prisoners. Hell, from the looks of things, Druaga's forces had free rein to eat whoever the fuck they wanted to.

It was fitting that The Source bathed this cave in a glow not unlike that of blood, because soon it was going to be drenched in it. For perhaps the first time since becoming a vampire, I didn't mind that thought at all.

My hair burst aflame and my skin charred, but still, I held on. I wasn't ready to give up yet, not if there was a chance I could still have my pound of flesh. I let the anger that was Dr. Death feed me, using Sheila's death as a fuel source. The only question now was which was stronger – my rage or Calibra's magic? Powerful as I was, I had limits. I just had to hope not to hit them before...

And then I was free. In an instant, the heat evaporated and I fell to the ground. The fuck?

I looked up and, as my eyeballs stopped steaming, saw that Calibra's body was covered in multiple spots of blood, including a hole just above her right eyelid. The wound closed almost immediately, such was her ability to heal, but the bullet had been enough for her to lose concentration.

With any luck, I would live long enough to thank the shooter. For now, it was time to add some bloody icing to this cake.

I launched myself at her, using everything my still healing body possessed. It would have been enough to plow through a concrete wall and keep going.

That was assuming I connected, which I didn't. It was almost unreal how fast she was.

A backhand caught me midair, shattering my jaw and sending me flying away, over the still prone form of Meg and into a platoon of Jahabich. Shit! I'd forgotten about her. I was failing friends left and right this day.

Well, no more!

Okay, fine. No more, just as soon as several tons of rock monster finished shit-stomping me. I was a lot stronger and tougher than them, but flat on my face with a bunch of them pounding my backside – and yes, that sounded wrong to me, too – didn't leave a lot of leverage for a counterattack.

My flesh parted, then healed again with every blow, but my senses were still keen enough to hear the sounds of battle around me. Fists, guns, blades, magic – all of it rang out in a cacophony of chaos.

Then it all became muffled as a club fist slammed into my back and became lodged in my flesh. I was dragged to my feet, where my head was immediately engulfed by the mouth of a Jahabich.

Ewww.

Fucking gross. Useless, too. Had I been my normal self, this fucker would have bitten my noggin clean off. Instead, it was a minor effort on my part to send the top of its head sailing off into the distance.

I was still being swarmed, but the asshole had stupidly given me a fighting chance and I used it to pulverize those nearest me.

Much as I hated to admit it, there were different degrees of evil in this hellhole, and it was probably wise to align myself with the asshole who was the lesser one in the grand scheme of things. I needed to get to where Alex and his buddies were battling it out.

Another explosion rattled the cavern. Shit! Make that I

needed to get to them before they accidentally blew the cave up around us.

My claws extended and I started shredding my way through Jahabich like they were made of lettuce instead of rock. As if I already wasn't particularly fond of salads.

Now where was ... of course. In the center of things. I caught sight of Alex as he twisted a mage's head clean off, discarding the pieces as if they were nothing.

To Alex's left, Gaius, Zyra, and a few other members of the First whose names I didn't catch were taking apart everything they could get their hands on.

To the other side stood Yehoshua, Kathryn, eyeless freak, and Druaga. The sage had that shit-eating grin on his face again, but otherwise wasn't doing much, save throwing out the occasional creepy old man hiss at anything that got close. Druaga looked bored, but then most everything seemed to be giving him a wide berth. Can't say I blamed them. All of a sudden, Calibra felt like only the second scariest thing in the room.

Yehoshua dispatched two Jahabich, then looked my way, one brow raised questioningly, but then he gave me a brief nod. Note to self: team up with that guy if possible.

Things were looking promising. What Alex's forces lacked in magic, they made up for with guns ... lots of them. Several of the Magi had managed to get shields up, but many more lay dead or dying. The Jahabich definitely had the numbers advantage, something they were using with brutal efficiency. But the more Jahabich that joined the fray, the less were left to act as prison walls, which meant more reinforcements for our side, even if they were sickly and beaten down.

A beam of red-hot magic caught my attention, lancing out and reducing at least three of the vampire elite to ash. It was Calibra. Despite her forces being slowly driven back, she was holding her ground, her back to The Source and a disturbingly calm look on her face. Either she was planning something or she was an idiot.

I really hoped for the latter, but I wasn't about to bet my

life savings on it. Nevertheless, if she was distracted enough, then maybe I had a chance to step in and do something useful, like extract her fucking spine and shank her with it.

Yeah, that might be ever so slightly satisfying.

Her eyes found and locked on Alex in the fray. "Die, Macedonian!" A lance of power flowed out from The Source to her, igniting her body in a red glow that made even Christy's bad moods seem tame in comparison. She released the spell, a supernova compared to the run-of-the-mill death rays everyone else was throwing around. Ten feet wide and hot enough that it singed my eyebrows from where I stood, it burned a path toward Alex, instantly disintegrating everything in its path – both friend and foe.

Alex saw it coming. He stopped fighting and held his arms wide open as if he'd just spotted an old college buddy. Holy shit! This was it. Calibra was going to do half of our job for us. Sadly, it was the half we'd been hoping to save for last.

Instead of turning him into a pile of crispy critters, though, the spell stopped about two feet from him as if hitting an invisible barrier. The tremendous bolt of power continued to push ineffectively toward the vampire leader until it finally fizzled away to nothing.

Surprise shone on Calibra's face for a moment, but she quickly covered it up. She nodded ever so slightly, a knowing look appearing upon her face as Druaga stepped in front of Alex.

"Did you think I would not be prepared for you?" Alex shouted over the din.

A buzzing noise began to sound inside my head, as if a million cockroaches were nesting in my frontal lobe. A moment later, Druaga's voice filled my mind and presumably the minds of everyone here.

Well done, vampire. You promised me worthy sport. It is not often that my allies are able to deliver upon such boasts.

Color me gobsmacked. For all the planning and fretting I'd done with my friends, I never once thought to ask a death god for help. Who'd have guessed all Alex had to do was convince one insanely powerful immortal to kill another?

Much as I despised him with every fiber of my being, I had to give him kudos. There was a fucker who thought ahead.

Come, witch. See if you are worthy to face one who has conquered countless worlds, enslaved billions, and been witness to the very act of creation itself.

At the very least, it looked like Dru had brought enough ego to this fight. The self-absorbed monstrosity probably called out his own name during sex.

Two of Druaga's four eyes swiveled in their sockets toward me.

Ah, Freewill. I am glad you remember your offer to mate with my kind. Perhaps once I dispatch this nuisance, you may fulfill your vow.

Shit!

I was just about to yell out that I was kinda already married, but Calibra spared me the indignity as her voice echoed throughout the chamber. "You are a fool to waste your allies so carelessly, Macedonian. Or did you think I would not be prepared for you?" she mocked.

Again she reached out to The Source and let loose with a spell of such tremendous power that it caused the very ground beneath us to rumble. It was so bright as to almost be painful to look at. Bitch had pulled out all the stops and fired her own version of the wave motion cannon at Druaga.

This one didn't appear to be as easily dismissed as her last blast, but the gecko from Hell wasn't exactly a lightweight. He held his arms out wide and his eyes glowed. A crackle of power appeared before him, stopping Calibra's spell in its tracks.

It was pretty goddamned impressive, kinda like that time Thanos took on Odin.

Despite looking like something that could have blasted its way through a mountain, little by little, Druaga started to force Calibra's spell back.

Oh yeah! Bitch should have watched more movies. She might've learned the painful lesson the Japanese knew: you do not fuck with Godzilla!

Sweat stood out on Calibra's brow, evident even in the near blinding light of the spell pouring off of her, but despite The Source backing her up, it looked to be a losing battle on her part. Now, if only Druaga would do us all the favor of killing Alex next, then my job here would be so much fucking easier.

However, rather than slump down in defeat or beg for mercy, like someone sane might do when clearly outclassed, Calibra actually smiled.

What the...?

She disengaged one hand from her spell and began gesturing with it.

What the hell was she doing?

A bright flash of light appeared about twenty feet over her head like a miniature sun, brilliant enough so as to overpower the perpetual red gloominess that hung over everything.

A bolt of what looked to be lightning lanced from it toward Calibra. Rather than vaporize her, though, it wrapped itself around her body as if tethering itself to her.

Then, without warning, a much larger blast of energy shot out from it and struck Druaga. His voice snarled inside my head and he raised a hand to attempt to fend it off.

It was a mistake.

His attention divided, his counter-spell could no longer hold against Calibra's. Before he could mount a defense against both, the monstrous cascade of power emanating from her slammed into him and engulfed him whole.

The snarl in my head turned into a scream, so loud I was certain I'd pop a blood vessel, then Druaga's body exploded in a blinding blast of multicolored light.

I had no way of knowing if he'd actually been vaporized or just banished back to the land of the lost, but when the light cleared, he was gone.

Apparently, my thought process was in need of correction. You didn't fuck with Godzilla, not unless you brought the Oxygen Destroyer with you, which Calibra seemingly had.

All around the cavern, a keening hiss rose up. With Druaga gone, so too was whatever tether kept his forces here. The lizard men who'd come charging in alongside the vampires all abruptly began to melt.

Gross to watch, but probably not particularly fun to experience either.

Calibra had just done the impossible. She'd defeated a god and, in doing so, probably us as well. But how?

The answer came a moment later in the worst possible way imaginable.

The energy attack, which had come out of the miniature sun, dissipated and the light emanating from it dimmed considerably, allowing me to see the source of the power.

It was Tom.

79

PLAYING TO A PACKED HOUSE

om was still wearing his human glamour. It looked intact, save for an ugly gash in his chest from which power appeared to be crackling forth.

Shit! Calibra had somehow tapped into the Apollo's Prism and was using it, and my friend, as a weapon of mass destruction.

"Fuck you, bitch!" he shouted down to her.

Or maybe that was weapon of ass destruction. Whatever the case, I'd lost track of him when we'd arrived and foolishly let myself hope that he was okay. I couldn't have been more wrong had I tried. And that made yet another friend of mine this bitch had victimized.

Enough was enough, but how? She'd defeated a fucking god, for Christ's sake. Even worse, her victory seemed to rally her troops and they began fighting back in earnest.

She wasn't finished yet, though. That lance of energy was still present between her and Tom. More than ever, I began to suspect I was right – that it was a tether between them, a way for her to control the massive power sustaining his body.

Calibra herself looked winded from the amount of magic she'd just expended. The glow around her had faded away to nothing. Using Tom as her personal Death Star seemed to be her fallback, though. More bolts of energy flew from the gash in his chest, utterly vaporizing any of Alex's troops unlucky enough to be hit.

She wasn't finished with the surprises yet either. She had at least one more party favor up her sleeve. "***SERVE ME, YOUR TRUE MASTER!!***"

The compulsion went out wide. It washed over me, doubling my vision for a moment, but fortunately, this new Dr. Death physique of mine seemed to be a bit more durable when it came to not getting my head psychically blown off. That was a plus.

But it was a small plus at best, as a portion of Alex's men opened fire on their own number. Even more were rooted to the spot, making them easy prey for mage and Jahabich alike.

"***THE WILL OF THE FIRST IS YOUR WILL!! REMEMBER WHERE YOUR LOYALTY LIES AND RESIST!!***"

Whereas Calibra's compulsions had an odd grace about them, Alex's were raw, unadulterated power. Dust fell from the cavern rooftop as his counter-command blasted through the place. He and the rest of his coven had no doubt been hard at work insulating their people as best they could, and the results showed. Many of those who Calibra managed to ensnare shook her off. As a nice side effect, several mages in my line of sight fell to the ground clutching their heads, knocked for a loop.

Calibra pointed Alex's way and more energy flew from Tom's body, but it had been anticipated. By the time it struck, there was nothing standing in the spot she was aiming for save the rocky floor.

Most of the First Coven regrouped, this time closer to Calibra. Even the blind weirdo somehow stayed in step with them.

It was high time for me to follow their lead.

The battle between lizard god and White Mother over, the Jahabich resumed trying to ruin my day, necessitating me returning the favor several times over.

As I smashed heads and tore arms off, working my way

back in her direction, I spared the occasional glance to check on how things were going. The game of cat and mouse continued – Calibra using my roommate against the First Coven with them scattering, then regrouping slightly closer than before.

If this kept up, they'd be within striking distance soon and that seemed to be the plan. I couldn't help but notice the majority of Alex's troops were busy dividing their time between creating rock gardens and planting Magi corpses in them. The big guns themselves were reserved for Calibra.

Strong as she was, I doubted she could fend off all of them. So much the better if I got there in time. Hell, I'd happily hold her down while the Dracs took turns shitting in her mouth, if that's the way they wanted to play it.

First things first, though. Meg started to stir from where she lay. I still had no idea if we could save her, but that didn't mean I should stop trying. I'd already failed Sheila in the worst way possible, something I would need to live with for the rest of my life. Tom was in serious need of saving, too, but first I needed to keep the former witch from turning.

I changed direction slightly as I continued to press forward, leaving a trail of dead or dismembered Jahabich in my wake.

Meg sat up just as I cleared their ranks. Calibra was still preoccupied trying to flash fry the Dracs, so that left me with a clear shot to her.

"Huh? What happ..." was all Meg managed to get out before I clobbered her again. I really hoped Christy was able to help her, because I was starting to feel kinda bad about continually punching her lights out.

Speaking of Christy, with any luck she was making good progress on her spells. She'd asked me to keep Calibra occupied and, well, if this wasn't a hell of a distraction, I didn't know what was. With any luck, she'd show up on the scene soon and make with the Jahabich-ending magic.

For now, though, I definitely had enough to keep me occupied.

There! Another missed blast from Tom – still cursing out Calibra midair – and Alex's minions were within striking range.

"You miscalculated, witch," Yehoshua said, stepping into flank with Gaius.

Alex stepped forward and drew his sword as the rest, crazed sage included, spread out to surround her. "Indeed. Those who fail to learn from history are doomed to repeat it. This time, however, the First shall ensure you do not slip away like a thief in the night upon your defeat."

Calibra merely laughed. "For all your vaunted leadership, you truly are blind, Macedonian, even more so than the sages you keep locked up in your caves. For they see the truth. No matter how long you have kept them under your thumb, they have never stopped knowing where their true loyalty lies. Is that not right, my love?"

There came a sudden black blur of motion, then Yehoshua let out a gasp as the blind weirdo appeared behind him and stabbed him through the back with his double-tipped dagger.

The elder vamp's eyes opened wide in surprise as the sage revealed himself to be a Judas in disguise. To his credit, Yehoshua refused to cry out and give his attacker the satisfaction. Instead, he simply put his hands together as if in prayer before bursting aflame from within and turning to dust. The only other member of the Dracs, aside from James, that I considered to be worth a damn was gone.

Goddamn it all!

The Seer of the Mists began to laugh as the hood over his face slipped away, revealing that his eyes had grown back in. With the holes in his face filled, I realized with no small degree of horror that he looked disturbingly familiar.

That's when it hit home. He was in the vision Calibra had shown me, the one whose neglect had caused the accident that had created her.

That meant he was old, older than everything here save her, which made him far faster and more powerful than I'd have ever guessed. This was driven home as the bearded creep launched himself at both Zyra and another Drac in the time it took me to process all of this.

Calibra let out a long, hearty laugh. "I should thank you, Macedonian. I may be the First, but you have unwittingly returned my second to me after all these long years."

Son of a bitch. Alex had explained to me a while back that the cave sages were a holdover from the time of Ib, but I figured he meant they were groupies who somehow managed to plea bargain their way down from an immediate dusting. If what I was hearing was correct, at least some of them – this guy definitely – were present at Calibra's rebirth. The first vampires ... the true First Coven, if you would.

There came a flash of light and the unnamed Drac was dusted. Then it was Zyra's turn. The Seer powered her to her knees and slit her throat with his dagger, taking her head clean off.

Three of the Draculas gone in the space of a minute. That left seven, including Alex and James. Almost down to half strength. There were no doubt gonna be some vamps who woke up tomorrow surprised to learn they'd just gotten the mother of all promotions.

That was assuming there would even be a First Coven tomorrow, something that was now sorely in doubt.

But not if I had any say in it ... or something like that anyway.

I launched myself forward, closing the distance faster than most people could blink. Calibra heard me coming, but turned too late to do anything about it. She caught my shoulder in the back, enough force behind it to tip over a semi. That sent her stumbling forward, where Gaius and two other members of the Dracs awaited her.

Unfortunately, in my rush to do something, I'd left myself open for third eye not-so-blind guy. He socked me good on the side of the jaw, knocking me down. It wasn't enough to keep me there, though. I rolled to my feet just in time to catch his wrist before he could slice my face off.

Ugh!

Talk about strong. But I was currently no lightweight myself. Besides, this guy's biceps didn't hold a candle to mine. It would be plain embarrassing for a buff hunk like me to lose to this emaciated asshole.

After a few moments of back and forth struggle, it became clear we were pretty evenly matched with regard to power, which didn't help much since he had a massive edge in experience ... even if most of that experience involved huffing paint fumes in a cave.

I contemplated my options. A solid punch to the nuts? Always a classic, but not nearly as effective against ancient zealots.

Throwing dirt in his face? Nah. It was probably safe to say his blind-fighting skills were off the charts.

Wait! This guy wasn't used to seeing, which meant maybe ... err ... I could stick my tongue out at him?

While I was busy contemplating whether funny faces were an effective combat tactic, he stepped back and drove a kick to my chest, knocking me on my ass.

Sadly, he wasn't the type to quip one-liners before finishing off his foe. He straddled me – answering the question of whether he and his buddies wore anything under their robes, eww – then raised the dagger above his head, preparing to add a fourth kill to his record this day.

I was quick to defend myself, but someone else was quicker. Thunder, or something like it, rang out in the cavern before he could bring the blade down, and the seer's stomach exploded, spraying me with intestinal goo.

He'd been hit by something of a large caliber, almost like the bullets found in a...

"I can't leave you alone for five fucking minutes."

I leaned back and saw the upside down, from my vantage point anyway, form of Sally striding my way, a comically large gun in her hand.

The seer leapt back to his feet to face her. Unfortunately,

Desert Eagle or not, she was dealing with a vampire who would be healed in seconds at most.

Or would have healed, if I didn't pick that moment to punch skyward with everything I had, smashing my fist into his ancient nuts and sending him careening off me. Before I could make my next move, though, I realized Sally had brought reinforcements. A red lance of magic cut through the air from the same direction she had come. It hit the asshole midflight, bisecting him. He came crashing back to the ground in two pieces, his lower half quickly turning to dust.

Sally stepped in and offered a hand to help me up. "Get your ass moving and let's see if we can't unfuck up this mess you caused."

It was so nice to have friends who cared.

80

PIT STOP

First thing on my list was to ensure that number two got eighty-sixed.

I grabbed hold of the formerly eyeless, now dickless, weirdo by the back of his robes. His body had been cauterized below the waist. Fine by me – I didn't fancy being showered in crazy guy innards.

As for what to do with the still-cackling fucker, that was easy, especially since Calibra was having a grand old time zapping people with my best friend.

"Sorry to break it to you, number two, but you're a piece of shit." Still holding the nutball, I spun, built up some momentum, then let him fly.

Calibra looked up at the last moment and let out a scream of outrage, but it was too late. The deadly magic was already flaring out of Tom's body. I'd never thrown anything so far or straight in my life, but luck was with me. Calibra's secret weapon slash boyfriend hit the energy blast in much the same way a moth might fly into a bug zapper.

With a flash of light and crackle of high voltage, number two got erased from the equation.

Calibra turned toward me. "You killed my second."

"Sorry, bitch, but that's just another name for the first fucking loser." Then I dove for it as a bolt of energy came

583

flying my way. I had to admit, this new body of mine was mighty handy when it came to dodging after one-liners.

Thankfully, James and his platoon of vamps picked that moment to appear at Sally's side and open fire, forcing Calibra back on the defensive.

We weren't home free by any stretch of the imagination. Still, every man, woman, and monster was fighting with everything they had. I even saw Grulg, chained up as he was, take out a few Jahabich who'd wandered too close. Bad as his situation looked, even he seemed to know it could only get worse if Calibra won.

As for the queen bitch herself, she was none too pleased at the arrival of my reinforcements. "***KNEEL!!***"

All subtlety was gone from this compulsion. I was pretty sure that if she threw out enough of them, the entire cave would collapse in on itself. That would certainly be a round-about way of winning, but it wouldn't leave much left for a victory celebration.

Once my teeth stopped rattling, I spied many of the combatants – vampires, humans, mages, and even a few other things – down on their knees. James, Sally, and their group, however, remained standing.

Fuck yeah!

Judging by the surprised looks on their faces, even they hadn't expected it.

Fortunately, Sally was never one to let an opportunity for snark pass. "What is the sound of one hand telling you to go fuck yourself? Oh yeah, this." She raised her middle finger and flipped Calibra the bird.

Hah! The first part of Christy's spell crafting had worked. Now to see if the other had a shot in hell. If so, we could end this.

Alex's people once more began to lay the pressure on Calibra, while most of James's group broke off to engage the other myriad enemies. It gave me a chance to approach my friends.

James looked me over for a moment and nodded in approval. "Most impressive."

"At least until he opens his mouth," Sally replied.

I let out a derisive snort. "I've already had enough fists in mine, thanks."

"As well as other things, I'm sure."

"Wonderful to see you too," I said to her. "Where's Christy and the others?"

"The shooting gallery is right behind us." She hooked a thumb over her shoulder. Beyond, I could see Calibra's rock palace, or the remains of it anyway.

"Looks like you guys rocked the Casbah."

"And then some." She beckoned me to follow. "Let's go."

I found Kelly and Veronica helping Christy along, although she didn't seem happy for the assistance. A pair of vamps from James's crew had stuck around to guard them from any Jahabich who got too close, but from the looks on the younger witches' faces, they were more than aware they were basically packages of chop meat being guarded by hungry wolves.

Sally, being the perceptive type, told the bloodsuckers, "Go help James."

The two, both probably much older than her, basically scoffed at her order. Even in the face of ultimate evil, some vamps couldn't stop being assholes. Sadly, thanks to Christy's workings, I couldn't compel them to get the fuck out of my face. Oh well. Sometimes you gotta use the carrot instead of the stick.

"Listen, guys, I appreciate you watching out for my friends, but pissing off The Wanderer's pal as well as the Freewill isn't going to win you any brownie points in this mess." When in doubt, appeal to a vampire's sense of not wanting to tick off their betters. Remembering my newly buff self, I cracked my knuckles to emphasize the point. They exchanged a quick glance, then took off to join the battle, leaving us alone for the moment.

"Thanks," Christy said. "I really didn't want to have to kill those guys. Will you stop trying to help me! I can walk."

"Barely," Kelly chided before turning to me. "Yeah, thanks. I had a feeling those creeps were about a minute away from breaking out the barbecue sauce."

"Don't blame them," I said. "Calibra didn't exactly keep her prisoners well fed. Well, okay, you can probably blame them a little." I turned toward Christy. "Are you okay?"

She nodded, then pulled away from her two helpers as if to emphasize the point.

"Good. Because if you're going to do that spell of yours, it *really* should be now."

"Meg?" Veronica asked.

I gave a single shake of my head. "I was too late."

Kelly kicked at a small pile of rocks on the ground. "Shit!"

"Is she...?" Christy asked.

"Yes and no," I replied. "They killed her and threw her in. She came back out and..."

"And what?" she demanded.

"And I decked her before she could turn. She's lying back there, out cold. I don't know if there's anything you can do or not, but I had to try."

"Wait, you punched Meg?" Kelly asked.

"A couple of times, actually."

"Oh, she is going to be pissed."

"She's going to be a slave to her White Mommy if you don't do something," Sally said.

"Don't call her that," Christy warned, then addressed everyone. "Go get Meg and bring her back here to me. I don't know if there's anything we can do for her, but we can at least ensure she has the same chances as the rest of us when this spell goes off."

"Any idea what those chances are?" Sally asked.

Christy shrugged. "Let's just say I hope you didn't make any good plans for tonight."

"Nothing quite like going out with a bang," I remarked.

Sally laughed. "Closest you're going to get to the real thing."

"Sorry, can't hear you over the sound of how awesome I look now." I stepped back and took a deep breath. We could snipe at each other later, if we survived. "Okay, rest break is over. We'll retrieve Meg and buy you whatever time you need."

Christy nodded. "Keep them off of us. We need to get near The Source, set up the spell right on its shore for this to work."

"Isn't that a little too close?" Sally asked.

"If this backfires, then everywhere on the planet could be a little too close."

"Point taken."

"Good. After you get Meg, I need you two to find everyone you can and get them here."

I glanced at the chaos behind us. Magic, gunfire, and screams of pain echoed all around. "Easier said than done."

"Try. Even if this works perfectly, I don't know what will happen. We may need to send ourselves out of here in a hurry."

"I don't think there's going to be a second bus, if you get my drift," Kelly added. "Get your roommates, find Sheila, and get your asses back here ... oh shit! How are we gonna get out of here with her?"

I looked down at my feet, unable to tell them that wasn't going to be a concern any longer, when Sally said, "Don't worry about Xena Warrior Templar for now. We'll figure it all out after we find her."

"Listen, guys," I said. "I have bad news."

"Tom!" Christy gasped.

"No. It's Sheila, she..."

"Tom," she repeated. That's when I realized she was looking over my shoulder at the battle behind us. Oh no!

"TOM!"

She pushed past me. I tried to grab hold of her arm but quickly jerked my hand back as a red glow enveloped her, making touching her akin to sticking my hand on a hotplate.

"Don't," I warned. "We'll save him. I promise..."

"You fucking whore," Christy snarled, her eyes focused on Calibra, who was still using her boyfriend as the world's deadliest piñata. "You goddamned bitch!" She let loose a scream of rage that rivaled anything that could come out of even Gan's mouth.

I was at a loss what to do, but thankfully, Sally wasn't. She stepped forward and raised the butt of her oversized gun. "Sorry about this."

Christy, still facing away from us, made the barest of gestures with her hand and a bright blue surge of power nailed both Sally and me, knocking us to the ground.

"Oh shit!" Kelly cried out, but she was a second too late.

With a flash of light and a snarl of anger, Christy vanished from in front of us.

81

TOTAL FUCKING CHAOS

The stun spell didn't have much effect on me, other than putting me on my ass. I recovered in time to see Christy reappear in the middle of the battle.

"Goddamnit!" I cried, slamming my fist into the rocky ground and gouging a good chunk out of it.

I glanced over to find Sally still twitching. She'd be okay, but I couldn't afford to wait for her. I turned to Kelly and Veronica, standing there with their mouths hanging open. "You two, make sure Sally's fine and then start that fucking spell. I'm gonna go get Christy."

"We can't," Veronica said, her voice near panic.

I so didn't need this right now. Fine, comfort giver it was. "Sure you can. I believe in you guys. You can do anything you set your minds to."

"It's not that, idiot," Kelly snapped. "We literally can't do it. We only know part of the spell. Christy's the only one who knows how to complete it. Harry did too, but he's..."

"Not going to be able to help much," I finished. Fuck! "Why didn't she teach you the rest?"

"Sorry, there hasn't been much time for study hall lately."

Well, if that wasn't the croutons in this shit salad, I didn't know what was. "Just fucking great! What do we do now?"

Kelly put her hands on her hips. "Oh, I don't know. Maybe keep Christy from dying?"

She had a good point and, of all of us, I was currently the best candidate for the job.

"Lay down some covering fire, but stay back." Kelly nodded, then I added, "And try not to hit me."

"No promises," she replied with a grin.

I turned back to the battle, debating how best to fuck up everyone's day. As tired and beaten down as Christy was, she was throwing some serious magic Calibra's way and not being too careful about it. I watched as two of Alex's men got ashed when they tried to flank Calibra and got hit instead.

"Cocksucking bitch!" All the while, Tom continued to curse in midair, sending out blasts of energy at Calibra's command. It was only a matter of time before one of them was headed Christy's way. I needed to...

"What the hell is that?"

"Huh?" I glanced back over my shoulder to find Kelly pointing toward The Source. I was about to tell her to stop gawking at the giant spooge pool when the light in the cavern changed ever so slightly, the red hue becoming a bit softer.

What the...?

I turned toward The Source and what I saw caused me to momentarily forget my mission. A brilliant white glow shined right below the surface, growing brighter as whatever was causing it moved toward the shore. A moment later, a dome of blinding white energy broke the surface, seeming to push the magical orange goo away on all sides.

No way. It wasn't possible.

Yet somehow, it was.

"What the fuck is she doing in there?" Kelly asked from behind me.

I was at a complete loss of words as Sheila became visible from within the aura. Not only was she standing, somehow whole again, but she looked pissed. The energy pouring off of her was easily the most powerful I'd seen it, so intense that she was somehow able to keep the primal energies of The Source at bay around her.

"Is she one of them?" Veronica asked nervously.

"I don't think so," I replied. The Jahabich possessed the forms, but not the powers of their former hosts. Decker hadn't been able to perform magic, and I doubted Starlight needed blood to survive now. If Sheila's powers were intact, then that meant she was, too, or so I had to hope.

Unfortunately, we weren't the only ones noticing her emergence.

Several of the mages still fighting saw her, too. Multiple lances of magical energy flew out and hit her aura, dissipating harmlessly against it as she continued to wade toward dry land.

Calibra turned and saw her, genuine surprise on her face. "*NO!!*"

The entire cavern shook from the compulsion's power and several of the creatures fighting – both vampire and mage – dropped unconscious as it washed over them. Christy wasn't one of them, though, and she used the distraction to hammer home another blast, a smaller version of the spell that Calibra had used to fuck up Druaga's day.

Calibra raised a hand at the last second and a protective dome of purple energy sprang up around her. She smiled from within, having apparently recovered from the drain of battling a death god.

That wasn't good.

She pointed a hand toward The Source and once more began to draw power from it. Her smile turned into a laugh as its power added to her own, allowing her to fend off Christy's attack. We'd squandered our opportunity, allowed her to get back on her feet, so to speak. And now we were going to pay for it.

But it seemed a certain witch was going to be served her check before the rest of us.

Energy crackled around both of Calibra's hands, breaking my voyeuristic malaise. I rocketed forward, not quite as fast as Christy could teleport, but pretty damn close.

"Insignificant insect of a witch!"

I reached Christy just as Calibra let loose with a bolt of energy, managing to throw us both out of the way just in time. I landed atop her, shielding her with my body. "Are you fucking insane?"

"Get off me, Bill. She hurt my baby and she's hurting Tom. Now it's my turn to hurt her."

"All you're going to do is..."

"*DIE!!*"

I glanced up, certain the compulsion was aimed at us, but instead saw that Calibra was throwing a spell at Sheila, still a few feet from shore. The massive blast of power met her aura, the proverbial irresistible force versus the immovable object.

The power at Calibra's command was insane, so intense that it didn't dissipate upon hitting the faith aura. But neither did it penetrate. Instead, it began to push Sheila back further into The Source.

Calibra wasn't finished yet, though. She smiled and then gestured Sheila's way.

"Bite me, you dried up bitch," an angry voice cried from high above us. "I'm gonna enjoy skull-fucking your ... ARGH!"

"Oh God, no," Christy whimpered as Tom convulsed.

I got back to my feet, but it was too late. A crackling bolt of plasma flew from Tom's body and slammed into Sheila's aura, adding its fury to the spell she was just barely fending off.

It was as if a bolt of lightning hit a tanker full of rocket fuel. The energy from the Prism reacted with the aura of faith, and a storm of white-hot power exploded from it. The entire cavern rumbled as if a giant was awakening beneath our feet. Then a shockwave of energy raced from the site of the impact in a three-hundred-sixty-degree arc, slamming into us all and sending bodies flying ass over teakettle.

What the fuck? I'd never felt anything like that before. The force of the shockwave aside, it had actually been kind of numbing, as if someone had created the magical equivalent of Novocain and picked that moment to test it out.

The effects had to have been delayed, though, because by the time I opened my eyes and sat up, I felt like a bus had run me over.

And no wonder, too.

I couldn't help but notice the lack of brawny muscles or toned abs on my body. Talk about a poor time to be myself again. I tried to summon the rage that had been bristling inside of me, eager to get out, and found it missing. Don't get me wrong. I wasn't exactly happy at that moment, but the voice whispering in my mind to kill and maim had gone silent.

And that wasn't the only thing.

The entire cave was quiet. Gunfire, magic, head-smash-ings; all of it had seemingly ceased. That, or I'd gone deaf.

"What the hell?" Christy asked shakily from my side.

Okay, not deaf.

"I don't know." I gave my head a shake to clear it, then looked up. Calibra was doubled over, her hands on her knees. As for Tom, he was nowhere to be seen.

It was the same all around us – like a giant hand had punched each of the combatants in the solar plexus. Not even the Jahabich were unaffected. I spied a few close by, standing still as ... statues. The normally malevolent glow of their eyes was barely a pinprick, as if someone had shut off their pilot light.

"Out of my way, *now*," Christy growled with such intensity that I found myself obeying.

She raised a hand toward Calibra and a few red sparks appeared at her fingertips, but nothing more.

"No," she cried. "This can't be happening. Not now!"

"What have you done?" Calibra growled, but it wasn't aimed at us. Instead, her gaze lay in the direction of The Source.

Shit ... Sheila!

My worry was unfounded, though. Amazingly, she was still where she'd been, looking a bit dazed but still in one piece. All around her, The Source pulsed in color, one moment its normal orange hue, the next a flat mud brown that made it look more like a cesspool than the gateway for all magic in this world.

Her aura was barely visible around her, more a nightlight than a shining beacon, but she was alive. She saw me looking her way, waved groggily, then began working her way back to solid ground again.

Calibra, on the other hand, wasn't in quite as jolly of a mood. She turned toward us, a look of pure rage on her face. The murderous intent I'd seen before was still there, but things had changed. The tether of energy that had connected her to Tom was gone. In fact, there didn't appear to be any power crackling off her at all. Her hair, previously raven black, was now streaked with white. Something strange had just happened, although I didn't have a clue as to what that was. "What have you done?" she repeated.

I managed to drag myself back to my feet as she approached us, but she backhanded me aside. It wasn't as earth jarring of a blow as I'd been expecting, but it was still more than enough to send me tumbling.

I landed, stunned, unable to do much more than watch as Christy faced her. The two witches pointed their hands toward one another and again nothing happened save the barest of sparks flying forth.

Out of juice, but not out of the fight, Calibra did the next best thing. She grabbed the younger witch by the front of her blouse and decked her. Christy's eyes rolled back in her head, and this time Calibra slapped her – the sound ringing in the eerily silent cavern.

No.

She did it again, this time even harder.

No!

That did it. Once more, I felt the red rage inside of me, a small ember at first, but rapidly growing into a five-alarm blaze.

I shook off the blow and prepared to launch myself at the queen bitch when a thunderous report sounded, deafening from its closeness.

A chunk of Calibra's upper arm blew off and she staggered back, releasing Christy, who fell to the ground unmoving. I turned and saw Sally striding our way, weapon in hand, and a look on her face every bit as angry as I felt inside.

I reined myself in for the moment. Christy was far more important than making sure Calibra got her just desserts. She was still breathing, but had been messed up pretty badly. Still, alive was the important part. That was going to be more than I could say for the yabba dabba douche who'd laid hands on her.

I turned toward where Calibra stood clutching her ruined arm. Sally joined me on one side of her while Sheila, finally free from The Source, raced up on the other.

From off to our left, Alex and James stepped past a column of still unmoving Jahabich and approached as well.

"Shall we draw straws?" I asked. "Or does everyone want a piece?"

"That last one sounds pretty good to me," Sheila replied.

I smiled at her, glad to see her alive and whole again, but then had to ask, "How did you not drown?"

"No clue. Maybe I had some unfinished business."

Sally made a gagging sound. "Oh, will you two just get a fucking room already?"

"I'm thinking we should carve the cake first," I replied.

Alex stepped forward. "This is First Coven business, Freewill. An oversight that is long overdue to be corrected."

I was tempted to argue, but fuck it. So long as this bitch was dead, who really cared where the killing blow came from? "Age before beauty." I started to make an "after you" gesture, but then stopped dead in my tracks.

The wound on Calibra's arm was knitting itself back together, the process growing faster by the moment.

Oh no!

Something caught my eye from behind the two Dracs – multiple orange glows.

"Look out!" Sally cried, but to no avail. One of the Jahabich slammed its club arm into the side of James's head, sending him to his knees. The others came back to life just as quickly, falling upon him and Alex.

Though I was pretty sure of what I would see, I quickly glanced toward The Source to find it back to its normal color. Whatever had disrupted everything was over, passed, which meant...

A shockwave of power burst from Calibra, knocking Sally and me away. Sheila's aura sprang to life, protecting her, but Calibra was ready for that. Quick as thought itself, she kicked out. Her leg ignited upon contact with the faith magic, but such was the force of the blow that Sheila went flying ... straight into the arms of a gaggle of Jahabich.

Calibra was in the fight again, which was bad for us.

But if she was back, then maybe that meant...

I turned toward Christy and focused. Her pain and suffering. Ed, casually blasted away. Tom, killed, reborn, then used as little more than a pawn. Sheila, broken and discarded like an unwanted toy. I thought of all the friends who'd been hurt or worse. I saw their faces in my mind and let my heart break in anguish over what had already been done and what was likely to come if we failed.

When I looked down at myself again, my hands were wicked claws and thick, veiny muscle stood out under my skin.

Good timing, too, because Calibra was heading my way.

"No more words," she said. "I am going to tear you apart with my bare hands."

"The hell with that shit," I replied. "I've got plenty of words left." I closed the distance between us and lashed out, raking a furrow across her midsection. "Not the least of which is fuck you!"

82

FIRST TO DIE

I didn't know a great deal about magic. Hell, I didn't know a great deal about fighting either. But in both cases, I figured hitting the bad guys hard enough so that they couldn't mount an effective defense was a sound strategy.

Slashing, punching, and kicking, I brought the battle to the matron of both vampires and mages, hoping I'd wear her down enough for ... I dunno, maybe for her to die of old age or something.

Maddeningly, Calibra healed almost as fast as I could wound her. It was like trying to stab a lump of Silly Putty to death. Throwing her into The Source was a potential solution, but she was attuned to it. For all I knew, I'd chuck her in and the bitch would part it like the Red Sea.

No, this was best done the old-fashioned way. A stake, or my fist, through her heart. I wouldn't rest easy until I saw that she was good and dusted. None of that half-assed turning away while she was dying shit that heroes loved to do in the movies. Fuck that noise.

Pity that Calibra had other plans. She caught my fist as I tried to flatten her stupid fucking nose and crushed it. We're talking crumbled bag of potato chips here. Goddamn! Oh, and it really fucking hurt, too.

I was no slouch in the healing department either right then. So the second she let go of the deflated balloon of skin that had been my hand, it immediately rebuilt itself. Freaking weird feeling. Imagine reconstructive surgery followed by months of intense physical rehabilitation all taking place in the space of a few seconds. And then imagine it happening again as she lashed out with her own claws and gutted me where I stood.

That took the wind out of my sails and I went down to one knee. It was only for a moment, but that was all she needed to turn the tide against me. I went from offense to defense in the span of a heartbeat. Calibra wasn't exactly the hand-to-hand expert that Alexander was, but she was strong and unthinkably fast.

Bones broke, skin parted, and many contusions were had as she gained the upper hand. It was unbelievable. Before I'd met her, the only person who'd stood toe to toe with my Dr. Death form had been Alex, and I only had his word to go on for that. Hell, this body had practically torn Turd a new asshole when we'd fought. I hated to admit it, but I'd let myself get taken in by the same arrogance I'd attributed to other vamps.

I'd believed myself invincible.

I was wrong, and if I didn't turn things around soon, I would be dead wrong.

It was only a matter of time. Already that drink I'd taken from the mage seemed like ages ago. No matter how strong the vampire, there's only so much abuse anyone can take. If I hit my limit before I somehow clawed this chick's face off, I'd turn back to myself. And if that happened, I might as well save everyone the trouble and throw my own ass into the goo.

No! That was quitter talk.

There were too many lives at stake, including one that hadn't even begun yet.

Call me a stubborn dickhead, but I wasn't about to let them down.

Calibra had just finished using her claws to take a chunk out of my shoulder. She spun, meaning to bring them around again for another go – turning herself into a living Cuisinart.

It was the only chance I was going to get. I mustered my strength and stepped in, taking advantage of my greater size and wrapping my arms around her in a bear hug. It wouldn't hold. She could snap my arms like matchsticks, but not before I could sink my teeth in and...

Feel my mouth ignite as a red glow sprang up around her.

I staggered back a step, my body singed from head to toe.

"You didn't think I was serious about using only my bare hands, did you?" she asked with a smile before plunging a glowing fist into my stomach.

Well, that was certainly a new one, being torn apart from the inside while having the wound instantly cauterize itself as it went. I imagine this was what it would be like to be gutted by a lightsaber, if lightsabers had clawed fingers that seemed to like grabbing hold of organs and squeezing until they popped.

Calibra's eyes glittered as she amped up the power, throwing some of that blue energy into the mix to help ensure I was too busy twitching to do much about my situation.

Hmm, what was that smell? Oh yeah, that was me being barbecued from the inside out. Go figure, I kinda smelled like chicken.

Regardless, I wasn't overly eager to sample a bite.

Mustering what little control I had over my muscles, I

grabbed hold of her wrist to try to yank her out of me. Pity she still had a free hand, which – now that both of mine were occupied – she placed upon the side of my face, almost lovingly.

It didn't last. She tightened her grip, almost to the point where I was certain she'd rip my ear clean off. However, it wasn't my ear she had in mind. She elongated the nail on her thumb and I barely had time to gasp in panic before she plunged it into my right eye.

Pain exploded in my head as she filleted my optic nerve and began to dig deeper. My healing was just barely keeping up with the fire in my gut. If she poured power straight into my brain, too, there would be nothing I could do save accept ending my adventures and turning into a fine white powder.

It might have been the effect of having my grey matter poked with a skewer, but I could have sworn I heard laughter coming from somewhere deep inside of me. I had a moment to imagine some small remnant of Dr. Death's personality enjoying the show as I proved that, even with his power at my disposal, I still wasn't good enough.

I...

Calibra's gaze wavered from mine and an instant later she yanked her thumb out of my head with a disturbing sucking noise. Oh well, whether alcohol or fingers, what was the difference how those brain cells died?

She grabbed hold of something inside of me – my spine, I think – then spun around, dragging me along with her.

Her free hand flashed out and snatched at something. When it came back, I saw she was holding a Desert Eagle, complete with the tip of a trigger finger still attached to it. Shit!

"Sally!" I glanced around with my good eye and saw her cradling her injured hand.

"Did you really think it would be that easy?" Calibra scoffed. She dropped the gun, then grabbed hold of Sally's throat.

My partner was lifted off her feet, her eyes bulging from

the pressure. Calibra was apparently through playing around. All she had to do was close her fist. With her level of strength, she could pop Sally's head right off.

No! I'd failed enough friends this day. No more!

This was the perfect moment, the one I'd been waiting for. It was time to win this once and for all.

I let go of Calibra's wrist, freeing her hand to roam through the recesses of my broken body. Forcing my arms to obey me, I reached down into my right pocket – tattered, but still intact and ... shit! Where was it?

Oh wait, that's because I'd put it in my left.

Duh!

There! My hand closed upon the small metal vial Gan had so helpfully returned to me when we'd met up in the woods near the Boston Prefecture. Being somewhat preoccupied with other concerns at the time, I'd pocketed it for a rainy day – perhaps knowing I'd soon need it against a category 5 storm named Calibra.

Still holding it by my side, I popped the top with my fingernail.

"Two for the price of one," Calibra purred. "First her, so you can watch, then you."

I spat a wad of blood into her face. "Sorry, bitch, but there's only one person who's going to be on the bottom of this threesome, and it ain't either of us."

Before she could retort, or finish fricasseeing me from the inside out, I emptied the contents of the vial into my mouth and swallowed.

There wasn't a lot, barely enough to taste, but Gan had insisted that was fine. It wasn't quantity so much as quality – a drop from each of the vampires at her command, including herself.

The blood hit my stomach and I realized my wannabe paramour had understated her case. With Dr. Death's power at my disposal, I was the physical match of ancient vamps such as Alex or Vehron. This blood, however, was like lighting a grill with liquid oxygen. I had no way of knowing the combined ages of all the donors, but if it was under two thousand years, you could have colored me surprised.

Calibra mirrored my shock once I slammed a fist into the side of her stupid witch face, hard enough to rip the bottom of her jaw clean off.

Her arm pulled free of me and she simultaneously dropped Sally, who'd been exploring whether blue was a good color for her complexion.

It really wasn't.

Calibra staggered back a step, her body glowing, then someone threw themselves at her knees from behind and she went down on her ass.

"Meg?"

The witch looked up at me from her prone position, awake, and still herself for at least the moment. "Please don't hit me again."

"Are you ... you?"

"I don't know. I think so."

"Good enough."

I took a moment to drop to one knee next to Sally, who was just now starting to regain her normal color. "You okay, Smurfette?"

She gurgled, her neck still healing, but managed to hold up a mangled hand and flip me off.

"You know, with half your index finger missing, it looks like you're pointing at the ceiling. Kinda dorky, really."

"Meg!" Kelly and Veronica were racing in to help, but I had more important matters for them to attend to.

I hauled Sally to her feet. "Get her back to her sisters, now, then see what you can do to help Christy." I turned to Meg. "You, try not to change."

"I'll do my best, but this feels really weird."

"Do what you can. If you feel yourself changing, get away from them. I'll see what I can do about pulling Mommy's leash off of you once and for all."

That was all the time I could spare.

Calibra was getting back to her feet, her face already regrowing the parts I'd clubbed off. It was time to see if I could make that damage a bit more permanent.

I doubted the boost from the blood milkshake would last long. There'd been precious little of it, but with any luck, it would be enough. I closed the distance between us and brought all my strength to bear. There was no time to waste. No more clawing at each other like the supernatural version of a slap fight.

Every blow I threw was done with the intent of killing this fucking witch and sending her to whatever Hell she was thousands of years overdue in visiting.

83

HEAD GAMES

Calibra wasn't stupid by any stretch. She saw that, perhaps for the first time in her long life, she was physically outclassed. But that still didn't make the job easy.

She managed to parry me, if just barely, as I went after her chest ... and not just in the interest of seeing her tits again either.

"Kick her ass for all of us, Bill!"

I caught a glimpse of Tom. He was standing with Ed on the very fringe of the battle. Amazingly enough, both were alive and apparently doing their best to keep out of the way of beings more than capable of kicking their asses. Tom's chest was still sparking energy, but at least he wasn't shooting out death rays anymore.

Reinvigorated, knowing I had a cheering section watching me, I threw them a quick thumbs up, then raked a clawed hand at Calibra's face.

She uttered something unintelligible and a purple half dome of energy rose up between us, but not before I'd taken a chunk out of the arm trying to block me.

It was a quick and dirty spell, only half formed, but it would serve to cockblock me long enough for her to get something more substantial going. I needed to make sure that didn't happen.

I extended my claws to their maximum and tried to force my way through. I'd seen enough science fiction to know that force fields could only take so much before they overloaded the generator. Fine, maybe the odds of Calibra blowing up were pretty slim, but let a guy hope.

That didn't happen, but the walls of the magical barrier began to bend under my assault, allowing me to inch ever closer to my target.

Her eyes met mine and momentarily flashed ... orange? That was a new color. Maybe it meant...

"*MOTHER!*"

Oh, that's what it meant.

Jahabich from all over the cavern disengaged from whatever they were doing and began marching my way. In the end, her unwanted children were her last hope. Kinda ironic in a way. Sucky, too, at least for me.

Heavy footsteps sounded behind me – Jahabich closing in from my six. I braced myself for whatever they could hit me with.

But then there came a screech, like that of metal scraping against rock, followed by several thuds. I risked a quick look over my shoulder to find three dead Jahabich on the ground and Sheila standing over them as more converged on us.

"I've got your back. Finish her."

Oh, I really could have kissed her right then – if I wasn't sweaty, covered in gore, and it wouldn't have gotten us both killed. Instead, I flashed her my most grateful smile and turned back to the task at hand ... just in time to catch a knee to the crotch, one moving with enough force to upend a truck. Sadly, Calibra wasn't out of the fight yet, and definitely wasn't above fighting dirty. The pain, immense as it was, only lasted for a moment before my healing took over, but what a long moment it was.

The stars finally cleared from my eyes and I saw that the dome was still up in front of her, but a multi-hued ball of energy had formed in her hands. Strong and fast as I was, she had me point blank. There was no way I could dodge before she blew a hole in me wide enough to step through.

I braced myself for it and threw everything I had into one last-ditch attack, hoping to at least take her with me.

And then the power of both spells abruptly dissipated as the tip of a sword erupted from her stomach.

Calibra's eyes opened wide in shock, more so when the blade was given a twist for extra measure.

Truth be told, I wasn't sure whether to be relieved, angry, or terrified when Alex lifted his head over her shoulder and smiled at me.

"Well done, Freewill."

"A tactical mistake, my dear Ib," he whispered in her ear. He continued to work the blade in her while wrapping the claws of his free hand around her throat. "You focused your forces solely on one foe, allowing them to disengage from an equally dangerous adversary."

I was flattered. All it took was for me to master my Freewill power and then amp myself up above and beyond my limits for Alex to acknowledge me as a peer, however temporary that might be.

And temporary it definitely was. Already I could feel the boost from the blood wearing off.

"In case you're wondering," I said to him, "I'm not going to argue about who gets the honor. Dead is dead in my book, no matter who writes the last chapter."

"Wisely said. However, there is also the matter of this place and the power she has been drawing upon," he replied casually, as if he'd just strolled in for a quick bite of lunch.

"Not disagreeing in the least," I offered, keeping one eye on Calibra. If she so much as blinked the wrong way, I would tear her arms off and shove them in different openings. "But maybe we can talk about real estate after she's dead."

"Not to belabor the point," Sheila said from somewhere behind me, "but any minute now would be just dandy."

I glanced back to find her still fighting the Jahabich, and she wasn't alone. James, along with several other vampires, had formed a rough circle around us to stave off the Jahabich, who seemed desperate to save their master. Gone was their normal method of fighting as one cohesive unit. Now, it seemed that each individual was making a play at it, only to be replaced by another when that one was destroyed.

Cries of "*Mother!*" echoed throughout the cavern, sounding more like pleas for mercy than anything.

"What she said," I replied, hooking a thumb Sheila's way.

"Wait," Calibra gasped, coughing up blood. Fast as her healing was, Alex was ensuring it didn't have a chance to take hold. "I am the only one who can control The Source. I am one with it. Destroy me and you shall never know its secrets."

Alex let out a laugh, almost genuine sounding. He let go of her throat to pull something out of a pocket. It was a small flask. He gave his sword one more twist in Calibra's gut, causing her – and subsequently the Jahabich – to cry out, then he yanked it out of her. Lifting the blade, he proceeded to coat it with whatever was in the flask.

He then bent down to her ear again. "Do you honestly think I don't know that? I am Alexander of the First. I am lord and master of all the covens of this world and all the vampires within them ... including you."

With that, he severed her head from her body with one clean swipe. I let out both a whoop of joy at the sight, as well as a massive sigh of relief. For a second there, I thought he might actually consider joining up with her. I mean, wasn't that what the bad guys usually did?

A howl of pain rose up from every Jahabich present as they abruptly ceased fighting, almost as if stunned at what had transpired and unsure of what to do next. It echoed for several long seconds before fading away, along with the last of their resistance.

"Much better," Alex remarked.

I found it odd that none of the Magi seemed to race to their precious White Mother's side. Maybe the whole vampire business had freaked them out.

If so, then this next part was the topper on that cake. Calibra's body burst aflame and melted into a puddle of goo. Not the usual way vamps went, but then she was a unique case.

It took me a moment to realize the problem.

Her body was no more, but her head was still there, staring creepily up at us, the eyes darting back and forth.

That's when it hit me. "No! You can't be serious."

Rather than answer, Alex sent out a compulsion. "***TO ME!!***"

It was wickedly powerful, but seemed to be focused elsewhere. He held up a hand and snapped his fingers, loud in the suddenly quiet cave.

From the back, near the tunnels leading in, someone began pushing their way forward. It took me a few moments to make out any features among the sea of creatures still present, but then I caught a glimpse of his face.

"You have got to be fucking kidding me!"

Colin stepped past James, nodded once to his former boss, then walked up to Alex and presented him with a jar of blood. It was eerily similar to the ones I'd seen in a certain bedroom closet. Alex removed the lid, picked up Calibra's severed head, and placed it inside, where it stared out at us with a look of horror upon its face.

"A fitting trophy to replace those lost to me," he said softly, looking at his new prize almost reverently. Then, as if not enough salt had been thrown in my wounds, he threw me a wink.

Such an asshole.

84

SHOWDOWN AT THE EARTH'S CORE

The circle around us widened, giving me a greater view of the area. The Jahabich had indeed disengaged from the battle. They stood around, still very much alive, but unmoving. It was almost as if they'd crashed and were waiting for someone to reboot them. Sadly, the guy with the keys to the server room was worse than any virus I could imagine.

I looked around and realized the answer to my question on where the Magi were. Turns out the vast majority of them were dead. Though I couldn't see the entirety of the cavern from my vantage point, the bodies littering the floor were evident. Many had been torn to pieces, which brought to mind a certain little psycho who I hadn't seen since the start of this debacle. I had no idea where she was, but I had a feeling the little ragamuffin wasn't so easily disposed of.

For now, though, I had bigger fish to fry.

The remains of the First Coven gathered around Alex, although I can't say their faces were entirely happy ones. Still, they kept their opinions to themselves. That is, until James stepped forward. "Is that wise, Lord Alexander?"

Alex, for his part, seemed enraptured by the newest addition to his bookshelf. It took him a moment to realize he'd been addressed. "Ah, Wanderer. Why do you say that?"

"Calibra ... Ib is infinitely dangerous. She hid among us unseen for countless eons."

"Right under your nose, if I recall correctly," Alex remarked, still staring at Calibra's noggin.

"Yes," James replied uncomfortably, the dig definitely not lost upon him. "Be that as it may, I will remind you of recent events with the Destroyer. Ib might be neutralized, but that does not mean she will remain so. She still has followers, believers. The Magi, if they learn of this..."

"Will be dealt with accordingly. Speaking of which," Alex turned his gaze toward James, "there is the matter of your absence."

"I was held prisoner."

"As I am well aware, just as I am also aware that Ib's machinations have been moving forward for some time now. I am sorry to say, Wanderer, but before I can accept your counsel again, we must be certain you are yourself and have not become yet another of those machinations."

There it was, Alex's genius on display – sowing doubt among the rest of the Dracs that perhaps James's word could not be trusted. Mind you, that was total fucking bullshit, especially since he was advocating killing the very same person he'd be going out of his way to save if he was a Jahabich. Despite this, none of the other Draculas spoke up in James's defense. Fucking cowards.

"So be it," Alex said before I could open my mouth. "A glorious day, my brothers and sisters. The false goddess has fallen. We now control that which she so jealously hoarded. Once we plumb the mysteries the so-called Source has to offer, we shall remake the world in our own image. None shall stand against us. An eternity of peace is within our grasp. A new era begins today."

"No!" Sheila stood from where she and Sally had been trying to help Christy. She put her hand on the grip of her still sheathed weapon.

"Shining One," Alex replied, sounding entirely unperturbed by her challenge. "You have my gratitude for your assistance. Know that the word of Alexander is law. As such, I grant you the thirty-day reprieve from persecution that was agreed upon." He glanced down at the still unconscious Christy. "You and your allies may leave this place. None shall stand in your way and no harm shall come to you. Unless, that is, you choose to break your bond."

The threat was obvious, but Sheila was ready for him. "Me? You're the one who broke your word first."

Alex raised an eyebrow, seeming genuinely curious. "A serious accusation against my honor. Did I harm you when last we met? Have I or any of my people moved against you in this battle? I think not."

"What about the Templar, you bastard?"

"The Templar?" he asked. "I have not seen them since the Destroyer fell."

"You're a liar," she said, drawing some serious shade from the other Dracs. Toadies they might be, but they didn't take kindly to smack talk.

"I caution you," Gaius said from behind Alex, "speak your next words carefully, Shining One."

"I don't need to speak carefully," she spat before addressing Alex again. "You had the Templar killed. Had them turned into monsters like yourself."

"I did no such thing," he replied.

I stepped over next to her. "It's true. I saw it. They were all turned."

"Not by my hand."

"Maybe not." I pointed a finger at Colin. "But you don't need to get your hands dirty when you have your fucking lackey around."

Alex turned to Colin, who looked as if he desperately wished to be invisible at that moment. "Is this true?"

"My l-lord," Colin stammered. "I thought it best to contain the potential threat they represented."

"*IS THIS TRUE?!*"

"Yes," Colin blurted out robotically.

Something akin to actual annoyance appeared on Alex's

face. I got the impression a certain greasy vamp had been acting on his own authority again. "Why would you do this?"

"Victory is ours, my lord," Colin replied. "We need not apologize to lesser beings for our actions. We..."

"You know that my word is law and yet you thought to impugn my honor?"

"No, I..." He turned to James. "Wanderer, please."

James simply crossed his arms and said nothing to his former assistant.

"Kneel," Alex said.

"My lord?"

"***KNEEL!!***"

Colin dropped to his knees. Alex didn't put him fully under, however. Though his legs weren't under his control, the look on his face said he was painfully, and terrifyingly, aware of what was happening.

Alex turned to Sheila. "Despite what my Prefect here would have you believe, I do offer my apologies. What happened was not by my command. Though he has served my people well for four centuries, such slights cannot be overlooked. As recompense for his dishonorable actions, his life is yours."

Sheila wasn't having any of it, though. "I don't want his life. I want..."

"Fuck that," Sally said abruptly. "I do." She stood and drew the sword from Sheila's side. "Mind if I borrow this?"

Sheila seemed to be taken by surprise and didn't immediately move to protest. As for Sally, though her hands were already blistering from the touch of the weapon, she didn't seem to mind. If anything, she was smiling.

"What are you...?"

"Something that's been overdue for a very long time," Sally interrupted. "Wouldn't you agree, *Uncle Colin*?"

Uncle Colin?!

I barely had time to process this before she stepped up and drove the blade straight through his chest. Her blow was true and he didn't even have time to scream before he burst aflame and turned to dust before our eyes.

"Say hi to Jeff for me." Hands now charred and blackened, Sally turned away from his ashes and handed the sword back to Sheila. Without breaking stride, she strolled over to my other side, a big grin still on her face.

"Let me guess," I whispered to her. "You enjoyed that?"

"You have no idea."

In most movies, revenge ultimately leaves the hero feeling hollow and empty inside. Don't believe the hype. Sometimes seeing an asshole get what they deserve feels mighty tasty indeed.

"Justice is served," Alex decreed. "As I was saying, you may leave now with your friends unharmed and unhindered. If you continue to press the matter, however..."

The threat hung in the air between them for several seconds.

"Oh fuck, did I miss it? I wanted to see you guys kill..." Tom's words faltered as he pushed his way to the front of the crowd and laid eyes on Christy. "Oh shit!"

Smoke still pouring from the gash in his chest, he dropped to her side and began cradling her head. "Oh shit!" he repeated. "Babe, wake up! It's me."

Sheila gritted her teeth as she continued to glare at Alex, but then she looked down at Tom and then at Christy's battered form. With an air of resignation, she sheathed her sword and gave a single nod.

Alex had won.

Ed joined us a few seconds later, following in Tom's footsteps. He threw Sally and me a grateful nod, but then joined the others by Christy's side.

"The ... anomaly will come with me," Alex said upon seeing him.

"What?" I replied. "Fuck that. He's..."

"One of us now, or so I am led to believe. His life now belongs to the First, to be judged by our laws accordingly."

Ed stood back up. "Fuck that shit."

"*SILENCE, CHILD!!*"

The compulsion was nothing compared to what Alex could normally do – something barely said out of the corner of his mouth, but more than enough to control a vampire of Ed's age, a normal vampire anyway.

"And I repeat, go fuck yourself."

Gaius made to step past Alex, no doubt intent on a beat down for the whelp who dared talk back. I readied myself to tear his fucking head off, but Alex merely held out an arm, blocking his way.

"Curious," Alex said, sounding more bemused than put out. He took a long breath through his nose, then added, "Not a Freewill, at least not like any I have seen before. No, something else." He turned to a few of the nearby soldier vamps standing guard. "Bring him."

This was bad. Sheila couldn't do anything to stop him, not without our friends being sentenced to death. And with Christy out of action, so too ended our plans for her spell.

There was nothing we could do, save hope to live to fight another day once our thirty-day *protection* was up. It was like back when I was first turned into a vampire, except one-third the length.

Wait!

Back when I was first turned ... something about that was niggling at the far corners of my mind. It took me several seconds of racking my brain, but then I realized what it was.

It was a long shot, but maybe we still had a chance.

"Where are you going?" Sally asked as I stepped away.

"Oh, you know me. It's time to do something stupid."

"This should be entertaining."

◆———➤———◆

I found Grulg encircled by several soldiers all pointing their weapons his way despite him being shackled. He looked worse for the wear, definitely not helped by the massive battle that had just been fought, but he was alive. Leading Alex here had been the key to his survival, we both knew that. But that was finished now, which meant soon he would be, too. After that, it was only a matter of time before Alex learned of my peace treaty with the Feet and had it declared null and void.

That was, unless he was overruled.

"Excuse me," one of the guards asked, "what are you doing?"

"Fulfilling a promise. Now, if you fuckers don't mind, kindly ***BACK THE FUCK OFF!!***"

One of the benefits of being merged with Dr. Death, besides looking like a stud, was being able to throw out compulsions that rivaled Alex's in power and definitely beat his in style.

Vamps and humans alike in the immediate area all did as told, giving me some space to step in. The compulsion had the secondary effect of alerting everyone else in the cavern to what I was doing. Oh, well. If you were gonna do something idiotic, you might as well have an audience present.

The crowd parted and I found Alex staring at me quizzically. "And you are doing what, pray tell?"

It was show time. "As per the peace set forth in the Woods of Mourning between myself and ... Big C, leader of the Feet, I am freeing this unlawfully detained prisoner."

Hmm, that could have been more dramatic. Still, what came next, snapping Grulg's chains, filled in any gaps my words might have left.

Gan's vial of blood hadn't been the only secret discussed in the unnatural woods of Boston. Despite knowing he would be tortured, Grulg realized that Calibra needed to be destroyed. He'd agreed to help on the condition that we pretend to take him prisoner so that he would maintain his honor in his people's eyes, whether or not he lived to return to them. I'd planned on acting on this much sooner, but none of us had foreseen getting separated from Alex so quickly.

Of course, I also didn't foresee what I was about to do next.

I owed the big guy for all the beatings he'd had to endure, and now it was time to repay the debt.

"Peace?" Alex asked. "No such offer was sanctioned by the First."

"Not yet," I replied.

"Oh?"

Behind him, I saw Sally's eyes open wide in realization of what was coming. She always was a smart cookie, that one.

"I'll make it official once I'm in charge," I said. "Alexander of Macedon, I challenge you to fair combat for leadership of the First Coven."

85

DUELING BEAT DOWNS

From the look on Alex's face, you'd have thought I'd declared myself King Dick and commanded everyone to get on their knees and start sucking.

"Surely you must be joking."

"No joke, asshole." I was already taking a boat ride down shit's creek. Might as well toss my paddles overboard while I was at it. "You and me right here, right now. Winner becomes master of the Draculas."

That last one was meant to be salt in the wounds. I mean, the Dracs was their nickname amongst the rabble, but it was a nickname they were known to loathe. From what I'd been told, you didn't say it in their presence lest you wanted to end the day being vacuumed up.

Alex was every bit as egomaniacal as the rest of his crew, maybe more so, but where I was concerned, he seemed to have an odd sense of humor. As a result, rather than racing forward with a roar of rage, he grinned. "You do realize, Freewill, that the First Coven has no master. We are equals, each having a say."

"Yeah, as I'm sure you realize that's complete and utter bullshit. Tell me, who kept all those Freewill heads in their closet, locked away from the world?"

His veneer of amusement faltered slightly. "I warn you, you are treading toward dangerous waters."

"That's okay. I do a mean doggie paddle. And while we're on the subject of heads, who's going to ultimately be in charge of Sabrina the prehistoric witch's noggin? Don't tell me that's going to be a group effort. From the looks on your buddies' faces, they're all thinking she should be planted on a beach somewhere at high noon."

"Dr. Death," James warned, but I ignored him. We were well past caution here. Even now, with pecs I could've bounced baseballs off of, I was mindful of how dangerous Alex was. Magic or not, he gave me more nightmares on any given day than Calibra did. Yet, here we were.

All of my and my friends' best plans had fizzled, leaving me with a choice – walk away, live to fight another day and leave the most potent weapon in the world in Alex's hands, or do whatever I could to stop this asshole without putting my friends in additional danger. Hey, at the very least, they could return home with a good story about their buddy Bill's last stand.

Mind you, that wasn't a particularly great comfort to me.

"The rules of normal covens do not apply to the First," Alex said. "Now, I say this one last time, stand down or I will have you put down *permanently*."

"Who is to say the rules of fair combat do not apply?" James suddenly asked. "Have not duels been fought in the past among us? Have not hopefuls fought to the death to secure a place in our ranks? While I cannot abide by the Freewill's wish to be master of the masterless, or even to be a member of our esteemed number, I do think it is his right to challenge any of us to fair combat and for that challenge to be upheld honorably."

Yes! Just when I thought James had been effectively castrated, he'd jumped right back in. Even if Alex still held to his earlier decision, that James was a piece of shit until his identity could be proven, I could see the doubt worming its way not only through the rest of the Dracs, but many of the other vampires standing around, too. There was no way Alex could compel them all to forget, especially with a small group still protected by Christy's spell. Turning me down or ordering me executed would be a serious loss of face to him. Though he probably didn't have anything to worry about from anyone still left standing, that doubt would fester and eventually he would need to start watching his back.

Either that, or kill everyone who...

"The Wanderer speaks true," Kathryn said. She took a step back from Alex, trying to look cool and detached, but not really fooling anyone. Yeah, the First Coven was a group of equals. My ass it was.

Alex narrowed his eyes at James and, for a moment, I was afraid for my friend. However, then the calm demeanor returned to his face and he turned toward me. "So be it, Freewill. I had hoped to rule this world with you..."

"By your side?"

"As one of my subjects. However, I see that an example must be made. A pity – I had thought you different from your brethren. They, too, sadly thought themselves above our laws. Now you will join them in the annals of forgotten history."

"Heh, you said anal."

Even Grulg let out a pained sigh behind me. That's the problem with supernatural terrors these days – no sense of humor.

I turned to the big ape. "Any last minute advice?"

He nodded. "*Yes. Do not die, Freewill T'lunta.*"

Well, now that I had *that* going for me...

Alex drew his sword. Fuck! He was going to be tough enough to beat unarmed, but now the odds were even less in my favor. I considered asking Sheila to borrow hers, but then I glanced over and saw Sally's hands, still red and raw. Yeah, maybe not the best of ideas.

Rather than immediately run me through, though, Alex tossed it to the side where it clattered uselessly against the ground. "I can think of no fairer combat than hand to hand," he said. "Would you not agree?"

And there it was again, that twisted sense of what vampires considered fair.

Oh well, in for a penny...

I raced forward, hoping Alex's arrogance would render him unprepared for a frontal assault.

There was arrogance at play here, all right, but apparently it was mine as he effortlessly parried my clumsy slash to his face. I threw another blow, missed, and found myself launched over his shoulder. I landed on my back and skidded to a stop at Sally's feet.

She looked down and sighed. "Got him right where you want him, champ."

"I don't suppose you have any useful advice."

"Pretty much what Grulg already said."

"Thanks. You're a real peach."

"If you wish to yield, Freewill," Alex said from behind me, "I would suggest doing so now, while I am still in a forgiving mood."

The snickers from the crowd told me that so far I wasn't exactly winning them over with my skill.

I popped back to my feet and saw I wasn't wrong. Minus the Jahabich, almost every being in the cavern had gathered and formed a wide circle around us. Holy shit, I even saw money exchanging hands. For Christ's sake, we were battling to determine the fate of the fucking world and some people were trying to make a fast twenty.

Sadly, my cheering section was in the minority. Most of my friends were – rightfully so – hovering over where Christy still lay. I could only express a silent hope she was okay and that, whatever happened to me, she and her baby would go on to lead long, boring lives.

Alex, meanwhile, waved me over, Bruce Lee style. Physically, I was his match, maybe more so, but he made up for it with experience. I couldn't hope to beat his skills, but maybe raw brute force could give me the edge. I just needed to time it right.

I again rushed him, trying to use what little advantage my speed might have given me. In doing so, I managed to rip his shirt a little with one slash. Hey, that almost counted as a hit. He parried with an open palm strike to my solar plexus that knocked me into the waiting arms of the other Draculas – right where I'd been hoping to go. Sadly, it left me unable to do much more than drop to my knees, wheezing.

Just like a fucking asshole to pull out a ninja nerve strike during a fistfight. Thankfully, my super-accelerated healing allowed me to get my wind back in record time. I leapt to my feet, braced myself to charge Alex again ... then turned back instead and grabbed the nearest Drac. Ah, it was Gaius, the troll-faced fucker. I couldn't think of a more fitting donor to my cause.

I caught him by surprise and, before he could mount a defense, dragged him to me. I didn't have time for anything fancy like the classic neck chomp, so I just prepared to bite whatever body part was closest, which thankfully wasn't his crotch.

My teeth had just barely grazed the surface of his skin, however, when my forward momentum ceased. A hand, impossibly powerful, grabbed hold of my hair ... then sank its claws into the back of my skull for greater purchase and yanked me back.

"No," Alex said, all humor gone from his voice. "I will not allow that."

I was lifted high above his head and then, much as Calibra had done to Sheila, he brought me down across his knee, snapping a lot of bones I had otherwise grown rather fond of. It was as if an electric shock ran through my body and then my bottom half became completely numb.

I rolled off his knee to the ground and he kicked me in the side, sending me tumbling toward the middle of our makeshift squared circle.

Once again, my healing was up to par. It only took a second or two for my spinal cord to spontaneously reattach itself, sending a secondary jolt – equally as uncomfortable – through my body. Unfortunately, that was more than enough time for Alex to fall upon me.

With a series of expertly placed slashes, he severed the ligaments of my arms and legs, rendering them useless meat logs. There was just no getting around it. Alex made even James look like an amateur by comparison. There was none of the clumsy fighting that other elder vampires did, relying only on their power to win a fight. He knew exactly what he was doing and where to hit to take me apart.

Moving with both precision and speed, he flayed me alive while the cheers of the crowd increased to frenzied howls. He was the master of the First Coven, leader of all vampires, and now it was becoming painfully obvious why. I couldn't help but think he'd been holding back during the battle with Calibra, letting her shoot her load before acting, letting the rest of us tire ourselves out while he remained fresh.

Smart guy. Much smarter than me apparently.

He parted skin and muscle while I could do nothing more than watch, re-crippling me every few seconds before I could heal. At last, in a spray of blood, my sternum was revealed. At that point, shock was setting in. Pain, blood loss, it was taking a toll on me, but in a way that left me feeling a bit detached. So I watched in fascination as he set to work carving it out of me.

His goal became clear. He was going to gut me in front of the crowd, then pluck my heart right out of my chest like he was Mola fucking Ram, while I turned to ash beneath him.

Kind of cool, I guess, if one were on the viewing end.

"Fuck this shit!" Sally stepped from the crowd behind Alex, her big-ass gun back in hand. She raised it, took aim, and then there came a blur of motion as James appeared by her side. He disarmed her handily, gave her a single shake of his head, then dragged her back to the sidelines against her will.

I threw him a smile, although I wasn't certain if he saw it. Though I doubted Sally would see things his way, I appreciated what he was doing. He was saving her life. Things might be over for me. Alex might have secured supreme power for himself, but at least she would be alive, she and the rest of my friends.

I had no way of knowing what kind of hell on Earth awaited them, but I had to think that together they stood a chance of surviving it.

It was all I had left.

"You fought well, Freewill," Alex said, tearing the bony plate out of my chest. "Indeed, I am sorry things have come to this. Know that, despite everything, I was quite fond of you."

I opened my mouth to say something dignified, like how I was pretty sure he was fond of my cock, but a high-pitched scream drowned me out.

Oddly enough, it wasn't coming from me.

86

PROPS TO THE PROPHECY

At first I thought the keening wail might be from one of my supporters, seeing as how I'd gotten my ass soundly beaten, but it seemed to be coming from everywhere and nowhere at once.

Judging from the look on Alex's face, he heard it, too.

The thing was, I recognized the voice making it, which was impossible because its owner no longer had the capacity for sound ... other than maybe the occasional thud as she clonked around in her fish tank. That's when I realized Calibra's voice was crying out in my mind, loud and clear – a scream of pain, anguish, fear, and perhaps most of all, outrage.

Alex stood from where he'd been carving Freewill flank steaks and looked around, leaving me to enjoy the gruesome sight of my body knitting itself back together. You haven't truly lived until you've had a chance to watch your own ribcage regrow.

NO! You must stop her!

The psychic conniption became coherent words and a moment later, Alex focused on something in the direction where The Source lay.

"STEP ASIDE!!"

The crowd parted in front of him, and I beheld the cause

of his and Calibra's concern. Sheila stood at the edge of The Source, her sword drawn.

That in itself wasn't all that unusual. What caused my breath to catch in my throat, however, was who she had the blessed weapon pointed at – Tom.

I'd thought I was done for. Between my embarrassing defeat and the blood loss, my body was struggling against turning back to normal again. All of that went out the window once I saw my best friend in this world about to be inexplicably skewered by the girl I once thought to be my world.

Horror, rage – all of it coursed through me, bringing with it a wave of adrenaline that got me back on my feet even as my wounds were still healing.

What the ever-living fuck? Had she gone crazy or something? I'd been working to fix things, stop Alex. Sure, I'd been doing a shit job of it, but it was all in the name of saving her and the rest of my friends.

So why this and why now?

The agony of my battle with Alex, followed by this ... betrayal, left me in neither the condition nor the mood to fight Dr. Death's anger.

The assembled crowd, including the most powerful vampires on the planet, watched stunned as this unfolded, stepping aside for me much as they did for Alex as we marched toward The Source.

"Stop!" I yelled.

Alex, perhaps thinking I was speaking to him, turned to me, his eyes pitch black. "I hereby suspend our duel, Freewill, but do not seek to interfere in this, otherwise I will be forced to..."

I ignored him. "What the fuck do you think you're doing?"

Sheila turned to me, sadness and regret in her eyes, but

also resolve. Though she spoke softly, I could hear every word with painful clarity. "I'm sorry, Bill. This is the only way."

"I will warn you once and only once, Shining One," Alex said, stalking toward her with deliberate steps. "If you do not stand down from whatever it is you are doing and leave this place immediately, I will declare our truce null and void. Neither you nor your friends shall leave here alive. Do not cross me, girl."

Had she challenged Alex to a fight, or stepped in to help me with mine, I would have supported her to the end and beyond, but this ... dragging my best friend to the shore of this magical abomination, seemingly with the purpose of killing him, left me with serious concerns as to her state of mind.

In short, insane as it might be, I wasn't sure I wanted to stop Alex.

Alex, however, didn't see things that way as I caught up to him. He spun back toward me, so quickly I didn't see him move until he already had his hand around my throat. "Your insolence grows tiresome. I should have killed you after the first report of your existence. It is an oversight I shall rectify n..."

A shrill shriek reverberated across the cavern. Distracted as he was, Alex was caught off guard by the blur of movement that crossed directly behind him. Gan stopped a few feet away and shook off her hand, sending drops of blood flying.

Alex crumbled to his knees, releasing his grip upon me. I backed up a step and saw what had been done. She'd hit him with a drive-by attack that had severed both of his Achilles tendons. Insanely strong as he was, even he couldn't remain on his feet after something like that.

"The time of the prophecy has come," she said to him, her voice that of the woman she would never grow to be. "You will not interfere with my love's destiny."

Okay then, good to see the crazy was in full effect.

"Prefect Gansetseg?" Alex asked, eyes wide. "What is this treachery?"

"What you call treachery, Lord Alexander," she replied, "I call a changing of the guard. The old ways die today and in their place a new order shall rise, one that I and my beloved shall rule hand in hand."

I was sorely tempted to mention that she was on her own on this one, but Alex was a step ahead of me. "I have tolerated your impetuousness for too long. *TO YOUR KNEES, WHELP!!*"

Needless to say, he seemed a wee bit surprised when that didn't happen.

"I am not the one currently on my knees, false conqueror. Nor shall I ever bend them to you again." She stepped in, claws at the ready.

Gan was fast for her age, but not nearly at Alex's level. Normally, she would be no match for him, but she'd caught him unawares, especially with the news his compulsions were no longer worth dick as far as she was concerned. His throat vanished in a mist of red, and he dropped to all fours, gasping.

I merely stood there gawking as she continued to lay into him, too flabbergasted by the sheer amount of balls weighing this crazy little girl down. After a moment, though, she looked my way and said, "Go, my love. This is your time. Make me proud."

I spared a glance back toward the vampires and whatnot watching this spectacle, but I needn't have bothered. None of them looked like they wanted any part of this. Go figure, it was only at the end of the world that the assembled members of the vampire nation decided to play it passive aggressive.

That's when I remembered what I was trying to stop. Shit! I spun to find Sheila raising her sword. Tom wasn't fighting back for some reason. He stood there calmly, as if allowing this. What the fuck had she done to him?

Trusting Gan to keep Alex busy, I raced past them with

everything I had and managed to drag Tom out of the way at the last possible moment.

My roommate landed on his ass, while Sheila hit nothing but air. When she recovered, she found me standing between her and her intended target. "I don't know what's gotten into you, but you need to stop it now."

"Don't you understand?" she replied, sounding desperate. "This needs to be done."

"Yeah, I understand. It's been a long day for us all, but there are much better targets here to point that at."

"No, you don't. Didn't you see it earlier? The energy from his body. It hit me when I was standing in ... *there*. Everything stopped for a moment. Calibra, you, the mages, even me. It was like ... what do you call those things that disrupt electrical power?"

"An electromagnetic pulse?" Tom offered from behind me.

"Yeah, that."

"So?" I asked.

"So, don't you see? That was one measly bolt of energy and it brought everything here to its knees. We need to do that again, but with more, a lot more. Don't you get it? We can still stop this."

I did get it, but this was crazy. Coming down here, we knew that sacrifices might need to be made. But to outright murder one of our own? And for something that might not have been anything more than a momentary glitch? That was a step too batshit, even for me. "You don't know what that will do, if it will even work."

"No I don't," she agreed. "But we need to try, and we need to do it with everything we have and hope it's enough to shut this place down for good."

"You'll kill Tom, that's the only thing certain here. Are you willing to do that for nothing more than a guess?"

"Christy didn't know what her spell would do either. The only thing any of us know for sure is what will happen if we let that monster have this place."

She had a point on that last one. Mind you, that assumed Calibra was cooperative, which she probably wouldn't be. It could be years, centuries, or never before Alex plumbed The Source's mysteries. He was a lot of things, but a mage wasn't one of them.

Yeah, maybe I was grasping at straws, but so was she.

"It's okay, man, I..." Tom's hand fell on my shoulder. "Whoa! You are fucking rock hard ... and just to clarify, I'm not talking about your dick."

I glanced at him out of the corner of my eye, not willing to let Sheila out of my sight. "What the fuck are you still doing here? Run before she runs you through."

"I know what she's going to do. I'm cool with it."

"What?! Is your brain leaking out of that hole in you? Why would you even say that?"

"Because..." He lowered his voice. "Don't think I've gone all pussified saying this, but it's because of Christy. She's hurt. She can't finish this, but I can ... for her. I mean, I ... y'know."

"Love her?"

"Yeah, that's it."

"That's why you can't do this," I argued, keeping between the two of them. "She needs you. *Your daughter* needs you."

"Daughter? I thought she didn't want to know."

"I found out when Calibra was torturing her. I kinda saw inside her stomach. Hard to explain."

"Thanks for ruining the surprise, asshole."

It was all I could do to keep from decking the fucking idiot. "There won't be a surprise if you're dead!"

"Who said anything about dying?" he replied. "So I have to live as a doll for a while. I can deal. Eventually, Christy will figure something out."

"You don't know that." I turned to Sheila. "Neither of you do!"

"A daughter," Tom mused from behind me. "How awesome would it be if she grew up to be a lesbian porn star?"

"Seriously?!" I spat.

He grinned that dumbass grin of his at me, but then his expression grew serious. "But she needs a world to grow up in if that's going to happen, and this is the best way to ensure it."

"It's your choice," Sheila said and I could tell by her voice that she was close to tears. "But if we're going to do this, it has to be now."

"I'm in," he said resolutely. "For Christy and for my little girl."

I looked in his eyes and saw something I never thought I'd see – the serious adult buried somewhere deep inside of him looking back at me. Tom had been physically grown for some time now, but he was finally a man, making a man's decision.

Sheila was right. It was his choice to make. They both were right.

The thing was, I just couldn't bring myself to let them do it. I'd already watched once as my best friend died. It had almost sent me over the edge, almost made me give in to the monster clawing away inside my head. I didn't want to go through that again. I didn't want to go back to Christy and explain how I could have saved him, yet chose not to.

Maybe if we had more assurances. If we knew for a fact this would work, then...

Oh, who was I kidding?

I'd been willing to sacrifice myself. But this, this I couldn't allow, even if it meant that in doing so I was fulfilling my part of that goddamned prophecy. That, in choosing this path, choosing to save my friend, I would become the champion of the very darkness I had fought so hard against.

"Sorry, bud," I whispered.

"For wh...?"

I popped him in the face before he could reply, knocking him to the ground.

Then I turned to Sheila, eyes blackened and claws extended.

"You're going to have to get through me first."

87

THE MAIN EVENT

"**Y**ou do know you didn't actually knock me out, right?"

Fucking moron. "Stay down!" I ordered my roommate.

In front of me, Sheila's aura ignited, bright and powerful. Whether the poison was fully out of her system or The Source had somehow given her a recharge, she was back to full. Oddly enough, that seemed fitting.

"Get out of my way, Bill."

"No."

"Why are you doing this?"

"Why? I'm doing this for my friend," I said. "I'm doing this for Christy and her baby."

"And you think I'm not?" she snapped. Tears stood out in her eyes, but her gaze hardened. "Now move."

"No chance."

"You can't stop me."

I tried to keep my voice steady, despite feeling torn apart. I was screaming inside my own head, but in two distinct voices. One was devastated by what was about to happen, while the other howled for blood. "I guess it's time for us to find out one way or the other."

Sheila charged me, her power flaring up.

We'd done this dance before and I knew how it usually played out. Mind you, that was before I'd put on a hundred pounds of supernatural muscle.

I braced myself as the aura of faith slammed into me like a freight train. The power singed my skin, but my healing compensated. It hurt like hell, but the new me was far more resilient than the old. I held my ground and tried to push my way through it. Her power protected her, but if I could get past it, it would take only the barest of efforts to incapacitate her.

Kill her!

A wave of fresh rage filled me from deep inside, as if tapped from an unknown wellspring. Despite the white magic around me, all I saw was red. The small part of my mind still thinking logically shouted out a warning. Despite being beaten and absorbed, some of Dr. Death's alien consciousness remained. It was influencing me even now as it probably would forever more.

But right then, I didn't particularly care.

With a snarl, I pushed forward, deeper into the aura even as my skin fried right off my body, only to regrow with every step. Another few feet and I could end this before it even...

It was arrogant of me to think it would be so easy. Sheila raised her sword and her eyes glowed white as she added its latent power to her own, sending me flying back aflame.

I'd thought something like this might happen, though, so I'd planned ahead and purposely kept myself between her and her target.

The downside, for Tom at least, was that I slammed right into him. But at least Sheila wasn't going to get a free swing before I could get back to my feet.

"You can't win this," she said, approaching.

"That the best you got?" I asked. "If so, then you're dead wrong."

Big words for someone whose epidermis currently looked like an order of extra crispy KFC, but my dander was up and there was no way I was showing either fear or doubt.

"Get off me, asshole!" Tom cried out.

"Oh, shut up." I stood and considered my options. If we kept playing this game the same way, she was right. I was already nearly running on empty. I couldn't keep this up forever. And even if she didn't choose to outlast me, all she had to do was sidestep and change my trajectory.

I needed a new plan, but what?

"Stand aside. I won't warn you again." I saw the same resolution in her eyes as I felt in my own. "I won't let this world fall to darkness."

"One innocent life for many, eh? You can't really believe there isn't another way."

"I'm sorry, but there isn't."

With that, the words were finished and we rushed each other again. This time, however, I didn't just stand there pushing against the tide. No, that was a losing strategy.

Instead, I brought my strength and speed to bear, trusting in my healing to keep me in one piece as I swung a clawed hand at her. She parried expertly, if just barely in time, and sparks flew as my talons glanced off the blade of her sword. I hadn't won by any stretch, but my attack had put her on the defensive, keeping her from focusing enough to channel more power through her weapon. I needed to keep it up. As deft as she was in the art of fighting, her skills couldn't entirely compensate for my speed and strength.

I spun and lashed out again, this time catching her on the shoulder. However, where my blow should have rent flesh, all it did was tear her shirt and leave the barest of scratch marks. It had been like clawing through tar, her goddamned power protecting her.

Sadly, I didn't have a similar advantage. Where my blow failed to do any real damage, hers didn't.

She slashed me in the side, cutting deep and sending the fiery agony of faith coursing through me. I staggered as I clutched the wound, and she caught me in the side of the head with a roundhouse kick. The blow itself was nothing, but backed by her aura, it was like a molten hot pile driver slamming into my noggin.

I went down hard but managed to roll back to my feet despite wanting nothing more than to pass out for a good long while.

Damnit!

As expected, she'd knocked me out of the way only to rush Tom – who again stood there with his arms wide as if he couldn't wait for her to snuff out his stupid life.

No way was I letting that happen.

I dug my claws into the rocky earth and ripped loose a good-sized chunk. Praying that my dodgeball skills had improved since our fight with the mages up top, I flung it at Sheila.

Direct hit!

Though it didn't penetrate her aura, the force of it was enough to knock her off her feet. She landed on the hard ground, dazed.

It was a temporary reprieve at best, though. This was like *King Kong versus Godzilla*. I was reduced to throwing rocks at a foe who could blast the shit out of me at will. Worse, I was already breathing hard from the effort.

"Hey."

What the...? I turned my head to find Sally standing only a few steps away. She reached into her jacket, pulled out another of those black-bladed daggers, and tossed it to the ground at my feet. "This might help."

I stared at it incredulously for a long moment. "You said you only had the one."

She shrugged. "I lied."

"You fucking bitch."

"That I am," she replied with a smile before backing up. "But I'm also your partner, even when you don't like it."

I was stuck on what to do. On the one hand, this proved she'd been plotting to kill Sheila all along, even after we'd spoken about it. It was a heinous abuse of my trust. The flip side, though, was she'd given me the means to end this and save Tom. Could I ignore such an opportunity?

No, I couldn't. There would be a reckoning when this was over, but first I had to finish this, and now I had what I needed to do that.

The cut on my side was taking longer to heal than it should have, possibly a side effect of taking a faith-imbued sword in the gut. Needless to say, it would be in my best interest to not let her carve me like a turkey again. I looked at the knife in my hand and swallowed hard. No. Now it was my turn to do the carving.

I plucked another rock from the ground, then strode over to where she was climbing back to her feet. Tom stepped in front of me before I could get to her. "Seriously, dude, you're kinda being a dick about this."

I effortlessly shoved him to the side. "Fine. I look forward to you bitching me out about it for years to come."

"C'mon, man," he called after me. "This is the chick you've been in love with for, like, forever."

Maybe so, but whoever coined that phrase about only hurting the ones you loved turned out to be disturbingly apt. Who knows? Maybe it had been one of those blind cave weirdos making another prophecy. Stranger things had happened.

Sheila got to her feet and faced me, her aura strong around her. She saw the knife in my hand, looked me in the eye, then nodded once. Our die was cast; this was destiny.

Despite everything, we hadn't been able to avoid it. What I could do, though, was make it quick. I'd stop her if I could, but if it came down to it, I wouldn't let her suffer. I owed her that much.

The look on her face seemed to echo mine, and I had an eerie feeling she was thinking the same thing.

So be it.

When next we came together, it was with a resolve to finish this. Faith magic met raw physical force. My side hurt like a motherfucker and reintroducing it to her power didn't help, but I soldiered on.

She swung at me, but I used my superior reflexes to dodge. I stepped in to do the same, but her skills allowed her to compensate and keep me from driving the point home.

My skin constantly burning and re-healing, we met again – speed versus skill, strength versus magical power.

I backed up, ready to attack again. I'd been planning on going low and daring her to try to go high to counter. Before I could make my play, though, Tom jumped on me piggyback-style, almost knocking me off balance. "You are seriously making me reconsider your position as godfather."

"Yeah?" I snarled. "Well, here's an offer you can't refuse." I slammed the back of my fist into his nose, sending him flying once again.

He landed behind me, cursing up a storm. I had to admit, knowing I couldn't hurt him physically definitely eased my guilt over it.

However, he'd done what he'd set out to do, distract me so Sheila could act. Stealing my plan, she came in low, swinging her sword. I tried to leap out of the way, but was a hair too slow. Her blade took a sizzling chunk out of my calf muscle and I went down to one knee.

She stood over me and raised the sword over her head. "I'm so sorry."

"Me too," I replied, then threw the pulverized remains of the rock I'd grabbed into her face. Faith was good at keeping a killing blow at bay, but I'd been willing to bet it didn't do shit for dust in one's eyes.

Sheila cried out and backed up a step, allowing me to bring up the dagger. She was able to block me in time to prevent a killing blow, but I still managed to bury the blade deep in her upper arm. I felt her humerus shatter from the impact, which she apparently didn't find particularly funny at all.

Before I could pull the weapon out and try again, though, the fucking brittle metal snapped, leaving me with little more than a useless hilt.

With a cry halfway between anguish and rage, she reared back with her good arm and drove her sword forward. She'd been aiming at my chest, but I managed to stand up and catch it in my gut instead – not as bad, but not exactly a walk in the park either.

She was injured and badly bleeding, with the blade of a cursed dagger nearly bisecting her arm. I, on the other hand, was stuck like a pig. White fire lit up my insides and I coughed out what felt like a gallon of blood as my innards tried to escape the torturous magic.

I shoved her away from me. It wasn't nearly as powerful as it should have been, but it was enough. She went skidding back to the very edge of The Source, thankfully taking her sword with her. I tried to take a step, but then doubled over, hoping against hope that I had enough in me to come back from this wound.

Sadly, I wasn't certain I did. I looked down at my bloodied hands and, sure enough, they seemed smaller than they'd been.

If Sheila was able to heal herself before I could, this fight would be over and Tom would die. I couldn't let that happen. I needed to dig deep, find everything I had left and...

"ENOUGH!"

What the...?

Still holding my guts in, I turned to find Alex back on his feet. Bloodied and with his clothes in tatters, he held Gan aloft by the throat. She clawed at his hand, but to no avail. Despite her new powers and the advantage of surprise, she'd been no match for him in the long run.

"You dare think yourself my usurper?" he spat at her. "That your lineage is superior to mine ... MINE!? I am Alexander of Macedon, the once and future ruler of this world. None shall stand in my way, especially not a foolish girl with delusions of grandeur."

He tossed her in the air like a sack of potatoes, then let loose with a monstrous punch – so hard that the crack of bones being pulverized echoed throughout the chamber. Gan's limp form went sailing over the heads of vampire and Jahabich alike until she was lost to my sight. The implication was clear, though. There was no way she could have survived that. I didn't hear an impact, which told me what had landed was little more than dust.

My heart wanted to go out to her. She'd been an ally. Hell, she'd adored me, followed me around like a lost puppy, and saved my ass more times than I really cared to admit. I was too tired to feel much of anything for her, though, aside from pity.

As horrible as it was for me to think, I couldn't help but wonder if perhaps it was for the best. Despite her innocent-looking exterior, in the end, her aspirations were every bit as dark as Alex's, maybe more so.

Suddenly, I felt tired, oh so tired. I looked down to find that my wound was indeed sealing itself, forcing out the white-hot energy, but it cost the last of my reserves. I could feel myself shrinking, the fab turning back to flab.

Alex stalked up next to where I kneeled on one knee. He spared me a quick glance, his expression unreadable, but it was safe to say I was probably no longer on his BFF list. Then, he turned his attention beyond me, toward The Source.

"And now, Icon, we finish this."

88

THIS IS HOW THE WORLD ENDS

"Know that you have sentenced yourself, your friends, and everyone you have ever loved to die," Alex said. "You have chosen to spit upon my mercy and, as such, shall be shown none."

Sheila was just now getting back to her feet. Even in the glow of The Source, she appeared dreadfully pale and every bit as tired as I was. Her aura was still alight around her, but it seemed to be pulsing, almost as if it were an effort for her to keep it going.

Her eyes locked with mine and rather than hatred, fear, or even pity, I saw in them resolve. Then she actually smiled at me before turning her attention back to Alex. It was a sad smile, though, as if she'd known all along that we would eventually reach this place. The last defender of humanity ... the only one left to stand against the darkness, and she was about to be snuffed out forever.

Her death, however, wouldn't save Tom, Christy, Sally, or any of my friends. Alex had said as much, and – as he liked to tell us – his word was law. With her defeat, the prophecy would be fulfilled. I would, in theory anyway, win our final battle, but in doing so, Alex would reign supreme. I couldn't beat him. He'd proven that much. The eternity of darkness that was prophesied upon my victory would descend upon mankind, but it wouldn't be by my hand. I was merely its catalyst, a pawn of fate used to usher in a new era of hell on Earth.

Tom got back to his feet not too far away. For all the dumbass things he did and said, in the end he'd seen what I could not. He'd understood the implications of Alex winning. It was only now that I saw it too. Either way, his fate was sealed, but at Alex's hands it would be an empty death. At Sheila's, there would still be hope.

And that's what I needed more than anything right then, far more than I needed Dr. Death's rage to empower me.

I fought against the anger that had blinded me to reason – pushed it back, deep down inside where it truly belonged – and cried out, "Hey, asshole!"

Alex turned and stared down at me quizzically.

"Made you look."

Okay, maybe fate had something more grandiose in mind than that, but it was time I put my money where my mouth was.

Speaking of which...

"What foolishness are you talking about now, Freewill?" Alex asked.

"Oh, just this."

Thankfully, he was still within reach. It was nothing fancy on my part. No, that wouldn't have done shit against him. I simply threw myself at his feet, wrapped my arms around his legs, and bit his ankle.

He'd proven I couldn't stand toe to toe with him, but maybe it was a different story down on my hands and knees.

I crunched bone, getting only the barest amount of blood in my mouth before I was grabbed by the scruff of my neck and yanked away. I tried to swallow, but Alex wrapped a hand around my throat and squeezed so hard that my air was immediately cut off. Oh well, it hadn't been enough for more than a short boost anyway.

Craning my head as much as I could, I looked and saw

Tom making his way toward Sheila's position. So I did what I do best: be a dick. Despite being certain my head was about to pop right off, I looked Alex straight in his furious eyes and smiled.

Oh, and I might have raised both hands in a one-fingered salute, too.

I definitely wanted his attention on me, at least for a few more seconds.

After that, it wouldn't matter. Either Sheila and Tom's plan would work, or it wouldn't. Regardless, I wouldn't be around to see what happened next.

Alex's eyes turned black as night, finally matching each other, and I knew he wasn't about to waste any more time with me.

But maybe he had time for someone else.

He stumbled a step as something plowed into him from behind.

His grasp on me momentarily loosened, albeit not enough for me to swallow. A collective gasp rose up from the crowd as Sally leapt up onto Alex's back. Her claws were extended and she raked them across his eyes, leaving deep gouges, for the second or so it took for them to heal.

"What?" she asked, looking my way. "You didn't think I was going to let you die alone, did you? Misery loves company."

Indeed it did, and that's what I was going to have. Sally was no match for Alex. Try as she might, she barely fazed him with her attacks.

He reached back with his free hand, grabbed her by the hair, and yanked her over his shoulder with seemingly no effort whatsoever. He held us both out before him, glanced between us for a moment, then smiled as he pulled his hands apart. "You two are truly quite the team. Therefore, it is only fitting your ashes be allowed to mingle."

Uh oh. Sally and I were close, but I had a feeling that was about to be put to a ridiculous extreme.

I braced myself for the feeling of our skulls being crushed

against one another, but instead something slammed against the side of Alex's, a fist with a lot more behind it than I was capable of at the moment.

James!

Alex staggered and lost his grasp upon me. Even with the pressure gone, my throat still felt like a toilet paper tube that had been compressed into a ball of wet cardboard. Still, I swallowed anyway, hoping that even a single drop got through.

It did.

All at once, a fire erupted in my stomach and I could breathe again.

Before Alex could recover, I threw a punch into his gut with everything his stolen strength had given me. He doubled over and James drove an axe-handle blow down onto his back, sending him to his knees.

"What are you doing?" I asked.

"Committing career suicide, obviously." He must have seen me looking over his shoulder, because he said, "Do not worry about the others. They will not interfere. This is ... beyond their capacity for bravery."

"Wait, why are *you* interfering?"

"Because your duel with Alexander is over," he replied, continuing to hammer his former boss. "Sad to say, but you lost."

Sally kicked Alex in the face. It didn't do a lot, but probably made her feel a helluva lot better. "Are you going to just stand there and gawk, dipshit?"

"She is correct, Freewill," James said. "We will not be able to hold him for more than a few moments. Your destiny awaits at the shore of that strangest of tides. Go now and fulfill it ... in that unique way only you can."

I flashed them a smile of gratitude, then turned and raced to where Sheila and Tom once again faced each other, the viscous waters of The Source lapping at their feet. One arm was hanging useless at Sheila's side, but she was able to hold her sword up with the other. When she heard me approaching, she turned and pointed it toward me.

"Please," she gasped, tears now streaming freely down her face.

I stopped and smiled. "Fine. Since you used the magic word, I hereby concede our battle."

"What?"

"You heard me. You win."

"Once a loser, always a loser?" Tom replied with a grin.

"Fuck you, buddy." Then, I turned back to Sheila, who still looked confused. "Go on. Do what you need to do to bring about that light that's supposed to happen when you win."

"Or," Tom added, "in the words of Optimus Prime..."

"Let me guess," I said. "Light our dorkest hour?"

"Darkest."

"Not when you say it."

"Dick."

"Around you, always." I stepped forward and held out my hand to him. "Good luck, man."

"Don't worry about me. I'll be fine. Just don't dress me in any of those stupid Ken doll outfits." Nevertheless, he took my hand and shook it before pulling me in for a hug.

I wanted it to last forever, but then I heard the sounds of battle behind us and I realized our time was up. I pulled away and stepped back.

Tom nodded at Sheila, but she still looked my way.

"It's okay," I told her.

She turned the sword back toward Tom's chest, where he was still leaking energy.

Before she could strike, he said. "Tell Christy I love her."

"I will."

"Good," he replied, looking past me, over my shoulder, "because we *really* should get a move on."

Sheila hesitated, though. The resolve, the surety that her Icon powers gave her, suddenly melted away from her tear-stained face. "I don't know if I can do this."

"Sure you can," I told her. "I have faith in you."

That did it. She gave me a single sad nod, steeled herself, and then cried out, igniting her aura with everything she had left.

Just before she plunged the weapon into his chest, Tom said, "Oh, and let her know that Cheetara is an awesome name for a girl."

The blade hit home. Sizzling, white-hot magic pierced his chest and the immense otherworldly energy within it.

"NO!" Alex shouted from nearly directly behind me.

But then his cry, along with everything else, was lost as both Sheila and Tom were engulfed in a blinding flash of power.

I closed my eyes against it, for all the good it did. So brilliant was it that I was certain it would melt my retinas even from behind my eyelids.

After what seemed an eternity, the light abated, seemed almost to pull back, and I opened my eyes in time to feel a torrent of wind at my back strong enough to almost shove me off my feet. Where my friends had stood was now a white sphere of energy. I watched as it collapsed in on itself, almost seeming to suck in air from all directions.

And then it exploded outward again, sending a shockwave that hit me like a giant fist.

The wind was knocked completely out of me and I landed on the rocky ground, hoping it was over.

Just when I thought it was, though, horrific wailing cries pierced the air.

⟨——————•———————⟩

It came from all around me, rising in pitch until I was certain I would go mad. I lifted my arms and covered my ears, but to no avail. Whatever I was hearing was happening at least partially in my head ... a high-pitched keening as if a thousand voices were crying out at once.

Then, above it all, came one that was distinct.

No! What have you done?!

It was Calibra again, her voice echoing in my mind much as Harry Decker's had back when he was a skull, but infinitely louder. Her outrage turned to fear, then to a roar of seemingly infinite pain, growing louder until I could feel my teeth vibrating from it.

Something popped in my head and I became dimly aware that blood was pouring out of my nose.

Much more of this and I was going to rip my own heart out just to make it stop.

I was mere moments away from seriously considering my threat of self-harm when the fevered pitch from all those voices began to grow distant – almost as if they were screaming from the other end of a tunnel. Then, as if it were a car radio that someone decided to turn down, it faded away until once again all was quiet.

When I finally opened my eyes, I saw nothing but stars. I blinked several times to clear my vision, then realized I wasn't seeing things. It was some of those bioluminescent crystals shining down from the ceiling of the cavern. That was odd. I hadn't noticed them before.

I sat up and realized why. The light had changed. Gone was the perpetual blood-red glow. In its stead, the crystals gave off a twinkling twilight.

I pulled myself to my feet to get a better look around, or at least did after the third try. It felt as if I'd been run over by a dump truck. Every inch of me hurt.

At last, my head cleared and I remembered what had happened and who had done it.

Tom!

Sheila!

I started toward where The Source lay, but then heard movement behind me.

Not thinking much of it in my beaten down state, I turned, only to be greeted by Alex's eyes staring daggers into my own.

He did not look happy.

His hand shot out and once more wrapped itself around my throat. Then he echoed the words Calibra had spoken in my head.

"What have you done?"

89

DUST IN THE WIND

I expected my head to be torn right off, but Alex wasn't gripping me with the strength he had before. In fact, it wasn't nearly the same.

Was he playing with me?

Unpleasant as it was to be choked, I could still draw enough breath to respond. "The ... usual. Fucking things up for guys like you." It was an empty gesture on my part, useless against a vampire like Alex, but I pulled my arm back and socked him in the jaw nevertheless.

It was a solid blow, against myself anyway, and I felt something crack in my hand.

Fuck, that hurt!

Amazingly enough, though, Alex's head snapped to the side. He released me and staggered back a few steps. When he looked at me again, a trickle of blood was leaking out the side of his mouth.

He wiped it with his hand and stared at it incredulously. "You..."

That was pretty much my reaction, too. I was as surprised as he was, but not as much as with what happened next.

He balled his hands into fists, no doubt preparing to dole out some serious hurt upon my personage. I should have moved to defend myself, but I was too busy staring at him. What the fuck? Maybe it was the fucked up lighting, but his arms, normally toned and looking like they were made for smacking the shit out of guys like me, appeared all withered and veiny.

He noticed it, too. "What is this?" His voice came out choked and surly, almost as if he'd decided to smoke a century's worth of cigarettes in the last few seconds.

Whatever was happening wasn't finished yet. His hair turned from blonde to grey, then began to fall out. His skin cracked and became brittle.

"Noooooo!" he croaked just before his eyes collapsed in on themselves. His skin turned to dust and melted off his bones, which then crumbled into a pile before me, before withering away to nothing.

Holy Indiana Jones and the Last Crusade, Batman! What the fuck had just happened? Whatever the case, my heart leapt into my throat as I stared at the pile of moldy remains.

Wait a second.

No fucking way!

My heart really was beating a mile a minute.

My heart was actually beating!

Just to make sure I wasn't tripping on some bad cave dust, I placed two fingers against the side of my neck. Sure enough, I found a pulse, strong and steady, as if it had been there all along.

Movement registered beyond where Alex's remains lay. I turned to look, but couldn't make out many details. All at once, it seemed like it was way too dark and everything was … motherfucker! Everything beyond a few feet had suddenly become blurry, as if I were nearsighted again.

I instinctively reached for my back pocket … only to find nothing but a melted lump of crushed metal and glass. Goddamn it! Those were three-hundred-dollar frames!

Fuck my life!

I squinted, compensating for my shitty vision as best I

could. My ears were able to confirm what I struggled to see, though – that more of the same was happening all around. Vampires were crying out, only to be silenced as their bodies aged and crumpled.

In a panic, I looked down at my own hands, but they appeared normal. A bit bruised, but otherwise they were just my hands – the ones I had seen every day for years as I'd programmed, played video games, or touched myself in inappropriate ways.

"I would not worry if I were you, Dr. Death."

I spun toward the sound of the voice and saw James walking toward me with Sally by his side. My heart leapt for joy at seeing they'd survived, but then a lump caught in my throat.

James's hair, normally brown and looking like it was ready for a fashion shoot, had already turned grey. "Near as I can tell," he said, "all of those present are reverting to their natural ages. Since you are, in actuality, still in your twenties, I believe the effects will be barely noticeable."

"But how?"

"The Source. You and your friends did it. The wellspring has been closed. In doing so, it would seem that whatever made us what we were has been sent back to wherever it belongs. Unexpected, perhaps, but not an entirely poor outcome, I would say."

I gasped as his once toned arms began to shrivel. "There has to be something we can do. Maybe we can..."

He held up a hand to silence me. "Time waits for no man. It catches up to us all eventually. If anything, I have had the privilege of living far beyond my normal years. I have seen wonders few men alive have and now ... this. Trust me, my friend, I have no regrets."

He turned toward Sally. She smiled at him, and I spied a tear or two fall from the corners of her eyes, which she tried to wipe away before I noticed. She stepped in and kissed him on the cheek, before turning away.

"It was truly an honor knowing you," I said miserably. It seemed so inadequate for everything he'd done for us, but it was all I had.

"The pleasure was all mine, Freewill." His body began to age rapidly. Just before he fell to the ground, however, he said something that I couldn't help but laugh at.

"You truly were the terror that flaps in the night."

"Are you okay?" I asked, stepping up to Sally.

When she turned toward me, I saw that she'd changed ... albeit not all that dramatically. Some women just aged well and Sally was apparently one of them. Her skin had lost some of its youthful sheen and I caught the barest hint of crow's feet when she smiled at me, but otherwise, she looked pretty darn good.

"How bad is it?" she asked, trying to read my face as I looked her over.

"Remember the ending of *Old Yeller*?" I replied solemnly. "Well, you might want to consider a trip out behind the wood shed because daaamn."

"Ass." She punched me in the arm, proving she was indeed still in good shape. "Come on; let's find the others."

We passed multiple piles of bones before coming to a familiar-looking glass jar ... one now filled with nothing but cloudy liquid, as if dust had mixed with the blood inside.

Good riddance to bad rubbish.

The vampires weren't the only ones affected by whatever had happened. We passed by dozens of Jahabich, but gone was the ominous glow in their eyes. If anything, they seemed to be nothing but inert rock now.

If so, then that meant...

"This way!" Sally said, dragging me along.

As we go closer, I caught sight of a figure that appeared to be crouched over another.

"I'm sorry," the one on top said, seemingly to herself.

"Veronica?" I asked.

"Back off!" She spun in a panic, then brought her hands up in a warding gesture. I expected to be blasted, but nothing happened save a few red sparks that fell from her fingertips before fizzling to nothing. Recognition filled her features and she immediately looked embarrassed. "Sorry. I'm a little on edge. Didn't hear you coming."

"What happened?"

She stepped aside to reveal Meg, now a lifeless statue lying upon the ground.

"This," she said sadly. "One minute she was her, and the next this. No matter what I tried, I couldn't..."

I put a hand on her shoulder. "It's not your fault."

"We couldn't save her, could we?"

"No. I don't think we could have." I looked back at Sally and saw her wiping her eyes again. Though I couldn't know her thoughts, she was probably thinking about Starlight. It wasn't fair, but at least she was now free from Calibra's control, along with all the other souls that had been trapped here. "Where are the others?"

"Just over there," Veronica said. "I'll come with you."

We found Ed and Kelly standing guard over Christy, and they weren't alone.

"I don't have the proper equipment to do a full exam here, you know," Dave complained from where he was crouched over Christy. "Hell, I can barely see my hands in front of my face."

"You're going to see my fist in your face if you don't shut up and get back to work," Kelly warned.

"What she said," Ed added before he turned and saw us approaching. "Bill!"

He ran up and greeted us both warmly, hugs all around, at least until Sally said, "Watch those hands, mister."

He backed up a step, looking her over. "Sorry."

"You forgot to add 'ma'am,'" I replied, before ducking another swing from her.

"Do it and you both die," she said.

I leaned in toward Ed. "She's got the looks, but she needs to work on the MILF attitude a bit."

"As if either of you losers would get that lucky," she replied with a sniff before leading us over to where Dave was treating Christy on threat of an ass-beating.

As we neared them, Sally suddenly cocked her head to one side. She bent down and retrieved a gun that had been dropped by one of the many combatants. Before I could ask what she was doing, she turned and pointed it my way.

What the fuck?!

Just as quickly, she lowered the barrel. "Oh, it's you."

"Yeah, it's me! You going senile in your old...?" I heard the crunch of gravel behind me and turned to make out a massive shape walking toward us from the gloom.

It was Grulg. He'd survived, sorta anyway. Maybe it was a trick of my eyes being back to their normal sucky selves, but I could have sworn he looked ... translucent.

"Did someone invite the snow ghost from Scooby Doo?" Ed asked.

Whatever he was, hopefully it wasn't some spirit of vengeance here to take revenge for all the beatings he'd endured to maintain the lie of being our prisoner.

He stopped just short of us and took a deep breath through his nostrils. "*Freewill T'lunta no more. She-T'lunta no more.*"

"So it would seem," Sally replied.

He nodded. "*War over. No more enemies. No more stealing ... what is word?*" He reached out and tapped my chest with one meaty finger. Though he might've been see through, he sure as hell felt solid enough, almost knocking me on my ass.

"Um, heart? You were stealing hearts?"

"No, stupid," Sally said. "Remember what Calibra showed us? I think he means souls or spirits. That's why your people hated us, isn't it, Grulg? Vampires were a perversion of nature, stolen spirits combined with human souls."

Grulg nodded. "*She-T'lunta smart.*" He then turned to me. "*Freewill T'lunta brave. Would have made good cubs.*"

Sally let out a pained sigh.

"Grulg must go now. Can feel pull back to where Grulg and his people belong. Will miss this world. Good grubs, but time to go."

"Thank you," I said.

Grulg nodded, then faded away to nothing. From the sound of things, it wasn't going to be just him either. Even so, I had a feeling it might be a while before I went camping again, just to be safe.

"Stay down. You're in no condition to..."

"Get away from me before I hex you into another dimension!"

We found Kelly helping Christy to her feet despite Dave's protests. Fuck it all. The rest of this weirdness could wait a few moments. I needed to know she was all right.

A bloody bandage was tied around her head and her face was black and blue, but she was awake and seemed alert.

"Hey, you," Sally said.

"Hey, guys," she replied weakly.

I looked at Dave. "How is she?"

"In need of an attitude transplant," he replied. Then, after I glared at him for a few seconds, he added, "It looks worse than it is. Although I think she's going to make some orthodontist very happy in the coming months."

"I think we managed to fix the worst of it before..." Kelly trailed off.

"Before what?" Christy asked. As Dave had said, she was at least a couple teeth short of a winning smile. Still, it was a small price to pay for having pissed off the mother of all mages.

"I actually have no idea what happened," Kelly admitted. "One second, it was chaos and fighting. The next, *poof!*"

Christy's eyes opened wide in panic. "Oh my God! Kala, the spell..."

I stepped in and put a hand on her shoulder. "Taken care of."

"What?" She turned and looked around, taking in the

dead Jahabich, the piles of bones, the confused humans still milling about. "How?"

I glanced toward Sally, a question in my eyes. She nodded. Yeah, there was no point in beating around the bush. "We stopped it, all of it, just like we planned, but..."

"Tom?" she asked. "Where is he? Did that bitch hurt him? If so, I swear..." She gestured with her hand to no effect, save a spark or two falling to the ground. "What happened to my magic?"

"I was kind of wondering the same thing," Kelly added.

"Does anyone else suddenly have a pulse again?" Dave asked from the edge of our group.

I, along with everyone else, ignored him. "That's what I'm trying to tell you. Tom and Sheila, they did a very brave thing. They figured out a way to stop the..."

"The Source!" Christy cried out, pointing. "What happened to The Source?"

I'd been so caught up in, well, being alive – and not just metaphorically – that I'd forgotten about it. I followed her gaze. Gone was the pool of orange glowing jizz. In its place appeared to be nothing more than the granddaddy of all mud puddles.

"What's that?" Kelly asked.

I squinted, but couldn't see anything aside from a big blotch of brown. "What?"

"There's someone in there!" she cried.

There was?

I hated to admit it, but watching what had happened when Sheila's powers combined with the energy inside of Tom, I hadn't even dared to hope that anything was left of them. It had just seemed so ... impossible.

"Let's go," Sally said, leading the way.

Christy, though looking halfway to death's door, somehow found the strength to follow us as we made our way to the shore of what was once the gateway of all magic in this world, now closed, hopefully forever.

Once we got close enough, I made out something. Was

hard to tell without my glasses, but it appeared to be a big-ass lump of mud.

Except, as we neared it, I realized it was sobbing softly. At first, I thought it might be some new form of Jahabich risen from the muck, but then, as we gathered around, I realized I was mistaken.

It was Sheila, covered head to toe in grime, but somehow alive.

The wound on her arm was still bleeding badly and at first I thought that was the cause of her pain, but then, as I stepped up to help her, I saw how wrong I was.

In her arms was the charred plastic form of a Max Adventure doll.

I knelt down in front of her. "Tom?"

She looked up, tears streaming down her face, and gave her head a single shake. Then she threw herself into my arms and dissolved into tortured sobs.

It was only after several seconds of shock that I realized I was crying just as hard as she was.

Christy joined us, the look on her face one of utter despair. She held out her hands, and Sheila placed the doll in them.

"What happened?" she asked after she was able to get herself under control.

I explained it to her – Sheila's theory after being hit with the prism's energy, Tom's decision upon finding her unconscious. My attempt to stop them only to realize at the last moment that they were right. Finally, Tom's resolve to do this for their child so she would have a world to grow up in.

For a long moment, Christy refused to look at either of us. I felt shame – shame because I tried to save him, shame that it had been a selfish decision on my part, and shame because in the end, we had saved the world, but left her unborn child fatherless.

After what seemed like an eternity of misery, though, she stepped to Sheila and looked her in the eye. "I forgive you."

They embraced for a long moment, both of them crying hard. Then, Christy pulled back and turned to me. Guilt at everything I'd done ate away at my insides as I looked into her eyes, and I opened my mouth to tell her again how sorry I was. However, she raised a finger to my lips to silence me.

"You were there with him at the end?"

I nodded.

"Good. You were his best friend and I can't think of anyone else I would have rather had by his side."

There were several long minutes of tears, followed by hugging and more crying, and then finally laughter. The grief was real, but it was mixed with triumph. Tom's sacrifice hadn't been for nothing.

The prophecy was fulfilled. Alex and Calibra were both dead. The side of light had won. Oddly enough, it seemed the other prophecy had been met, too, albeit not quite as expected. Aside from our friends, there weren't many mages still alive in the cavern, but it was obvious, from watching the few survivors desperately trying and failing to perform magic, that the effects weren't limited to us. In destroying The Source, Sheila had severed the Magi's connection to their power, effectively destroying them as foretold, just in a much less genocidal manner.

Though we couldn't be certain, Christy seemed to think that, with The Source gone, the effect would spread. Whether it was days or weeks, soon enough, every mage on the planet would have to start taking the bus to work and dealing with their problems in ways that didn't involve zapping things.

That was fine, though, because she also didn't think there would be much need for fending off supernatural threats anymore. The gates were closed and sealed tight. Sure, some godlike beings could probably force their way through, but it would be like breaking through a concrete wall armed only with a toothbrush.

Sadly, our resources for magical healing seemed to have joined the rest of our abilities.

After we'd had our chance to get the tears out of our system, for now at least, we turned our attention to patching up our friends. Thankfully, we had Dave with us. He wasn't an idiot by any means, and eventually he realized that shutting up and doing his job would ensure he, too, didn't need medical attention.

Sheila and Christy would both need hospital stays when this was done, but we managed to get them stitched and splinted as best we could.

Of course, that still left the issue of actually getting them to a hospital, which meant the very real problem of getting the fuck out of here.

"So ... anyone got a really big shovel?" Kelly asked.

"I don't know about the rest of you," Ed replied, "but I don't fancy living out the rest of my days as a Morlock."

"Still beats being adopted by the Feet," I added, to which he wholeheartedly agreed.

"We'll be okay," Sally said after a few moments.

"Suddenly an optimist, are we?"

She shrugged. "It's weird, but I was remembering what Calibra told us about becoming a vampire, essentially two souls fusing into one. Well, it's hard to explain, but yes, that driving force in my head always pushing me to do ... not so nice things. It's not there anymore. Doesn't mean I'm applying for sainthood anytime soon, but I find myself actually feeling hopeful."

"Does that mean you won't pull anymore knives on me?" Sheila asked with a weak laugh.

"Relax, hon, I only have so much pocket space in these jeans."

That set the group to laughing. Amazing how quickly

things could become water under the bridge, especially in light of what we'd accomplished.

"But, anyway, I wasn't talking about hope. I was serious when I said we'd be okay." She turned to me. "Remember that other thing Calibra said, the part about a natural tunnel leading out of here? Anyone up for visiting Damascus?"

"Oh yeah," I replied. "But there's dozens of caves in the outer chamber. Going to take us a while to find the right one."

"I don't seem to have any pressing engagements at the moment," she said.

Christy looked up from the rock where she'd been sitting, silently staring at the doll that had been Tom, and wiped her eyes. "That won't be necessary."

"What do you mean?" Sally asked.

"Look around us."

"It's a cave."

Christy shot her a pained look. "The ambient light."

"Yeah?" I asked. "Crystals, glow worms, psychedelic moss?"

"Energy from the ley lines," she replied. "Their source is cut off, but, much like a damned up river, it takes a little bit of time for them to run completely dry. I'm willing to bet there's enough residual energy left in them to power the portals leading out of here."

I gestured toward Sheila. "Will it work for all of us?"

She looked down at her heavily bandaged arm held in a makeshift splint. "I have a feeling it's not going to be an issue this time."

"How will we know where we'll end up?" Kelly asked.

"Offhand," I replied, "anywhere topside has gotta be an improvement."

There were nods all around, but then Christy stood up.

"There's just one small catch," she said. "They probably won't work for long. So I would suggest we don't dawdle."

Sheila and Christy were the most injured of our group. Dave, Kelly, and Veronica went ahead with them to the outer chamber while Ed worked with a few of the military types Alex had brought, so as to help round up any other stragglers for us to lead out of here. Vampire, mage; none of it mattered anymore. There were just people here now and most of them were scared and confused.

Sally suggested she and I make a circuit of this place before catching up to the others, to ensure there weren't any loose ends.

I really wanted to get the fuck out of there, but that was topped by my desire to never want a repeat performance of any of this ever again, so I agreed.

"Slow down," she said. "I'm not as young as I used to be."

"Looks like you're holding up pretty well ... for someone of advanced age."

She held up the gun she was carrying. "You do realize this thing is loaded and I still know how to shoot, right?"

"So..." I said, turning serious. "How are you doing, really?"

"It's a little weird, the whole spontaneous aging, but it somehow feels fair."

"Fair?"

"Yeah. I mean, I got to spend the last thirty years or so in the prime of my life, with more money and energy than I knew what to do with."

"Most of that was as Jeff's slave."

"I know," she replied, "but I won't lie and tell you it was all bad. This ... well, this is just balancing the books."

"What now?"

"I don't know. Maybe I'll try tennis, find myself a hot young stud of an instructor that I can corrupt."

"Well, I don't know how to play tennis," I said as we

passed a circle of former Jahabich, "but I am always open to being corrupted."

She laughed. "You have the young part down at least. Still need to work on the hot stud piece."

"Bitch."

"You know it. Besides, don't you have a former Icon who you should finally be asking on a date?"

It was about as gentle of a put down as Sally was capable of. I thought about that one. "I don't know. We've been through a lot."

"Don't blame her. Fate put you on different sides of the coin."

"Maybe."

"Think about it," she said. "I hate to point it out to you now, but life is short. Too short for regrets."

I didn't quite know how to answer that. "We'll see. After everything, who knows what she'd say? I don't even have my massive pecs to flex anymore."

She eyed me up. "Don't sell yourself short. You didn't get off too badly in the deal."

I looked down at myself, something I hadn't thought to do since we'd destroyed The Source. I mean, I assumed I was just me.

I was, but I'd somehow changed, too. I wasn't sporting Dr. Death's physique, not by a fucking long shot, but judging by my waistline, I seemed to have dropped a good twenty pounds. Not too shabby. "How?"

"I was wondering that myself," she replied, "but after hearing what Calibra had to say, I think our bodies might have been less dead and more in a kind of stasis while we were vamps. Anything we did or ate could've still affected us. It just did so at a much slower rate."

I considered this, remembering how I'd seemingly dropped a pant size after my three-month sojourn in a Swiss prison cell.

"And now, with that stasis gone," she continued, "our physical forms are catching up to what they would have been. Hence why anyone over a century old basically turned into a pile of bones."

"So if we stayed active, we'd be in good shape. But if we sat around on our asses..."

Sally held up a hand to stop me. She was looking at something off in the distance that I couldn't make out. I so needed to consider LASIK when we got back home. "What?"

"Sat around on our asses, or spent most of our time on our backs," she said.

"Huh?"

"Never mind." She turned to me with a predatory smile, eerily reminiscent of her old self. "Come on, I think I see that loose end I was looking for."

I followed her, past where the Jahabich had once stood as living cages, back toward Calibra's former castle. "What are we looking for?"

"Not what. Who."

"Stay back," a voice warned from somewhere up ahead. It was thick and throaty, like the owner had led a harsh life of cheap liquor and too many smokes.

I caught up to Sally. The person before us was cowering against the wall of Calibra's castle, bag in hand. Apparently, she'd been in the process of trying to sneak out when Sally spotted her. Whoever she was, she was a mess – grossly overweight, jowly, bad skin, sallow eyes. Ugh! Not even beer goggles were going to help this chick.

Then I noticed her hair, stringy and unkempt. She was going grey, but the deep red it had once been was still evident. "Firebird?"

"Going somewhere, Betty?" Sally asked with a grin.

Firebird snarled at her, but there was very little threat behind it. "What the fuck did you do?"

Sally ejected the magazine from her gun and casually checked it before sliding it back in with a click. "Oh, you know me. Can't leave well enough alone."

"Look what you did to me, you whore!"

"Me?" Sally asked innocently. "You're the one who

laughed while I kept up with all those classes over the years. Remember? Jazzercise, aerobics, Pilates, all of it."

"Jazzercise?" I asked.

"It was the eighties," she snapped. "A weird time even for vamps." She turned back to Firebird, the gun barrel casually pointing her way. "I guess you should have listened to me ... about a lot of things."

"Doesn't change what you were, what you've done," Firebird spat.

"No, but it definitely changes who we are now. Me, well, see for yourself. You, on the other hand, would be lucky to get by with fifty-cent blowjobs behind a truck stop ... *would* being the operative word." She leveled the gun at Firebird, who cowered pathetically at the sight of the weapon.

Though a part of me would have loved to see her pull the trigger, I put a hand on her shoulder. "It's over, Sally, Lucinda, whoever you are now." She glared at me, her eyes hard, so I quickly continued. "You said it yourself. Look at her. You won. All she had going for her were her looks, and those are gone and never coming back." I glanced again at Firebird. Yeah, *definitely* not coming back, not even with a team of plastic surgeons. "This is the best revenge you could ever ask for, letting her live out the rest of her miserable life."

Sally stared at me for several seconds, but I held her gaze. Finally, she lowered the gun. "You're right. This is the best revenge for me."

"Good, because I..."

"But *this* is the best revenge for Starlight."

Before I could react, she shot Firebird in the head. Her brains splattered on the wall behind her and she slumped to the ground dead as a person could be.

"The fuck?!" I cried when the echo from the shot had died down.

"Rest in peace, Alice." Sally tossed the gun to the side, then turned and walked past me. "Coming?"

I gritted my teeth in frustration, then turned to follow. Truth be told, I felt very little sympathy for Firebird. That surprised me, but at the same time didn't. Dr. Death might have been gone, but perhaps it would take some time for all of his influence to be forgotten. "I thought you said the part of you that told you to do bad things was gone."

"That was the last echo of it," she replied. "The thing I needed to do to settle the score from that old life. Now it's over and I can move on."

I let out a heavy sigh, but didn't argue the point. "Is it? I mean, over?"

"I think so," she said as we headed toward the tunnel leading to the outer chamber. "There'll be hell to pay up above, a world left in chaos, but at least there's still a world to return to. It'll take some time for the higher ups to get used to the fact there are no longer monsters dictating things from the shadows, but humanity will survive. And so will we."

"So what's next?" I asked. "Aside from getting out of here."

"A long shower, a nap, then maybe a few days at the beach. I have some tanning to catch up on."

"That's it?"

"Taking it one step at a time, Bill. I think we all need to."

"Says you," I replied. "I have a feeling Ed and I are going to return to find overdue rent bills waiting for us."

She laughed. "That's one other thing I'm going to do."

"What?"

"I have a card with your name on it. It's about time I gave it to you."

"A card?" I asked. "You do realize it's not my birthday."

"I mean a bank card." Then, when I looked at her incredulously, she added, "You've earned it."

"You're finally giving me access to coven funds?"

"Some of it anyway," she replied with a chuckle. "There's no coven anymore, but that doesn't mean those accounts just disappear. Would be a shame to let them go to waste, and even I can't spend that much on my own."

"I'd be willing to bet on that one."

"And, as usual, you'd lose."

Now it was my turn to laugh. "What do you say we get the fuck out of here?"

"Best plan you've had all day."

With that, we entered the tunnel leading away from this place.

We didn't speak again until we'd rejoined our friends, but we didn't need to.

The future was uncertain, but it was finally ours to do with as we pleased.

90

THE HATE MAIL
INDUCING EPILOGUE

I looked at each of my friends as we stood around the headstone in a moment of silence.

It was three years to the day since we'd sent Calibra and Alex to whatever hell they deserved. Though the world as a whole had chosen to mostly forget the strange events that had nearly consumed it, we hadn't.

Ed was the only one missing from our core group, but it was more than forgivable. I knew he was there in spirit. Flying out from California so soon after moving was asking a lot. In the days following our victory, Tom's sister had come back to New Jersey for her brother's funeral. She'd matured quite a bit following her ordeal as one of the undead, as had most of us. While in town, she and Ed had started a dialogue, a sort of mini Vampires Anonymous, if you will. Soon, they were doing more than talking and things had moved forward from there. Now, they were busy setting up an apartment close to Silicon Valley where Ed had landed a cushy gig thanks to his stint as President of Iconic Efficiencies.

Tom would have understood, although that still wouldn't have stopped him from making some snide comment about Ed porking his baby sister.

That thought brought a smile to my lips as I took in those present.

Kelly stood hand in hand with Vincent, the now former Templar. He and the others of his order had reverted back to human following The Source's destruction, much to their surprise. Some had continued with their cause, seeing it as a sign from God. Others, such as Vincent, had moved on – in his case, starting a relationship with a girl he might have burnt at the stake just a few years prior.

Veronica stood next to them. From what I heard, she was now a college student working toward a degree in physics. Kinda hilarious, considering all her time spent breaking the laws of nature.

Dave looked bored. Go figure – his days as a blood-sucking fiend hadn't done much for his personality. We still occasionally gamed together, but he'd been busy lately trying to find funding for his continued attempts at cashing in on the little progress he'd made deciphering vampire blood. Word on the street was some shady venture in Argentina was potentially interested in letting him set up a lab. If that happened, I'd have to make it a point to avoid any future vacations to South America.

He tried to subtly glance down at his watch, but caught an elbow to the gut instead from my former coven partner.

Sally had changed her hair, opting to lose the multi-hued stripper locks in favor of something a bit more professional – probably the work of Alfonzo, who she'd made it a point to entice back to New York. She had an image to maintain, after all.

Much to both my chagrin and amusement, upon our return to Manhattan, she'd set to work re-establishing the suicide hotline that had once been used as a means to supplement Village Coven's supply of blood.

This time, however, it was legit. That didn't mean Sally hadn't benefited greatly from it, though. As Sally Carlsbad, CEO of the nonprofit Pandora's Light Foundation, she established herself as a media darling, helping the hopeless in the time of their greatest need.

I volunteered there in my spare time. It was partially to help make amends for having started Armageddon in the first place, but mostly because she was still Sally. A part of me would always consider her my partner in crime, even if she was now old enough to be my mother – something I took great delight in reminding her of, despite her retaining a mean left hook. Regardless, it was always fun to trade barbs when she wasn't busy, which, in all fairness, wasn't often enough.

Indeed, the phone, chat, and email lines had buzzed nonstop in the days following the end of the Apocalypse. There were so many people whose lives had been left in shambles and there she was, like an angel sent from heaven to help them ... and get her picture in the *New York Times* at every possible opportunity.

Speaking of angels, the moment of silence ended and Christy gave a nod to the little girl standing by her side.

Tina Cheetara McIntyre stepped forward and placed an unopened action figure at the base of her father's monument. It was quite the piece of work, a massive headstone topped with a marble representation of the Autobot Matrix of Leadership. Below it was the inscription "He helped light our darkest hour." I'd argued for "The Power of Prime compels you!" but Christy ended up shooting that one down. That was fine. I had a feeling Tom would've approved either way.

As for Christy, she looked sad, but otherwise in good health. I saw her and her daughter – my godchild – quite often, and knew they were doing fine. Turned out that Tom really had been more than meets the eye. Despite his constant dumbass behavior, he'd secretly taken out a massive life insurance policy at some point after learning of Christy's pregnancy, listing her as the beneficiary. Considering his age and good health at the time, he hadn't had any trouble getting covered, much to his insurance agent's chagrin after the end of the world almost happened.

Wherever my friend was, I was certain he was laughing about that one.

More words were spoken. Most were about the bravery of my best friend, but there were a few stories of his idiocy as well, to lighten the mood. Then the service broke up.

Sheila walked over to me from where she'd stood during the memorial. "Hey, you okay?" She shakily raised her left hand and put it upon my arm. She'd suffered some pretty major nerve damage from our battle, enough so that it would never be the same again, but it didn't seem to bother her much. She claimed it a small price to pay for effectively saving the Earth from the supernatural horrors gleefully running amuck upon it.

"I'm good. Just remembering."

"Me too," she said. "I don't know about you, but I'm not ready to head back to the office yet. Up for a walk around the block with your boss?"

I smiled and looked up, noting the clear sky and warm sun shining down upon us. "Nice day for one. Why not?"

Hopskotchgames had closed up shop for good after everything that happened. Though Manhattan hadn't suffered nearly the same devastation as Boston, nor the same loss of life, it had taken a beating, and many areas were still in the process of being rebuilt.

In the wake of it all, Sheila had retaken control of her company, refocusing Iconic Efficiencies toward helping businesses rebuild in the wake of disasters like that which had occurred. Needless to say, business had boomed. Though I wasn't hurting for cash following my Village Coven windfall, I'd accepted an offer of employment nevertheless. It wasn't quite the snazzy position Ed had gotten, but as Chief Technologist, I was kept busy enough — both fixing clients' programming snafus, of which there was never a shortage, as well as developing our new branded line of network recovery tools dubbed Freewill Suite 1.0.

As for Sheila and me, there wasn't much to tell. We remained close as coworkers, but not in the way I had once wanted to. Despite what Sally had advised, the circumstances of our *final battle* had left an awkwardness between us that we didn't really talk about.

Still, I mused as we walked through the cemetery together, there were days when I couldn't help but think we'd both taken the easy way out. Part of the problem was that old habits died hard. While I could talk to her now without sputtering like an idiot, it was always about business-related topics. Every time I thought to break the ice, maybe clear the air between us and see if we still had a chance, I found myself backing down.

I'd definitely changed in some ways from my ordeal as a vampire, but in others I was very much the old me. Without Dr. Death egging me on in my mind, it seemed I kept coming up with excuses to put things off until tomorrow.

The funny thing was, I got the impression it was the same with her. Go figure. Two fools who had faced hell together and lived to tell the tale, but, after everything, were still afraid of each other.

Without a proper impetus to push us together, something even the end of the world couldn't accomplish, it seemed a status quo that would never change.

"So how's your meeting schedule look?" she asked, making small talk, neither of us in a hurry.

"I'm booked at two and three, but otherwise, it's not too bad."

We exited through the gate, turned, and began walking down the sidewalk, next to the high concrete retaining wall that surrounded the cemetery.

"You're lucky," she said after a minute. "The Halsford account is up for renewal. They want to meet at five today."

"Assholes," I replied.

"Yes, but high paying assholes."

I chuckled. "If they've got the budget, then I guess we're fated to deal with them."

"Fate is a fickle thing," an unfamiliar voice replied from seemingly out of nowhere, "but I believe you know that already."

I nearly jumped out of my skin at the unexpected interruption. Judging from the look on Sheila's face, her too.

There, atop the retaining wall, just above our heads, sat a figure seemingly cloaked in darkness. I almost had a heart attack, but then realized that was only because their position put the sun in our eyes, casting them in shadow.

"Excuse me?" Sheila asked after the shock had passed.

"I said, fate can be a funny thing, as I am sure you are both aware." The figure pushed off the wall and landed nimbly before us, revealing herself to be a girl roughly in her mid-teens, wearing what looked to be a school uniform. She was pretty, with Asian features, long black hair, and a pair of dazzling green eyes that stared back at us ... or, more specifically, at me.

Something in my gut twisted as I noted the SpongeBob earrings she wore.

No fucking way.

It was impossible.

"It can't be," Sheila whispered, echoing my thoughts.

I wasn't sure whether to run or piss my pants at the ... I had no idea ... ghost, maybe ... in front of us. For a ghost, though, she seemed pretty goddamned solid.

It's just a coincidence, I tried to tell myself. *Nothing more.*

However, that illusion was shattered when she said, "It has been far too long, beloved."

◄———— ✶ ————►

The girl turned to Sheila and bowed slightly. "Shining One."

Sheila, for her part, was as gobsmacked as me. "I ... that's not me anymore."

"If you say so, Shining One."

"Gan?" I asked, daring to say her name aloud.

"Of course, my love."

"But, how? I mean, I saw Alex. He killed you. He..."

A look of annoyance crossed her face, older and more filled out, but possessing that same arrogance I remembered. "I will admit to overestimating my chances against Alexander. However, gravely injured though I was from his blow, it merely incapacitated me for a time."

"But The Source," Sheila said. "All the vampires, they aged, turned to dust."

She had a hell of a point. Unless Gan had access to the fucking skin cream of the gods, she looked way too good for a girl of over three hundred.

Gan shook her head once and looked away, a thoughtful expression upon her face. "That, I cannot say. All I know is I awoke surrounded on all sides by the Jahabich. Despite feeling curiously frail, I prepared to battle them, but they were already dead. I was forced to climb over their bodies to freedom, causing further harm to myself that I saw, in my confusion, did not immediately heal."

Sheila and I glanced at each other as she spoke. From the look in her eyes, the hair on her neck was standing up as much as it was on mine.

"I was surrounded by the dead, injured, but still alive, and that was when I realized I was somehow mortal again."

"So what did you do?"

"What little light was fading fast," she continued, "so I took whatever supplies I could scavenge from the dead and sought to find my way out. I do not know how long I searched. Hours, perhaps days, but eventually I found a tunnel that did not terminate in a dead end."

"You were all alone down there?" Sheila asked, horrified.

Gan's eye's glittered at us. "Indeed, Shining One, but fret

not. My father prepared me well. I did not give in to despair as others might have. There was only resolve, to escape and be reunited with my love."

"Uh, yeah," I said. "Listen, Gan. I'm truly sorry we left you. I didn't know. If we had any idea, we would have..."

"Worry not," she replied with a dismissive wave of her hand. "My will to live was stronger than any of the obstacles that stood in my way, of which there were many. Eventually, I emerged into the light, far from home, but free."

Sheila put a hand over her mouth. "Oh my God! You must have been terrified. I mean, a little girl, all alone in..."

"I am a woman!" Gan snapped before composing herself again. "Alone I might have been, but my father's heir I still was. It was a minor matter to access the vast resources at my disposal."

"Vast resources?" I asked.

"Yes, both my own and those formerly possessed by the First Coven. As daughter to the Khan and Prefect of his lands, I had access to all he knew."

I let out a sigh. "Let me guess. Including all of his bank records?"

"Indeed," she replied. "I am, I believe is the saying here, filthy stinking rich."

Of course she was. "But how did you..."

"And," she continued, "with such resources at my disposal, it has been a simple matter to keep tabs on you, my love."

"Hold on. You've been spying on me?"

"Not personally, but through my many paid associates."

Fucking not-so-little bitch. "Fine," I growled, not really all that surprised. "But why wait until now?"

"For you," she said as if I were a stupid child. "In the past, you have shown ... *reluctance* to my advances. In an attempt to assuage that, I thought it worthwhile to learn your culture, perhaps discover the cause of your hesitation toward our divine union."

"Listen, Gan..."

"I purchased a residence here, brought over my servants, and enrolled in school ... a fascinating social experience, if entirely infantile. I even recently attracted a would-be male suitor. However, the fool seemed incapable of understanding that my indifference toward him was not, in fact, a sign of interest."

"A boyfriend?" I asked, probably sounding more hopeful than I intended.

"His advances became tiresome, so I snapped his neck."

"What?!"

"Fear not, my love. It is unlikely his remains will ever be discovered. It was quite the bother, though, for I was rather fond of the dress I was wearing at the time."

This was insane, although not as insane as she was. Where the few other vampire survivors I knew of reported feeling sane again, as if a deep seething hunger had been removed from them, Gan was still somehow Gan, leading me to believe that whatever spirit had once been in her hadn't been steering the ship.

"That is serious, Gan," Sheila said. "Very serious."

Gan shrugged as if she couldn't have cared less. "I am aware of the laws of the land, Shining One. As I have already mentioned, I have been studying your culture. I find it interesting, if tedious at times, but that is also why I am here."

Again, Sheila and I looked at each other wide-eyed. "Um, you didn't, oh, I don't know, frame us for that murder, did you?" I asked.

She laughed at that, loud and musical. "And that is why I love you so, Dr. Death. You are always able to make me laugh. It is a trait I find so rare in this world. It is why I shall return in three years' time to make you mine once and for all."

"Wait, what happens in three years?"

"Have you not been listening, my love? I am aware of your ways now, the laws of your people, the cultural taboos you feel bidden to uphold. Though I have existed for centuries, I am aware my physical age does not match my long life. I have finally realized that is the cause of your hesitation. It has been three years since Ib was defeated, since I began to age as a mortal again. That puts this body at a physical age of approximately fifteen of your years. In another three, I shall be eighteen, which, if I am correct, is the age at which both your legal establishment acknowledges me as an adult and at which your silly taboos cease to have any hold upon your urges. As such, I will return at that time so that we might be joined forever and begin anew our plans to subjugate this world."

Holy shit! What a fucking nutcase. If I was hearing her correctly, that gave me just a few years to figure out how to fake my death and assume a new identity so far away I...

"What I don't understand is how you're aging at all," Sheila said. "How could you have survived when none of the others did?"

At this, Gan grew quiet for a moment. When she at last spoke, she almost sounded embarrassed. "I do not know. I survived where others perished. Perhaps fate was not finished with me. Or perhaps, despite everything, there is still a little bit of magic left in this world after all." She let out a sigh, then locked eyes with us again. "Regardless of that, I am here as a courtesy."

"A courtesy?"

"Yes," Gan said to me. "I am no fool. I am well aware of your fondness for the Shining One. As such, I am here to convey my wishes that you enjoy one another's company in the time you have left. Be happy, my love, for that is how I remember you and how I wish to find you once I return."

I had no idea how to respond to that, but Gan wasn't finished yet. She turned to face Sheila. "Have a care, Shining One. Treat my love well, but know that I shall return and make him mine. It is fate and fate cannot be denied."

She spun on her heel and walked briskly away, leaving both of us to stare after her with mouths agape. We watched until Gan finally turned a corner and disappeared from sight.

After a few more minutes of numb silence, Sheila said, "I think I'm going to cancel the Halsford meeting tonight."

"Huh?" I asked, still too horrified to form coherent thought.

"I said I'm canceling my meetings for the rest of the day. You should, too. I don't know about you, but I could use a coffee."

I let out a breath of laughter. "Fuck coffee. I could use a drink, maybe three."

"You buying?"

"What?"

"Well..." She looked away for a moment as if not sure what to say, but then she turned back to me. "I was wondering if you were planning on drinking alone or if you wanted company." The sun glinted in her eyes and, for just a moment, they sparkled as if silver.

The realization of what I'd been thinking earlier, that without a catalyst we'd be stuck in neutral forever, sank in and I smiled. "I could probably use some company."

"I'm glad to hear that."

"But, I have to warn you."

"Oh?"

"If it gets late, I'm gonna want dinner, too. And if so, I might..." Holy crap, was I actually going to say it? "Want, no, *insist*, on buying some for you, too."

"Insist?" she asked with a smile.

"You heard me."

"I guess it's a date, then ... isn't it?"

I thought about it for a moment, then laughed some more, this time truly feeling it. "Considering we only have three years until the end of the world *again*, I think it is."

"Hmm, I don't know. I mean, you are a married man."

"While I can't say for certain, I'm pretty sure everything we did down below counts as an annulment. If not, I can maybe nail a dead squirrel to a tree somewhere."

"Fine, I'll give you that one. You're on."

I reached down and took hold of her hand. It trembled

in my grasp for a moment, but then she squeezed mine back and we turned to continue along our way.

As we walked off into the brightness of the day together, I had to wonder whether the next few years would be enough.

I had no way of knowing, but I sure as hell would do my damnedest to ensure they were.

THE END

Bill Ryder's story isn't over yet! To be continued in…

Strange Days (Tome of Bill – 9)
Read on for a sneak preview

BONUS CHAPTER
STRANGE DAYS

Tome of Bill - 9
(Bill of the Dead Saga)

"Look at what I can do, Uncle Bill!"

An unexpected shiver ran down my spine at my goddaughter's words, as if someone had driven a dump truck over my proverbial grave.

There'd been no alarm in her voice, nothing to give me cause to shit a brick. For all I knew she was doing nothing more than playing with her dolls, yet that sudden feeling of barely contained panic only grew worse.

The hell?

I was watching Tina for the weekend while her mother was away on business, and though I couldn't exactly claim to be an expert when it came to babysitting, this wasn't the first time I'd done so.

It's not like anything weird had happened to cause such an intense feeling of dread, and trust me, I know weird. Hell, I'd once had a front row seat to the apocalypse and lived to tell the tale.

At first glance, I wouldn't blame anyone for not believing that. Fuck it. *I* barely did. I'm a near-sighted, thirty-one year old programmer of average height and ... *slightly* below average build. One might not think from looking at me that I'm anything special like, say, a former vampire who'd once saved the world – and no, I'm not being metaphorical. I may not be that old, but I've seen some shit.

Since those days, my threshold for what I considered to be disastrous had been upped ever so slightly.

But that was the past – dead and buried, so to speak.

It had been five years – right before Tina's birth, as a matter of fact – since anything seriously out of the ordinary had happened to me. Yeah, there had been one *minor* incident about two years ago, something I really didn't like to think about, but I'd long since chalked that up to the universe throwing out one last *fuck you* before letting me get back to my regularly scheduled life.

Maybe that was it. The anniversary of the barely averted end of the world had recently passed. I had company flying in for a reunion of sorts, but otherwise there'd been no fanfare to mark the date. It was possible that survivor guilt was worming its way through my subconscious, causing the knot of unease in my gut.

"Come see, Uncle Bill. I can make fire!"

Or maybe not.

Please be playing with matches, I said to myself, racing toward the guest room.

I looked in at the familiar contents: bookshelves lined with toys and action figures – a sort of shrine, if you will, to its former occupant, Tina's father and my best friend, Tom. He hadn't been quite as lucky as me when it came to surviving Armageddon, something I still occasionally struggled to let go of.

Dwelling on the past could wait, though, as my eyes locked onto his daughter, the small girl with brunette pigtails sitting in the center of the room.

I *really* should have been a lot more startled to see a ball of green flame floating above her outstretched hand. Shit like that wasn't normal, at least not anymore. But again, there was that strange feeling in my gut. I could almost taste the weirdness in the air, making the sight before me unexpected but not entirely surprising.

Mind you, that didn't mean I wasn't terrified out of my fucking skull.

Tina giggled and flicked her hand, causing the ball of unnatural fire to bob up into the air before landing again an inch or so above her palm.

So much for a nice boring day.

"Um, hey, Cat," I said carefully, using my nickname for her. "What'cha got there?"

She turned to me and smiled, her eyes momentarily lighting up the same color as the fireball dancing above her fingertips. It was all I could do to keep from pissing myself.

Memories from an earlier time raced through my mind – clashes with the Magi, the collective name for the warlocks and witches who'd once dwelled in the shadows of this world. If memory served me right, their spells had a tendency to be color-coded according to purpose. Green, if I recalled correctly, wasn't from the friendly side of the Crayola box. Not by a long shot.

We closed the door, destroyed The Source. This shit doesn't exist anymore.

Except that, despite my brain's insistence to the contrary, it apparently did.

Tina, for her part, continued to smile the innocent grin of a child too young to understand she was playing with the magical equivalent of a cruise missile. "Isn't it cool, Uncle Bill?"

"Yeah, cool is ... one word for it." Did I mention that talking to kids wasn't one of my specialties?

"I was thinking about the man in that movie we watched. The wizard ... Ganny."

My left eye twitched for a moment. "I think you mean *Gandalf,* sweetie. Trust me, there's a difference."

She shrugged, unconcerned. "Yeah, that's his name. I thought about him and then it just appeared."

I was tempted to ask how, but then remembered she was

a preschooler, still at an age where shows about talking hamsters were considered high entertainment. Besides, I already knew at least part of the *how*. Tina's mother was a former witch, after all.

But she wasn't anymore. *No one* was ... or at least that had been my assumption up until this moment.

How is this even fucking possible?

Sadly, any answers would have to wait as Tina got to her feet and faced me.

"Wanna play catch?"

A better person would have done ... *something*: called 9-1-1, grabbed the fire extinguisher, or maybe even tried to wrestle the magical death ball away from Tina. I, however, froze as every instinct in my body refused to process whatever the hell was happening.

So this is how it ends. A five year old was going to do what a legion of monsters had failed at: kill me with extreme prejudice.

But then, just as she was about to lob the orb of fiery doom toward me, it winked out of existence. It didn't fade, or pop, or any dramatic shit like that. It was as if a light switch somewhere had simply been turned off.

"Oh poop!" she cried before covering her mouth, as if she'd said something dirty. "Sorry."

Considering the litany of colorful words dancing on the tip of my tongue, I wasn't about to call her kettle black. Besides, I was too busy counting how many years had been scared off my life.

Oddly enough, though, freaked out as I was, I realized that strange feeling in the back of my head, the one that had struck when Tina first called out to me, seemed to fade away in the same instant her spell had. Of course, no longer being in the line of fire probably didn't hurt matters either.

I pushed all that aside, however, because of one simple

fact: whatever the hell was going on, I was in *way* over my head.

Fortunately, one upside to surviving the end days was knowing others who had, too – people who I could talk to about this stuff without sounding batshit crazy.

My first instinct was to call Sally, my old partner in crime. Though she might not have been as spry as she'd been in those days, she had a sharp mind and an ability to cut through bullshit like a hot knife through butter.

But this wasn't just about me. A little girl, barely old enough for kindergarten, had just conjured a ball of energy containing enough eldritch power to seriously fuck up my insurance premiums. Keeping this from her mother made me a piss-poor godparent. If she found out after the fact, I'd deserve whatever verbal ass-kicking came my way.

She'd been called away at the last minute, filling in for a sick colleague at some trade convention. Busy as she was, though, I had a feeling this was worth the interruption.

I pulled out my phone and dialed her.

"Hey, Christy. It's Bill. I think we have a bit of a problem."

⬥━━━━━ ⌘ ━━━━━⬥

Strange Days
Available in ebook, print, and audio

AUTHOR'S NOTE

This is how the world ends, not with a bang but a few strokes of the keyboard.

Okay, fine, that was lame. But hopefully I saved anything good I had to say for the story itself. I mean, heck, nobody reads these author note things anyway, right?

So anyway, here we are at the end of the Tome of Bill, or at least this chapter anyway. And what a ride it's been. I can only hope this novel gave you many a thrill in this multi-book roller coaster I've attempted to build.

I likewise hope that you found the ending of this chapter of Bill's life to be satisfactory. Mind you, that isn't to say you had to like it. Let's be honest, there was no way I was wrapping up this storyline without at least a few people cursing me out under their breath (or aloud, or via email, or showing up at my front door). However, my goal was to answer some burning questions and end things in a way that's fitting. At the very least, I tried my damnedest to avoid a *Battlestar Galactica* or *Quantum Leap* type ending that leaves you shaking your fist at the sky while screaming "What the ever-living fuck was that?!"

With any luck I succeeded. Regardless of whether I landed this plane safely or drove it into the side of a mountain with all hands aboard, though, I had a hell of a time flying it and an even better time conversing with all the wonderful people I've met during the journey.

This has truly been a game changer for me in so many ways and I am humbled if I have been able to entertain you.

Fear not, though, for Bill's story isn't quite over, not yet anyway. Don't worry. I've given him a few years to enjoy his victory.

Emphasis on a few. Too bad evil doesn't rest easily, especially when Bill's ass is so darned kickable. Stay tuned for the next chapter in Bill's journey, as the Tome of Bill continues in the *Bill of the Dead Saga*.

I hope you'll stick around for the ride.

- Rick G.

ABOUT THE AUTHOR

Rick Gualtieri lives alone in central New Jersey with only his wife, three kids, and countless pets to both keep him company and constantly plot against him. When he's not busy monkey-clicking words, he can typically be found jealously guarding his collection of vintage Transformers from all who would seek to defile them.

Defilers beware!

Also by Rick Gualtieri
THE TOME OF BILL
Bill the Vampire
Scary Dead Things
The Mourning Woods
Holier Than Thou
Sunset Strip
Goddamned Freaky Monsters
Half A Prayer
The Wicked Dead
Shining Fury
The Last Coven
BILL OF THE DEAD SAGA
Strange Days
Everyday Horrors
Carnage À Trois
The Liching Hour

FALSE ICONS
Second String Savior

Wannabe Wizard
Halfhearted Hunter
Deviant Dark Dryads

HIGH MOON
The Girl Who Punches Werewolves
The Girl Who Fights Witches
The Girl Who Hunts Fairies
The Girl Who Defies Fate